# A Horde of Fools

The Dark Ages Saga of
Tristan Saint-Germain
Book 3

Robert E. Hirsch

W & B Publishers
USA

W & B Publishers

For information:
W & B Publishers
9001 Ridge Hill Street
Kernersville, NC 27284

www.a-argusbooks.com

ISBN: 9781942981855



Book Cover designed by Melissa Carrigee

Printed in the United States of America

# Dedication

I dedicate this story, due to its incredible improbability and actuality in human history (for the greatest part), to each and every innocent victim of hate-filled intolerance and violence brought on by arrogance, xenophobia and mob rule.

That the most cataclysmic events in history are often engineered by men of decent heart in the name of righteousness is a bloody testament to both the blinding power of misguided conviction and the ignorance of the masses. Such was the wellspring of the Peasants' Crusade led by Peter the Hermit of Amiens, France (Kuku Peter) and others– a murderous rampage of hatred and subjugation that bared its ugly fangs at the end of the 11th Century... and whose venom lingers within us to this very day.

# PROLOGUE

The Year 1096: ***"Your vision of godliness has but ushered... rivers of blood."***

Thick clouds began boiling and carving black scars into the skies along the road leading out of Civetot, as though warning the two armies below that the narrow pass sitting between them would soon spell doom– and shortly be awash in blood. Yet, consumed by that single-minded obsession that comes to possess men upon the arrival of hatred and intolerance, both camps dismissed nature's foreboding prophesy. Casting celestial omens aside, their full focus rested solely upon wreaking havoc on the other, thus decimating the foreign, godless foe awaiting somewhere ahead within the rocky, barren landscape.

One army represented a violent confederation of renegade Christian knights and violent peasants who had traveled to Byzantium, unsanctioned by the Church. Dreaming of killing Seljuk Turks and commandeering their fabled Muslim treasure, they now marched into the mouth of a steep gorge just outside Dracon, near Civetot. The other army was a deadly troop of Seljuk gazis, archers, and footmen, crouching in wait– hidden along both ridges and outcrops of that same gorge, as well as at the opposing end.

As the anxious but confident Turks awaited their unsuspecting prey, nary a man moved or whispered. Rather, it was the horses that shifted and stamped, issuing whinnies and nods, tossing their heads, chomping at their bits with impatience. Then, as on signal, their ears pricked vertical in unison as from the distance came the low, rumbling cadence of men approaching on horse and on foot, over twenty thousand in all, bristling with instruments of war. Driven by the promise of glory and plunder, lost in idle chatter, they marched through the gorge– content that only a two day march lay ahead before seizing their prize, Nicaea, the capital city and treasury of Sultan Kilij Arslan's empire.

Half an hour later as advance elements of the Christian force penetrated the depths of the gorge, the sky erupted into a seething mass of armor-piercing arrows, raining from ridges, slopes, and the far mouth of the pass. By hundreds, Christian troops collapsed dead atop each other in strewn heaps like so much cord-wood, while thousands of others raised their shields, scrambling for cover. But then came the Turkish gazis' light-cavalry charge, thundering through the pass and into their midst with blinding speed, howling and gabbling, rushing forward with sabers raised.

Moments later men were grappling with each other in savage exchanges, Christians groaning beneath the weight of chain-mail armor while staving off the oncoming crush of Islamic warriors and horseflesh. Turks streamed forward, knotting themselves into the chaotic mass of dead and dying while being repulsed by thousands of survival-obsessed Christian men-at arms struggling to repulse the Muslim ambush. Terrified horses struck out with deadly, steel-shod hooves, even those having lost their riders plunging wildly into the chaos. On the ground, Christian footmen hacked and hewed in a tangled scrum, some screaming and exhorting their comrades, others urinating in their breeches or seeking escape– all cursing the miscalculations and arrogance of commanders who had led then into this debacle of inconceivable dimension.

An hour later the madness abated as the valley of blood was abandoned to the mutilated casualties of holy war. The gorge fell still then for the rest of the day, save for the occasional movement and groans of the slow-dying wounded, or the confused spasms and whinnies of perishing horses.

As evening arrived, dusk began its shadowy descent, symbolic almost of some dark shroud slowly dropping over the slain. Then the crows gathered. Slipping in from the hills, converging in huddled flocks, they began to pick through the mountains of human carrion littering the valley floor. Holding an ear to the distance, speaking in hushed tones, this ghoulish gathering of destitute Byzantine and Turkish shepherds, women, and children fumbled and groped about in the fading light, picking through the heaps of dead for anything of value.

"Don't fool with the footmen!" hissed a father to the pack of children trailing hesitantly behind him, terrified by the dead. "It's only the knights on either side who've anything worth a shit... and be sure to check their goddamned saddles, too!"

"B-but I'm afraid, Dada," one of the little girls stammered, paralyzed by the ghastly scene surrounding her. A sliver of moon had risen and its pale light now made the faces of the dead look ashen, but alive; their contorted faces were frozen in those perverse, opened-mouth expressions peculiar of the violently murdered. Their mouths agape in hideous contortions, it seemed at any moment they might yet arise, shrieking in fury at those disturbing their sleep. Trembling, the girl began to bawl.

"*Dammit, Thekla!*" swore the father. "Quit fussing and get busy, for we'll not see another windfall like this for the rest of our years!"

Taking his younger sister by the shoulder, an older brother comforted her. "Come with me, no need to be scared," he said, leading her to a dead knight laying before them, still positioned in his saddle, his leg trapped beneath the girth of his slain horse. "These fellows are dead as rocks," he whispered, trying to convince himself as much as her. Still, in the distance, there came the isolated moans of the mortally wounded, those who had not quite yet taken their final breath.

Straining through the sparse light, the brother examined the knight and horse laying at his feet. Man and beast, still attached, lay frozen like some stone sculpture that had been set on its side. The knight's dead face carried an expression of exclamation and his hand still clung to his sword, which was poised in a raised position as ready to strike, though in truth it lay supported by the ground. Picking through the knight's hauberk and gambeson, he felt something. *What's this*, he thought, palpitations racing through his heart.

"D-do you hear that, Dandelo?" shuddered the girl, pointing, then grabbing onto her brother. "One of the d-dead men is m-moving over there!"

Ignoring her, the boy gasped with delight. "Look here, a silver ring… *and a gold besant!*" Holding them to the moon, he showed the prizes to his sister. "I'll share them with you, Thekla!"

"The hell you say!" barked their father, jumping to his feet, snatching the discoveries from his son. "These'll go into the family till, by damn. Now go find more before these other bastards out here beat us to it!"

So it went throughout the night. Christian-Byzantine and Turkish-Muslim paupers alike looting and picking over the dead, caring neither about the race nor the religion of butchered corpses now offering a glint of hope in the form of baubles and trifles. Indeed, the slain noblemen and knights on both sides were born far more fortunate in life than these paupers, so there was not the slightest measure of pity from those now picking pockets. In life these slain lords and knights had feasted on entitlement, squabbling like hogs at the trough over the riches of the earth, vast tracts of territory and power– while the destitute had been forced to scrabble for crumbs. But now God had wantonly balanced the scales, exacting retribution upon those greedy creatures of privilege while laying a trove of possibilities at the feet of His poor, His struggling, and His disinherited. Whether true or not, such at least was the interpretation of those looting the dead.

"Aye," exclaimed the father, coming across a palm-sized golden crucifix encrusted with rare gems stuffed within a crusader saddlebag, "these bastards purport to fight for either God or Allah, and have been paid in kind! Damn their thieving souls for razing the land and trampling the innocent who seek only to feed their families while hoping but to live yet another day, eking out a living from this sorry earth!"

# Chapter One

## God's Deadly Snare

It is purely a ruse of God that man pretends to learn from mistakes of history, and it is this deception alone that has doomed every generation of humanity since the dawn of time to ceaselessly recreate cataclysms of similar disastrous vein. Yet, oddly, men do not simply blunder into this snare. Rather, they are led, willingly– much like those bleating herds of hoofed victims following the jingling lure of the Judas goat.

Given that God has blessed mankind over all other creatures of this earth with superior intelligence, one might be tempted to believe that intelligent leaders of men would clearly recognize when they were repeating the same follies of their ancestors… but that would be to discount pride. Ah, *pride*– that irreversible, self-destructive foible of humanity! It alone ensures that each man born upon this earth, regardless of origin, era or circumstance, believes himself more clever and capable than those who came before him.

Accordingly, history is littered with the graveyards of those too weak to withstand the crushing tide of narcissism running especially rampant within the souls of the privileged and the powerful. Insisting that their own sanctified vision, twisted though it may be, is the only course to follow, these demagogues of authority and self-appointed divinity spare no consideration to consequences inflicted upon others– especially the weak.

There is no better example, perhaps, than what began in November of the year 1095 in Clermont, France. From his pulpit there, Pope Urban II, Holy Father of the Roman Catholic Church, delivered an incendiary plea to the faithful knights of Western Europe to take up arms against Islam in the East and recapture the holy city of Jerusalem for Christianity. This fateful plea, conceived of political roots but guised in spirituality, was to unleash a flow of blood between Christians and Muslims that was to unleash centuries of bloodletting and hatred, culminating in profound suspicion and distrust that even to this very day, a thousand years later, has abated very little.

Such is the consequence, then, of free will... and superior intelligence.

## Chapter Two

### Kuku Peter

April of the Year of Our Lord 1096 marked the launching of the single most bizarre cross continental expedition in the history of humanity: an intended 1,864 mile trek overland on foot from northern France to Jerusalem, which stood at the time beneath the political, spiritual, and military hammer of Islam through conquest by the Seljuk Turks. On this date a wild-eyed little monk of Amiens, France wearing woolen sack cloth and riding barefoot atop a donkey led a horde of over twenty thousand out of that city to make war against Islam in the name of God.

The strange dress of this charismatic monk was further accentuated by his own hairy physical appearance, featuring a long beard trailing to his waist and filthy, disheveled hair tumbling in knotted strands to the back of his shoulders. Yet, the unlikely collection of misaligned hopefuls following the lead of this monk were little concerned about his tramp-like appearance, for they perceived him to be a 'divine vessel of the Lord.' Highly disparate to say the least, this horde of 20,000 adherents included certain members of the lower nobility, villagers, unemployed men-at-arms, adventurers, and monks and nuns who had left their monasteries and convents. The mix was further populated by criminals, the diseased, the elderly, and even included a certain number of the mentally ill. Its greatest mass, though, was comprised of peasants of Flanders and other nearby regions who had abandoned the fields, thus freeing themselves from beneath the brutal boot of subsistence servitude to French nobility. So destitute and ignorant were these particularly coarse people, and so confining had been their entire existence, that most had never set foot beyond the boundaries of their masters' fiefdom where they had slaved since birth.

Also following in the wake of this strange, feral-looking holy man were three knights. The first was Sir Walter Sansavoir, lord Duke of Boissy-sans-Avoir in the Ile-de-France. Sansavoir, being uncommonly pious when matched against other French noblemen, fell beneath the thrall of Peter the Hermit's preaching in the Rouen area of Normandy. Taking everything the itinerant evangelist said to heart, Sansavoir fervently swore himself to poverty while gathering around him eight other knights of similar ilk, along with a sizeable contingent of Frankish foot. Having adequately enjoyed the entitlements of aristocracy in youth, Sansavoir's growing and inextinguishable faith convinced him with age that God had other intentions for him than flaunting family title and living off the backs of serfs. So it was that, in seeking a more altruistic direction in life, he began following the preaching of the ascetic little monk from Amiens, soon even becoming his military lieutenant.

The second knight was a certain Geoffrey Burrel, also a nobleman, but of extremely inconsequential rank. Having long resented his low station within the aristocratic framework of France, he had spent his recent years seeking fortune as a mercenary– thinking not to enrich himself through the highest bid as much as through plunder. His efforts falling on barren ground, he next slipped into a long period of indolence resulting in the near depletion of his already modest purse. Hearing that French zealots in the northern French city of Rouen were organizing a massacre of Jews, a race he found abominable, Burrel made his way there to participate in the anti-Semitic pogram as a matter of amusement. Afterward, having satisfied his bloodlust but also having piffled away his final denier, he happened by chance across Sir Walter Sansavoir who was recruiting men-of-arms for Pope Urban II's Holy Crusade to recapture Jerusalem.

"Ay, an unemployed knight like yourself would be welcome in my ranks," said Sansavoir, knowing nothing about Burrel. Still, this fellow had military experience, spoke well, and exuded confidence. "Yes then," Sansavoir insisted, certain that Burrel would prove useful in battle, "join me in reclaiming the Church of the Holy Sepulchre from the hands of heathen Turks!"

Burrel knew nothing about the Islamic faith, nor did he care one feather about Jerusalem as it was heavily inhabited by Jews. Yet, he *had* heard many tales of unimaginable Turkish wealth throughout Asia Minor, Armenia, and Syria. Smelling opportunity, Burrel waxed eloquently about his own undying love of God to the gullible Sansavoir, then joined Sansavoir's cause on the condition that Sansavoir appoint him next in command.

The third man accompanying Sansavoir and Burrel was completely unknown, and had appeared from nowhere, it seemed. A knight, as identified only by the armor he was wearing upon joining the march, he claimed to have 'lost his horse.' And though he carried a sword, he seemed to hold more favor for the ominous hard-wood staff he carried about at all times. Looking at the disorganized mob of runaway peasants surrounding him, realizing they had little experience in battle therefore no hope in war, the horseless knight quickly petitioned the fiery-eyed monk of Amiens to be appointed military leader of these very poorest elements of the horde. "I see you have a small contingent of soldiers here marching under Sir Walter Sansavoir," he said to the monk, "but what of these poor farmers filling your numbers? Their only weapons are shovels, forks, and other farm implements they've carried from the fields... but I can train them to turn these humble tools into deadly weapons, I swear it!"

"Huh?" said the monk. "But what makes you think such a thing?"

"Well, look here!" the horseless knight said, grasping his staff, swiveling it with remarkable dexterity, then suddenly reversing it into a dizzying spin, ending with its sharpened point nudging the monk's throat.

Impressed beyond words, the monk clawed at his beard, shouting, "Aye... aye, my man! You shall indeed prepare and organize my paupers, for with skills such as that you can turn this untrained rabble into a dangerous troop! But tell, what's your name, sir, and from where do you come?"

"My name and origin matter none, for as of this moment I'm... *reborn!*" the horseless knight proclaimed, falling suddenly to his knees. Flinging his shield aside, he removed his helmet and pushed back the hood of his knee-length chain-mail hauberk from his head. Next, wriggling out of his hauberk entirely, he stripped the quilted gambeson beneath it from his torso and removed his breeches. Kneeling there naked, cupping his testicles with one hand while crossing himself with the other, he then swore, "I'm so struck by your adherence to the blessed state of poverty that I, too, shall now adopt sackcloth and bare feet, just as you have!"

Animals behave on instinct, whereas men embrace the gifts of reason and logic bestowed through the infinite generosity of God, Creator of all. But to balance the scales and to temper man's arrogance, God included with reason and logic a snare called 'impulse.' Next, He ordained that half of humanity would harness and put to good use the gifts of reason and logic, but that the other half would be easily tempted into the snare of impulse–as was the case of this horseless knight.

"Though you be reborn and your name does not matter," nodded the monk, "alas, I must call you *something*! So what shall it be then, sir?"

The knight considered the question, tilting his head with reflection. Then, gazing skyward as being directed by Heaven, he said, "Call me 'Tafur,' after the coarse little wooden shields carried by peasants who are so disgracefully forced to die for their greedy masters, yet given so little by them to protect themselves!"

Two days later the monk came across the man now calling himself Tafur as he and five of his peasant recruits stood about a campfire, a crude brand poking from its white-hot bed of embers. "Say there, you men, what's about?" asked the monk.

Looking up, Tafur replied, "The knights and nobles of this crusade have elected to wear a scarlet cross emblazoned across their fine tunics, but we here have no tunics... only these humble woolen rags. Thus, as befits our station on this earth, we have sworn to mark ourselves for *life* in honor of this crusade and Christ." Next, wrapping his hand in damp rags, he reached into the fire, grabbed the brand by its short handle, and stuck it against his forehead. Crying out with the agony of a wounded beast as the thin meat of his skull sizzled and simmered into the sign of a cross, he withdrew the brand, then stepped aside as the other men each followed his example.

Such was the fervor and devotion that this evangelizing little monk of Amiens was able to draw from others. Known only by his zealous followers as Peter the Hermit, he was looked upon by these adoring masses as a divine light placed on earth by God Himself to lead the poor and dispossessed toward salvation. But the Hermit's rabid fervor for God, coupled with his inviolable belief that God spoke to him directly, also made him known derisively in some quarters as 'Kuku Peter.' In particular, it was the high nobility who eyed him with scorn; it had become his habit to tell noblemen to their faces that they would be spending the remainder of eternity in Hell due to their greed and licentiousness. Moreover, the high clergy of the Catholic Church considered him a threat of sorts, as he commanded such adulation and reverence from the masses of France's and Germany's poor.

It is probable that as a youth the Hermit received some form of scholastic education, as evidenced by his sharp wit and astounding ability to incite passionate, even hysterical responses to his preaching. Scribes of the day recorded that his torrential flow of words had the same effect on listeners as sparks on bone-dry tinder. To his audiences, everything he said seemed like something divine, and many even pulled the threads from his tunic or plucked the hair from his donkey, treating these keepsakes as though they were holy relics.

That a man of such humble means and filthy appearance could muster such a massive following might seem ludicrous. That he could muster such for the intent of going to war, however, would seem impossible. Yet, this was precisely Peter the Hermit's purpose, as well as that now of his burgeoning following.

As the Hermit neared Germany riding at the head of this ragtag army, he turned from atop his donkey and gazed back at the endless train sprawling behind him in a two day march. "Ho, there, Tafur," he shouted, which was the primary timbre of his voice whether conditions warranted or not, "behold God's peasant army and swell with pride in the name of the Holy Ghost!" As he said this, his eyes darted left and right in a ceaseless, circuitous motion, which was a habit that had seized him during childhood, and never left him. "And bless you for training the peasants of this mass how to wield their staffs, forks, and scythes as deadly weapons!"

Tafur, who was now dressed in sackcloth and also riding a donkey, which he had acquired by mysterious means, glowed at hearing such praise. "Aye," he replied, "and know that I've by now recruited three thousand of the most able among them as the core of your peasant troop. In their passion, they've zealously adopted the same title of 'Tafur' as I have. And to my humble surprise, they refer to me now as their King of the Beggars!"

"Ah, praise Heaven!" replied the Hermit, not realizing that it was Tafur himself who had actually invented his title of 'King of the Beggars,' insisting that his recruits honor it. "So are they to serve under Sir Walter Sansavoir who's been recruiting men-at-arms all along the path to Germany?"

"Certainly *not*," sniffed Tafur flatly. "His knights carry shields, helmets, chain-mail armor, and lances and swords atop their war horses, and his footmen wear leather gambesons and carry bows and swords. No, we Tafurs shall fight the heathens in sackcloth and humility, bearing only humble staffs and farm implements as weapons. Our armor shall be prayer!"

This pleased the Hermit, but as he signified the cross over Tafur's head, he happened to notice several knights riding at them from the German border. "Look there," the Hermit pointed, "it's Walter Sansavoir fallen back from his advance march to check our progress."

When Sansavoir's party pulled alongside the Hermit and Tafur, the Hermit proudly pointed to the rear and said, "Look yonder, the army of God grows in number each day, Walter."

"An arousing sight," agreed Sansavoir, whose military contingent had actually been preceding the Hermit's horde by two days since leaving Amiens; Sansavoir was scouring the territory ahead for the purpose of recruiting additional men-of-arms along the roads of France en route to Germany, a task in which he had been very successful.

Next to Sansavoir rode the knight he had recruited in Amiens and appointed as his main lieutenant, Geoffrey Burrel. Looking at the motley columns behind the Hermit, Burrel shook his head, sneering. "Would be to our advantage, Peter," he grunted, "if your pitiful rabble had decent weapons at least to take down the Turk."

"Watch your mouth, Burrel!" objected Tafur sourly, his eyes drawing down into a scowl. "These men of mine'll fight as well as your own despite being poorly armed. Never confuse lack of armor with lack of courage, you damned piker. Indeed Burrel, *temper your tone*," he scolded.

"These men come to champion Christianity just as we do," snorted Sansavoir, casting Burrel a shrug. "So don't belittle them. Armor or not, they serve the Lord."

Burrel felt the reproach, yet continued to chortle to himself while slipping Sansavoir a dubious look. *You're too virtuous for your own damned good, Sansavoir,* the look said.

"Amen," replied the Hermit, agreeing with Sansavoir. "No worries about the Tafurs, Burrel. The Lord promises them both victory and favored places in Heaven. *God* shall be their armor! And you and Sansavoir, with your knights and footmen, shall be their shields, Burrel." Looking at Sansavoir, he then added, "Yes, Walter, just imagine that growing army of yours marching ahead of this company, man. You left Amiens with but a handful of knights, but along the way God's trumpet has garnered a full battalion of knights and several thousand more footmen. By the time we leave Germany for Constantinople, that number will multiply yet again!"

"Perhaps, but I question the motives of many of these soldiers I've picked up along the way," groused Sansavoir. "Assembling about the campfires at night, I hear much talk of booty and plunder in the East, but I rarely hear mention of God or the Church of the Holy Sepulchre in Jerusalem. And that disturbs me, Peter... God may not be pleased."

"Typical military jabber," replied the Hermit, passing off Sansavoir's concern. "No, I'm confident these soldiers you've recruited wish to rid Jerusalem of the heathens just as we do!" Then, gazing about, he said, "I've not seen my nephew, Innocenzo, in several days now. Did he by chance slip up ahead with your advance troops, Walter?"

Before Sansavoir could venture a reply, Tafur spoke. "No, he didn't slip ahead," he interjected snidely, shaking his head, "for there's no *females* with Sansavoir's military bunch. But one of the ox-men mentioned to me earlier today that Innocenzo was to the rear of our own train assisting two young women with their cart." As he said this, Tafur brows lifted with contempt. "A loose axle or some such thing… *or so the teamster claimed.*"

Spinning his donkey about, the Hermit began trotting through the teeming files of people following, parting them as a ship's prow parts the waters ahead. "I go to check on him then, and on God's flock!" he shouted back to Sansavoir, bouncing up and down in tandem with his donkey's clumsy canter.

The sight before him would have filled any other man with discouragement, especially one headed to war. Urging his mount through the crowd, he came across nothing that even remotely resembled a capacity to wage battle. In particular, there were endless streams of women and children trekking forward at a snail's pace. While the mass of travelers also included thousands of men, their weaponry consisted of little more than farm tools and sticks sharpened and tempered after being plucked from the forest. There were many elderly, too, some of whom were lame.

As Peter maneuvered his donkey through the crowd, he came across an aged blind man who, with one hand grasping at the air before him, stumbled forward while poking a cane at the ground in a metered, staccato rhythm. "Ho, there, blind crusader!" Peter shouted. "Be not afraid, God will be your eyes, I say!"

Recognizing the Hermit's voice, a smile crept over the old man's face as he continued plodding forward, never slowing a step. "My only fear, friend Peter, is whether there are enough days left in this decrepit old body to reach the gates of Jerusalem!"

As the man spoke, Peter's donkey was encircled by a throng of fawning onlookers. "Look, Peter the Hermit's here!" they shouted, gawking like crows huddling atop fence posts.

"Oh, our Lord's holy shepherd!" rasped an old man shouldering his way through women and children to get closer.

"Aye, God's voice upon this earth!" yelled another.

A coarse woman surrounded by her four young children bustled toward the Hermit, rudely shoving those next to his donkey aside. Clutching at the tail of his tattered tunic, she shouted, "Peter, we saw God's signs, and though they mystified us at first, after hearing you preach in Flanders, we understood! My husband and I then immediately gathered our brood and are now following you to Jerusalem, precisely as you urged! Remember me, Peter, my name is Estelle! Estelle Dupuis!"

"Ah, certainly… *Estelle*," Peter nodded, emphasizing each syllable as though the name held special meaning. "Yes, of course, I'll remember you for recognizing God's messages from above." Forming his fingers into a claw, combing them through his filthy beard in reflection, he then happened to notice that the woman's belly was swollen to bursting with child. "But ho there, Estelle Dupuis," he shrugged, "that baby there is nearly arrived, huh?"

"Aye, Peter," the woman beamed, "any day now!"

The signs of which Estelle Dupuis spoke had been seen by all of Europe the previous year. Many, especially the poor and ignorant along with the superstitious, had interpreted them as messages from Heaven sent to sanctify the Hermit's fervent proselytizing about the coming holy war. For those many in France who possessed little more in life than their Catholic faith, Peter the Hermit was seen as a beacon of hope and a vessel of the Lord.

To the Hermit's good fortune, as he had begun preaching his Peasants' Crusade, it appeared that nature itself conspired and colluded to augment his appeal to the masses. As things happened, either by chance or by celestial design, nature had begun to thrust a timely confluence of harsh and strange conditions over Western Europe. The peasants had already suffered famine, drought, and plague over recent years– causing many of them to see the Hermit's beckoning as an escape from these hardships. At that same time a mysterious series of meteorological occurrences also began to fall over the land, starting in 1095; these included a meteor shower, an aurorae, a lunar eclipse, and a comet. Many of the faithful poor translated these events as divine signs directing them eastward with Peter the Hermit to battle Islam.

Seizing opportunity, the Hermit capitalized on nature's improbable intervention. Yet, it is also quite possible that he did, in fact, actually accept these signs as a direct communication from God because from the very day of his birth, Peter possessed a pontifical certainty about things– especially the divine.

This, of course, calls into question the very formation of the human soul during that mystical period between conception and birth. Every human begins as a microscopic creature curled within a woman's womb, and for a period of nine months floats about in the womb's waters as the body takes human form. There are those who insist that during this process of physical formation, the temperament, spirit, and intelligence of a fetus are likewise shaped within these womb waters. Moreover, these same people insist that whereas one fetus may be bathed in the waters of ignorance, calamity, or disarray, another may be bathed in the waters of certainty and divinity. In other words, an infant's destiny is not simply flung to the wind, it is pre-determined. Those embracing this concept believe the compass is already set in a different way, also. They think newborns are destined to take one of two directions, to lead or to be trampled; and those who lead are further destined to accomplish one of two things, raise up all those within their sphere, or lead them to destruction.

Which leads back to Peter the Hermit who, apparently, had been bathed in the womb waters of certainty and divinity. His predestination as told by God, according to himself, was to lead others– not to glory or prosperity, but to salvation… which is what he had set about doing by embracing the monastic vow of poverty and orating the Gospel to the masses. Peter of Amiens adopted an utterly ascetic life and wore pauper's garb while preaching barefoot from the back of the humble donkey. Moreover, it was said he had not washed his feet or hair in years, and that he refused all meat, fruit, and bread, with wine and fish comprising his only sustenance.

In his divine certainty, Peter the Hermit now gazed at the flock of worshipers closing in about the rump of his donkey and listened to them and the pregnant Estelle Dupuis rattling on about celestial signs. He, naturally, found nothing extraordinary about their blind faith in him. *Truly*, he thought, *this was exactly as it was meant to be... just as God had ordained.*

"I seek Innocenzo, my nephew!" he shouted to the gathering mob, impervious to their adulation. As none were interested in the Hermit's nephew, they continued to press closer, hoping only to touch this little holy man as questions about the Holy Land and the Muslims precipitously began to pour from their mouths like water bursting from a freshly pried spring.

"There's a city just ahead, Peter!" exclaimed one old woman. "Is it Jerusalem?"

## Chapter Three

### A Horde of Fools

Aside from his zealous followers, Peter the Hermit had cultivated opponents and detractors who thought him an imbecile, such as the man who came riding hard toward the head of the Hermit's train on the morning it crossed into Germany. "Ho there, Peter of Amiens!" the man shouted, driving his horse nearly into the Hermit's donkey, then wrenching back on his reins at the final moment, causing the Hermit's donkey to buck and bray with terror.

This agitated Tafur, but even more so Walter Sansavoir who quickly spurred his horse toward the unannounced rider and called out, "Stop, fool! What in thunder do you think you're doing? And who the devil are you?!"

"Jurgen Handel, agent of the Vatican," the man declared, dismounting and snatching the reins of the Hermit's donkey. Though he was German, he spoke French with only a trace of accent. "I've come directly from Rome, sent by his Holiness, Pope Urban II." Slipping a hand into his sleeve he retrieved a sealed document, and shoved it at the Hermit. "Here, read it!" he said.

Peter the Hermit accepted the parchment and slowly read its contents. Stroking his beard with his free hand, he read it a second time. Finally, shaking his head, he said flatly, "Oh, but Odo de Lagery and I go back a good ways... long before he became Pope Urban II. Because of that alone he should know better than to waste time relaying threats such as this! Ha, he's already sent two other emissaries and even a delegation of archbishops before you, you know. And we've sent them on their way, eh, Tafur?"

Placing a palm over the burled end of his staff, Tafur nodded. "Yes, and with very few words," he smirked, a glimmer of malice seeping into his expression.

"Oh sir, and I'll send you back to wherever you came from even *more* quickly," barked Sansavoir, pulling his sword from its scabbard.

"Make short work of him, Walter!" yelped Burrel.

Standing beneath the shadow of Sansavoir's imposing war-horse, the papal agent named Handel carefully measured the knight for an instant. Yet, there was lacking in Handel's eyes the least sign of trepidation, which surprised Sansavoir a bit. Nor did Sansavoir imagine that within this man's boot was concealed a dagger, one he had wielded many times with great facility and little reluctance. But on this particular day, it was not Handel's purpose to spill blood. Turning, he pointed to the long trail of humanity and carts extending back into the hills. "This is pure madness!" he bristled. "Look at these damned people– they've no provisions, no means, and there's no order amongst them. If you intend to fight the Turks with that motley horde, you're but leading them to imminent doom, can't you see that!?" Turning, he directed a troubled glance at Sansavoir, pointing a finger. "And *you*, if you be Walter Sansavoir, shame on one who should know better!"

"Eh?" said Sansavoir, puzzled. "I've never seen you in my life. How is it you guess my name, or condemn my actions?"

"I condemn no one without taking account of circumstances or hearing reliable report," replied Handel, his tone sharp. "I can only assume the Hermit's sapped your brain, for as a knight you should be well practiced in war; so says the Pope, and so says the Church. You were supposed to depart France with Bishop Adhémar of Le Puy who Pope Urban has placed in charge of this crusade and who all knights are to obey in all matters as though his commands came from the Vatican itself."

"Bah!" groaned Sansavoir. "Bishop Adhémar's muster date for the main force isn't scheduled until August, and the way Raymond of Toulouse, Robert of Normandy and the other French noblemen are squabbling and procrastinating, they'll be lucky to take leave of France by September or October. I'll not wait around that long while our Latin pilgrims are being molested by dark heathens in the Holy Land!"

"Aye," agreed Tafur, "God's army will not tarry."

"You were to wait, Sansavoir," insisted Handel, ignoring Tafur. "But a question, then. How is it you can you believe for an instant that this pack of paupers and fools can stand up against even a brood of piglets, let alone the goddamned Turks!"

Walter Sansavoir possessed a pure heart, one solely devoted to the service and adoration of God. "Saints of Heaven! I'll not tolerate such language!" he erupted, incensed at hearing the Lord's name blasphemed. Then he raised his sword.

"No need for that, Walter!" intervened the Hermit, flagging him off. "Though his tongue goes astray from time to time, Jurgen Handel here is himself a Benedictine monk. And beware, Walter, he's far more dangerous than he appears."

"*What*, you say?" said Sansavoir. "You know this man, and claim he wears the cloth? But he's not dressed as a monk, nor does he speak appropriately for a man of God."

"Indeed," agreed Tafur, "there's nothing about this piker that resembles a man of the cloth!"

"Oh, but he *is*, for we've met before," the Hermit replied dryly. "He doesn't wear the black robe because he's been absolved from wearing it, as well as from shaving his crown in the tonsure of the Benedictines."

"And how's that?" muttered Tafur.

The Hermit issued a wry smile, and tugged at his beard. "Because he's a member of the Benedictine Underground," he said.

"The Benedictine Underground?" echoed Burrel. "He's a… *spy*? But–"

"Ay, a spy," the Hermit interrupted. "And on more than one occasion, a papal assassin as well... huh, Handel?"

"I proudly serve Pope Urban, and served Pope Victor before him, and Gregory before that," Handel replied, his tone as frigid as his expression. Spitting at the hooves of the Hermit's donkey, he continued. "And yes, perhaps I've been up to my chin in intrigue and dagger work, but I've never left a wake of damage such as the bunch of you now manufacture. You're leading these people to slaughter, and the Holy Father commands you to stop before it's too late! These damned paupers won't have a chance in Hell against the fury of the Turks. It'll be like releasing lambs into a ravening pack of wolves!"

"Odd words coming from the mouth of one who's so coldly stuck others with your point in dark streets and back alleys,

Handel," sneered the Hermit, "and whose reports have sent many others to the gallows."

"You'll not ensnare me with your moralistic jabber," snapped Handel. "Though not upon my knees or through prayer, I serve the Church in my own way. We are besieged by violent enemies coming at us from every quarter these days, so stop wagging your tongue for once and open your ears, Hermit. Heed the words Pope Urban has inscribed upon that document you're holding. Stop this march. Turn these peasants around and lead them home. Leave the fighting to the knights of Europe."

"We *are* the knights of Europe!" shouted Tafur, brandishing his staff with menace as he nudged his donkey closer to Handel.

Raising the Pope's document to the sun with one hand, the Hermit's fingers slowly curled, crumpling it with deliberate drama. "What we do here in the name of the cross," he declared, "is for God alone to determine, Handel, not for *you* to decide, not for *Rome* to decide!" Dropping the wadded document to the ground, he slipped a hand beneath his tunic and, retrieved a folded parchment, holding it high for all to see. "This letter I carry on my body at all times was dropped from Heaven by God himself," he proclaimed, "and it alone is the only document to which I'll adhere!" Waving it about like a banner of war, his expression grew more impenetrable than granite.

Handel had been instructed by Rome to apply reason during this meeting with the Hermit, but Handel's temperament had gone afoul even as his horse was approaching the peasant army and he caught first glimpse of the Hermit bouncing toward him from atop his donkey. Now as Handel stared at the immovable Hermit, the fire of his disdain simmered even more hotly. Dropping all pretense of diplomacy, he allowed his full scorn to surface. For him, the Hermit had long represented an intolerable threat to the Church, and he had loathed the puny evangelist of Amiens from their very first encounter years earlier.

"Oh you *wretch*, posing as a preacher," Handel began, his face reddening. "We've all heard about your infamous letter from God, but those of us with brains know it's but a ruse devised to net the ignorant of this earth. Yea, though you pretend to embrace the poor of the earth, in truth, my own dark heart is more inclined toward the dispossessed than yours. You're an opportunist, tapping into the desperation of these people like some starving leach, playing on the hopeless repetition and dreariness that poverty's forced upon their backs. Judas priest, man, you feast on their ignorance and superstitions without conscience! Have you no shame?"

"Hold your tongue," said Tafur, dismounting his donkey and moving toward Handel.

"Yes, enough of your mouth!" echoed Burrel, grinning, anticipating fisticuffs.

"Nay, Handel, I give them hope," said the Hermit calmly, though his eyes were beginning to work back and forth. "I offer them salvation. Tis not *this* life that matters, but the next."

"*Scheisse*!" Handel swore, lapsing for an angry instant into German. "Then why does the Church feed the poor and try to shelter them from the greed and rape of the nobles if not to make existence more tolerable in this life? Why then do we establish infirmaries in our monasteries for the ill and diseased of the earth, or tend to lepers? Certainly not so perverse preachers like yourself can lead the children of God to slaughter in some ill-devised race to butchery as you're doing here!"

"Hold, there!" interrupted Sansavoir, flushing at the collar. "Your words are offensive! This isn't the Hermit's crusade, but *God's* crusade. Best then that you silence yourself and climb back on your horse! Be on your way, I say!"

Ignoring Sansavoir's outburst, Handel gave the approaching Tafur a wave of warning and continued. "Aye, Hermit, but let's even for a moment lay aside the doom of these sheep you're herding toward slaughter. Let's talk instead of the havoc this ramshackle mob of yours wreaks wherever it goes. There've been reports of violence and criminality, even abductions and rape. It's also said the Jews of every town now tremble at your very approach. Yes, and your roaming horde thieves food and livestock from God-fearing folk everywhere they march, even ripping the planks from barns and villagers' homes for kindling and firewood. Christ, man, your mob's become a swarm of locusts devouring all before them, terrorizing every region they invade!"

"God's army must eat," said the Hermit, "and God provides."

"Oh, so now in the name of God you encourage hooliganism, huh?" Handel fired back, his throat filling more with spite as each word tumbled from his mouth. "God's bells, man, has Satan himself seized your miserable goddamned soul?"

Sansavoir, who considered taking God's name in vain as among the most vile of cardinal sins, second only to missing Sunday worship, flushed at Handel's words and angrily spurred his horse onto Handel who was still afoot, knocking him to the ground. "Oh, I've warned you once already about such blasphemy!" Sansavoir shouted, the veins of his neck turning to purple roots.

Meanwhile, Tafur had moved to within inches of Handel and now raised his staff. "Oh, I'll knock some sense into this fool!" he shouted.

It seemed that Handel had crumpled beneath the crush of Sansavoir's horse, but as Sansavoir leaned over to spot him, Handel appeared from nowhere, knocked Tafur aside with a jolting fist, then jumped up behind Sansavoir on his saddle, snaking one arm about his neck, and with his free hand thrusting the edge of a dagger blade across the knight's throat. "Another word from you, Sansavoir, and you'll meet your Creator, by God!" Handel rasped.

This raised the fury of Tafur who now lay on the ground with bloodied lip, as well as that of Burrel and the other knights who had been listening to the escalating exchange with growing agitation. Pulling their swords, they reined their horses forward, surrounding Handel who was by now tightly planted behind Sansavoir, his dagger poised to dissect Sansavoir's gullet on further provocation.

"Drop the knife or we'll gut you like a spring hog!" shouted Burrel.

"Oh, but death is the entrance into great light!" responded Handel. "Sansavoir and I shall meet that light together, then." As he said this, it was difficult to determine which was greater within his expression, pallor or serenity. This confounded Burrel and the other knights, creating a moment of uncertainty.

In the midst of their hesitation, the Hermit's eyes shifted wildly in their sockets and his hands began to shake uncontrollably as he ranted, "Hoo-oo! Hoo-oo!" Then, going stiff as seized by some invisible force, he stared straight ahead, his open palms facing upward as though waiting for those first precious drops of rain after an unbearable drought. After several moments more, he burst into a series of incomprehensible, guttural sounds and began to tremble there atop his donkey as caught in the grips of some horrific seizure– prompting the surrounding knights to swiftly dismount, fall to their knees, and fold their palms in prayer.

"Hold all!" Tafur motioned wildly. "A vision approaches! God speaks to Peter!"

Handel, still positioned behind Sansavoir with his blade at the knight's throat, watched, bewildered. "*What's this*?" he snorted, easing the blade from Sansavoir's neck.

"He communes with God," Sansavoir replied, as though nothing on earth could be more natural.

After interminable moments quaking atop his donkey, the Hermit issued a final shudder and fell still. Next, sitting there as though nothing whatsoever had occurred, he looked at Handel, raised his letter from God, and proclaimed, "God wills that I lead this march against the heathens. Who am I to deny God's will? He's once again directly commanded that I lead this troop of his holy faithful against Muslim wickedness, defeat their godless armies, and march straight into the gates of Jerusalem while celebrating His name!"

"Amen!" agreed Sansavoir.

"Amen!" echoed Tafur and Burrel, even louder.

"Amen!" cried the surrounding knights, gaining their feet, poking their swords to the sky.

Witnessing the exalted expressions on the faces of all surrounding him, Handel blinked slowly, as a frog blinks, trying to digest what had just unfolded; he sat there behind Sansavoir motionless and mute, as one struck by lightning.

"So then, Brother Handel, put your weapon away and return to Rome," said the Hermit, glancing over at Sansavoir. *Forgive Handel's actions*, the glance said. "And," he continued, "instruct his Holiness that no man shall interfere with this labor that God has thrust onto my shoulders, not even a pope! Remind him also that it was himself, Odo de Lagery, who called for this war against the heathens. So you see, I'm but heeding his call."

Handel, defeated, gave a half nod and slipped from Sansavoir's horse. But instead of quickly vacating the area as any other man would have done in such a situation, it seemed his feet became rooted there beside Sansavoir's mount, his mind slipping into the netherworld, chasing wild suppositions of some sort, perhaps. Indeed, that is precisely what had happened. Oblivious to the Hermit and the hostile knights surrounding him, Handel thought himself staring down an endless dark corridor with neither light nor door at its end. Within this corridor thousands of peasants and paupers silently streamed toward the blackness at the far end. Handel shuddered then, placing a palm to his forehead as if dispelling a cloud. "Oh, but God in Heaven, I beg You… show mercy on these women and children," he whispered to no one.

"Be on your way, then!" shouted Sansavoir, kicking at Handel from atop his horse.

"Yes, on your way!" repeated Tafur who had regained his feet and was now poking the tip of his staff into Handel's chest.

Jolted from his vision, Handel's eyes shifted from empty space onto the ground at his feet. Growling with disgust, he dug the heel of his boot into the dust with odd, nearly ceremonial gestures, as if crushing the approach of some horrid insect. "*This* is what awaits these peasants to whom you offer salvation by fighting the Turks, Hermit."

"Did you not hear me?" scowled Sansavoir. "Be gone!"

"Absolutely," muttered Handel, mounting his horse. "My work here is futile so I'll report such to the Vatican." Casting a final gaze at the Hermit as he turned to leave, his eyes turned to slits and he said, "KuKu Peter, may God Almighty damn you to the fires of Hell for what you've wrought on these ignorant masses, as well as for the trials you're about to place before them!" Glaring then at Sansavoir and Burrel, he added, "May God likewise punish you two despite your cloaks of piety for assisting this madman." Finally, turning to Tafur, he said, "Should you ever poke me with that stick of yours again, you sniveling lout, I'll shove it up your goddamned ass!"

Mounting, Handel kicked the flanks of his horse and made south.

## Chapter Four

### Innocenzo

Peter the Hermit's nephew, Innocenzo, was a handsome but thick-skulled young lout of twenty-two who had taken to the road with him several years earlier. The Hermit was not absolutely certain the lad was actually his true nephew, but the youngster had shown up on his own seventeenth birthday claiming blood relationship to the Hermit through an alleged illegitimate sister of which the Hermit knew nothing except through Innocenzo's tale. In a moment of faith the Hermit took him in, shortly thereafter determining it appropriate for his newfound nephew to one day take religious vows and become a monk.

Unbeknownst to the Hermit, however, Innocenzo had at the tender age of thirteen discovered the pleasures of female flesh on being seduced by a certain lusty aunt of his who happened to possess an insatiable appetite for young boys. Fortunately or unfortunately, the pleasures of that promiscuous encounter, which actually extended over a period of months, convinced Innocenzo early on that there could be no greater goal in life from that point forward than plowing the soft furrows of femininity.

It would seem odd that young Innocenzo, a womanizing huckster, would agree to an existence on the road in the shadow of a rabid moralist who was especially offended by carnal sin. Nonetheless, Innocenzo, not being especially bright intellectually but possessing a keen nose for opportunity, knew before introducing himself to Peter that the Hermit drew crowds– crowds filled to brimming with females of every age, shape, and need imaginable. Innocenzo further perceived that the Hermit was able to manipulate many of these females by the very gaze of his wild expression or the rising and falling timbre of his voice– all committed in the spirit of faith. Since these particular women could never hope to seduce or compromise the Hermit himself as he was adamantly earnest about both chastity and celibacy, the next closest thing for these desiring followers was the Hermit's new-claimed nephew, Innocenzo. Subsequently, Innocenzo soon craftily adopted the Hermit's most powerful preaching phrases, storing them on the tip of his own tongue to draw in vulnerable women in search of spiritual fulfillment or uplifting.

As was his habit then, while the Peasants' Crusade trekked toward Germany, Innocenzo kept well out of eyesight of his uncle, and well tucked between the lusty thighs of women, young and old, along the tail-end of the march. Though his pleasant appearance had generally provided decent fortune in snaring women while working the shadows of the Hermit, this new holy crusade for Innocenzo was like hitting an inexhaustible vein of gold.

On this particular night, Innocenzo had fallen into the unexpected pleasure of finding himself nestled within the confines of a hay-cart– between two bawdy, buxom young sisters of Flanders. The evening had begun with Innocenzo attempting to mimic his uncle's rhetoric on the topic of the spiritual hereafter. As there was a full moon that night casting a lustrous blue hue down across the landscape, Innocenzo imagined that this ethereal gift of nature could not help but enhance his well rehearsed sermon. Quickly, though, he discovered the two young ladies were actually about as interested in the after-life as he was. Having established this commonality, it did not take long before the three were engaged in naked frolic within the bedding of a hay-cart.

What Innocenzo did not know that night was that his uncle had sent out a search party for him. As Tafur and three of his zealous adherents went from area to area seeking Innocenzo, they eventually came near his nest. "We seek the Hermit's nephew!" growled Tafur to a peasant family huddled in a ditch alongside the road, poking his staff into the father's back. "Have you seen him about?"

"*Wh-what?*" snorted the man, looking up in half-sleep, irritated at being so rudely disturbed. Making out Tafur's branded face in the meager light, and seeing him surrounded by a coven of rough cohorts of his newly formed peasant army, the man drew back. "Y-yeah" he muttered meekly, pointing to a hay-cart just thirty feet away.

Peering hard through the light of the moon, Tafur discerned the pale form of bare white buttocks frantically rising and falling above the swell of hay spilling over the cart sideboard. Then came the soft moaning of a female, accompanied by the girlish laughter of another.

"Dammit," growled Tafur, "are you *sure* that's Innocenzo in the cart there?"

"Yes, certain," grumbled the peasant, "and he's been thumping about like a March hare all damn night. Shit, my family and I can barely sleep with all that thrashing about going on next to us!."

Motioning to his men, Tafur stalked to the cart. Reaching down with both hands, he roughly extracted the naked Innocenzo from the cart while the other men held him in place. "Your uncle wants you!" barked Tafur. "*Get your goddamned clothes on.*"

"You... you won't t-tell him about this, will you?" whispered Innocenzo, cowering as he covered his privates with one hand, groping over the sideboard for his clothing with the other. Tafur frightened him, but less so than did the moralistic wrath of his uncle. "He'll have you whip me again, Tafur– but afterwards, he'll then also look upon *you* with disfavor for bringing my fornication to light!"

"*Yeah, yeah, I know!*" Tafur snarled, recalling the last time he had dragged Innocenzo before the Hermit for promiscuity. As Innocenzo had said, after ordering Tafur to administer a brief whipping to his nephew, the Hermit next turned his fury against Tafur and the men who had discovered Innocenzo copulating with a nun from Dijon. "Now get your ass moving, dammit," Tafur ordered, disgusted. "I'm tired of wasting yet another night chasing you down as you spray your damned seed all along the road to Jerusalem while your uncle plays at keeping a blind eye, thinking he'll yet turn you into a damned monk!"

# Chapter Five

## The Vatican

Pope Urban's call to war against the Turks was directed solely at the Christian knights and men-of-arms of Western Europe, primarily from France, Germany, and Southern Italy. Unbeknownst to him, his incendiary speech so inspired Peter the Hermit that the itinerant little evangelist immediately embraced this holy crusade with filial fervor– and began raising a people's crusade of his own to fight the Turks. "The Lord beckons us east!" he preached from atop his donkey, working the back roads as well as the cities of the Clermont and Amiens regions. "No longer can we allow the Holy Land to be ruled by the godless! The trumpet beckons. It's war against the Turks, the Pope says, and war against Islam!"

By January of 1096, only two months after Pope Urban's speech, the Hermit had amassed over three thousand followers– a good number of whom had participated in the attack against the Jews of Rouen scarcely a month earlier in a violent anti-Semitic riot that saw many Jews massacred. Pope Urban, by design, had fanned the flames of intolerance to make the Muslims seem like a sub-human species; it was a strategy meant to arouse and inflame European knights against Islam, but at no time did the pope aim his strategy against Jews. Nonetheless, as could only be expected, the flames of intolerance began to spread beyond Urban's control, consuming *all* populations that were non-Christian... in particular, Jews.

Although the Hermit's growing following was filled with many different segments of the French population, the vast number of peasants with wives and children in tow gave impetus to the description of this roving horde as the 'Peasants' Crusade.' Spurred by early success in recruiting followers, the Hermit intensified his preaching, and the more passionate he became, the larger the crowds grew; the excitement he ignited caused such a stir as to generate mobs and riots that frightened village and town officials wherever he appeared. By February the Hermit's labors had tripled his original numbers of January. Toward the end of March as he finalized preparations to depart Amiens, his ranks had nearly tripled yet again and continued to swell as the Hermit began his march across France toward Germany.

Those of good sense witnessing the assembly and movement of this unruly horde quickly grew disturbed. The thousands of peasants within the Hermit's flock had spontaneously dropped their farm chores and abandoned the fields, which alarmed the land-owning nobility who abruptly found themselves lacking for laborers. Moreover, the French, German, and Southern Italian knights who had actually been tasked by Pope Urban II to carry out the war against Islam feared the Hermit's rabble would impede and interfere with military progress. Yet greater apprehension was experienced by villages, towns, and cities standing in the swath of the Hermit's approach. Like some parasitic infection spilling over the landscape, the Hermit's ill-provisioned, unmanageable mob became a blight to every region visited. Subsequently, as the creeping tentacles of their advance laid waste to everything in their path, a hue and cry arose in France as the Peasants' Crusade began to raise fear while gaining a reputation of outlawry. It was Pope Urban II himself, engineer of the Holy Crusade, who became the most alarmed by the genesis of this rogue, unsanctioned army.

The Pope and Peter the Hermit had come to know of each other many years earlier in France while Urban was a noted Benedictine monk serving as archdeacon of Rheims under his original name of Odo de Lagery. Odo had initially been struck by the unusual monk's reputation as a fiery orator, as well as by his passionate devotion to God. Moreover, the Hermit seemed to possess an uncanny ability to forecast certain events before they actually occurred. This conferred upon him an aura of mysticism that engendered cult-like devotion amongst the more vulnerable and superstitious elements of the population. Nevertheless, as Odo became more acquainted with Peter the Hermit's over-zealousness and affinity for drama, his admiration for the bizarre little evangelist waned; Odo began to view him as a fanatic. This fanaticism generally manifested itself within the accepted parameters of Church doctrine, but it also created a threat of sorts; that a dirty, barefoot monk riding on an ass might carry more sway with the poor and ignorant masses than would a high bishop presented certain dangers to the order of things.

As time progressed, Odo's extraordinary talent for logistics and political strategy resulted in his rise to Grand Prior of the Benedictine Monastery in Cluny France, then to Cardinal-Bishop of Ostia, near Rome. From there he was appointed First Counsel to Pope Gregory VII and served as de facto head of the Vatican's College of Cardinals. Peter the Hermit, meanwhile, continued to ply the roads of France and Germany preaching on his donkey.

Despite the great gulf dividing the two clerics, Peter the Hermit developed over time an undying veneration for Odo de Lagery, often mentioning Odo in his orations, or emulating him as God's finest example of Christian grace. He had even gone so far as to predict Odo's ascendency to the papacy at a time when such was considered folly. In the end, precisely as the Hermit had forecast, Odo de Lagery was handed the papal tiara, and now reigned supreme over Western Europe as Pope Urban II, Holy Father of the Roman Catholic Church.

As increasingly disturbing reports about Peter the Hermit and his Peasants' Crusade continued to stream into the Vatican, Odo became more and more distressed. Perceiving disaster of unprecedented magnitude, Odo deemed it essential to bring an immediate halt to the radical monk's misguided support of the holy war against Islam. Through papal authority and Vatican mandate, Odo began issuing communications to the Hermit demanding that he end his participation in the Holy Crusade altogether. Undeterred by such demands, such threats from Rome only served to further fuel the Hermit's ardor, especially after the contentious encounter with Jurgen Handel at the German border.

"Holiness," reported Handel upon returning to Rome, "the little nut simply refused to be cracked. Despite all reason and common sense, that thick-skulled lout's bound and determined to tramp his way on foot 1,800 miles across the entire continent to Jerusalem with that army of beggars he's assembled!"

Odo already knew Peter the Hermit was hopelessly crippled by his own obstinacy and inflexibility. Worse yet, the fanatic monk had convinced himself that he actually possessed a direct line of communication to God. Thus beleaguered and outmaneuvered by the irascible Hermit at every turn, Odo realized it was time to abandon diplomacy, threats, and even prayer as the means to disband the Peasants' Crusade. In their place he now fell to a final strategy– which was to summon his most trusted and faithful Vatican confidante for a private meeting.

"May God help us," lamented Odo as young Bishop Tristan de Saint-Germain entered the private quarters of the Lateran Palace. "Oh, what insanity that fiery little evangelist has unleashed. Now *other* renegade evangelists are following Kuku Peter's path, trying to raise peasant armies of their own! Reports are streaming down from Germany about two new fanatics named Gottschalk and Volkmar who have now also raised up thousands of peasants, the homeless, and derelicts of all brands! Gottschalk and Volkmar have begun their marches south through Germany even as I speak, and their roving hordes are targeting all Jews in their path. God in Heaven, I *never* anticipated losing such control over my own crusade against the Turks!"

Bowing, Tristan acknowledged the Pope's concerns. "Indeed, Holiness," he bowed, "I just finished reading Handel's report."

As he said this, Tristan could not help but be struck by the Pope's frustration and expression of urgency– if ever God had placed a man upon this earth who was a pillar of calm, that man was Odo de Lagery. But the flush now filling the pontiff's cheeks seemed to be undermining that rock-solid calm– causing Tristan to survey, for a moment, the great figure standing before him.

Tristan de Saint-Germain and his younger brother, Guillaume, had been sent to the Benedictine Monastery of Cluny, France as young boys during the same period Odo de Lagery was there serving as Claustral Prior. The two brothers had been turned over to the Black Monks by their mother in 1073, an unfortunate development brought on by the execution of their father by William the Bastard of Normandy for treason. As fate would have it, Odo de Lagery quickly detected that Tristan possessed frightening intelligence and perception for one so young. Taking the seven-year-old beneath his wing, Odo began harnessing Tristan's phenomenal gifts for the benefit of the Benedictine order; over time Odo maneuvered him toward a monastic future.

As Odo continued to rise within the Church, he continued to groom and elevate his young prodigy who by now was thirty years of age. Just one year earlier Odo had appointed Tristan to the prestigious positions he himself had once held before becoming pope: Bishop of Ostia and First Counsel to the Pope.

After a moment of assessing Odo's uncharacteristic demeanor, Tristan went to one knee, genuflecting, then kissed the papal ring. "Forgiveness, Father, I spoke without even issuing a greeting." Then, despite the gravity of circumstances and the worry lines etched across the Pope's face, as Tristan arose, the faint trace of a smile slipped into his expression. It was a wry look, as when one grasps some twist of dark comedy.

"So, Tristan," Odo shrugged, "you somehow find humor in this latest outbreak of madness by Kuku Peter?" Though Odo was frowning, the question carried no trace of disapproval. Odo loved the young bishop as his own blood, and their relationship was, in fact, as father to son. "But," Odo continued, "you *do*, of course, realize the implications here, n'est-ce pas?"

"Forgive me, Odo, Holiness, yes, I do," Tristan replied, his smile dissolving a measure, yet lingering. "Since my boyhood at Cluny, the Hermit has never ceased to dumfound me. Just when I conclude that he has finally reached the absolute *pinnacle* of absurdity, he then out-trumps himself by devising something even more inane, such as this so-called Peasants' Crusade. Whatever bile it is circulating within that feral brain of his, it has finally cannibalized whatever sparse sense he once possessed. Though the man cannot even wield a stick, he now believes himself to be a general?"

"Oh, but he was once a soldier," said Urban, shaking his head, "and now claims that during his brief time in the army he became well familiar with the art of war."

"Ah, but of course. He claims *many* things. Indeed, he claims *everything*."

"Yes, but now his claims are weaving a disaster of divine proportions," sighed Odo with a flap of his hand, ill feelings flaring up again in his throat. "What is he *thinking*, gathering this mob of paupers to fight the Turks? Worse yet, Sir Walter Sansavoir has joined him!"

"So states Handel's report," nodded Tristan. "There's no knight more devout in all France than Sansavoir, but they say he has been infected by the Hermit of late… and become a zealot." Shrugging, his eyes narrowed before continuing. "But I thought Sansavoir intended to travel to Jerusalem with Bishop Adhémar of Le Puy who you've appointed as leader of the crusade. Bishop Adhémar, Raymond of Toulouse, and the southern force of French knights are not due to depart France for yet another three months."

"Sansavoir *did* intend that very thing... at first," replied Odo, "but then refused to wait. August 15th was my original muster date for Adhémar's march, but it appears the noblemen and their retinues will be delayed due to difficulties finalizing property affairs, raising money, collecting troops, and such."

"How long will they be delayed?"

"No idea as yet. But now on top of Sansavoir's early departure, it's been circulating that he just recently experienced a heavenly vision. Apparently, it was revealed to him by the Seven Archangels themselves that Peter the Hermit has actually been *touched by God.*"

"Oh, the Hermit is certainly touched, but not by God," remarked Tristan. "But if the Hermit and Sansavoir refuse to wait on the main military muster, they will gain a considerable lead on both the northern and the southern forces of French knights, depending on when each departs." Crossing his arms, he fell into reflection. "Hmm, the Peasants' Crusade will be traveling slower than the military contingents due to the large number of women, children, and elderly. But still... the Hermit will arrive in Constantinople long before either of the two French armies."

"Before the Germans and Italian-Normans as well," said Odo, unable to mask concern.

"That must mean the Hermit and Sansavoir intend to… engage the Turks *alone?*" said Tristan, raising his shoulders with revelation. "But, oh," he said, his tone filling with mockery, "I am *certain* God has already advised the Hermit *directly* on the issue. Well then… unfortunately, I fear there is little else to do but pray for those poor souls he leads into battle."

"No, no... more than prayer is required," said Odo, a spot of flush appearing above his brow. "Which is why I sent for you, Tristan. The Hermit's march is taking the old northern pilgrimage route down through Germany, into Hungary and Bulgaria, then on to Constantinople. According to Handel, the peasant army has just recently crossed into Germany and will be making a long layover in Cologne."

"Oh? to what purpose?"

"So the Hermit can preach and raise yet more followers, I'm told. It has finally dawned on him, evidently, that he needs a far, far bigger war chest if he hopes to make it all the way to Jerusalem. Our German agents claim he has begun the chore of raising money and begging for alms. That, fortunately, should hold him in place for quite some time." Here Odo extended his hand toward Tristan, unrolling his fingers as if to reveal an answer to the Vatican's plight. "Which is why I am dispatching you north immediately... to intercept him before he departs Cologne. You might, at the final moment, be able to dissuade him from this twisted quest of his. But after what Handel told us about his encounter with the Hermit's bunch at the German border, I want you to take your brother and his Tuscan battalion to accompany you, along with the Danes, naturally… as a precaution."

Tristan failed to absorb this final bit about Handel, his brother's Tuscan battalion, and the Danes. The truth was, he had balked strongly at Odo's very first mention of going to Cologne to stop the Hermit, and was still recovering from the jolt of it. Staring at the floor, he shrugged, offering a troubled glance. "*Dissuade him from marching to Jerusalem*?" he asked. "Oh, but Odo, Father, you know as well as I that Kuku Peter has never been dissuaded from *anything* in his life, by *anybody*. He has gone so far, now, as to even belittle your own Vatican mandates ordering him to disband his army, thus openly defying your own papal decrees. You ask the impossible of me… unless, of course…" Pausing, he gave Odo a curious look. "Are you directing me to arrest him and drag him back to France?"

"Heavens no!" Odo replied. "Our couriers have already reported mass chaos surrounding the peasant march. Taking the Hermit by force would only lead to more bedlam– open rioting even. Remember, he also has Walter Sansavoir at his side now. Sansavoir and his men aside, Handel claims the Hermit has also surrounded himself with a band of peasant hooligans. No, no... I want no force, no violence. I simply need you to make one final effort at making the Hermit understand the logistical impossibilities of his expedition, and the dangers posed to his followers. If nothing else, appeal to Walter Sansavoir's sense of decency. Come up with anything you can think of, Tristan, because… I have simply exhausted all other options at this late point. And once the Hermit leaves Cologne, the die is cast. All hope of retraction will be forever lost!"

Considering carefully the plaintive tone carrying Odo's plea, Tristan looked at his mentor and de facto father in life. "This business with the Peasants' Crusade has rattled you to the core, has it not, Holiness?" he asked. "And yet, I did not fully recognize it at first. Well then, I apologize, Father. I failed to realize it carried such weight. I thought your main concern was the military campaign against the Turks."

"Yes, it still is, Tristan… and everything was going so well," said Odo, his voice lifting a bit. "With God's blessing, our crusade has now been joined by Bohemud of Taranto and his Italian-Normans, Stephen of Blois, Robert of Normandy, Robert of Flanders, and a host of other noblemen of note. Incredibly, even our old German enemy, Godfrey of Bouillon, has placed the scarlet cross over his tunic." He offered up a weak smile then, but the effort was soon trumped by the return of his frown. His voice dropping in a weary, disjointed manner, he murmured, "Lord knows, Tristan… the path was set and we were dead on course, but now Kuku Peter has injected himself into this war and lured all of these… *these…*"

"Innocents?" said Tristan, completing Odo's thought.

"Yes, *innocents*. I specifically raised the call only for the knights of Europe to fight the Turks and recapture Jerusalem. Against my authority, the Hermit has enlisted peasants in droves who are anything but soldiers." An unhappy foreboding arose in his throat then as he continued. "And who alive could have ever imagined that *women* and *children* would be dragged into this thing by the thousands? Handel has even reported the Peasants' Crusade's ranks to be filled with the sick and the elderly. Oh, but how in God's name could the Hermit for one minute believe people such as that can make war against... *anybody?*"

"Aye," Tristan assented, "a grand fiasco in the making." Crossing his arms, he slipped into an uncomfortable silence, then asked, "What of the original mission you assigned to me, Father? I was to join Bishop Adhémar and Raymond of Toulouse as they march through here en route to the southern tip of Italy. We were to sail together across the Adriatic for the final muster in

Constantinople before attacking the Turks. Am I, then, no longer to serve as Direct Papal Liaison and First Expeditionary Scribe? And what of my brother, Guillaume? Even now he is mobilizing the Tuscan knights under the banner of Aunt Mathilda Medici of Tuscany. He *also* was to join Bishop Adhémar and Raymond of Toulouse as they march through Italy."

Urban raised a hand to his brow, as confused, slipping into a moment of disquiet while taking on that worn appearance of a man beyond his years. "Yes, yes…" he muttered, dropping for an instant into the appearance of– senility. Rolling several possibilities about in his head, his thoughts managed to coalesce. "Tristan," he said, "you and Guillaume can still, if fortune favors, retain your original mission as hoped. The French knights have yet to even assemble and will not be arriving in Italy until September, maybe October." Stepping back to calculate, he nodded, smiling weakly. "Yes, after your business with the Hermit in Germany, you and Guillaume would easily have time to return to Italy... and meet Bishop Adhémar as originally planned."

Tristan tried to return the smile, but it formed poorly on his lips, dissolving. Knowing Odo as he did, Tristan suspected there was more to this improbable mission to Cologne than had yet been exposed; whenever devising a strategy, it was always Odo's practice to create a back-up plan, one anchored with multiple alternatives to counteract the eventuality of the unexpected. Acutely aware of this, Tristan looked at him squarely. "And if I should *fail* to turn the Hermit back from Cologne, Odo," he asked, "what is it that you will require?"

Odo's eyes took on a nearly mournful appearance as he absorbed the question. He wished to sweep it aside, but moving closer, placed himself in front of Tristan. As his hand slipped to Tristan's shoulder and his gaze dropped directly into Tristan's eyes, however, Odo saw himself in miniature within the reflection staring back at him. *Oh,* he thought, *but how well my Tristan knows me.*

Diverting his eyes so as to block his own reflection, Odo replied, "If the Hermit refuses to turn back, Tristan... I will need you and Guillaume, along with his Tuscan knights, to accompany the Hermit and his mob overland. All the way to Constantinople." As he revealed this, his eyes gazed into space; just as he had no wish to see himself reflected in his young bishop's eyes, nor did he wish to witness the reaction on Tristan's face. "Once there in Constantinople," he continued carefully, "you *must* convince the Hermit to await our main crusader force– which should only be a month or so, *hopefully*. Indeed, it is absolutely *critical* that he not invade Turkish territory until the real crusader armies arrive!"

When one has spent every waking moment of the past year preparing for something, and it unexpectedly and recklessly comes undone, an internal collapse occurs, knocking one off kilter only to reel into a bramble of confusion. This is precisely what was occurring now within Tristan, and his mind began to race about, vexed, for possibilities. Finally, he found his tongue. "Constantinople is... over a *thousand* miles overland from Cologne, Father," he stammered. "Am I hearing you correctly? You wish for me and Guillaume to follow Kuku Peter's horde across the entire continent to– Byzantium?"

His cheeks coloring, Odo fell still. After a time, he finally shook his head yes. "There is *another* fear," he said. "These reports I am receiving describe the Peasants' Crusade as a growing blight wherever they march. Being ill-provisioned and poor, they are causing havoc wherever they go... thieving, pillaging. Then, too, there is an element within their midst that has been seeking out Jews– setting fires, assaulting and terrorizing. Should the Hermit refuse to turn back from Cologne, yes, I then need you to shadow his march– keep his crowd from running *completely* amok. The Jews aside, it will do us no good for the Peasants' Crusade to alienate our own Christian flock from our holy crusade before even arriving in Byzantium.'

Now it was Tristan who fell still. His eyes narrowing, his thoughts fell back on Handel's report describing the his encounter at the German border with the Hermit and Walter Sansavoir. "But Holiness," he said, treading lightly, "Peter's peasant horde now exceeds thirty thousand, with more joining each day. There is no way that me, Guillaume, and 600 Tuscan knights could control them, especially with Walter Sansavoir's accompanying army at their side. Worse yet, even if the Hermit somehow actually makes it to Constantinople with his rag-tag bunch... *what then?* Guillaume and I will never be able to keep him from leading his paupers immediately to war should he refuse to wait on your main armies. And zealot that he is, I dare wager he has no such intention of waiting."

Odo rubbed at his forehead, grasping for the best way to reply although he had already anticipated the eventuality of this very question. Still, having to actually communicate the solution to the individual he was burdening it with was more difficult than expected. "If the Hermit refuses yet again to listen to reason in Constantinople," Odo said, "then possibly… *hopefully*... Emperor Alexius will intervene. Yes, he could provide troops to help you hold the Peasants' Crusade back." But even as he said this, the words seemed to drive the color from Odo's cheeks, only augmenting the uncertainty of future developments.

Tristan offered a deferential tilt of the head, but pressed on. Like Odo, Tristan also examined every possible angle of a future strategy. It was, after all, Odo himself who had cultivated this skill within his young liege as a boy. "But," insisted Tristan, "if the Emperor should choose not to intervene... what *then* is your final command, Father?"

This, ultimately, was the question Odo neither wished to answer, nor to even face. "W-e-l-l," he said with cautious deliberation, closing his eyes, "I pray things will not come to that. But if they should, Walter Sansavoir has amassed certain military muscle during the march…" Here, Odo paused, eyes still closed, and shook his head. "Not nearly enough to protect the flock of innocents following the Hermit, mind you… but there will be other Christian military confederations arriving early in Constantinople also. If the Hermit's rabble army attacks the Turks prematurely, the combined military force of Sansavoir, the independent confederations, and Guillaume's Tuscan knights might give the peasants a– *fighting chance*... at least until Bishop Adhémar and the main crusader armies arrive."

So stunned by these words that he found himself grappling for a reply, Tristan was struck silent, trying to fathom the future bedlam of the scenario Odo had just described.

"Handel will be accompanying you," continued Odo, opening his eyes finally though they seemed vacant now. "Although he despises the Hermit, Jurgen Handel is a good ally in a tussle. As you well know, the man possesses many skills that may prove useful in narrow straights."

Odo then shook his head with distress, placing a trembling finger to his forehead. Tristan, despite still reeling from his own unanticipated reversal of fortune, was touched by this action; he had never once during childhood, nor throughout the most trying of circumstances since, ever seen Odo so consumed with woe and uncertainty. Indeed, of all men on this earth, Odo de Lagery was made of granite, fearing no person nor any challenge standing before him.

What Tristan failed to comprehend, however, was the actual depth of Odo's predicament. Tristan understood Odo's apprehension about potential ravages committed by Kuku Peter's army. He also understood Odo's heartfelt concerns about the women, the children, the elderly and diseased, and the helpless constituting much of that ill-devised army. What Tristan did not grasp at the moment, however, was the existence of a more private, heartfelt issue looming over Odo's head– and that was his angst over the safety and well-being of Tristan himself.

Odo, as lifelong mentor and father-figure, well realized Tristan's faithful and passionate service in preaching the Holy Crusade throughout Italy and France. Moreover, he knew that Tristan's entire focus of late had been preparing for the great march with Bishop Adhémar of Le Puy and the French army. But when it is the father who becomes the very root of shattered aspirations to the son, the weight is nearly impossible to bear. Thus, on this particular day, Odo was dissolving from within; his heart was bursting because of his own decision to dispatch Tristan after Peter the Hermit.

Setting his regrets for Tristan aside, Odo returned to the peasants. "Oh, these misguided fools following the Hermit," he muttered, his barely audible voice breaking the silence that had descended across the room. "Though carrying God in their hearts and believing themselves to be following my directive to free Jerusalem, they have set themselves on a path of extinction. Their imminent misfortune shall forever haunt my conscience, Tristan, should they actually make it beyond Constantinople and into the realm of the Seljuk Empire. Such a thing would poison my soul for the remainder of my years, following me even to the Day of Judgment! Tristan, you *must* shelter them at any cost… especially the women and children." He fell silent then, burying his face in his hands, slowly rocking his head and shoulders back and forth as when one surrenders hope.

Tristan stood there quietly, faithfully awaiting further instructions– but Odo said nothing more. "So be it, then, Father,"

Tristan acknowledged, determining that additional discussion would serve little purpose. "I will begin preparations immediately," he continued, "and will notify Guillaume of the changes to our plans upon my arrival in Tuscany." Bowing dutifully, he turned to leave, feeling the entire weight of Odo de Lagery's guilt beating at his own brow. *Indeed,* he thought, *Odo is correct... faithful as the Hermit's thousands may be, without military support they shall be doomed the moment they encounter the Turkish onslaught.*

"Oh," called Odo as Tristan reached the door, "there is one other thing."

"Yes, Father?" Tristan said, turning.

"Though I have informed you of this mission only today, it has been rolling about in my thoughts since the Hermit first departed the city of Amiens in France. Thus, thinking ahead, and due to the uncertainty and danger now facing you, I have sent for your mother in France."

"*My mother?*" replied Tristan, his shoulders slipping as his voice dropped low. His eleven year separation from her at age seven had carved a gaping hole in his heart as a boy, leading to a vaporous but pervasive loneliness that even to this day came after him in moments of solitude, or restive sleep. He had worshipped his mother, Asta of the Danes, as a boy, and loved her still to the ends of the earth despite now only seeing her on rare occasions; she had years ago sequestered herself behind the restrictive convent walls of Marcigny-sur-Loire.

"Yes," Odo nodded, gathering a smile in hopes that this last news would lift Tristan's spirits. "I thought you might wish to see her should things unravel, forcing you... into a long absence and a march to Byzantium. She will be waiting for you in Canossa where you will join Guillaume on the way north to Cologne."

# Chapter Six

## A Private Prayer

After his meeting with Odo, Tristan left the Vatican complex, making his way down a series of back streets to locate Jurgen Handel who maintained a secret residence along the Tiber River. As he walked, he happened to notice the form of a rather short individual trailing behind him. He first thought it to be a young boy due to the individual's tiny stature, but in slipping a furtive glance backwards, he discerned that it was a man. Though the individual's face was half concealed by a slouchy hat of some unfamiliar fashion, Tristan saw that the little fellow possessed a pointy beard.

Rolling several possibilities about in his head, Tristan at first suspected the odd-looking fellow was shadowing him, but dismissed the suspicion as over-thinking. Besides, he reasoned, the foot traffic was always heavy along the riverfront with so many people frequenting the popular area, and many people took the same long path as Tristan was now taking.

Nonetheless, after making his third turn down winding streets, Tristan noticed the figure was still trailing him. This caused Tristan to stop, with the intention of confronting him, but as Tristan spun around, the small man casually turned down another street and soon disappeared. Thinking this too happenstance, Tristan switched to the other side of the street and concealed himself, thinking that if this individual was indeed following him, he would soon reappear. After several minutes of waiting, the man did not resurface– and Tristan thought nothing more of it.

Continuing to seek landmarks he had been given to locate Handel's residence, Tristan was unable to orient himself to the exact location of Handel's hidden dwelling. After wandering about for nearly half an hour, he then happened across an ancient cathedral tucked into the cul-de-sac of a hidden side street. The small cathedral had been fashioned of crude stone in the early Romanesque style, but oddly, Tristan had never even known of its existence. Curious, he examined it for a short while, trying to guess its origin. His feet, tired from wandering about so aimlessly, and his mind spilling with uncustomary confusion after his meeting at the Vatican, Tristan entered the old church.

*I'll say a prayer for Odo*, he thought. *I've never seen him in such a state of distress. Yes, and I'll reflect a moment over my own sudden turn of events involving the Hermit and Germany.*

Tristan loved Odo de Lagery more than any man on earth, trusting him beyond reproach. Nevertheless, his mentor and boyhood savior now seemed surprisingly unanchored on the issue of the Peasants' Crusade– like some ship-wrecked sailor clinging to a spar in a raging sea. Yet, Tristan found it difficult to believe that the fate of the Hermit's peasants seemed to now outweigh Odo's focus on Christendom's great military campaign against Islam. It was not that Tristan failed to share Odo's concern about the inevitable victimization of these peasants, but recapturing Jerusalem from the Turks had been Tristan's sole focus for over a full year now, beginning with the secret trip he and Handel had taken to Constantinople; Odo had sent the two East to listen to and evaluate the pleas of Emperor Alexius Comnenus who was seeking military assistance against long-standing Turkish incursions into the Byzantine Empire.

Dipping his finger into the font of holy water as he entered the vacant, dimly lit church, Tristan remarked how cold the water felt– as though he was unwelcome here in this place of worship despite his high position in the Church. He admonished himself, then, for thinking such. Strange, disconnected thoughts had been intruding upon him since birth, for some reason, and this trait was a peculiar foible of his that he despised, yet could not suppress. Others did not endure such an affliction, it seemed, and Tristan envied them their simplicity. Acknowledging this weakness of his, he still could not help also noticing the echo of his own footsteps as he made his way down the center knave– hollow, foreboding, as warning him of some ill future occurrence. Going to his knees after entering the first pew, his eyes next fell across the life-sized crucifix hanging behind the altar. It looked frighteningly real, and

Tristan imagined for a moment that the eyes of the carved Jesus moved, dropping a measure to gaze down at him.

*I must stop over-imagining,* thought Tristan, shivering the tiniest bit. *Yet, that face there on the cross, so artfully chiseled into an eternal mask of agony and sorrow by some long forgotten craftsman…it is peering down at me in a most direct and piteous fashion.*

Solitude has a peculiar effect on men; solitude in a silent, abandoned place of worship magnifies that effect, forcing the mind to wander into regions long forsaken. Accordingly, the devastating isolation of the ancient stone cathedral began to worm its way into the repressed regions of Tristan's conscience, poking its head into corners and crannies long abandoned. His beloved mother, Asta, came to mind. Now stowed away behind the walls of a French convent resolving to serve the remainder of her life as a Benedictine nun, she was but forty-three years of age– but even beneath the concealing folds of her nun's tunic, scapular, wimple and cowl, her beauty still radiated with undeniable grace and luster. Nonetheless, her promising youth had been twisted by the perversity and ambitions of men's designs, which finally drove her to seek refuge behind the cloistered walls of sanctuary where no man could enter. Although Asta had willingly sought this refuge, just as he himself had voluntarily taken his Benedictine vows, Tristan still felt that there was something sad about the course she had chosen. Still, he was beyond pleased at the prospect of soon reuniting with her in Canossa.

His mind next wandered back to Saint Germain-en-Laye, the place of his and Guillaume's birth. *Oh,* he thought, *those early years were peaceful, but then how rapidly came the descent of our idyllic existence there with mother and the Danes. Had things not turned so black, which direction would my life and Guillaume's have taken had we not been sent to the monastery?*

The vision of Saint Germain-en-Laye eventually faded, and despite his attempts at beginning prayer, one face after another continued to intrude, reeling one after another like water rolling over the steps of mill, forcing the wheel into ceaseless motion. Tristan envisioned Odo de Lagery as a younger man, and this vision was followed by faces of teacher-monks at Cluny. Tristan was then struck by images of Canossa and King Heinrich's penitent suffering there in the snow and ice of Countess Mathilda

Medici's mountain fortress. Next, memories of Duke Robert Guiscard's bloody rape of Rome by his Norman and Saracen troops surfaced, as did Tristan's momentous flight with Pope Gregory from the Vatican in the midst of rioting anti-Gregorian mobs. Visions of his own illicit operations as a former member of the Benedictine Underground next began to intrude– traveling in disguise, plying information from secret sources... the assassination with Jurgen Handel of a Greek Orthodox nun and the murder of a Byzantine nobleman at the Inn of the Sparrow.

Then, in a moment of epiphany, a single face emerged from the fog of his memory, erasing all others. It was the face of a beautiful young Romani woman named Mala whom he had first met along the road to the Cluny monastery when he was but seven years of age, and she was ten. The Danes, members of his mother's personal guard, were taking Tristan and his brother to the Black Monks, and along the path rescued Mala's Romani troupe of gypsies from Norse raiders. Mala's people were migrating from Spain into northern France to escape the Moorish invasions of the Iberian Peninsula. He hadn't realized it back then, but that night when he and Mala first gazed upon each other, fate had thrown two children together into a ceaseless cycle of recurring separation and reunion over the years to come.

Though they were but children at the time, Mala had been profoundly impacted, drawn in by his sensitivity and phenomenal intelligence, prompting her to affectionately dub him 'smart boy." Whenever she called him that, he would blush timidly, though he knew she was not mocking him, but adoring him. He adored her also, though he did not entirely grasp the reason, other than she was beautiful. Odd as their young relationship was, it was providential... they had already fallen in love, it seems, though too young even to comprehend what love was. But then came Tristan's 'miracle' on the Mount of Monte Cassino... after which Tristan took the black robe, embracing its accompanying vows of piety, chastity, and celibacy.

She had then begged him on many occasions to abandon the Benedictine order, and had even borne him a son, although the infant died within days of entering life. This was an excruciating memory of ten years gone by, and because of it Tristan had determined that the ordeal of this illegitimate and deceased child was God's judgment against him for violating his sacred vows.

Indeed, Tristan had bitten into the forbidden apple of carnal knowledge, and God's vengeful hammer had been merciless to him, merciless to Mala, and merciless to the infant.

Rolling prayer beads between his fingers, he tried to push Mala's face from his mind, but her eyes refused to dissipate, causing him to reach into a hidden pocket of his vestments to fish about for a moment. Soon his fingers extracted a small silver ring. It was crudely fashioned of a less than mediocre grade of Moorish silver, but it was the only possession in life Tristan had retained from boyhood. Mala had given it to him that first night along the Seine River as a gesture of gratitude for her and her people being saved by the Danes. Although he was but seven at the time, Tristan had cherished and carried the ring with him nearly every day of his existence since receiving it. Now rolling it about in his palm, a flood of memories began to consume him… and he suddenly ached to see Mala again.

*What could she be doing this very moment while I kneel here thinking about her,* he asked himself. *What lies deep within her heart, now?*

He allowed himself to dwell on the questions despite knowing that any future together had always been, and was still now, impossible. It was this ugly realization that finally dispelled Mala's image and prodded Tristan to begin his prayer. The prayer he quietly communicated, however, did not end as intended. The first words he uttered were, "Lord, give me strength as I move forward with the Holy Father's new mission, which is fraught with impossibilities and risk." A moment later his words inexplicably veered, and he found himself whispering, "Heavenly Father, forgive me for my past trespasses against You, against my earthly father in this life, Odo de Lagery, and against the Benedictine Order of Black Monks. Above all, forgive me for the terrible suffering I caused Mala, who has possessed my heart since my boyhood. I pray also that the son Mala and I conceived, and she brought into this world for such a short time, now sits at your side. He did not deserve such an unfortunate beginning as I thrust onto him. Most of all, forgive me for this love I still carry for Mala. It confuses me, and I cannot escape it despite daily prayer, or even despite having set her aside. Therefore, I pray that you protect me from my own weak heart. Amen."

He stood then, lost in thought– until the furtive rustle of fabric toward the rear of the church pricked his ears. Turning, Tristan caught movement and the vanishing slip of some slight shadow. In that tiny instant the shadow froze, and Tristan caught a glimpse of a slouchy hat just before the figure bolted, fleeing out the door.

"Who are you!" Tristan shouted, straining to make out details through the obscurity of the dimly lit cathedral. "*Why are you following me!?*"

But there came no reply. The figure was gone.

# Chapter Seven

## King of the Beggars

Within the human race there are those who, upon birth, deviate from the general mass of humanity by evolving into... predators. With cold calculation, weighing circumstance and the weakness of those standing about, these particular humans perceive and treat others only as prey. It is a simple equation really, predator status being achieved through only one of two fashions. The first is through power, whether inherited or seized, which enables one to establish the rules by which others must live. Power enables one to control and manipulate circumstances in such a manner that others can be handily exploited to advantage. By creating, administering, and enforcing self-serving laws, expectations, and norms, the powerful fill their pockets while greedily perpetuating the authority of their own position to the detriment of others.

The other means of achieving predator status is cultivated by and springs from those who are unafraid to violate the rules invoked by that first pack of predators, the powerful. More precisely, this next species of human predator comes from the dark underground of criminality. While most individuals fearfully follow the expectations and rules enforced by the power-controlling hierarchy of a society, criminals shove aside such fear. Thus they easily victimize their prey through surprise, operating in the shadows while boldly violating the norms. In truth, the power-possessing predators are far, far more deadly and destructive than the lowly criminal; the infection they spread is vastly more widespread and everlasting. Yet, in a human foible of puzzling dimension, it is the criminal that is more feared by the general population. The horseless knight who had adopted the name Tafur and scorched a fiery crucifix brand to his forehead was a perfect example of this paradox. Having long ago been stripped of his own fear of the powerful through their own abuse and cruelty, he had evolved from an innocent peasant boy into a violent and hardened outlaw. Now, finding himself within Peter the Hermit's gathering horde, Tafur quickly perceived that those joining the Peasants' Crusade were, for one reason or another, easily manipulated– and even more easily incited. Watching how Peter the Hermit maneuvered, and witnessing the astonishing effect of his machinations, Tafur reasoned that he, too, might be able to amass a following of his own from within the Hermit's very flock. Such a trick would require guile and cunning, of course; to undermine the Hermit too early in the game simply would not succeed as the Hermit yet held entirely too much sway over his masses. Still, by attaining that first crumb of authority, Tafur determined that he could at least *begin* mining the fields of exploitation. So it was that after taking the task of turning simple peasants into warriors from the shoulders of the Hermit, Tafur began in earnest to collect his own core of devoted followers.

"I seek courageous men dedicated to God to join my ranks!" he bellowed day after day, fishing the peasant mobs. Appealing simultaneously to a man's vanity as well as his spiritualism proved an effective pull, especially amongst the more ignorant, or those of weak character; within the first two weeks of departing Amiens, Tafur had recruited nearly a thousand fellow 'Tafurs.' Thus, proclaiming himself 'King of the Beggars' and naming his recruits 'Tafurs' in his own honor, he labored tirelessly at pulling others into his net. By the time the Peasants' Crusade crossed into Germany and was making its way into Cologne, Tafur had more than doubled his initial numbers.

To his satisfaction, Tafur discovered that the peasant warriors he was enlisting, without exception, shared his own hatred of the nobility. Also like Tafur, regardless of the fact these men were joining Pope Urban's holy crusade, it seemed they distrusted the higher echelons of the clergy; this explained why so many of their grain chose to embrace a monk like Peter the Hermit rather than highly placed bishops or archbishops. There was yet a third element of kinship shared by Tafur and his following– a nagging hunger for violence to sate long dormant leanings of resentment, fury and intolerance.

As pertains to Tafur himself, in addition to his venom for the nobility and the high clergy, he had also begun to hate Jews at a young age, beginning with the Jewish treasurer of a certain Lord Cartier who was master of the territory in which Tafur was born. An early incident involving this particular Jewish treasurer was actually the catalyst of Tafur's flight from southern France, which caused him to be in the Amiens area of France when he first encountered Peter the Hermit. Tafur had slipped north to Paris, and it was there that he heard rumblings amongst the lower classes that there would be an attack on the Jews of Rouen that December, and had traveled there to Normandy to take part in it. After satisfying his long simmering bigotry during a shameful week of anti-Semitic rioting, he happened across Peter the Hermit preaching outside Rouen. Learning from Peter that Pope Urban had declared a holy war against the Turks, it then for some reason became Tafur's objective in life to wreak violence against Muslims, whom he imagined in his tiny brain were another heathen race not dissimilar to Jews. Of course, he had never once in his lifetime even encountered a Muslim, nor did he know the first thing about Islam itself. No matter, he decided, they were *heathens*.

Now, as the Peasants' Crusade entered Cologne, Tafur decided it was time for him to begin doing a bit of preaching himself. "There's a large population of Jews in Cologne," he informed his forehead-branded zealots. "They refute Christianity, which is an abominable sin against God as well as an affront to each and every one of us now going to risk our own lives in this war against Islam. Let *us*, then, become the instruments of God… and begin cleansing the road to Jerusalem!"

## Chapter Eight

### Tafur's Secret

Tafur, born of humble roots within the Duclos peasant clan of Lyon in southeastern France, had begun to despise the nobility early in life. Blessed with the sharp wits of his mother, Paulette, he perceived his surroundings with unusual clarity, even as a boy. Given the name of Lucien at birth, his family was stuck in that bottomless precipice of hopelessness and poverty common to all peasants of that era in Western Europe. The injustice of it all became evident to young Lucien by the time he was but six or seven years old, when a slow, simmering resentment against the entitlement and abuses of the aristocracy began to take root in his head. Then, at the age of nine, this resentment turned into unadulterated hatred. It was at this time that a certain Lord Cartier incidentally took notice of a large-breasted, somewhat attractive peasant wench living within the midst of the mongrel serfs scraping a living upon his feudal estate. That peasant woman was Lucien's own mother, Paulette Duclos.

Lord Cartier showed up unexpectedly one afternoon at the family's shanty, claiming he was there to bring Lucien's father several bottles of special wine made from the Cartier vineyards. "Ah, Monsieur Duclos," crowed Cartier, throwing a leg over his saddle to dismount, "a small gift to show my appreciation for your hard work in my fields."

Lucien's father, Henri Duclos, had little idea that Lord Cartier even knew who he was, as Cartier had never spoken to him before nor even acknowledged him. Being both naive and dimwitted, Henri broke into movement, helping Lord Cartier from his horse. "Certainly, my Lord," he said, his heart bursting with newfound honor, his face beaming in a toothless grin. "Come have a seat at our little table beneath the apple tree just there and I'll share the first bottle with you immediately… uh, if you have the time, sir?"

This struck Lucien, who was standing nearby watching, as odd. His father had never had a decent thing to say about *any* nobleman, and here he was inviting the most arrogant of the entire region to share his table.

"Oh, sure, sure, I've plenty of time," clucked Cartier, a middle-aged man of fifty, paunchy and balding. He took a seat then beneath the apple tree and gazed about, as looking for someone. "And say there, Duclos," he said after a while, "why don't you invite your missus to have a swig of this fine product with us, huh?"

"Yes sir, a splendid idea," replied Henri. "She's just in the shack there. I'll fetch her."

As his father disappeared into the shanty, Lucien stepped closer to Lord Cartier, having rarely seen such fine garments so close up. Compared to the rags he and his family wore, Cartier's apparel hung stiff and proper, giving him the air of a king.

"Hey there, boy," said Cartier gruffly, "what the hell are you looking at?"

"Y-your trousers, sir… and your jacket. I was just–"

"Dammit, it's impolite to stare, you little piker. Don't they teach you little bastards any manners out here? Now get along! Scat!"

Mortified, Lucien tucked tail and slipped behind the woodpile, out of view. Moments later he heard his parents, and peeked over the stack of wood as they settled in at the table across from Lord Cartier.

Cartier quickly changed mood, breaking into jovial jabber while Paulette remained demure, and stone still. Henri commented only from time to time, listening mainly, and on occasion cackling with affective laughter at Cartier's stilted jokes. After several goblets of wine, Henri's tongue finally loosened and he began to blather insipidly about his labors in the fields and his knowledge of livestock.

Maintaining his position behind the woodpile, Lucien watched and listened. Although Lord Cartier was directing his words at Henri, his eyes never left Paulette– and there was a look in his eyes that Lucien had only seen amongst the hungry... as they gazed longingly at the feasting fare of the nobility.

Cartier's own aristocratic wife, it seemed, was a pasty woman of bony frame. For Bernard Cartier, then, the voluptuous peasant woman sitting across from him caused an immediate stir within his breeches. He had first spotted her pendulous breasts spilling from her tunic as she was leaned over picking herbs one day, and was even further aroused by her firm rump. After making several inquiries, Cartier learned that her name was Paulette and that she had been married off to the older Henri Duclos after the sudden death of her peasant parents of the pox. She was but thirteen at the time and had no other means of survival. Still, being raised a faithful Catholic by her pious parents, she remained faithful to Henri and bore him a son whom she adored above all else in life. Lucien returned this love, valuing his mother as his only blessing in life.

As Lucien continued to watch, his father's face grew red with wine as he clumsily opened a second bottle, then yet a third. Cartier, in the meanwhile, had moved next to Paulette and was now ignoring Henri's ceaseless babbling about the manor's herd of oxen. Soon Cartier was touching Paulette on the shoulders and neck, pulling her near, nearly dragging her onto his lap. Paulette politely rebuffed these advances, to Cartier's irritation and Henri's drunken ignorance, and ended by pushing Cartier away, standing, and leaving the table.

Irate, Cartier jumped to his feet and grabbed her. Thrusting a hand into the top of her blouse, he groped a breast, plying it forcefully, squeezing her nipple so hard she cried out in agony. "Ha, shut up you little bitch!" laughed Cartier, dragging her toward the shanty. "You know what I want, and I know what *you* want! Ya, you'll even be wailing for more once I start poking your little honey-hole!"

Furious, seeing his mother's terror, Lucien charged from the woodpile, taking a run at Cartier's legs in hopes of tackling him so his mother might escape. The effort failed, and Cartier swung about with the back of his hand, knocking the nine-year-old to the ground with a broken nose.

Instead of fleeing Cartier, Paulette ran to Lucien. "Oh, Lucien!" she cried" "Oh, my poor boy!"

Pushing her aside, Lucien jumped to his feet to go after Cartier again, but Cartier was on him before Lucien could steady himself. A wink later Cartier delivered a swift kick to the boy's abdomen, followed by a boot to the head. The last thing Lucien remembered was the cries of his mother being dragged into the shanty and the voice of his drunken father muttering, "*Wha-what's th-this*?"

Thus began Cartier's regular visits to the Duclos shanty. Thinking it his right, Cartier would show up unannounced at different times of the month to ply Paulette's flesh. Whenever Cartier arrived, Henri would bow, then take his son by the hand and walk away while Cartier rutted about inside the shanty, forcing Paulette to perform one bestial act after another. From the distance, father and son could not help but hear Paulette's shame-filled pleading.

This went on year after year, but one day shortly after Lucien turned fourteen, Lord Cartier showed up with another man as the family was splitting wood outside the shanty.

"This is Simon, my treasurer," declared Cartier to Lucien's father. "He's a Jew. Still, he's done an especially good job for me this year, earning me unexpected returns… so I'm rewarding him today with your wife's crack." Cartier grinned then, and motioned to Simon. An instant later the two men grabbed Paulette and began dragging her inside the shanty.

As father and son listened to her struggling and heard the two men's lurid abuse of her from the woodpile, Lucien fumed. "Father, are you going to do *nothing?!* Bad enough that Cartier himself shames mother, but now a *goddamned Jew*?"

"Watch your mouth, boy!" retorted Henri, shaking his head. "And just what the shit do expect me to do here, huh? Yeah, you little bastard, you'd be quite happy to see me in an early grave, wouldn't you?" Then his father stormed off, just far enough so as not to have to hear his wife's shrill objections emanating from the shanty.

Groaning with disgust, Lucien was of the mind to take a plug of firewood and burst into the shack, catching Cartier and the Jew by surprise– but the poor and helpless are impotent against the privileged. Hot tears filling his eyes, Lucien stalked into the forest.

A week later, to Lucien's dismay, Cartier's treasurer showed up by himself, brazenly insisting that Paulette again service his lust. "Ah, your round ass was so pleasing to me last week during our little tryst with Lord Cartier, Paulette," snickered Simon, "that I've come back alone to relieve my hunger and poke both of your holes a while!" He then twirled the waxed tips of his mustache and added, "And if you find this objectionable, I'm certain Lord Cartier will take it out on your husband's back... or your son's!"

Luciens's mother, who had always abhorred the visits of Cartier, protested vehemently at Simon's demand which she found even more offensive. Yet, fearing violent consequences for Lucien, she followed Simon into the shanty, bared herself, stooped over the table, and spread her legs as Simon commanded.

Enraged, Lucien listened from outside for a few moments, his temples pulsing so hot and fast he could scarcely breath. Then, in one of those moments of wild desperation that seizes the life-long abused, he gathered his shepherd's staff and stormed inside the shanty. Simon the Jew, so lost in his frantic rutting of Paulette from behind, neither saw nor heard Lucien's approach. Seconds later the treasurer lay dead on the floor, his skull bashed to raw meat by the hands of an adolescent son gone berserk.

"*Oh my God!*" screamed Paulette, covering her nakedness "*What have you done?* "Lucien! You must flee! *Run, son*, and never come back or Cartier will have you hanged!"

By then shocked by his own actions, and terrified of the gallows, Lucien embraced his mother, unable to imagine life without her. "N-no, Mama! I won't leave you here!" he shouted.

Pushing him away, her eyes filling with tears, she dragged him to the door and pointed to the forest. "*Lucien, you must! Run, boy, save yourself!*"

Heartbroken, confused, Lucien understood. Without saying a word to his father who had heard the commotion and was now approaching the shack, Lucien exchanged a brief look with him, then dashed into the cover of the trees. Behind him he heard the wailing of his mother and the cursing of his father.

He slept that night, chilled, beneath the cover of a massive oak. Though his fury had quelled, his resentment of Cartier grew more bitter than ever, as did his seething hatred of Simon the Jew. In his restive sleep, this poison brewed even more intensely, and when he awoke that next morning, Lucien's scorn of the two men had turned to venom against all nobles, and all Jews.

Lucien wandered about for three more days in the forest, festering and fuming until, overcome by hunger and despair, his adolescent confusion led him into Lyon to seek solace and counsel from Archbishop Duchamps, the highly devout high cleric of the city. Duchamps was respected by the wealthy and beloved by the poor. He preached hope to all, promising that Heaven awaited those who performed God's will on earth.

Slipping into Lyon under cover of darkness, Lucien meekly rapped on the back door of Duchamp's rectory. "So now, what's this?" the archbishop asked, surprised at receiving a visitor so late in the evening.

"I'm Lucien Duclos," snuffled Lucien, the image of defeat. "Do you remember me?"

"Yes, yes, of course, I remember you well, lad… come in, come in," replied Duchamps, ushering him inside.

In truth, Duchamps barely remembered the boy. What he did remember was the boy's mother, Paulette. Indeed, he had wondered more than a few times what it might be like to nuzzle his face between her full breasts, or plant himself between her thighs.

"I've s-sinned," muttered Lucien, warm in the shelter of the archbishop, but tumbling into tears. "I've killed a man!"

"*What?*" cried Duchamps.

"Y-yes," wept Lucien. "He was just a Jew, but still, I know the commandments say–"

"A *Jew*?" shrugged Duchamps, relaxing a measure. "Well then, lad, you must have had a reason, huh?"

Lucien spent the next half hour reciting his story to Duchamps, who intermittently nodded with empathy while offering blessings. Shaking his head, he said, "You mean to tell me Lord Cartier has been violating your mother all these years? And then invited a *Jew* to do the same? Oh, such horror! Though you shouldn't have killed that filthy Jew, lad, I'll hide you for a time until we sort out what to do next."

"Thank you," said Lucien, voraciously devouring food set before him by the archbishop's servants.

"Yes, bless you, lad, for the suffering you've endured these years," said Duchamps, making the sign of the cross, "as well as that of your poor mother." He then made a gesture to one of his servants, a little man named Bourgeois. "Bourgeois," he said in a low voice, "get this boy some more potage." Then, leaning into Bourgeois' ear, he said something else that Lucien did not hear, as he was busy stuffing bread down his gullet.

The next morning Lucien wandered into the bishop's library, drawn by the small collection of books; the only book he had ever seen before was at the Lyon cathedral during Sunday mass. Lucien could not read, of course, but he began browsing through illustrations within Bishop Duchamps' Bible, and lost himself there until hearing a ruckus outside. Slipping to a window, he peered between the curtains. To his unbridled shock, he saw the arrival of a coach accompanied by a troop of soldiers. He next saw Lord Cartier step from the coach along with Archbishop Duchamps who was urgently pointing at the house. Unbeknownst to Lucien, Lord Cartier was a huge financial contributor to the archdiocese of Lyon– a gesture that Archbishop Duchamps was not about to jeopardize.

*"My God, this damned bishop has betrayed me to curry favor with my mother's rapist!"* moaned Lucien. Scarlet with disappointment and rage, Lucien dashed out the back entrance of the house and faded into the streets.

Aghast at the archbishop's betrayal, Lucien fled the Lyon region and never returned, becoming in one fell swoop a homeless vagabond and a wanted criminal at the age of fourteen. Though it would be simple to think him wicked or misdirected, in truth he had now been forced by the powerful to evolve from an innocent boy into a creature of survival, inclining day by day toward the abandonment of normalcy and civility. Thus cast aside, he spent the next ten years scraping about to simply survive.

***

As one year of struggle melted into another, the hatred Lucien felt for the nobility, Jews, and high clergy continued to ferment and ripen until, by age-twenty-four, it had hoarded itself to bursting like the pulsating sac of some horrid spider.

Feeling lost, he began considering death a more welcome proposition than the misery of his sparse existence. In the midst of this turmoil, fate intervened one night during a fearsome storm as Lucien found himself wandering within a valley of the Pyrénées Mountains along the border of Spain. Seeking shelter beneath the cover of a massive stand of trees near a curve in the road, he covered himself with his stolen mantle. Two hours later he was awakened by the whinny of a horse approaching from the direction of Spain. Struggling to see through the darkness, he managed to determine between jagged flashes of lightning that the horse was hobbling along, injured. He next perceived that the rider, a knight, also appeared hurt.

At first believing the knight a nobleman, Lucien went to him in the downpour, thinking to rob and kill him. Seeing from his humble armor that the injured man was a mere warrior and not an aristocrat, Lucien took pity on him and said, "Say there, knight, let me help you get beneath the cover of these trees and out of this storm!"

After dragging the knight beneath the trees, Lucien noticed the man's severe wound; blood was emanating profusely through his leather gambeson from his stomach.

"I've b-been fighting the M-Moors in Spain," the man muttered, only half conscious. "I was w-wounded over a m-month ago, but the wound continues to purse open and refuses to h-heal. I've n-not much longer to live, I f-fear. I'm heading h-home to be buried by my f-family... not far from Cluny."

"Perhaps I'll help you get home," said Lucien, feeling an unfamiliar pang of compassion. "Besides, I've nothing else to do…nor anywhere else to go."

"Oh, bl-bless you, lad," groaned the knight. "But if I should die along the way, p-perhaps you would deliver my sh-shield and armor to my w-wife? She h-has very little to her name. Perhaps the s-sale of this chain-mail, sword and sh-shield will help feed our children."

"Certainly," replied Lucien, thinking back to the destitution of his own mother. Taking his mantle from his own shoulders, he covered the man as rain continued pelting them both. "Best we get some sleep now," he said, wiping rivulets of rain from his brow.

When Lucien awoke in the morning, the knight was dead, as was his horse. Stripping him of his chain-mail hauberk, gambeson, and helmet, Lucien determined that he would, as promised, deliver the knight's armor to the man's widow. Carrying this heavy equipment along with the knight's shield, however, quickly proved to be burdensome. In a moment of discouragement, Lucien decided it might be easier if he actually wore the equipment instead of hauling it in his hands and over his shoulder. To his satisfaction, the knight's garments fit him suitably, and as he began trudging his way toward Cluny in southern France, he from time to time began to fancy himself a knight, especially after several peasants along the road mistakenly took him for a man-of-arms. Being thus greeted with respect was a new experience for Lucien, which pleased him to no end, causing his head to swell. After several more encounters with peasants and pilgrims showing deference along the road, Lucien determined there was no need to return the armor to the knight's poor widow.

Shortly after making this decision, and still being in Burgundy, a bevy of peasants near Cluny waved at him from the distance, apparently recognizing the shield. "Ho there, Jacques Boulon!" the men shouted, mistaking Lucien for a man of the area. "We thought you still in Spain fighting the Saracens!"

Lucien balked, struck by the realization that if people of this area recognized the coat of arms on the shield, he might well be arrested for theft– perhaps even unjustly accused of murdering this Jacques Boulon and absconding with his armor.

*Ah, I'll not surrender this armor*, he vowed. *But best I leave south France and go north where no one will recognize my acquisitions or accuse me of thievery.*

So it was that Lucien decided to make a bee-line toward Paris, where he lived in hiding for several years, sleeping in the streets and taking menial tasks just to afford bread in order to survive. Again disgusted with the lot life had cast him, he finally abandoned Paris and headed toward northern regions of Flanders and Normandy where he heard there might be work. His only possessions were the armor, sword, and shield he had acquired in southern France, and he still posed from time to time as a southern knight who had lost his horse in battle against the Moors. Knowing little about parrying the sword he wore on his belt, he continued to carry his stout shepherd staff, the very one he had killed the Jewish treasurer with, and had also used with great ability to protect himself over the years. Indeed, he had become so skilled with it that, in his deft hands, the simple staff had become a lethal weapon.

Having trekked to Rouen to purposely join the mobs persecuting the Jews there, he happened onto the evangelization of Peter the Hermit. Seeing so many thousands of similar humble roots as himself, and tiring of posing as a knight, he decided that this Holy Crusade of Pope Urban the Hermit was preaching might offer opportunity– while also satisfying that dark, parasitic disease that had been infecting his heart over the years: *bitterness*, and the need to take it out on others. Having found neither satisfaction nor pleasure in life over his difficult years, he had learned along the way that watching others suffer, for some reason, eased his hatred.

Abandoning the name 'Lucien' in Amiens on joining the Hermit, now calling himself 'Tafur,' he reveled in his status as 'King of the Beggars.' Before long he found something he had never possessed in life: purpose. With the fever of single-minded obsession, he placed his entire store of energy into training peasants how to defend themselves and fight with staffs and farm implements. These peasant men, thinking Tafur a former knight, master of war, and man of spiritual fervor, quickly bowed to his will. This gave Tafur something else he had never possessed in life: power.

As with all men savoring that first' pungent taste of power, Tafur knew there was only one direction for him now– the acquisition of *more* power. Thus began his quest to reach Constantinople with Peter the Hermit's Peasants' Crusade, then march forward over a carpet of Muslim corpses to Jerusalem... where he would find enough Jews to finally sate his thirst for Semitic blood.

# Chapter Nine

## Jurgen Handel of Bavaria

Immediately following Tristan's ordination into the Benedictine order, he had requested to join and was accepted into the elite Benedictine Underground. Thus began a year of intensive training within the clandestine, subterranean infrastructure of Monte Cassino Monastery beneath the callous tutelage of Brother Dieter Muehler and company. From there, Tristan entered the dangerous realm of continental espionage as a field agent, at times operating beneath the wing of Jurgen Handel, a hardened monk who had already spent twelve years working the dark, violent underbelly of Church intelligence. But Odo de Lagery had deemed Tristan's phenomenal intelligence and talents too valuable to either risk in the world of the Benedictine Underground, so he had quickly moved Tristan to the open stage of the Vatican. Now, ten years later, Handel still stalked the shadows. Highly revered by peers and superiors, plying his trade from one country to the next with unparalleled proficiency and ingenuity, he was assigned only to missions of high sensitivity or extreme significance... such as now with Bishop Saint-Germain.

"Proud of you, lad," said Handel as the teamster driving them to Tuscany finished loading his wagon with their trunks and possessions. "You've done well for yourself, though I wouldn't for one moment wish to trade positions. I don't think I could tolerate the damnable ass-lickers that you're forced to deal with in your position."

"Nor I those in yours," Tristan grinned, amused by Handel's jagged edges.

Tristan admired Handel as a master of his craft, but also respected him profoundly as an individual; despite the brutality of his work Handel was a good man, principled and grounded. Now barely forty, he had been born and raised in Bavaria, possessing that rugged Teutonic presence common to Germans. His hair was blond, his eyes sky-blue, and he was easily two hand widths taller than the average Italian. His stature, though lean, concealed unusual strength. Handel also possessed extraordinary agility and hand speed, which made him dangerous with his fists, and especially lethal with a dagger.

Although Handel had taken his vows at eighteen, possessing a keen hunger to do God's work, he had never actually aspired to spend his years behind monastery walls copying manuscripts or wallowing in devotional duties. He became, consequently, an ideal candidate for the Benedictine Underground. On completing his training at Monte Cassino, he soon became one of the most resourceful and wily papal agents of the entire continental network. He was intelligent and judicious, but also possessed the icy temperament of an assassin.

"Very well, gentlemen," the teamster grunted, "the wagon's loaded and the oxen grow impatient. Let's be on our way. 'Tis a long ride to Canossa!"

Accompanied by a papal escort of forty Vatican guards, twenty to the front and twenty to the rear, Tristan and Handel left Rome behind, taking the road north toward Tuscany; they would meet Guillaume and his Tuscan brigade there, then proceed together to Cologne, Germany to parley with Peter the Hermit. The trek to Tuscany was a trek Tristan and Handel had both made many times over the years. In Tristan's case the trips were generally for diplomatic purposes, made in the company of a papal delegation or personal entourage. Handel, on the other hand, worked as a lone wolf, traveling the roads alone. It was pleasurable for him, therefore, to now share company and conversation with Tristan along the long road north.

The two had first met when Handel was a young monk and Tristan was but a boy studying at Cluny Monastery in France. In fact, it was during those early times that Handel had predicted that Tristan would end by becoming a Black Monk, even suggesting that there might be a future for him within the Benedictine Underground. From there they had experienced numerous other encounters, both by chance and by Vatican design; just the year before they had been sent together by Pope Urban on a clandestine mission to Constantinople. Although their politics differed profoundly, as did their motivations and duties, Tristan and Handel had always found each other's company engaging; over time and despite intermittent political bickering, they had become quite close.

As on their trip to Constantinople a year earlier, the two soon found themselves swapping banter about the European nobility, conditions endured by the peasants, and the rise of Italian city-states. Inevitably, though, the bulk of their conversation centered on Pope Urban's approaching holy war.

"Bishop Adhémar of Le Puy was a wise appointment for leader of the crusade," mused Tristan as they traveled north. "Since the Pope's decree that Bishop Adhémar of Le Puy be obeyed in all things by all crusaders, Adhémar now has full authority to keep things in order, though he is already revered by all French knights."

Handel, who rarely missed the mechanics of things, voiced opinions with more rawness than others. "Adhémar was picked only because of his high noble birth and endless family connections to the power structure of France's most influential aristocracy," he said. "Moreover, Adhémar's attached at the hip to Count Raymond of Toulouse, the wealthiest and most powerful lord of all southern France. And Judas priest... Raymond's treasury is four times that of King Philippe! High nobility is the bucket from which Urban is drawing his military force for this war. Every top echelon nobleman that's recruited attracts a full retinue of money, resources, and lesser nobles, not to mention troops and support personnel. So Adhémar's selection by Urban was merely a point of strategy, not virtue. Fact is, old Adhémar's a rather righteous old bastard in my view, overly rigid and inflexible. Still, he's a wise pick. Note though, he's forbidden by Church law to actually fight in battle as he's a cleric. Consequently, Raymond of Toulouse still vies to be anointed the overall military commander of the crusade, though he's over sixty and prone to illness." Handel snickered then and said, "Did you know he still carries that goddamned eyeball of his around with him everywhere he goes?"

"The one he lost fighting the Moors in Spain?" asked Tristan.

"Oh no, his story's changed, haven't you heard?' smirked Handel. "Raymond now claims it was extracted by the Turks during his pilgrimage to Jerusalem for refusing to pay the exorbitant tax they've imposed on Latin pilgrims! So he carries it about now as testament to his suffering. Whether by the Moors in Spain or the Turks in the Holy Land, who *knows* how he lost the damn thing? Like everything else going on, his changing of the story is just another of the bizarre developments arising since this declaration of a holy war."

"Indeed," agreed Tristan, "such as Godfrey of Bouillon. Who could have imagined he would join Pope Urban's crusade after all those bloody years battling the Gregorian Vatican during the Investiture War? It was Godfrey who so angrily vowed to place my aunt Mathilda of Tuscany in shackles and shave her hair to the scalp. Stranger yet, how about Bohemud of Taranto? He and his Italian-Normans have for decades been engaged in vicious war against the Byzantines– but by taking the cross, Bohemud will now be *helping* the Byzantines fight the Turks!"

"Aye, the paradox of war... yesterday's enemy, today's friend," grunted Handel scornfully. "Yeah," he muttered with certain bitterness, "let's now hold hands and simply forget all the friends and allies who were slaughtered back then, as well as the innocent peasants standing in the way who were trampled without mercy. As I said, this crusade is creating some odd bedfellows. Bizarre twists, too... and I fear there'll be more to come." Then Handel went silent, trying to make sense of it all.

"You mentioned earlier that in Cologne," said Tristan, interrupting Handel's ruminations, "we are to be given an update on the movement of Christian forces involved in the crusade. Will it be the Underground providing this news?"

"Yes," nodded Handel. "Agents from throughout the continent are already beginning to converge at the Benedictine monastery in Cologne. By the time we arrive, they should all be there." Handel paused then, and looking over at Tristan, asked, "Remember your days with the Underground? You know, traveling about in secret, changing disguises, never knowing where you'd be sent or what country you'd end up in."

"Of course I remember," Tristan nodded. "It was all a bit shocking at first, though. I had no idea in the beginning how much intrigue was involved in Church politics... or violence."

"Yeah, I recall your innocence caused a bit of a clumsy start," chided Handel. "But you soon got good at it... *damn* good at it." Thinking back, he chortled, recalling Tristan's first mission.

"Hunh! I remember that night in Rome... the Inn of the Sparrow when we had to kill that Byzantine nun. Shit, I nearly met my end at her hands when you froze up! Still, we managed to kill that wily bitch, and you probably saved my life dragging me out of there that night. And you know… damn, I'm not even sure I ever thanked you properly, lad."

"Oh, but Handel" objected Tristan, "it was *you* who killed the nun, not *we*! I just happened to be there."

"Certainly you 'just happened' to be there,' Handel grinned, "*pinning her down, struggling to pull the dagger out her damned hand... leaving me to do the dirty work, eh?*"

"But she was stabbing you, Handel!" Tristan insisted. "Yes, it was a clumsy start for me and I froze up at the Inn of the Sparrow... but how could I have possibly guessed she was an assassin herself? Anyway, *you* drove the dagger into her throat, killing her... not *me*."

"Oh, had you not been there, yes, she would most likely still be alive, and *I* would be dead." Then Handel's eyes took on a slight glimmer as his mouth curled a measure, forming that particular smirk he delighted in issuing when smugly driving home a point. "Yes then, lad, if it makes you feel better, *I* was the one who killed her… *entirely* by myself."

The incident at the Inn of the Sparrow had been a shocking and pivotal moment in Tristan's early days with the Underground, and he had long since tried to bury it. "So, Handel, your thoughts on our visit to Cologne?" Tristan said, channeling the discussion into more comfortable waters. "How do you think it will end?"

"An absolute and total waste of time! Once we get there the Hermit'll tell us to kiss his hairy ass. Then he'll start waving that damn letter from God telling him to lead the peasants to the Holy Land in our faces. Which reminds me, Tristan, have you ever seen God's hand writing?"

"No, of course not."

"*I have*," said Handel. "Yeah, in the Hermit's letter. And it shames me to say, but our Lord scribbles in the hand of a goddamm five year old!" Handel brayed then at his own humor, but only for a moment. His smile evaporating, scorn returned. "Who in Satan's Hell but Kuku Peter would dream up of scribbling a letter, then claim it dropped in his own lap directly from Heaven, written by God Himself!?"

"Aye," Tristan agreed, "who but the Hermit? Such a thing borders on sacrilege, actually. But you never finished, Handel… how do you think this thing with the Hermit will end? I mean, should he refuse to turn back and we end by having to follow him east."

"Judas Priest, Tristan, you *know* how it's going to end. We'll have to drag ourselves overland across the entire damned continent while his peasant horde plods along at a tortoise's pace. Then, when the Hermit and his beggars get to Constantinople, they'll try to take on the Turks with sticks and dirt clods and *we'll* end up trying to save his filthy ass along with his army of imbeciles. Let's just pray we get out of this thing with our goddamned heads still attached to our shoulders, huh?"

Tristan was thinking much the same, only in less coarse terms. But Tristan had long ago learned to overlook his friend's gruffness; it was more than balanced by Handel's strong sense of justice, as well as an extraordinary awareness of all that circulated around him regardless of place or circumstance. Tristan appreciated these qualities and respected Handel's opinions despite his bluntness and penchant for baiting others. "So then," he continued, "do you think the Hermit can actually drag this peasant army of his with thousands of women and children all the way to Jerusalem on foot? Grace of God, the distance from Amiens to there is nearly two thousand miles!"

"Oh yeah, he'll drag them that far, even if it kills them… and it probably will, one way or another. If the trip itself doesn't do it, then the Turks will." Shaking his head, Handel took on a look of disgust. "As always happens in cases like this," he said, "the man *starting* the shit will get to *walk away* from the shit, unscathed, somehow, while his dumb-ass sheep end up rotting in graves far from home. Dammit, and us too if things go badly!"

"I have doubted from the beginning that I will be able to keep him from leaving Cologne and marching to Constantinople. Still, I pray once he gets to Byzantium, we might be able to convince him to wait for the French knights to arrive before launching against the Turks. What do you think, Handel?"

"Ha, good luck! No, not likely."

"Well then," Tristan pressed, "If we can't stop the Hermit, what about Sansavoir? He at least has a more seasoned grasp of war, I would think. Certainly he understands the distinct advantages of awaiting additional manpower and better weaponry."

"Sansavoir's a fool," said Handel curtly, "as evidenced by his attachment to the Hermit. As also evidenced by his early departure from France to fight the Turks."

Seeing that Handel was offering little hope, and conceding no ground, Tristan continued. "Then what of Emperor Alexius? Might he not intervene and force the Hermit's peasant army to hold in Constantinople until Bishop Adhémar arrives?"

"Bah!" grunted Handel. "And just what emperor have you ever encountered who gives a rat's ass about the fate of peasants, huh? Besides, you know my opinion of Alexius... he's a snake of divine dimensions!"

Tristan shrugged, knowing well that Handel distrusted Emperor Alexius and held him in low regard; it had long been a major area of disagreement between Tristan and Handel. Handel also despised Greek Orthodox Christians for breaking with the Roman Catholic rite during the Great Schism of 1054, whereas Tristan was in complete accord with Pope Urban's policy of détente with the Eastern Church. More than on any other point, however, Handel had from the very beginning disagreed, and vociferously so, with Tristan on getting involved in a crusade to help the Byzantines in their struggle against the Turks. Nonetheless, even knowing this, Tristan said, "Handel, when you and I undertook our secret mission to Constantinople, I found Emperor Alexius to be a reasonable man with a legitimate cause. I also saw value in mending fences between Roman Catholics and the Greek Orthodox rite. After all, they are still Christian despite breaking from Rome years ago."

"You'll never win me over about Alexius, lad," snorted Handel, "so quit peddling duck shit my direction! I tried to warn you about Alexius and the Greeks when the Pope sent you and me to their capital the first time. But thanks to your overly altruistic heart, and then your filial ties to the Pope, Alexius has succeeded into now dragging *us* into fighting the Turks in the Holy Land while *he* sits on the crack of his royal ass back in Constantinople. Then–"

"Ah, no!" objected Tristan. "Odo insists that once our main forces arrive in the Byzantine Capital, Emperor Alexius will himself take command of the combined crusader and Byzantine forces and lead them against the Turks. After all, it is *us* helping the *Greeks*, not the reverse."

"Sure, the Pope's told you, me, and everyone else that… because he *believes* it," said Handel. "But you just wait, lad, I'll kiss your ass if Emperor Alexius ever raises a sword to the Muslims. No, he'll sit on his duff while *we* reconquer Byzantine territory lost to the Turks, and then he'll demand that we turn it all back over to him as lost Byzantine territory! Then, if we're fortunate enough to get beyond that, he'll be waving farewell to us as we press on to retake Jerusalem...a place he doesn't give a shit about! Dammit, I advised Pope Urban time and time again to leave things alone in the East, but it was you who had Urban's ear, and pulled us into this fray."

"Handel," said Tristan, having endured that particular accusation from Handel time and time again since their return from Constantinople, "we have *always* disagreed on this war, and forever will, apparently. But regardless of what you believe, the Greeks are still Christians, and the Turks continue to encroach into their empire! Nor should the Turks rule Jerusalem, the most sacred city of all Christendom. Moreover, they have no right to molest Christian pilgrims as they travel to the Holy Land to worship."

"Ha!" Handel snarked testily. "The Turks molest Christian pilgrims going to Jerusalem no more so than the nobles of Europe molest Christian peasants right here at home... robbery, torture, exploitation, rape! As to the Turks being a threat to the West? No. They're only a threat to the Byzantine Empire… and damn the Byzantines to hell anyway for abandoning the True Church!"

Tristan sighed, then shook his head, issuing a slight chortle as Handel continued to drone on against the Byzantines, because at that moment it occurred to him that poor Handel had fallen into a paradoxical snare of confounding proportions. Ironically, despite vehemently opposing the Pope's Holy Crusade, Handel had now been placed in a position of fighting an enemy he did not see as an enemy, the Turks– while assisting a man he thoroughly despised, Peter the Hermit.

*Ah, but Handel still willingly agreed to participate in this mission to Cologne, then possibly on to Constantinople and*

*Jerusalem,* thought Tristan with admiration. *Indeed, despite his political stand, Handel is a faithful Benedictine soldier of Christ. And despite that streak of cold bloodedness that bares itself from time to time, he may be the best man I have ever met.*

## Chapter Ten

### La Gran Signorina of Genoa

In the year 1096, the city of Genoa was an independent Italian city-state, and along with Venice, Pisa, and Amalfi was one of the so-called 'Maritime Republics,' flourishing with prosperity in trade, shipbuilding, and banking. Its name was derived from the Latin word meaning 'knee,' from its geographical position at the middle of the Ligurian coastal arch of northwestern Italy along the Mediterranean. The designated president of the city was the Bishop of Genoa, but actual power was controlled by a privileged corps of the city's wealthiest individuals. Sitting at the pinnacle of this elite group was a foreign woman known by most only as la Gran Signorina.

She was a bit of a mystery to the Genoese, surrounded by ceaseless rumors and misconceptions as to her actual origins. Her skin, though smooth as porcelain, was a shade darker than that of the local populace, so she was initially thought by many to be Byzantine, possibly mixed with Armenian or Arab blood. Others guessed she might be from much farther east, the Indus Valley floodplain region, perhaps. Some went so far as to insist that she was a Saracen beauty who had miraculously escaped the harem of some powerful Turkish emir in Medina or Baghdad. Yet others claimed she might actually be from Egypt. Despite such conflicting presumptions there was no disagreement, however, concerning the fact that at age thirty-three, she was an exotic presence whose beauty eclipsed all the women of Genoa, and perhaps all of Italy.

The one thing known for certain was that years earlier she had appeared in Tuscany from nowhere, and shortly thereafter been quickly and mysteriously married to Lord Vincento Balducci, wealthy military commander and nobleman of Tuscany. This unlikely union had initially created scandal throughout northern

Italy as Lord Balducci was already betrothed to another at the time, a woman of elevated family heritage and wealth belonging to the highly regarded House of Bertucci. Upon Lord Vincento Balducci's untimely slaying during the Investiture War, his beautiful young wife inherited his vast fortune. Within a year she abandoned Tuscany, accompanied by a strange old woman who always wore black, claiming to be an aunt; the two moved to Genoa where the young widow risked her inherited fortune in the construction and shipping trades of that region. Despite early doubts by bankers and established trade magnates of the city, the beautiful new arrival proved to be extraordinarily adept and clever in business, and within several years had quadrupled the original capital her deceased husband had bequeathed her. By the year 1096, the foreign beauty had become known as 'la Gran Signorina,' amassing one of the largest fortunes within the combined cities comprising the Italian Maritime Republics.

Despite her devastating appearance and immense wealth, it was rumored that some vaporous, intangible melancholy possessed la Gran Signorina. This melancholy, accordingly, hung about her neck like a stone, which seemed to explain why she was so driven, and rarely smiled. Like the caramel sheen of her skin, this in itself generated yet more rumors.

Although la Gran Signorina was a widow, nobody within Genoa attributed her sorrow to the death of her husband, Lord Vincento Balducci. After all, everyone in Italy had always known he was both vain and petty, therefore impossible. This, of course, caused many to wonder how he had snared one so beautiful and talented into marriage in the first place. Consequently, many Genoans suspected that the source of la Gran Signorina's sadness could be attributed to some unrequited love of younger years. Others suspected it may have originated during a devastating childhood during which she must have lost or been separated from the rest of her family except the old bitty dressed in black who accompanied her wherever she went. Since the old woman's death years earlier, la Gran Signorina was now most often seen alone save those occasions when accompanied by either her financial adjutant or her business partner, the elderly Count-General Bertucci.

In any case, la Gran Signorina was admired and loved by all along the Ligurian coast due to her beauty, generosity to the poor, and contributions to the commerce and well being of the port city of Genoa. As spring of 1096 waned, she sat within the heavily guarded confines of her palatial sea-front estate going over trade invoices with her financial adjutant, an officious but faithful little accountant named Salvetti.

"Here, Signorina," said Salvetti, "the deed to your new property in Constantinople. My congratulations! According to these documents, the Greek furnishings included within possess not only monetary value, but historical worth as well– having belonged to the lineage of Byzantium's royal family."

"Thank you," she replied. "I'll need the estate this coming year for entertainment purposes, but after that I'll want you to negotiate its re-sale."

"Eh?" squeaked Salvetti, going falsetto. "You bought this magnificent property only for others' entertainment... for a short while? Oh, *irrealizzabile!* But upon whom would you lavish such attention, if I may inquire?"

"You may not."

"Of course," Salvetti replied, disappointed. He well appreciated his good fortune in being one of the rare Genoese who could get close to la Gran Signorina, being her financial adjutant; he even enjoyed a bit of local notoriety because of this. Yet, like the hound constantly starved for the master's touch, Salvetti hungered for even more of la Signorina's attention. Disappointment filling his expression after her curt denial of his request, he initiated discussion over shipping documents for cargo destined for Tunis, but was interrupted by the ring of a small bell.

Having been thus announced, a coachman entered the room, bowed, and set a note on the table before la Gran Signorina. "For you, Signorina." the man said, bowing. "The gentleman is waiting just outside."

"Grazie," she said, reading the note, motioning toward the door. "Yes, I've been expecting him for several days now. Please have him come in." Looking over at her adjutant, she said, "We'll go over the Tunis figures you've prepared tomorrow morning, Salvetti. I've other things to attend to first."

"Will you require my presence during the meeting you're about to hold?" asked Salvetti hopefully.

"No. This will be a private meeting, Salvetti."

Bowing, Salvetti turned to leave the room, but just as he reached the door, he nearly collided with an odd looking man coming from the other direction. The visitor was odd in that he was actually far smaller than Salvetti, who was himself quite short. The visitor also possessed a pointy beard that elongated his already thin face, and his strange appearance was further accentuated by a black hat, slouching to one side. This combination of features struck Salvetti as a tad comical, though there was not the least trace of humor within the little man's expression. Tipping his head, Salvetti started to issue a greeting but the man ushered him into the hallway, then abruptly closed the door on him.

Removing his hat, the visitor approached la Gran Signorina, bowing, then took a seat. "Good morning, my Lady," he said.

"Good afternoon, Fazio. You're overdue."

"Yes, apologies, Signorina, but getting information from within the walls of the Vatican is at times like... extracting water from stone. Especially information about the *Bishop*."

La Signorina looked at Fazio for a moment, considering his unusual appearance, smiling at the pitched timbre of his elfin voice. Slight of frame, a thick, curly mop of black hair sprang like a tangled thorn-bush from his crown, then trailed down his temples, turning into a sharp beard. He reminded her somewhat of Pan, the Greek god of nature, and she couldn't help but in her mind envisioning him springing up on goat legs at any moment– to dance while blowing into a pipe flute.

"Fazio, did you happen to see the Bishop while making your rounds of private inquiries?" she asked, dismissing her amusement.

"Yes, I came across him several times, actually. I followed him about a bit, thinking his actions might reveal this or that."

"He didn't notice you, I hope."

Looking slighted, Fazio shook his head. "Ah, *no*, Signorina, when Fazio chases the scent, the prey is unaware! But a little bad news, I fear. I regret to say that everything I learned about the Bishop's plans during my previous visit to the Vatican has– changed."

"*Changed*?"

Placing his elbows on the desk, knitting his fingers together, Fazio fussily scooted his chair closer. "Si, Signorina. To begin, the Bishop has made a rather hasty and unexpected departure from Rome under heavy guard with some other gentleman. The two left on horseback but were accompanied by an ox-man driving a large wagon which was *fully* loaded with enough valises and trunks to accommodate a trip of over a year or more. It appears the Bishop and his traveling companion will be away for quite some time."

"What? But this makes no sense whatsoever," she said, issuing that sigh that occurs when one precipitously discovers that what was previously certain has now come unraveled. "The Bishop was to meet Adhémar of Le Puy and Raymond of Toulouse in several months as they march through Italy. This has been well publicized, Fazio. So tell me then, why would he now leave Rome ahead of that important engagement for an unexpected trip that you suspect could last such a long while?"

"Ah, I was unable to learn exactly *why* he left, my Lady, though I grilled all my sources to the very bone."

"Well then, who was this other fellow in the Bishop's company?" she asked.

"Ah, I dug deep trying to unearth this man's identity… but a total and complete mystery. Nobody seemed to know *who* he was. A veritable phantom."

"Well, Fazio, it seems I'm paying you handsomely to go to Rome for the purpose of learning *nothing*, and then paying you again to come back to Genoa to *tell* me nothing."

Staring into his lap, Fazio tugged at his beard a moment, feeling la Signorina's irritation. Looking up, he pulled together a half-smile. "My Lady, despite not learning the *why* of the Bishop's departure, I *did* manage to learn that the Bishop will most probably be making a stop in Tuscany before going to wherever his final destination may be. His brother resides there, as you already know, as it's also the kingdom of the celebrated Countess Mathilda Medici, the adoptive aunt of both the Bishop and his brother."

She frowned at the mention of Mathilda Medici, a woman she loathed. "Ah yes, the scheming Countess of Tuscany, confidante of our last three popes and champion of the Vatican against its former military enemies like King Heinrich of Germany and Godfrey of Bouillon. She's always been and still is neck deep in the Vatican's secret activities and affairs. That, then, begs the question, Fazio: was the Bishop wearing his clerical garments, or was he in disguise?

"*In disguise,* Signorina?"

"Yes, Fazio," she replied, impatience seeping back into her tone. "Years ago the Bishop was a member of the Benedictine Underground, often traveling incognito. Perhaps this is a covert affair of some sort the Pope has devised. Diplomacy and espionage are one and the same, you know."

"Oh, I *s-e-e*. But no, he was in full bishop's regalia, and as I said, had a full military escort."

"Good, Fazio," she said, sounding satisfied for the first time since his arrival. "Then it should be easy enough for you to locate him in Tuscany and track wherever else he's going after that. After all, he's the Bishop of Ostia and First Counsel to the Pope. People in Tuscany will easily recognize him wherever he goes. But then, I also have a contact planted in Mathilda's court at Canossa. He might be able to help you ferret out what this trip is about."

"Ah, *eccellente*, Signorina, and Fazio here promises to stick close to him and keep you informed through messenger!" As he said this, he opened his right palm and pressed it flat across his heart in a gesture of faithfulness.

Nodding, she reached across her desk for a blank bank note. Scribbling her signature across it, she said, "Fazio, take a day of rest, then travel to Tuscany. As things change while you follow the Bishop, try to learn whether Constantinople is still anywhere in the mix and let me know immediately. Hai capito?"

"Yes, I understand," said Fazio, standing to accept his payment. "But... one more little thing, Signorina."

As he said this, an odd instant of hesitancy slipped into his voice. She expected him to continue, but instead he fell silent and stood there, shuffling his feet. "Well, Fazio?" she said. "I certainly don't have all day."

"Just s-something that..." Fazio stopped mid-sentence as tiny shimmers of perspiration began to spot his forehead, and a shadow of apprehension slipped over his brow. "S-Signorina," he stammered, "it troubles me to tell you this, but in all of my digging in Rome, I happened by chance to unearth some completely unexpected news… a deep, deep secret about the Bishop, I fear. I thought perhaps you might wish to… *know of it*?" Here his expression went blank as he offered a tepid shrug.

"*Y-e-s*, Fazio?"

"I shudder to say such a thing openly," Fazio continued with trepidation, "but it seems that the Bishop, shortly after being ordained a monk ten years ago, had a… *lover*." Fazio took a breath then, having finally freed himself of the words he had been holding since his return to Genoa. "The Bishop kept this affair hidden from his superiors," he continued, confidence returning by degrees as each word slipped from his tongue, "but then this mistress of his apparently became... *pregnant*." Here Fazio paused, measuring la Signorina's reaction. "Yes," he then continued, "and she bore the Bishop a *child*."

When Fazio had said the word 'lover,' he felt la Signorina's gaze begin to alter, almost imperceptibly at first. When he had followed shortly thereafter with the word 'pregnant,' her eyes had narrowed. Now, as he had just uttered 'and she bore him a child,' her eyes suddenly went dark. Still, she said nothing, though her bottom lip began to tremor the least bit.

"Do you wish me to... continue, Signorina?" asked Fazio.

"Yes, finish what you've started," came the reply, insistent but flat.

"Very well, my Lady. This child the woman bore presented a problem to the rising young monk, of course. It had been determined since the monk's boyhood with the Benedictines, apparently, that he would be groomed to become a powerful presence within the Church. Even now many claim that one day the red cope shall be draped over his back and the papal tiara placed on his head."

"Yes, yes, I've heard the whispers," she nodded. "But *F-a-z-i-o*... how is it you came upon such a fable concerning the Bishop, a lover and a child?"

There was something cryptic in the manner she drew out his name, and it unnerved Fazio a bit. Nonetheless, he continued. "While I was in Rome, Signorina, I happened across an old acquaintance of mine by the name of Antonelli. Years ago he was employed by the Countess Mathilda of Tuscany at one of the Quattro Castilli… I believe it may have been the fortress of Monteluccio, actually. My friend Antonelli was a jailer there."

As she looked at him, her brows furrowing, Fazio's voice dropped low as if fearing someone else might be in the room, listening. "Since the Bishop is the adopted nephew of the great Mathilda of Tuscany, and is like a son to the Holy Father, Pope Urban II, just the mention of what I'm about to say could cost a man very dearly. *Capisce,* Signorina?"

"Yes, of course, Fazio. But go on."

"Very well, but first a bit of a caveat. Since what Antonelli was telling me about happened so long ago, and also because things have been kept secret for so long, it's difficult to tell whether everything my old friend whispered in my ear is *completely* accurate. After all, he was drinking a good bit the night I spoke to him in Rome. Yet, he's neither clever enough nor ill-willed enough to invent such a story."

"And you, Fazio, were you also drinking?"

"Ah, no, not a drop!" replied Fazio, appearing wounded by the question. "Fazio never drinks when on the hunt, Signorina! But to continue... while Antonelli was tending jail years back at Monteluccio, a fortress owned by Countess Mathilda Medici, it seems that the Bishop was imprisoned there once beneath my friend's supervision."

"Imprisoned?"

"Yes, my Lady…for a period of thirty days. But not imprisoned as a criminal, evidently, but to perform some severe kind of penance under the orders of the Cardinal-Bishop of Ostia." Here Fazio's eyes widened and his voice fell to nearly a whisper. "The Cardinal-Bishop of Ostia at that time was none other than Odo de Lagery, who now reigns in the Vatican as Holy Father of the Catholic Church."

Fazio expected some sort of reaction after divulging this, but la Signorina only stared back at him with frigid, expressionless eyes.

"About this penance that was issued," Fazio continued, "the Bishop was locked naked in a cell, was given only water and bread, and was ordered to scourge himself on the back every few hours for an entire month. It was a bloody business, apparently, and by the time the Bishop had completed his penance, he could barely stand, or even speak."

"Quite interesting… if *true*," she said, quietly folding her hands on the desk. "Fazio, what then was the source of such brutal penance?"

"Ah, the jailer was never told," said Fazio. "In fact, Antonelli was prohibited from talking to the Bishop, or even entering his cell to feed him bread or offer water slack his thirst. That duty was left to the Bishop's own brother, who was the only one in the castle allowed direct contact with the penitent. But know this, as the Bishop suffered through this hellish ordeal, he fell from time to time into fits of sorrow and half consciousness. During these spells he would rant pitifully from time to time about this *woman* he loved… but had apparently forsaken, perhaps? Antonelli heard all this from the other side of the cell door, so it was a bit unclear."

"But Fazio," she said, her voice growing distant, "the Bishop wouldn't have been the first holy man to fall victim to sins of the flesh. Prior to Pope Gregory, concubinage and promiscuity had reached a point of abuse amongst the clergy. Many priests and monks had become common whore mongers and flesh peddlers, and even had multiple wives."

"Ah, yes, but there's more to the Bishop's story, my Lady. The agony imposed by the constant scourging and his loss of blood caused him to fall into bouts of loud raving. At times he would cry out things about an infant his mistress bore. This baby apparently *died* somehow, which caused the Bishop infinite grief and guilt."

Her eyes showed no emotion, but la Signorina's face seemed to grow ashen as she heard this. "Did the jailer mention how this infant died?" she asked.

"No, the Bishop's ravings were often incoherent and unintelligible. But Antonelli told me that *he* believes there's a possibility that the infant was… *murdered*."

"What!" la Signorina cried, her voice catching fire. "Oh, impossible, Fazio! To what purpose could such a thing have possibly been done!"

"T-to avoid scandal, my Lady?" stammered Fazio. "Oddly, shortly after this penance, the Bishop did begin to quickly rise within the Vatican. Probably because all trace of scandal, meaning the child, had been… *erased*?"

"Do you mean to suggest that the Bishop and the Pope colluded to–"

"Oh, no, no!" interrupted Fazio, frightened to the bone. "I'm only telling you what my friend the jailer *suspects*. Oh, I beg you, Signorina, don't put words in Fazio's mouth! Two such powerful men as Pope Urban and the Bishop of Ostia, my God in Heaven! I could end up at the end of a rope if–"

"Calm down," she snapped, gazing about the room, collecting her thoughts. Finally, her eyes still brimming with agitation, she looked at Fazio. "But tell, then," she said, "what did the jailer believe ever happened to the woman?"

Fazio said nothing at first, fearing he had already said too much. As la Signorina's eyes bore into him, however, he finally whispered, "I shudder to say, but she, too… just *disappeared*. Possibly murdered also, Antonelli suspects."

"Ah no! Such a thing is also not possible, Fazio! I never wish you to utter such a horror again as long as you live!"

"*Si, si, my Lady!*" bowed the tiny Fazio, his terror augmented by la Signorina's outrage at his last statement. "Oh, Dio mi salva! Fazio is so stupid! I sh-should never have even *mentioned* any of this Antonelli business. I only did so because you show such interest in the Bishop! I th- thought you might wish to know these things I heard. But ho, the jailer was drinking the night we talked! Perhaps it's all simply wild conjecture on his part, eh? Yes, I may have simply fallen victim to an old friend's overly lively imagination… and wine!"

"Rumors are a wicked thing, Fazio. I know. I've been the victim of such fabrications my entire life. And the *imagination* of wagging tongues is far more damaging than the actual truth of things. Fazio, I warn you... never utter these lies again! Do I have your word that you'll never give voice to such poison as long as you live, to *anyone*?"

"Si, Signorina!"

"Very well, then," she said, returning to the promissory note she had begun signing before Fazio had begun revealing his story. Completing her signature and marking the note with her ring, she said, "Here, take this to the Banca di Genoa for a job suitably done in Rome." As she handed it to him, she gazed at him with eyes so penetrating that it sent a shiver skittering up Fazio's spine. "The *extra* I've included in this bank note," she said coldly, "is to ensure that you hold your tongue on this Antonelli business in the future. As you said, Fazio, such talk could cost a man like yourself *dearly.* Even the *idea* of such talk could be… *dangerous.* Capisce?"

"Yes, Signorigna, certemente!" said Fazio, accepting the bank note, then quickly leaving the room. It was not until he gained the outside and was entering his coach that he sighed aloud, "*Il cielo me!* What ungodly Pandora's box have I opened this day?"

## Chapter Eleven

### Mala, the Romani

As Fazio's coach clacked down the cobbled boulevard of la Gran Signorina's estate, she watched from the window as it disappeared around a turn and out of sight. "Oh, Mala, the boy would be ten years old this month had he lived," she whispered to herself, quietly drowning in that vacant despair that overcomes one when past injury is suddenly dredged from its grave. Although Fazio had not intended to do so, he had unwittingly unearthed in la Gran Signorina a past torment of crippling dimension. Indeed, of all burdens a human being might shoulder in a lifetime, the most crippling is– a hurtful secret.

*`Mala, Mala, oh what would your son look like now,* she wondered, finding that her real name sounded strange to her after years of only being known as la Gran Signorina.

Thus, silently lost to trying to envision her lost infant as a growing boy, her memory dragged her back to a frozen mountain pass atop the Alps where the little wagon she and her companions were taking to Tuscany had become stranded in ice and snow.

She was eight months pregnant at the time, carrying the child of a young monk whom she loved above all else on this earth. His name was Tristan de Saint-Germain. They had met as children, but even then their young hearts had somehow become tethered in one of those rare communions of the soul that binds two strangers, inexplicably, for life. But the bond was shattered by a series of misinterpretations fueled by jealousy and the gossip of others; she had mistakenly been led into believing that he had betrayed her for another woman. In a heartbroken furor that wounded her beyond repair, she had furiously abandoned him, leaving no word of her whereabouts or intentions.

Neither knew at the time that she was already carrying his child. Eight months later Mala found herself bloated with pregnancy and in a state of destitution, unable to earn the income she had previously generated as a popular Romani folk dancer traveling the cities of France. Discouraged, living on the edge of starvation, she and her faithful old woman companion, Duxia de Falaise, teamed with a man named Fernando to travel to Italy. The purpose of the trip was to seek assistance from the wealthy and powerful Countess Mathilda of Tuscany, Tristan de Saint-Germain's adoptive aunt. Midway through the Alps they became trapped in a blizzard that crippled the wagon and froze their two ponies to death. Suffering from severe hypothermia and frostbite, the three struggled to stay alive. Then, in the midst of this frozen horror, Mala's water broke and the child she was carrying came early. In the end, God showed no mercy on her infant, the product of an illicit union between a Romani street dancer and a Benedictine monk. The baby froze to death after only a few days of life. The cold also then took Fernando's life.

Mala and the old woman would have perished, too, but a German named Jurgen Handel happened upon the scene while leading a military supply train across the mountains. Finding the two women unconscious and on death's doorstep, Handel managed to save them despite their deteriorated condition. In one of those freakish coincidences that fate throws onto the table from time to time, it so happened that Handel himself was also on his way to meet Countess Mathilda Medici; he was delivering arms and munitions to Tuscany sent by her northern allies, rebellious German princes who like herself were fighting against King Heinrich during the Investiture War.

Handel carried Mala and old Duxia to Countess Mathilda's fortress at Canossa, then went on his way; Mala never saw him again. The countess immediately arranged a full funeral service for the dead infant and Fernando which was officiated by Bishop Odo de Lagery who happened to be visiting Canossa on Vatican business at the time. Mathilda and Odo both believed Fernando to be the father of Mala's lost infant, but in a later secret conversation, Mala shared the truth. Horrified, Countess Mathilda rebuked Mala, accusing her of fabricating the tale for purposes of extortion, insisting that her adopted nephew would never engage in an illicit sexual affair. Odo, however, eventually accepted Mala's story due to the efforts of the old hag, Duxia de Falaise. Mathilda, still refusing to believe or even discuss the issue further, held the story close at hand, never sharing it with a soul. Odo also kept the story secret, but determined he must confront Tristan with it. Tristan was devastated and shocked upon learning of Mala's pregnancy and the full circumstances surrounding the death of his unknown son. After a fiery dispute with Odo, and despite Odo's objections, Tristan decided to renounce his Benedictine vows and seek out Mala, because he loved her above all things in life at that point… even God.

In the meantime, an Italian nobleman named Vincento Balducci, who had been there during the rescue of Mala and Duxia on the mountain pass, sought out the beautiful Mala at Canossa and became hopelessly smitten by her. Recognizing that Balducci was a wealthy aristocrat, old Duxia de Falaise maneuvered Mala into accepting his sudden offer of marriage. "Tis a new life this man offers, security from hunger and poverty for us both," she insisted. "Besides, though you love that monk of yours, look what he's done to you! A future with him is impossible, for he's owned by the Church! By marrying Balducci, you and the monk can both go on with your lives. But Balducci must continue to believe that the father of the child you lost is the dead Fernando. Truly, *no one* must ever learn that the real father is Tristan de Saint-Germain!"

Thus it was that by the time Tristan finally located Mala, she was on her way to wed Lord Vincento Balducci. Although Tristan caught up to her coach and begged Mala to flee with him, it was Duxia de Falaise who drove him off, accusing him of once already destroying Mala's life, and now yet again trying to sabotage her revived future with an aristocratic husband.

"God, my Lord and Savior," Mala whispered as she remained by the window, reliving the events of ten years earlier, "they say You drive all things. Why then have You put me and Tristan through such trials? Why would you throw us together as children, welding our hearts into one, if You did not intend for us to forever love each other?"

Then, stepping away from the window, she remembered Fazio. "Oh, my tiny spy, though what you've been told by the jailer is much twisted, you have still managed to strike a vein... rooting out things long buried."

## Chapter Twelve

### Tristan and Guillaume… Forever

As Handel and Tristan continued to travel north, their discussion of the approaching crusade deepened each day, and though words grew testy on occasion, the two relished the exchange. Finally, as they neared the foot of the Tuscan mountain atop which the impenetrable fortress of Canossa stood, they crossed a picturesque brook. “Handel,” said Tristan, motioning the ox-man and accompanying guards to halt, “would you mind if we paused here a moment?”

Looking about, Handel saw that they had reached the last farm before ascending the steep trail up to Countess Mathilda’s fortress. “No, certainly not,” he said. “It’s a nice spot. I’ve passed through here quite often, actually, but given it little consideration.”

“A humble spot, this,” said Tristan, pointing to the quaint stone cottage across the brook, “yet my favorite little corner of the entire world.”

“Really?” chortled Handel, curiously amused.

“Indeed. Each time I pass here, this pastoral setting transports me to another mindset for some reason, changing my entire ethos– for a short while, at least. This spot reminds me that peace does actually exist… for a fortunate few, anyway.”

“Ha!” laughed Handel. “Sure, it exists, for those who seek it. But we’re neither one of *that* grain, my friend. Whether you acknowledge it or not, you’re a driven man. But go ahead and enjoy the landscape a moment, then let it pass. You’ve an entire world out there to save yet, eh?”

Dismounting, Tristan took a seat on a stack of large rock piled beside the brook while gazing at the flocks of geese and swans lazily navigating its waters. In the distance, a herd of sheep foraged along the lush meadow surrounding the stone cottage, and a little beyond that, goats were pulling at the grass, watching over recently born kids kicking and scampering about, bleating playful communications to each other.

From his saddle Handel watched Tristan, whose focus seemed lost to the serenity of the agrarian landscape now surrounding him. "So," he chided, "you don't harbor secret designs of one day retiring and becoming a damned farmer, do you, lad?"

"No," Tristan answered, "but whenever the politics and violence of the world overcome me, my thoughts incessantly gravitate back to this place. The tranquility of it seems to pacify the torments of my soul, for reasons I yet fail to comprehend. But you know, Handel, I certainly would not mind owning this little property some day. Later in life, perhaps. It would be a placid setting to spend one's last days."

"Ah, but I think that's within easy reach," nodded Handel. "Your aunt Mathilda owns this place. She leases it out a year or so at a time to local shepherds for next to nothing."

"Oh?" Tristan shrugged, surprised. After a few minutes more of staring about, he stood, dusted the back of his vestments, and mounted his horse. "Let's go then, Handel. It's yet a good climb up the trail to Canossa."

It took them a while to make the full ascent up the treacherous trail to the fortress, but as they cleared the final rise, Tristan spotted his brother and aunt standing outside the gates. Waving, he gazed about with anticipation for Asta, but she was not in view.

"Hail, Bishop of Ostia!" shouted Guillaume as Tristan and Handel dismounted.

After the two brothers embraced, Tristan reached up, grasping Guillaume by the shoulders. "Ah, but let me look at you, Brother. I declare, war has turned you into a beast of a man, Guillaume! You now have the frame of a blacksmith, yet you still stand more handsome than Adonis himself."

Like Tristan, Guillaume was remarkably handsome, his brilliant grey eyes possessing the same startling Scandinavian clarity as those of Tristan and their mother, Asta. But unlike Tristan, Guillaume's full mane of hair was Nordic-silver, identical to Asta's, whereas Tristan's was blond. At age twenty-seven, Guillaume de Saint-Germain was barely three years younger than his brother, a head taller, and far more muscular. Though raised in the same monastery as Tristan, he had never captured Odo de Lagery's attention as had Tristan. Nonetheless, he did enjoy the good fortune of becoming the favorite of their adoptive aunt, the Countess Mathilda Medici of Tuscany, celebrated female warrior and ardent supporter of the Gregorian Papacy. Just as Odo de Lagery had mentored Tristan during boyhood toward the Benedictine order, Mathilda had mentored Guillaume, but toward weaponry and military strategy as she defended the Vatican against the attacks of her cousin, King Heinrich IV of Germany, during the Investiture Wars. By age eighteen, Guillaume had already developed into a seasoned military commander and unquestioning champion of the Vatican.

"Oh, Tristan, my dear, dear, Tristan!" exclaimed Countess Mathilda, hugging him, kissing each cheek. "Oh, and I see you have that rascal, Handel, with you!"

"Good afternoon, my dear Countess," grinned Handel, unclasping his mantle, bowing with impish exaggeration. "I've missed you terribly this past year! Furthermore, I–"

"But where's Mother?" interrupted Tristan, looking about.

"In her quarters," nodded Mathilda. "She arrived from Marcigny with a bit of cough, and though she wished to await you at the gate with myself and Guillaume, I insisted she stay out of the wind." Rifling a quick glance at Guillaume then, which Tristan caught, she followed with an awkward, albeit brief drop of expression. Then, dismissing it, she continued. "Ah, but so *very* good to see you and Handel again!" she beamed. "Oh... if only it weren't under such dreadful circumstances. Damnation, I say, to that horrid little worm, Kuku Peter, and his unsanctioned march. Ay, but perhaps you'll stop him in Cologne!"

The last comment surprised Tristan, who was under the impression that he and Handel were the only two possessing details about the mission to Cologne. "Aunt Mathilda, you *know*?" he asked.

"Yes, certainly, and so does Guillaume," she replied. "Odo sent the details north via the Underground even before telling you and Handel back in Rome, and also informed me that Asta would be arriving to bid you and Guillaume farewell. Besides, he didn't want you to have to be the one to disappoint Guillaume with the bad news about not marching with Bishop Adhémar, Raymond of Toulouse, and the southern French knights. He knew Guillaume was so looking forward to that, as were you. Besides–"

"Well, actually," interjected Tristan, looking over at his brother, "there is *still* a chance Guillaume and I may be able to do as originally planned, if I can manage to convince the Hermit to turn back."

But Tristan's tone carried lack of conviction, and neither Guillaume nor Mathilda swallowed it. "Oh no, I'm certain we'll end by following the Hermit overland to Constantinople," replied Guillaume, offering a glum shake of the head.

Tristan nodded reluctantly, then followed with that squint one collects when chasing answers. "So Guillaume," he said, "are you amenable to leading the Tuscan battalion over a thousand miles to Constantinople, if need be, shadowing the Hermit and his Peasants' Crusade?"

"Well," shrugged Guillaume, "I'm not ecstatic, if that's what you mean. But there's no way on earth I'd let you take on something like this alone, even if you *are* now Bishop of Ostia and Pope's Counsel. Besides, you've not forgotten the vow we swore as boys when King Heinrich and the Germans were besieging the Vatican, have you? We promised that as men we'd both become devoted Christian soldiers, and until the very end of our days on this earth we'd stand together, you and me."

"Ha, I *do* remember that day!" grinned Tristan, thinking back. "It was a dark time, but young as we were, we *did* stand together, did we not, Guillaume?"

Mathilda beamed, listening to her nephews reviving that seminal moment of fraternal solidarity. Then, turning to Handel, she said, "Oh, but things would be much simpler had his Holiness simply allowed you to stick a blade between Kuku Peter's wretched little ribs when you approached him crossing the German border! I read all about that meeting in Odo's letter."

"Ah, but Countess," chided Handel, "the Hermit was surrounded by knights. Would you have had me meet my end, not amongst friends, but in the midst of Kuku Peter's rabid imbeciles?"

"No, no, of course not!"

"But where are the uncles?" asked Tristan, glancing about.

The uncles Tristan was referring to were not uncles by blood, but by circumstance. They were the last three remaining members of Asta's original Danish Guard, clansmen of her father, Guntar the Mace; he had assigned them to protect and serve Asta upon the day of her birth. They had also helped raise Tristan and Guillaume until the boys were sent to the Black Monks of Cluny, then reunited with them after an eleven year separation. They had followed Asta to England after her arranged marriage to the despicable Lord Desmond DuLac, the boys' uncle, then helped her flee the ill-fated marriage and England during a night of violent rebellion.

"The Danes have been here visiting Mother," said Guillaume, "but left this morning to muster the Tuscan Knights. They'll be meeting us in three day's time. And by the way, Orla's son, Hroc, is coming with us. He's eighteen now, and as fearsome a warrior as God ever put upon this earth. He's no longer little Hroc, though. He's as big as a bear now."

"Ah, Hroc Five-hands, now grown!?" exclaimed Tristan. Then, after several minutes more of banter, Tristan settled into the business at hand. "So, Guillaume, what of the military arrangements for this expedition?"

"Aunt Mathilda has allocated us two hundred horse and nearly four hundred foot, including archers, signalmen and support. Then, too, she's included a full war chest ample to finance nearly a year. Also–"

"Nearly a year... *that's it?*" interrupted Handel, his shoulders raising to his ears. "Christ, this isn't some goddamned little hare hunt we're going on, you know!"

"*Handel*!" hissed Mathilda, crossing herself. "*Must you use such horrid language?*"

"Indeed, can you not find more suitable words?" scolded Guillaume, who was not quite as pious as Walter Sansavoir, but equally devoted to God and offended by anyone blaspheming the Lord. Turning back to Tristan, he said, "Surely a year will suffice to get us to Jerusalem and put the Turks to retreat, n'est-ce pas?"

"Well," Tristan replied, "remember that Handel is far more cautious than his actions indicate. Nevertheless, I must confess, the Muslims are far more advanced in art, education, culture, and weaponry than we in Europe like to believe, a mistake owed to a foolish Western bias that they are dirty and primitive simply because of the shade of their skin and the alien nature of their religion. In truth, they are extremely intelligent and aware, and–"

"Whoa, hold a minute," objected Guillaume. "You've preached this crusade throughout the cities of Italy and France for over a year, Brother, yet now you praise the enemy?"

"I am but giving an honest appraisal, Guillaume," Tristan countered. "This is no time for self-deceit about enemy weaknesses, nor for self-inflation about our own capabilities. The Muslims are a threat, truly, but their success is owed to their own advancements, not ignorance or inability to fight. Never forget that centuries ago the Moors would have swallowed France if Charles the Hammer had not chased them back south of the Pyrénées. Yet even now the Moors hold North Africa and continue to control half of Spain, and were it not for Duke Guiscard and the Normans these past decades, the Saracens would still control Sicily and the entire southern peninsula of Italy. But Moors and Saracens aside, it is the *Seljuk Turks* we will be fighting. They, of all the Muslims, are the most aggressive and violent, spreading terror amongst Arabs, Persians, and Africans of all Islamic sects. They've already consumed over two-thirds of the former Byzantine Empire, and continue like rats to gnaw away at the current Byzantine borders! What happens then when Constantinople falls? The Turks will eye Spain, Italy, then France! Where then will Christendom stand?" As each word spilled forth, Tristan's passion rose without him even realizing it, as did his voice.

His brother did not miss this, and was impressed by it. "Well spoken," said Guillaume. "I understand."

"Yes, *well spoken*," echoed Handel, that wry smirk of his surfacing. "Indeed, spoken in the same certain, fiery fashion of... Peter the Hermit himself, I might add."

"Oh Handel, such a vile thing to say!" huffed Mathilda. "For shame! I'll not have such indecent comparisons made on my property. You should be flogged for saying such a thing!"

"Indeed, *I should be flogged for saying such a thing*," echoed Handel in perfect mimicry, a corner of his mouth tilting upward. He found amusement in extracting inflamed reactions from the great Countess of Tuscany, whom he adored.

Seeing Handel's expression, Mathilda threw both hands to the air like startled birds, and laughed aloud "Oh, Handel, you *weasel*, once again deliberately agitating me, then finding humor in it!" But there was no anger in her face.

## Chapter Thirteen

### Canossa

After stabling horses and stowing baggage into the arrivals' private quarters, Guillaume led his brother to Asta's chamber. "Tristan, over these past two days," he said, "I have for the first occasion in life had the opportunity to spend extended time with our Mother, and gotten to know her a bit. I will confess, I've gained a better grasp of her... position... you know, when she sent us away so many years ago as small boys."

Pleased by these words, Tristan nodded. Asta had, since sending her sons to Cluny as children, always been a point of contention between the two brothers. Tristan had missed her terribly from that first moment of separation, but Guillaume was only four at the time; he had quickly forgotten his mother, and as he grew older, even harbored certain resentment over having been abandoned. Tristan, being seven at the time, did not forget Asta, and in fact grieved her absence throughout the eleven years of their separation. Moreover, he better understood the impossible circumstances that had necessitated Asta's decision to send the boys to the Black Monks of Cluny. "It warms me to hear this coming from you, Guillaume," Tristan acknowledged. "You tethered yourself to Auntie Mathilda as a boy, considering *her* your mother. God's grace to Mathilda for all she's done for you, but *Asta* is your true mother... and always has been."

"I suppose," conceded Guillaume. "In any case, I thought you should know that the rift between Asta and me has been bridged."

"There was never any rift with Mother," said Tristan. "The rift was only within yourself, Guillaume."

Guillaume felt the reproach, thinking Tristan's words harsh. Nevertheless, having no wish to incur dispute under the circumstances, he remained silent. *So odd*, he reflected, *the only words Tristan and I have ever crossed have centered on two women... Asta of the Danes, and Mala the Romani.*

As Guillaume ushered Tristan into their mother's quarters, Tristan moved to her quickly, enveloping her in a filial embrace. Reciprocating the affection, Asta flushed pink, throwing her arms about Tristan's neck, murmuring, "Tristan, oh Tristan, my dear, dear son!"

But the tenor of her voice was weak and thready, and within their embrace Tristan could feel that her breathing was labored, which caused him to pull back– examining more closely her face. The remarkable beauty of it was still evident, yet lay queerly veiled. Her hair, cheeks and neck being concealed by her nun's wimple, Asta's face resembled a mask– but unlike past visits, that mask appeared pallid, even ashen. Her eyes, once so lucid and stunning as to mesmerize, appeared ghostly– punctuated by tiny rivers of scarlet, palpitating lines. Then she coughed.

"*Dear God!*" Tristan heaved, alarmed, staring into her face as a funereal silence slipped over him, followed then by a tone of bitterness as he shuttled her immediately onto a nearby divan. "Mother, you are ill!" he scolded. "Why in God's name would you travel such a distance, and especially over the Alps in such condition?!"

"I had to," rasped Asta. "On receiving the Pope's message, my heart filled with despair over you and Guillaume! It was a mother's intuition turned dark and disturbing, I suppose, on hearing of the Pope sending you both to Germany, and later to this approaching holy war in the East. Then too, unknown to the Pope, I was already dreadfully ill back in Marcigny-sur-Loire... thus, I feared never to see you and Guillaume should I not make this journey. Sister Superior refused to release me at first, but caving to my violent objections, she put me in a coach under the care of two of our infirmary nuns, Sisters Angélique and Gisèle." The coughing came again, in sporadic bursts, and she gazed at Tristan with doleful eyes. "I've already told Guillaume, Tristan... I have but a short while left on this earth..."

Appalled, Tristan shot Guillaume a blank stare, then dropped next to Asta, grasping her hands. "Oh, but that cannot be!" he gasped, feeling his blood go cold from the roots of his hair to the tips of his fingers.

Tristan's words tumbled out in a passion, taking on a melancholy so solemn as to force Guillaume to look away. Then Tristan, confused, still refusing to believe Asta's words, was seized by that mournful, stricken half-laugh of the bereaved. Reaching out, he clasped Asta's head to his breast, cradling it ever so gently.

"Ah, Tristan," sighed Asta with resignation "I have been laboring with the ill and abandoned of Burgundy this past year– lepers, and those deteriorating with consumption and pox. It was God's work, and I relished it... but it has extracted its toll on me." Gathering a weak smile, she tightened her grip on Tristan's fingers, pausing slightly. "But be not sad for me, Son, for this has been a while coming, and long anticipated. The glory and mercy of God await me shortly in Heaven, and I welcome such peace for my earthly fate has been unkind in so many ways... and I am weary from it."

"I'll leave you two," said Guillaume in a low voice, excusing himself, feeling his heart beginning to swell. "Mother and I have shared time already, Tristan, and the two of you have much to discuss."

As Guillaume closed the door behind him, Tristan and Asta collapsed into each other's arms again, and Guillaume heard his brother slip into sorrowful whispering as Asta, in turn, whispered back, striving to soothe his fracturing heart. Asta and Tristan's love had always constituted an inviolable bond, one that Guillaume had not shared in equal measure... yet Guillaume now felt an unexpected wave of emotion coming at him– not for himself so much, but for his brother and his mother.

***

Over the next three days Tristan and Asta spent much time in prayer, sharing stories, even discovering moments of laughter together. It was a time of contentment for all, in fact, as Countess Mathilda's army of servants spared no effort in preparing exquisite meals of pheasant, swan, goose, trout, and roasted hog for the guests. Asta was unable to attend many of these festivities, but appeared whenever feeling fit enough to leave her chambers. And though she said little during those occasions, her eyes glimmered with pride and adoration watching her two sons interact with each other, Handel, and Mathilda at the table. Tristan and Guillaume had been the joy of her life upon their birth into this world, and for Asta, even these many difficult years later... nothing had changed. Thus her sojourn in Canossa, despite her failing condition, was a joyous time for her.

"It's a long and arduous journey you men are undertaking," bemoaned Mathilda one night as they dined, "and if you fail to turn the Hermit back in Cologne, I'll not be seeing you three for a year at least. Perhaps even longer, if we're to believe Handel, here. That means you'll be stuck eating nothing but lowly camp fare along the long road to Jerusalem, so best that you eat to your heart's content now! Indeed, so let's make the most of each other's company while we can!"

Heeding Mathilda's advice, they spent hour after hour dining at leisure, sharing recollections of earlier times, and discussing what the future of the crusade might hold. It was during one of these dinners that Tristan inquired about the farm at the foot of the mountain. "Aunt Mathilda," he asked, "what would I have to do to acquire deed to that little piece along the brook at the foot of the mountain?"

"Huh?" she said, surprised. "But Tristan, what's your interest in it? The land is rocky and the cottage is but a hovel."

"Perhaps so," replied Tristan, "but that little plot possesses my heart, and it has for a good while now. It holds meaning to me."

"Oh, but I could've never guessed such a thing," shrugged Mathilda, the wealthiest, most powerful woman of all Europe. "Especially since you now stand upon the grand stage of Europe, working in the Vatican, visiting Paris, Berlin, Vienna, and such. That property is but a trifle. All you need do is ask and it's yours, Nephew, for it means little to me, dear."

"Ah, wonderful," Tristan replied, a broad smile filling his face. "If you don't mind then, would you hold it for me? When the crusade is done, I should like to establish a summer retreat there, perhaps."

"Yes, certainly," Mathilda smiled, content that Tristan appeared so pleased, yet puzzled why the small plot held so much meaning to him.

## Chapter Fourteen

### The Grave

The brief visit at Canossa was a pleasant time for Tristan while in the company of Asta, Guillaume, Mathilda, and Handel. When caught alone, however, Tristan would slip away to a gated, abandoned area behind Saint Nicholas Cathedral. There, his mood inevitably darkened. A graveyard stood there, and in the far corner stood a modest granite headstone upon which was carved the inscription: *Un-named Infant of God.* Tristan spent hours there, seated on a marble bench erected in front of that grave and another simply marked: *Fernando.*

Tristan remembered Fernando, a husky, dark Romani who had always despised him out of jealousy over the beautiful Romani girl, Mala, whom they both loved. Tristan had defeated Fernando in that mutual endeavor to acquire her affections, but after that short-lived victory, time, circumstance, and even Fernando had conspired to later defeat Tristan. In the end there were *no* winners in that ill-fated triangle. Now, as Tristan glanced at Fernando's stone, it seemed to him that Fernando lay in that grave moldering in a state of contentment, knowing that though he had lost Mala to Tristan, in the end Tristan had not won either, but had paid a devastating toll.

More than anything, though, it was the infant's grave that drew Tristan's attention. He sat staring at it for hours on end, rising only to kneel from time to time. *God, have mercy on this infant,* he prayed... *for he was innocent of my sins and all other sins. Although he died before he could be baptized, I pray that You pardon the original sin that all beings are born with as they enter life upon this earth. Lord, I would spend all the days of eternity suffering the fires of Hell if only you promise to be merciful and accept my son into your Heavenly realm. Amen.*

On his last full day at Canossa, Tristan determined it important to bring his mother to the infant's grave site. Sick as she was, he swaddled her in blankets and had servants litter-carry her to the cemetery, propping her upon the bench located before the infant's tomb. Tristan had told Asta years earlier about his fall from grace, Mala, and the ill-fated birth of their newborn son. Now, knowing that Asta was ill, that she had never been to Canossa and would likely never return there, he felt compelled to unite his mother and his son– even if only for a moment.

"I've often thought it was the infant who bore God's punishment for my own illicit actions," he confessed to Asta as they sat there together contemplating the grave site. "And God continues that punishment by channeling it through my unbearable grief for my unfortunate son. It's a terrible burden, Mother. Then too, my profound feelings for Mala have never completely... dissipated. And that, too, hurts deeply."

"Indeed," rasped Asta, gazing thoughtfully at the inscription carved into her only grandchild's stone, "God shows his wrath in hurtful ways... yet, in the end, somehow, He remains a just God."

"Oh, but I wonder, at times, Mother. The infant did nothing to deserve such a fate. Punish me forever for my trespasses, yes– but the child was innocent, even denied the opportunity of baptism, and thus denied eternal salvation and Heaven."

"Yes, as dictated by Saint Augustine of Hippo's judgment about the Limbo of Infants many centuries ago..." shivered Asta, pulling her blanket about her neck. "But trust in God, Tristan. Never lose your faith in Him, Son, for without it, you shall be lost."

"I feel lost already now, Mother– at times," replied Tristan, shaking his head, cradling his chin into a palm. "As I stare at this grave, as I contend with learning of your illness, and as I depart for some ill-devised mission to stop a madman, I feel as though I am but wandering about listlessly, stumbling about in some accursed fog. More and more, things begin to make less sense to me in this life."

Extending a hand from beneath her blanket, Asta fumbled about, clasping her fingers around those of Tristan. "Hold strong your faith, Son," she whispered. "We know nothing of God's plan... until the very end. It will all become clear then, and only then." She coughed then, and began to quake, falling into a slight seizure. "Bless you, Tristan, for bringing me to the grave of my grandson," she said, struggling. "It is a blessed moment, this – you, me, and the child together."

Considering these words, Tristan's eyes filled with admiration. "How is it, Mother, that despite all the struggles God has thrust onto your shoulders... you remain so resolute and faithful. I find myself, even as a bishop, faltering at times."

"God gave me life, Tristan, placing me into a world of position and prestige as a child... like yourself. It was a garden, really, until the heavy boots of men tramped through it. For me, it was first William the Bastard– betraying and executing my father for opposing my marriage as a twelve-year-old child to a man thirty years my senior. Next came Roger de Saint-Germain. Yet, from such dark roots sprang you and Guillaume, the loves of my life... God's true purpose for my existence, I've since decided. In the shadow of Roger came Desmond DuLac, my next husband... and yes, by my choice perhaps, yet not happily so because earlier men had left me no other options. Still, because of Desmond DuLac's evil I ended a sister of the Benedictine order. So you see, Tristan, it is never God who tramples the garden, nor sets it afire. It is always the greed and hunger of men... *privileged men."*

Tristan sighed with assent, yet a part of his expression teetered with disquiet as his eyes fell to the grave at his feet. Seeing this, something flicked Asta– forcing a feeble convulsiveness onto her body. It lasted but an instant– then disappeared like a glimmer. "*What is it, Mother?*" Tristan said, his voice falling low.

"Tristan," she whispered, her eyes imploring, "vow to me that you will never abandon your faith... no matter what falls, no matter what life brings."

Tristan nodded. "Indeed," he said, simply. Then, despite remarking how warm the breeze felt, he perceived that nature was beating at Asta; she was still trembling beneath her blankets. "Yes, Mother, a blessed moment, this... you, me, the infant," he said, caressing her shoulder. "But let me take you from this wind and back to your bed." Motioning to the servants standing nearby, he instructed them to return Asta to her quarters. *Ah,* he then whispered, crossing himself as he watched Asta's departure with sadness... *and now, God, You are soon about to rip yet another fragment from my already depleted heart...*

# Chapter Fifteen

## The Human Heart

One is inclined to suppose that of all of God's creations, the most complex would be the human mind. That, however, would be a grievous error of judgment. By far, the more complex creation is the human *heart.*

Whereas it is true that the mind possesses unparalleled brilliance that has propelled humanity forward through the darkness of prehistory and primordial ignorance, it is the heart that has both created and solved the more intricate challenges of humanity's struggle to exist. The mind seeks stability, operating on logic, identification of patterns, and recognition of consequences. The heart, however, often defies such anchored reasoning, overwhelming rationality with that oppositional bludgeon known as 'emotion.' And the wildly swinging pendulum of emotion frequently leads men into taking the most difficult rather than the least complicated course of action… which easily leads one to the very precipice of self-destruction, if not beyond. Thus the rash heart out-trumps the level mind, by-passing it almost at will through detours of impracticality, impossible hope and runaway dreams.

The ill-fated love of Tristan de Saint-Germain and Mala the Romani was a perfect case in point. Raised by a zealously pious mother, taught by a corps of teacher nuns, then raised within the very nest of extreme reformist Benedictines since the age of seven, Tristan's mind should have quickly and indisputably directed him into a monastic future. Despite the crush of his combined circumstances, Tristan's young heart retained the wherewithal as a boy to resist the inclination of becoming a Benedictine monk. In other words, his heart resolved to outmaneuver his logical direction, his religious surroundings, and those attempting to direct him into the clergy.

But then, as hearts are so apt to do, his heart veered wildly. After years of resisting the pull of ordination as a monk, Tristan's heart then swamped itself, switching direction after his cathartic episode atop Monte Cassino which came to be known as the 'Miracle of Monte Cassino.' Then too, the strange episodes of the ghostly cathedral bells taking over his consciousness during moments of high trauma added to the equation of Tristan's shifting heart. Indeed, both the episode atop Monte Cassino and the tolling ghost-bells during Tristan's two flights from Rome defied all tenants of logic and reason... therefore, they could only have occurred as matters of the heart, later forcing themselves to be *accepted* by the mind.

The damnable complexity of Tristan's rash, unsettled heart had not ended there. After finally and willingly following his heart into taking the vows of celibacy and chastity while donning the black robe, an earlier swing of his heart's pendulum remained intact... and that was Mala, the beautiful Romani girl he had first met as a boy. Whatever that mysterious fixation and mutual adoration was that had befallen the two children, following them through adolescence and into young adulthood, had somehow been chiseled in stone, refusing to dissipate.

Within a year of ordination, despite now being a reformist Benedictine monk, the swerve of Tristan's own heart once again flung itself against the jagged edges of reality. To begin, his ordination into the Benedictines had defied his life-long love for Mala. Next, his love for Mala in turn defied his vows to the Church. Nonetheless, that very next year he had pursued Mala despite those vows. His mind repeatedly warned him that he would forever be possessed by the Church, yet he allowed his heart to lead him toward Mala, into temptation and violation of his Benedictine vows.

Later, when his illicit love for Mala turned to shambles through no fault of his own and their newborn son was taken by God in the Alps, Tristan performed an excruciating penance and returned to the Church. For years he shoved thoughts of Mala aside, as she had married Vincento Balducci, and went about his religious responsibilities duteously. Still, his love for her burned ever secretly and fervently within the depths of his heart.

Years later after Balducci's death, Mala offered herself to Tristan once again as la Gran Signorina of Genoa, with no expectation of marriage or of Tristan abandoning the Church. It would have been an easy play for him, yet the same heart that had bound him to her now shifted yet again... he refused her, pledging his allegiance once again to the Church, and according to Mala, holding true to the expectations of Odo de Lagery, his de facto father.

Thus the very things that could have simplified Tristan's existence, establishing at least a modicum of certainty in the flow of his life, were sabotaged by the oppositional arcs of Tristan's own heart as it swayed one direction, then the next. Had he ever simply followed his heart completely in one direction or the other, life might have taken a clear path forward.

Nonetheless, it was his own shifting heart that led him asunder time and time again, dancing first here, then there. This, of course, was by no means a trait unique to Tristan de Saint-Germain. Rather, it is characteristic of many within the human race who are born without the gift of 'certainty.' Therefore, this instability of the heart is a common snare in which half of humanity entraps itself. By way of comparison, one need simply refer back to the womb waters of certainty in which Peter the Hermit was bathed between conception and birth. Never led astray or confounded by the shifting pendulum of an irresolute heart, Kuku Peter knew and forever followed only one direction.

So it is that by bestowing free will and superior intelligence upon mankind, God balanced the scales by adding the heart... thus also ensuring infinite weakness and confusion.

The day after bringing Asta to the grave of his and Mala's deceased newborn, Tristan went there again, alone. Reaching into his vestments, he withdrew the silver ring Mala had given him when they were children. Staring at it wistfully as he had done so many other times since first receiving it from her as a boy, his heart filled with regret and sorrow… not only over the death of their newborn child, but also over the loss of other things that might have been. He imagined vignettes then, of him, Mala and their son together on the small farm at the bottom of the mountain, warm in each others' company as a loving family. Then, realizing the child had never even been named or baptized, he dismissed the thoughts as sinful, and began to ponder – *Indeed, God is putting me on trial once again, but I have chosen the Church. Therefore, I must remain strong and keep Mala in my past.*

At the very moment this thought was creeping into Tristan's mind, a great distance away Mala was kneeling alone within the great cathedral of Genoa, thinking of him. She had gone there to light a candle for her lost baby boy, as she did every Wednesday; the child had passed on a Wednesday atop the frozen heights of the Alps. But each time she made this visitation commemorating her lost son, she could not help but also think of Tristan. *Why did he refuse me a year ago,* she wondered. *I made no demands, nor did I set any conditions.*

In truth, she knew the answer, and had confronted Tristan with it in a moment of anger that same night he rebuffed her. *It's Odo de Lagery!* she had told him angrily. *He has molded you into his own image. You were but a child and he craftily manipulated you for the benefit of the Church.*

Mala, for that reason, often found herself at odds with the Church though she was still drawn to it. She fully understood the reformist movement was a necessity of sorts; so many of the Catholic clergy had become abusive in terms of money, power, and promiscuity. Then again, she also felt the reformers were incorrigible in their own way, having become merciless and inflexible in their quest to cleanse the landscape, especially with their own clerics.

Of everyone within the power structure of the Church, there were two individuals she resented above all. The first was Countess Mathilda Medici of Tuscany, from whom she had sought assistance during the most devastating period of her life. Mathilda had rejected her, accusing her of profiteering and attempting to destroy Tristan's brilliant future in the Church. Even though her son was buried there at Mathilda's Canossa fortress, Mala had long since refused to go there due to the personal venom existing between the two women.

The second individual was Odo de Lagery, now enthroned as Pope Urban II. Irrespective of the fact she had enabled him to buy his way into the Lateran Palace years before, she had done that for Tristan, not for Odo. She knew Tristan loved Odo and would give his own life for the man who served as his father during boyhood at the Cluny monastery, then later in Ostia and Rome. Yet every time she envisioned Odo de Lagery, it was with bitterness.

So as she knelt within the Cathedral of Genoa, it was Tristan who possessed her thoughts. *Yes, I'll see him soon again,* she promised herself. *Indeed, upon receiving word from little Fazio, I'll go to Tristan once again, but this time it will be far from the Vatican and far from the scabrous reach of Odo de Lagery... far to the East, in Constantinople.*

# Chapter Sixteen

## Little Fazio

Each human enters life equally naked by being one day rudely expelled from the sheltered haven of woman's womb. Each newborn then equally gasps for air in a humble and helpless beginning, blinking in terror as it enters the world. But then, after breathing that first gasp of air, all equity abruptly ends as each infant launches forward under circumstances predetermined or cast down by genetics, family, and fortune. Whereas some are born into this life blessed with the gifts of fine appearance, intelligence, and means, others arrive bearing burdensome crosses they must drag about the rest of their days.

Benito Fazio was of this latter group, his curses being his tiny stature and his larynx.

He had thought himself like other children until the age of four when he realized those of his same age had grown twice his size. By age eight, that time when cruelty amongst children blossoms, he became the butt of snide remarks and pranks as girls shunned him and boys began poking at him. Worsening matters, the sound of his voice developed unnaturally, taking on an elfish quality. When looking at and talking to young Benito, then, one felt nearly disoriented, as confronted by something unreal. Indeed, his tiny stature forced one to stare, then on hearing him speak, one could not help but snicker.

It is nearly impossible, of course, for those living a life steeped in regularity to fathom the struggles of those suffering from abnormality– nor is it of much interest, actually. Little Benito, subsequently, became isolated in childhood, finding himself lacking playmates or friends. By adolescence he was still but half the size of his peers, and the elfin quality of his voice had become even more pronounced, therefore more ridiculed. These shortcomings incurred several consequences. To begin, he soon abhorred and avoided females as it seemed they invariably traveled in gaggles of three or four, and on encountering Benito, these girlish gaggles would point, giggle and squeal, creating theatre– which humiliated him, drawing even more unwanted attention. Next, Benito withdrew into himself, which only further exacerbated an already lonely existence. And finally, he began to especially resent those whom God had blessed with handsome countenance, position, and public respect.

"Why couldn't I have at least *one* of those things?" he lamented time and again, wondering why a select few had received so many gifts in combination while he had received none.

Such was his state of mind as he clandestinely followed Bishop Saint-Germain north, reconnoitering his activities for la Gran Signorina. As the papal train entered one town after the next, Fazio watched enviously as the Bishop was much admired and hailed by all he encountered. Bishop Saint-Germain had already earned somewhat of an early celebrity status as a boy due to his phenomenal intelligence and close association with Odo de Lagery, becoming known as the 'Wonder of Cluny.' This touted status only elevated with maturation into manhood, reaching a pinnacle when he became renowned for the 'Miracle of Monte Cassino' and, more recently, for so passionately proselytizing the Pope's holy war. Now, at age thirty, young Bishop Saint-Germain was wildly lauded throughout Italy, as well as throughout Germany and his native land of France.

*Oh, but to have a position such as Bishop of Ostia or to be First Counsel to the Pope himself,* wished Fazio. *Oh, to be so remarkably handsome and applauded by all!*

Notwithstanding, there was something more elemental nagging at Fazio about Bishop Saint-Germain. Bad enough that the man seemed to have everything in life, but to have committed two abominable crimes such as his friend the jailer, Anonelli, had intimated. Worse yet, of all things, to be rewarded in the end by the Vatican and the Church!

*Men such as him laugh at the rest of us fools, and the world,* simmered Fazio as he trailed Bishop Saint-Germain's retinue north toward Canossa. But there was yet another burr poking at Fazio– la Gran Signorina's keen interest in the Bishop. It baffled him. He had difficulty understanding why she had so vehemently defended him back in Genoa, and he now began to fret over it because he admired and respected la Gran Signorina above all other people; she had treated him so well from the very beginning, and also paid him handsomely over the years. Thus, despite her massive wealth and untold influence opposed to his own meager existence, Fazio felt a compelling compunction to protect her from the likes of Bishop Saint-Germain.

Thus imbuing himself day by day with loathing for Bishop Saint-Germain, Fazio trailed him into Tuscany, then on to Countess Mathilda's stronghold at Canossa. The fortress had been tightly secured during the bloody Investiture War against King Heinrich IV of Germany, but the return of peace had prompted Countess Mathilda to re-open her gates to accommodate pilgrims wishing to lay alms at the altar of the Cathedral of Saint Nicholas; beneath it were buried two reliquaries containing holy relics, one holding filings from the chains that had bound Saint Peter just prior to his execution by the Romans, and the other holding a bone fragment of Saint Jerome's forearm.

Posing as a pilgrim, Fazio easily gained entrance to the fortress and set about seeking la Gran Signorina's informant, a blacksmith whose shop was reportedly located next to the fortress stables. Investigating this location but finding no one, nor even signs of recent activity, Fazio called out to a stable boy pitching hay nearby.

Looking up, the lad was immediately struck by Fazio's small stature, as well as by the high tenor of his voice. Squinting, he stared hard for a moment before setting his pitchfork aside and stepping closer to examine this most curious of visitors. "Ah, if you're looking for Valentino the smithy," he said, his eyes raking over the diminutive figure standing before him, "you'll not find him this week, for he and his son are off to a funeral two valleys over."

Masking discouragement, Fazio peered toward the stables, thinking to adopt a new tactic. "So there, lad, from the smell of things, I see you're tending to a full slew of lathered horses... must be those fellows who recently arrived from Rome, huh?"

"Ay," the boy nodded proudly. "And Bishop Saint-Germain himself is in their party!" Did you know that, eh?"

"Ah, so I've heard. But tell, word in Rome was that he was soon to be headed south to sail off to the Pope's holy war. What's he doing so far north?"

"Ah, no idea, really," the boy replied, more and more amused by the aberrant sound of the visitor's voice. "I did hear one of the soldiers mention something about Germany... Cologne, I think." At this, a light seemed to dawn on his expression; he had heard tales of dwarves before, but had never actually seen one... now, eyeing Fazio from head to toe, he was certain that this little fellow was, indeed, a dwarf.

"If you stare any harder at me, you little piker, your damned eyeballs will cross, then stick that way forever!" snorted Fazio. Then, setting aside his irritation, he fished into a pocket and withdrew a small silver coin. "Here boy, it's yours if you can tell me anything else of interest concerning Bishop Saint-Germain's visit here."

His eyes turning to saucers, the boy shuffled about with yearning for several seconds, thinking to fabricate some bit of false information. But then he remembered something his grandfather had mentioned the last time the Bishop was at the fortress. "Well, sir," he said, "every time he visits, the Bishop makes several visits to the Canossa graveyard, just yonder behind the Cathedral of Saint Nicholas."

"Eh? Now that's a worthless observation," grunted Fazio, passing off the boy's effort.

Undeterred, the boy pressed on. "My grandfather's the cemetery caretaker, and he told me the Bishop *always* visits one certain grave, and prays over it... the grave of an un-named infant. I thought that interesting, odd even... don't you?" Then, quick as a wink, the boy snatched the coin from Fazio's fingers and bolted, having already calculated that the odd little fellow baiting him could never catch him, thus posed no threat.

Caught by surprise, Fazio thought at first to chase the lad down, but quickly determined it best to not draw attention to himself within the fortress. "Goddamned little piker!" he swore beneath his breath, abandoning the stables. Still, the boy's words pricked Fazio's curiosity a tad, so he crossed the square and made his way to the back of the Saint Nicholas Cathedral, finding there an elderly man pulling weeds and raking leaves from around gravestones. "Say there, good fellow," called Fazio, "dare I venture to guess you're the caretaker of this graveyard?"

"I am," nodded the man curtly, as wishing not to be interrupted from his labors. "I've tended these stones for nearly thirty years. But what's your interest in that, huh?"

"Oh, it's just that I'm so very impressed!" lied Fazio. "Ay, I've rarely seen a graveyard so well manicured! Then too, it seems I just met your grandson there in the stables." Saying nothing of the boy's theft, Fazio continued spinning words. "Yeah, the boy was bragging about all your good work here."

As intended, Fazio's word's softened the caretaker. "Indeed," he said, looking up, "I work my fingers to the bone each day tending to these resting places of the dearly departed." Crossing himself, he continued. "May they rest in peace. As to my grandson, yes, that's him in the stables. And a little rascal he is, too!"

"Oh, a good lad, that boy!" Fazio exclaimed, still saying nothing of the coin theft. "And so full of interesting stories."

"Oh?"

"Yeah, such as telling me about Bishop Saint-Germain spending so much time here at the cemetery whenever he visits Canossa. And as I recall, the boy said something about a certain grave... an infant's tomb?"

Hearing the Bishop's name, the old man smiled. "Oh, a saint, that man! Come along, yes, I'll show you." Leading Fazio to the tomb inscribed 'Un-named Infant of God,' he pointed. "Ay, whenever the Bishop visits Canossa, he prays over this grave. As a matter of fact he was just here this morning... with his mother, who happens to be visiting."

"*His mother?*" asked Fazio, puzzled. "Is this infant a family member, then?"

"Oh no, not at all."

"Hmm..." shrugged Fazio, "that's odd, then. And too, it's such an inauspicious marker. No name, even?"

"Ah, the poor child died, evidently, before being named.

"Oh, *unfortunate,* that..." Fazio mused, his mind edging toward disconnected suppositions, one of which kept leading him back to his friend, Antonelli the jailer. "Well then, sir," he continued, "dare I suppose you have any idea where this infant came from, or how it happened to be buried here in the fortress of la Gran Contessa Mathilda?"

"Oh, 'twas a long while back," sighed the caretaker, "but yes, I still remember. A German caravan was on its way here to Canossa one winter, and while traversing the Alps came upon a small box-wagon buried in ice. Breaking through the ice, the Germans discovered two women within the wagon ... they were both on death's doorstep, I was told, frozen near to death. With them in the wagon was this infant who's now buried here... frozen solid, dead. The younger woman in the wagon was the baby's mother, apparently, and the older woman an aunt. Oh, and there was a dead man in the wagon as well." Raising a hand, the caretaker motioned to the adjacent stone marked 'Fernando.'

Fazio gave the stone a brief glance, then looked back toward the infant's marker. "There's... no date on either of these gravestones," he remarked, raising his shoulders with curiosity.

The caretaker nodded. "The two women in the wagon were unconscious when the Germans discovered them, and may well have been unconscious for days. Neither one knew when exactly the infant died, or the man. Ay, neither had any recollection of anything, really. So the Germans revived the two women, strapped the two corpses atop a wagon and brought them here to Canossa. Anyway, Countess Mathilda agreed to bury the infant and the man here within the fortress. I was instructed to dig two graves and dedicate two stones. It all happened rather quickly, actually, so time was short. As things happened, the Cardinal-Bishop of Ostia, Odo de Lagery himself, was here at the time visiting Countess Mathilda. It was him, actually, who ministered the burial mass and gave final words here at the gravesite."

"*Really?*" muttered Fazio. "Quite generous of both Countess Mathilda and the Bishop of Ostia to make such grand gestures to... complete unknowns. And stranger yet that Bishop Saint-Germain has taken an interest in this infant's grave, too."

"I suppose so," nodded the caretaker, his brow furrowing. "A strange thing though... since you mention generosity. In the end, that generosity was short-lived. Shortly after the burials, the Countess went into a rage at the two women who survived."

"Huh?" said Fazio, struggling to knit sense out of the details the caretaker was now divulging.

"Yes, and the Cardinal went into a rage at them also," the caretaker continued. "He stormed out of Canossa shortly thereafter, as a matter of fact. "And as I recall... the two women also quickly left, fearing that Countess Mathilda might imprison them... or worse."

"And what became of them, then?"

"Oh, God only knows... they simply disappeared. Poof! Gone. Hell, they could both be dead for that matter, huh?"

Those who earn their bread spying on others and unearthing private information are easily inclined to caving in to hunches and suspicions, even at the cost of truth. Absorbing the words just uttered by the caretaker, Fazio began falling into this very trap. Despite being unable to contrive factual connections, he imagined foul play– which seemed to fit handily into the story Antonelli had shared. Squinting, he placed a finger to his forehead while summoning a slight shrug. "Sir," he said, "you say you've been here thirty years or so... but this incident you're describing, did it by chance occur... ten years ago, or very close to that time?"

Reeling back in time, the caretaker closed his eyes, calculating. Soon his eyes reopened as he nodded, surprised. "Why yes, almost ten years exactly!" he exclaimed. "*But how could you guess such a thing?*"

Saying nothing, Fazio took his leave, confident that secrets long buried were beginning, slowly, to coalesce. Thus convinced, he began to presume an ill-fated connection between Bishop Saint-Germain and the unnamed grave. *No*, he thought, following his suspicions down the spiraling trail of misdirection, *that infant did not freeze to death in the Alps, but was likely murdered... as was, later, the mother. After all, according to Antonelli, and now the caretaker, she simply vanished, never to be seen or heard from again. Oh, but that Bishop is a vile predator clothed in lamb's wool, and la Gran Signorina is falsely attracted to him.*

*But if there is truly a God, things right will come right...and should the opportunity ever present itself, I will expose the Bishop's true character and his crimes to la Gran Signorina... and to the world.*

# Chapter Seventeen

## Brothers in Arms

On the morning of departure from Tuscany, Tristan anticipated that exchanging his final farewell with Asta would be more than he could bear. Thus, struggling against the wounds of her future absence, he wrapped her in an extended, grief-stricken embrace. But Asta held strong, and her affirmative spirits helped to lift Tristan through the impossibility of seeing his mother for the last time. Then, her eyes taking on a strange glimmer, she gazed up from her bed, squeezing his hand tightly. "Tristan," she said with solemnity, "do you remember our last day together in Saint-Germain-en-Laye when you were but seven? That day I sent you and Guillaume away with the ox-man and the Danes to the Black Monks of Cluny?"

"Yes... of course," Tristan replied. "It was a day that crushed my soul, Mother... and still chills me when I think back on it. But why do you ask?"

"On that day I asked you to keep an eye to your younger brother, for he was only four years old– neither as clever nor as cautious as yourself."

Thinking back, Tristan nodded. "Indeed, those were your exact words." he murmured.

"As we now part once again," Asta continued, "I will unearth, and repeat that same request from the past. Guillaume is *still* not as clever nor as cautious as you. Worse yet, his naked fearlessness will invite peril in this deadly war against Islam that awaits. Will you, then, on God's word... promise to keep an eye to your younger brother, Tristan?"

"Yes, Mother," assented Tristan, nodding with certainty.

"Be on your way then, Son. And Godspeed to you both."

Thus having uttered the last words she would ever say to her beloved first-born, Asta of the Danes kissed Tristan on the back of his hand, crossed herself, and sent him away... so he would not be there to witness as she herself fell into trembling. As happens to all mothers just on the threshold of sending two sons off to war, she had arrived at that moment of bursting with dread–already suspecting that fortune would be neither so kind nor happenstance as to spare them both from being unscathed.

Moments later Tristan was gathering Handel, and the two descended the fortress trail to meet Guillaume at the foot of the mountain where he had assembled the Golden Knights of Tuscany and accompanying foot soldiers. Although the knights were not suited in battle regalia, they looked formidable in formal uniform with bright gonfalons and pennons streaming in the breeze from the ends of their lances. After so much talk over the past year, as Tristan eyed this sight, it was the first time he actually felt the palpitation of oncoming war. As a cleric he was forbidden from fighting, of course, yet he felt confident the Turks would be put to route upon facing such military splendor as the Tuscan knights, even though this small force was but a tiny fraction of what was to soon emerge from the shadows of Christendom.

"Ah, such magnificent troops!" he declared to Handel as they approached Guillaume at the fore of the first phalanx.

"All troops are magnificent at the rest position," quipped Handel, "when there's no blood staining the blouse, nor brains streaming from head gashes and bashed helmets. Ay, and lacking that final gaze of stupefied horror just before taking that dying breath, crying out *how in Hell did I get dragged into this!?*"

Tristan was about to scold Handel for these remarks but just then caught sight of the Danish uncles sitting astride their mounts beside Guillaume. "Ho there, Orla! Crowbones and Guthroth, greetings!" he shouted, riding up to them, exchanging raised fists and slaps on the shoulders.

"Damnation, Boy, and we hear they've raised you to bishop since we last met!" exclaimed Orla, who like the other Danes had called Tristan "Boy" since birth. Orla was a big man, immensely taller and far stouter than the southern Europeans of France and Italy, and though now nearly sixty, still cut a fearful figure with his intimidating size and brutish frame. Yet, beneath his full, reddish-gray beard and behind the glint of his fierce blue eyes, a hint of his old mischief was still evident.

"Ja, just look at those fine holy vestments you're now wearing!" laughed Crowbones, Orla's brother who was equally enormous and often mistaken for Orla's twin though he was four years younger. Crowbones was missing his left arm, severed at the elbow in England during battle with raiding Scotts. His real name was Ivar, but as a boy he had spent much time with his pagan Finnish grandmother who was adept at reading bird bones to forecast the future. He adopted her craft while young, and still carried a leather pouch containing the desiccated bones of a crow about his neck. Neither he nor Orla had ever consented to being baptized, and both still clung to the old Viking beliefs though Christianity had long since been forced upon most of the Nordic people.

"J-ja, ja... you'll n-next be p-pope!" repeated Guthroth the Quiet, the third uncle who was cousin to Orla and Crowbones, and twelve years younger. Guthroth the Quiet had acquired his moniker because he was born with a stutter; speaking had become, since childhood, a source of embarrassment. As a boy, it had also been the source of frequent beatings from his father who thought him thick-headed and was embarrassed by his son's speech impediment. From an early age then, Guthroth preferred to remain silent, though in reality he was far more clever than others imagined.

Then Hroc, Orla's son, nudged his horse up to Tristan, issuing a shy wave of the hand. Like his father and uncle, Hroc was massive, though his face was boyish. Looking at him, it was difficult for Tristan to believe that this youngster was a ruthless warrior who had killed his first adversary by age fourteen and sent hundreds of others to their grave during the Investiture War against the Germans.

"Hail to you, Uncle Tristan," Hroc said respectfully. Just as the Danes were not uncles by blood to Tristan, nor was Tristan uncle to Hroc by blood. Nonetheless, old Nordic clan tradition expected younger men to address elder men who were closely tied to family as such.

Interestingly, Tristan's Danish uncles were actually Normans. The Normans of France were originally Danes who during previous centuries had raided and terrorized the French, eventually forcing them to pay exhaustive tribute known as Danegeld. Weary of paying such tribute, King Charles the Simple of France had ended by ceding a portion of northern France in 911 to the Danish clans of Hrolf Ragnvaldsson in exchange for promises to leave France in peace and keep other Vikings from attacking its borders. This Danish territory became known as 'Normandy' due to the Nordic influx.

Within a century the incoming Danish settlers had abandoned Nordic traditions, adopted the French language and customs, and formed a French society of their own. A sparse handful of throwbacks steadfastly refused to adopt either French culture or Christianity, however, and fiercely clung to their Viking roots, which cost them alienation amongst both the Normans and the French. Tristan's uncles were such men, and thus represented the final remnants of a passing breed.

After presenting Handel to the Danes and sharing a few more exchanges, Guillaume nodded to his signalman. The bugler trumpeted a series of blasts that signified the 'forward march' command as Guillaume tipped his pennon and spurred his horse.

Thus began the first leg of the Holy Crusade for these brothers-in arms, joined together in a common endeavor by the politics of the Church, but tied to one another even more strongly by kinship, loyalty, and faith in each other.

# Chapter Eighteen

## Moving North

When men of strong will and character gather, opinions are bound to be voiced– and also to collide. As the Tuscan force marched north toward Cologne through the Apennines and the Alps, conversation and disagreement flourished amongst the men in Tristan's circle. Handel continued to challenge the very validity of the Pope's crusade while Tristan and Guillaume continued to defend it, Guillaume even more adamantly than Tristan.

Although Tristan was the cleric, Guillaume's adherence to Church dogma was far more rigid than his brother's. Moreover, Tristan's keen intellect and sensitivity forced him to assess things more profoundly than Guillaume, thereby forcing questions to arise. Further reinforcing Guillaume's spiritual inflexibility was the fact he had never committed a single trespass against the Church. This single factor in itself made it inevitable that he would interpret things as black or white whereas Tristan drifted from time to time within the margins of gray, as prescribed by his previous carnal indiscretions with Mala.

More interestingly, the opinions of Orla and Crowbones gave these verbal disputes yet another slant. As pagans, they clearly understood war for defense or conquest, but simply could not fathom going to war over– religion. Subsequently, the exchanges among the men often became quite heated. Young Hroc remained nearly as silent as Guthroth the Quiet, more out of deference to elders than embarrassment of speaking, as was the case for Guthroth.

"Tristan, how is it that this bizarre little preacher, Kuku Peter, can call himself a man of God?" asked Guillaume one day as they worked their way through the mountains. "Isn't he the same little fellow who was imprisoned and scheduled to be executed by Lord Truffault of France for seducing Lady Truffault? Wasn't it him you saved from certain hanging that day we found him by chance in Truffault's dungeon? And yet now he preaches to thousands about the sanctity of grace and adherence to God's commandments?"

"Yes, he's one and the same," Tristan replied. "I managed to save him from execution only by invoking the name of Odo de Lagery to Lord Truffault as the Hermit's dear friend and protector. A distortion of the truth, I fear, but the innocent should not suffer for the sins of the guilty. In truth, Guillaume, the Hermit was innocent of the charge of promiscuity with Lord Truffault's wife. It was actually his young nephew, Innocenzo, who was cleaving Lady Truffault's crack. But the Hermit refused to give Innocenzo up, so he took the blame. In any case, though I question his sanity at times, I must confess that the Hermit earnestly avoids both temptation and sin."

"Perhaps, but now he leads entire families of peasants as an army to battle the Turks for Jerusalem? Pray tell, Brother, what power can such a clown hold over so many others?"

"The power of lies," interrupted Crowbones, waving his stub of an arm in the air with authority. He had never actually spoken to or listened to Peter the Hermit, but had come across him along with Guillaume that day at Lord Truffault's manor, and thought him to be a madman. Moreover, Crowbones had come across similar charismatic Christian preachers of the day, and thought them all to be charlatans.

"Ja, and the power of Christian *trickery*," added Orla, who eyed Christianity and such preachers with even more suspicion than his brother. Both Danes found it difficult to believe that people could swallow such mystical nonsense as did the Catholics. "Though you two lads so adamantly reject the old Viking beliefs," Orla snorted "you Christians have your own magic and myths, but you proudly declare them as 'miracles.' Ha! You even have your own sorcerers, too, but call them 'saints.'

"Careful with your words," said Guillaume, glancing with disapproval at the two older men. "It's only by the Christian mercy of Aunt Mathilda of Tuscany and the Pope himself that you make a living beneath their banners despite refusing baptism." Guillaume loved Orla and Crowbones, but it disturbed him that as family, they still clung to their Norse beliefs.

"Oh, but let them speak!" quipped Handel, amused that Guillaume had become miffed. "I say our two heathen companions here are no worse than the Byzantines who at least were baptized in the faith, yet now shun the Roman Catholic rite!"

Orla laughed. "Odin's ass, Guillaume!" he exclaimed with false indignation. "May we not speak our minds in our own safe company of friends and clan, or must we now walk on eggshells? *You*, Guillaume, should have become the monk, not Tristan, for you're far more inflexible!"

As with much that Orla had to say, Tristan found the accusation humorous. "Yes, easy there, Brother, *I* am the cleric here," he chortled, "and I take no offense from our pagan uncles."

"Nor we from you, Boy," remarked Crowbones, winking at Orla, "even though you're now a Catholic holy man of the highest order. Indeed, perhaps one day your fellow Catholics will even anoint *you* a saint, huh? Should that happen, however, Crowbones and I will, of course, consider you a *sorcerer*."

Listening from behind and becoming somewhat agitated by this banter was Guthroth the Quiet. Unlike Orla and Crowbones, Guthroth had consented to being baptized after being miraculously spared from certain death at the hands of Desmond DuLac's troops years earlier in England. Giving the Christian God full credit for sparing his life that bloody day, Guthroth had become a convert, though the endless, quirky details of his new faith still confused him to no end. "Sh-shame on you, Orla and Cr-Crowbones, y-you should both be b-baptized!" he blurted, unable to wrangle his tongue. "*Y-you'll end up in H-Hell, you two!*"

This surprised Handel, who had assumed Guthroth was still pagan like Orla and Crowbones. Moreover, Tristan had warned Handel that Guthroth never spoke. "Ho! A miracle!" Handel shouted with mock reverence. "*God has loosened the mute's tongue!*"

More surprised than Handel by this unexpected burst of loquacity from Guthroth were Orla and Crowbones, who exchanged looks, then brayed with laughter at their younger cousin's blathering about the threat of damnation. This in turn tickled Tristan, and even caused the devout Guillaume to slip into a grin.

"Bones of God!" cried Orla. "Guthroth the Quiet is now Guthroth the Preacher! Oh, but how in hell will he save souls with his preaching if no one can understand a damned word he says?"

Guthroth's face reddened at the barb, and he attempted to fire off a retort, but his words tangled on his tongue, frustrating him even more. Seeing this, Hroc nudged his horse close to Guthroth's and whispered, "Ah, they but jest, Uncle Guthroth. It's said in fun only. In truth, they much admire you."

This soothed Guthroth, who held great affection for Hroc. It was through Guthroth's guidance that Hroc had become such a ferocious warrior, in battle often forging savagely through the enemy as the ox-driven plow violently turns the earth. Yet, when Hroc's sword was sheathed, he was charitable, especially toward Guthroth.

Tristan happened to witness this exchange between Guthroth and Hroc, and it warmed him. Being in the company of these men, kinsmen, was far different than being jostled within the stilted climate of the Vatican where cardinals and other high clerics ceaselessly jockeyed for position through subterfuge and connivance. Humor and affection existed here amongst these men, and though the teasing and poking could be pointed at times, Tristan knew the bonds holding himself, Guillaume, Handel and the Danes together were inviolable. Truly, a man could actually drop his guard here and be himself for a moment without fear of being outmaneuvered.

## Chapter Nineteen

### Orla and Crowbones

Although the conversation during the march north to Cologne was often peppered with debate and disagreement, it was also filled with that laughter and merciless raillery inherent of any fraternity of closely related men cast together and put upon the road. Handel had known Guillaume for years, but had spent little time with the Danes. After several nights of sharing the campfire, Handel found them to be both amicable and honorable. Despite their pagan background, Handel also found them like-minded on many issues, in particular as concerned loyalty, justice and defense of the helpless.

"I've a question for you," said Orla to Handel one night, poking at the embers of a late night fire. "It seems you aren't too happy with defending these people surrounding the Hermit, huh?"

"Don't misunderstand," Handel replied. "I've been against this crusade from its inception, and foresee nothing but disaster in the end. Then too, I despise the Byzantines and especially distrust Emperor Alexius. As to the Hermit, I wonder at times why God would unleash such a curse upon the earth as that hairy little scorpion! As I've always said, it's the sheep that will suffer, get slaughtered and gain nothing by this so-called holy war in the East. To hell with the men who've joined the Hermit, they should know better… but dammit, they've dragged women, children, the elderly, and the infirm into this thing, putting them at risk by exhorting them to fight the Turks. Sheer lunacy, I say. Still, by taking my religious vows I agreed to become a shepherd, so I'll do what I can to protect the helpless sheep, which in this case will be those incapable of defending themselves." Standing, Handel dusted his breeches. "It's late, gentlemen, so I leave the fire to you."

Turning, he disappeared from the meager circle of light afforded by the waning fire, after which Crowbones said to Orla in a low voice, "A good man, that Handel, huh?"

"Ja," replied Orla, "and sensible."

The two brothers sat there then in a comfortable silence, gazing at the fire, warm in the glow of its embers, as also in each other's company. They had shared their entire un-rooted existence together. From birth, circumstances had forced them into a life of violence, bloodletting, and war. While most boys entering adolescence had never shed the blood of another human being, Orla and Crowbones were already seasoned warriors and had lost count of the men they had slain by age thirteen. They had fought the French, the Flemish, fellow Normans, Saxons, most recently the Germans, and were now on their way to fight the Turks, a race which to them was completely unfamiliar.

Perhaps it was this history of roving and ceaseless wars that prompted Orla to look over at his brother, whose eyes were peacefully lost to the fire. "You know, Crowbones," Orla said, "we're not getting any younger, eh?"

Crowbones said nothing at first, his gaze still hostage to the glowing embers. Although the two brothers had barely spent a day of their lives apart, the question sounded odd to Crowbones. They rarely spoke of personal thoughts; men of such rough hew rarely do. "No," Crowbones finally answered.

Orla had been hoping for more of a reply, but seeing that Crowbones was not going to add to the discussion, Orla continued. "Ja, lately I've been thinking about when we were boys coming up together. It was a good time, ja?"

"Hunh!" Crowbones grunted. "All I remember is fear as a child. Then by the time we were half grown, it was time to fight, remember? Nothing's changed since those days except the enemy every five years or so. I started to grow tired of war in England, as you know, Orla. But when we escaped there we came to Italy to fight the Germans, and now we're on our way to fight the Turks. Do you never get weary of fighting, Orla? Does the smell of blood never burn your nostrils at night as you seek sleep? It does mine, at times."

"But all I know is fighting... just like you," shrugged Orla. "We've no trade, no skills other than defending ourselves and slaying enemies. But tell, I haven't seen you casting your bird bones of late. Have you given them up?"

"No," answered Crowbones with a tilt of his head. "I rolled them two nights ago."

"Ja? Well what did they say? And why've you said nothing about it?"

"I said nothing," Crowbones said, finally lifting his eyes from the fire, "because I'm unclear on what to make of them exactly. Though we've survived every war we've fought, and they've been many, the original Danish Guard is down to you, me, and Guthroth. According to the lay of the bones the other night, they prophesized that of the six of us at the head of the Tuscan force, most of us will... never see Jerusalem."

"Huh?" said Orla, his expression dropping. Disturbed, he stared at the fire with glum reflection, then said, "Well, that'd be me, you, Hroc, Tristan, Guillaume and Handel. Did the bones say *which* of us wouldn't make it to Jerusalem? Swine's head! *Most* would mean at least *four of us* aren't going to reach Jerusalem, then, huh? Maybe even more."

"Ja..."

Orla shook his head, narrowing his eyes as trying to peek into the future, refusing to dismiss the bones since he believed in them; his brother's predictions had been accurate too many times over the decades to disregard, especially on the threshold of war. "Roll them again, Crowbones," urged Orla. "Maybe the outcome will be different than the other night, eh?"

"*Orla,*" chided Crowbones, "the bones don't *change.* Just because one doesn't like the prophecy, one can't simply erase it by rolling them again. Ja, they might tell a bit more than on the previous roll, but the prophecy itself can't simply reverse itself."

"*Roll the damned bones!*" insisted Orla, growing uneasy.

"Very well," sighed Crowbones, taking the leather pouch from his neck, spreading his mantle flat on the ground beside him. Delicately dumping the desiccated bird bones into his palm, he shook them for several seconds, then rolled them across the mantle. Leaning forward with squinted eyes, he stared for a long while.

"Well, dammit," said Orla, a plume of impatience furrowing his brow. "What about it? What do they say?"

Crowbones gave no reply at first, but eventually muttered, “Same thing… most of us will never see Jerusalem.”

“Anything more?”

“No.”

Orla sat back, crossing his legs, and stared into the fire. “You know… if it’s my turn to go,” he said, “I wouldn’t be sad.”

“Huh?” said Crowbones, having never heard such talk from his brother.

“Ja, when our younger cousins Fairhair and StraightLimbs were slain in England, I lost something that day. Then you lost your arm, too, and I’ve worried about you losing the other ever since. I keep picturing you unable to even feed yourself. Then my wife was killed as was yours, along with your kids during our escape from Engand, and I lost a little more of myself. And finally, when I lost my son, Knud, to the Germans, I...” Here, he failed to finish and simply shook his head. A few moments later he added, “You know, I should have treated my son Knud *better*, Ivar. But my eyes were always on little Hroc.”

Seeing the glaze in his brother’s eyes, Crowbones thought back on the events Orla had just reeled off, and thought it strange that the loss of his own arm would be in the mix of such catastrophic occurrences. “Ja, you’ve lost much along the road, Brother, but the loss of my arm has been on your mind? Nah, it’s no big thing. And if I lose my good arm, I’ll simply lap my food like a dog.” Then he grinned a bit. “You know, you’re beginning to talk like a woman, Orla. It’s a good thing no one else is here by the fire to hear this shit. I’d be embarrassed by such a thing!”

“Maybe so,” Orla chortled, feeling his brother’s poke, “but if your bones are right… even more reason then to talk about what’s important for once, you and me, huh?”

“Ja… maybe so.”

# Chapter Twenty

## Toward Cologne

As the peasant horde marched east toward Germany wreaking havoc wherever they went, Tafur found himself surrounded by a fanatic following of nearly three thousand peasant warriors, their ranks increasing by the day. His ragtag troops included a mix of adolescent boys and oldsters, but most were capable men of prime age hardened by unforgiving labor in the fields of French nobility. This hardening was not restricted to backbone and sinew, but included a seething resentment over the lot life had cast onto their backs.

Their existence, until of late, had been one endless stream of deprivation, mistreatment, and humiliation. But now they had unchained themselves, abandoning their masters' shacks and shanties, running loose along the road to Germany. As serfs most had never traveled beyond their lords' feudal estates, had cowered when spoken to by nobility, and had constantly feared the forfeiture of even what little they and their families possessed.

But now, like abused, collared hounds long confined to leashes and tiny spaces suddenly unleashed, they were roaming the countryside, wild with newfound freedom, taking what they needed– as well as what they wanted. On first leaving Amiens in the footsteps of Peter the Hermit, tempered by his preaching and insistence on civility, these men had remained somewhat orderly. But Tafur, behind the Hermit's back, ignited their imaginations, playing on their hatred of aristocracy and fury against the feudal world of France that had turned them into slaves. Each night he lured recruits to his fire, spewing hate against noblemen and Jews. And when his venomous preaching abated, he then conducted a secret ceremony, passionately exhorting the more radical listeners to apply the fiery brand to their foreheads as he had, marking themselves forever as a soldier of God's army.

"We'll not wear scarlet crosses on our garments like these goddamned noblemen!" Tafur yammered. "No, we'll *burn* the mark of the cross onto our foreheads for all to see, and for Jews and Muslims to fear! Don't be timid! Step forward, I say!"

On one particularly fruitful night, Tafur succeeded in swaying nearly a hundred men to take the brand. Standing by the fire, he had each approaching candidate repeat a vow of his own creation. Being uneducated, Tafur's vow was an odd mingle of spiritual hocus-pocus and mysticism so absurd that anyone of reasonable intellect would have laughed. Nonetheless, eager peasants even more thick-headed than Tafur lined up as instructed and repeated the vow in devout reverence, their eyes closed, their arms folded across their chests in 'X' fashion. They had never been a part of anything, nor ever belonged to any brotherhood. This initiation of fire, for them, was akin to being knighted... yet even more sacred.

An hour into that evening's ordeal, one man who had stepped up to Tafur suddenly balked. He was timid and faint of heart to begin with, but the smell of burnt skin and the sizzle of the white-hot brand against human flesh now made him queasy to the point of illness. "*I d-don't think I can do this!*" he stammered.

"Do it or be branded a coward!" shouted Tafur. "And the King of Beggars will take no cowards in God's troop!"

"N-no," the man stammered, backing away, unfolding his arms.

"What's your goddamned name, you piker?" bellowed Tafur, so all could hear.

"M-Marcel…" the man mumbled, trembling. "Marcel Dupuis. My w-wife has four children, and a baby due any day now… I'd b-best get back to where they're sleeping. Estelle will be worried, she doesn't know I'm here."

"Run then if you must, Marcel Dupuis," Tafur smirked, "but I thought you came along to kill Jews and fight the Turks!"

"Yes, I c-came to fight the Turks, but really... I've n-nothing against Jews…"

"Jews, Turks, all the same! Both heathen, both godless! But run to your wife, little man. But I warn you, in the morning you'd best turn about and go back from where you came. You'll be no good for us here. And if I see you again, I'll have my men turn you out!"

Tafur had no authority to dismiss anyone from the Peasants' Crusade, but once men of no authority acquire a taste of power, they begin to seize things.

"But I c-can't go back, you know that!" protested Dupuis "And my w-wife… she'd be furious. *She's* the one, after all. who put us on the road to Jerusalem."

"Ha, sounds like she's got bigger balls than you, Dupuis! But again, if I see your milky face again, we'll have you tarred, then run a pole up your ass and parade you around as a coward! Best then that you start packing. Now move along, you're holding up the line! There's better men than you waiting to take the fire!"

Faced with Tafur's ultimatum, knowing his wife, Estelle, would scald him for being expelled from the crusade and raising the wrath of the Tafurs, Dupuis closed his eyes, forming his arms back into an 'X.' "*I'll t-take the fire!*" he shuddered stepping forward. "Give me the oath…"

Two hours later, his forehead searing with pain, Marcel Dupuis quietly returned to his sleeping wife and children, as would a pup with tucked tail. It was not until morning that Estelle discovered the cross scalded into her husband's forehead. "Oh, Marcel!" she cooed, embracing him with unadulterated affection. "I was *hoping* you'd take the brand and join the Tafurs. You look suddenly so... *dangerous*, husband! And that cross above your eyes will serve as a war blessing, like some holy amulet, when we and the children attack the Turks!"

Three days later Marcel Dupuis' pain had subsided for the most part, and his cross began to scar and scab over the tiniest bit. And oddly, he felt like a new man. Whereas he had always been stoop-shouldered and reticent, it seemed he stood more erect, even discovering a little swagger in his step. More importantly, whenever encountering other Tafurs, he passed a secret signal. That simple exchange of gestures, boyish as it was, emboldened him. He was a part of something now– something big, something meaningful. Whereas he had been ignored since leaving Amiens, others in the march now began to give him looks, and at times these surreptitious glances were filled with trepidation, even though Marcel Dupuis was no more frightening than a woodchuck.

A week later, Tafur approached him. "Come along, Dupuis," he said, "I need your help today."

"Yes sir!" Dupuis replied, seeing that Tafur had already assembled ten others; they were a brutish lot, making Dupuis feel out of place. Still, their fearsome appearance made Dupuis swell with courage. *Ah,* he thought, *in this crowd I'll be taken for a ruffian, too, despite my thin, bony frame.*

A ruffian Dupuis was not. Still, all men like be considered tough and dangerous, especially the weak. Stepping into their midst with his shovel, the only weapon he had managed to scavenge from his master's estate, he followed them as Tafur led them away from the road.

"So then, King Tafur," Dupuis gibbered, "where is it we're headed, sir?"

Pointing over a rise, Tafur replied, "My scouts reported a prosperous enough looking German farm just on the other side there. We're going to hijack the livestock, clean out the garden and cellar, then tear down the shanty and barn for camp wood."

Having been molded upon the iron anvil of strict Catholicism, Dupuis hesitated a step, wishing suddenly to find an excuse to absent himself from Tafur's raid... but as Tafur's dull eyes gazed at him, along with the other branded men listening, Dupuis wilted. "Yes, sir!" he said, snapping to his idea of attention, issuing a feeble attempt at a salute.

Half an hour later he and the raiding party led by Tafur descended on a small farm. The only people in sight was a man currying a mule, and what appeared to be his son, carrying a bucket from the well. Without a word the Tafurs spread out, and within moments were chasing chickens, gathering the four cows confined in the pen adjacent to the stick-barn, and herding a tiny flock of nearby sheep. Their actions, so brazen and unexpected, failed to register to the German farmer at first. Realizing then that he was being plundered, taken aback, he watched saucer-eyed for a short while before finally bursting into movement and yelling at his son to flee.

So vastly outnumbered and outmanned, it would have behooved the farmer to step aside and silently accept the unjust fate that had befallen him that day. But those with little, facing loss of it all, will charge blindly even into an entire pack of savage hooligans which is exactly what the farmer did. Grabbing a pitchfork leaning against the stable post, he charged toward the man who seemed to be leading the pack. Meanwhile, instead of fleeing across the field, the young boy ran into the house to warn his mother.

The enraged farmer was on Tafur within moments, cursing, waving his pitchfork in wild arcs, thinking to put Tafur on the run. Laughing, Tafur knocked him to the ground handily with a double-motion of his shepherd's staff, then struck him across the temple with it. Next, while Marcel Dupuis stood there aghast, the others began pummeling the man with fists and feet. Buried beneath such a brutal barrage, screaming for mercy, the farmer was soon a bloody mess.

Then came the wail of a woman. It was the farmer's wife, running out the door of their shanty with her son to see what was happening. Frantic, her eyes darted from one man to the next, down at her bloodied husband, then back to the intruders. Next her hands flew to her face and she pointed across the field, pushing her son that direction. "*Raus! Raus mein sohn!*" she screamed.

"Well, well… *what have we here?*" snickered Tafur, fueled by the terror flooding her eyes.

The woman was in her thirties, perhaps, possessing a face that could turn away a mule. Still, she was heavy-breasted and stout. Slowly loosening the cinch of his trousers, Tafur gestured to the others. All knew what to do except Marcel Dupuis, who stood there making the sign of the cross. As the men moved toward the shanty, he sensed what was about to unfold, and did not wish to be a part of it.

Then, as horrific screams of a woman being repeatedly violated mingled with wild voices of men shouting and hooting emanated from the shanty, Marcel fell to trembling. "*O-oh, but God in Heaven,*" he shuddered, "*by joining these beasts– what have I done!?*"

## Chapter Twenty-one

### And Thus... Asta of the Norman Danes

Following the departure of Tristan and Guillaume from Canossa, Asta's condition deteriorated yet further. Mathilda, along with Sisters Angélique and Gisèle who had accompanied Asta from the Marcigny convent in France, tended to her lovingly for three days... but on that third evening called for a priest to administer final rites, determining that God would shortly claim her soul.

Against expectation Asta clung to life throughout the night while, to Mathilda's dismay, adamantly insisting that Mathilda place her in a coach bound back to France. "Oh, by the Saints, but that's impossible!" objected Mathilda, torn between reason and Asta's tearful but furious pleas to return across the Alps. "To do so would be to pronounce your death sentence!"

"God demands that I cross the Alps!" clamored Asta, her resolve driving her toward delirium. "*God demands it, Mathilda!*"

Unable to subdue Asta's furor, and rattled by her invocation of God's will, Mathilda had a coach readied along with Sisters Angélique and Gisèle and a guard detail. "Tend to her carefully," fretted Mathilda as the coach departed, "for this woman is surely favored by our Lord and Savior!"

Wrapped in blankets, shivering, fading in and out of consciousness, Asta tried to lose herself in prayer during the journey. The fragility of her condition, however, was further exacerbated by the Via Francegina, the ancient, rocky trail connecting Italy and France; the alpine path allowed moments of sleep along rare smooth stretches, but mostly forced the coach to bobble and lurch recklessly, tossing Asta from one side of the coach to the other. Despite this pummeling, Asta began slipping toward blackness– welcoming its warm, cathartic embrace. Feeling herself dropping, gradually, she soon lost all sense of coach wheels buffeting against stone; it seemed her pain dissipated, too. As her descent deepened, from nowhere snatches of her past began breaking through this blackness, unearthing moments of comfort, but also of dread as she felt herself careening back through time. Then, as when theatre curtains part, light emerged, appearing first in sparse, mottled patches, then radiating into clarity as suddenly Asta envisioned herself as a small child– seated atop the lap of her father, Guntar the Mace; his throat had just erupted into laughter and his eyes were brimming with paternal adoration. This vignette was followed by milky images of Mielikki, the pagan Finn who served as Asta's nursemaid upon birth, later continuing as Asta's personal attendant and surrogate mother. Mielikki was dressing her, brushing her long tresses, preening and fussing over them as would any doting mother. But just as Asta began to revel in Mielikki's motherly affection, a cold finger touched her heart and the image shattered. In its place Asta found herself grown– pointing furiously, banning Mielikki from the household, accusing her of trying to drown three-year-old Tristan.

Cutting through even her state of unconsciousness, Asta suddenly felt hot tears streaming down her cheeks, and the crush of heartbreak lumping in her throat as Mielikki turned one final time to plead forgiveness before vanishing back into the past. Asta imagined swiping tears from her eyes then... when she removed her hands from her cheeks, she discovered the Danes standing before her, and felt the warm shelter of their protective devotion... Orla Bloodax, Ivar Crowbones, sensitive Guthroth the Quiet, handsome Sigurd Fairhair, and the ever awkward-looking Halfdan StraightLimbs.

But the dreamy solace of their guardianship lasted only a short while, dissipating as the image of Roger de Saint-Germain broke forward, standing beside her at the altar of marriage, leering at her hungrily though she was but twelve years of age... and next he was assaulting her tiny, girlish frame with lust-driven, forced copulation, night after night, despite Asta's howls of revulsion and pleas for mercy.

This ugliness played over and over for what seemed an endless course, until finally broken by the image of two infants– her sons, Tristan and Guillaume. But no more had her heart lifted at seeing them, than came images of Roger de Saint-Germain's execution for treason and forfeiture of all rights and property, followed by Asta's marriage of necessity to Desmond DuLac and the loss of her two sons to the Black Monks. Sorrow ensued, and from there she relived the misery of England beneath DuLac's boot until the hope-filled face of Jack Forest the Saxon appeared, offering a far-fetched dream– until his own slaughter during the Gamekeeper's Revolt before her own eyes and within the very saddle they shared while trying to flee to Scotland.

Shuddering to escape the glacial despair of that moment, Asta struggled to gain consciousness, but ended, instead, enduring and reliving again the perilous escape from England that had cost so many innocent lives. Finally, as she ceased struggling against herself, all grew still; she found herself sequestered behind the convent walls of Marcigny-sur-Loire as a nun of means within the Benedictine Sisterhood.

Throughout this reeling kaleidoscope of images, faces, joy and angst from the past, as Asta's heart both soared and bled, one thought overshadowed all other thoughts– eternal salvation. *Bring me finally home, God my Father*, she mumbled subconsciously, over and over... *bring me finally to Your side*.

There was little that Angélique and Gisèle could do for Asta but hold her in place and pray as she slipped in and out of awareness, rasping and chattering sporadically, at other times lying motionless, as dead– so pray they did, day and night. Then, as in answer to their fervent pleas, the unimaginable occurred in the midst of the Alps just as the coach topped an especially high mountain pass. Asta awoke from her stupor, sat erect, and directly addressed Angélique and Gisèle. "Tell the driver to halt immediately," Asta commanded, lucidly, "for I wish to take a look."

"A look?" asked Sister Angélique, glancing at Gisèle, stunned.

"Yes, *here*!"

Puzzled, the nuns shouted to the driver, then watched as Asta peeled from beneath her blankets, struggling her way out of the coach.

"*Heavens,*" pleaded Sister Gisèle, alarmed, "be careful, Dear!"

But Asta was not listening. Moving forward, her eyes took on an odd glint as she began looking about, as driven with purpose. Finally, she took a seat along a jagged outcrop of rock hugging the mountainside.

Watching Asta as she continued assessing her surroundings, it seemed to both Angélique and Gisèle that Asta's face had filled with an air of... expectancy. But as they waited, nothing happened. Still, the two nuns, the driver and the accompanying guards remained patient and watchful; they found Asta's unanticipated recovery surprising, if not startling.

Finally, after a good while, happening to spot something on the ground, Asta stood. On closer inspection, she saw the object was a skull, bleached and worn... of a small horse, she imagined. In actuality she was correct. It was the skull of a small Icelandic pony... one that had many years earlier met its demise atop this very pass. Indeed, this particular pony and one other had frozen to death while stranded atop the pass in an ice storm, pulling a small box wagon with three people making their way from Lyon, France to Italy.

There are occurrences so happenstance and unlikely in this worldly existence as to refute the realm of probability. When such rarities unfold, humans are forced to set aside denial and disbelief, while also being forced to acknowledge that the impossible has actually arrived. By way of explanation, humans excuse these unlikely occurrences as phenomena, sorcery or... miracles. Being devoutly Catholic, Angélique, Gisèle and the others watching Asta determined then that they were witnessing a miracle– in the form of Asta's recovery. This was a miscalculation; history is actually *filled* with moments of unexpected, inexplicable recovery from injury or illness, therefore such occurrences may not be as miraculous as supposed. The real phenomenon developing before their eyes was that Asta had somehow been 'awakened' at this particular time and at this particular location, filled by a strange expectancy of unknown origin... and for no identifiable reason.

Staring intently at the weathered skull, Asta's brow furrowed as her eyes narrowed, launching into reflection. Thus she remained, motionless, lost to the skull for good while until, suddenly, she floundered, bolting a step as appearing overcome. Grasping her breast with one hand, she dropped, uttering the Pater Noster in Latin while raising the other hand to the sky.

Scuttling to her side, the nuns and guards surrounded her, propping her up. "*Asta!*" cried Sister Angélique. "*What is it?!*"

"I feel the... specter of tragedy haunting this rise," rasped Asta, struggling for breath, "as if fate took something atop this pass."

"Took something?" asked Sister Gisèle.

"Y-yes, yes... from *me*... and my *son*... a part of our hearts, as carving it from our breasts." Then, her imploring eyes boring deeply into those of Sister Gisèle, Asta whispered with urgency, "Saint Augustine of Hippo declared that without baptism, infants shall not be free of condemnation from original sin... thus suspended into the Limbo of Infants, thus *denied* the Kingdom of Heaven. But God is infinitely more merciful than men... therefore I struggle against Augustine's pronouncement! Am I a sinner, Gisèle? A fool?"

But it was Angélique who answered. "Oh, but beware, Asta, for such thoughts border on *blasphemy!*" she interceded, her tone stark with certainty. "Augustine is a holy saint, and a pillar of our faith!"

Asta's expression dropped with resignation. Still, hope refused to flee entirely. Her eyes filling with resolve, she shook her head a tiny measure, saying, "Surely our Lord would not refuse entrance into Eternal Paradise to an innocent, newly born infant?"

Seeing Asta's piteous expression, Angélique faltered; regret began etching itself into her face over her insistence about the infallibility of Saint Augustine of Hippo. "But, of course," she then added softly, her heart astir, "though a saint, Augustine was also but a... *man*. Thus his edicts are earthly, not Heavenly. Only God, Asta, could determine for certain such a thing as a Limbo for Infants, or Heaven for infants denied the rite of baptism."

"*Y-yes*," whispered Asta, her lips forming the tiniest trace of what Angélique imagined was a smile. "I was thinking... the same..." Nodding, she gazed into space, and murmured, "Oh, but did you hear what Angelique just said, my dear... *Tristan?*"

Hearing this, Angelique clucked with contentment, beckoning Gisèle and the guards to hoist Asta back into the coach.

"Yes then, Dear, let's be on our way back to Marcigny," soothed Angélique, caressing Asta's cheek as she assisted with laying Asta upon her back across the cushioned coach seat. "There now," she continued, covering Asta with sheep skins, "best that you close your eyes and rest. But raise your head just a bit while I cushion it... I believe that would be more comfortable, don't you, my Dear? Come along now, Asta, up with your head then, won't you help me out just a bit?"

But Asta did not move. Nor did she answer.

Thus it was that one of God's most blessed and beautiful creatures, Asta of the Norman Danes, faithful servant of the Church and loving mother, passed from this life... filled with hope that man, indeed, did not know 'everything' about God, or death, or the Kingdom of Heaven. God may well have, during her final moments, cast upon her a ray of light at the very place her illegitimate grandson was born and shortly thereafter perished. Then, too, Asta may have simply been struck by that profound, inexplicable intuition sensed by and given only to women who have given birth– that mysterious maternal instinct so deeply rooted as to defy reason. Or indeed, far-fetched as it sounds, this entire incident entailing the final moments of Asta's existence might well have been little more than a collusion of– coincidence.

Regardless of all prospects in question, in truth... such things can never be determined for certain.

## Chapter Twenty-two

### The Mob Appears

As Tristan, Guillaume and the Tuscan battalion neared the edge of Cologne, they came across isolated packs of paupers in large numbers camped along the side of the road. These people appeared bedraggled and spent, and as Guillaume's troops marched along the road, the soldiers were quickly besieged by hundreds of women and elderly folk begging for bread, money, or anything else the soldiers might be willing to surrender. Many of the children mobbing the troops brazenly snatched things from the saddles of the knights and the backpacks of the footmen, creating an immediate ruckus.

"Swine's head! Who are all these damned beggars?" shouted Crowbones, kicking at a boy who was attempting to pull the leather pouch he so treasured from his neck.

"The ass end of the Hermit's camp here in Cologne," said Handel, kicking out at several other boys pulling at his boots. "I crossed their path when I tried to turn the Hermit back while crossing the German border. But you've seen nothing yet. These are but the stragglers camping outside the city, and few in number compared to the main force."

Continuing to cut a swath through the crowd, the Tuscan battalion soon came upon a circle of people assisting a woman who was sprawled on the ground, groaning and wailing as an old woman tugged at her loins. "Push, Estelle!" the old hag shouted. "The baby's breached! Push, by God, or we'll lose it!"

"Push, wife!" whimpered a slight man standing to the side, trying to keep his other four children from bawling and pushing near.

"Saints of God," Guillaume called to Tristan, "people in such condition as this pregnant woman on the ground have come on foot like this all the way from Amiens, France?"

"Aye," said Tristan, "without provisions or means of survival, simply spurred on by the call of the Hermit."

"Still, despite their squalor, there's an odd but palpable euphoria in the air."

"Most certainly," answered Handel, frowning. "It's that foolish euphoria bred by utter ignorance! Intoxicated by these early moments of abandoning their shackles, knowing nothing of what awaits ahead, and failing to understand the distance to Jerusalem, these fools believe themselves *liberated.* But like the grown hare confined to a cage since birth, then suddenly released to the wilds, their future is slim indeed! Doom awaits."

As Guillaume's troops progressed closer to the city, the crowds grew thicker and their mobbing of the Tuscan force increased to such a point that Guillaume's men had to resort to force at times to keep the masses off them. The sights also became more appalling, as many came into view who were half naked, diseased, and covered with boils and blisters from weeks of trekking beneath the bare sun to get to Cologne, then getting stuck in the open for several weeks more.

Some carried others upon their backs from place to place while some dragged others about on litters fashioned of barn wood or tree limbs. Packs of adolescent boys, appearing to be orphans, roamed about at will like packs of stray dogs, harassing others or falling into savage fisticuffs amongst themselves; the raucous actions of the more aggressive boys served only as fuel to embolden the others. In other spots along the roadside there were couples, half dressed, openly copulating, while others stood about watching or cheering. Beyond this, a group of bawdy women began exposing their breasts to the troops, lifting their tunics above the waist, baring their bushes and cracks in efforts to prostitute themselves. "Come taste the fruit!" they enticed. "Come get a poke!"

"God forbid," whistled Guillaume. "What is this Hell on earth we've come across here in Cologne, Tristan?"

Before Tristan could respond, Handel shouted, pointing a finger to the side. "Dammit, look there!"

The Danes gazed in the direction Handel pointed, taking sight of a group of eight people, heavily covered, following behind an individual tinkling a bell as he led the group. "*Lepers,*" Orla whispered. Looking at Hroc and Crowbones, he continued in a low voice, "The Christian preachers call upon lepers now to fight their God's wars? Oh, but the foolishness of this religion has no bounds!"

"You must remember, Father," said Hroc, "Uncle Tristan and Handel are holy men of the Christian faith, and they are good men. It's this strange Hermit who's gathered this helpless rabble to fight the Turks, not the Pope, nor the Church."

The remark surprised Orla, as did its defensive tone. "I'm well aware of the difference, Hroc," he replied sharply. "Still, who ever heard of enlisting beggars and derelicts to march and fight half way across the world?!"

"Ja," agreed Crowbones, "it makes no sense. I understood the fight in Italy against the German advance during the Investiture Wars, but *this* thing? So far away in Jerusalem?"

The commotion caused by the arrival of the Tuscan troops continued to escalate, finally becoming so unmanageable that Guillaume commanded the battalion to clear the road and make haste toward a distant hill. Some of the more hardy of those along along the road tried to run after them, but within half an hour fell back out of sight.

Reaching a clearing on the back side of the hill, the knights dismounted as the footmen dropped to the ground, exhausted from fighting off relentless crowds of peasants and beggars.

"I could have never imagined such a thing," said Guillaume to Tristan. "How on earth could these people take to the road like this with nothing to carry them over?"

"The promise of heavenly rewards from a madman," said Handel, shaking his head with disgust.

"A madman, indeed, to create such a roving riot as this," said Orla. Then he happened to look over at Guthroth who stood a distance away, eyes glazed. "Hey, what say you, Guthroth?" Orla shouted. "What do you think of that tangled mess? Like a bad dream, eh?"

Guthroth glanced up, acknowledging the question, but said nothing. Instead, it was Hroc who answered. "He agrees, it's like a bad dream, Father," said Hroc, sparing Guthroth the effort of answering. "And I, even in war, have rarely seen such a pitiful sight as on that road!"

"Aye," said Handel, "but as I said, it'll get far worse. You're seeing but the ass-end right now. According to the report that was delivered to me in Canossa, the Hermit had upwards of twenty-five thousand or more following his footsteps as he crossed into Germany, and is expected to pick up another five or ten thousand while here in Cologne where he's preached in previous years and cultivated a large following. Beyond here he's not as well known, so hopefully his recruiting drive will finally peak. God knows, the more people he attracts, the more problems for the main crusading effort– and for us, dammit!"

As Handel talked, the Danes exchanged looks, shaking their heads. "This Hermit has attracted that many thousands to go to war?" whistled Orla. "Women and children? Peasants with no swords, lances, or shields?"

"These damned people must be as mad as the man they're following," muttered Crowbones.

"No, they're not mad, just ignorant," said Handel. "Some are hoping for salvation while others simply seek adventure. But *trouble* is what they'll find... and trouble is what they'll create, as well!"

"I saw no signs of the Hermit on the road, Handel," said Tristan. "Where would you suppose he and Walter Sansavoir might be?"

"I'm sure KuKu Peter's in town begging for money," replied Handel, "and beating the drum for yet more rats to load on his sinking ship." Then he kicked at the ground. "Damn his twisted soul."

"Aye, I'd guess he's probably in Cologne, too," agreed Guillaume, "but no point taking the entire battalion into the city just to get mobbed again. Tristan, best that you and I go in alone in a day or so. Let's pitch camp for now, and we'll try to locate him later. And though we have our doubts, who knows... perhaps as the Pope intends, you can sway him into ceasing this unsanctioned march of his."

Handel shook his head. "Don't bother, I say. It'd be easier if the entire city of Cologne was on fire and you attempted to distinguish it with a shot of piss. *I* know it, and Tristan knows it, too."

"Handel," said Tristan, "I may well know it, but I also know my instructions coming from Odo were very clear. I have to at least make the effort."

"The Pope already knows what the Hermit's answer will be," scowled Handel. "Sure, in his heart he hopes for a miracle, but changing the Hermit's mind is beyond the realm of miracles, so we may as well prepare to move on to the second phase of the Hermit mission... which is to follow his hairy ass across the whole damned continent while convincing him to hold off fighting Turks until the main armies arrive. But seeing as you're hell-bent on going into town, I'll tag along,"

"Absolutely not," said Tristan. "You are the *last* person the Hermit or Sansavoir need to see, especially in light of your previous encounter with them at the border. Ha, you would be less welcome than the Plague!"

"Probably so," chortled Handel. "Truth is, they're probably the last two faces *I* need to see right now, too. I'd wring the Hermit's little rat's neck, but then Sansavoir's band of numbskulls would skewer me in retaliation, eh?"

"Exactly."

"And us, Boy?" asked Orla. "Shouldn't we at least come along? Considering the chaos we just encountered, the city might be even more treacherous than the road."

"No, Guillaume and I will go it alone. To do otherwise would only stoke the fire."

## Chapter Twenty-three

### City under Siege

As Tristan and Guillaume made their way toward Cologne, havoc stirred by French peasant squatters continued to increase in intensity. Within the limits of the city proper, chaos became even more pronounced; the streets were burgeoning with thousands of peasants aimlessly milling about, as disoriented or lost, while others harangued shopkeepers and residents. Along the edges of boulevards, other mobs of French arrivals sat clustered in massive huddles, staring idly about at the vast circus of their own devise now encompassing the entire commercial district of Cologne.

There were those also who, overcome by drunkenness, stumbled here and there, blithering nonsensically about this or that to anyone passing by, or even within earshot. Worse yet, the streets were heavily punctuated by unconscious bodies sprawled about, many victim to drink, others to sheer exhaustion. Yet, in their comatose state these hapless souls slept soundly, oblivious to the filth in which they slumbered– excrement filled streets thick with passing horse dung, as well as human excrement discarded from resident German chamber pots or defecated and urinated publically by masses of shameless French peasants who had nowhere else to relieve themselves.

Sporadically, Tristan and Guillaume came across wavering attempts by groups of the Cologne Guard to maintain order, but the swell of newcomers flooding the city was too much. The enforcement officers may as well have been attempting to hold back the raging rush of a frothing sea.

"Ho, there! We seek Peter the Hermit!" Guillaume shouted to a cadre of guards who were heavily involved in a wild mệlée with a pack of delinquent French adolescents.

The guard closest to them, in the midst of thumping one of the boisterous lads over the skull with a baton, looked up, squinting. Holding his victim at arm's length long enough to spot Guillaume's military garb and Tristan's clerical garments, he jerked a nod over his shoulder. "Büro des Oberburgermeisters, five blocks down," he grunted. Turning, he resumed the beating as other guards fought off his victim's friends.

Tristan and Guillaume traveled the short distance as instructed, but with each block the Hermit's people became more dense and their agitation at the Cologne militia grew more animated. Then, above the clamor of the mobs, Tristan recognized the Hermit's voice mingled with other shouting voices ringing back and forth in German. Dismounting, Tristan and Guillaume pushed through the crowd blocking the entrance of the Burgermeister building. Those blocking their path were at times listening, at times booing, and at times cheering– depending entirely on the cadence of Peter the Hermit's speech, which they could hear from their position outside. Eventually managing to force their way through the door and into the meeting hall, Tristan and Guillaume stood elbow to elbow within the packed audience, which appeared to be thoroughly enjoying what could only be described as a comedy of rage.

Had the scene not been so boisterous, Tristan and Guillaume might have noticed that they had picked up a follower shortly after attaining the center of town. But bedlam ruled, so the two brothers had no idea they were being watched. In truth, this same dark, bearded figure of exceptionally short stature had been slipping about in their wake since arriving at Canossa. Now, as the Saint-Germain brothers stood side by side, the tiny man took up position just behind them, pulling the brim of his pointy black hat so that it fell over his eyes. Meanwhile, the wild spectacle unfolding at the front of the meeting hall continued to careen out of control.

"Leave the city or at least quell the damage being done by your herd of beggars!" shouted a Cologne magistrate, poking a finger into the Hermit's chest as Walter Sansavoir poked the man back. Sansavoir, surrounded by knights, could have easily knocked the German official back with a single blow, but he showed restraint as the man was elderly; his old face was beet-red with perspiration, and it appeared as though his agitated heart might fail at any given moment.

Just behind Sansavoir stood another man, Tafur, deigning not to copy Sansavoir's restraint. Tafur was swinging a long, burled staff in hand, thumping a different city official about the shoulders and head as several other men in sackcloth held the German in their grips. Then Geoffrey Burrel, who thought little of abusing the weak, stepped forward and punched the man squarely in the face. Oddly, others in the meeting hall seemed to pay little heed to the beating. Of those who did take notice, none objected, not even the local Germans.

Innocenzo stood to the far side of Sansavoir, listening to neither the angry magistrate nor his uncle. Ignoring their ongoing tirade at each other, Innocenzo's eyes were, instead, scoping the vast hall for young women, of which there was an abundance. Just at the moment he caught a certain young fraulein's eyes and began exchanging flirtatious signals with her, he spotted Bishop Saint-Germain. Embarrassed, Innocenzo ceased his philandering and threw his arm to the air in recognition; the Bishop had spared his and his uncle's life from the fury of Lord Truffault in France years earlier, and Innocenzo had since that day considered Bishop Saint-Germain a hero.

"Goddammit, we'll send for King Heinrich's troops and they'll kick your filthy ass back to France!" screamed a Cologne burgermeister, so furious at the Hermit that spittle flew from his mouth like water from a fountain. "Your mob's not welcome here anymore, and neither are you, you smelly little French bastard!"

"Nay, I say, the children of God are welcome everywhere!" sneered the Hermit, his eyes rolling back in his head as his hands waved about like pennants in a tempest. "And if *I'm* not wanted, then why do your own Colognese citizens shower me with gifts and surrender their jewelry for my war chest?! Oh, angels of Heaven, many are even joining my crusade to Jerusalem!" This retort he bellowed with such dramatic flair that his amused German supporters cheered, clapped and whistled, drowning out the angry burgermeister's futile attempts to reply. The French within the crowd, failing to understand a word of the dispute as it was being conducted in German, joined in the raillery regardless, timing their outbreaks to the tempo of German applause and the facial expressions of Kuku Peter.

"You're like cow shit in the city wells!" shouted another burgermeister at the Hermit, "spreading your stink amongst our people! Worse yet, you're draining the city's resources and luring our citizenry off from their labors and responsibilities with your promises of delivery from eternal damnation! But it's all horseshit, and you damn well know it!"

"Ho, but I have a letter from God, you *doubter!*" the Hermit roared, reaching into the top of his tunic, pulling out his treasured parchment. "Behold, words written by God himself! Directing me to lead French and Germans alike to defeat the heathen Turks!"

As the Hermit waved his letter above his disheveled head of hair, so crusted with filth that individual fibers hung in clumps rather than strands, a hush descended across the entire hall, punctuated only by an occasional coo or sigh of elation. Tafur then, as on signal, broke the silence and yelled, "Behold! Look! A sacred vision approaches!"

To this point the Hermit had been speaking in German, acting little different than the infuriated magistrates and burgermeisters with whom he was feuding. But as the room fell quiet upon seeing his letter from God, and as Tafur shouted his proclamation, the Hermit suddenly transformed. Without provocation or cause, he began to quake and tremble. In a foreign and guttural tone, he issued a strange, bestial sound. "Hoo-oo! Hoo-oo! Hoo-oo!"

Those standing closest to him, the German city officials, grew frightened and began backing away, having never heard such an unearthly sound coming from a human. This created an opening, a staging space so to speak, and put the Hermit in clear view of all in the room. But those standing further away, the Hermit's supporters and enthralled Colognese who had come to hear the Hermit speak, drew nearer instead of retreating– many clasping their hands with reverence or directing their faces upward with closed eyes.

"Hoo-oo! Hoo-oo!" came the Hermit's bestial sound again, causing an even more sepulchral silence to drop over the entire hall… such that people could hear their own breathing. Next his pupils dilated, turning to embers, further terrifying the city officials. Then, leaning forward from the waist only, craning his neck forward like a goose, he uttered a bleating sound, like that of a complaining field goat. This he repeated several times, while pointing with stilted exaggeration to a man standing to his left. Abandoning German, he broke into French. "You th-th-there!" he cried, still bleating in the manner of a goat. "You will kill a heathen for Christ and sit next to the Lord's throne! Hallelujah, thou chosen child of God!" His eyes then shot to the person standing to the man's left, an obese woman so overcome with wonder that she no longer seemed to be of this earth. "Y-y-you there, *b-b-i-g woman*," he bleated, "you shall stand firm before the Muslim horde and call out God's name! Hallelujah, thou blessed and saintly sister of us all!"

The woman, who was born fat, ugly, and ignorant, and worsening her pitiful state through a lifetime of gluttony and indolence, had never once in her entire existence been the center of anyone's attention– not even that of her own parents. But now, having suddenly been pointed out by Peter the Hermit, and having hundreds of people ooh-ah and point because of the Hermit's prediction that she would turn the Muslim horde, she flushed red as perspiration and palpitations began a wild assault on her face and frame. "*Aiee! Aiee*!" she squealed, her hands flying above her head like fluttering pigeons released from the cage. She began to run about in a fit of blind frenzy within the slight available space surrounding her. Haphazardly, her huge, jostling torso knocked a helpless old man to the ground. Next, as she careened off an equally obese woman standing nearby, she bowled over an entire huddle of spellbound onlookers as her seizure of ecstasy seemed only to heighten.

"The chosen of God!" affirmed Tafur, knocking people aside with his staff and running into the small clearing to kneel before the woman as she continued her delirious gyrations. "Aye, she's the chosen instrument of God against the Turks!"

"And what of me?" proclaimed another large woman, stepping forward, thrusting a newborn infant above her head with both hands. "Do you remember me, Peter?! I'm Estelle Dupuis, and this infant was just born to me on the road outside Cologne! My husband and I are making our way to the Holy Land, so we've named this infant– *Jerusalem*!"

Staring at her, his eyes ablaze, the Hermit made the sign of the cross over the child. "Oh, yes, I remember you, Estelle!" he shouted. "Yes, you shall hold that child against the advance of the enemy exactly as you are now, and placing your other children beside you in a circle, you shall cry out, *Jerusalem! Jerusalem!* The enemy will begin to fall from their horses, seeing they have no hope before an infant of God… then the earth shall open and devour their wicked souls!"

Certain observers, primarily women, became so overcome by this unanticipated outbreak of holy drama that they collapsed on the floor, falling into trances, their lips riffling with whispering sounds that might be made by slithering reptiles of unknown species. Others in the crowd dropped to their knees, folding their palms in prayer or lapsing into fits of weeping or singing. In the midst of this clamor, the Hermit moved to a different person, pronouncing some special and sanctified prediction while bleating that 'this one' or 'that one' would do something extraordinary upon confronting the Islamic heathens in the Holy Land.

This latest drama the Hermit had pulled from thin air was at first spoken entirely in French and reserved for his French followers, but next he switched back to the German tongue and started pointing at individuals wearing German garb, uttering audacious forecasts of their bold actions against the Turks. As each prediction precipitated into an augmenting outcry of jubilation from the crowd, more and more Germans within the hall and outside pledged themselves to the march of the Peasants' Crusade to the Holy Land.

Guillaume, having never before witnessed Kuku Peter's fits of preaching, was as entranced as others in the room. Feeling an overwhelming tide of evangelical fever rising in his chest, his eyes followed every move and changing expression that fell across the Hermit's face. "*God in Heaven*," he whispered, nudging Tristan, "I've never seen such a thing in my life! The man's a puppeteer, and is either a saint or a sorcerer! I feel a change sweeping through me as if I'm unworthy and need to prove my love for God!"

"He is neither saint *nor* sorcerer," Tristan whispered in return. "Though I believe him to be earnest in some ways, he is an actor, Guillaume, albeit a good one. Ah, but we'll not make any progress with him in the midst of such theatre! Best we leave, ask one of Sansavoir's knights outside where Peter's encampment is, and go there in the morning."

Shrugging, Guillaume gave his brother a look of objection. “But, must we leave just *now*?”

“Aye, Guillaume, immediately... lest you yourself get swept away into Kuku Peter’s madness like these others!”

# Chapter Twenty-four

## Tristan Speaks

That next morning Tristan and Guillaume sought the Hermit who, they had learned, was encamped at Walter Sansavoir's military bivouac on the opposite outskirts of the city along the road to Mainz. Unlike what they encountered along the road and in the city, there was order in the camp, which was made up of Sansavoir's collection of knights and footmen recruited in France and along the German road to Cologne.

Shortly after entering the camp they happened onto Innocenzo, who seemed lost, wandering about while looking rather out of place in the midst of weaponry and soldiers. "Bishop Saint-Germain!" he shouted upon recognizing Tristan, running to him, dropping to a knee and kissing his bishop's ring. "I spotted you at the town hall meeting last night– oh, and was heartily hoping to catch you again while here in Cologne! But tell, what brings you this far north, Bishop?"

"We are here to see your uncle," replied Tristan, who still harbored doubts about Innocenzo's sudden and dubious appearance into the life of Kuku Peter just three years earlier. Tristan was also aware of Innocenzo's weakness for female flesh and his reputation as a young rooster. Still, Tristan had always found the young man quite likable.

"Ah yes, yes– then come along with me," said Innocenzo, ushering them deferentially in the direction from which he himself had just come. "Uncle Peter will be most pleased to see you, I'm certain!"

Several minutes later Innocenzo led them into a large tent where they found Walter Sansavoir standing next to Peter as he sat on a camp stool stuffing himself with smoked fish. Also standing next to Peter were the two men Tristan had seen beating the

German magistrate the night before during the Hermit's tumultuous town meeting.

Looking up as they entered, the Hermit jumped to his feet, grasping Tristan by the hand. "Aha!" he crowed, motioning them onto empty camp stools, "Young Bishop Saint-Germain and his handsome brother, Guillaume, imagine that!" Next, motioning to his cohorts, he continued with, "And I believe you two already know Sir Walter Sansavoir here, commander of the formal military faction of the People's Crusade." The Hermit far preferred to refer to his movement as the 'People's Crusade' rather than the 'Peasants' Crusade'; although he had taken a vow of poverty himself and considered the poor as God's favored flock, he felt his crusade was far more inclusive than only peasants. "And this other fine knight standing with Walter here is Geoffrey Burrel, leader of Sansavoir's footmen." Next he pointed to Tafur. "And this is my own immediate right-hand-man, commander of the peasant army. His name is Tafur… his men call him the Beggar King."

Sansavoir and Burrel stepped forward to shake hands. "Greetings, Bishop," said Sansavoir. Both knights had met Tristan once before in Normandy, and both had been impressed by his fiery preaching of the crusade. "We heard you speak in Rouen," Sansavoir nodded. "Twas your own words that caused me interest in what the Hermit was preaching in Flanders, and I've been with him since. Along the way, I came across Burrel, here, and enlisted him in the Hermit's service also."

"Truly?" replied Tristan, thinking it ironic how one's own actions at creating solutions could circle back, becoming the root of future problems.

Tristan then turned to shake hands with the rough looking man who had burned the mark of the cross across his forehead, expecting that he would step forward to shake hands as had Sansavoir and Burrel.

But Tafur, staff in hand, held position– staring sullenly at Tristan and Guillaume through heavy lids. "I'm a former knight," he said, his eyes raking over the fine fabrics of Tristan's bishop's vestments, which made his heart swell with bile; they reminded him of that hated cleric of his youth, Archbishop Duchamps, who had betrayed him as a boy to Lord Cartier so many years ago. Tafur was further offended by the rich fabric and dressings of Guillaume's ornate officer's uniform designating him a nobleman.

"*But*," Tafur blenched sourly, "like the Hermit, I've recently forsaken the pursuit of worldly appearances in favor of clothing more like the Lord Himself wore during his humble presence on this earth."

"I see that," replied Tristan, "and commend you for such."

"As do I," said Guillaume politely, despite thinking the man rude.

"I lead the peasant warriors," Tafur continued, his cheeks going thin. "They're becoming deadly of late with staffs and farm implements, under my tutelage."

"You've been to war, then?" asked Guillaume. "As a knight, I mean."

"Of course," lied Tafur. "But these peasants have limited means, due to the greedy habits of their masters, the nobility. It's my role, then, to teach them to wield shovels, staffs, and forks... as they have nothing else to fight with."

"Shovels, staffs, and forks against the Turks?" Guillaume queried. "But you shall be vastly out-armed, then. The Turks are famed for swift light-cavalry assaults, and deadly archer maneuverability while riding full tilt on speedy ponies. I fear you may be in for more than you imagine. Then too... I've never in my life heard of a peasant army."

"Ha!" interceded the Hermit. "Were the Israelites not an army of former slaves? Was David not a mere shepherd boy taking on Goliath? Where's your faith in God, lad? Shame on you! *Do you doubt the power of God's Heavenly intervention?!*"

"My faith in God stands firm," replied Guillaume coldly, displeased by the Hermit's insinuations. "Yet, God neither expects us to abandon common sense, nor wishes us to depend entirely on miracles."

Reaching over, Tristan gave Guillaume a look. "Do not inflame," he whispered. Then he stepped forward to offer a blessing over the Hermit, but the little man's gross breathing nearly made him swoon. Backing away, Tristan began extending his blessing from a reach– but Peter had already moved away. He was now eyeing Guillaume, much as a farmer inspects his livestock, stooping, probing at shoulders and limbs. Guillaume, who also felt palpably ill in such close proximity to the Hermit, expected Peter at any moment to reach out and pry his mouth open to inspect his teeth as one does to determine the age of horses.

"Ah, yes, good to have another crusade preacher in our midst, Bishop Saint-Germain," said the Hermit to Tristan though his eyes were by now boring in on Guillaume from beneath thick, bushy eyebrows. "Yes, lad, I remember that day I met you down in Cluny. You were in the Treasury Tower counting money for Odo de Lagery when he was Grand Prior there." Glancing over at Sansavoir, he laughed. "Ha! And Walter, this lad was only but about nine or so at the time! Imagine that, and working in the Treasury Tower of Cluny Monastery, the greatest center of wealth in all Christendom, and working for a future pope. Such things this young man has done in his few years, and now already Bishop of Ostia and Pope's Counsel!"

"Aye, I too remember the day you visited Cluny," Tristan said. "You were there to inform Odo de Lagery he would one day be pope... which he refused to believe, as did everyone else at the time. But the pendulum swung, time took a twist and a turn, and just as you predicted, he is truly now Pope Urban II."

"Ah, good lad, such a sharp memory you have!" clucked the Hermit. "Not only did Odo not believe me, he became angry. Hmm… then you must also remember what I told you in the stable that day, huh? I said you had an *aura* about you, and that you'd one day sow the seeds of war and lead Christendom to glory. And here it is, twenty years later already, and the undercurrent claims it was *you* who finally swayed Odo de Lagery to put the wheel in motion on this long talked about war against Islam. God bless you, lad! Christianity owes you a great debt!"

Tristan, slipping into a reminiscent vein, recalled the incidents Peter the Hermit had just recited, privately conceding the Hermit had uncannily foretold both events. He marveled a bit, too, in retrospect, that the strange little preacher could have conjured such ideas at that early date.

The Hermit sat down and resumed devouring his smoked fish, as if suddenly alone in the tent. Tristan began to speak on several occasions, but seeing the Hermit so voraciously poking at and swallowing gobs of fish he had raked into his fingers, he stood there in silence, repelled by the crudeness of the Hermit's table manners. Soon he felt Guillaume nudging him. Looking to his side, he saw Guillaume glancing at him. *What are you waiting on,* the glance said.

Then, for no apparent reason and without warning, the Hermit jumped from his stool, as if returning from another world. Pointing his finger at Tristan, his eyes wide as saucers, he shouted, "*Ah, but it's just hit me!* You've been sent by Odo de Lagery, haven't you, lad? Oh, but he stoops to a new low, the Holy Father! Last time, he sent that damnable Jurgen Handel to hound me, but now he sends one I revere!" Approaching Tristan, the Hermit circled him twice, sniffing from time to time, as would a hunting dog following scent. "O-h, y-e-s, and even now I seem to smell the odor of that foul Bavarian all over you, lad. Aye, that damnable spy, Handel, is right here with you somewhere in Cologne, isn't he?!"

This caught Tristan off guard, but Guillaume was yet more surprised. *How could the Hermit possibly guess such a thing?* Guillaume wondered, perplexed.

"Yes, he's here in Cologne, but I told him you would not wish to see him, especially after your last meeting," Tristan said, knowing it would be fruitless to deceive the Hermit. Even if the Hermit had simply happened onto a lucky guess about Handel, he would eventually run into Handel over time in Cologne.

"Oh, and you're damned correct, Bishop!" snapped Tafur. "Handel isn't welcome in this camp, and should I catch him here, I'll sic my men on him! That lout attacked me for no reason at the border some time ago."

"Aye, and even put a dagger to my throat, threatening my life!" grunted Sansavoir angrily.

"He attacked *both* of you?" said Guillaume, having already heard Handel's version of the incident. A slight smile creeping over his lips, he continued. "Funny thing," he smirked. "Handel tells us, Sansavoir, that you rode rough-shod right over the top of him on your horse." Turning, he looked at Tafur. "He also said that *you,* sir, were about to assault him with that stick of yours. Handel is many things, but I've never known him to lie. In any case, you're both alive and survived his so-called 'attack.' As for you, Tarfu, I'd not make idle threats to Handel, ever. You'd look a bit odd walking about with your own stick stuck up your hind end."

"My name's *Tafur*, not Tarfu," replied Tafur with heat, drawing his face down into a scowl. "And I find your tone insulting."

"Aye, your voice is full of stink and scorn," said Burrel, taking Tafur's side. "Condescending and full of shit, I'd say!"

"Now, now, lads," chided the Hermit, "we're all fellow crusaders, are we not?" Having said that, his brows drew together before continuing. "Let's get back to Odo de Lagery, Bishop. It occurs to me that if Odo sent you here with Handel, then you're not here as a friend, *are you?* Well then… spit it out. Be done with your little errand about commanding me to return to France, then be on your way! You'll not be turning me back!"

"Guillaume and I saw you yesterday evening with the magistrates and burghermeisters," said Tristan, unmoved. "Obviously you have turned the city on end with your army of crusaders, such as they are. We saw many of them camped on the road as we came into Cologne. Peter, their ranks were filled with the old and infirm, children, harlots, a woman giving birth, and even lepers. Truthfully, do you not see the *condition* they are in?" Turning to Sansavoir, Burrel, Tafur, and Innocenzo, he asked them the same.

Innocenzo had said nothing since entering the tent, and had become uncomfortable during the sparring session that was developing. He admired Bishop Saint-Germain, but was not about to contradict his uncle. Choosing to remain tight-lipped, he continued to stare dumbly at his feet.

Sansavoir, who had traveled in advance of the Hermit, knew only that the peasants and others had managed to make it from Amiens to Cologne in just less than three weeks. He had thought little of their hardships; he and his troops had adequate food and supplies. "The Hermit's followers are doing just fine," he said. "I see no problem. Besides, they are fueled by piety... uplifted by hope."

"Indeed," agreed Tafur, who had begun to resent Tristan from the moment he entered the tent. "Look at me, Bishop, do I look forlorn?" he sneered. "No, my condition is fine."

"But you are a man in your prime," said Tristan, straining to remain patient, "as are Sansavoir and Burrel, as are the Hermit and Innocenzo. The walk from Amiens to Cologne is but a short journey compared to going on foot all the way to Constantinople. There are thousands of women, children, and elderly in your midst, and you have the entire continent yet ahead of you. The other day as we approached your train, we saw people begging for bread, people without shoes, and people without even mantles or other cover at night or against the rain."

The Hermit shook his head, looking Tristan in the eye. "You're looking at this all wrong, Bishop," he said. "Aye, I know you're clever, and as a boy was touted as the Wonder of Cluny, but allow me to give you a simple... analogy. Imagine in your mind for a moment... *Hell*. Can you picture it, lad?"

"Yes, certainly, I have imagined Hell more than you might think," replied Tristan.

"As have I," agreed Guillaume, wondering where the Hermit was leading.

"*Now*," continued the Hermit, "look at the condition of these people traveling with me and compare it to everlasting suffering and burning in the fires of Hell. Aw, they're in good stead compared to those burning in hellfire! Next, imagine Heaven as you walk through the gates of Paradise." His dark eyes widened into a look of sheer enlightenment and shifted toward his supporters, satisfied he had squelched the issue with a rhetorical hammer.

"Well, spoken, Peter!" Sansavoir exclaimed, as Burrel shook his head in agreement.

"Ah, you've made it so clear now!" asserted Tafur, shaking his fist in the air.

"Indeed, well spoken, Uncle Peter!" said Innocenzo, smiling to mask his confusion.

Knowing the Hermit talked in circles, knowing he also excelled at confusing others, Tristan plowed forward. "Congratulations, Peter, but you've said absolutely *nothing*. I asked you a simple question, not a deep theological question. I asked whether you saw the condition of your followers. It was a yes-no question, yet you launched off on some visual tour of Heaven and Hell. Now again, I ask the same question."

The Hermit was accustomed to mesmerizing others, leading them into confusion, or infuriating them to the point of incoherence– but not to being challenged. He sat there a moment stroking his beard, then repeated word for word what he had already said.

Again, Sansavoir exclaimed, "Well spoken, Peter!"

"Indeed!" agreed Burrel, "A brilliant analogy!"

"Aye, aye, well spoken, Uncle Peter!" chimed Innocenzo, still confused.

Guillaume, witnessing this, looked at Tristan and shrugged, unable to believe what he was witnessing. There before him stood one man saying exactly nothing, and the other four congratulating him for it. "The question *was*," Guillaume interjected, adopting Tristan's tactic of reason and remaining on topic, "do you not *see* the condition of your followers? Or perhaps all of you here simply don't *care* about their condition… whether they starve, whether they have shelter from the weather, or whether they die. If that be the case, then *I* have a question. How is it that any of you can hold yourself up as representatives of God, who says 'the shepherd should tend to his flock?"

The Hermit gave Guillaume a vigorous shake of the head. "Oh, so you're just like those German magistrates last night who are too dull-witted to comprehend the *b-i-g* picture, eh? These magistrates see people in the streets and they equate it to disruption, while failing to see that the *real* issue here is… *Islam*. Let's go back to my analogy that neither of you seem yet to grasp. Look at the condition of my followers in Cologne, then imagine their condition in Hell… *forever*. Which is worse, eh? Ah, *now* do you see their condition here in Cologne compared to burning in Hell? Far better here than in Hell forever, huh? Next, imagine their condition in Heaven. You then begin to see that they are, with this bit of discomfort getting to the Holy Land, earning an eternal reward in paradise! So to answer your yes-no question, Bishop Saint-Germain, yes, I *do* see the condition of my people– and it's sound as granite. The crusade to Jerusalem's not just a holy war, but also an individual act of penance for the remission of all earthly sins… so said Pope Urban II himself at Clermont to the thousands of nobles and knights in attendance. Although he may have preached such a principle to recruit the aristocratic warrior class for this crusade, paupers and peasants *also* have the same right to perform their own personal act of penance! Indeed, the gates of Heaven are open to all, not just the fortunate of this world."

"Well spoken, Peter!" shouted Sansavoir and Burrel simultaneously.

"Yes, do you two hard-heads not see the reasoning of it all?" declared Tafur.

"Uh, yes, well said," muttered Innocenzo, his effort to show enthusiasm waning by the moment.

"Bishop, you'll not deter me from this holy mission of defeating the Muslims and taking Jerusalem back," insisted the Hermit. Reaching into the top of his tunic, he started to withdraw something.

Suspecting it was the infamous 'God letter,' Tristan waved his hand. "Hold there," he said, "we have no need to see your letter from God, Peter. We saw it last night at the meeting. And truthfully, we reject its authenticity. We– "

"Oh, but it's *truly* a letter from Heaven, Bishop Saint-Germain!" interrupted Innocenzo, spurred to life at seeing God's letter; moreover, at last something had been said that he understood. He had seen and touched the letter, and on the Hermit's word alone was willing to wager his life that that each word, though scrawled in childish script, had been scriven by the blessed hand of God Himself.

As to Tafur and Burrel, it is dubitable whether they actually held credence for the Hermit's claim. What is certain, however, is that Walter Sansavoir accepted it purely and conclusively as a divine document written by God and delivered to His earthly messenger, Peter the Hermit. Thus, what occurred next was the product of that volatile tinderbox spawned only within the brain of a man consumed by righteous indignation and religious fanaticism. Though Sansavoir had been relatively calm to this point, all composure fled at hearing Bishop Saint-Germain's refutation of the Hermit's letter from God; he flew into an absolute, blind rage. "Holy Jehovah!" he bellowed, incensed, the veins of his neck turning purple. "*Do you call the Hermit a liar, Bishop Saint-Germain!?* By God, I'll not have it! He's divine, I say, and so says God also!" Balling his fist, spewing spittle as his fury allowed for nothing at that point but incomprehensible snarling, he charged at Tristan with complete disregard for his bishop's vestments, his papal appointment, or high position within the Church.

This in turn precipitated in Guillaume, despite an instant of disbelief, an instinctual reaction; he pulled his sword, gave it a half turn, and swiftly struck Sansavoir across the skull with the flat of the blade. "*Hold there*!" Guillaume shouted. "Have you gone daft, man!?"

Sansavoir's charge toward Tristan terrified Innocenzo, in whose mind attacking a bishop was tantamount to earning a sentence straight to Hell by the Almighty, Himself. Regardless, Innocenzo was also a coward, abhorring violence in any form; it frightened him. Cowering behind his uncle, squealing girlishly, he shrieked, "Sakes Alive! This is madness!"

"Ungh!" Sansavoir groaned, his eyes swimming in liquid at the instant of taking Guillaume's blow. Staggering about as a man drunk, he went cross-eyed, teetering side to side before slumping to the floor, unconscious.

"*What's this?!*" shouted Burrel, jumping backward, surprised.

Tafur, spurred to action, surged forward, spinning his staff. In a show of blinding agility, he next made a series of swift parrying maneuvers, coming directly at Guillaume, cursing as he moved. Guillaume, not expecting such a brazen, skilled attack from a man holding only a staff, retreated several steps, barely dodging several well aimed blows from Tafur. Then, quick as a cat, he happened to catch Tafur at the end of a missed parry, deflected the staff tip, and shoved the point of his sword to Tafur's throat. "No, no," he warned, "*put it down!*"

Feeling the tip of the blade pressing against his Adam's apple, Tafur froze. Scowling, he dropped to a knee, laying his staff to the ground.

"Oh, outrage!" shouted the Hermit at Guillaume. "You've attacked the devout knight Walter Sansavoir with such brutality, and now threaten to slit God's loyal soldier's throat! Back off of my man Tafur, Guillaume, or I'll have God pass a sentence of damnation upon you!" Reaching behind him, he then swatted at Innocenzo who was still crawling up his back, terrified that Guillaume might next come after him and his uncle. "And get off me!" the Hermit yowled.

"In the name of Rome, my brother's a high Vatican bishop!" exclaimed Guillaume. "By God, one doesn't attack a high cleric, especially the First Counsel to the Holy Father himself! Damnation, man, what breed of wild boars are you people?!"

The commotion in the tent drew the attention of knights outside, and the tent quickly filled with Sansavoir's men, some tending to Sansavoir who was slowly gaining consciousness while others began to corner the Saint-Germain brothers in the back of the tent.

"Get them!" shouted Burrel, pulling his own sword. "Take them down!"

"*Stop there!*" yelled the Hermit. "Hold, I say. Don't harm these two men. We've had but a little dispute here and Sir Walter got carried away... but all's well!" Turning to Tristan, he said. "Get out, both of you. As I'm a generous man you'll still be welcome here in my camp, but *never* utter another word to me about turning back this holy tide of Christian righteousness. We're marching to Jerusalem, Bishop, and we're going to turn back the Turks!"

"Very well," said Tristan, keeping a wary eye to the knights surrounding him and Guillaume, "but know one thing. We have a battalion of Tuscan knights and footmen outside the city, and when you leave Cologne, we intend to accompany you all the way to Constantinople… if indeed you even make it that far. And then we shall follow you into the territory of the Turks should you foolishly refuse to wait for Pope Urban's main crusader armies."

"What?" asked the Hermit, his eyes flaring with confusion. "You're *joining* my march?"

"Certainly not!" snapped Tristan. "We will march separately. And never will we heed any commands coming from you or any of these imbeciles you have gathered! We answer to no one but Pope Urban who has commissioned us to protect you from *yourselves*, and in the end, from the Turks if need be!"

"Then bless you, lad, you'll be like a guardian angel," said the Hermit, ignoring Tristan's irritation while setting his own aside. "I'll scold Sansavoir as soon as he gains his senses and his head clears. Ah no, he shouldn't have tried to attack you, Bishop. It was a poor decision, but be patient with him… he's a bit quick tempered, I fear, when it comes to me, and when it comes to God."

"Indeed," said Guillaume, his eyes drawing down to slits, "I'm exactly the same when it comes to my brother... and when it comes to God!"

"Well said, lad, well said!" nodded the Hermit. Then, reclaiming his position on his stool, he began stuffing fish into his mouth as though nothing whatsoever had just transpired within the tent; it was one of those damnable practices of his which so confounded and confused others– abandoning one action, even a conflagration such as the one that had just occurred, to suddenly launch into something completely unrelated... which in this case was his dinner. “Innocenzo!” he barked. “Fetch me more wine to wash down this fish, then go feed my donkey, poor beast!”

## Chapter Twenty-five

### A Visitor

After filling Peter's goblet with wine, Innocenzo abandoned the tent and caught up to the Saint-Germain brothers before tending to his uncle's donkey. "Oh, my deepest apologies!" he implored. "I'd never have imagined that Sir Walter would try to lay hands on you, Bishop Saint-Germain! I–"

"No worries, Innocenzo," interrupted Tristan. "None of that business in the tent was your doing."

"Agreed," said Guillaume, "your hands are clean, Innocenzo. But you know, I'd always thought Sansavoir a genteel knight… but I'll no longer swallow such gristle. As to that other fellow with the branded forehead, he appears off kilter. Still, I confess, he's agile with that staff of his. I was fortunate to catch him as I did."

"Sansavoir *is* a good man, I assure you," said Innocenzo, "but since taking up with Uncle Peter he's become fanatical about this crusade, and he'll brook no disagreement against my uncle whatsoever. Still, it's a terrible action he took in the tent, and I want no association with it. As for Tafur, he's dark and angry at the world, resenting anyone who has even the slightest snatch of happiness in this life. I've never trusted him, and in truth, I believe he's a criminal."

"Oh?" said Tristan.

"Yes. Worse yet, rumors circulate that he's been undermining my uncle behind his back– but Uncle Peter refuses to believe it. He insists Tafur is driven only by piety." Pausing, he looked at Tristan. "As for me, I'm happy to learn you'll be following us to Constantinople, Bishop Saint-Germain. Though Sansavoir's recruited a good number of practiced men-at-arms for the Peoples' Crusade, I feel better knowing that you'll be bringing the Tuscan knights along. Some of these men Sansavoir's dug up are questionable, I fear, and the ideas that Tafur is drilling into the heads of his peasant troops are enough to give me the willies. So, yes, you and your bunch are a welcome addition for certain."

"Well, good to know at least one person in this camp appreciates us," said Tristan, clasping Innocenzo by the shoulder. "We'll be on our way, Innocenzo, but Peter has not seen the last of us, I assure you."

"Oh, but should you try to stop his march again," said Innocenzo, swelling with concern, "I'm afraid things will only get worse. Tafur would think nothing of calling in his branded hooligans, especially after the way he was just humiliated in the tent by Sir Guillaume. He prides himself as invincible with that staff of his, you know."

"No, no," said Tristan with assurance, "I can see Peter refuses to be stopped, and actually suspected it from the very beginning. Still, there is now a different tack I must take, Innocenzo, and perhaps you can help my cause."

"But, how?" asked Innocenzo, doubt filling his expression. "With all due respect, Bishop… I'll not go against my uncle, nor be involved in deceiving him."

"Deceit is not my goal, Innocenzo. *Saving* him, and you, and these thousands of others is what I must now drive at. Aye, I must now convince him not to engage the Turks until Bishop Adhémar and the sanctioned crusaders arrive."

Hearing this, Innocenzo breathed easier, nodding with contentment; the Bishop's proposal made sense to him. Although Innocenzo knew nothing of war, he had already developed suspicions about the capacity of the Peasants' Crusade as a viable combat force. "Oh, Bishop, a wise idea, that. I'm no general, but from the very onset I've wondered about the wisdom of bringing all these women and children along. Also, I've been frightened by the very idea of attacking the Turks without the Pope's military. So yes, yes, I'll certainly try to get into my uncle's ear if possible. But you know… he's not always open to suggestions from others, especially when God has given him explicit instructions."

"So then, Innocenzo," shrugged Guillaume, "you really believe God talks to your uncle?"

"Yes, *certainly*, Sir Guillaume. My uncle is divine, you know."

At this, Tristan and Guillaume exchanged a dubious glance, and took their leave. Innocenzo started to make for the stables, though what he really wished to do was make his way back across town to the other camps where women were to be found– but the Hermit had demanded Innocenzo remain in Sansavoir's camp after recently being caught fornicating with a German miller's wife– and nearly getting killed by her cuckolded husband. Regardless, Innocenzo had never been one to give up if a woman's crack was within grasp, and now his mind was centered on two other women– the two promiscuous sisters from Flanders he had been rutting when Tafur had caught him just outside of Cologne

Thus lost, grasping about for excuses to cross over to the other side of Cologne, he felt a light tap against his back. Turning, he glimpsed a short figure standing there. "Yes, lad, what is it?" he said.

"I'm no *lad*," the man barked in a high pitched voice. "My name's Fazio, and I'm twice your age, you piker!"

Taken aback at seeing the little man and hearing his elfish lilt, Innocenzo stared, open-mouthed. "Oh, pardon… s-sir. I didn't notice your beard at first, only your…"

"*Size*?" said Fazio, softening his tone at noticing Innocenzo's pleasing face.

"Yes," Innocenzo replied, reddening.

"It happens often to me," Fazio nodded. "But tell, those two men you were talking to… wasn't the one wearing clerical vestments the Bishop of Ostia?"

"Yes."

"Ah, he's well known throughout Europe, and some claim he may well become pope one day. My, then... you must be a fellow of high stature to talk to someone like that with such familiarity. I saw him place his hand on your shoulder as though you were a relative or close friend, huh?"

This pleased Innocenzo to no end. "Yes, yes, we *are* somewhat close, you could say."

"Hmm… but he's such a long way from Ostia and Rome. Has he come all this way just to see *you*?"

"Yes, I suppose," Innocenzo replied, feeling more important with each exchange, "and to see my uncle, Peter the Hermit."

"What? Your uncle is the renowned preacher, Peter the Hermit?" asked Fazio, feigning surprise. "Well now, I'd say I was certainly correct in assuming you're a man of substance. It would therefore be my pleasure to take you for some German ale at a little place I've begun to frequent since my recent arrival in Cologne."

Innocenzo happily accepted the invitation, but then hesitated, shaking his head. "No, I'd best not… my uncle wants me to remain in camp," he said. Then he added, "He might need me at a moment's notice. You see, he depends on me heavily, you know."

"Ah, but the place I'm talking about is only two blocks from here, my friend, at the very edge of this very camp, in fact. So there... how could you disappoint a fellow traveler such as me? After all, it's not every day I get to meet a relative of Peter the Hermit, or a friend of the Bishop of Ostia!"

"Indeed," smiled Innocenzo, his head swelling. "I suppose not! Yes, then, if it's not far from here and you're willing to pay, I'll go… but only for a short while, huh?"

***

Within the Hermit's command tent, he and Burrel tended to Sansavoir who by now had nearly cleared his head. "Ungh…" he muttered, probing at the knot rising on his scalp. "*Wh-what happened?*"

"You tried to assault Bishop Saint-Germain, you numbskull," said the Hermit, shaking his head with disapproval, "and God saw to it you got your just reward, Walter. Never do such a thing again, for you're fortunate the Lord only gave you a bump on the noggin instead of striking you dead. God in Heaven above, Walter, what were you *thinking*? Bishop Saint-Germain's the Pope's man, for Christ's sake!"

Clumsily gaining his knees, Sansavoir stood. "Y-yes, a foolish thing… I understand, Peter. I don't know what came over me. It'll not happen again."

"You understand nothing," snorted Tafur, still simmering from his exchange with Guillaume. "A shame you didn't manage to give that bishop a taste of your fist!"

"Tafur," scolded the Hermit. "No more such talk in my tent. One simply doesn't lay hands on a high cleric! Or *any* cleric for that matter." As he said this, he felt himself flushing beneath his beard. He had thought Tafur more respectful of the cloth and collar, but this was yet another indication that he may have misjudged the horseless knight. Though the Hermit did not wish it, he was beginning to hear tiny alarms going off in the back of his brain, warning him to keep a closer eye to his peasant commander. "Should the Bishop return, which he surely will," declared the Hermit, "I'll expect you both to treat him with more decorum."

"Bah," Tafur snuffed, turning to stalk out of the tent. "That bastard's come only for one thing, Peter, to sabotage your crusade! Can't you see that? And he'll not be content until he sees it in shambles, dammit!"

As Tafur left, the Hermit gave Sansavoir a shrug. "There's an anger that's sprouted from somewhere and taken root within Tafur's spirit," he muttered, "and I don't quite understand it. Let's hope he can contain it until we meet the Turks. Then, maybe, it'll serve a better purpose, eh?"

Stamping his way from the Hermit's camp, Tafur's blood was up now, and he made a line for his own camp, assembling several of his men. "Dupuis," he said, "I've received word that Count Emicho has arrived in Cologne from the north. He's making his way south toward the Balkans and on to Constantinople just as we ourselves intend to do. He's heard of our riots back in Rouen against the Jews months back, and has sent word he wishes us to join him later today."

"Huh?" said Dupuis, scratching at the brand blistering on his forehead; it had never properly healed since inception, and was now infected. "Count Emicho of Leiningen?" asked Dupuis. "Butcher of German Jews?"

"Ay, the same," nodded Tafur. "And he's organized a little foray into the Jewish quarter later in the day. Even as I speak, he's gathering Cologne citizens to join his troops. Start rounding up some of the others and we'll make for the commercial district."

This daunted Dupuis. He had overheard Tafur and the others talking about the earlier Jewish pogrom in Rouen back in December, and the tales had chilled him. The mobs had actually murdered hundreds of Jews, including women and children. Thinking back to the recent raid on the German farm, Dupuis shivered. Tafur and the others had not actually killed the German farmer, but undoubtedly crippled him for life. As to the farmer's wife, they had gang-raped her over and over and over, committing one bestial act after another on every part of her body.

Dupuis had refused to enter the shanty as this had been going on, but was eventually forced by others to enter and watch. An hour into the brutality, Tafur asked Dupuis whether he would like a go at the woman's orifices. What Dupuis did not understand at the time was that Tafur's question was not a 'question'... it was a command. Minutes later, the woman's rump propped in the air by three other men, Dupuis was forced to strip and mount her. He became so terrified, knowing God was watching, he was unable to get stiff. This caused raucous amusement amongst the other Tafurs, ending in taunting that endured the remainder of the day. "You'd best do better next time, Dupuis," warned Tafur, "or you're *out*, you little slug!"

Thinking back at the incident, Tafur shuddered a bit.

"Goddammit," barked Tafur, jolting Dupuis from the memory of the farm, "did you not hear me? I said start rounding up the others and let's be on our way!"

The others needed little prodding. Born into the helpless, impotent ranks of French peasantry, being since birth tied to spade, fork, and oxen, they had a lifetime of fury to shed. Breaking from their masters' fields had opened the world to them, and they were now drunk with empowerment... and unlike Dupuis, they had forgotten God somewhere along the road from Amiens.

"King Tafur," said Dupuis in a low voice so others did not hear, "could I first inform my wife, Estelle, of my absence? She just days ago gave birth to our son, Jerusalem, along the road into Cologne. She'll be worried if I'm not to be found in camp."

"Christ, Dupuis," spat Tafur with disdain, "are you not your own man, or is that a crack running up the front of your crotch? To hell with your wife, man! Need I find you a bonnet and apron so you can walk about like a goddamned woman? That brand seared into your head marks you a warrior, Dupuis, so get to it!"

Dupuis' head dropped with shame as the men standing around him began to snicker at Tafur's injurious darts. "Yes, sir," he muttered, issuing his pitiful salute.

After leaving, however, he circled around and slipped back to his wife despite Tafur's barbs. "Estelle," he said, "I'm headed into town with our men. We've a little job to do." As he said this, he bristled a bit, brandishing his newly acquired staff like an instrument of war. Secretly, he was hoping she did not spot his apprehension, nor guess what was about.

Cradling her newborn, Estelle's eyes shone with pride as she looked at her husband. She was twice his size and had always run him about as one might herd a favored old goat. Still, he had changed since taking the brand and becoming acquainted with Tafur, whom Estelle perceived as the most manly of men on earth. "Oh, I'm so proud of you, Marcel," she beamed, moving a hand to his forehead, touching the infected cross-scar as one gingerly touches another's wound. "And God is, too."

Hearing this, Marcel's conscience overcame him. "*God?* Oh, but Estelle, Estelle. I came along thinking to do God's work, but I don't know now… I just don't know any more…"

"Huh?" said Estelle. "But what's that supposed to mean, Marcel? Of course you're doing God's work!"

Marcel shook his head. He had never told Estelle about the German farm, but simply could no longer remain silent about the task now at hand. "Estelle, this work we men are about to do… Tafur has got us going after Jews today."

"*Jews?*" asked Estelle, rocking her infant a bit. "Ah, then… if Tafur has ordered it, then so be it," she nodded, passing her hand over their baby's forehead, then kissing it. "Do what the man says, dear, for he's nearly as touched by the Holy Spirit as Peter the Hermit himself. Yes, and I'll tell you this, Marcel, if tiny Jerusalem's skin here were not so tender, I'd burn a cross upon his forehead to match your own… and could he walk, I'd send him along with you today."

## Chapter Twenty-six

### The Benedictine Underground

After leaving the Hermit's camp, Tristan and Guillaume proceeded to the Benedictine monastery of Cologne where they were greeted by the monastery abbot, an elderly Benedictine named Herman Schwartz. "Ah, been expecting you," the old monk said. "Come along, they're waiting on you in the conference hall." Ushering them forward, he then led them through the main building followed by a cloistered courtyard, ending in a network of back-buildings. Entering the largest of these and taking them down a series of narrow corridors, Abbot Schwartz finally came to a thick, triple enforced door and knocked on it in code. Moments later a coded response returned, and the door opened. "Step in," said Abbot Schwartz, "they're waiting on you." Turning to leave, he tipped his head. "Pax Vobiscum, my brothers in Christ."

Tristan and Guillaume found Handel and the Danes standing about a table where five men wearing the garb of various vocations sat huddled in conversation. Tristan knew these men, despite their non-descript appearance, to be monks of the Benedictine Underground. They were among the most educated, linguistically skilled, and diplomatically capable men of Europe– and also among the most ruthless.

Nonetheless, despite their secretive and often dubious tasks, agents of the Underground were first and foremost Black Monks of the Benedictine Order. Most had taken their sacred vows with the intention of serving God through prayer or service to the destitute of this earth, both material and spiritual. Owing to specific skills or personal attributes identified by superiors, these particular monks were side-tracked for duty within the Benedictine Underground, the Vatican's most secretive branch of operations. Being some of the most talented clerics in all Europe, they had been accumulated from a vast network of monasteries stretching from England, to Spain, to Scandinavia, to Italy. Once identified and selected, they had been sent to the mountains of southern Italy to undergo training within the secluded confines of Monte Cassino Monastery, established around the year 529 by Benedict of Nursia, founder of western monasticism. Each candidate then underwent intensive training in language, diplomacy, and political science. The most promising were then schooled in espionage, self defense, and even assassination, becoming clandestine agents within the largest, most effective network of communication and information gathering in all Europe– in service to the political activities and needs of the Roman Catholic Church.

"Welcome," said Handel as Tristan and Guillaume entered the room. "So how did you fare with the Hermit… if I need bother to ask?"

"As expected," replied Tristan. "Though realizing what sort of inflexibility rules the man's mind, I will continue to peck away at his hard-headedness while here in Cologne."

This caused a swell of grumbling amongst the men at the table, all of whom were aware of the Hermit's fanaticism. To the man, they loathed him. "The Hermit listens to no one but himself," grumbled one of the men at the table. "The fool believes himself to be divine."

"What have we missed?" Tristan asked, brushing the comment aside.

"Nothing," Handel replied. "Actually, we've been trading greetings and small talk while waiting on you and Guillaume, so let's begin." Turning, he nodded to an older man, dressed in the manner of a pilgrim, to begin the first report.

"I'm Brother Harold Hood of Manchester, England," the man said. "There'll be little help from England in this crusade. Since the Bastard's death, his two sons have engaged in a blood feud." The *Bastard* the monk referred to was William of Normandy, later to be known as William the Conqueror. "Son Robert controls Normandy and plans to join the crusade," the monk continued, "but son William is now king of England, and has rejected it. As you all know, Pope Gregory several years ago rebuked the Bastard for excessive violence and greed, and the Bastard in turn became hostile to Rome. His son, William Rufus, maintains those hostilities. As a result–"

"Brother Hood," interrupted Tristan, his brows drawing together like purse string, "you said you came from Manchester? You labor in northwestern England then. Might you by chance then be familiar with a place dubbed DuLacshire, or a nobleman by the name of Desmond DuLac?"

"Yes, certainly," said Hood.

"Damnation!" declared Orla. "*You know Desmond DuLac?*"

Startled by this outburst, Hood nodded. "Yes, rather I know *of* him. He's notorious in the Manchester area where it's well known he's hated by all Saxons of North England, as well as by the neighboring Scotts. But I must inquire... how is it you know of Desmond DuLac here, so far from England?"

"He is my... uncle," Tristan said, looking hard at the Danes who appeared ready to erupt, "but we will speak to you later about that." Shaking his head at Orla, he waved a low hand at Crowbones and Guthroth, who like Orla, had turned scarlet at the mention of DuLac's name. "As you were saying, Brother Hood?"

"Due to the English king's resentment toward the Vatican, only a handful of loyal Normans and French from England proper will be joining the crusade. There will be certain others, but I fear they are but rogues and renegades who've earned the disfavor of King William Rufus' Norman hierarchy that's now choking Saxon England." As he finished, he gave Tristan a questioning look. "Yes, Bishop, I'll be happy to speak to you and your men about DuLac after this meeting."

Handel pointed to the man seated next to Hood, a burly young Spaniard. "So then, Brother Francisco, what of Spain?"

"Over time," began Francisco, "the Reconquista in Spain has become a complex web of intrigue and betrayal, but also intermarriage of Muslim and Christian royal blood. Within this framework, the on-going war against the Moors to reclaim the Iberian Peninsula continues. Fortunately, and of late, the Christian effort is gaining momentum. As a result, the Pope has forbidden Christian knights of Spain from joining this war for Jerusalem against the Turks. Taking soldiers who fight Muslims in one place and moving them to another makes little sense. In light of the Holy Father's mandate, then, there'll be *no* Spaniards joining the crusade against the Seljuk Turks."

Tristan was already aware of this strategy, as he had helped draft it. Several of the other Benedictine agents in the room, excluding Handel and Francisco, were not, however. Though the policy made sense to some, it was disappointing to others, causing a flurry of questions and discussion.

"Enough," said Handel. "The Pope has made the determination, so it shall stand. No point in kicking a dead mule!" Turning, he yielded the floor to the next monk, a German dressed as a town burgher. "Brother Oberhoffer, what can you tell us about the German effort?"

"King Heinrich, after many bloody years fighting the Gregorian papacy in the Investiture War, has no heart for this crusade," said the German. "Though he has finally laid down his weapons against the Vatican, he also refuses to assist the Vatican in any manner. Yet, his great ally against us in those wars, Duke Godfrey of Bouillon, has taken the cross and pledged on behalf of Pope Urban. It was Godfrey, as you may recall, who slew the Church's champion, Rudolph of Swabia. But this avowed former enemy of the Vatican has now sworn allegiance to Pope Urban's crusade and has agreed to help the Greeks of Byzantium."

"Aye," said Handel, "and this strange change of heart by Godfrey has confused many, including myself. Godfrey has no outstanding history of piety, has been a despoiler of papal lands, and even took part in the siege of Rome years back, threatening to place Pope Gregory in chains. The question, then, Brother Oberhoffer, do you and the rest of the Underground here in Germany believe Godfrey of Bouillon can now be trusted?"

"Handel, a year ago I would have flatly said no," replied Oberhoffer. "The smell of blood was yet too fresh from the Investiture War. But now I'd have to say yes, he can be trusted… entirely so. Though many claim he's joined the crusade simply because it's become the fashion of his northern French neighbors, he's taken the crusader ideal to heart and set aside his bitterness with Rome. But there's another development also. You'll be glad to learn, at the final hour, Godfrey's brother, Baldwin of Boulogne, has *also* declared for the journey to Jerusalem!" Scooting back on his stool, Oberhoffer beamed a little.

His news surprised all in the room, causing a brief commotion during which the five Benedictine agents exchanged thoughts on how the two former enemies would add favorable military muscle to the Christian cause. Handel listened to the exchange for several minutes before again bringing the men back to order, motioning to the monk from southern Italy, realm of the Italian-Normans. "Bohemud of Taranto has always been our staunch ally," said Handel, "but what of his past issues with the Byzantines, Brother Minelli?"

"Emperor Alexius and the Byzantines are greatly displeased with Bohemud participating in this war," replied the Italian monk. "As we all know, Bohemud's father, the deceased Duke Robert Guiscard the Wily, carved his Norman Empire in Southern Italy decades ago by wrestling it away from the Byzantines. Then Guiscard and Bohemud began invading the Greek coastline and the Balkans. Much blood, over time, has effused between the Italian-Normans and the Byzantines."

"But surely," said Handel, "the Emperor recognizes that Bohemud and the Normans are ferocious in battle and will be formidable assistance against the Turks, doesn't he?"

Minelli shook his head no. "That makes little difference. Emperor Alexius has always despised Bohemud, and now fears Bohemud is using this crusade purely as a ploy to get his Norman army in the midst of Byzantine soil… only so he can then *turn* on them."

"Well then, Minelli, what *is* that likelihood?" asked Handel.

Minelli shook his head. "I honestly– have no idea. Our agents have slipped in and out of Bohemud's court, digging here and there to uncover any possible word of such a conspiracy. But we've found nothing... so only time will tell. Still, we dare not refuse Bohemud and the Italian-Normans. They'll be far, far too valuable militarily against the Turks."

This ignited more discussion amongst the monks, and ultimately, a division of opinion arose which soon became heated. As they argued on the merits and risks of Bohemud's assistance, the Danes themselves began to speak amongst themselves about what had been said by the monks.

"Bones of God," Orla complained to his brother, "this Christian alliance is fraught with liabilities, conspiracies, and bad blood! And we'll be thrown in the midst of all this confusion and distrust, eh?"

"Ja," nodded Crowbones, waving his stub, "it sounds as though we'd best only count on ourselves, then, when the iron starts flying."

After several minutes Handel took the floor again, and addressed the only monk who had not yet presented his information, a Frenchman from Provence. "Brother DuBuisson, what's the latest word on the departure of the northern and southern French armies? There's been much confusion and many delays, we hear."

"The news isn't good," replied the French monk, looking glum. "The Pope had originally ordered an August muster of the combined forces, but that obviously isn't going to happen now. Only Hugh of Vernadois will be ready to depart by then, and he has but a small force. The large northern force from Normandy and Flanders will not depart for another two months after that. The worst news is that Bishop Adhémar and Raymond of Toulouse will not now be ready to depart until late November or early December."

"*What*?" cried Handel. "Dammit! Then by the time the last of the main forces gather in Constantinople, it'll be goddamned March or April before we're assembled to attack the Turks... almost a year from now!"

Tristan also grew alarmed. Elbowing Guillaume, he said in a low voice, "And the Hermit will arrive in Constantinople two and a half months from now according to Handel's latest calculations."

"That's early August... long before the main French forces even depart France," Guillaume replied, dismayed. "You'd hoped to talk the Hermit into waiting a month or so for the main forces to arrive before going into battle, but there's no way on earth he and Sansavoir will agree to wait half a year or more. We and the Tuscan Battalion will have no back-up whatsoever then from the main crusader force if the Hermit insists on taking on the Turks as soon as his mob arrives in Constantinople!" Discouraged, he glanced over at the Danes who had already come to a similar conclusion and were sullenly shaking their heads, complaining amongst themselves.

"Well then," sighed Tristan, feeling gutted, "we will have to depend on Emperor Alexius keeping the Hermit and Sansavoir under control and within the borders of Byzantine territory. He, then, is our final and only hope should the Hermit refuse to wait."

As those around the table talked, Handel's irritation only grew at the news of Bishop Adhémar's and Raymond of Toulouse's late start. The Pope's first hope in his Hermit strategy was that Tristan could persuade the Hermit to dismantle the Peasants' Crusade. Knowing that was not going to occur, Handel now suspected that the Pope's next alternative, convincing the Hermit to wait on the main crusader forces, had now also collapsed. "Judas Priest!" he swore. "The damned French nobles need to get their heads out of their asses and get moving! With a start like this, we Christians couldn't beat a flock of newborn lambs, let alone the goddamned Turks!"

Such violation of God's name in the midst of clerics might have normally caused a stir within a coven of monks, but the five agents sitting at the table were a different breed of holy men, tempered by the misdeeds of others and hardened by the twists God threw down upon his faithful.

Handel's anger at the French nobility for delays masked his real fury, however, which was directed at the Hermit... who ultimately had created the precarious position that the Tuscan force was now facing. After fuming a while longer, Handel finally settled. With a look of resignation, he dismissed the Benedictine agents from the room. "Thank you, Brothers, for holding up Mother Church," he said as they filed out of the room. "You've done a fine job and traveled a long distance. Pax vobiscum." After all the monks but Brother Hood of Manchester had streamed out the door, Handel flung himself onto a stool and buried his chin in his left hand while crossing himself with the right. "May God help us," he said. "That dumb-ass Hermit and his mob of imbeciles have somehow mobilized and managed to march with more speed and organization than the best goddamned armies of Christendom!"

## Chapter Twenty-seven

### Brother Hood of Manchester

When the other Benedictine agents had filed out of the room, Brother Hood closed the door and returned to the table, taking a seat. Meanwhile, the Danes had already taken a place with Handel at the table, and were impatiently awaiting the English monk.

"Bishop Saint-Germain," said Hood, "you mentioned that Desmond DuLac was your uncle, yet I saw embers in the eyes of these men here at the table when I spoke his name. Please tell, what has passed between DuLac and your bunch?"

"It's a long, twisted tale," sighed Tristan. "It was DuLac, brother of my father, Roger de Saint-Germain, who married my mother, Asta of the Danes– just after Roger's execution by William, Bastard of Normandy. Refusing to accept me and my brother Guillaume, aged seven and four at the time, we were sent off to the Benedictine monastery at Cluny while he, my mother, and these men here serving as her personal Danish Guard moved to England."

"Your father, Roger de Saint-Germain, was beheaded for... treason, as I recall," said Hood. "Plotting with King Philippe of France to overthrow the Bastard in Normandy?"

"Yes," Tristan nodded. "But it is now known that it was his own brother, Desmond DuLac, who helped revealed the plot to the Bastard."

"Well then," nodded Hood solemnly, "that explains the bad blood."

"No, that explains nothing," interceded Orla. "Roger de Saint-Germain was as foul as his brother, DuLac, if not more so! We held no affection for him. He was a worm of a man and knew no loyalties. Worse, he mistreated Asta who was forced to marry him when she was but twelve years, and him over forty. He impregnated her within a fortnight with child though she herself was but a child, and mistreated her horribly, doing the same to these two boys as they came along. Truly, we Danes would have celebrated his execution were it not for the fact that the family name was disgraced and Asta lost all rights to her husband's property, inheritance, and the manor at Saint Germain-en-Laye. Her entire life, and ours, was reduced to shambles."

"Ja," said Crowbones, "but DuLac had coveted Asta since her marriage to his brother. After Roger's execution, DuLac offered to marry her and take her to his ill-gained territories in England to keep her from groveling in the dirt as a pauper. She agreed only if he would send a high sum of wealth to the Benedictines at Cluny to educate her sons, and also bring the Danish Guard and their families to England with her. There were about eighty-five of us in all, including the women and children. In a word, she sacrificed herself for us all."

Guthroth wished to speak, but his face was turning red as the story was being revealed, so he knew the anger rising at his temples would only cause him to bumble his words. Hroc, seeing this, placed a hand on Guthroth's shoulder. "Uncle," he said, "we feel your rage."

"Once in England, DuLac was a complete ass as usual," Orla continued. "Asta despised him for refusing her sons, as did we Danes. But there were other things. In the end, we rebelled, killed many of his troops, and fled England with Asta."

"Brother Hood," said Handel, who had not been involved in any of this history but knew it well, "you're well acquainted with Brother Dieter Muehler who oversees the entire Underground operation from beneath the subterranean tunnels and caverns of Monte Cassino?"

"Yes, of course. He commands the entire network."

"Dieter Muehler and I grew up together in Bavaria," said Handel, "and joined the Benedictines together as young men. He's my best friend on this earth. The mutilation he now bears upon his face, the burns and scars that he conceals by wearing a veil… that ugliness is all the work of Desmond DuLac. When Odo de Lagery was Bishop of Ostia he sent Muehler there under cover to engineer Asta's escape from England. But Muehler was captured by DuLac and a Norman nun, a spy from the convent of Rouen. They tortured him to the edge of death. Asta managed to pry him loose from DuLac's dungeon and took him with her and the Danes as they fled north to Scotland, then sailed to France."

"I didn't know any of this," said Hood, appalled by the story. "I understand your fury now. Yes, DuLac is noted for being ruthless and bloodthirsty. During the Harrying of the North, as the native Saxons rebelled against French and Norman cruelty, DuLac committed genocide against the Saxon population, and spoiled the land. Even now, thirty years later, his name is uttered as a curse by them all." Here Hood shook his head and gave Tristan an odd look.

Sensing reticence in the monk's eyes, Tristan asked, "What is it, Hood? Is there something you wish to say?"

"Yes, but it won't be pleasing to you or to these men here."

"Well, spit it out," said Handel. "We're not a bunch of damned old women."

"You remember that I said there'd be little help from England in this crusade except for a few rogue Normans or Frenchman who'd lost favor within the Norman Court of the Bastard's son?" asked Hood.

"Yes, what of it?" nodded Tristan.

Hood placed a hand to his chin and scratched at the stubble of pale whiskers shadowing his lower face. "Desmond DuLac is one of them," he said.

At this, a gasp arose from the room as Tristan, Guillaume, and the Danes stared at Hood, stunned. "*DuLac is coming to Constantinople?*" asked Orla. "Oh, but the gods set snares for the wicked, though long in coming! We'll have his ass on a pike, huh, Crowbones?"

"Ja! And his balls!" hissed Crowbones.

"You'll do no such thing," interjected Hood. "Though DuLac has been dismissed by King William Rufus, he carries a formal letter of blessing from the Archbishop of Canterbury as well as a Letter of Commendation and Protection from King William Rufus himself."

"*What?*" said Guillaume, confused. "But you just said DuLac had fallen out of favor with King William Rufus."

"Ah, a king's ploy!" groaned Handel, shaking his head. "What better way to get rid of a problem than by shipping it off to get skewered by the Turks? Then too, by unloading his snakes,

Rufus also appears to be making a gesture of assistance to the Pope's crusade, false as it is!"

Tristan agreed. "A clever move by King Rufus." Looking at Hood, he asked, "How many troops is DuLac bringing with him?"

"I'd guess about two hundred knights and maybe half a thousand foot," replied Hood. "King Rufus has cleaned out the pantry so to speak, and filled DuLac's ships with the disgraced, the dishonored, and the disavowed of England."

"His contingent is about the size of our own Tuscan force then," remarked Guillaume.

"Brother Hood," said Tristan, "when is DuLac expected to arrive in Constantinople?"

"He and his force left the west coast of England ten days before I departed Manchester for Cologne. Their route is to sail south down the Atlantic, cut east at Gibraltar, slip through the Mediterranean, then north up the Aegean and into the Bosporus Straight to Constantinople."

"He'll be arriving in Constantinople well earlier than the main crusader forces, then," said Tristan, performing calculations in his head. "Early August maybe."

"Same time as the Hermit and us," interjected Handel. Staring at the floor, he grasped about for possibilities. After some time, a light broke on his brow, and he said, "Look here, as much as he's hated by all of you, DuLac's early arrival could be a damn blessing in the end."

"What the hell did you say?" shrugged Orla, thinking perhaps he had misconstrued Handel's words.

"Look," said Handel, "just take a deep breath and listen a moment. If DuLac shows up early like the Hermit, then at least there'll be another Christian army there to join us if the Hermit and Sansavoir get stupid, still refusing to wait on the main crusader force to cross into Turkish territory."

"*Us fight alongside DuLac?*" yawped Crowbones, waving his stub in the air with heat. "Ha!" he roared. "Swine's ass! There's a better chance of me growing a crack between my legs and declaring myself a street whore!"

"Ja," agreed Orla, "the only reason we'd fight alongside DuLac would be to stick an ax in his skull from behind!"

"J-ja, J-ja!" snorted Guthroth angrily.

"Dammit," said Handel, "I know DuLac's a bastard, but fighting alongside him is no damned different than Godfrey of Bouillon now fighting for the Pope, or Bohemud of Taranto now fighting for the Byzantines! If we find ourselves stranded and alone with the Hermit's paupers against the Turks, DuLac may well be a salvation." Turning, he looked at Tristan. "Tell them, Tristan. Now dammit, don't you agree?"

Tristan, though he had not seen DuLac since age seven when being sent from his mother, had harbored a lifelong, simmering bitterness toward the man. But Tristan was also a seasoned strategist, and fully comprehended the analogy that Handel had just offered about Godfrey of Bouillon and Bohemud of Taranto.

"We will sit on this for a time," Tristan said, gazing at the torrid expressions on the faces of the Danes. He knew Guillaume had never quite developed the same poison over DuLac since he was so young when Asta had sent them to the Black Monks, but to the Danes, DuLac was the embodiment of evil and the object of their full hatred. "Yes, Tristan repeated, "we will sit on this for a time."

The Danes grumbled amongst themselves, and Orla was about to object mightily when the door burst open as Abbot Schwartz hobbled into the room, his limbs skittering, his face ashen. "Come quickly! There's rioting in the streets! People are being murdered!"

# Chapter Twenty-eight

## Count Emicho of Leiningen

Tristan and the others hurried out the monastery gate, and upon gaining the street were met by chaos. People were running about in confused packs, some shouting for blood, others screaming for mercy. Forty or fifty bloodied corpses already littered the street, laying face down in pools of blood or sitting with backs propped against building walls, their heads bludgeoned, legs splayed. Women ran wildly about, clinging to their infants and frantically herding children forward while being chased, stoned, or taken to the ground by angry pursuers.

Men also were being tackled and taken to the ground, then beaten by attackers wielding clubs and knives, their hands already scarlet with blood. In the midst of the mayhem, a man on horseback, whooping and hollering like a banshee, dragged a body tied to a rope through the street, scattering fellow rioters like flocks of chickens. Yet, as the helpless were being massacred on the public street of Cologne within the very shadow of a monastery, there seemed to be a back-current of festivity and glee. The groans of suffering and wails of agony were so mingled at times with laughter and excitement that it was impossible to fathom exactly what had broken out amongst these people.

So surprised and perplexed was Tristan's group in witnessing this bedlam, they stood in place trying to make sense of it until Abbot Schwartz's frenzied pleas brought them to action. "Help these people! Help them before they're *all* slaughtered!" he begged, pulling at Orla and Crowbones with urgency.

As he supplicated, a group of fifteen or twenty people bolted toward the gate, mostly women and children, their faces so full of dread and legs so full of flight they no longer appeared human–but resembled a stampeding herd of sheep fleeing a charging wolf-pack. Still confounded by what they had stepped into, Guillaume and the Danes pulled their swords while Handel reached into his boot, extracting his dagger. If nothing else, they could see that those being pursued were helpless, and neither Guillaume nor the Danes were going to tolerate such a gross imbalance.

"Let's go!" shouted Guillaume. "Get between these women and children and those chasing them!"

Tristan and Abbot Schwartz, having no weapons, began grasping at those who had made it as far as the sanctuary of the monastery gate, hurrying them behind its walls as Guillaume and the others confronted the attacking mass of rioters.

Those at the head of the charging mob were so fueled by passion they failed to realize at first that the men now standing in their path were heavily armed. Accordingly, as they had run into no defensible opposition since beginning their rampage half an hour earlier, they blindly shoved their way through, swinging fists, clubs, and canes while others brandished knives and other implements.

Jolted by this oncoming crush, Guillaume and the Danes at first tried to repulse the mob without inflicting injury, as it included several women and young boys– but then a man leaped forward and flicked his knife at Handel's face, opening a razor cut across his right cheek that quickly pursed open like yawning red lips.

Without a word, Handel swept up with his dagger, catching the man's navel, then eviscerating him to the top of his sternum. Not knowing what struck him, the man's eyes rattled, like eggs cast in a bowl, then grew still as he leaned forward into Handel, dead.

"Damn you!" shouted Handel, not waiting for the body to tumble on its own. Shoving it aside, he attacked the next man before him, who himself carried a long dagger. The rioter was not nearly as deft with it as was the Underground monk, and he, too, quickly fell as Handel shot his free hand to his own face to stop the flow of blood from his cheek. "C'mon then you filthy bastards!" he snarled, eyes afire.

Seeing this, and feeling the full brunt of the mob's assault, Guillaume and the Danes realized these people fully intended to kill anyone standing in their way. Following Handel's lead, they switched to the offensive as a matter of survival, and immediately drew blood. The mêlée heightened as a group of seven or eight men dressed in sackcloth attacked them from the side, wielding forks, staffs, and scythes. Guillaume recognized the two men leading this pack, Tafur and Burrel, the men he had met earlier in Sansavoir's camp. Though close, it seemed neither of the two recognized either Guillaume fighting in front of them, or Tristan who was standing to the rear by the monastery gate.

"*Tafur, Burrel, what's this?*" yelled Guillaume, as confused as he was furious.

An instant later the two vanished, lost in the scramble. Advancing step by step, Handel and the Danes inflicted gaping wounds on the pack of peasant attackers, shifting the momentum of the fight. Having lost sight of Tafur and Burrel, Guillaume joined the Danes' attack. Taking a position beside the devastating blade of Hroc whose massive body was plowing forward like some angry young bull bolting from the pen, Guillaume advanced.

In Hroc's path stood Marcel DuPuis, his eyes full of dread, crouching as he struggled to back out of the fray. Despite the frightening brand recently emblazoned across his forehead that had filled his heart with expectancy and bravado, he now felt faint. He had never once in life engaged in an actual fight, and the sight of Hroc and the Danes surging toward him, weapons flaying, filled him with terror. "*O-oh!*" he wailed. "*God help me! What's this mess I've gotten tangled in*?!"

Around him, others also quickly came to the realization that they themselves were now under attack. Beginning to unravel, the mob dropped away, cowering while looking to each other for support or leadership– but finding neither.

"Get back! Get back or we'll take your heads!" bellowed Orla as Crowbones, Guthroth, and Hroc formed a wall beside him, their bloodied swords flailing at all within reach.

"Yes, back up!" shouted Guillaume. "We've no wish to kill you! Nor will we allow you to kill these others! Stop, I say!"

"Oh, traitorous knight!" yelled a man from the back. "You kill the good people of Cologne and God's own crusaders from France as well!"

It was Tafur, and as Guillaume looked at him, Tafur's eyes were ablaze with hatred.

"There's not a true crusader in this entire mob!" retorted Guillaume, setting his eyes on Tafur, pointing his sword. "And we'll kill any person, *man or woman*, who advances!"

Hearing this, a wave of muttered threats washed through the crowd, but the grumbling fell away as none dared to move forward. Yet, they refused also to back away any further, so the two hostile camps stood there glowering at each other in motionless silence, as awaiting an artist to place the final stroke on this painting for which they now seemed to be posing.

The two sides remained in place for several long moments until, from the distance, the thunderous clatter of hooves against stone pavers broke the quiet. The sound advanced, until finally a large contingent of German knights on horseback appeared; the mob slowly parted, ushering the riders forward. Leading the horsemen was a nobleman so haughty in countenance that Handel could smell his arrogance from where he stood.

Slowly reining in his horse before the line of armed men who had quelled the rioting mob, the nobleman turned his horse ceremoniously. Next, riding it with deliberation in a slow track, back and forth, he stared with cold, condescending eyes at the objects of his obvious displeasure– Guillaume, Handel, and the Danes. Finally, sticking a fist to his hip, he said, "Why do you interfere with these people who are simply trying to cleanse filth from their own streets?"

Handel stepped forward, spitting at the horse's legs. "Quite a little show you're putting on for this ignorant rabble!" he snorted, his face full of contempt. "Ha, just look at you dancing around on your pony, as leading a parade!" Handel had despised men such as this from youth, and wholly blamed them for turning God's garden on earth into a barren desert of misery for others. "Do you, then, *lead* this pack of street butchers?"

Unaccustomed to being spoken to in such a manner by those in common garb, the man scowled. "Yes, I am Count Emicho of Leiningen," he said, "and you stand in the way of this pogrom. Also, as I look about, I see you and your bunch have killed some good German Christians here, as well as faithful crusaders following Peter the Hermit of Amiens."

"Aye!" agreed Tafur, stepping out from the crowd, emboldened by the arrival of Emicho's troops. "These bastards have killed French and German crusaders alike and don't deserve to live!"

"Agreed, take them prisoner!" shouted Burrel.

Marcel DuPuis, watching Emicho's manner and seeing a full complement of German knights in full array mounted behind the count, also stepped forward. "Yes! Arrest these traitors!" he shouted, shedding all trace of the fear that had crippled him just moments earlier. As he said this, many within the mob shouted approval, boosting Dupuis' confidence even more. "And hang them from storefront hooks up yonder, I say!"

Dupuis did not mean any of this, but had stepped up only to restore his fading credibility amongst the other Tafurs. Nonetheless, his spurious bravado was lost to the crowd. They had already turned their attention to Guillaume, who had stepped to within inches of Emicho's horse, sword in hand. "*What's this?*" he shouted. "Are you indeed a Christian knight or simply a well dressed imposter?" He, unlike Handel, wore the military dress of nobility as did Emicho. "No right-minded crusader of the Pope would engage in the slaughter of women and children!"

"Perhaps so," replied Emicho, his voice level but cold, "but in this case we're not committing slaughter, we're scouring rats from this city. We've just burned down the Jewish quarter, and the surviving vermin made a run for the monastery. And we had them under hoof and foot until you chose, for some unknown reason, to interfere. *Unacceptable*. And lest you retreat, in a moment my knights and their horses will trample you into the very pavement upon which you stand!" Raising his hand, he signaled his troops forward.

"Let's join them!" cried Tafur, raising his staff and waving it about, exhorting the mob to once again catch fire.

Interrupting Tafur's tirade, a voice rang out. It carried such volume and authority that Guillaume was not even aware that it belonged to his own brother; Guillaume had never in his entire existence heard Tristan raise his voice in such fury. "I am the Bishop of Ostia, Tristan de Saint-Germain!" Tristan bayed. "I am First Counsel to Pope Urban, and also First Scribe and Papal Liaison to the Holy Crusade, commissioned to document every detail I encounter on this holy crusade to Jerusalem! And these men you now threaten are direct emissaries of the Holy Father, Pope Urban II!"

Hearing this, spotting Tristan's Vatican attire, Count Emicho shriveled a fraction, though refusing to make it evident to the ruffians of the crowd or the knights behind him. "Hail then, Bishop of Ostia Saint-Germain," Emicho answered, "and praise be to the Holy Crusade of Pope Urban! My army and I are passing through Cologne on our way south, in fact, to join the Holy Father's knights in Constantinople for the war on Islam. And this man riding next to me is Bishop Hess, my Archbishop of Leiningen."

Tristan looked hard at the archbishop, finding it difficult to swallow that a cleric of such high stature would condone such action in the face of the Church's official position on the status of Jews in Europe– which was to leave them in peace.

The archbishop nodded back in greeting, but looking rather dour, said nothing. Returning his gaze to Count Emicho, filled with indignation, Tristan stepped forward. "Why are you leading this riot?" he asked. "What have these poor people done that you and this crowd hunt them down like rats in the cellar?"

"These people are *J-e-w-s*," said Emicho, "the very race that killed Christ! Though many of us in France and Germany now travel to risk our lives fighting the heathen Turks, the filthy Jew vermin remain here in peace and prosperity with complete impunity. It's time to either rid all of Europe of them, or force them into conversion. Today, with citizens of Cologne and certain parties of the Peasants' Crusade, I marched into the Jewish quarter which is not far from here, and offered the Jews that choice, but most refused to convert."

"Nay!" shouted Handel, pressing his palm against his bloodied cheek to hold the hemorrhaging in check. "The Church has long since prohibited forced conversion, and though it doesn't condone Judaism as the true faith, it also prohibits pogroms against the Jews. Canon law legislates that they be allowed to freely build their temples and worship within their own faith. *You*, therefore, are violating ecclesiastic law!" Handel then pointed an accusatory finger at Archbishop Hess who had continued to sit upon his horse, stiff-lipped and silent during the exchange. "And *you*, so-called Archbishop of Leiningen, do you dispute canon law? Speak up, man, have you nothing to say here?"

"The eradication of Jews may be frowned upon by the College of Cardinals," interrupted Emicho, his voice full of retort, "but it's no crime in the eyes of God. As I traverse Europe and the Balkans on my way to Asia Minor, I fully intend to bury every Jew standing in my path who refuses to convert. God himself has instructed me to either eliminate them, or save their souls! And when I reach Jerusalem, it's my hope to– "

"*God has spoken to you directly*?" antagonized Handel, his voice turning sing-song, brimming with ridicule. "Oh, but how is it *possible* that God chooses only to speak to the *buffoons* of this world, and not the rest of us? And–"

"Be on your way, Count, and take these hate mongers with you!" interrupted Tristan, his voice still ringing with uncharacteristic bluster. "You are not welcome here, nor is your intolerance. But know this, you and this hateful episode will be the first entry in my official documentation of this crusade for the Pope!"

Emicho sat there on his horse, weighing this threat issued by the Bishop of Ostia, of whom he had heard much over the years from his own home cleric, Archbishop Hess. Emicho passed his archbishop a questioning look, and the archbishop, in turn, whispered something in Emicho's ear. Emicho then shrugged, motioning to his knights. "Very well, Bishop Saint-Germain," he said, "out of deference to you and your papal office, my army will end today's work and continue south. But know this, the Jews of Maintz and Worms shall have no such consideration." Turning his mount, he signaled for Archbishop Hess and the German knights to follow.

"Damnation," Orla whispered to Crowbones as the rioters, in turn, began to melt away, "I didn't know Boy carried such muscle. We could have shortly been crow feed under those German hooves."

Crowbones nodded. "Ja, that bishop's robe Tristan wears is more effective than armor, it seems." He snickered then. "Perhaps we should get one for ourselves instead of these heavy-ass hauberks on our shoulders, eh?"

## Chapter Twenty-nine

### Aftermath

"You're a bloody mess," Orla said to Handel, handing Hroc a damp rag. "Get him cleaned up a bit, son, but go easy."

"It didn't go quite to the bone, just through the flesh," squinted Hroc, dabbing at Handel's face, loosening black blood that had caked the cheek.

"You were pretty damn quick with that dagger of yours, and cold," Orla muttered. "You had that first fellow gutted before he knew what pricked him. We may have to start calling you the Bavarian Ice-man."

"Had to be quick," Handel replied, wincing as Hroc dug deeper, "or I'd have been dead. You, too, maybe."

"J-ja," said Guthroth, watching Hroc who was now working into the gash on Handel's face. "Q-quick thinking, H-Handel."

"This is going to leave a bit of a scar, I'm afraid," said Hroc. "Of course, as a monk you're not too worried about attracting women are you, Handel?"

"No, nor men," Handel grinned. But the effort was painful; his grin turned to a groan. "Argh!" he cried, placing a hand to his cheek.

As the Danes tended to Handel, Tristan and Guillaume spoke to Abbot Schwartz about the Jews now hiding in the monastery. "I'll keep them here within our walls for the next few days until things simmer down," said Schwartz, "but I worry about the Jewish quarter. I saw smoke coming from that direction when we entered the street; looks like three years ago when Count Emicho came through Cologne."

"This happened before?" asked Tristan.

"Yes, everywhere Emicho appears, he persecutes Jews and incites the local population against them," Schwartz replied.

"He insists God has promised to make him emperor if he succeeds in either killing or converting all Jews in Germany. There'll be dead laying all about in Cologne's Jewish quarter today, I fear. Far more than what's now in the street fronting the monastery. I'm sure most didn't have time to get out."

"Perhaps we'd best take a look, see if we can help," said Guillaume.

"No, it'll be far too dangerous yet," warned Schwartz. "Wait until tomorrow."

"That'll be too late to help should there be survivors," said Guillaume.

Tristan agreed. "We can ride back to camp, bring a good-sized contingent of the Tuscan knights with us."

"Aye," nodded Guillaume. "I'll post them as sentinels throughout the quarter overnight to keep the Colognese and the Hermit's crowd from getting in."

It was late afternoon by the time Tristan and Guillaume returned with the Tuscan Knights, dressed in light armor, bristling with weaponry. The streets, though littered with over four hundred corpses settled in various positions of repose, appeared to be void of troublemakers. Many of the bodies lay abandoned, while others were surrounded by huddles of relatives tearfully holding the heads of their beloved dead in their laps. Most of the mourners wept quietly, but some uttered that mindless wail of the bereaved, overcome with grief and confusion at the senseless horror that had descended without warning and without cause.

"Check the buildings, or what's left of them anyway," instructed Guillaume, motioning for his men to enter the charred hulls of shops and living quarters in search of survivors.

As the men scattered, poking their way through the remains of what was once a thriving center of trade and commerce within Cologne, they came to one terrible scene after another. Babies lay charred like little black dolls, their hands and arms extended forward, frozen in final cries of agony as death overcame them. There were women and children huddled in corners holding onto to each other, also burned – resembling lignite sculptures crafted by some demonic artist who had expertly captured the actual expression of terror at the precise moment of realization that death had arrived. Picking their way through one dreadful vignette after another, some of the Tuscans issued groans of repugnance and anger, some crossed themselves in prayer, while yet others began to retch with revulsion, sickened by the carnage wreaked upon humans by fellow humans.

Orla, as he walked with Hroc from one horrid spectacle to the next, shook his head with disgust, unable to comprehend any of it. "These people were not enemies, they posed no threat, they paid their taxes, and they contributed to the commerce of this town. Yet they were singled out, though I swear I can't tell any difference between them and these other damned Germans. Christian butchery, I say. But why?"

"According to Uncle Tristan," said Hroc, "many Christians blame the Jews for killing Christ."

"Well now, Christians believe Christ is immortal, don't they? And if one's immortal, you can't be killed, I'd think! Besides, if Christ arose from the dead, then the Jews didn't really kill him in the first place then, eh? So what's to be mad about at Jews? But another thing, I thought the man the Jews crucified was the son of God, not God himself."

"They're one and the same, with a third entity: the Father, the Son, and the Holy Ghost," said Hroc. "They call it the Holy Trinity."

"Bah!" snorted Orla. "More fairy tales. And to think Christians actually belittle our own Norse myths. Don't you see the absurdity of it all?" Hroc offered no answer, which Orla found odd. Looking at him, he said, "Hroc, I notice lately you seem to know a lot about Christian beliefs lately. Has Guthroth been preaching to you since his conversion?"

"No, Father. He says little on the subject. But fighting the Investiture War, supporting the Pope, Uncle Tristan, and Uncle Guillaume, and being in the employ of Countess Mathilda… I can't help but be touched by their beliefs. Christianity's begun to interest me somewhat."

"Eh?" grunted Orla. "Well shit, I'll not tell you what to believe, Hroc, but look around and ask what Christians *really* believe, not what they *claim* to believe or what they're *told* to believe by their holy men." Leaving Hroc's company, displeased, Orla shortly encountered Crowbones. "Dammit," he muttered, "Hroc just told me he's interested in Christianity."

"Ja, probably because of Guthroth, huh?"

"Naw, he's come up with this on his own, I think."

"Ha, imagine that," Crowbones mused, passing his brother a wry look. "He's *your* son, isn't he? There's never been a more thick-skulled man on earth than you, Brother, so let it be... he's no different than you, in the end. Besides, pagan worship's nearly dead now, even in the Norse territories ever since the final conversion revolts were suppressed. You and me, we're becoming relics, Orla. Besides, we may have escaped baptism, but it might be to Hroc's advantage to become Christian, don't you think?"

Scowling, Orla refused to respond– and walked away.

## Chapter Thirty

### A Document for History

As the Tuscans and Danes rounded up survivors, Tristan and Guillaume walked from one empty black shell of a building to another, gazing about at the dead. "As I told Count Emicho," said Tristan, "I intend to document this horror in full detail as my first entry into the Papal Crusade Report, and cite Emicho specifically as the instigator of this massacre."

"And don't fail to mention the Hermit's people participating in the massacre," said Guillaume. "Did you see Tafur and Burrel? It appears they were at the head of the peasant crusaders we encountered today. Makes me wonder just how deep the Hermit's involvement is in this mess, or whether as Innocenzo said, Tafur's the problem, and not to be trusted."

"I have no idea," said Tristan, "but I will confront the Hermit directly on the issue. I saw neither him nor Sansavoir in the fray, so maybe they are clear of it. I can only pray that is the case."

"You know," said Guillaume, "this report of yours to the Pope on the Holy Crusade, you've mentioned it a time or two, but given few specifics. What does it entail?"

"As Papal Scribe of the Crusade, it will be my responsibility to document all aspects of the crusade that I personally witness or learn of through others, including dates, places, and events. More importantly, I am to record the conduct and behavior of all individuals providing impact or leadership during the course of the expedition. As you know, I was originally assigned to travel with Bishop Adhémar's group like yourself, but things changed. Still, with my commission as scribe, I will record the events of the Peasants' Crusade… at least until Adhémar arrives in Constantinople. War opens the gates to greed, massacre, and other behavior contrary to Church doctrine, and war of the magnitude of this crusade is especially volatile. This crusade is in itself, after all, a Church-sanctioned call to arms, so the Pope is concerned about abuses. He expects our armies to conduct themselves according to expectations of decency and Church doctrine."

"*Decency?*" shrugged Guillaume. "Ha, a rare commodity when the iron starts flying! So in truth, is the purpose of your report to provide an accurate written history of the expedition, or to hold the leadership accountable?"

"Both, in equal parts," replied Tristan. "It has been well established that history is written by the victors, which means history is too often distorted to shed favorable light on those writing it. Whether we win or lose this crusade, Pope Urban has charged me, along with others, with writing a truthful, uncolored version of this war... whether it remains noble or whether it turns heinous. Upon our return from Jerusalem, I will spend my first weeks in Rome reviewing my entire Papal Crusade Report with Odo. It, combined with the reports submitted by other designated scribes, will become official Church history."

"And what of those who *do* behave heinously?" asked Guillaume. "Consequences for ill conduct in war have never been passed on anyone except the defeated."

"Guillaume," said Tristan, adopting an authoritative tone, "since Pope Gregory VII's coronation twenty-three years back, and through the continued implementation of his reforms, the Church has struggled to free itself of the control and abuses of the nobility, as well as from the abuses and woeful conduct of our own clerics. Though there have been no consequences in the past for heinous conduct during war, Pope Urban, the College of Cardinals, and I are now looking to change that, just as the Church has reformed other past abuses."

"Sorting what's necessary and what's unavoidable in war will be no easy task," frowned Guillaume, shaking his head. "War, though often necessary, by its very nature turns things inside out. Though the commandments clearly dictate 'we shall not kill,' turning bloodshed into a sacred act is not uncommon, as in the Investiture War, or even in this crusade against Islam. It's a tricky proposition you're stuck with here."

"Yes, but some things are *clearly* wrong in war, such as today's massacre at the hands of Emicho. Besides, today was not even war, but butchery within the borders of Christendom itself. Regardless, the murder of innocents, the helpless, and the unarmed under any circumstances is legitimate cause for excommunication, do you not agree?"

"Y-e-s, perhaps," said Guillaume, giving the question thought. "Indeed," he then said with more certainty. "It's a lofty goal you seek with this report of yours, Tristan, and I pray you make it work."

That evening Guillaume and the others remained at the monastery with a squadron of Tuscan knights and footmen to block townspeople from attempting to extract Jews sheltered there. He also stationed a faction of troops within the Jewish quarter to protect those residents who for one reason or another refused to abandon the area. As hoped, the night passed without incident.

Tristan, meanwhile, retired to the monastery scriptorium; in the flickering light of candles he began to record the events of the day, first describing in detail the meeting with the agents of the Underground and the information they had gathered. He had just completed marking down final comments by Handel and Brother Hood of Manchester when a knock at the door drew his attention. It was Abbot Scwartz. "Bishop Saint-Germain," he said, "a courier arrived just moments ago. He claimed to be a guard in the employ of Mathilda of Tuscany, said he was accompanying your mother across the Alps to France." Extending his hand, Abbot Schwartz handed Tristan a message. "He instructed me to deliver this to you," he continued, "it's a message from a certain Sister Angélique of Marcigny-sur-Loire."

"Yes, thank you," replied Tristan, feeling the approach of dread as he reached to accept the message, bracing himself for grievous but anticipated news. Then, as tiny tremors slipped onto his lips, he began to read: *'Bishop Saint-Germain, it is with prayerful sadness that I inform you of the passing of your mother while traversing the Alps. Please know that God filled her final moments on this earth with a strange but evident grace before calling her to His side. Also, please know that her final thought in this life was about you... the last word she uttered was your name. We are currently still on the road and shall be taking her body home to Marcigny-sur-Loire to be buried in our convent cemetery. My heartfelt condolences, Sister Angélique.*

Though Tristan had known from the moment of his and Asta's final farewell in Canossa that the arrival of such news was inevitable, Angélique's words struck Tristan like a death knell. Feeling faint, his thoughts dissolving into vaporous threads, he threw a hand to his head. Then, sending Abbot Schwartz from the room, he buried his head into the crook of his arm as it sprawled across the table, and began to heave with sobbing. "Oh, but Mother!?" he wept, losing himself to her memory. "Asta! Dear, sweet Mother!"

Just as had happened to him at age seven upon first being separated from Asta so many years before, Tristan felt a wave of inconsolable sorrow sweeping over him. Indeed, that first separation had created in his boyish soul a pervasive loneliness that had haunted him throughout his life, remaining intact somehow even after their eventual reunion. That gaping theft of her presence from his childhood had been a bitter lesson, teaching him that 'certainty' does not, in fact, exist. Rather, stability and happiness could be crushed in the blink of an eye by those in power, or by circumstance, or even by mere chance. And this harsh realization at such a young age had never left him; it clung stubbornly to him over the years, slinking about in the backwash of his thoughts, holding at bay any hopes of final or complete quietude.

He realized at this moment, too, that he should immediately notify Guillaume and the Danes... but his heart would not allow it. No, he first needed time to mourn alone, without interruption, without sharing; Asta was, first and foremost, *his.* Thus, for the next hour Tristan grieved and prayed, marveling over Asta's existence and her strength– wishing he but possessed even half of her resolve, half of her faith, half of her selflessness.

When finally the well was dry and tears were spent, Tristan sat up, staring at what he had been transcribing before Abbot Schwartz's knock at the door. Shaking aside grief, by degrees, he resumed recording where he had left off'; describing the street riot, he reconstructed the massacre of Cologne Jews led by Count Emicho.

It was well past midnight when Tristan penned his final words and stood to seek sleep within the monks' quarters. As he started to leave the scriptorium, though, he realized he had written nothing about the sights he had seen on the road entering Cologne.

He had also neglected to document the Hermit's fiery meeting with the Cologne burghermeisters and magistrates, or the fact that Tafur's thugs and Geoffrey Burrel were actively involved in Emicho's massacre of the Jews. More importantly, he had not written a word concerning Peter the Hermit's refusal to disband his march to Jerusalem.

Despite the long and eventful course of the day, despite the news of Asta's passing, and despite his weariness, he returned to the table and began writing again; it was nearly dawn when he finished. Standing, his hand happened to slip into his vestment pocket– and he felt Mala's ring. Taking it out, he held it to the candle light, giving it long and thoughtful consideration. Finally, placing it to his lips, he closed his eyes.

*Ah, but I'm so far from home– and in such a wicked place,* he thought. *It would be good to see Mala's face again, at least... or even touch her hand.*

## Chapter Thirty-one

### A Reckoning

Even as Tristan held Mala's ring late into the night, thinking of her within the confines of the scriptorium, Mala was thinking of him– from the confines of a coach snaking its way overnight through the mountains toward Canossa. She was on a mission– one that had been long in coming.

After burying her newborn son within the graveyard at the fortress of Countess Mathilda Medici ten years earlier, Mala had sworn she would never return; nor would she ever speak again to the great Contessa after being so poorly treated and stung by her accusations. During the most destitute and hopeless period of her life, and eight months pregnant, Mala had been on her way to seek assistance from Mathilda of Medici, as Tristan's aunt.

On hearing Mala's claim that Tristan was the father of her deceased child, Mathilda had flown into a rage, accusing Mala of extortion and attempting to ruin her nephew's name. Disheartened, humiliated, ashen with defeat, Mala had then abandoned Canossa in the company of Lord Vincento Balducci, who shortly thereafter proposed marriage. After Balducci's slaying in battle against the Germans, and her subsequent inheritance of his considerable wealth, Mala's life turned– blessing her with unimaginable investment opportunities, success, and riches far, far beyond even what Vincento Balducci had bequeathed her upon his death. Truly, as la Gran Signorina of Genoa, she was among the wealthiest and most powerful figures in all Italy.

Still, of all poisons brewed upon this earth, there is none as enduring as personal poison... especially between women. After more than a decade, Mala had never overcome her bitterness toward Mathilda Medici... yet now she was headed into Mathilda's own lair, full of purpose, brimming yet with venom. Her intent, however, was to shed it, as it had for too long now eaten at her soul.

This unanticipated journey to Canossa had all begun shortly after Benito Fazio informed her of Bishop Saint-Germain's unexpected departure from Rome. Months earlier, Mala had already been orchestrating a trip to Constantinople for the express purpose of encountering Tristan there upon his arrival with Bishop Adhémar and the French crusaders. Tristan knew nothing of her scheme, nor would he have approved, undoubtedly– but Mala's intent was to disguise the meeting as pure chance. In truth, her shipping empire was heavily involved in Byzantine trade, and she often traveled to Constantinople. Moreover, she was on friendly terms with Emperor Alexius himself. Thus... the stage was set.

Benito Fazio's news, however, and Tristan's mysterious disappearance from Rome, altered everything. Mala was still convinced that Tristan would ultimately end in Constantinople with the crusaders, but now she had no concept of his whereabouts, route of travel, or arrival date. Thus, she became frustrated, and with each passing day waiting on word from Fazio, this frustration grew.

Compounding circumstances, she then began to experience a series of dreams– about her deceased infant. In these dreams, she, Tristan, and the child were a family. The touch of these dreams was so vivid, so palpable, that when she awoke from them, it took a good while to realize it had all been ethereal and false– which drove her into troughs of anguish and melancholia. Dissolving into spells of unbridled weeping, she would close her eyes, trying to recapture the dream... but impossible.

After nearly two weeks of such angst, she then began to think of God... and her old deceased companion, Duxia de Falaise. "God punishes the innocent!" old Duxia used to bray. "Each time people like you and me rise, even if for a moment, He drops his merciless hammer onto us, smashing hope! Aye, the hammer of God is a cruel instrument, wielded by a cruel God!"

But Mala refused to blame God for her misfortunes, especially bringing her Tristan as they were children, only to bury him in a monastery. No, there were other culprits who had engineered her and Tristan's failed love. There was Odo de Lagery, taking young Tristan beneath his wing, manipulating and directing the boy for the benefit of the Church, along with Pope

Gregory VII, and the cardinals of Rome. Then, too, there was Mathilda Medici, la Gran Contessa of Tuscany– swaddled in piety and self-righteousness, also directing Tristan as a boy toward a monastic life. And finally, there was the Church itself.

More than anything, it was the Gregorian Church she blamed, because with Pope Gregory VII came the renewed mandates about clerical chastity and celibacy. Priests had been marrying since the advent of the twelve disciples, and centuries thereafter. But with Gregory and the Benedictine reform movement, rigid morality had become an obsession, albeit as political as spiritual. Indeed, it was the tentacles of Gregorian reform that had tangled young Tristan in a vice-like grip, then suffocated him, forcing him to throw himself onto the altar of sacrifice for the sake of Odo de Lagery, the Benedictines, and the Gregorian Church. After days of such wrestling with herself, she concluded that, no, it was not God who had taken Tristan, but the Gregorian Church and those individuals shouldering its power.

As her coach jostled through the night, following the winding trail, Mala finally slipped toward sleep, wondering where her Tristan could be. *Is he well? Do I still haunt his heart as once I did, though in the end he again chose the Church? Will he ever break free of the Gregorian vice?*

***

It was dawn when the coachman drove his team up the steep approach to the fortress of Canossa. "Gran Signorina!" he called loudly on slowing the pace, nearing the open gate. "We've arrived!" Showing documents to the gate guards, he said, "The great Countess is expecting us, as my Lady has been in communication with her."

"Aye, we know," replied one of the guards. "And since Countess Mathilda has never had the pleasure of yet meeting la Gran Signorina, she's well pleased to finally make her acquaintance. So come along to Huntsman Hall, then, have a bit to eat and shake the dust from your boots. The Countess is occupied in the cathedral yonder, saying her morning prayers. She'll be done shortly and–"

"That won't be necessary," interrupted Mala, stepping from the coach, walking directly toward the cathedral."

"B-but Signorina," stammered the guard, "la Contessa doesn't allow interruption of her prayers!"

Offering no reply, Mala continued walking.

Shortly, on entering the expansive cathedral, she saw the form of a woman, Mathilda, praying along the first row of kneelers. Moving directly there, Mala took a position on the adjacent kneeler, making the sign of the cross. But instead of praying, she said, "Contessa, I have traveled a good distance to meet you. How appropriate, then, that it would be in a church... as I have heard you are the holiest of all women in Italy."

Looking over, Mathilda sped up the final words of her Pater Noster, then crossed herself. Struck by the sheer elegance of the visitor's garments and jewelry, the sheen of her olive skin, and the stunning delicacy of her face, Mathilda whispered, "La Gran Signorina of Genoa?"

"Si," replied Mala.

"Oh, but I've heard much about you over the years," Mathilda smiled, keeping her voice low and reverent, being within a cathedral. "But come along then, we can talk outside and get to know each other a bit, finally. If only you knew how pleased I am to finally meet you!"

As Mathilda stood, Mala remained in place, reaching out to nudge Mathilda back onto her kneeler. "Actually," she said, also keeping her voice low, "I would prefer that we both remain here... in the shadow of Christ."

Mathilda awkwardly returned to her knees. "Certainly... if you so wish, Signorina."

Looking closely at Mathilda, as cataloguing each feature of her face, Mala then removed her own head covering, which was veiled on each side. Her head and face thus exposed, she turned a bit, offering a more open view of her own features to the countess. Then, after a period of silence during which Mathilda grew more and more puzzled, Mala said, "Dear God... even though I bare my face, you still fail to recognize me... *don't you?*"

"Recognize you?" said Mathilda. "No, of course not, my dear, we've just now had the first occasion to meet."

"Oh, but not so, Countess. We met ten years ago. Do you not remember?"

Mathilda shook her head, her smile fading to uncertainty. "But had I met one as beautiful as yourself, Signorina, I would certainly recall it."

"Oh, but it was a hard day when we met, and I was not well, Contessa. I was half dead from frostbite, as was my old companion, Duxia de Falaise. Our wagon got caught in the ice and snow atop a God forsaken mountain pass in the Alps... on our way to you. Yes, it was there that my loyal friend Fernando froze to death... along with my newborn infant, who lies in your own Canossa graveyard. I'd be dead myself had a German not come along, leading a wagon train. He saved me and Duxia, my dearest friend in life. His name was Jurgen Handel, I learned later, but have not heard nor seen any trace of him since, though I've inquired."

A blow to the temple could not have struck Mathilda more violently than did the words flowing from Mala's voice. Shifting back on her kneeler, dismay flooded Mathilda's face as she started to stand.

But again Mala reached over, settling Mathilda to her knees. Her voice softening, she said, "Please, Contessa, stay with me just a bit longer. There are things I've held close to my heart for such a long while, but must now rid myself of... or go mad. Do you recognize me now?"

"Y-yes... oh, yes," murmured Mathilda, turning pallid, reconstructing their exchange of ten years past.

"I merely came to beg assistance back then," continued Mala, "but you shunned me... and threatened me... accused me of scheming against your adopted nephew, Tristan de Saint-Germain."

"*Yes*!" Mathilda snapped, on hearing Tristan's name. Gathering her wits, she stiffened. "Yes, yes, and I'd do it again! I couldn't have known at the time that you were actually pregnant with his child, nor even imagined such a thing, until he himself confessed to it! Still, what you did, and what he did– was carnal and immoral, a violation of the flesh against God! Tristan performed harsh, bloody penance for his sins, administered by Odo de Lagery! But what punishment, then, did *you* serve!? None, I'd say, though repentance was in order!"

Her eyes turning cold, Mala's mouth tightened. "Was the death of my newborn son not enough penance for you, Contessa?

Was his infantile, angelic face frozen stiff to my bare breast not enough penance, either? God in Heaven, woman, what are you made of?! I've heard that you yourself once lost a child... does that child not haunt your dreams, or your heart?"

"God took my child, for whatever *just* reason He sought," scowled Mathilda. "So be it! Just as he took yours, Signorina."

"I am Mala. Mala! I was Mala ten years ago to you, not 'la Signorina'... and I am Mala *now* to you, at my own insistence! Only the clothes have changed, along with wealth, and power! But let me correct you, Contessa... *God did not take my child!* It was the freezing snow and ice of the Alps that took him. And thieves who stole the last money I had in France, forcing me to come to you in Italy for help. And two other things killed him... the first was my own fear and desperation that drove me to seek your help back then. Having been reduced to paupers, we three were starving to death with no way to turn– which led us to foolishly cross the Alps in mid-winter. We did this based on the single hope that a woman known for godliness and generosity, la Gran Contessa of Tuscany, might offer us a new beginning. Oh, but such foolishness on my part! And the second thing that killed my son was the Gregorian Church! Oh yes, that nest of overzealous reformers' new ecclesiastic laws that a monk could not marry the woman he loved, nor have a family, nor live a normal life!"

"Oh, but blasphemy!" hissed Mathilda, recoiling with anger.

"*Not blasphemy, but indoctrination!*" retorted Mala, her voice rising to the top of its timbre, echoing against the vast cathedral walls. Then, taking a deep breath, she laughed the tiniest bit; it was a wry, bitter laugh. "I am going now to the graveyard, Contessa, to see my son after these many years. That sac of poison boiling in my heart has burst, finally, and I'll hate you no more. But know this. I am soon to depart to Constantinople to meet the crusaders. No, in truth... to meet *Tristan*. Just as God did not take my child from me, God did not take Tristan from me. O-h no, rather it was you, and Odo de Lagery, the Black Monks, the Vatican, and the Gregorian Church. So when he arrives in Byzantium, and I am there to meet him, I will do everything within my power, and with God's own blessing, to take him back from all of you... because I love him, and God meant from the very beginning for us to be together!"

## Chapter Thirty-two

### Fazio and Innocenzo

The bonds of human friendship are founded on commonalities, shared attributes, or interests that run with similar vein. Yet, on occasion, two people of completely different thread take a liking to each other for less evident cause. Such became the case with Innocenzo and his newfound acquaintance, Benito Fazio of Genoa. Whereas Innocenzo was young and clean-shaven, handsome, thick-headed, obsessed with women, Fazio was bearded, middle-aged, droll in appearance, and cared not one farthing about females. While Innocenzo was full of life, possessing more than a dash of panache, Fazio leaned toward broodiness and was withdrawn, lonely.

Despite his head crawling with such scorpions, Fazio had, since meeting Innocenzo, begun to venture from his shell. He found Innocenzo's company gratifying, and was strangely drawn by his new friend's innocence, as well as by his boyish good looks. There was an uncommon gentleness about Innocenzo, and he lacked that rush to judgment so inherent of others. Simply put, he accepted Fazio, and seemed untroubled by Fazio's abnormal appearance or the queer sound of his voice; he even openly introduced him to others, including his uncle, acting as though he had known the little fellow for a long while. Fazio was unaccustomed to such receptiveness, especially from a person as likeable as Innocenzo.

After that first afternoon in the tavern together when Fazio was milking Innocenzo for information, the two continued to drink together at the same establishment. For Innocenzo's part, he was at first simply bored. Unable to farm the fields of femininity while restricted to his uncle's camp, he harvested moments of amusement from Fazio's company. In truth, Fazio's conversation suited Innocenzo far more so than that of the military men of the camp. As time elapsed, Innocenzo then actually began to look forward to Fazio's company, discovering Fazio was well traveled and full of interesting tales. More importantly, it seemed he could be trusted as friend and confidante.

As for Fazio, for whom having an intimate friend was novel, he found himself pouring his heart out to Innocenzo. Sharing the loneliness and mistreatment of his youth with Innocenzo became cathartic; Innocenzo would listen with full attention, cluck with sympathy, then soothe Fazio's rumpled feathers with compliments about his wit, keen sense of perception, and travels.

So it was that Fazio soon began to seek out Innocenzo each morning within hours of awakening. Without realizing it, an odd sense of possessiveness about Innocenzo quietly began to cultivate itself in Fazio's subconscience, and Fazio began to resent intrusion by others. Innocenzo came to notice this, yet did not seem to mind. Their friendship, then, became a communion of circumstance. Fazio had always been adrift, constituting an island unto himself. Innocenzo now found himself in similar straights, trapped within the confines of a military camp and men-at-arms whom he did not in the least understand. In short, the two became inseparable.

Over the days their conversations evolved from the exchange of idle gossip and story bending to more profound topics such as beliefs, hopes, and the pursuit of happiness. After consuming a good amount of ale one particular afternoon, Fazio ventured far out on a limb. "Innocenzo," he asked, "have you ever been with a man?"

"Of course," Innocenzo laughed, suspecting nothing. "I've been with men all my life, such as now. Look around you, I'm *surrounded* by the damned creatures, all wearing hauberks and helmets!"

Seeing that Innocenzo had missed his point, Fazio leaned forward, lowering his voice as the tavern was brimming with guests. "No, Innocenzo," he said, "I mean, have you ever *lain* with a man… you know, *fornicated*?"

The question had come at him so unexpectedly and so out of context, Innocenzo was not certain he had heard it correctly. "*Wh-what!*" he asked, caught between a snicker and a snout full of ale.

"Sh-sh!" Fazio warned, looking about anxiously. "No need to draw attention!"

"Fazio," said Innocenzo, setting his mug aside, leaning closer. "Did you just ask me whether I'd ever… *fornicated with a man before?*" Then, heavy with drink, he could not keep from breaking into a raucous snort.

As others began to look their way, Fazio's eyes widened and he pleaded, "Please, Innocenzo, keep it down, for Christ's sake!" Dropping his tone, shrugging with frustration, he said, "Oh, never mind. It was a stupid question, so just forget it!"

Too late. The spring had been sprung. Innocenzo's eyes rose to the top of his forehead in curiosity, and he whispered, still snickering the least bit, "But Fazio, men don't have a… *crack*."

Looking about, content that others had returned to their own conversation, Fazio replied, "Sure they do… you know… their *butts*."

His expression going blank, Innocenzo's innocence overcame him. "*Wh-what?* M-men *do that* to each other?" Sitting back, he shook his head, unable to accept such a picture. "Oh, but Fazio, you jest, *right?*"

"Ah, no my friend," Fazio replied quietly. "It's called *buggering*. Yeah, you see, one guy sticks his poker up the other guy's… well, *you know.*"

Innocenzo said nothing at first, trying to envision what Fazio was describing. Then it hit him, and he blinked. "Up the other guy's… *ass?*"

Fazio nodded, the corner of his mouth curling. "It's not so strange as you might think, Innocenzo. You see, I myself, like many other men, find no pleasure in women. Oh no, I'd *far* rather bugger a fellow than a woman. For example, in *y-o-u*… now, *there* I could find pleasure."

Staring at Fazio, his eyes crossing, Innocenzo twittered, feeling the nascent germination of discomfort. "Ah, no… I could never imagine doing such a twisted act, Fazio! Besides, that'd be against the laws of God and nature– *wouldn't it?*"

"Oh… so say some," Fazio said, passing off the objection as nugatory. "In ancient Greece it was a time-honored practice, Innocenzo. And in many, many other cultures as well. You … might wish to try it *once* at least before casting stones, lad. If you're curious, as I am, I have a room upstairs in this very tavern."

Although a hungry look then slipped into Fazio's eyes, he shrugged with meekness. "*Eh?*"

"You have a room upstairs?" asked Innocenzo, his interest pricked.

"Yes indeed," Fazio replied, failing to understand that Innocenzo was heading in another direction entirely.

"Well then," Innocenzo smiled, "let me ask you something. Just *how good* of friends are we, Fazio?"

"*Very* good friends," answered Fazio, feeling a swelling between his loins.

"In that case," said Innocenzo, his eyes drawing down, "I wonder if you might be willing to hike across town and do me a slight favor… you know, over to the peasant camp along the west road into Cologne"

"Certainly," said Fazio, feeling that anticipation of the spider at feeling those first palpitations of something probing the web. "To what purpose?"

"There are two young sisters there from Flanders who I met before arriving in Cologne. The Bordillon sisters, Marie and Jeannette. They were taking a fancy to me, you could say… but now I'm stuck here in my uncle's camp. I wonder if you might not bring them here. You know, maybe allow me the use of your little room upstairs, huh?"

"*What!*" cried Fazio, his face caving with disappointment.

Seeing Fazio wilt, Innocenzo saw his opportunity with the Bordillon sisters evaporating. Still, his craving for female flesh had gone un-itched for weeks now, which to him was intolerable. His mind grasping at straws, he snatched the goblet sitting before him and took a long, deep swallow, emptying its entire contents in one swallow. "Fazio… I'll tell you what," he murmured slowly. "Though I'll not let you *bugger* me, or whatever that word was you said, I'll consent to letting you dally with my privates a bit…uh, if you agree to bring those girls across town. There now, what do you say?"

Fazio stared across the table at Innocenzo, and in the haze of alcohol, Innocenzo's young face drew him in. "Yes… *done*," said Fazio, taking a final drink. "Now follow me then, lad, and let's go upstairs for a short while."

## Chapter Thirty-three

### The Hermit Moves Forward

Fazio and Innocenzo aside, two other men came to know each other quite well while in Cologne– Tafur and Geoffrey Burrel. Their liaison was not a friendship, rather more of an ill-mannered accord, as snakes are solitary creatures ever wary of their own species. The two men had met only once in Amiens, France, then again near the German border during Handel's dispute with the Hermit and Sansavoir. Being encamped with each other in Cologne, however, they crossed paths frequently.

From the onset, Tafur distrusted Burrel for the simple fact he was a minor noble, having brought a small retinue of vassals in his wake. Just as one wolf smells the scent of another, Tafur perceived that Burrel was underhanded, possessing a dark side that could not be trusted. But unlike himself, Burrel quietly worked the shadows rather than publicly stating his intentions or taking charge of others. Indeed, Burrel's specialty was subterfuge.

Nor had Burrel taken a liking to Tafur; Burrel's arrogance forced him to consider Tafur base and ignorant. Still, in recognizing that Tafur's hatred of Jews matched his own and that Tafur was undermining the Hermit just as he himself was undermining Walter Sansavoir, Burrel did not mark Tafur as a competitor, simply as one to scorn. Tafur's view of Burrel was much the same.

When Count Emicho of Leiningen had arrived in Cologne, the two men found themselves standing next to each other as the German count issued his strategy to raze the Jewish sector later that afternoon. Grinning with contempt, Burrel leaned over and said, "Ha, Tafur, what the hell good are you going to do with a stick? I can loan you one of my lesser swords… for the day at least."

"If you want," sneered Tafur, "I'll show you right now what I plan to do with my stick, you horse's ass!"

Taking immediate offense, Burrel motioned to several of his men listening to the exchange. Without a word, they grabbed Tafur and took him to the ground. Before they could do more, they were suddenly swarmed by fifteen or twenty agitated peasants swinging shovels, scythes, and staffs. They, too, had been listening to the exchange.

Startled by the speed with which the peasants reacted, Burrel interceded to save his men who were already profusely bleeding from their faces and hands, saved only by helmets and hauberks. "Hold there! Stop I say! Enough!"

Rising from the ground, Tafur dusted himself, spitting on Burrel's boots. "You or your men do such a thing again, and I'll be less inclined for mercy. The men under my command outnumber your little party two hundred to one, and I've taught them how to use their farm tools. So, Burrel, best you save your piss and vinegar for the Jews today, I'd say."

Although from that moment Burrel disliked Tafur even more, he gained a begrudging measure of respect for the Beggar King. "Aye," he grunted, "the Jews."

***

On being informed by Tristan of Asta's passing that next day, Guillaume dropped to a knee, crossed himself, and slipped into prayer. Though his bond with Asta had never been cemented because of his young age at separation, he had set aside questions that had long hung in the balance about her motivations in sending him and Tristan to the Black Monks of Cluny. Now, his only hope was that she would find peace in Heaven... a sentiment he felt she sorely deserved.

The news of Asta's death had far more impact, however, on the Danes. Orla, Crowbones and Guthroth had been her protectors since the day of her birth. From that early moment they treasured her, hoisting to the very pinnacle of their purpose in life. "Oh, damnation... but such a sad day," lamented Orla, his great blue eyes turning glassy as he thought back to Asta in the innocence and beauty of her early girlhood.

"Ja," snuffled Crowbones, "such an angelic child, so full of life, bursting with happiness and joy... until the year of Guntar's execution and her marriage to Roger de Saint-Germain." At this he flinched, nodding with disgust as his jaw tightened. "Life took a turn for her then, as it did for all of us."

Young Hroc had only vague memories of Asta during his boyhood in England, but looking over at Guthroth as Tristan shared the news, he could see that his uncle was deeply, deeply wounded. Although he said nothing, on hearing the news Guthroth's shoulders had dropped a measure, in unison with his eyes. He issued a long sigh then, which conveyed an entire lifetime of reverence for Asta of the Norman Danes. Guthroth had lost his mother as a boy, had no sisters, and had never married; for him, Asta had been the sole female of his entire existence. Simply put, he had from that first day she opened her eyes at birth adored her– to the ends of the earth.

Seeing that Guthroth was overcome, yet knowing that he would say nothing, Hroc placed a hand on his uncle's shoulder. Like Guthroth, Hroc himself remained silent; over time, the two had come to understand each other so well that they now shared the ability to commune in complete silence. And on this particular morning, their communion was especially heartfelt.

***

Over the next week Tristan made several trips into the Hermit's camp, but went alone in light of the scuffle between Guillaume and Sansavoir during the first visit. Not wishing to add fuel to the fire, Tristan advised his brother to remain in the Tuscan camp during these parleys. Oddly, however, Tristan noticed that Sansavoir, Burrel, and their troops were suddenly nowhere to be found. Despite their absence Tristan still decided it best to go to the Hermit's camp alone, seeing no benefit to Guillaume and Tafur being in the same company either.

Having abandoned making direct demands or pleas for the Hermit to stop his march, Tristan's visits were now aimed solely at swaying him into recognizing the logistical challenges incurred by a war against the Turks without wagons, mule trains, and weaponry provided by the main crusader forces. Although Peter listened with evident interest in Tristan's detailed layout of these issues, he would shake his head after a time, insisting, "God has told me nothing about *waiting*, Bishop Saint-Germain. If anything, he's spurred me forward by adding another seven-thousand recruits from Cologne and filling my war chest to bursting! Indeed, is that not a signal to go forward with haste?"

Tafur was invariably present during Tristan's visits, but spoke infrequently. Standing behind the Hermit like some watchful crow crouched atop a stump, his dark, disapproving eyes stared narrowly at Tristan each time he spoke.

Although Tristan had from the very beginning suspected there would be little chance of dissuading the Hermit from his Jerusalem quest, he now knew for certain the Hermit could not be deterred, and dispatched a message to Rome indicating such. He also then doubled his efforts at focusing on the importance of waiting for the main military forces of France, Italy, and Germany to arrive in Constantinople before leading the peasant army into Turkish territory.

Supporting this effort was Innocenzo, urging his uncle to weigh and consider the idea. "Aye, Uncle Peter, a capital idea that," he said time and again, nodding with assent. "I've *never* thought we should go into battle without the full array of courageous and experienced Christian knights at our side." For Innocenzo, it was a simple matter of arithmetic. Whether God was on their side or not, Innocenzo presumed the odds of fighting the Turks would be far improved in the company of a fully armed and capable multitude of the pope's knights and footmen.

Simple as that might sound, others in the Hermit's camp failed to grasp that equation, such as Tafur. Tafur had convinced himself the Turks would have little chance against his army of peasant crusaders, especially in combination with the added military muscle of Sansavoir's and Burrel's uniformed troops. Accordingly, in contrast to Tristan, he lobbied the Hermit for an immediate attack on the Turks on reaching Constantinople.

The Hermit swallowed Tafur's reasoning whole heartedly at first, believing first that to delay would be contrary to God's will, and believing next that Tafur's army of beggars had developed, truly, into a deadly military force. Yet, with time, Tristan's reasoning began to chip away at Tafur's advantage. Sensing a swing of the pendulum, Tristan next tried to convince the Hermit that, should he hold off attacking the Turks until the arrival of Bishop Adhémar, the Peasants' Crusade could greatly augment the Pope's ultimate strategy of a single, massive force confronting the Islamic enemy.

In time, the Hermit became less and less averse to the concept of waiting. Then too, Innocenzo's echoing of Tristan's strategy was ceaseless the moment Tristan would leave the Hermit's camp. Finally, after several days, the Hermit gave the slightest of shrugs, and said, "As I think about it, Bishop… it might not hurt to hold off a while for the purpose of greater armed strength. Perhaps that's what God intended all along, eh?"

"Very possibly," agreed Tristan, well contented.

Still, Tristan knew there was a huge obstacle looming in the path of the Hermit's concession. The Hermit had not been privy to the late arrival dates presented to Tristan by the Benedictine Underground. Consequently, the Hermit was under the impression that 'waiting a while' would be a matter of weeks, or perhaps a month or so at most. Nonetheless, hearkening this concession from the Hermit, Tristan continued to hammer home the idea of waiting to attack, as did Innocenzo.

One area of contention, nonetheless, did arise as the days passed, and that was the Jews. "A violation of rightful behavior," insisted Tristan, refusing to let the topic rest. "And Peter, let it be known, the Jews of Cologne claim that your own crusade is the root of these violent pogroms against them."

"Not true!" retorted the Hermit, indignant about the charge. "It was Count Emicho who incited this recent riot here in the city. *You* know that! It's been well publicized. Besides, though I've no love of Jews, I've also never encouraged attacking them!"

"Perhaps so," said Tristan, "but the Jews here insist the pogrom that occurred back in Rouen last December was a result of your inflammatory preaching. Many of those who rioted there and killed French Jews joined your ranks and are now with you here in Cologne. After that bloodletting in Rouen, the French Jews sent word to their brethren here in Germany to expect trouble as you and your people moved this direction, and these fears have now been confirmed precisely as predicted."

"Hold there, Bishop Saint-Germain!" declared the Hermit, his eyes beginning to shift back and forth. Looking over at Innocenzo, he said, "Nephew, bring forth that satchel yonder beneath my pack." Innocenzo returned shortly, satchel in hand,

and the Hermit said, "Pull out some of those letters, lad, and show the good Bishop here what they contain."

Innocenzo stuffed his hand in the satchel and started handing letters to Tristan. "Letters from the Jews of France, mainly Normandy and Flanders," he said, "intended for their Jew peers here in Germany, requesting that they help feed the Peasants' Crusade."

Tristan read the contents of several letters, then looked up at the Hermit. "Oh, but these letters are full of fear and intimidation," he said. "This is extortion. After so many Jews were killed in Rouen and other parts of France, naturally the French Jews would beg their German brethren to cooperate with you… either that or *die*."

"I can't control every member of my following," insisted the Hermit. "There are many in my crusade, and they come from different walks of life. So yes, there are some who despise Jews… but *I* can't change that, so what am I to do? There's a much bigger issue here than dead Jews, and that's erasing Islam from the face of the earth! You continue to lose sight of that, it seems, Bishop. Yes, you continue to get distracted!"

"No, most certainly not," insisted Tristan. "But I've also recently learned that you invited Count Emicho into your camp last week, and am certain you were already aware of Count Emicho's anti-Semitic hatred at the time." Next Tristan pointed directly at Tafur who happened to be present, and whose eyes had drawn down to slits at Tristan's first mention of Jews. "And your so-called 'King of the Beggars' there was in the midst of the massacre, as was Sansavoir's next in command, Burrel. Worse yet, they encouraged Count Emicho to attack me and my entire party at the monastery for trying to stop the massacre of those helpless people."

"They were *J-e-w-s*," hissed Tafur, breaking his silence. "And Jews are never helpless. They taint and destroy all they touch. They're a disease, Bishop, a foul, slow-growing race of parasites slowly devouring all of Europe. If they're not eradicated, we'll all be speaking Hebrew within the decade! But I dare say you've never had to deal with them directly, shunted away in that fat life of monasteries and the Vatican, eh!? How easy for you, then, to take their part!"

Tafur's barb was, in truth, on target. Still, Tristan was about to launch into Tafur's intolerance– but the Hermit interceded. "Enough, Tafur!" he snapped. "Aye, Bishop, I was aware of Emicho's reputation, but I didn't participate in his purge here in Cologne, nor did I encourage any of my people to join in with his ravaging of the Jewish quarter. Tafur has his own reasons for hating Jews, I suppose, and so might Burrel… but that's really none of my affair. Furthermore, I can't very well stop what others do!"

"Yes, but you can *discourage* it," said Tristan. "Did you do that, at least, Peter?"

The Hermit looked at Tristan as though he'd lost his mind. "What words are these, Bishop?" he blurted. "You *know* I only preach about Christ, salvation, and the ever-after. In the name of God, far be it for me to waste my time talking about Jews one way or the other!"

"Then you said *nothing* to Emicho on the topic of anti-Semitic pogroms, nor to Tafur and his hoodlums, nor to Burrel?" Tristan pressed.

"Of course not! Both Tafur and Burrel are on their way to risk their lives in the fight against Islam as faithful Christian knights, and I'll not castigate such loyal heroes who sacrifice all in service to the Lord!"

"*Loyal heroes*?" gasped Tristan. "But their hands are bloody from the butchering of women and children, Peter, and you know it! I beg you, pray tell what perverse breed of hero commits such acts as that?"

"Nay, no more talk of Jews for we'll never agree," said the Hermit, dismissing Tristan's remark with irritation. "If you truly intend to follow my crusade to Constantinople as you've threatened, there's no sense in you and I fighting over things we can't control. So there it is, simply put, huh? Now go gather your brother, Handel, and whoever else you've dragged here to hound me, and tell them to prepare to march. Sansavoir's impatience has already set him and Burrel onto the road to Hungary and the Balkans a week ago, and I plan to follow now in two days."

## Chapter Thirty-four

### Worms

So began the march out of Cologne. Although the city leadership had objected to the rabble of the Peasants' Crusade and the resultant damage they inflicted upon their city, there were also thousands amongst the citizenry who either enthusiastically contributed to the Hermit's war chest or decided to join his crusade. So it was with great fanfare over 25,000 French and 7,000 German crusaders beneath the Hermit's leadership departed the city in late May, taking the road south to Maintz on their way toward Vienna, then on to the Balkans.

Tristan's group and the Tuscan force, under Guillaume, shadowed the Peasants' Crusade by two day's march. "As there's no military threat to the Hermit's mob here in Western Europe," reasoned Guillaume, "there's little point in getting tangled up with them. Otherwise we'll simply end up policing their hooliganism, which is inevitable in light of their numbers and lack of preparation for this march."

Handel agreed. "Yes, and though the Hermit now has his war chest, I doubt he'll be spending much of it to feed or clothe these poor bastards following him to the ends of the earth."

Though none within the Pope's party, including Tristan himself, were enthused about following the Hermit's train along the arduous trek toward the Balkans and on to Constantinople, they faithfully took the road for Maintz. Their original plan of joining Bishop Adhémar and Raymond of Toulouse in Italy, then sailing to Constantinople, would have been a far simpler proposition than this extended overland route trailing the Hermit. Nonetheless, although their journey to Jerusalem had now suddenly become far more arduous, at least the Hermit had indicated to Tristan that waiting on the main crusader forces before engaging the Turks was now a strong possibility. This, alone, kept Tuscan spirits afloat.

Entering Worms, their encouragement was quickly shattered when they came upon horrors committed several days before their arrival. Passing through the city, they traversed a devastated area that had been turned to ash and rubble, much resembling the Jewish quarter of Cologne after the anti-Semitic uprising.

"Oh, that bastard, Emicho!" hissed Handel. "He did exactly as promised back in Cologne. He precedes us by a week's march, and is devastating every Jewish quarter along his route!"

"Why does he hate these people so?" asked Orla, who possessed no understanding of historical friction between Judaism and Christianity. "They're neither dark-skinned like the Saracens, nor are they Muslims. They don't even talk a different language than their fellow Germans."

"It seems to be an issue of Emicho's interpretation of faith," said Guillaume, "though I don't myself understand it. Unfortunately, it seems he doesn't stand alone on hatred of Jews."

"No," objected Handel, "it's not an issue of faith for Emicho, but of hatred. More than that even, it's an issue of exploitation and plunder!"

"Huh?" said Crowbones.

"What in hell do you suppose Emicho does with the goods of all these people he butchers?" said Handel. "Hell, he confiscates their jewels, their gold and silver, and anything else of value, then loads his saddle bags to bursting with this loot as he moves toward Constantinople. This crusade isn't about God for him, it's a goddamn treasure hunt!" Then he looked at Tristan. "Ah, are you beginning yet to see the evil being hatched by your crusade, my friend? Oh yes, and there'll be a dozen more vultures just like Emicho… or a hundred!"

Tristan nodded, though not in agreement. "Handel, bad fruit settles in every barrel. You have no right to defame all those noble knights and men-of-arms who will be taking up this fight for faith and the preservation of Christianity. Emicho is wicked, agreed, but he in no way represents the Christian ideal put forward by the Holy Father's crusade. It surprises me that one as clever and fair as you would so quickly jump to generalizations."

"Bah! Things *are* what they are, and though you may see good in this crusade, don't be so blind as to objectify the bad. As Pope's scribe, it's your duty to accurately chronicle all that you witness on this march. I but hope you go into *great* detail on what we've witnessed before even coming across the first Turk, eh?"

"Certainly, Handel,' replied Tristan, "with precision and honesty. And mind you, there will be consequences at the end of it all. I vow it on the word of Odo de Lagery himself."

"Look there," said Guillaume, pointing to a man approaching them in bloodied clerical vestments. "Isn't that the archbishop we saw riding with Emicho in Cologne during the riot?"

"Indeed, it's Archbishop Hess, Emicho's man," said Handel, his hands turning to fists as he dismounted. "Probably tallying up the dead for his master like the lapdog that he is!"

"Wait a minute!" implored Tristan, seeing that Handel intended to turn his furor onto the German archbishop. "The man looks distraught– and has blood on his face. Let him speak, Handel."

As Archbishop Hess approached, he grasped Tristan's leg, moaning with woe while crossing himself, red with shame. "Oh, Bishop Saint-Germain!" he wailed incoherently. "Such slaughter and indignity have I witnessed here in Worms! Far worse than in Cologne! Mothers slashing their children's throats to save them from Emicho's knights, entire families locking themselves in their houses carrying out suicide pacts before the roofs caved from fire or before the troops and townspeople could break the doors down!"

"What in hell happened here?" demanded Handel.

"After arriving in Worms," sobbed the archbishop, "Emicho's men dug up a trampled body that had been buried a month earlier. They carried it through the streets claiming the Jews had murdered the man by boiling him in water, then poured the water into the city wells to poison the gentiles! None of it was true. Still, Emicho managed to stir the populace, and he then led the rampage himself!"

"Where's Emicho now?" asked Tristan, about to request that Guillaume mobilize the entire Tuscan force marching in their company to attack the German nobleman's troops.

"He's further south in Maintz, committing the same atrocities!" wailed Hess.

"And why aren't you with him, you bishop bastard?" asked Handel. "Aye, you were riding right beside him in Cologne as he killed Jews and you said *nothing!*"

"I feared for my life," Hess mumbled, choking with shame, falling to his knees. "Do you not see these bruises and knots on my face? After Cologne he set upon me in a fury for not speaking up against the bunch of you! Oh, but I've sinned so grievously, and I've drunk the intoxicating poison of politics these past years just to attain my bishop's mitre. I sided with King Heinrich against the Vatican during the Investiture War since it was him who appointed me Bishop of Leiningen, on Emicho's recommendation. I've cowardly blessed Emicho's actions ever since, but no more! No more! I've abandoned his crusade, and upon my return home shall renounce my bishopric in Leiningen… for I am not worthy."

"Oh, but stop this public confession!" commanded Tristan, dismounting his horse and pulling Hess in his arms. "Make your confession to God only, Archbishop, through a priest of the Church within a confessional, but not here on this open street." Leading Hess away a distance, he began to pray over him. Looking up, the archbishop continued to intermittently weep while begging forgiveness from the Bishop of Ostia, whom he knew to be a man of stronger conviction and righteousness than himself.

"Well now," said Handel to the Danes, jerking a thumb over his shoulder at Hess, disgust washing through his face. "That's the *first* good thing I've seen come of this grand crusade–a sinner of the high Church shedding his collar!"

## Chapter Thirty-five

### Maintz

Several days later the Tuscan force arrived in the city of Maintz. As Archbishop Hess had said, after Worms Emicho had trained his dreadful gaze on the Jews of Maintz, whose quarter now lay in ash and a shambles of demolished buildings.

"Odin's ass, this man Emicho has a sickness!" exclaimed Orla as they slowly rode through heaps of refuse and piles of bodies stacked one atop another.

"Ja, Father," said Hroc, "and it seems his hatred never slackens. I can make no sense of it."

"Nor I," muttered Crowbones. "Emicho claims to be a crusader on his way to holy war, but the Turks must not be the only enemy he had in mind."

Shortly, as they neared the end of the Jewish quarter, they yielded to several men who were gathering corpses and placing them in stacks like cord-wood. They appeared to be Jews. Noticing the approach of the Tuscan battalion, they broke into flight.

"Stop there!" shouted Guillaume, chasing one of the men on horseback into the chest-high corner of a collapsed building. "We mean you no harm. We're Tuscans just passing through. We just came from Worms and saw this same devastation. What happened here?"

"Indeed," said Handel, pulling alongside Guillaume, "what excuse did Count Emicho use here in Maintz to set off this slaughter?"

"No excuse," muttered the man, nervously shifting about from one foot to the other, weighing whether to bolt or scramble over the wall at his back. "He just came in and commenced killing us all."

Tristan approached. Seeing his Bishop's garb, the man spat. "Damn all of you bishops!" he shouted, pointing a quaking finger at Tristan. He made an obscene gesture then and let loose a string of profanity, but none could tell whether the man was cursing or sobbing. It was a mixture of both.

"Watch your tongue there," snapped Guillaume, "this is Bishop Saint-Germain of the Vatican you so shamefully disrespect, and he's done nothing to warrant such disregard."

Tristan glanced at Guillaume, waving him off. Dismounting, he went to the man, grasping him by the shoulders. "We tried to stop Emicho in Cologne," he said gently. "We are not your enemy, and our hearts are with you."

Tristan's tone was so sincere and heartfelt that the man sagged a bit, and looked into Tristan's face, repentant. "I-I'm sorry," he snuffled, barely able to hold himself up. It's those bishop's vestment's you're wearing."

"And what of them?" asked Tristan, steadying the man as he spoke.

"Here in Maintz we heard about the trouble up in Worms, that Emicho was coming our way. We immediately sought sanctuary within the palace of Archbishop Rothard here in Maintz. He agreed to protect us, but only after negotiating an exorbitant fee which we gladly amassed and paid. When Emicho entered the city, the Archbishop did nothing to protect us though, and quickly fled his palace for his own safety. Emicho and his men then set about killing nearly every Jew of Maintz; men, women, children, even newborn infants. Only a handful like me and the others you saw a moment ago escaped. We ran like cowards and left our families behind!" At this the man dropped to the ground, hugging Tristan's knees. "Archbishop Rothard took our money, then abandoned us! But then, like a coward, I also abandoned my own wife and children who now lay dead in yonder pile!"

"That filthy bastard, Emicho," growled Handel, shaking his head. "And Bishop Rothard, too. Aye, Tristan… another sterling entry in your report to the Pope about the righteous behavior of our European nobility within his Holy Crusade, eh?"

Ignoring Handel, Tristan comforted the man a while longer, saying prayers over his family. Then, as he mounted his horse, a commotion stirred at the end of the street. From nowhere a procession of nearly five-hundred German peasants appeared, coming toward the Tuscan unit. At the head of this procession walked a goose. Walking as geese walk, the fowl would advance slowly, then stop and peck about for a while. Then it would advance again, look about, and waddle off to the side, stopping again. Oddly, it appeared that the peasants were carefully following the disconnected movements of the goose.

"What the hell is this?" muttered Handel.

As the curious procession inched its way forward, following the actions and direction of the goose, the Tuscan battalion moved aside, allowing it to pass. When the head of the procession neared, Tristan noticed the peasants were following a heavily bearded monk in sackcloth, not dissimilar in appearance to Peter the Hermit. "Greetings, Brother," Tristan said. "Pray tell, what is this gathering behind you, and why are you following this goose?"

Glancing up while still trying to keep his attention on the goose, the monk made the sign of the cross on seeing Tristan's holy garments. "This is no ordinary goose, Bishop," he replied, "but the *Holy Goose*."

Orla and Crowbones exchanged skeptical glances. Orla then looked over at Hroc and Guthroth, but their full attention was focused on the monk.

"The Holy Goose?" snorted Handel. "My God, man, what are you talking about?"

"We're following it to Jerusalem," the monk said, keeping sight of the goose. "One month ago I came upon the bird in our monastery stable and found myself in the midst of a miracle. There within the hay strewn about the stable floor, next to the goose, lay hay in the form of a cross, the head of which was pointing toward Jerusalem! Immediately recognizing this as a divine sign from Heaven related to the Pope's call to arms against Islam, I began gathering the folk of our town to join the march east! We had hoped to intercept Peter the Hermit and join his fold, but the goose isn't moving quickly enough."

Orla and Crowbones could not help at this point but to break into snickering. "But," nitpicked Orla, passing his brother a conspiratorial wink, "has it not occurred to you to place the goose atop a horse to quicken your pace? It's the goose, after all, that's holding you back."

"Ah, no," insisted the monk, "it was the Holy Goose who inspired the miracle, so we must follow him, not some horse that has nothing to do with the miracle!"

"But couldn't someone from your town have simply shaped the hay in your barn into the sign of the cross?" asked Crowbones. "A boy, perhaps, as a prank... or a fellow monk?"

"Of course not!" retorted the monk, taking offense. "Do you take me for a complete imbecile? I know a miracle when I see one!"

"But at the speed you're moving, you'll make Jerusalem in perhaps... *five years*!" brayed Orla.

"Enough," said Tristan, scowling at Orla and Crowbones. Turning back to the monk, he said, "Very well, Brother, God bless you and may you have a safe journey to Jerusalem."

This brought a reaction from Handel who by now could not stifle his own laughter. "Yes, a safe journey, Brother, and don't get too dizzy going to and fro, stopping and starting in meter with your Holy Goose!" Slapping his thigh, he then started heehawing uncontrollably.

"Have a little more respect," whispered Tristan with agitation. "These people are simple peasants and know no better. The superstitions of the poor run rampant, but their intentions are pure. Pity them, perhaps, but no need to ridicule them!"

"And the monk," said Handel, "shouldn't *he* know better, at least?" sniffed Handel.

"Let's be on our way," said Guillaume, "lest we get bogged down by this nonsensical parade. We'll be stuck here till dark at the pace they're moving."

The Tuscan battalion marched forward at Guillaume's command, but as they left the procession behind, Orla leaned over his horse and swatted Hroc on the rump. Smirking, he said, "Ah, the 'Holy Goose'! Ha! Even the Norse pagans of old could never come up with such twisted ideas as these Christians, huh, Hroc?"

## Chapter Thirty-six

### Hroc and Guthroth

At eighteen, Hroc had known little but being around men. He had lost his mother as a small boy during the Danes' flight from the English estate of Desmond DuLac, hated husband of Tristan's and Guillaume's mother, Asta. Hroc scarcely remembered his mother, and from the moment of her death had been under the care of his father, Orla, and his two uncles, Crowbones and Guthroth the Quiet. He had an older brother, Knud, whom he worshipped, but Knud was slain at age fourteen during the Investiture War while battling the Germans. It was Knud's heroic death while saving their father in battle that inspired little Hroc to one day become a fearsome warrior.

Hroc was little more than seven at the time his older brother was killed, and it was Guthroth who patiently began tutoring him in the craft of wielding sword, ax, and hammer, though the young boy could barely hold them up. Guthroth was also a master horseman, and taught Hroc how to maneuver his mount back, forth, and to the side, using its crushing weight and force as a battering ram. By age thirteen, already larger than most grown men of southern Europe due to Scandinavian genes, Hroc was a deadly opponent in battle and possessed no reluctance whatsoever in slaughtering the enemy.

Despite this merciless battle mentality he possessed a certain consideration for others, as well as a deeply rooted respect for his elders. This was evident in his dealings with his father and Uncle Crowbones, but especially so in dealing with his Uncle Guthroth. The two shared that special cohesive bond that develops only between a younger man and a patient mentor– a bond that is heightened even more by the sharing of common bloodlines.

Having spent nearly his entire life in the shadow of men, living in their military camps, fighting their wars, Hroc was now at an age when he had begun to wonder about himself a bit; he had begun to contemplate his own future. Though the presence and availability of females were a rare occurrence due to his war-like existence, he had begun to think about things like courtship, marriage, and the possibility of one day perhaps having his own children. He also wondered whether his entire life would be spent at war, as had happened to his father and uncles. He hoped not. He had already lost count of friends killed in battle, and men he himself had slain; most had died for naught, in the name of this man, or that idea, or this cause. In his mind, most of it had made little sense, especially when causes, conflicts, and alliances reversed themselves so swiftly within the unpredictable swirl of political winds.

So it happened that one night as Guthroth the Quiet sat alone by the fire, Hroc approached him. "Uncle," he said, "I've been thinking lately, and one of the things that confounds me is what to believe in. Would you mind telling me why you agreed to baptism when father and Uncle Crowbones refused it?"

Without looking up, Guthroth said, "W-we are different m-men, Hroc." Then he said nothing more.

Hroc well realized that Guthroth did not engage in long discussions, especially on abstract topics which forced one to delve into detail, having to explain and express many things with many words. Guthroth simply preferred to remain silent as talking, for him, was laborious. Nonetheless, Hroc continued; he trusted Guthroth and valued his opinions. Moreover, Guthroth usually made far more sense in far fewer words than anyone he knew. "I'm thinking about taking the water as you did, Uncle Guthroth, but first… I'd like to know what changed your mind."

This surprised Guthroth, and he looked up. "M-my life was s-saved in battle at the very m-moment of p-passing. At that instant, I th-thought about the Christian G-God that Lady Asta always prayed t-to. Death reached down for me… but I l-lived. It was the Christian G-God who s-saved me."

"Could it not have been a twist of timing, an accident?" questioned Hroc. "Or could it not have been the Norse gods that saved you?"

"No," replied Guthroth, staring back into the fire.

"I don't imagine father would be too happy if I agreed to baptism. But then, Uncle Tristan and Guillaume would be pleased, I suppose."

"Me t-too," said Guthroth, his eyes remaining lost in the flames. But Hroc thought he detected a tiny smile creasing his uncle's lips.

Guthroth offered nothing more though, and Hroc was about to leave the fire when footsteps approached. It was Handel. "What're you two doing up this late?" he muttered, half asleep.

"Having a talk about God, Master Handel," replied Hroc.

Handel chuckled. "Yeah, but then... I wager you're doing all the talking and Guthroth's doing all the listening, right? That's not a talk, that's a sermon!"

"No," replied Hroc. "Actually, my uncle has said quite a lot."

This tickled Handel. He had already figured out that Hroc covered for Guthroth whenever possible. "Well," he said, "what in hell brings up such a complex topic between you two on a night like this?"

"I'm thinking about being baptized," said Hroc, "but haven't made a final decision. Maybe you could shed some light. Though I didn't believe it possible at first, my Uncle Tristan told me the other day that you're a monk."

"Ha," Handel snapped, "I take offense to that!" But there was no offense in his expression, only a grin. "It's not so much how a monk dresses or how he acts, it's what's in his heart, and my heart is full. It often swells to bursting, especially for the poor and dispossessed."

"Oh? Even as an... assassin?"

"Yes."

"Mine, also... though I have never assassinated anyone."

"The hell you say," smirked Handel. "You've killed as many men as myself, Hroc."

"Ja, maybe so... but never clandestinely, only face to face."

"Murder is murder, lad. You're as huge as a goddamned bear, so what chance do most other men have against you, huh? And if it's not a fair fight, it's murder, I say. Whenever taking on a Goliath, my only chance, then, is to be clandestine! Still, as I said before, my heart swells for the poor and dispossessed."

"M-mine, t-too," added Guthroth, nodding at the fire.

"I've listened to the words of men my entire life," Handel continued, "and they're twisted, self-serving. The only words that make sense to me are the words of Christ… how to live… how to treat others."

"How to treat others?" echoed Hroc, shaking his head. "Oh, but as you just said, I've killed so many men already, and there'll be many more to come, I imagine. And just on this trip, I saw you take down your share back in Cologne… and that confuses me a bit, Master Handel, when I hear Christians preaching about the sinfulness of killing. Yet Christians kill all the time."

"Hroc," said Handel, "we kill animals to eat… but we must kill men, at times, to *survive*. But a question. Do you kill the helpless and the weak?"

"No," said Hroc.

"Do you kill for pleasure or profit?"

"No, certainly not."

"Well, you've surely learned by now there are those who slaughter the helpless… think back on the Jews in Cologne, and Worms and Maintz. There are men who kill for plunder, too. No, you and I kill only those who *need* to be killed… and there are many, unfortunately. Certain forms of killing are even sanctified, according to both the Bible and the Church." He shook his head then. "This crusade sanctifies killing the Turks. Though I've no heart for Muslims, I doubt we'll be killing them for God. No, we'll be killing them for the Byzantines… whom I despise."

"And why's that, Master Handel?"

"They broke from the True Church over forty years ago, Hroc, which is anathema to me. Better to be a pagan as you and your uncles and never take the water than to be a Christian and abandon the faith."

"I'm not sure I understand such a position as that," said Hroc, looking puzzled. "As I said, there are many things about Christianity that confuse me."

"It's a question of pure faith, Hroc. Does your father confuse you at times?'

Hroc had to chuckle. "Yes… often."

"Yet you accept him completely, and believe in him, huh? Aye, because you have faith in him. But simpler yet, if you're torn about baptism, there's but one question you need to ask yourself. Going back to what I said before about words… would you rather accept the words of any mortal man upon this earth without question, or the words of Christ?"

"It's difficult to accept the words of many men."

"*Most* men," said Handel, "and eventually you'll learn that *all* men are wrong, or misguided, or misleading at one time or another. Even the Pope, despite what the Church would have us believe about papal infallibility. So again, would you rather accept the words of men, or the words of Christ?"

"Ch-Christ!" declared Guthroth before Hroc could answer.

Handel looked over at Guthroth and shook his head. "Judas priest, Guthroth, if you're going to talk my damned ears off tonight, I'd best go back to bed for I'll need them in the morning!" Breaking into laughter, he stood then, evaporating into the darkness.

## Chapter Thirty-seven

### The Great… Walk

As history confirms, a good number of those following Peter the Hermit in the Peasants' Crusade were actually not peasants. These fortunate souls enjoyed the amenities of horse, mule, oxen or donkey traveling in wagons providing the luxury of adequate food and drink, covered shelter, and bedding. Unfortunately, however, the vast majority of Peter the Hermit's crusaders were destitute, forced to make the excruciatingly long trip by foot with little but what they could carry in hand or strapped to their backs.

The walk from Amiens, France to Cologne was a distance of 217 miles. An average group of people on foot, depending on age and health, is generally capable of maintaining 15-20 miles per day on foot when moving over an extended period of time. The first leg of the trip to Jerusalem, ending in Cologne, was therefore manageable for most despite the nagging presence of many children and elderly. Roughly speaking, the trek took most of them two and a half weeks. The distance from Cologne to Constantinople, however, was a daunting 1,200 miles. Bearing in mind that during the Eleventh Century most people of Europe rarely ventured beyond their townships or feudal territories, in particular the poor, a journey of this magnitude would seem impossible. Indeed, for many, it proved to be exactly so. To begin, the poor undertook this improbable expedition with neither planning nor resources. Though a heart may be filled to bursting with *faith*, the human body requires as a bare minimum: sustenance, appropriate clothing, and shelter from the elements. When not readily available, these things must be acquired whenever possible, and by any means necessary; for the destitute, this translates into thievery and intimidation.

The victims of such malfeasance, due to the massive numbers of those marching within the Peasants' Crusade, could do little to resist the crusaders' increasing habit of taking whatever and whenever they wanted. This inevitably precipitated into disputes with city officials and local militia, but small towns and large cities alike were quickly overwhelmed by the advancing crush of this massive army of bandits within a matter of days. As to the farmers and other isolated populations in the path of the Peasants' Crusade, they had not a prayer from the onset. Thousands watched helplessly as their homes and barns were dismantled, their fields and gardens stripped and trampled, and their entire store of livestock, fowl, and food was carried off by marauding crusaders.

Yet, this by no means meant those marching to Jerusalem ate regularly, for along the way many died of starvation, and some even of thirst. The military component of the Hermit's crusade, meaning Walter Sansavoir's army, was adequately provisioned and outfitted in comparison to the vast civilian component of the march. The military force also marched well ahead of the civilian train, concerning themselves little with the welfare of the mob marching in their wake. In the end, much discontent, difficulty, confusion, and rioting took root along the road to Constantinople among the thirty thousand plus crusaders marching with Peter the Hermit, especially as time elapsed. Also, the further the Hermit's hordes moved away from France and Germany, the more vociferous became their relationships with foreign, native populations– and the more violent became the resultant clashes.

Adding to the hardships imposed by hunger, lack of finances, and intrusion on foreign soil, was the issue of disease, generated primarily by complete disregard for sanitation and cleanliness. People urinated and defecated along the very roadsides where they marched, ate, and slept by the tens of thousands. Bathing and personal hygiene were nonexistent amongst this roving mob, due to a matter of practice as much as of a matter of negligence. Sickness also ran rampant because of rain, cold, and lack of shelter. The more prosperous travelers had tents, covered wagons, or other means of shelter, but vast numbers lacked even a simple blanket or mantle to stave off cold nights or raking winds. When the rains came, at times for days on end, the poor were as exposed and helpless as cattle caught in the open fields during violent, extended downpours.

But let us for a moment, in terms of this incredible venture, consider the human foot… a humble organ generally taken for granted for some reason, and whose value is so often neglected until the moment of incapacitation. The foot, in fact, is a complex structure of twenty-six bones, thirty-three joints, and many muscles, nerves, and ligament types. It is therefore susceptible to many dermatological foot conditions related to the skin, bones, and nails to include corns, calluses, bunions, ingrown toenails, hammertoe, arthritis, and vascular disorders. Moreover, fungal and bacterial conditions are easily developed and transmitted by the warm, humid, dark conditions created by footwear.

Ill-fitting footwear, whether too loose or too tight, creates yet another host of debilitating circumstances, as does *lack* of footwear. On this walk to Constantinople, many were barefoot, having worn out the shoes in which they had begun this ill-advised journey. Even those who did possess sandals, shoes, or boots suffered from foot disease, blisters, or boils incurred by the endless cobblestone roads they traversed, or worse yet, the rocky and unpaved terrain they so often encountered while trudging east. Those suffering most were undoubtedly the many field peasants and serfs who had begun the journey in shoes made not of leather, but of wood.

Shouldering all of these circumstances, and facing a litany of other consequences inflicted by a two thousand mile walk from France to Jerusalem, it is inconceivable to imagine, even, the number of foot injuries and ills that befell these people. One could begin by trying to guess the number of times people tripped, fell, or stumbled– then wondering how many toes, feet, or legs were broken, then further wondering how people managed such injuries during this era. Due to the wearing of inappropriate footwear or even the lack of footwear, one could then attempt to imagine how it was these people found the will and fortitude to plod forward day after day, week after week, month after month. Then too, there were the lame and elderly taking on a physical feat far beyond their limited physical capacities, let alone the many young children prone to playfulness and carelessness, thus prone to accidents.

All of this is to say, then, that this venture was a *long walk* for the many thousands who had initially given their feet little consideration, nor anything else for that matter, save for some, their burning faith.

## Chapter Thirty-eight

### Mala Looks East

"Grazie, Signorina! Si sono cosi generosi!" smiled the Archbishop of Genoa as he stood and bowed. "Never in history has our diocese ever received such a generous endowment! I assure you, we will use the funds as you have instructed, half going for renovations to Genoa's grand cathedral and the other half to be distributed amongst the Benedictine infirmaries of the city and outlying areas that care for the poor."

Mala offered a courteous but restrained smile of acknowledgment as the archbishop kissed the back of her hand, then accompanied him to the door. Once he was gone, she turned to Salvetti who was still seated at the table and said, "Thank you for adding the addendums to this contract ensuring each on-going phase of the cathedral renovation is inspected and audited. Also, it was good you insisted that each infirmary provide invoices on every expenditure made on their behalf from the archbishop's office. Such details did not occur to me, though they should have."

"Ah, but Signorina," Salvetti replied, basking in the warmth of her praise, "you pay me to guard your affairs, and I guard them like a wolfhound! Besides, this year's gift is far larger than what you normally contribute to the diocese. We need to make sure it's distributed wisely and not pilfered. Some bishops have sticky fingers when large endowments drop." Pointing to a stack of documents piled at the opposite end of the table, he continued. "So we'd best begin untangling that unwelcome knot sitting there, I suppose, eh, Signorina? Some serious decisions stand ahead, and we must start reassessing certain future renegotiations, I would think. Inevitably, this crusade Pope Urban has started may well interfere with many of your current operations, creating future trade complications."

As a mighty sea power of Europe, Genoa possessed one of the largest navies of the entire continent. It also boasted a flourishing maritime trade, extending its tentacles throughout the Mediterranean, the Adriatic, and along the European Atlantic coastline. Salvetti's concerns were not centered so much on these areas, but more toward the Black Sea and the Bosphorus Strait, gateways to la Gran Signorina's heavy volume of commercial traffic with the Seljuk Empire. Still, Salvetti was aware of the possibility that a holy war against Islam might also affect her exporting and importing with the Moors of southern Spain and North Africa. As with all wars, the period immediately preceding the actual outbreak of armed conflict created uncertainties, and Salvetti had already begun to fret over them.

"Of course, on the other hand," he said, putting a finger to his chin, "it might be best to simply sit back… you know, wait to see which way the wind shifts, eh, Signorina?"

"I'm not concerned," replied Mala. "War bears a cost, but also presents opportunities. *Many* opportunities. With thousands upon thousands of people on the move once war begins, there'll be an increased need for transporting livestock, munitions, men and supplies. My fleets will be busier than ever. This crusade will shortly create a desperate need for goods on *both* sides of the Bosphorus, so I foresee unimaginable possibilities. No, this is no time to hesitate, Salvetti."

"Ah, si… of course," said Salvetti, skilled at accounting for wealth but lacking the vision to generate it. In this, la Gran Signorina was unsurpassed, and he knew it. "So, you wish to keep our channels with the Muslims open then, when the fighting begins? Even with the Turks?"

"Yes, most certainly. Especially with the Turks. They'll be needing trade more than ever, and the transport of food and munitions."

"But won't that anger the crusaders and the Byzantines? And what of your efforts to solicit the Genoese navy's support for the crusaders to and from Constantinople and even in the Bosphorus? Won't that, in turn, infuriate the Turks? I fear playing both sides at once could promote retribution from both camps, Signorina."

"Though I solicit our navy's assistance for the Christian cause, I'm not viewed by the Turks as a military threat, only as a commercial presence. Besides, the Turks will be grateful to me for keeping our trade networks open with them… which is exactly what they'll be hoping for once they learn war is coming. As to angering the crusaders by keeping sea trade open with the Muslims, this is entirely a land war. They'll not be concerned about shipping going through the Bosphorus Straight."

Still yoked with doubt, Salvetti shrugged. "But what about the Byzantines? Sitting at the mouth of the Bosphorus Straight, they'll see your ships coming and going into the Black Sea."

"Ah, but this is not *their* war, Salvetti. Besides, don't believe for one minute that Byzantine ships won't be sailing into the Black Sea as usual. Their trade with the Orient is far, far too valuable to cut off simply because there's a war going on!"

This confused Salvetti even more, and vexation etched itself into his face. "But what do you mean 'this isn't the Byzantines' war,' Signorina? It was *they* who called on Pope Urban for assistance against the Turks."

"Yes, yes, of course… but I doubt Emperor Alexius intends to actively engage himself or his army in this war. I know him too well. He'll leave that to the Latins while the Byzantines remain at home."

Salvetti found this impossible. Shaking his head, he was about to contest such a preposterous assumption. Still, he knew la Signorina had a network of spies in Constantinople as well as in all other major maritime centers of trade. This fact, coupled with her keen intuition for shifts in the political fortunes of the continent, caused him to balk. Her espionage network and unique business acumen had always given her a jump on competitors, especially in the midst of political turmoil. "Yes, Signorina," he said with reluctant acknowledgment, "you're on the mark– Emperor Alexius would not wish to lose his trade to the Orient, even during war. Still, it makes little sense to me that he would continue trading with the enemy."

"Money drives this world, Salvetti, even more so than war," said Mala, amused by the expression of perplexity on Salvetti's face. "And this particular war is going to be rather interesting, so let me lay out the future landscape for you. To begin, reports have already surfaced about squabbling amongst Christian crusaders over leadership and logistics, and they've yet to even leave the continent. You need to realize then that once they actually begin to *move*, the inner discourse will get worse, especially once they arrive in Constantinople where squabbling will then also break out between the Latins and the Greeks. There are questionable and fragile alliances in place already amongst the crusaders, not to mention that the Byzantines greatly distrust Bohemud and the Italian Normans who they've been fighting for years. Consequently, Emperor Alexius is forced to allow them to march right through the entirety of Byzantium. These alliances were easily made, and will be just as easily broken. On top of everything else, there's that ridiculous Peasants' Crusade lurking about the continent, and it's bound to cause problems for both crusaders and Byzantines alike. Do you begin to see the *mess* that's developing here, Salvetti?"

Salvetti possessed only a vague awareness of the political details she was describing, but knew she had a far higher capacity for understanding such intricacies than he did. "Si," he agreed, "there appears to be a certain level of confusion."

"Just as there's division and distrust amongst the Christians," Mala continued, "the very same exists amongst the Muslims, perhaps on an even *greater* scale. For centuries now there's been this never-ending blood feud in the Muslim world between the Sunni and Shia factions, not to mention old feuds between the Turks and Saracens since the Turks conquered Baghdad. Even now there's endless bickering and war amongst the Danishmends, Manjujekids, Saltuqids, Chaka, Artuqids, and Akhlat-Shahs."

"Oh, Signorina," groaned Salvetti, "but how do you keep track of all these things?"

"It's business," replied Mala. "So you see, it's all quite simple. This war will turn into 'everyone for themselves.' In the end, nobody on either side will care what I'm doing or who I'm trading with. They'll be too occupied nipping at each other... plus they'll *all* need my services. Additionally, there are other merchants out there on both sides, exactly like me, who understand that trading and transport opportunities will flourish, not decline. Yes, Salvetti, wait and see for yourself. This war will be good for trade, so it will be good for Genoa."

"Ah, Signorina, I begin to see. But a question. Do we care, then, who wins?"

"Yes, of course we do! We would hope that Western Europe prevails. Listen closely Salvetti, I said *prevail* because no one will *win*, even if there's a victor."

"No one will win, even if there's a victor?" repeated Salvetti, confused. "Oh, but Signorina, you're talking in circles and continue to confound me more with each statement! How can nobody win if one side is victorious over the other?"

"*Salvetti*," said Mala, her tone beginning to scold, "do you really think anyone can actually *win* a war such as this? Over race, religion, culture? And over a city so sacred to Christians, Muslims, and Jews alike? No. Once this first episode is finished there'll simply be another one later, then another, and another. No race would surrender their most holy of cities, unless they're willing to disappear from this earth forever."

She was about to expound on this point when a servant rang a bell and entered the room. "Signorina," the maid said, "a messenger from Germany has arrived. I inquired whether the messenger needed to see you, but he simply asked me to make sure that you received this note." She then handed over a sealed envelope and added, "I believe the man said it came from Cologne, Germany."

"Grazie," said Mala, grasping the envelope, dismissing the girl.

"Do you wish me to leave, Signorina?" asked Salvetti, expecting also to be dismissed.

"No," said Mala, "this may pertain to you somewhat."

This comment intrigued Salvetti though he dared not say another word as she broke the seal on the correspondence and began reading the message. He had no way of knowing that the message was from the little bearded man who had come to the office over a month earlier, although he could see la Gran Signorina was deeply absorbed in the letter's contents.

'The Bishop has come to Cologne to negotiate with Peter the Hermit,' began the message. 'His purpose, apparently, was to bring the so-called Peasants' Crusade to an end, but in this he has failed. As a result, by the time you receive this communication, the Bishop will be on his way to the Balkans with his brother and the contingent of Tuscan knights and footmen who accompanied him to Germany. The Bishop's intent is to now follow Peter the Hermit's peasant crusaders to Constantinople. Anticipated arrival to that city, if nothing goes awry, will be early August. Please know that this information is well substantiated and comes directly from the nephew of Peter the Hermit himself, a pleasant young man by the name of Innocenzo whom I have come to know and have spent a good deal of time with here in Cologne. Having completed my mission and being well compensated for such in advance, I will soon be returning to Genoa. Should you need my services in the future, you know how to contact me. Your faithful ear to the ground, Benito Fazio.'

Mala read the note again, then looked at Salvetti. "It's early June, Salvetti," she said. "Please begin making preparations for a fleet of six of my ships to arrive in Constantinople by the end of July."

"*Six* ships, Signorina?"

"Yes, and notify Captain Moreno that he's to mobilize my Personal Guard and that they will be accompanying us to Constantinople as well."

"*Us*?" said Salvetti.

"Yes, you are coming to Constantinople with me, Salvetti. Also tell Captain Moreno that we'll be shipping full armor, weaponry, and horses for my Guard, and to bring along an extra twenty horses or so. We'll be setting up at the estate I recently purchased along the harbor of Constantinople."

Startled, Salvetti sat back in his chair, blinking several times in succession. "B-but Signorina, we're not going to w-war, are we?" he asked nervously.

"No, probably not, Salvetti. But if war were to come to *us*, we would certainly not wish to be caught off guard, would we?"

## Chapter Thirty-nine

### Hungary… and Dissent

As the Peasants' Crusade and Count Emicho's troops moved south through Germany, separately but along a similar route, the Rhineland Jews were crushed with barbaric efficiency. There were also two other large bands of crusaders that had formed in Germany, and they too were slaughtering Jews on their march toward Constantinople. The first of these was led by a priest named Volkmar from Saxony who persecuted the Jews of Magdeburg, then later the Jews of Prague in Bohemia. The second was a monk named Gottschalk who punished Jews throughout the Rhineland, Lorraine, and into Hungary. The only Jews spared the wrath of these roving hordes were those who either managed to flee or agreed to convert to Christianity, such as in Regensburg where the entire Jewish community was rounded up and driven into the Danube where a mass baptism was performed.

It should be noted that the official position of King Heinrich IV of Germany was one of tolerance toward Jews; he had even issued an order that Jews were not to be molested as crusaders marched through his realm. Despite this the anti-Semitic mobs little feared retribution since the local courts had no jurisdiction to pursue or take action beyond their own localities. Compounding this legal handcuff was the fact that the anonymity of these huge groups made it nearly impossible to identify or prosecute specific offenders. For these same reasons, the Catholic Church's official position of tolerance toward the Jews was also widely ignored, even despite the threat of excommunication.

The question arises: what was the cause of this hatred of Jews? There were, in actuality, many. The root cause, inarguably, was that many Christians blamed the Jews for killing Christ. Also, Jews were not viewed as fellow countrymen but as foreigners clinging to their strange traditions and faith. Igniting this intolerance yet more, at this particular point in history, was the Vatican's recent attempt to fan the flames of intolerance against Islam and the Turks. Though it may not have been Pope Urban's intention, the end result of his strategy was that vitriolic intolerance was fueled against *everyone* that was not Christian. Another nail in the Semitic coffin was the issue of money lending. Unlike Greek Orthodox Christianity, Roman Catholic law forbade usury and other forms of money lending for profit. This left money lending to the Jews, which caused widespread resentment against them throughout Western Europe.

Many members of the nobility found themselves going into debt to Jewish moneylenders to finance weaponry, manpower and travel for the crusade. Having thus armed themselves with Jewish money to fight heathens, many of these crusaders simply interpreted the murder of the Jewish race as an extension of fighting heathen Turks. In truth, an equal number of crusaders had been financially fleeced by high clerics of the Church paying pennies on the pound and mortgaging their estates for a fraction of their true worth. Either missing or ignoring this analogy, no collective hue and cry was raised against bishops and archbishops enriching themselves. This, for some reason, was reserved for the Jews.

There was yet another issue slinking in the shadows. It was believed in certain quarters that Jewish entrepreneurs were actively engaged in the abduction of Europeans for slave trade enterprises with Arabs and Turks. Muslims of North Africa, Spain, and the Near East paid premium prices for young, light-skinned males for sexual exploitation or castration as eunuchs, as well as for young light-skinned females to add variety to the harems of wealthy Islamic aristocrats. Younger children were especially prized. As these rumors and stories proliferated, it raised yet another black mark against Judaism.

Walter Sansavoir and his army, preceding the Hermit's army, actually marched their way through France and Germany without persecuting Jews, although a handful of his officers such as Geoffrey Burrel managed to slip away from time to time to join Jewish pograms. As an earnestly religious man who followed the commands of the Church, Sansavoir rode herd on his recruited army of knights and footmen, leading by example, constantly encouraging his troops to demonstrate moral behavior.

Conversely, Geoffrey Burrel subverted such modeling, encouraging both intolerance and infractions. Regardless, the march remained peaceful until Sansavoir's army reached the city of Belgrade in Bulgaria, sitting immediately across the Hungarian border upon the confluence of the Danube and Sava Rivers.

Bluntly, the military commander of Belgrade refused them entry into the city. Word had filtered to certain Bulgarian aristocratic circles about the approaching holy war, but not to the entire country. Even those who knew of it had heard nothing of crusaders marching across their borders. Growing suspicious, feeling threatened by the appearance from nowhere of such a large foreign army, the Belgrade military commander refused Sansavoir's explanations.

This, in essence, now meant Sansavoir's French crusaders were denied markets, food, and lodging areas to pitch camp. Burrel became incensed by this Bulgarian slight, and as Sansavoir struggled to seek a solution, Burrel began spreading dissension amongst his fellow knights. "These bastard Bulgarians have delivered not just a slap in *our* face, but have also affronted the Pope– and France as well, by damn! We risk our damned lives upholding Christianity, yet these Bulgarian vermin refuse us the slightest gesture of hospitality!? Well then, let's turn back for Hungary. But when we cross the river, we'll no longer *ask* for anything! We'll take it!"

Thus inflamed by Geoffrey Burrel, over half of Sansavoir's knights and footmen angrily crossed the water and began pillaging the countryside back on the other side of the Sava River in Hungary to seek food. Although some violence did occur, this pillaging was aimed more toward the purpose of re-supplying than the intent to kill foreigners. Nonetheless, this sudden and unexpected disturbance alarmed the Hungarians, and during the tussle, sixteen French crusaders were captured while stealing from a market in the city of Zemun. Angry Hungarians stripped the thieves and hung their suits of armor from the walls of the city to serve as warning to others to not plunder their vicinity. Many of Sansavoir's troops, already inflamed by Burrel, grew angry at seeing the French armor hanging from the city walls.

Again, Burrel came to the fore, seizing the opportunity to instigate yet more violence. "Look yonder, men, the people of Zemun have murdered our comrades and now hang their suits of armor on the walls like hunting trophies! No more restraint, I say! To hell with these goddamned Hungarians and Bulgarians alike!"

Half an hour later a full blown armed conflict broke out between the French crusaders and the city militia of Zemun. During this battle, some of Sansavoir's troops retreated back over the river and sought refuge in a church. Although they knew they were not welcome in Belgrade or even on Bulgarian soil, they were certain the Bulgarians, as fellow Christians, would respect the sanctity of church grounds. Frightened by what had broken out across the river in Hungary, thinking it would soon bleed over to Belgrade, the commander of the Belgrade militia ordered an attack on the church where the French crusaders were hiding. Circling it, his troops set the church ablaze, burning every man within alive.

Routed thus from Zemun and Belgrade both, Sansavoir and Burrel gathered their troops and quickly made south for the safety of Byzantine territory and the city of Niš. The commander of Niš was expecting the arrival of crusaders from Western Europe, but not for another half year or more. What's this?" he asked Sansavoir, spotting wounded men amongst the foreign troops now assembled beneath the city gate.

"We're French crusaders," Sansavoir answered, exhausted from the retreat from Zemun and Belgrade. "We ran into trouble across your border on the way here, and now seek your assistance– and markets as well. My men are spent and the horses are starving."

"*French crusaders?*" queried the Byzantine commander. "But we received recent reports from Constantinople that you'd not be arriving until next spring. According to communications from Rome, your pope claims his armies have been long delayed by logistics and such."

"Yes, yes," interrupted Burrel, his horse stottering with impatience, "so we're early, dammit! Are you going to let us in, or are we to bake out here in the sun all damned day?"

"Very well," grunted the Byzantine commander. Though irritated by Burrel's manner, he clearly understood that these men at the foot of the gate had come to fight the Turks, and that suited him enough to gesture to his gate guards. "Let them in," he ordered, "but keep an eye to them, dammit."

The French remained there four days, and despite Burrel's rudeness, were well received for the most part because of

Sansavoir. The Byzantine commander then escorted them further south where they were met by another Byzantine contingent that escorted them to Constantinople without further incident.

***

Peter the Hermit and the main force of the Peasants' Crusade were moving at a slower pace than Sansavoir through Germany and Hungary. Along the way, unfortunately, the Hermit gradually began to lose control of certain elements of his following. A good number of his people had participated in the murder of Jews in Cologne and continued this practice whenever possible during the march to Hungary. There were also many within the march who possessed nothing in life to begin with, and had simply joined the Hermit as an escape from their existence of dreariness and hopeless poverty. Certain others viewed the expedition purely from the viewpoint of adventure, especially stray knights and footmen who lacked employment, as well as young boys and men who had little to lose.

Inevitably, as in any great congregation of the poor and dispossessed, there existed a certain criminal element within the Hermit's horde that smelled endless opportunities for plunder from hapless victims along the road eastward, as well, even, from fellow crusaders more fortunate than themselves.

This combination of dubious and malicious motivations made for a volatile mix, something the Hermit had not anticipated. Naively driven by the tug of his own narcissism, he had deceived himself into thinking those following him to the Holy Land were entirely motivated by faith, salvation, and the fire of his own boundless spirituality.

More than anyone else in the Hermit's ranks, it was the devious Tafur who was the root of misdirection and misguidance. As a false knight, of course, Tafur had never been in command of anyone or anything. Now, as 'King of the Beggars' amongst his so-called Tafurs, he was basking in the authority he had cultivated… and hungered for yet more.

His burgeoning core of peasant warriors had evolved into an intimidating presence within the march itself, being comprised of the most malevolent and violent men of the entire horde. Their penchant for violence spread fear throughout the march, and it did not take them long to begin forcing their will upon others. Their actions included rape and plunder as well as torturing or murdering people both within the march and along the road to Constantinople. Increasingly, these outlaws openly looked to the sadistic Tafur for leadership rather than to Peter the Hermit. As much of Tafur's chicanery was committed behind the Hermit's back, Peter was not fully aware that his peasant commander was causing an erosion of order and discipline within the march, although he *was* getting the sense that Tafur no longer came to him for instructions or permission.

Subsequently, as the Peasants' Crusade moved forward with increasing criminality and violence, word circulated in advance of them. Many towns locked their gates and refused market access to the Hermit's horde. This aroused cries of retribution from Tafur and his followers, which in turn gave rise to civil disturbances and bloody clashes with locals. The Hermit did his best to quell such conflicts, but Sansavoir had taken the vast majority of knights and armed troops along with him in the advance march; without their military assistance, the Hermit's efforts to maintain order within his ranks became more and more ineffectual. At times Innocenzo, with the help of his new friend Fazio whom he had convinced at the final moment to join the crusade, attempted to assist his uncle in settling the masses. Fazio, so tiny in stature, was often ridiculed or beaten, and Innocenzo, a fear-driven coward, became increasingly apprehensive about hooligans such as Tafur and his henchmen. In the end, their efforts to intervene quickly became more and more tepid.

This growing unrest within his crusade as it moved through Hungary soon began to take a creeping toll on Peter the Hermit himself, sapping his once inexhaustible well of energy. More significantly, it chipped away at his certainty and his will. He began to feel the crush of discouragement descending on his normally unshakable shoulders.

Since leaving Amiens, France, after traveling all day, he had preached every single evening into the late hours of night. He might have alleviated this frenetic schedule during his stay in Cologne, but when not bickering with city officials, he had also preached day and night there to raise money and recruit more followers. That aside, he also found himself constantly herding miscreants, struggling to calm angry crowds, and quelling constant discontent amongst his flock.

Meanwhile, the very approach of the Peasants' Crusade was looked upon with more and more dread as his followers more and more began to ignore or even openly disobey him.

Peter the Hermit began to sense he was losing control of his own mission, which in turn began to drain both his mental perseverance and his physical stamina. "Oh, Innocenzo," he complained bitterly, his nerves drawing taut, "what's happening here? Is God abandoning me though I dutifully perform his labors?"

"It's Tafur and his like who are causing it, Uncle," replied Innocenzo, "yet you continue to treat him with deference."

"Aye," agreed Fazio, "Tafur is a disease within your flock, and if something's not done, he will soon take over the march…"

## Chapter Forty

### Zemun and Belgrade

Rumors of the Jewish pogroms and destruction being committed by the Peasants' Crusade had filtered across the German border to Hungary, creating apprehension as the great march approached. Nonetheless, King Coloman, recently crowned ruler of Hungary, agreed to allow the Hermit's horde to march through his country despite pleas of his subjects living near the German border, standing in the immediate path of the oncoming march. As he had hoped, the Peasants' Crusade made their way nearly through all of Hungary with little controversy and few disturbances.

This changed drastically when the peasant army reached the Hungarian-Bulgarian border at Zemun. Cautious city officials of Zemun, recalling the earlier pillaging of Walter Sansavoir's French military crusaders, insisted that any markets set up for the Hermit's march be set up outside the city walls. Furthermore, it was decided to lock the city gates to this huge influx of raggedy foreigners. So it was that as the Peasant's Crusade converged on Zemun, the marchers were informed they would be not allowed to enter the city itself.

This aroused immediate offense and agitation within the Hermit's ranks, which began to manifest itself as soon as the crusader masses began bartering for goods. Moreover, from their position within the market that had been erected beyond the city walls, the crusaders could not help but catch sight of the sixteen suits of French armor hanging from the ramparts of Zemun. This gave rise to grumbling, which in turn began to generate a combustible climate of resentment and retribution.

"Hey, but look there," insisted Tafur as he and his minions added tinder to the woodpile, "it's the French armor of Walter Sansavoir's men! What have these damned Hungarian people done to our fellow crusaders?! They've undoubtedly slaughtered the entirety of Sansavoir's force, and are hiding the corpses within the city– which is why they refuse to let us enter!"

Thus fomenting suspicion and goading others into believing the Hungarians had committed an atrocity against fellow Christians, Tafur and his renegades caused resentment to swell within the peasant horde. Soon the entire march was infected. Smelling trouble, several of the Zemun merchants grew fearful, packing their wares and closing their stalls. This further incited the mob, elevating their mood of suppressed rage to the brink of open fury. As with all conflagrations, it would now take but a tiny spark to cause an eruption, which in this case proved to be... a pair of shoes.

Two peasants lacking footwear began to wrangle with a young Hungarian boy who was tending his father's stall. Attempting to acquire a particular pair of shoes for next to nothing, one of the peasants tried to turn the Hungarian youth's inexperience against him. The youth, fearing his absent father's hand, remained insistent about the price and refused to give ground. As voices escalated, the father showed up. He was a large, brutish man and his temperament was as dark as the black woolen tunic covering his frame.

As frequently happens with men like this who have shouldered and bullied others since boyhood, his temper outweighed his judgment. Disregarding the mood of the mob, he shoved one of the peasants aside, grabbed the shoes from the other, and slapped him across the face. "Get your thieving fingers away from here or I'll kick your filthy French asses back where they belong!" the man raged.

At that very moment Tafur and three of his hoodlums happened by, and despite the vendor's massive size, Tafur swiftly swung his staff about, shoving its tip into the man's chest, pushing him back. "Who the hell do you think you are, you fat Hungarian bastard!" he shouted.

Surprised, but undaunted, the big man briefly sized up the four men now standing before him. Despite the crosses branded across their foreheads making them appear fearsome, the man had a trump card. Whistling, he called to his brother who was manning the adjacent stall, standing even larger than himself. As his brother stepped over, the first vendor turned, grabbed Tafur's staff, and pulled it free of his grip. "*We'll kick your little French asses*!" he bellowed, waving the staff in circles.

Tafur gave an imperceptible nod to the others, and without a word, he and his men lunged at both him and the approaching brother, taking them to the ground– but only briefly. The two massive Hungarians surged to their feet, rising like two great bears on hind quarters, flinging their attackers to the side like rag-toys.

Neither of the burly Hungarians had taken account of the fact that, at the time, their stalls were surrounded by over thirty other men carrying brands on their foreheads. As if on signal, every one of them instinctively swarmed into the mêlée, burying the vendors much as a swarm of bees would inhume an intruder. Seeing this, the vendor's son dove into the fray despite his diminutive size, which drew the support of three fellow vendors from nearby stalls. As they jumped into the fracas, they frantically called for help from other vendors as shoes, blankets, and stall tables toppled, flying in every direction.

The brawl spread like wildfire up and down the market aisles. Hundreds upon hundreds of crusaders viciously attacked any vendor within reach, overturning and looting stalls as the squabble over a pair of shoes erupted into a full scale riot. The Tafurs within the crowd, numbering several thousand, surreptitiously brandished weapons and turned the fisticuffs into a vicious outbreak of violence and murder as their rampage moved from the market area, spilling into the city of Zemun itself before the militia could manage to shut and lock the gates; they had opened them temporarily to provide escape for fleeing Hungarian vendors. Spotting their fellow citizens being murdered by the hundreds upon their own city streets, Hungarians began to flee the city through an eastern gate to the banks of the Danube. There 7,000 of them, many being members of the city militia, managed to regroup, massing themselves atop the summit of a steep hill to set up a defense. The crusaders, led by Tafur and his peasant fanatics, charged the slope. What followed was a bloody confrontation between Zemun militia defending the rise and attacking peasants climbing the rise, berserk with rage. As swords and pikes held the hill, axes, staffs, shovels, and forks attacked the hill, and in the see-saw confusion of it all, Hungarian women and children were caught in the midst, trampled beneath the battling surge of Hungarians and foreigners alike. Worse yet, the attacking peasants next began singling them out as marks, killing them indiscriminately.

While this bloody rampage escalated, within the city remaining Hungarians were chased down, women were raped, children and babies skewered by forks and staffs, and men's bodies mutilated by dismemberment and beheading. Within a matter of three hours, the entire city of Zemun had been overrun, and lost. The riot, now at its peak, would last four more days before running its course.

Meanwhile, as the bedlam escalated, the terrified people of Belgrade were watching events from atop their city ramparts across the river. Horrified, they began to realize that the rampaging foreign crusaders were now disassembling houses and building rafts to ferry their way across the Sava. Leaving everything behind, they began to flee their city in packs, seeking refuge in the forests. It so happened that a battalion of Pecheneg mercenaries had arrived in Belgrade a few days earlier seeking work in Bulgaria and Hungary. City officials, running for safety, as a last act bargained with them to remain behind for the purpose of maintaining order as the crusaders ferried across the river and entered the city. To the relief of the fleeing city officials, the Pechnegs began arming themselves, agreeing to convince the crusaders not to burn down or raze the city. It may have seemed a dubious decision, but the Pechenegs could see from their positions that the 'so-called' crusaders appeared to be little more than a mob of peasants running amuck, poorly armed.

Since departing Cologne, Guillaume had ordered his Tuscan battalion to march and maintain a distance of one or two full days behind the Peasants' Crusade. This distance was carefully maintained throughout Germany and Hungary, as Guillaume and Handel were both insistent about not getting caught up in the outlawry and hooliganism of the Hermit's mob. Guillaume's advance scouts had reported back on several clashes between the peasant army and towns along the route, which only confirmed to Guillaume and Handel that they had made the appropriate decision. Tristan, on the other hand, had become apprehensive on hearing these reports and suggested on several occasions that it might be wise for Guillaume's battalion to intervene– primarily to ensure the safety of the women, children, and elderly making up a good part of the Hermit's following.

"Hell no," insisted Handel, "we've no responsibility to protect thieves, looters, and murderers of Jews, I'd say!"

"Be reasonable," Tristan would insist, "the helpless are not the ones causing the trouble, but Tafur, Burrel, and others."

"No, I'll not do it," declared Guillaume, giving no ground. "Our commission from Pope Urban is to protect the Peasants' Crusade from the *Turks*, not from fellow Christians, and we're a good distance yet from the Turkish border. Besides, if the Peasants' Crusade would simply act civilized, they'd encounter no problems. Aye, let the Hermit control his own flock and the mayhem they breed. After all, *he's* the one who gathered them!"

In the end, Tristan realized Handel and Guillaume were correct. Yet, he frequently worried about the many members of the wayward crusade who were innocent of wrongdoing, especially the women, children, and elderly. Nonetheless, he decided to quell his requests for intervention– until the day the Tuscan force approached the Hungarian-Bulgarian border. Tristan and the others had no idea that the peasants had delayed to ravage Zemun, nor that, as a result of this action, they were now located less than an hour ahead.

As the Tuscan force unwittingly neared the rampaging Peasants' Crusade, one of their Tuscan scouts came riding hard toward their column just before dusk. "Fighting's broken out just ahead in Zemun!" the scout decreed.

"Aw, shit," groaned Handel, "yet another disturbance caused by the Hermit's crowd?"

"Nay, far more than a disturbance, Handel, it's a full battle!" the scout replied. "And the dead are piling up like cord-wood, by the thousands! There's a major fight going on upon a rise along the river bank outside the city. The Hungarians must have come out in force to attack the crusaders!"

In his haste, the scout had not taken time to learn how the fray started. In his defense, it was more than reasonable to assume that since the Hungarians had left the haven of their own city walls, they must have been on the offensive, and were therefore the aggressors. He was also mistaken in that what he witnessed was a battle, having no idea that it was, in actuality, a massacre.

"What?" queried Guillaume, stunned. "Thousands of dead, you say?"

"Yes!" the scout answered, looking harried.

"Well, you can bet your ass the Hungarians didn't start this shit," fumed Handel.

"*Guillaume*," pressed Tristan, alarmed, though his voice took on the tone of command. "I've tried hard to hold my tongue about intervening on behalf of the Peasants' Crusade, but now you best move your troops forward quickly! With thousands of peasants dying in this assault by the Hungarians, they surely need our help. The Pope would not abide by us remaining idle under such circumstances. Sound the attack and pull them from the fire, I beg you!"

Guillaume looked over at Handel, then at the Danes, but none offered counsel. "Very well, Tristan," nodded Guillaume. Motioning to his signalman to trumpet the attack, he and the Danes triggered their mounts forward in tight formation as the Tuscan knights followed. Behind them, footmen cinched their straps, secured their packs, and moved forward at a paced run, also remaining in tight formation. Handel, meanwhile, had not moved. Sitting there atop his mount, he shook his head with disgust, cursing the Hermit. Finally, he kicked his horse in the flanks and took off at a gallop. "*Scheisse!*" he muttered.

Half a mile ahead on a hill east of Zemun's city walls, a bloody struggle was raging between the Hungarians and the peasants. Darkness was beginning to settle over the landscape, and as the Tuscan force neared the rise, cries of battle could be heard, accompanied by the clanging of iron and the wailing of war.

Guillaume and the Danes were the first to charge into the chaos. In the blazing light of fires coming from the city of Zemun, which had by now descended into an inferno, they quickly found themselves embroiled in a hellish scene of confusion and mayhem on the hillside. Men were fighting and murdering each other, women and children were wailing and running amok, and the blaze burning the city had begun now to spread outside and crawl its way up the hill.

"What do we do!" yelled Crowbones, wrenching his horse one way then another, trying to make sense of what they had entered.

It was impossible to tell who was whom or what was what. Next to him, Orla caught sight of several Hungarian militiamen falling on a group of peasant crusaders armed only with staffs and pitchforks. Instinctively, he kicked his horse forward and charged directly into the midst of the fight to scatter the Hungarians, felling one quickly with his ax. As the entangled mass scattered, Orla saw in the fire light that one of the peasants was pulling his fork from the torso of a woman laying wounded upon the ground, desperately shielding an infant in her arms. Gazing up at Orla, her eyes half-lidded, nearly dead, she threw a hand upwards in a gesture for help. She then tried to cry out, but the blood gushing from her mouth drowned her words in a bubbling gurgle of scarlet horror. Before he could react, Orla next saw the peasant's fork come down again, this time puncturing clean through the wailing infant's back. The peasant, a Tafur, then raised his fork and the impaled infant to the fiery night sky with a shriek of triumph, waving the dead infant about as one would wave a victory banner.

Orla stopped dead, shocked, realizing that the Hungarian militiaman he had just slain had only been trying to defend the woman and her child. Most of Orla's life had been spent at war, thus bloodletting bothered him little. Over time he had seen soldiers butchered, mutilated and eviscerated, having contributed more than his own share to the murdering of other men. But the sight of this woman and infant being so needlessly and joyfully slaughtered was more than he could tolerate. Looking about with alarm, it next dawned on him that most of those at the very top of the rise were Hungarians, many being women and children– and they were being slaughtered by the peasant Tafurs. Furious, Orla spurred his horse at the man waving the infant back and forth, and with one sweep of his ax cleaved the man's head from his shoulders. "You murderous bastard!" Orla bellowed.

Crowbones had just slain two Hungarian militia men and another Hungarian not in uniform who came at him with a knife. Looking up, he happened to catch Orla's ax dispatching the peasant, having failed to see what the peasant had done to the woman and the baby. Confused, thinking Orla had either lost his mind or could not clearly differentiate friend from foe in the chaos of Zemun's flames, Crowbones spurred his horse to Orla's side and shouted, "What in hell are you doing, Brother! You've just killed a crusader!"

Hroc was nearby, and from his mounted position was bludgeoning anyone who appeared to be attacking peasants or people in French dress. Heaving his hammer left then right, skillfully maneuvering his horse as a battering ram, he created a deadly swath of destruction through the Hungarian ranks, as though scything wheat. In the dimming light, hearing high-pitched foreign cries underfoot, he suddenly became aware that he was also trampling over women and children. Cursing himself, he bulled forward into a wall of Hungarian militia.

Crowbones, still shouting, reached out with his only arm, grabbing at Orla's arm in an attempt to stop any further misdirected attacks.

Waving him off furiously, Orla cried hoarsely, "It's these bastards of the Hermit! *They're* doing the murdering here, not the Hungarians!"

Hroc was still advancing, crushing Hungarian skulls and trampling over militia who were trying to hold the hill when he felt a strong arm grab his wrist just as he was about to dispatch yet another Hungarian in his path.

It was Guthroth. "N-no, Hroc!" Guthroth stammered. "St-stop! These people of Zemun only f-fight for their l-lives!"

"What are you doing?" shouted Hroc, pulling his arm free. "These Hungarians have attacked the peasants and are murdering them!"

"N-no," insisted Guthroth, prying the hammer from Hroc's grip, "th-they've fled the city and are m-making for safety! Stop!"

By this time the main body of Tuscan knights and footmen had entered the half-lit chaos, setting themselves upon anyone who appeared to be wearing Hungarian garb. Distinctly aware that the Tuscan army that had been following them for the past month had now entered the fray, a hue and cry arose amongst the peasant crusaders. Thinking the Tuscans had come to help slaughter the Hungarians, the peasants began to run even more wild, murdering Hungarians with more fervor and confidence than before.

Handel was sitting atop his horse next to Tristan, glancing about, refusing to take action until he had deciphered what was occurring around them. Clapping a hand to his forehead, he realized, like Orla and Guthroth, that it was not the peasant crusaders who were in peril. Rather, they were the aggressors and had invaded the city and set it ablaze, murdering everyone they could seize. Tristan, simultaneously, came to the same bewildering conclusion and the two men looked at each other a moment, thunderstruck.

"God in Heaven!" Tristan cried, looking about as Tuscan knights and footmen slew one Hungarian after another. "*Wh-what have I done!?*"

"We've got to stop our own men!" shouted Handel, kicking his horse toward Guillaume and the Danes. "Do you see what's happening here?"

"J-ja!" hollered Guthroth. "We've g-got to end it! Hroc, c-come along!"

Orla and Crowbones joined them, as did Handel, and they desperately began shouting at and intervening with their own troops. Guillaume, meanwhile, had his signalman trumpet the cease fighting call. This confused the Tuscans at first, and it took several minutes to bring their fighting to a halt. The trumpet call did nothing, however, to still the Tafurs and other crusaders who continued to butcher the city population.

"Goddammit," cursed Handel, "we've got to end this, Guillaume! Set your troops against the crusaders *now* or regret your inaction till the end of your days!"

Guillaume, who had never once hesitated in battle– now did. His unassailable courage was momentarily undone by the impossibility of circumstances before him. Things were upside down and irrefutably inverted. Dumbfounded, he sat there staring blankly at Handel, torn over setting his troops upon the masses of French and German peasants and smattering of crusading men-at-arms in their midst.

It was Guthroth, bridling in next to him on his charging destrier, who shook Guillaume violently by the shoulders. "D-do it!" he shouted, his eyes afire.

Jolted from indecision, Guillaume surged forward, shouting counter-commands to his knights and footmen, who now became more confused than ever. Still, they followed orders and set themselves against the Hermit's horde. They tried to intervene with reason at first, but the passion of the Hermit's combined French and German mob refused to be quelled, and most quickly turned their bloodlust onto the Tuscans themselves. Thus snared, the Tuscan troops abandoned all restraint and tore into the peasant masses with a vengeance. Within minutes, hundreds of peasant warriors began to drop.

Tafur, caught in the midst of this bloody turn of events, found himself standing just twenty feet from Tristan. Seeing him, Tafur flew into a rage, focusing the entirety of his anger on Tristan because he believed him to be in command of the Tuscan force. "Oh, you murdering bastard!" Tafur screamed. "Such treachery coming from a man of the Church! Be damned, Saint-Germain!"

Tristan was still frozen atop his horse in stoop-shouldered silence, numbly staring at the dead strewn as far as the dwindling firelight allowed his eyes to see. But Tafur's ringing accusations brought him back. At the sound of his name, Tristan glanced aside, recognizing Tafur's hate-filled face. By now, however, the atrocities committed by the peasants had fully registered in Tristan's mind, and Tristan was lost to his own uncontrollable swell of fury. "Oh, it's you, you ungodly beast!" Tristan raged. "You, somehow, are behind this butchery!"

Tafur spat, violently grabbing the man next to him and pointing at Tristan. "Kill that bastard for me, Dupuis!" he shrieked with single-minded fury.

Marcel Dupuis was leaned over, withdrawing his dagger from the body of a young Hungarian boy who was the same age as his own eldest son. He had not killed the boy, but having lost his scythe, was merely trying to retrieve a weapon. Looking up on hearing Tafur's command, Dupuis followed Tafur's finger, shocked to see that Bishop Saint-Germain was the target of Tafur's order. Straightening himself, he gave Tafur a questioning look. "B-but– he's a bishop of the Church..." he muttered dumbly. Although he himself had shouted threats encouraging Count Emicho to hang Bishop Saint-Germain back in Cologne, it had all been for show. In truth, Dupuis had been brought up by his peasant parents to both fear and revere all men of the cloth.

"*Goddammit, Dupuis*!" screamed Tafur, "Did you not hear me! *I said kill that bastard now*!"

Since birth, violence had actually been at variance with Marcel Dupuis' decent character. Rather, he had always been a meek follower, which is how his wife, Estelle, had been able to so easily herd him about since the first days of their union. But on that fateful day Tafur had administered the brand of the crucifix on Dupuis' forehead, Dupuis had felt himself being swept into the thrashing current of something far beyond his capacity to resist. For the first time ever, as the white-hot brand had melted and seared his skin that night, Dupuis experienced a compelling surge of manhood, sensing himself included in something consequential. Yet, since taking the brand, he had also discovered himself in one crisis of conscience after another.

Shortly after the German farm incident when he had been forced to strip and mount the German farm-wife, he found himself in Cologne taking human blood for the first time in his life. He murdered an old Jewish woman on the day Count Emicho had swept into the Jewish quarter. He had spent the first part of that day running about, yelling and shouting, chasing terrified Jews. He did this only to satisfy his peers, yet deliberately refrained from actually injuring anyone. In the chaos of the day, his ploy seemed to be working. Then, at one point he inadvertently cornered an old Jewish woman in a shop.

"Run out the back door!" he whispered, pointing her to safety. "Be quick!"

Before the old woman could gain her feet, a stampede of footsteps ensued. Looking behind him, the shop filled with a dozen Tafurs. "Ha!" snarled one of them, a big man named Nardier, "finally you show some balls, Dupuis! But don't let us stop you, get on with it!"

Looking first at Nardier, then glancing down at the helpless oldster huddled at his feet. Dupuis swallowed hard. Shrinking even further into the corner, the woman muttered something in German that Dupuis did not understand, yet the very tone of it was clear. She sensed somehow that Dupuis was not a murderer, and was pleading for his intervention in the face of the thugs who had interrupted him from pointing her to safety.

"Here," said Nardier, grabbing at Dupuis' pitiful knife, replacing it with a long dagger honed to a razor's edge. "This'll do a far better job than your little piece of shit."

Dupuis looked down at the woman who was now curled in a ball, her eyes staring into his, imploring for mercy. Dupuis did not wish to hurt the old woman, but as the men behind him began chanting his name, egging him on, his cowardice allowed him no choice. In a moment of supreme weakness, he raised the dagger.

Frozen with fear as the old woman gazed up at him questioningly, he plunged the dagger through her heart. Hearing the knife crunch against rib-bone, he then thought himself on the edge fainting. But the men surrounding him began shouting approval and slapping him on the back. Moments later, after the others left, Dupuis found himself falling to his knees, his throat filling with vomit.

Now, standing between Tafur and Bishop Saint-Germain, trapped in yet another snare of Tafur's devise, Dupuis began imagining the fires of Hell itself lapping at his feet if he murdered a high priest. Terrified, Dupuis' feet remain nailed in place.

It would seem that Tafur, rendered so scarlet with rage and being in such close proximity to Tristan, would have attacked Bishop Saint-Germain himself... but he did not, choosing instead to continue his rant at Dupuis. Seeing that Dupuis refused to move, Tafur angrily struck him across the back of his head and shoulders with his staff. "*Goddammit, do it, Dupuis*!" he screamed.

Hopelessly hobbled by a lifetime of Catholic dogma preaching obedience and deference to all clerics, Dupuis knew without question that he was not going to lay hands on a high bishop of the Church. But suffering from the wrath of Tafur's staff, he made a quick series of steps forward to escape its punishing blows.

Spotting this move by Dupuis, which also happened to be in the direction of Tristan, Handel's lightning reflexes kicked in, and he flung his dagger, pinning it directly into Dupuis' heart. Guillaume, who had spied Dupuis' move toward Tristan at the same moment as Handel, spurred his horse in a devastating charge forward. Arcing downward with his sword before Dupuis could fall even from the fatal dagger wound, Guillaume swiftly half-severed Dupuis' neck from his shoulder just before crushing him with the weight of his charging mount. Killed instantly, Dupuis' head lolled to one side, hanging only by neck-bone and sinews, as his body was flung aside by the horse's rampaging hooves.

Horrified, Tristan looked down at the fallen body, knowing the man was actually trying to escape Tafur rather than trying to attack. "God in Heaven, have mercy on this lost soul," he whispered, waving his hand in the sign of the cross over the corpse.

Watching everything that had transpired, and despite being the root of Dupuis' death, Tafur continued wailing at the top of his voice, trying to get others to attack Bishop Saint-Germain. But frightened by Dupuis' sudden demise, Tafur's men quickly began to melt away, seeking easier victims.

Would you like me to shut him up?!" asked Guillaume, riding up to his brother, pointing his sword at Tafur.

"N-no," stammered, Tristan, his eyes glazed, his heart drowning in remorse for the dead man at his feet. "Let him rant. He may well… have reason."

"None of this is your fault, Brother," said Guillaume, shaking his head. "You thought you were helping these people, and asked us to intervene on their behalf."

"Oh, but it *is* my fault, Guillaume," Tristan whispered. "Odo sent me to save these pitiful serfs, but they have become a monstrosity… a monstrosity that I, too, have now become a part of!"

## Chapter Forty-one

### Reflection

It was well after midnight before things settled enough for the Tuscan battalion to pitch camp, which was established but a short distance from the Zemun gates. Meanwhile, Tafur and thousands of his marauders had begun to raft their way across the river to Belgrade. The Pecheneg mercenaries who had remained behind in Belgrade, Turkish nomads who had been selling their services to any bidders needing security forces in the Balkans, tried to assist this crossing at first, demanding only that the crusaders not burn the city.

Seeing they were Muslims, Tafur and his men turned on them, efficiently decimating their ranks. "Ah!" he seethed, hoisting a Pechneg's severed head to his men, "the first Turks to meet Christian wrath!"

"*Aye, the heathen bastards!*" howled those in his wake battling the Pechenegs and crossing the Sava, by now drunk with bloodlust, lost to the inebriation of cathartic euphoria brewed by that toxic blend of misperceived invincibility and misdirected aggression. "*Spare not a one of them black bastards!*"

By contrast, the mood in the Tuscan camp was funereally subdued. "*What a goddamned mess,*" growled Handel, raising his head, looking over at the Danes and Guillaume.

"Lower your voice," muttered Guillaume. "Tristan's just there beyond the fire... he doesn't need to hear such talk. He's already flogging himself over what's occurred here."

Indeed, Tristan's face was stamped with shame; his eyes were glazed, his throat too full to speak. Staring dully into space, seeing nothing, it was Asta who finally came to mind. In his weakest moments, during his rare inner collapses, hers had always been the only voice that could muster words meaningful enough to soothe the gaping wounds of his soul. *Mother,* he thought... *oh...*

*but look what I have caused.* He struggled then to reconstruct the features of her face, hoping to find solace in it... but she would not appear, which hurt him ever more.

"Ja, just look at him," whispered Orla to the others, shaking his head as he eyed Tristan from the campfire. "The image of utter defeat and woe..."

"He was only trying to do as the Pope ordered," mumbled Crowbones, "and couldn't have guessed what was really going on ahead of us here in Zemun… no more than we could." Looking at Guthroth and Hroc, he shook his head contritely. "Shit, now I'm wondering how many innocent people I killed on the hill tonight."

"Ja, me too," nodded Hroc, passing a hand over his forehead with reflection. "I've a sick feeling in my belly, and can't shake it. I thought to be doing the right thing as I so blindly charged in."

"Don't wallow in it, Hroc," grunted Handel. "The blame isn't yours, nor any of ours, including Tristan. It's this goddamn Holy Crusade that's turned everything upside down and inside out. Propagandizing hate, murdering Jews, thieving, murdering fellow Christians… all in God's name. Yet God shan't be found in this mess, because it's a sham– devised only to raise up the Byzantine Empire!"

"You tread on thin ice, Handel," said Guillaume, sitting rigid. "Surely you don't castigate the Pope over what's occurred at the hands of this Peasants' Crusade?"

"Guillaume," replied Handel, sensing a delicate moment, yet shoving it aside, "I respect your piety, as well as your allegiance to the Vatican. I too am loyal to the Pope. But tell, man... if I did something wrong, would you timidly sit there approving of it, or would you stand up and speak!? The fact of the matter is this, regardless of Pope Urban's ultimate intent, his hands are no longer clean– not back in Rouen, not in Cologne or Worms or Maintz, and damn sure not here in Zemun! Nor will they be clean in the Holy Land. In the end it'll be the many, many innocents who suffer, as always... and but a sorry handful of the fortunate-born who benefit from the carnage of this sanctified charade!"

"In the end, *Christianity* will prevail," said Guillaume, growing cross, refusing to concede. "And *that's* all that matters."

This further agitated Handel. He leaned forward to fire back a sharp reply, but Tristan stepped closer from the darkness, quietly taking a seat next to him by the fire. His face was creased with worry and his eyes were half-closed, locked in that state of apprehension arriving when one has taken an unfortunate action that can never be reversed. Saying nothing, he stared hard into the smoldering embers of the campfire, his expression as blank as his eyes. Finally, his voice low, he said, "May God forgive me... and may each of you forgive me as well. What have I wrought here? So many dead because I– *miscalculated*."

Out of consideration, no one responded. Nor did a single one of them look at Tristan, for fear of adding to his injury. Instead, they too only stared into the fire, as lost to the hypnotic lap of flames seeking oxygen between the tangle of logs.

Thus silence and discomfort descended over the circle of light until, of all men, Guthroth spoke. "W-we m-mis-calculated also, B-Boy," he spluttered. "Let it g-go, th-then."

This touched Tristan. Nothing more meaningful could have been said at that precise moment, in such few words, with such heartfelt clarity. And the fact that it was Guthroth who had spoken it gave it even more depth.

Then a sudden clamor arose from across the river as distant flames erupted into a roaring conflagration, its many tongues licking high into the night sky. "Listen to that ruckus," said Handel, fighting to suppress anger. "Our barbarians continue their rampage now in Belgrade and torch it to the ground! But word will soon reach the Hungarian king." Spitting into the fire, he shook his head before continuing. "We'd best make tracks out of here first thing in the morning."

"Indeed," nodded Guillaume. "Once King Coloman receives word of the massacre of his subjects, he'll have the entire Hungarian army on the Hermit's trail, and ours as well. We'll receive no credit from him for trying to stop the killing, only blame."

"Aye," agreed Handel, "and the Bulgarians won't be happy either when they find out Belgrade's in flames."

"We'd best make a forced march, in all haste," said Guillaume, gathering himself, sitting back on his haunches. "It'll take King Coloman several days to muster troops, and several more yet to march here to Zemun. We might could make it to the

Byzantine border before his troops intercepts us. He'll not cross and come after us... hopefully."

"And what about the Hermit's bunch?" asked Orla.

"To Hell with them, we'll leave their asses behind," grumbled Handel.

"No," said Tristan, still staring into the fire. "Despite what happened here in Zemun, we can't leave them to the Hungarians. Odo would not abide by us abandoning them. Besides, everyone in the horde did not participate in this butchery. A great portion of them seem to be missing, and I have yet to see any trace of Peter the Hermit or Innocenzo. I find it hard to believe *their* hands are dripping with Hungarian blood. The Hungarians are Christians, after all, and the Hermit would not condone killing fellow Catholics."

"Nor did we think he'd abide by murdering Jews!" snapped Handel. "Yet he didn't lift a finger to stop it, did he?"

"Perhaps," Tristan said, looking up Handel, "but if you abandon these people, then you abandon me… for I will not leave Zemun without them."

Handel stood, his ire escalating. "*Oh, so now we protect murderers and–* "

"We take them with us," interrupted Guillame. "I'll not leave my brother behind, so it's settled, Handel." He next looked at the Danes. "Agreed?" he asked.

"Ja, agreed," they replied, without exception.

## Chapter Forty-two

### Flight

As dawn's light broke that next morning the Tuscan battalion began ferrying across the Sava, but while landing the first set of rafts along the banks, an angry mob gathered, led by Tafur. "Traitors!" he shouted, waggling a finger at Tristan as he stepped ashore. "Oh, but how many of our good crusaders did your troops kill last night?!"

This precipitated an outbreak of bitter grumbling behind him as nearly two hundred men, most with crosses branded on their foreheads, began to wave crude weapons along with swords and pikes taken from the Hungarian militia and Pecheneg mercenaries. Atop the pikes raised high were lodged Pecheneg heads taken the night before.

Orla unsheathed his sword with his right hand, pulling his ax from his belt with the left. Guthroth and Hroc followed suit while Crowbones raised his hammer high in his only hand, pointing it directly at Tafur. As this was happening, more rafts came ashore and Tuscan troops swiftly formed a phalanx at the edge of the bank.

Rallying his men, Tafur issued a signal and the entire wave of men surrounding him began to advance. Bracing for the onslaught, Guillaume's wall of men crouched defensively, tightening their ranks.

Without a word, pulling his dagger from his boot, Handel stepped in front of the Tuscan wall and flung it at Tafur's head. Through no action of his own, Tafur was at that very instant jostled to the side by one of his own advancing men, and as the dagger whistled by Tafur, Tafur heard bone cracking directly behind him. Glancing back, he saw Handel's dagger protruding from the very intersection of the cross branded into the forehead of the man who had inadvertently taken Handel's dagger. At that same moment, Hroc stepped out beside Handel and launched his ax at the man standing beside Tafur. The ax, spinning with fatal precision, cleaved the upper half of the man's skull, one side of which split aside, dropping, as would a half lopped apple.

The actions of Handel and Hroc occurred so quickly, their effect being so devastating, that Tafur and all surrounding him froze in place. Seeing this, Guillaume issued the signal for his men to charge.

But just then a loud commotion broke out behind Tafur's men. As the crowd opened, then closed behind itself, Peter the Hermit appeared, haggard and forlorn.

Whereas it was true that Tristan was buried in guilt over his insistence that Guillaume intervene on behalf of the Peasants' Crusade the night before, there was one person even more racked with shame than Tristan– Peter the Hermit. When the riot had erupted, he had actually been several miles outside of Zemun, moving ahead. Receiving word of an outbreak of violence to his rear, he returned with Innocenzo and Fazio, only to discover a hellish scene of mayhem and destruction.

After the fighting had died down, he walked among the thousands of Hungarian dead after learning how the riot had started, later estimating that nearly five thousand Hungarians had been slain. In comparison, less than four hundred peasants were killed during the Zemun rampage, many at the hands of Tuscans. Weeping openly as he had walked among the dead, he fell to his knees from time to time to pray over the Hungarian corpses.

Innocenzo had followed him throughout the night trying to console him, as did Fazio, but their efforts were futile. The Hermit had launched into another world entirely– a place where he was being flogged by the angels of Heaven upon the pillory of self perdition and guilt. The pontifical certainty that had driven him forward from the day of his birth seemed a distant, vaporous thing now. Death itself would be better than having to now shoulder the burden of all the Jewish and Christian Hungarian dead left in his wake since leaving France back in April. "Woe unto the faithful servant of God," he moaned throughout the night. "Woe unto me!"

Having suffered this hellish penance throughout the night in prayer and grief, he now glared with fury at the two opposing camps as they faced each other, weapons raised. "Oh, that Christian should turn against Christian! How can this be?!" he shouted. His face a mask of scorn, he next turned to Tafur and growled, "Get your men back, you damned viper! Aye, you've done nothing but breed discontent and spill blood since the day we left Amiens!"

Tafur, unaccustomed to being the target of such ferocity from the Hermit, motioned begrudgingly for his men to retreat from the banks of the river. "This bishop friend of yours set his troops against us last night!" he snarled. "He's a traitor, I say!"

Seeing Tristan standing behind Guillaume, the Hermit moved forward, motioning for Tristan to approach. Despite Tafur's accusation, Peter knew Tristan would never commit such an act unless warranted. "My heart weeps for the victims of Zemun, Bishop Saint-Germain, Bishop," he said solemnly. "Come, let's pray for them and hold a mass for their innocent souls this morning."

"There is no time for prayer, Peter," blurted Tristan, surprised at hearing his own words. "We must leave quickly before King Coloman musters his army, which he is surely already doing."

Then Guillaume spoke. "Byzantine territory and the city of Niš lay one week's march from here, but there's no time to tarry, Peter. Gather your people quickly and prepare them for a forced march."

At this, murmurs of discontent broke out amongst Tafur's band as many felt there was more plunder yet to be had within the remains of Belgrade. Nonetheless, Tafur was wily enough to understand the impending threat of Hungarian vengeance, as was the Hermit. Together the two quelled opposition to the immediate evacuation of Belgrade.

Within the hour, Guillaume assembled his captains and various members of the Peasants' Crusade, including the Hermit and Tafur. Despite their mutual distrust and fury at each other, in the interest of self-preservation Guillaume and Tafur managed to agree on the terms of the forced march. "We'll make haste," said Guillaume, "stopping for no purpose but to rest for a few moments at night. My Tuscan troops will serve as rear guard in case we're pursued, but we shan't be delayed by slackers. Stragglers will be left to their own devices, I promise you!"

So began the grueling march to Niš. Day after day and night after night, the tens of thousands trudged forward, catching only an hour or two of sleep at organized pauses during the night. The pace was brutal, but all understood that the fury of the Hungarian army would soon be following them, and if caught, there would be no mercy. This, to say the least, was a turn-about for the peasant crusaders, many of whom had been looting and plundering at will since joining the march. These particular miscreants had also wantonly and indiscriminately left the bodies of Jews, Hungarians, and others in their wake. Still, none of these marauders wished to become casualties themselves, so they suffered through the forced march, driven by a mingle of panic and fear of dying in a distant, foreign land.

As promised, Guillaume held his Tuscan troops to the back, serving to protect the rear flank, and also to drive the Hermit's horde forward, often beating and whipping those who lingered or fell behind. This disturbed Tristan at times, but realizing the end purpose of such action, he bit back comment. Besides, it was not his position to interfere with Guillaume's commands under such circumstances– he had made that mistake back in Zemun.

Watching as his brother relentlessly drove the monstrous train of people forward to save them, Tristan's heart could not help but swell with admiration. Guillaume was, indeed, an admirable and godly leader. *Far more so than myself*, he thought, as Zemun still weighed heavy on his mind... and thoughts of Mala began to creep into his conscience. *Oh, but seeing her now would be sweet medicine for this tormented heart*, he thought.

Other thoughts also began to weigh on Tristan's conscience as the marchers struggled to keep pace, including his own motivations in life, and his quick rise within the Church. *Have I simply been deceiving myself?* he wondered. *Have I all along sought position and power rather than taking the cloth to perform God's work? And what of Odo? Was it possible that Mala was correct in accusing him of leaving me no choice from the moment he placed me beneath his wing? Did I become a monk, not for God, but for Odo de Lagery?*

These thoughts, for some reason, shamed him even more than Zemun, and he chased them off. Yet, images of Mala continued to appear. He had not seen her in over a year now, and as he wearily plodded forward, he tried to envision the caramel sheen of her pure skin, and the richness of her thick, raven tresses.

Thus reflecting ceaselessly about Mala, he became lost then… ten years back in time along the Loire River in a gypsy camp. He remembered that first night he had found himself sleeping with her in her wagon, though they had shared nothing but conversation, memories of childhood and adolescence, and affectionate embraces. Next his thoughts transported him outside the port city of Marseilles in another gypsy camp, where he and Mala had spent the most exhilarating and passionate week of their lives, discovering affection, love, and carnal abandonment. And finally, his thoughts took him to the foot of the mountain in back in Canossa. He saw himself and Mala sitting together in the shadow of a quaint stone cottage looking out over their small farm as sheep and goats grazed peacefully along the lush meadow.

"Tristan!" a voice called, jolting him from his reverie. It was Handel. "Hey, are you awake, lad? Be careful lest you tumble from your horse."

"Yes, I'm awake," Tristan mumbled, returning from the fog of Mala.

"I'm sorry about some of the things I've said to you," muttered Handel, his eyes cast down. "Though I berate this crusade, and you championed it– I've over-spoken at times. Especially to you. Fact is, lad… you're the best man I've ever met. And a fine friend."

"Thank you, Handel," said Tristan. "That means much, coming from you." Trying to summon a grin, he nodded with a shrug. "The fact is, Handel," he continued, "other than perhaps my brother, *you* are the best man I have ever met. And a fine friend as well."

Handel tipped his head, then kicked his horse forward, leaving Tristan to his thoughts… which returned immediately to Mala.

*Am I actually living this nightmare of a Peasants' Crusade?* he wondered. *Or is it in truth the last ten years that have actually been the dream… and when I awake, Mala will be there waiting for me, wondering why I have been asleep for so long?*

## Chapter Forty-three

### Into Greek Territory

After grueling days of forced marching, Guillaume ushered the Peasants' Crusade across the border into Byzantine territory. "Keep going until you make Niš," he ordered. "You'll find markets there, and hopefully some Byzantine hospitality. My Tuscan troops will remain here by the border for several days as a precaution in case the Hungarians should decide to cross."

So finally, after two and a half arduous months of struggling against hunger, lack of resources, hostile hosts, the elements, and their own scandalous indiscipline, Peter the Hermit's crusading horde wearily dragged itself into Greek territory. Though their numbers had been depleted by death, disease, starvation, battle, and a good amount of desertion, the majority of those who had set out from Amiens and Cologne somehow miraculously arrived intact.

As these French and German crusaders streamed across the Byzantine border, the exhausted Hermit rode back and forth on his donkey, exhorting them forward. "Behold, the borders of Byzantium!" he shouted hoarsely, barely able to speak or even hold himself up. "Constantinople is now within reach!"

As he did this, Innocenzo saw that Peter was on the edge of physical and emotional collapse. Running to him, Innocenzo pulled the Hermit from his mount, setting him on his back against the ground. "Oh, Uncle Peter, stop this!" beseeched Innocenzo. "You must rest. These people can cross without your encouragement!"

"Y-yes, yes, I shall r-rest a moment," the Hermit wheezed, nauseous and spent. "It's been s-such a long journey, Nephew, but behold… *By-zan-tium.*"

Moments later a woman cradling an infant in her arms approached, surrounded by four other children. Seeing the Hermit in such a state, she knelt, taking his hand in hers. "Oh, holy shepherd of us all, it's me, Estelle Dupuis. Do you remember me, Peter? I had my fifth child on the road outside of Cologne. My husband and I named him Jerusalem."

Gazing up, the Hermit thought back to the German border where he had first seen the woman, and listened to her prattle on about the celestial signs which caused her and her husband to gather their children and join the Hermit's crusade. "Yes, dear Estelle," he said wearily, "I remember you and all your children… especially little Jerusalem there. But tell, where is your husband? I used to see him at Tafur's side from time to time, but haven't seen him since the mess back in Zemun."

"Oh, Marcel, my dear Marcel," replied Estelle, clasping her hands, gazing skyward. "Such a good soul, my Marcel. On the trek from Amiens he joined Tafur's bunch and had a cross burned into his forehead, Peter, to show his love of God." As she spoke a glimmer of pride pierced her eyes, but then she shook her head. Cradling her infant in one arm, she slowly made the sign of the cross with her free hand. "My poor Marcel…" she began. "He was killed in Hungary, at Zemun… by the Tuscans, I was told! Tafur said he was killed at the very feet of Bishop Saint-Germain, the bishop being the one who issued the command to kill Marcel!"

"Oh, poor woman," said the Hermit, burying his head into his palms, trying to imagine how she would now manage with five children and no husband in a foreign land. "Oh, my poor dear Estelle… but then, perhaps we should find a way to get you back to France."

"No, certainly not!" declared Estelle. "My children and I are still impatient to fight the Turks, Peter. Just as you prophesized, I'll hold my little Jerusalem up in my arms and turn the Turks away as they tumble from their horses in wonder and fear! Yes, yes... I now live only for that very moment!"

The Hermit closed his eyes, shaking his head the least bit as if to object, but an instant later he was out– unconscious from sun exposure, despair, and fatigue. This prompted Innocenzo to wave Estelle, her children, and others away. "He's fine!" he told concerned and curious onlookers. "He's merely resting a moment. Move along." Innocenzo then remained there with him for half an hour, cradling his uncle's head in his lap until Fazio came along.

Theirs had, indeed, developed into the strangest of relationships and arrangements. Each had, since Cologne, continued to look at the other to satisfy the need for companionship and intimacy, though Innocenzo's love of women had diminished little. "What's happened here?" asked Fazio. "Has he taken ill?"

"No, he's just exhausted," said Innocenzo, motioning to Fazio. "He's bled dry, poor soul. But come, help me move him into some shade."

"Certainly," replied Fazio, giving Innocenzo a hand. The two litter-carried him beneath the shade of a distant olive tree, and sat there talking as the Hermit slept. "He'd best slow his pace," warned Fazio. "I've been watching him. No man can continue as he's been doing since Cologne."

"Aye, well before Cologne even, Fazio... since leaving Amiens. It's these people more than the pace, though. They've become belligerent and defiant. My uncle tries to keep order, but come to find out, many in our company are criminals and opportunists, just like Tafur. They care little about Jerusalem, or God."

"And you, Innocenzo," asked Fazio, "how much do *you* really care about Jerusalem and God?" Though the question was blunt, Fazio knew Innocenzo would not take offense. The two had become close enough to share the most honest of exchanges. Even so, and despite the fact that they had dallied about at night together from time to time, Innocenzo had yet to allow Fazio to fully consummate their physical relationship as Fazio had hoped.

"Honestly," said Innocenzo, "I care little about Jerusalem, Fazio. It's so far away, so full of foreigners." He paused then, weighing his next words. "Still, even though I may not show it, and even though I know I'm a sinner, I *do care* very much about God. I suppose my uncle's taught me a thing or two about devotion along the road. I've never met a man more devoted to God. It makes me wish he was my… *real* uncle."

"Huh?" said Fazio.

Innocenzo shook his head ruefully. "I've been lying about it so long, I'm finally glad to tell someone the truth, Fazio. Sad to say… I invented the whole story about the Hermit having an unknown illegitimate sister, and her being my mother. At the time

I was penniless, hungry– had no place to go. Asking few questions, he took me in."

"Ah, a good man," said Fazio. "Funny thing, in Italy I'd always heard he was nothing but a crackpot. Seems he actually believes in everything he does, which is more than I can say for the two of us, huh?"

"Yeah…" nodded Innocenzo. "Anyway, let's stay here with him then, and let him rest a bit."

As they sat there quietly watching the masses file by, Fazio started to think of his own long journey which had begun in Rome, then back to Genoa, north to Tuscany, on to Cologne, and finally here to the borders of Byzantium. This had occurred all for the purpose of following the Bishop of Ostia, a man he suspected of unmentionable crimes against a child, a woman, and God. Though Fazio was not himself a pious man, he was offended that a man such as the Bishop could commit such horrendous acts while escaping justice and rising to such high stature within the Church. As often occurs with men, it mattered none that Fazio was completely mistaken about Bishop Saint-Germain due to the misperceptions of an old friend named Antonelli. No, in Fazio's mind, Bishop Saint-Germain had already been judged guilty of unpardonable acts of sin… and therefore deserved to suffer.

## Chapter Forty-four

### God's… Justice

It is pertinent at this particular juncture, the Peasants' Crusade crossing into Byzantium, to revisit the progress of Count Emicho of Leiningen. When Odo de Lagery as Pope Urban II declared his Holy Crusade against the Seljuk Turks at Clermont in 1095, he unleashed a massive wheel of motion– the undercurrents of which affected the entirety of Western Europe. Though directing his war plea to a specific corps of knights and noblemen of Christendom, Pope Urban fired the passion of others beneath his spiritual influence as well. Subsequently, charismatic evangelists, itinerant preachers, and clerics of questionable motive were easily able to enlist the poor and ignorant of the continent into taking on the impossible in the name of God. Thus the unexpected proliferation of improbable entities such as Peter the Hermit, Volkmar, Gottschalk, the Holy Goose, and a litany of other freakish developments too numerous to cite.

Pope Urban had also fired the passions of stray knights and nobles, some being altruistic, others being driven purely by mercenary ambition. In any case, Pope Urban, regardless of the purity or impurity of his true intent, unwittingly became the catalyst of movements he never imagined nor controlled. Many of these movements were commandeered by misfits, malcontents, and demagogues– such as the notorious Count Emicho of Leiningen.

The Eleventh Century was an era steeped in hopeless ignorance and wild superstition, while simultaneously being driven by the virtuous quest for faith and hope. This created circumstances under which the general population was easily led, and even more easily misled. The Eleventh Century was also a period of brutal intolerance, as testified by the European belief that those of heathen faith, in this case the Seljuk Turks, needed to be exterminated.

To be fair, it must also be noted that adherents of Islam were faring little better themselves during this age on the issue of tolerance, as evidenced by their own ceaseless, brutal foreign conquests accompanied by merciless in-fighting between their own Shia and Sunni factions. Muslims conquered and converted by the sword, thinking no more of Christians than Christians thought of them.

In terms of western intolerance, as already evidenced by the movement of the Peasants' Crusade, Count Emicho of Leiningen, Volkmar, Gottschalk, and others, the brunt of continental bigotry quickly focused on Jews; in particular, the Jews of Germany suffered. Through the political, cultural, and religious haze of Pope Urban's Holy Crusade, great contradictions arose between the practice of 'Godliness' versus the perception of 'Godliness.' In following these first waves of crusaders who pre-empted the muster of Bishop Adhémar of Le Puy's legitimate crusader force, one can easily get lost in the exploitation, brutality, injustice, and havoc wreaked by them while blazing their early path to Constantinople.

In the end, though man may hunger for justice, justice is open to interpretation, therefore liable to perversion. It is only God who determines true justice, and only God who administers it appropriately in the end... which circles back to the progress of Count Leiningen of Emicho as he made his way toward Constantinople. Having tarried in Germany, wreaking one malicious attack after another on Jewish communities, Count Emicho's army actually fell behind the slow-moving pace of the Peasants' Crusade. Arriving at the Hungarian border along the Danube laden with Jewish plunder about two weeks after the peasants' rampage in Zemun, Emicho most likely intended to continue his rapacious attacks upon the Jews of Hungary. The fact he was now on foreign soil seemed to little deter his ambitions. Nonetheless, when he attempted to cross the Hungarian border, he was refused entry.

This happened for a number of reasons. To begin, his reputation for brutality as he and his troops had moved through Germany preceded him. Although the Hungarians themselves possessed no great love of Jews, they objected to any parts of their cities being set afire or razed. Moreover, word of the massacre at Zemun and Belgrade by the Peasants' Crusade had circulated throughout the country by the time Emicho arrived. Compounding the Peasants' Crusade's reputation, German peasants following the two German clerics Volkmar and Gottschalk had also plundered their way into Hungary. Large groups of foreigners entering the country, therefore, were now perceived as a threat, thus no longer welcome in Hungary– especially if they claimed to be a part of the Holy Crusade.

Infuriated at being halted at the Hungarian border, Emicho brazenly laid siege to the border fortress of Wieselberg for nearly a month. Despite showing certain military aptitude and employing sound strategy, Emicho was finally attacked by superior forces when King Coloman angrily dispatched his army to Wieselberg. Coloman had tired of French and German crusaders molesting his realm, and having been unsuccessful in his attempt to intercept the Peasants' Crusade before it escaped into Byzantium, he did manage to mobilize his vast army against Emicho. During that ensuing campaign, the Hungarians brutally routed Emicho's forces while slaughtering most of his troops, forcing Emicho to flee for his life. In disgrace, he fled back to Germany while several of his key lieutenants managed to make their way to Italy. After floundering about for a time, those making it to Italy eventually encountered a later wave of crusaders just starting their journey to Constantinople, and joined their ranks.

In the end, despite power, privilege, and wealth, Count Emicho of Leiningen ultimately, as would so many others of his ilk, encountered God's final justice. How men like him could never grasp that they had simply been *born* into fortune and had not earned it is a peculiarity of the privileged classes. How they could deceive themselves into believing they were entitled to trample over others through divine right is an even deeper mystery. And how such misdirection could be clothed in the garments and symbols of righteousness and religion is completely beyond comprehension.

In any case, once Count Emicho of Leiningen was chased back to Germay, he waited out the remainder of his years in solitude and disgrace… humbled, finally, not by man's justice, but by the hammer of God.

## Chapter Forty-five

### The Plains of Niš

As the Hermit's masses streamed into Byzantium, their unexpected arrival coupled with their wild appearance took the local Greeks by surprise. Pouring in by the tens of thousands, this riotous mass of filthy humanity seemed an endless flood of barbaric invaders who threatened to ensconce the entire landscape– like some foreign plague cast down from the north.

While it was true that most in Byzantium were aware of the Roman Catholic Pope's impending Holy Crusade, they were not expecting the arrival of forces for another half year or more. Moreover, what the Byzantines were expecting was an army of Christian knights, noblemen, and footmen. In truth, the Byzantines could not have in their wildest imagination envisioned anything as preposterous as a peasant crusade heavily laden with peasants, Tafurs, women, children, and elderly arriving in their land.

As things unfolded, however, it was not the surprise and dismay of the Greeks that created the greatest stir. Rather, it was the horrid conduct of the newly arrived foreigners that unsettled the native population.

Unbeknownst to Guillaume's force holding at the border, shortly after entering Byzantium, the Hermit's masses soon set about looting their way south to the outskirts of Niš, one of the major towns along the southern route to Constantinople. Upon their arrival there, the military commander of the city directed them south in the direction he had taken Walter Sansavoir, and even negotiated an escort to Constantinople on the condition that the Peasants' Crusade leave the area immediately. Although he had welcomed Walter Sansavoir, this second wave disturbed the city commander; he had received reports of their conduct while approaching Niš. Also, their sheer numbers were intimidating.

Peter the Hermit was more than agreeable with the commander's terms, but a rowdy gang of his German recruits began drinking heavily while the Hermit was occupied with negotiations. These particular Germans were belligerent by character, evidently, and were now especially short-fused after their arduous forced march. Heavily intoxicated, they got into a vociferous dispute with locals outside the city. Aroused, their arrogance bursting with xenophobic bravado, they set a cluster of Byzantine mills afire. These mills represented the primary source of income for those living outside of Niš, so their destruction by foreigners sent emotions spiraling out of control, giving rise to an outbreak of rioting from both sides.

The unsuspecting rural Byzantine residents, all of whom became terrified and many of whom were brutalized, were soon fleeing toward the gates of Niš, seeking safety. As these streams of bloodied victims circulated stories of violence, theft, beatings, and rape, the city officials and military commanders grew furious. From their ramparts, perceiving a lack of organized knightly or foot-troop formations amongst the violent intruders, Niš mobilized its entire military garrison and ordered it to make a foray against the hostile mob.

Despite the poor selection of weaponry and lack of formal military muscle such as Walter Sansavoir existing within the crusader ranks, a good number of military footmen and independent knights were present within the Hermit's horde. Also, many of the peasants and villagers who had begun the march as lambs now thought themselves to be lions, especially the Tafurs. So it happened that as the Niš militia confidently charged out of the city gates, they encountered a resistance proving to be far more violent than anticipated. Causing additional confusion for the Byzantines was the fact that women and children were intermingled within the masses of men whom they had come out to fight. Being a civilized race, the Greeks were hesitant at first about attacking these perceived innocents. Shortly, however, the Greeks discovered that they would have to press the attack regardless of who stood in the way, or else suffer heavy casualties.

A brutal battle ensued then, blood running deeper by the hour. Finally, the Byzantine militia being far more disciplined, outfitted, and supported by heavy cavalry, broke the back of the Peasants' Crusade and set them to rout, even capturing the

Hermit's war chest and claiming it for their own. Thinking themselves soon to be annihilated by the Greek assault, thousands of Latin crusaders fled the plains of Niš and made for the nearby hills and mountains.

"Oh, Innocenzo," wailed the Hermit, "we've come all this distance only to be massacred within the borders of the very people we've come to save!" Kneeling, he looked skyward. "God in Heaven, what is this?!" Tearing at his ragged garments, pulling hair from their roots, he cried, "I listened to your command, Lord, and gathered this flock to perform your labor in Jerusalem, but they've turned into wild beasts and now you're having them slain!"

In the midst of this rout, Guillaume's Tuscan battalion, having retired from the Byzantine border, was now nearing Niš. Once again an advance scout came riding hard toward the head of Guillaume's column. "Trouble ahead!" the scout wheezed. "Battle's broken out between the peasants and the Byzantines!"

Guillaume nor any of the others could scarcely believe their ears. "Goddammit!" shouted Handel. "*Are you shitting me?* Now what the hell have those imbeciles started?"

Tristan, hesitant to say anything, gave Guillaume a look of desperation. "This bodes ill for the Greek-Latin alliance, Brother," he said. "Though we need not get involved on behalf of the Hermit's people, we had best at least quickly learn what has occurred– and mend relations lest Emperor Alexius gets involved."

"Dammit, here we go again," said Handel. "But Tristan's right. We don't want the whole damned alliance unraveling because of the goddamned Hermit!"

By the time the Tuscan force arrived at the scene, there were mounds of dead strewn over the battlefield, mainly French and German crusaders, along with a good number of women and children. Seeing from their ramparts a full battalion of foreign knights arriving on the scene, a squadron of Niš cavalry galloped from the city gates, and approached. "I'm the city commandant," said the man leading them. "Who are you, and what's your business here?!"

"I am the Bishop of Ostia, Tristan de Saint-Germain, official envoy and First Counsel to Pope Urban II," replied Tristan.

Hearing this, and noting Tristan's vestments and bishop's crosier, the commandant relaxed a measure, and shrugged. "Then… you're not with these wild people who crossed our borders this week past?"

"No," Tristan replied. "We've been following in their wake since Cologne, Germany, but we represent Pope Urban and the Vatican. They, on the other hand, do not. They are not sanctioned crusaders of Rome, and only represent themselves." Gazing about at the dead littering the plain, he continued. "But tell, sir, what happened here?"

"Approaching Niš, this pack of savages lay waste to the countryside and abused our citizens. We agreed to have them escorted south on the condition they leave immediately for Constantinople, which they claimed was their destination. This was agreeable to their leader, a little pauper calling himself Peter the Hermit. But before leaving Niš, a wild bunch of Germans got into fisticuffs with some of our millers. By the time it was over, the Germans had set fire to an entire cluster of mills, from which this entire region grinds wheat, barley, and rye for bread. Then, too, they ravaged the population, raped our women, and set houses and barns afire. Furious, and having issued warnings before this outbreak, we sent out the militia and attacked them. As you see here on the field, which we've not yet had time to clear, they've lost a good three or four thousand from their ranks. We lost nearly a thousand ourselves. These bastards, though poorly armed, fought like devils!"

"What about Peter the Hermit," asked Handel, "did he survive?"

The commandant pointed to the distance. "As far as I know, he fled into the mountains there with the others. We didn't pursue him because, in his defense, he tried to keep his mob under control. But they're like a pack of wild boars: filthy, coarse, unreasonable and violent."

"We know," assented Tristan. "Yet, Commandant, you *are* aware, are you not, that they came to support your cause against the Turks?"

"So they claimed," replied the commander, "but who needs help such as that? Best they turn around and go home… especially with all those women and children in their midst, and old people, lame, diseased." The commander shook his head then as a look of regret dropped into his expression. “Bishop,” he said, “please know, we tried to go easy on some of the weaker crowd, but even they clawed us like cornered cats, insisting on fighting. Pitiful… it’s as if these damned people are driven forward by some invisible, suicidal force.”

Handel gave a shrug and spat. “More like they’ve been *led* by some suicidal force,” he said, suppressing his wish to curse. “But we need to round them up and get them to Constantinople, Commandant. They’re not about to turn around after coming this far. Would you allow us to search the hills?”

“Yes, I suppose the threat’s been crushed. Gather them up, establish camp in one of the nearby valleys. I think it best, though, that you come to Niš first thing in the morning and negotiate some sort of settlement with the city magistrates and mayor. As a military man, I understand these people wouldn’t dare confront us again, but the city officials are still angry. Some are demanding further retribution. Perhaps you could come put out a fire or two, eh?”

“Yes, certainly,” said Tristan. “And Commandant, know that I *do* understand how your city leaders must feel about the matter.”

Guillaume, who had said nothing to this point, spoke up. “Did a French military contingent not come through here ahead of the Hermit’s horde? A man named Walter Sansavoir?”

“Yes, a decent sort of fellow, that one,” replied the commander. “We sent him and his troops on to Constantinople with an escort. He mentioned there was a peasant army coming behind him, but we didn’t believe such contrived nonsense. Who in hell ever heard of such an army as that?”

“Very well, Commandant,” said Tristan, “if you have no objections and give us a few days or so, we will set about gathering them up. But a question. Does the emperor know yet about the Peasants’ Crusade coming his direction?”

“If he didn’t, I’d imagine he does by now with Sansavoir having arrived in Constantinople,” replied the commander. “I’m sure he’s explained things in detail to Emperor Alexius, though neither are yet aware of the battle that just took place here at Niš. Early this morning, I sent a messenger south to the capital.” The commander then shook his head. “Emperor Alexius won’t be happy, I assure you.”

"Nor should he be," said Handel.

Over the next several days the Tuscan battalion scoured the countryside. Peter the Hermit and Tafur initially thought that the majority of the peasant crusaders had been killed in battle, but in time realized the Greeks had allowed most of them to flee and seek cover in the hills rather than slaughter them. As things happened, Peter the Hermit was one of the last to be found by the Tuscans; he, Innocenzo, and Fazio had retreated into a cave situated within the side of a massive outcrop of rock. Hearing the Tuscans calling for him from the valley floor, and seeing Tristan in their midst, Peter came careening down a treacherous slope, impervious to fear of breaking bones or splitting his skull, and threw himself at the feet of Tristan's horse. "Oh, praise God! Praise God!" he yowled. "It's Bishop Saint-Germain, come to save us from the enemy!"

"The *Byzantines* aren't the enemy, you fool," grunted Handel. "If you'd keep a grip on these morons you've dragged across the continent, you'd know that!"

Later that day as Guillaume gathered the recovered masses into a valley where the Tuscans had made camp, he addressed them sternly. "We'll accompany you to Constantinople from here," he said. "But the first of you to cause trouble will meet the end of my sword. You've been nothing but an affliction since the day you French left Amiens and the day you Germans left Cologne, and you've caused us to be dragged with you across the entire continent. But a question: before we depart for Constantinople, which ones of you fools started this fight, attacking the Greeks, setting their mills afire?"

"It's *they* who attacked us," shouted a faceless voice from a distance. "We've come to help them fight the Turks, yet they launched an attack against us with their troops!"

Guillaume looked toward the voice, but no one stepped forward. Then Handel shouted, "Oh, but we know what you did in Cologne and all along the road, you bastards! But you can't loot and plunder these Greeks and expect them to roll over like the helpless Jews along your way, or the Hungarians you butchered in Zemun!"

No one answered, but many stood there sullenly, refusing to conceal their open hostility toward Guillaume's circle, though they had come to rescue them and take them south to their destination.

"Ah, yes," said Guillaume, his eye moving from one pack to another, "I begin to see the problem. You're rebellious, thoughtless, and unthankful. Well, I'll not lecture you, but I give you this one warning between here and Constantinople: We leave in two days, and the first one of you to cause dissension will be buried here along the road south, and with very few tears from Tuscany!"

## Chapter Forty-six

### The Hermit Falters

That next morning as the city militia continued the chore of clearing corpses from the plains of Niš, Tristan and Handel parlayed with city officials. After hours of negotiation spent primarily by Tristan and Handel attempting to explain and make sense of Peter the Hermit and his Peasants' Crusade, the city officials reluctantly agreed to provide a market outside the city walls before the crusaders' departure for Constantinople.

Tristan and Handel had learned from the Hermit the night before that most of his war chest had been captured by the Niš militia during the battle. Fortunately, Innocenzo and Fazio had managed to salvage a portion of it as they escaped. Thus, during the talks, Tristan promised city officials that the Hermit would reimburse all merchants for food and goods provided to the masses outside the wall.

As he did this, Handel passed him a skeptical look. "You've no authority from the Hermit to spend the last of his chest for this, do you?" he whispered to Tristan.

Tristan, whose face was already tinged pink with grievance after hours of trying to rationalize the creation of the Peasants' Crusade by Peter the Hermit, shook his head. Then, his jaws drew taut. "No, Handel," he said in a low voice, "if need be… I'll have Guillaume's troops *take* the goddamned money from him!"

This so stunned Handel that he dropped into silence, staring into his lap, uncertain for a moment whether he had actually heard Tristan correctly. Handel had never once during his entire acquaintanceship with Tristan ever heard even a hint of blasphemy from his lips. "Indeed," Handel muttered, "I... believe you."

As Tristan and Handel left the Niš negotiations and rode across the plain leading toward the valley camp, the Byzantines had finished stacking corpses and were now lighting them afire. It was a gruesome sight, and the smell of human flesh seared the nostrils. "Dammit," said Handel, his nerves jangling, "all these people lost for nothing!"

"Exactly my own thoughts–" Tristan began to say, but before he finished, he caught sight of Peter the Hermit in the distance, on his knees as Innocenzo and another man he failed to recognize stood over him. Approaching them, dismounting, Tristan at first thought the Hermit was praying. On closer inspection, he discovered the Hermit was sobbing. "What goes on here, Peter?" he asked.

The man who lifted his eyes and muttered a reply was not the irascible Hermit of old; this man's eyes were dull, his gaze bloodshot and unsteady, his voice thready. "Oh… *Bishop*… I've been here praying over the dead, *my* dead. So, so many of them that I brought from the west, only to be burned like rubbish on foreign soil so far from home." Choking with shame, he continued. "I didn't mean for things to happen this way. We three standing here have been trying to hold the mob back since crossing into Byzantium, and for weeks and months before that just trying to get here."

"Aye," agreed Innocenzo. "The mob's gotten more out of hand with each step forward out of Cologne." Looking over at Fazio, he said, "Hasn't it, Fazio?"

Fazio nodded surreptitiously, but said nothing. His eyes were glued to Tristan.

As the little bearded man nodded, looking at him, Tristan perceived a glint of contempt in his expression. "Do I know you, sir?" he asked.

"No, most certainly not," replied Fazio, placing his hat over his face, concealing all but his nose and beard.

Tristan sensed something familiar in this image the short man now presented, but so much had transpired since that night he came upon the ancient cathedral along the back streets of Rome, Tristan failed to make a connection. Turning to the Hermit, Tristan said, "Peter, I am sure you mean what you are saying, but why did you so stubbornly fail to consider such things while luring these people from their lives in France and Germany? Too late now…

what is done is done. I spoke for you within the city to the Niš officials, and promised to pay the city merchants for food and supplies for your people with the remainder of what you have left your war chest." Shaking his head with certainty, Tristan then added, "There will be no argument on that point, Peter. Do you understand?"

"Y-yes, yes, of course," the Hermit answered in a hushed voice, his expression still glazed, his voice picking up a tremor. Staring up at Tristan, he lowered his voice even more so no one else could hear. "I… I begin to become afraid, Bishop," he stammered. "I no longer have control over this mob. They drive *me* now, not the reverse."

Tristan sensed the Hermit was begging for counsel, but Tristan had little to give. Still, he spoke low also so the others would not hear. "After all this hardship and distance, these people will refuse to turn back should you suggest it. They would hang you, Peter… and well they should, I suppose. They are *here* now, and will expect to very soon fight the Turks. You manufactured this madness all on your own, and it is shortly about to devour both you and the thousands you have dragged here. Unfortunately, there is nothing I can do at this point. Odo and I, Handel, we all tried to turn you back, but–"

"*I know, I know*, but God *spoke* to me, I tell you!" the Hermit asserted. "He *commanded* that I do it and…" Stopping mid-sentence, he dropped his head, despair consuming every feature of his face.

"There is no way I could possibly know whether God truly spoke to you or not, Peter," Tristan said, suppressing contempt, "but at this point there is but one alternative… you *must* delay these people crossing the Bosphorus into Turkish territory until the main force of Christian knights arrive. Together then, with help from them and Emperor Alexius, we may be able to contain your crusaders in Constantinople… *then* perhaps even convince them to return home."

The Hermit shook his head without looking up. "No, you were right a moment ago. They'll never turn and make tracks for home." Pausing, a spark of hope lit his thoughts. "But yes, yes, I may be able to hold them back from the Turks for a few weeks, perhaps even a month if need be."

Tristan shook his head, deciding there was no point in further disguising the truth. Sighing, he took a deep breath. "Peter, the main forces will not muster here for at least another six or seven months, maybe even more."

These words struck like a hammer blow to Peter's skull. Shocked, he struggled to his feet. "*Wh-what did you say!?*"

Tristan repeated himself.

In the Hermit's mind, this was a coup de grâce, and it hit him like the fall of an ax to his neck. Refusing to accept what Tristan had just repeated, Peter's shoulders heaved with denial as his eyes closed with painful deliberation. It looked as though he was raising his hand in prayer for a moment, but his fingers slowly interlocked into a ball and shook.

Tristan then heard what he thought was a whimpering sound, though the Hermit's expression barely changed. "Well then, Peter," Tristan continued with discouragement, "there is little left to do but pray. When we arrive in Constantinople, you and I will go immediately to the Basilica Hagia Sophia. You will go to your knees there at the altar, and confess your sins of pride, Peter… and I will pray for the Lord's understanding of what you have manufactured this past year."

## Chapter Forty-seven

### Byzantium

Byzantium was the sole surviving remnant of the classical Roman Empire. As Rome's dominion in Western Europe began to dissolve from the Fifth Century forward, only the eastern portion of the empire remained intact. Even by the Eleventh Century the people of the Byzantine Empire thought of themselves first and foremost as Romans, as the immediate and sole inheritors of the Roman Empire's past glory, power, and culture. In truth, they were more Greek than Latin.

Byzantium's struggle against the Muslims originated in the Seventh Century as the Muslims of Arabia, the Saracens, launched a series of invasions resulting in Byzantium's loss of many eastern territories. The struggle next centered on control of Asia Minor, much of which was also lost to the Muslims as the Byzantine Empire began to spiral into deterioration. By this time, however, the Muslims in question were no longer the Saracens of Arabia but the Seljuk Turks who had originated from the Hsiung-nu tribes on the northern edge of the Gobi Desert and the Altai Mountains in Central Asia. As these Turks over a period of centuries had begun to move west off the steppes of Central Asia, in the Tenth Century they embraced Islam and established themselves around Bukhara in Transoxania under their khan, Seljuk. Later, one branch migrated to India while the other struck west and entered military service as mercenaries under the Abbasid Caliphs of Baghdad, the spiritual leaders of Islam. The fierce Turkish horsemen, known as gazis, eventually followed a Seljuk Kahn, Tugrul Bey, and conquered Baghdad in the year 1055, thus wrestling power from the native Saracens. From there they made incursions into Anatolia, Armenia and other Byzantine territories.

Just as it appeared the Byzantine Empire might collapse beneath the Turkish hammer, a young aristocratic general named Alexius I Comnenus came to power in a bloodless coup engineered in 1081 by his mother, the powerful Anna Delassene. Somehow, Alexius managed to at least halt Turkish aggression along the eastern frontier. Nonetheless, to the north, the Turks ranged freely across Asia Minor, capturing and maintaining a tight grip on the fortified city of Nicaea, located immediately across the Bosphorus Straight, just twenty miles or so from Constantinople itself. To the far south, the Seljuk Empire extended as far as the great city of Antioch, once controlled by the Byzantines, and on to Jerusalem.

Realizing that Byzantium could never hope to dislodge the Turks without outside assistance, Alexius looked to the west which, due to history, heritage, and religion, seemed to be a natural ally. Despite the Great Schism of 1054 which resulted in the division of Christianity into the Eastern Orthodox rite and the western Roman Catholic rite, Alexius appealed to Pope Urban II for military assistance. This was a bold maneuver, as during the Investiture War the Byzantines had supported King Heinrich's cause against the Vatican. Although Emperor Alexius had never actually sent troops or engaged in combat against Gregorian Catholics, he had provided spies, intelligence, and finances to the German king. It is probable that any other Catholic pope under such circumstances would have rebuffed Emperor Alexius' plea. To Alexius' good fortune, Pope Urban II possessed acute political judgment, being a clever tactician and strategist. He was willing to forgive the past in order to cement the future. In response to the Byzantine pleas, Urban strongly lobbied the College of Cardinals and high clerics of Gregorian Europe, opening a state of détente with Byzantine Christians after nearly half a century of dispute and discord. The greatest single element of this détente was to join the Byzantine military effort against the aggression of the Seljuk Turks.

So it was that former enemies joined hands and Pope Urban II called upon all the faithful knights of Western Europe to march to the aid of their fellow Christians in the east while simultaneously reclaiming the Holy Land from the boot of Islam.

Thus, according to ecclesiastical history, developed the First Holy Crusade.

## Chapter Forty-eight

### Handel's Revelation

The capital of the Byzantine Empire, Constantinople, was located atop an isthmus jutting into the Bosphorus Straight. This straight connects the Black Sea and the Mediterranean, thereby straddling the European and Asian continents where it could exploit the pulsing trade route to the Orient. Constantinople was also the greatest Christian city in all the world by the year 1096, and its staggering size literally dwarfed the western capitals of Paris, London, and Rome. As such, Constantinople was far more opulent, far more exotic, and far more wealthy than anything the crusaders had ever witnessed in the West. On entering the city gates, Western Europeans could not help but be astounded by the architecture, the vast number of monasteries and palaces, and the amount of gold and silver worn by citizens and available in the markets, as well as by the luxurious clothing of the inhabitants and the richness of the food.

After making Constantinople, Guillaume's battalion began pitching camp outside the city walls, not distant from the camps of the Peasants' Crusade and several independent military groups that had been filtering into Constantinople early to join the Holy Crusade. In the midst of the Tuscans' final efforts to pitch troop tents, Tristan intercepted two men seeking Handel, both dressed as dock workers. "Yes, in the tent just over there," said Tristan, "unpacking his things. Come along, I'll take you there."

As the men entered the tent, Handel looked up and grinned. "Ah, Brother Marcus, Brother Franc," he said, extending a hand in greeting. "I wondered how long it'd take you to find me once we got here."

"Oh, not long," replied Marcus, "for the entire city's abuzz with the arrival of Peter the Hermit this morning. More are still filing in by the thousands, setting up camp far, far beyond the capital gates. Also during these last weeks, military contingents of different western European origin have been showing up too, along with deteriorating remnants of several peasant crusades from Germany."

"Be glad you didn't have to make this march as we did, Marcus," Handel groaned, turning to Tristan. "I introduce you to Brothers Marcus and Franc of the Underground," he said. "They were posted here shortly after you and I left Constantinople from our meeting with Emperor Alexius two years ago."

"Aye, and it's quite a city!" said the younger monk, Franc. Before taking a seat, he examined Tristan's vestments, then extended his hand. "You must be Bishop Saint-Germain," he said with deference. "I've heard much about you, and also that you made your start in the Underground immediately after ordination."

"Yes, at age eighteen, which is not far from your current age I venture to guess?"

"I'm twenty now," said Franc. "I was ordained at seventeen. I'm from Bavaria, the same town as Brother Handel."

"Yes," nodded Handel, "I've known Franc since he was a wee lad."

Franc smiled, looking at Handel with near adoration. "It was Brother Handel who first talked to me about becoming a Benedictine," he said. "After my ordination, on his recommendation, I was shortly sent to Brother Dieter Muehler at Monte Cassino for training." As he spoke, the young monk beamed with that same pride Tristan had possessed on joining the élite Benedictine Underground.

Tristan acknowledged the smile, happy for the young man. "And how is it you became so fortunate as to be stationed in the majestic city of Constantinople?" he asked.

"Oh," replied Franc, flattered that the Bishop of Ostia would show interest, "I was included with those lucky others who came here when Brother Muehler ordered that we triple our espionage efforts in Byzantium, you know… shortly after you and Brother Handel returned from your negotiations with Emperor Alexius."

As Franc said this, Tristan's expression dropped as his eyes shot to the ground, When his eyes raised again, they were afire, as was now the color of Tristan's complexion. "Brother Muehler ordered the *tripling* of espionage efforts here in

Byzantium?" he said, setting his jaw square, hitching both fists to his hips.

Seeing the abrupt change in Bishop Saint-Germain's demeanor, young Franc glanced over at Marcus, then at Handel. His face going pale, he looked back at Tristan and stammered, "Perhaps I… m-misspoke, Bishop Saint-Germain. I'll say no more."

Flushing red, Tristan turned to Handel. "What is he talking about, Handel? What is going on here, and why do I know nothing of it? I refuse to believe that the Holy Father would issue such an order and not inform me of it as his First Counsel."

Handel himself turned crimson, then took a seat on a stool and slapped the table. "Ah, hell!" he sighed. "The Pope didn't inform you because he… doesn't *know*. Muehler issued the order without Vatican authorization."

"*What*?!" Tristan barked with uncharacteristic agitation. Dumbfounded by what he was hearing, he blurted, "Handel… that just can't be! I mean, I am well aware we had a handful of spies here during the Investiture War when Emperor Alexius and King Heinrich of Germany were making alliances against the Vatican, but why would we *triple* the number of spies now that we ourselves are forming an alliance with the Byzantines? Does Muehler simply not understand the concept of détente, nor its intent!?"

Handel didn't answer at first, but after shifting about on his stool, he muttered, "Dammit, lad, as Muehler and I have both said time and time again, Alexius and the Byzantines aren't to be trusted. Now that we're tied to them in this war against the Turks, we've even *more* at risk than before, believe it or not! But worst of all, the Pope's developed a blind spot with the Byzantines. He so passionately seeks détente with the Greek Orthodox Church now that he's abandoned caution. Muehler refuses to mimic the same mistake, so he increased espionage on the Byzantines without permission because he… suspected the Pope would reject such a proposal. But goddammit, I'm in agreement with Muehler... hell, it was my idea in the first place! But now that I'm laying things on the table, Tristan, *you've* developed a blind spot about the Byzantines, too!"

Marcus and Franc shuddered a bit as Handel fired this accusation, expecting Bishop Saint-Germain to lash back at him.

To their surprise, he did not. Instead, he stared quietly at Handel a long while, then said, "Very well, what is done is done, and I can only presume that Muehler's intent was *cautionary*, not resistive or devious."

Handel sighed with satisfaction, and gesturing to Marcus and Franc, said, "Very well, gentlemen, fill us in on Constantinople then."

"To begin," said Brother Marcus, "Emperor Alexius has very much since his coronation after the Comnenus take-over coup been under the influence of an eminence grise… his mother, Anna Delassene."

"What?" questioned Handel. "How's that possible? We never saw, met, or even heard a word of her during our first visit here two years ago."

"Because your visit was both impromptu and brief, Handel," said Marcus, "and she happened to be out of country at the time. That's neither here nor there, as we've since learned it was she who engineered Alexius' rise to power through early maneuvering, then through coup d'etat. My point is this, she holds much authority within the Byzantine court, and even at times challenges Alexius."

"Openly?" asked Tristan.

"Ah, no," replied Marcus, "the old spider's too clever for that! Rather, she prefers to rely on her skills of motherly manipulation, constantly reminding him of her role in moving him to the throne. Oh, and she's got old Patriarch Nicholas deep in her pocket too, you should know."

"Aye," added Franc, "and to show you just how wily she is, she's managed to maneuver Alexius into doing something highly irregular. He's crowned her *Augusta* in place of the rightful claimant, his own wife, Irene Doukainia of the all powerful Doukas family."

"But in Byzantium, the Augusta is the Empress," said Tristan, "which is always the emperor's wife."

"Not in *this* case," replied Marcus, "so keep that in mind at all times. Although Anna Delassene arranged the marriage of Alexius to Irene of the Doukas bloodline, she despises the Doukas family because of previous intrigue and bloodletting. The marriage was arranged only as a political ploy to broker an alliance between the two powerful, feuding families. The Augusta despises her own daughter-in-law and strips her of her rightful functions and authority. As to the daughter-in-law, Queen Irene, she says little though her expressions speak volumes. Watch her eyes closely, for her tongue rarely wags."

"Bear in mind also," added Marcus, "that the Augusta had a heavy hand in selecting Patriarch Nicholas, the highest cleric of all Byzantium."

"Brother Marcus, are you telling me that Alexius does not run his own kingdom?" asked Tristan.

"Ah, now there lies the mystery," Marcus replied, inclining his head in puzzlement. "There are undercurrents of a struggle now rising between Alexis and his mother. After years of drama, and manipulation, Alexius has begun to weary of his mother's interference. In other words, there's a certain level of tension in the royal court."

"And there's even more tension *beyond* the court," interjected Franc, straining at the leash to pass along his own information to Handel and Bishop Saint-Germain. The young monk was acutely aware that Jurgen Handel was a legend within the Benedictine Underground, as was Bishop Saint-Germain within the Vatican; being within the vaunted company of such lauded figures was an occasion, and he intended to be noticed.

"Of course," said Handel dismissively, "the Turks."

"Ah no, far more than the Turks," said Franc, shaking his head. "There've been recent rebellions in Thrace, Crete, and Cypress. Then, too, major religious struggles have broken out between the emperor and the growing Paulician and Bogomil sects of the Balkans who refuse to recognize the practices, power, and authority of the Greek Orthodox Church. There's been bloodshed in the Balkans and martyring amongst the Paulicians and Bogomils, and it appears to be growing in severity, not decreasing."

"I see," said Tristan, knowing that religious uprisings could quickly morph into inextinguishable infernos. "We weren't aware of so many rebellions or such deep religious conflict going on here in Byzantium."

This brought a smile to young Franc's lips and he began to say more, but was interrupted by Marcus who said, "Then too, there's the issue of Bohemud of Taranto and the Italian Normans."

"Yes, we *are* aware of that issue," said Handel.

The Byzantines and Italian-Normans had been bitter enemies for decades. Under the leadership of Duke Robert Guiscard the Wily, the Normans conquered southern Italy and other territory from Byzantium. Guiscard and his son, Bohemud of Taranto, then crossed the Adriatic and invaded other Byzantine possessions. Whereas this protracted and bloody invasion was unsuccessful in the end, it had caused Emperor Alexius to seek an alliance with King Heinrich of Germany against the Gregorian Papacy during the Investiture War since the Normans were allies of the Vatican.

"But I can certainly see where Alexius would fret about allowing Bohemud of Taranto onto Byzantine soil," Handel continued. "The Italian-Normans are a violent and bloodthirsty lot, and have allied themselves with the Saracens of Sicily on more than one occasion to fight the Byzantines."

"Yes," agreed Marcus, "and Emperor Alexius feels Bohemud has ulterior motives, and may maliciously turn his army against the Greeks. Yet, the emperor is in a corner... he can't refuse Bohemud's services for fear of offending the Vatican and Pope Urban. Historically, the Italian-Normans have always been and still are the Church's most staunch military allies, other than Countess Mathilda of Tuscany. Alas, but Bohemud is not the only other crusader who concerns Alexius."

This comment caught both Tristan's and Handel's curiosity. "He has no history with the other knights of Western Europe," said Tristan. "Who, then, gives him concern?"

"It's an odd thing, but our agents in Alexius' court and among his military have intimated that all Alexius ever really wanted from the west was a mercenary force to help fight the Turks. But the Pope has mobilized major nobles from France, Italy, and Germany; strong personalities with strong appetites for territory. Alexius wishes only to reclaim former Byzantine territory from the Turks throughout Asia Minor, but fears that if the nobles of Western Europe defeat the Turks, they will then lay claim to the territory themselves rather than turn it back over to the Byzantine Empire."

"And well advised he is to do so," nodded Handel, who for the most part distrusted nobility of any strand. "And mind you, our greedy bastards might well do exactly as Alexius fears."

"And finally," said Franc, injecting himself back into the conversation, "there *is* the matter of the Turks. It was Alexius who prevented the total collapse of Byzantium at the hands of the Turks, but he still finds himself surrounded by them, and periodically they continue to raise their ugly heads to gaze upon Constantinople and Byzantine wealth. In particular, he fears Kilij Arslan who rules the Sultanate of Rüm from his capital of Nicaea, right across the Bosphorus Straight from Constantinople. Kilij Arslan and Emperor Alexius are currently under a treaty of peace, but the truce is fragile."

"So what's keeping Arslan from invading Constantinople, then?" asked Handel.

Franc put a hand to the soft stubble of his young chin as his already florid complexion gained pink. "At the moment," he nodded, "Arslan, who is a Shia Muslim, is engaged in a bloody feud against the Danishmends, who are Sunni Muslims." His bright eyes darkened a fraction and he added, "But when that fire's out, Alexius suspects Arslan might well start making designs on Constantinople again."

"As you see," said Marcus, "Alexius is a man sitting not atop a single fire, but atop many, many fires."

"Indeed," said Handel. "Bishop Saint-Germain and I will be reporting to the emperor as soon as we get things sorted out here at camp, and this information you've shared will prove valuable during our exchanges with him. It'll also prove useful as we await Bishop Adhémar and the European knights."

Marcus and Franc stood and took their leave, after which Handel turned to Tristan. "It seems we've entered quite a tangled web here in Constantinople, lad," he said. "Now tell me truthfully, is this good information to know as we enter Alexius' lair, or would you rather we be ignorant of it all?"

Tristan nodded, realizing that Dieter Muehler had taken a risk in intensifying espionage efforts upon Byzantium without the Pope's knowledge, but it had been a well calculated maneuver. "Yes, Handel," Tristan assented, "it is good information to have in our pocket, even if Odo would not approve of how it was acquired."

## Chapter Forty-nine

### Emperor Alexius I Comnenus

As Tristan and Handel were escorted by royal guards to the imperial palace and into audience with Emperor Alexius, each held his own interpretation of the briefing received earlier that morning from the two monks of the Benedictine Underground. Tristan felt hopeful the turmoil surrounding Alexius might actually facilitate the Pope's policy of détente with the Greek Orthodox Church and Byzantium. In Tristan's estimation, despite the theological differences dividing the two Christian churches, it was important that they now seek common ground, closing the gap that had divided them over the past half century.

Handel, on the other hand, distrusted Alexius even more than before, and viewed the emperor's effort to drag Western Europe into a fight with the Turks as a self-serving deception that would inevitably evolve into a never ending malignancy– one that would eventually cause the Roman Catholic Church irreparable harm. All the same, being a good Catholic soldier, he resolved to play the good diplomat.

As Handel and Tristan approached the majestically adorned, elevated imperial throne, Emperor Alexius posed there at ease, but with regal splendor, sitting erect with an elbow propped upon each arm of the throne chair, hands folded in his lap. To his immediate right sat a dignified woman in opulent but sophisticated dress, her face creased with age, her eyes squinting with condescension. Upon her head sat a golden crown embedded with dazzling patterns of inlaid diamonds and emeralds. Tristan and Handel supposed her to be the Byzantine Augusta, Anna Delassene, mother of the emperor.

To Alexius' left sat a much younger woman, also opulent in dress, but wearing on her head a small tiara. Though her eyes were focused directly on the two Latin guests as they knelt before the emperor, her expression seemed distant. She appeared distracted, as having little interest in politics; unbeknownst to Tristan and Handel, the fire of her once passionate heart quelled after being forced into the royal marriage by Augusta Anna, whom she loathed. Thus, whenever her glance happened to fall onto the old empress, it seemed a tiny seed of bitterness touched her tongue before turning away. Tristan and Handel surmised correctly that this was the emperor's wife, Irene Doukainia of the Byzantine Doukas dynasty.

To the side of Augusta Anna's throne stood Nicholas III Grammaticus, Patriarch of the Greek Orthodox Church. Surrounding him were huddled three elderly Byzantine bishops, each carrying a severe expression about the face. Such dour expressions were not uncommon of high clerics of the era, but Handel determined quickly that the bishops appeared displeased about this arrival of two clerics from the West. *Damn their tired old asses to Hell*, he thought.

"I heartily welcome you back to Constantinople, Bishop Saint-Germain, and very much congratulate you on your rise within the Vatican," said the emperor, smiling. "And we welcome you, also, Brother Handel. It seems impossible that nearly two years have transpired since our last meeting. So much has occurred since that time. Above all, I must sincerely apologize for such a humble welcome without heraldry or gifts, but I must confess... we were not expecting you for some time yet, Bishop Saint-Germain."

"Indeed," said Nicholas Grammaticus, "such a delightful surprise." He forced a smile then, but there was little sincerity within it. "As the emperor says, you are most welcome here, both of you." He next looked over at the emperor and motioned toward Augusta Anna. *Introduce your mother*, the motion said.

"During your last visit you missed the pleasure of meeting my mother, Augusta Anna Delassene," said Alexius. "She was away on a diplomatic mission of importance at the time."

Tristan and Handel bowed respectfully. "Your absence during our last visit was our own misfortune, Empress," said Tristan. "Please know that we are most honored to finally meet you, and that the Holy Father of the Roman Catholic Church sends you his formal regards and blessings."

As Tristan spoke, the old woman's glacial eyes raked over him from head to toe. His appearance pleased her, especially the brilliant clarity of his grey eyes, his deep rich voice, and his fine form which she was able to guess despite his flowing bishop garments. But her pleasure was not evident, for her eyes remained cold, her expression unchanged. Nor did she make a gesture, or even nod.

"And this is my wife, Queen Irene Doukainia," said Alexius, motioning to the woman on his left.

The queen also was pleased by Tristan's appearance, especially now that she had a closer look. He vaguely reminded her, in posture and movements, of a young captain of the Royal Guard who once possessed her heart before becoming queen– and haunted her memory still. Losing her air of disinterest, she smiled, tipped her head, and said, "My affectionate regards to you, Bishop Saint-Germain, and to…" She paused awkwardly then, having forgotten Handel's name though it had been given to her in an earlier briefing.

"Brother Handel," said the empress, her voice dripping with disdain for her daughter-in-law. "The man's name is *Jurgen* Handel, Irene… from Bavaria."

At no time had Handel's origin been mentioned during his first trip to Constantinople, nor since his recent arrival, and this piqued Handel's curiosity. *Ah, this old bitch is good*, he thought. *In the short time we've been here in the capital, she's already acquired personal details about us.*

"Ah, yes," said Queen Irene, her eyes smoldering at the empress, "my regards to you also, Brother *Handel*."

Alexius, disregarding the silent exchange of glares now occurring between mother and wife, looked at Tristan, whose company he had rather enjoyed during the initial visit to Constantinople. "Bishop Saint-Germain," he said, "tell me a little about this Peter the Hermit who has unexpectedly arrived in my capital with this massive horde of… *crusaders*? I have heard a tidbit or two from the knight, Walter Sansavoir, who arrived here before you. But, he seems to be in league with this unusual monk, and somewhat subservient to him. I would appreciate, then, another opinion– especially in light of the incident that was reported about my city of Niš."

"Quite simply, Majesty," interrupted Handel, "the Hermit is a madman, for only a madman would lead tens of thousands of non-combatants across the continent on foot to fight the Turks."

Alexius nodded, unable to mask a certain level of agreement. "I confess, I have never seen nor even heard of such an army as he leads. And you, Bishop Saint-Germain, what is your assessment of the man?"

"Let me make clear, Excellency, that Pope Urban has been extremely displeased with the Hermit from the very inception of this Peasants' Crusade," said Tristan. "He called only upon the knights of Europe to come to your assistance, not peasants, villagers, or their families… nor any of these other hangers-on who have followed the Hermit this long distance here."

"We here in Byzantium know you are extremely close to Pope Urban, Bishop Saint-Germain," said Alexius. "If the Pope rejects this Peasant Crusade, how is it possible that the Hermit's army and your group of Tuscans traveled and arrived here together with them? Because of that, it appears to all in Constantinople that your party is connected with Peter the Hermit."

"*Y-e-s*, Bishop," said Augusta Anna, "please explain your association with this man and his pitiful rabble." As she said this, Patriarch Nicholas leaned over, whispered something in her ear, then stood back, folding his arms. "His entire expedition appears, to some, as little more than a ploy to rid Western Europe of riff-raff and criminals," she continued, "and that you and your Tuscan troops have served as their escort."

"Brother Handel and I," replied Tristan, carefully choosing his words, "along with my brother's Tuscan battalion, were tasked by Pope Urban with convincing the Hermit to turn back from this venture in Cologne, Germany. The Hermit refused. So it was that I, Handel, and my brother's Tuscan troops still had to make our way to Byzantium... so we simply ended by taking the same path to Byzantium as the Hermit's group. Again, we are not associated *with* the Peasants' Crusade. But I will add this– now that we are here, I feel it my duty to convince the Hermit and his army to not engage the Turks until the arrival of Bishop Adhémar and the armies of Europe... for obvious reasons, Majesty."

"Yes, no doubt, any attempt to fight the Turks with a mob such as the Hermit has recruited would be disastrous," agreed Alexius. "But my latest communications from Rome indicate that

Bishop Adhémar is not due for another six months or more," said Alexius.

"Indeed," frowned the empress. "So tell us, Bishop Saint-Germain, over this next half year, what exactly are we in Constantinople supposed to do with this mob of indigents who have swarmed our borders?"

As she said this, Patriarch Nicholas nodded, placing his hand deferentially upon the empress' forearm as the three high bishops surrounding him exchanged glances of disapproval while murmuring amongst themselves.

"Pope Urban's hope, and mine, Empress Anna," Tristan replied, "is that Emperor Alexius will *contain* them here in the capital. I believe we all agree that they have no hope in battle against the Turks should they refuse to wait on the main crusader forces of the Pope."

"Any person of reasonable God-given intelligence would recognize that," said the empress crossly, leaning forward, wagging a finger. "Which then begs the question, what ridiculous presumption encouraged this hairy little preacher to raise such an army in the first place?" Tristan did not answer at first, nor did Handel. The empress waited a few moments more, but noting the blank expressions on Tristan's and Handel's faces and receiving no response, she pressed forward. "*Need I repeat the question, gentlemen?*"

"Empress Anna, Emperor Alexius," said Tristan slowly, choosing his words even more carefully than before, "the Hermit believes he has a direct line of communication with God. He also claims that God has commanded him to lead an army of peasants and commoners against the forces of Islam... as a gateway to penance and eternal salvation."

"A direct line of communication with God?" asked Patriarch Nicholas, his brows arcing as the expressions of the bishops around him filled with sneers. "As in experiencing a vision here or there on occasion?" he asked, willing to accept the occurrence of rare miracles or isolated incidents of spiritual mystery.

"No, Patriarch Nicholas," said Handel. "More as in *daily* conversation and written communication. In fact, he carries a letter on his person from God… instructing him to carry out this crusade of his."

Nothing else Handel could have said would have had a more unsettling effect on Patriarch Nicholas and his bishops. They were overcome with looks of disbelief, followed by a wave a grumbling. The empress, too, was incredulous. The emperor and the queen, however, appeared slightly amused. "Bishop Saint-Germain," said Alexius, suppressing the smile that broke for an instant across his lips, "do you and Brother Handel *accept* such claims?"

"Certainly not," huffed Handel.

"There are mysteries in this life," said Tristan, taking a more diplomatic tone, "that far surpass man's feeble ability to grasp or analyze. No, I myself do not accept the Hermit's claims, nor does Pope Urban, the College of Cardinals, nor the high clerics of the Roman Catholic Church. Even so, the reality of the matter is that our continent is full of people who *do* believe the Hermit's claims, as evidenced by the tens of thousands who have undertaken this impossible journey to the very gates of your city. It is *their* reality, then, that confronts us, regardless of whether spawned from the realm of reason or the depths of absurdity."

"Ah, a sensible point of view," nodded the emperor. "Please know, Bishop, I myself have already put a little thought into the arrival of these hordes to my capital. Your reasoning is not that far from my own. I find this entire Peasants' Crusade to be ludicrous, yet I must deal with it, and carefully so. Just as I have done with other crusader groups arriving unexpectedly in recent weeks, I have sent word to the Hermit that his people must remain *outside* the city for purposes of maintaining order within my capital. However, I will allow them entry into the city after a formal ceremony in which my entire court shall welcome Peter the Hermit. That ceremony will take place here at my palace tomorrow morning."

The empress shot her son a glance of disapproval, but quickly stifled it.

*Ah, the old bitch didn't know this*, thought Handel. Then, as if to rub it in, though he himself was equally put off at the emperor's idea, he said, "Excellency, such a generous gesture, and an undeniable diplomatic coup!"

"Yes, I do it in the interest of harmony and as a gesture to Pope Urban," said Alexius. "Though he may disapprove of the

Hermit, I am sure he would not wish us to mistreat these Christian crusaders who have espoused his call... even such as they are."

"A very reasonable approach," said Tristan. "You will then also, I pray, try to dissuade him from entering Turkish territory until a more appropriate time?"

"Yes, most certainly. I will also ensure his people have markets available. But tell me, Bishop, can either you or Brother Handel explain the actions of the Hermit's crusaders at Niš? I regret that so many of their numbers were killed by my militia of that city, but was told it was unavoidable due to the horrid behavior of these people."

"Undoubtedly true," said Handel. "Without going into detail, let me simply say that this mob has created a *number* of disturbances along the route to Constantinople."

"Unfortunate, but understandable to a point," said Alexius, who avoided mention of the death of his own subjects during the battle at Niš. In truth, he was less concerned about them than he was about the unanticipated arrival of so many foreigners to his capital. "Whereas such large numbers cannot help but create issues under any circumstances," continued Alexius, "I still find it odd that the Hermit fails to hold tighter rein over his following. After all, if he possesses the power to persuade so many to undertake the *impossible*, then surely he possesses the sway to moderate their behavior. Rest assured, I will make that impression upon him in the morning."

"Yes," scowled the empress, "rest assured."

"The journey here has been treacherous and long," said Tristan, "and there are those within the march with insincere motives, and others who have become rebellious, I fear. It is my hope that now in Constantinople, they will settle."

"Yes," said Alexius, "mine also. But if not, though I shall extend my arms in welcome tomorrow morning, I refuse to tolerate disturbances in my capital such as occurred at Niš. In any case, Bishop Saint-Germain, it is good to see you and Brother Handel again. As to the Hermit and his followers, we shall see what the future holds." Waving his hand, he called an end to the meeting and dismissed all in attendance except Tristan. "Bishop Saint-Germain," he motioned, "if you would kindly allow me a few moments of your time?"

"Certainly, Majesty," said Tristan, taking leave of Handel and following the emperor as he led him through a series of majestically adorned palace corridors. With each step away from the imperial throne, the emperor seemed more and more to shed the regal airs of formality. "Please know, Bishop Saint-Germain," said Alexius, amicably taking Tristan by the shoulders, "that we in Constantinople are strongly aware that you campaigned heavily on our behalf with Pope Urban despite much opposition, apparently, from certain members of the College of Cardinals who did not wish to support this alliance against the Turks. For that, I owe you a great debt."

"Thank you, Excellency," said Tristan, quietly wondering where the emperor was leading him. "In truth, though I admire many facets of the Muslim culture, I am deeply disturbed by their insatiable taste for military expansion. It is crucial, then, that the Byzantine Christians hold firm here in Constantinople and the Bosphorus Straight, for you are the very gateway to Western Europe itself. Your collapse would invite the Turks to mark Western Europe as their next target."

"Indeed, assisting us is a sound strategy for your own continent," Alexius replied. "But enough about the crusade. I wish to apologize for my mother. She becomes somewhat abrasive at times as concerns outsiders, and periodically forgets who actually runs the empire, as does Patriarch Nicholas." He issued a slight grin then, but it quickly dissipated. "Oh, and on another subject, I understand you will be staying here within the city as you await Bishop Adhémar's arrival, so please know that I will be granting you access to the palace for any and all services you might desire–baths, servants, dining, private needs, anything you wish."

This was an unexpected offer, and the emperor's comment confused Tristan. "Thank you for your generosity, Majesty, but no, I will not be staying within the capital. My brother, Guillaume, is in command of the Tuscan battalion from Italy sponsored by our aunt, Countess Mathilda Medici of Tuscany. His troops will eventually be in service to Bishop Adhémar along with Raymond of Toulouse as they open hostilities with the Turks. As I speak, my brother's unit is still establishing their bivouac outside the city walls. I will be staying there in camp with him while in Constantinople."

"Oh?" said Alexius. "But that's odd. I was told differently. An acquaintance of mine here in the capital has made arrangements for you to stay at a palace of my own former possession along the harbor."

"Oh, if only that were true," Tristan replied, amused, "but I have no connections here in Constantinople."

"Indeed? Truly, I *am* confused then," the emperor said, opening a door leading into a private chamber. "Then perhaps you were not aware that a childhood friend of yours anchored here in Constantinople weeks ago, and has been awaiting your arrival."

"*What?*" said Tristan, mystified.

"Why yes," replied Emperor Alexius, ushering Tristan into the room and motioning to the individual standing there in waiting. "Ah," he smiled, "yes, Bishop Saint-Germain, here she is, my primary trading partner of the western Mediterranean, la Gran Signorina of Genoa– the Lady Mala."

## Chapter Fifty

### Reunion

There are occurrences in life so surprising that, on unfolding, render one unable to grasp words, or even utter a sound. As Tristan looked across the room and saw Mala standing there, it was as though he had been struck by lightning. Blinking, he at first thought his eyes were tricking him. Next, realizing that Mala was truly standing before him, the floor seemed to buckle beneath his feet as his surroundings turned surreal. Finally, his shoulders sagged as though the air within his lungs had been knocked from him, and he could scarcely breathe.

Mala, though feeling a similar upheaval, managed to better maintain her calm. Smiling graciously, she stepped forward and gave Tristan a gentle embrace.

"Well," said Alexius, delighted by Tristan's surprise, "I had no idea until Mala mentioned it last week that the two of you have known each other since childhood. Ah, as they say, it is truly a small world after all, eh?"

"My dear Bishop," said Mala, kissing Tristan on both cheeks in the fashion of France, "it's been a good while since we last saw each other. I hope all's been going well in your world?"

Tristan stammered a few incomprehensible words before collecting his senses. "Mala!" he exclaimed. "God in Heaven! Is it truly *you*?"

The emperor, having only ever seen Tristan as a dignified diplomat in a state of full composure, chuckled at seeing Tristan in disarray. "Oh, but there are no friendships quite equal to those extending back to our lost days of youth and innocence," he commented, assuming from Mala's previous discussion that the two had grown up together, spending years as childhood playmates, perhaps. Of course, he had no way of knowing how tortuous or profound the bond between Tristan and Mala had really been. "Very well then," he continued, unaware that neither was listening to a word he was saying, "Lady Mala, I'll leave the two of you to wrestle over the Bishop's arrangements while here in Constantinople. But be warned, he has just informed me that he intends to camp with the Tuscans outside the city rather than at your new palace!" Laughing, he left the room.

A peculiar thing happens when unexpectedly stumbling onto a loved one after an extended absence, especially in the wake of bitter disappointments, personal trials, and tribulations. An inner collapse occurs, giving rise to an involuntary swell of succor inextricably mixed with a wash of high emotion. Finding Mala here, so far from Rome and everything familiar to him, then being able to hold her after his failed dealings with the Peasants' Crusade, was nearly more than he could bear. The deep hurt inflicted upon him by the Jewish pogroms, the Zemun and Belgrade disaster, and the outbreak at Niš suddenly conspired against him, and Tristan's heart gave way as he found himself on the edge of tears. So much had happened to him in the past year, and there was so much he wished to tell her, that it became a struggle to simply hold onto his emotions. Thus lost, he found himself simply murmuring, "Oh, Mala, Mala... I've thought of you so often these past months!"

## Chapter Fifty-one

### A Seafront Palace

Over the next hour Tristan and Mala exchanged news, describing their respective circumstances back in Italy since their last meeting of over a year past. From time to time Mala would embrace him with unabashed affection, knowing that Tristan would resist either from fear of God or fear of someone walking into the room. Still, she was so filled with joy that she took no offense, knowing that in his heart, Tristan wished to return her affection.

At one point Tristan reached in his vestments and fished out his most prized possession, the tiny silver ring of Moorish silver that Mala had given him during their first meeting as children. This, as hoped, made her squeal with delight. "Oh, but Tristan!" she spluttered, "You still have my ring?!"

"Of course," he answered, his heart beating like a rabbit diving for cover. "I carry it with me wherever I go. And on the day I die, it shall still be with me, Mala."

Taking the ring, she held it to the light. "Oh, but such cheap silver, this ring," she grimaced. "Yet, it was my greatest treasure as a child… and I gave it to you that night at the campfire along the Seine. It was the only thing I owned, but I wanted you to have it."

Tristan thought back to that time wistfully. "And to this day I cannot fathom why you gave your only possession in life back then– to *me*."

At this Mala laughed aloud. "Oh, but *smart boy*," she chided, "I told you why that very night– so you'd never forget me!"

"Oh, that dreaded moniker of 'smart boy' again!" huffed Tristan, feigning objection. "Will you never let it go?"

They chattered thus like adolescents for nearly an hour more until, finally, Mala called for her coachman. "Raphael," she said, "take us back to the rise and let me show Bishop Saint-Germain my new acquisition."

"Si, Signorina!" snapped the coachman, ushering them down the corridor.

Mala's 'new acquisition' sat along a high hill overlooking the harbor of Constantinople. Mala modestly described it as an estate, but it had once been the summer palace of Emperor Alexius prior to his construction of a more recent palace that was even more opulent, and of his own design. As Raphael dropped them off and guided his team of horses to the stables, Tristan and Mala were greeted by two men, one named Salvetti, her financial adjutant, and another named Moreno, captain of her personal guard of fifty Genoese knights.

"Bring wine immediately to the breezeway, Salvetti!" Mala laughed, still overcome with merriment at being in Tristan's presence again.

"Si, Signorina," replied Salvetti, unaccustomed to seeing such gaiety in la Gran Signorina's expression.

Mala gave Tristan a perfunctory tour of the waterfront portion of the palace, moving about with lively motions punctuated with girlish laughter. She then directed him to an immense roofed patio supported by massive marble columns directly overlooking the huge harbor sprawling out from the foot of the rise. Salvetti was waiting for them, filling two goblets with fine Byzantine wine.

"Oh, but another goblet so you can come join us, Salvetti," smiled Mala, motioning for her adjutant to be seated.

Salvetti had only met the Bishop twice before, and though he had never deciphered the relationship existing between Bishop Saint-Germain and la Signorina, he had come to realize the Bishop seemed to be the only person on earth who could coax such abandon from her. "Yes, certainly, it would be my honor," he said fussily, flattered by the invitation.

Tristan had never enjoyed the taste of alcohol, having developed a preference for fruit juices or buttermilk since childhood. And since that bout of drunkenness that had overcome him ten years earlier, sending him into a crippling period of melancholia on learning that Mala was betrothed to Vincento Balducci, he had shunned alcohol even more. Beaming with satisfaction at being in Mala's presence, however, he accepted the goblet handed to him by Salvetti, and drank willingly.

Quickly lost to the spirits of pleasure and festivity, the threesome remained on the breezeway drinking wine and engaging in conversation until well after sunset. That was when thousands of lanterns and torches of the great harbor below were lit, casting their reflections over the water, taking on the mystic aura of an entire constellation of shimmering stars. Meanwhile, Mala and Salvetti shared stories of commerce and merchant intrigue while Tristan recounted details of his dealings with Peter the Hermit and the Peasants' Crusade.

"Oh, Tristan, you poor soul!" whispered Mala, at times filled with horror, at times saddened by Tristan's accounts.

"Aye, Bishop, you've witnessed such monstrous behavior along your way east!" clucked Salvetti, especially touched by Tristan's accounts of the persecution of Jews launched by Count Emicho and the Tafurs throughout Germany. Salvetti was himself a Jew whose original family name was Salomone, but his grandfather had changed the name to Salvetti two generations earlier to feather his chances after migrating to Italy.

As more wine flowed and the conversation deepened, all sense of time elapsed until, unbelievably, the pale light of early dawn lifted from the east. "Heaven help us," cried Tristan, suddenly aware the entire night had passed. Standing, though his stance was unsteady from wine and fatigue, he gazed at the first rays of light as the edge of the sun peeked over the surface of the sea. "I had best go," he said with slurred speech. "Handel and Guillaume will be wondering what on earth happened to me."

"Certainly not!" insisted Mala. "You've been up all night, you've had too much wine, and you're exhausted!" She looked over at her adjutant and motioned for him to take their guest inside. "Salvetti, accompany him to the west chamber that's been prepared for his stay here in Constantinople, and make sure he's comfortable."

"N-no," objected Tristan, "I must get back to camp. My–"

But Salvetti had already grasped his unsteady hand, and supporting his shoulder, was escorting him inside the palace. Too tired to resist, Tristan complied. Shortly, he sensed himself being positioned onto the softness of lush pillows and covers.

Mala was tired also, but remained on the breezeway, determining that she would watch the full rise of the sun. Reaching for her goblet and taking a slight sip, she toasted the dawn and whispered to herself, “Oh, but it’s good to hear your voice and revel in your laughter again, Tristan… away from Rome. And far, far from the reach of Odo de Lagery.”

## Chapter Fifty-two

### An Invitation

It was early afternoon when Tristan awoke, and as he sat up in bed he fell victim to that momentary confusion confronting one following a night of excessive wine and merriment; it took several groggy shakes of the head to reconstruct the events of the previous evening. Contentment filled him then as he began dressing, realizing that circumstances had somehow fallen into place such that he and Mala happened to be in Constantinople together over the following months. He would be waiting on the arrival of Bishop Adhémar and the Pope's crusaders, and Mala had said her business in Constantinople would stretch until at least October or November. Good fortune aside, he hurried, feeling he must now report back to the Tuscan camp.

Salvetti met him as he entered the hall. "Ah, Bishop, I've set out smoked fish, sausages, roasted lamb, and four heritage varieties of Byzantine grapes for you," he said. "And," he quickly added, "la Signorina mentioned that you enjoyed fruit juice so I've also had the servants supply apple cider along with the nectar of crushed plums."

His tongue being parched from the night's wine, Tristan gladly followed Salvetti to the breezeway where Mala was waiting. "Come, Bishop," she said, motioning for Tristan to be seated, "and let's discuss your accommodations here in Constantinople. Alexius said you planned to camp with Guillaume and the troops… but really, I simply *insist* that you stay here with us upon the hill."

Sorely tempted to accept the offer, Tristan shook his head. "I thank you from my heart, Mala, but no." Slipping into thought, he grasped for an explanation. "I fear that me staying here might perhaps– prove a bit..."

"*Awkward*?" smirked Mala, finishing Tristan's thought, knowing well his compulsion for 'appearances.' "Come now, you didn't think it awkward when your Aunt Mathilda Medici hosted Pope Gregory for weeks and months at a time in Canossa, did you?"

"No, but–"

"And I dare say you think nothing of her hosting Pope Urban or certain cardinals of Rome at her estates in Tuscany for lengthy sojourns? So tell, does Mathilda deserve more consideration in such things than me?"

"No," said Tristan, bolstered a bit by this analogy, though he knew Mala held no fondness for Mathilda Medici. Yet, Mala's line of reasoning was sound. Many single, wealthy women of the aristocracy hosted high clerics of Europe during trips abroad. "But Mala," he half-heartedly rationalized, "I would feel that I was abandoning my brother and the Danes if I remained here… best that I stay in camp, then."

Mala had made the acquaintance of Guillaume, as she had the Danes. They were, in fact, the only other people besides Mathilda and Odo de Lagery who knew the true story of Mala bearing Tristan's child ten years earlier. The Danes, feeling that vows of chastity were simply another absurd Catholic creation, had thought little of Tristan straying from his vows at the time. Guillaume on the other hand, had castigated Tristan's trespass, and still harbored concerns about Mala's pull on his brother. Although he had chosen soldiering over monasticism, Guillaume's early years of tutelage with the Black Monks of Cluny and later years under the dogmatic religious thumb of Mathilda Medici had engrained in him an unshakable and inflexible adherence to reform Catholicism; so much so, in fact, that he had himself taken a vow of chastity on reaching the age of sixteen– a vow he had never broken. For Guillaume, dallying in carnal knowledge out of wedlock was a grievous sin.

Knowing this about Guillaume, and weighing Tristan's obsession with appearances, Mala switched tactics. "Salvetti," she said, "would you say that this palace is monstrously large?"

"Si, naturalmente!" replied Salvetti."

"And would you say it could certainly accommodate the Bishop's brother, a handful of Danes, and those who've accompanied them here?"

"Oh, but Guillaume's battalion is over five hundred strong!" interjected Tristan.

"Salvetti, you didn't answer my question," prompted Mala.

"*Si*," he nodded, "this is a former palace of the emperor, and accommodated his entire personal guard which is a thousand strong… half of them knights, the remainder footmen."

"I didn't show you the back acreage of the estate last night, Bishop," said Mala, feeling a bit nonsensical by her continuation of calling him by title. Still, she did it for Tristan's benefit, not her own… for the sake of 'appearances.' Continuing, she said, "There are barracks out back where my Genoan Guard is currently stationed, and room for many, many more, not to mention stables, training grounds, an armory, dining halls, and anything else men-at-arms could wish for." Tilting her head, she raised her shoulders in a slight shrug. "If you wish to deny your brother, the Danes, and the Tuscan troops such amenities, I can't stop you." Next, a slip of impishness settled onto her lips as she added, "Of course, men of such coarse caliber might well prefer to live out of tents, eat slop, and sleep on rocky terrain... I suppose?"

"Ah, but now I see how why you succeed so brilliantly in commerce and why they call you la Gran Signorina," said Tristan, bowing with feigned deference. "You make it impossible to say no." Smiling, he straightened himself. "I will convey your invitation to the Tuscan camp… and should they accept, then I also accept."

## Chapter Fifty-three

### A Royal Welcome

The welcoming and introduction of Peter the Hermit to the court of Emperor Alexius was a regal affair, accentuated with exaggerated pomp and religious overtones. Emperor Alexius, Queen Irene, and Augusta Anna sat upon their thrones surrounded by Patriarch Nicholas, twenty-five high bishops of the Greek Orthodox Church, high members of the Byzantine court, and a score of high ranking military commanders.

The palace hall itself was filled to bursting as royalty, the political hierarchy, and the wealthiest families of the city stood elbow to elbow, anxiously awaiting the arrival of the strange little monk of Amiens who had led over thirty-thousand peasants on foot all the way across the continent from far France. That such a thing could occur and that such a humble preacher wearing sackcloth and riding on a donkey could gather such a devoted following had created a stir within the city; more than anything, the throngs of influential Byzantine on-lookers were struck with–curiosity.

When Peter the Hermit entered the grand hall, they were not disappointed. Preceded first by a procession of two hundred Byzantine monks chanting Greek psalms, these followed by another two-hundred monks and nuns of the Peasants' Crusade, Peter the Hermit's unmistakable presence instantly silenced the crowd as he made his way down the aisle leading to the royal thrones, his pace deliberate and slow. His filthy hair was disheveled, his body was draped in ragged sack cloth, and his bare feet were so filthy as to be black, caked in mud and road dust. Holding a long staff, his long beard trailing to his waist, he approached with eyes raised to the ceiling, his lips riffling with prayer.

Overcome by his aura of spiritual humility, believing this bizarre little man to possess a mystical ability to preach and galvamize others, wide-eyed Byzantines stared, entranced, at this figure who had accomplished the impossible, leading so many people of no means all the way to Constantinople from Western Europe to battle the Turks for them.

"He carries the air of a humble saint," whispered a wealthy Byzantine countess, so fixed with the Hermit's appearance that she began to repeat herself.

"Aye," replied the nobleman standing beside her, "we are witnessing a living, walking miracle."

"Indeed," replied the man's wife, "and history in the making. With powers such as his, he might well turn the Turks and save the kingdom!"

Though those crammed within the throne room were of high blood, thus prone to pretentious airs, on this day they could not help but set dignity aside; straining and shouldering each other aside, they craned their necks while pushing to the very tips of their toes to get a closer look at the recently arrived curiosity of sacred repute. Never before in their lives had they witnessed such a cleric before, nor even imagined one of such unusual thread might exist.

On reaching the throne Peter the Hermit went to his knees, and began issuing the sign of the cross over Emperor Alexius, Augusta Anna, and Queen Irene. In response the emperor stood as Peter remained on his knees, and loudly proclaimed, "Peter of Amiens, servant of God, Constantinople welcomes you in the name of Byzantium and our Lord in Heaven!"

Next, as the Hermit gained his feet, one gift after another was dragged to the fore and placed before him as he graciously accepted each in turn. These gifts included a small chest of gold coins and gems from the emperor, a collection of religious relics including bones of two saints and slivers of the crucifix upon which Christ was crucified, and fragrances and oils. There also came a myriad of exquisite Byzantine goods of which the Hermit had no understanding. Despite having shunned such comforts, luxuries, and worldly possessions since becoming a monk, the Hermit remained genial, playing the honored guest for the purpose of diplomacy.

Innocenzo, standing next to him, could barely contain himself. His eyes large as saucers, he could scarcely wait to get his hands on the many goods upon returning to camp. "Holy chimes of Heaven," he whispered to Fazio, "just look at this hoard!"

After nearly an hour of such gift giving, the two hundred Byzantine monks began to chant on cue, leading the Hermit and his party to the Basilica Hagia Sophia, which was the largest and most beautiful cathedral in all of Christendom. Patriarch Nicholas offered a celebration of the mass, delivering a rousing homily in which he heaped praise onto the Hermit and his followers. Then, with the assistance of five high bishops, he administered communion to the emperor's party, Peter the Hermit, and all in attendance.

At the conclusion of mass, Peter the Hermit mounted his donkey and led his procession of nuns, monks, and priests back outside the city walls toward the peasants' massive camp. "Ah, praise God!" he clucked to Innocenzo and Fazio who were walking on each side of his donkey. "It's been a struggle, and our Lord has put me through my paces… but things have finally come right!"

## Chapter Fifty-four

### New Arrivals

As Peter the Hermit was being honored within the court of Emperor Alexius, an unexpected fleet of twenty-four ships approached Constantinople, entered the harbor, and dropped sail. "Ho there! From where do you hail?" inquired the chief oarsman of the armada of Byzantine dinghies that rowed out to tow them in for docking.

"From England!" shouted a deck hand leaning over the lead boat.

"And what's your business?" asked the oarsman.

"The Turks!" the deck hand laughed. "We've come to save your asses and clean your nest!"

Two hours later the vessels were moored and thick huddles of Norman and French men-at-arms swarmed off the ships like hungry locusts. Since William the Conqueror's invasion of England in 1066, it was the Normans who now ruled England, forcing their French language, their laws, and their will onto native Saxons. But these particular Normans, along with a mix of Frenchmen accompanying them, had been forced to leave England by their own Norman king due to criminality including tax theft, smuggling, and violations of fealty obligations to their monarch. In other words, they had been given the choice of deportation or imprisonment.

It is to be expected that sailors, after lengthy confinement aboard cramped quarters of small ships, become boisterous on finally landing at port. But as the chief oarsman watched the newly arrived Normans pile onto the docks and move toward the city, he noticed that these men were far more unchecked than others he had seen. Moreover, they exuded an unwelcome air of arrogance and aggression. "Shit," he said to the oarsman next to him, "first it's all these wild beggars from France and Germany running amok, and now a goddamned fleet of Normans piling in all the way from England added to the mix!"

"Indeed" replied the other oarsman, "and thousands more to come by next spring, they say. Soon Constantinople will be busting at the seams with foreigners, and will no longer be Greek!"

The two oarsmen watched the foreigners continue streaming off the ships, likening them to roosters, strutting about conspicuously as entitled to special consideration. As the oarsmen continued grumbling between each other, one arrival in particular caught their eye as he descended the gangway, positioning himself on the dock, hands hitched to his hips, nose high to the air. "Oh, but look there," huffed the chief oarsman, "and doesn't *he* think highly of himself, huh? He must be the master of these rutting bucks!"

Indeed, he was. His name was Lord Desmond DuLac, a Frenchman who had allied himself to the Norman invasion of England, and in exchange had received vast Saxon territory in north England by William the Bastard of Normandy. The Bastard had issued these estates not so much as a reward to the untrustworthy DuLac, but more for the purpose of manipulating him into quelling Saxon rebellions in the region and halting the movement of invasive Scotts from the northern border. DuLac, however, as was his nature, eventually fell afoul of the law and proved unable to rein in his own connivance and greed. After the death of William the Bastard, DuLac thought to take advantage of circumstances and began a series of illicit operations to enrich himself while undermining the new Norman king, the Bastard's son, William Rufus. After a period of corrupt success, DuLac's conspiracies were exposed and he fell under suspicion. Shortly thereafter he was placed under royal arrest and placed on trial. In the end, he was fortunate to escape England with his head.

Still, DuLac's behavior on the pier conveyed haughtiness rather than disgrace, and one would have thought him a king himself based on posture and overly affective gestures as he spoke to the two huge knights following him off the ship. The men were twins, Normans of pure Danish decent as evidenced by their blond hair, fair skin, and massive frames. Their ancestors were of the Gustafson clan, but as the Normans had begun adopting the culture of France, the family name was changed to the French adaptation of Gustave. These twin brothers, Pierre and Luc Gustave, were Lord DuLac's primary lieutenants and enforcers, and had over time picked up the same swagger of their master. Unlike Desmond DuLac who possessed noble rank, their arrogance was owed to intimidating size and a frightening presence, not position. Truly, anyone looking at the twins was immediately struck by their brutish hulk and fierce expressions.

"Shit," whistled the chief oarsman, "I wouldn't wish to tangle with either of those damned bulls!"

"Nor would I," agreed his subordinate, shaking his head.

DuLac and the Gustave brothers remained huddled on the dock in deep conversation for several minutes, then separated as DuLac said, "Luc, make your way around the city walls and find us an area to set camp for the troops. Then meet us back here at the ships by dark and make sure the men are ready to begin unloading horses and armor first thing in the morning. Meanwhile, Pierre and I shall look about, get our bearings, and make our arrival known to the Byzantine officials."

"Aye, Sire," saluted Luc, making his way off the pier, shoving his way through the throngs crowding the walkways leading away from the harbor and the city gate.

DuLac and Pierre Gustave took the opposite direction, and as they approached the massive city walls, soon came upon the sprawling, rag-tag encampment of the Peasants' Crusade. Both had heard vague rumors in England about a strange monk called Peter the Hermit and his proposed journey from France to Constantinople, but had thought the stories too preposterous to be true. After questioning several people of the camp, it soon became evident to DuLac that the rumors were true, and that the Hermit had successfully attained Byzantium with his unlikely following intact.

"Hard to believe, dammit, but impressive," mused DuLac. "So it occurs to me that we should meet this hermit character, Pierre. Though I see nothing resembling an army within this rabble, these many thousands might serve our own purposes of gathering Muslim plunder, eh?"

"Yes, my Lord, most certainly," replied Pierre, convinced that if there was any way to twist things to advantage, Desmond DuLac would uncover it.

As they headed toward the city gate, they heard a commotion coming from that same direction. Simultaneously, people raced helter-skelter from makeshift tents and shelters, forming two lines divided by a wide passage, as expecting the arrival of a procession. Then the clamor grew louder as people whistled, clapped, and cheered.

"What's going on here?" DuLac asked a bystander.

"It's Peter the Hermit returning from his welcoming from the emperor and mass at the Hagia Sophia," said the man.

"Hmm… the people seem quite happy about it all, huh?" remarked DuLac.

"Oh yes," the man beamed, "because maybe now we'll be allowed to finally enter the city gates."

"What?" said DuLac. "You've been denied entrance into Constantinople?"

"Thus far, yes," the man replied, raising to his toes to see above the crowd. "And we're not happy about it. Hopefully now that the Hermit's met with the emperor, we'll be received."

The noise of the approaching crowd drew nearer and the two lines constricted, closing in around Peter the Hermit's donkey as he approached. Without having to be told, Pierre started knocking people aside with his massive arms to make a clearing for DuLac as the Hermit passed. DuLac quickly stepped into the void to see the object of the crowd's adulation, but the sight puzzled him. He had supposed from the tales he had heard that Peter the Hermit would be some tall, imposing figure of a man, eyes ablaze with a thundering voice… but the man on the donkey passing before him was small and unimpressive; his head was bent forward and his shoulders were stooped, his face weathered and cracked. More puzzling yet, despite the jubilance and clamor of those surrounding him, he appeared somewhat diffident.

"Ho, there, Peter the Hermit!" DuLac shouted, falling in beside the Hermit's donkey as it plodded forward. "I'm Lord Desmond DuLac, just arrived from England to fight the Turks in response to Pope Urban's call for crusaders."

"Ah, bless you," muttered the Hermit without looking up, but raising his hand to signify the cross.

"I'd like to discuss joining forces with you," said DuLac.

"Ah, you'll want to talk to Sir Walter Sansavoir or Geoffrey Burrel, leaders of our military contingent, or to my man,

Tafur, leader of the peasant contingent," replied the Hermit, his eyes finally settling on DuLac as his donkey tossed his head with irritation at the mob closing around. "They'll be meeting at my tent at nightfall so I can brief them on my meeting with the emperor. You're welcome to join us there, for I'm sure Sir Sansavoir will be happy to see more troops join his command."

"Excellent!" shouted DuLac, despite having no intention of serving beneath anyone's command but his own. Leaning toward his lieutenant who was following beside him, he whispered, "Ah, and we're off to a promising start, Pierre. This little fellow and these other fools should be easy enough to turn, eh?"

## Chapter Fifty-five

### Joining Forces

As dusk settled over the peasant camp and torches were lit, Peter the Hermit measured the faction of men assembled before him. He had sent word to Walter Sansavoir, Burrel, and Tafur to bring their lieutenants, and also to other crusader contingents that had recently arrived in Constantinople, but not related to his own march. These groups included survivors of the ill-fated German peasant crusades of Volkmar and Gottschalk of Germany, a military German and Italian faction under the command of a certain Rainald of Broyes, and other small independent military units that had refused to wait on Pope Urban's main forces. It also now included Desmond DuLac and his host of French and Norman outcasts from England.

Combined, these different groups now comprised a population of over 50,000 foreigners camped outside the walls of Constantinople. Although half of Peter the Hermit's people were women, children, and elderly, the other groups were comprised only of fighting men. In essence, a very sizeable military force had unexpectedly converged on the Byzantine capital. Intimidating as it appeared, however, it was a fractured force lacking both leadership and a common vision. This impromptu confederacy, in truth, was more akin to a herd of stray bulls than to a real army.

"The emperor plans to open the gates to the city to us in the morning," announced the Hermit after taking an inordinate amount of time simply getting the men to settle. Even after saying that, many of those in the gathering paid little attention, being occupied in side-talk. As they had arrived in Peter's camp, many had entered animated discussions about their long journey to Constantinople, or the prospects of Turkish plunder. Yet others had already begun to bicker over who should be in command and who should have authority over the other.

Although their time together was yet sparse, hostility had already arisen between the Italian-German force under Rainald of Broyes and the French troops beneath the command of Sansavoir. Rainald's army was made up of Lombards and Longobords of northern Italy and Alemanni from the adjacent border of southern Germany. Further contributing to the fractured climate was the fact that the French themselves had begun to splinter. Geoffrey Burrel had begun the crusade subordinate to Walter Sansavoir, yet had been conducting a surreptitious campaign of cultivating his own base of support from within Sansavoir's recruits. After the debacle in Zemun when French armor was hung from the walls and French soldiers were burned within a Bulgarian church, Burrel ditched all deceit, openly usurping authority from Sansavoir. Burrel, being far more violent and aggressive than the pious Sansavoir, was now considered by many French crusaders as the more bold, decisive leader.

"Before opening the gates," the Hermit continued, "the emperor's representative will give a brief orientation on Constantinople and Byzantine law for purposes of keeping order. I suggest each of you attend, and make your people listen. It's important that we maintain a good relationship with the people of Constantinople, for we may be here a long while yet before attacking the Turks."

Hearing this, a pall fell over all side-talk, followed shortly by an outbreak of complaint and grumbling.

"A long while yet before attacking the Turks?" demanded Rainald of Broyes. "What in hell do you mean by that?"

"Emperor Alexius has strongly counseled me that we should wait for Bishop Adhémar and the main crusader armies!" shouted the Hermit, struggling to be heard above the discontent now spreading like wildfire amongst the military commanders and their lieutenants. "And though I dread telling you this, according to the latest communication Emperor Alexius has received from the Pope, Bishop Adhémar and the amalgamated crusader forces won't be arriving here until after December or January– at the very earliest."

Swapping looks of disbelief, a chorus of anger arose from nearly all present, even Walter Sansavoir.

"By damn, that's nearly half a year!" shouted Rainald. "And just what the shit are we supposed to do for that length of time, sit on our goddamned asses? *Jesus Christ!* We barely had the finances to get this far, let alone now supporting ourselves for another six months or so! Besides, my men and I have been here a good three weeks before your own arrival, and we're impatient to take on the enemy!"

"Damned right!" exclaimed Geoffrey Burrel, pointing angrily at the Hermit. "Me and Sansavoir have been stuck in this damned camp for weeks before your own arrival here too, and we're tired of being ill treated by these damned Byzantines. They don't even allow us knights to enter the city to worship and pray within their cathedrals but a handful at a time! Who ever heard of treating guests in such a manner, especially military allies?!" Then he looked over at Walter Sansavoir, calling him down. "You've said a hundred times you were impatient for battle, Sansavoir! Hell, that's why the entire lot of us left Europe in advance of the Pope's muster date of August 15th, which is two weeks off yet, and has now apparently been *further* delayed!"

Sansavoir, who rarely disagreed with the Hermit, shook his head. "Aye, Peter, I'm itching to engage the Turks, and see no way we can wait half a year or more."

"But listen to reason!" implored the Hermit. "Don't you see the wisdom in waiting for additional troops?"

"Look about you, Hermit," snorted Rainald of Broyes decisively, "we've gathered a formidable force here! So pray tell... you left Europe early also, but now you suddenly hesitate! Speak up, dammit... what are you afraid of, and just what the hell's going on here?"

"Aye, I marched early," replied the Hermit. "And yes, we've assembled a strong army amongst us here– but I've come to better understand the power and threat of the Turks since meeting with Emperor Alexius. I think it wiser at this point to proceed with caution! The emperor insists we've little chance against the Turks as things stand now, and he knows them far better than we do. More importantly, he refuses to commit Byzantine resources or troops until the arrival of Bishop Adhémar. Though the emperor has issued a formal welcome this very day and will open his gates to us tomorrow, he's of the opinion that we don't officially represent Pope Urban."

"To hell with who officially represents who!" shouted Rainald. "We came here to fight Turks, not lay about!"

"Damnation!" agreed Tafur, who had remained quiet to this point. "We don't need the Pope's permission to defend Christ! As King of the Beggars, I say the Tafurs are ready to fight now!"

"We don't need Adhémar and the others!" chimed Burrel, who like Rainald of Broyes and most of the other early arriving and independent military confederations, had intentionally left before the Pope's muster in order to get a jump on Muslim plunder and territory. "Goddammit, we don't need the Byzantines either!"

"Watch your tongue there, Burrel!" shouted Sansavoir, incensed with his blasphemy. "If you're a soldier of God, then show some respect to Peter the Hermit who's a monk of God! Though we may not agree with the Hermit, I'll not tolerate taking God's name in vain!"

Burrel glared at Sansavoir, fighting the temptation to draw his sword– but Sansavoir's lieutenants still outnumbered his own, so he bit his tongue.

DuLac, who had only listened until now, stepped forward, bowing to the Hermit and smiling diplomatically at the leaders assembled at the fore of the gathering. He had assessed already during this first day in the camp that much division existed amongst the crusader contingents, and smelled an opportunity for him to step into the void. Taking on the voice of reason, he said, "Peter the Hermit may well hold more information than we do, my friends, therefore we should at least *consider* his counsel. There are things at play here that we may not yet be aware of!"

"Aw, who the hell are you, and what the shit are you spouting about?!" grunted Rainald.

"My name is DuLac. *Lord* Desmond Dulac, actually, from England. And what I'm talking about is royal maneuvering behind the curtains... you know, Emperor Alexius. It's quite possible, after all, that he's deliberately constricting your actions and has issued ultimatums to the Hermit concerning your movement... information which the Hermit hasn't seen fit to yet divulge to everyone here. After all, hasn't the emperor already limited crusader access to his city in small groups?" Next, still fishing to decipher the mood of the majority, he shrugged toward the Hermit, as suddenly questioning Peter's credibility and strength of leadership. "Aye," he continued, "*who knows* what bargains Alexius and the Hermit may have cemented, eh?"

Whispers of agreement began rippling through the crowd as a swell of discontent escalated. “True!” shouted several voices from the back of the crowd.

Nonetheless, Sansavoir’s eyes drew down at this veiled accusation, and the large contingent loyal to him and the Hermit voiced their own displeasure. Seeing that opinions seemed split down the middle, and not wishing to yet alienate one half or the other until further testing the air, DuLac walked back his last charge. “But then, as I said earlier, perhaps for the moment we should at least throw the Hermit’s proposal of ‘waiting’ up for discussion.”

“Horse shit!” growled Rainald, not knowing DuLac but quickly sizing him up as a potential threat to his own designs for leadership. “My German-Italian force will *not* be ordered about by *any* damned foreign king! We’re not paid mercenaries fighting for hire, but men of faith fighting for the Christian ideal!” Looking at DuLac with contempt, he added, “You, sir, are welcome to sit on your ass as long as you wish before entering the fight. But not me and my troops!”

“Aye, *whatever* your damned name is, your bunch from England’s welcome to sit it out!” echoed Burrel. Burrel rarely agreed with Rainald since the two had already developed a severe distaste for each other, although both were equally egotistical and possessed an identical propensity for arrogance. “My French troops certainly aren’t shy about leading the charge against these Turks,” he continued, “which is why we arrived early!”

“Oh, no, no,” quailed DuLac, “don’t misunderstand me, my friends. We from England aren’t hesitant to fight, for as you well know, Normans are both fierce and fearless. Yet, you’ve heard the Hermit say the emperor *counsels* us to wait, but there may be more to the story.” Turning his gaze to the Hermit, he said. “Pray tell, Brother Peter, are there reasons *other* than the emperor causing you to hesitate?”

“Indeed,” replied the Hermit, raising his voice to be heard above the din of mutiny rising before him, “in the person of the Pope’s Counsel, Bishop Tristan de Saint-Germain who has followed me here all the way from Cologne... he also insists that we wait on Bishop Adhémar. I disagreed with him on this issue at first, but as I see things now, it’s solid counsel.”

"To Hell with Bishop Saint-Germain!" blurted Tafur, who happened to be standing next to Desmond DuLac and the Gustave twins. "He's a traitor! His and his brother's Tuscan force killed a good number of our men back in Cologne, and yet again at Zemun in Hungary! Or have you forgotten? To hell with the Saint-Germain brothers!"

At the first mention of the name 'Saint-Germain' by the Hermit, DuLac had stepped back, his eyes widening as if struck by an impossibility. Then, on hearing the name uttered a second time by the man beside him, along with the mention of a brother, a spasm of shock jangled both his memory and his nerves. "No, it… *cannot be!*" he whispered aloud, beginning to quake.

"*What's that*, Sire?" asked his lieutenant, Pierre Gustave, seeing that DuLac had turned pallid and was holding his chest.

DuLac did not hear him. He had already grasped Tafur roughly by the shoulders, and with desperation, demanded, "*Who's this Bishop Saint-Germain and his brother you speak of! Are they originally from north of Paris by chance?! Then from Cluny Monastery?*"

Feeling affronted, Tafur flung DuLac's hand from his shoulder, as he did not like being manhandled, especially by any man in the attire of nobility. "Keep your damned hands to yourself, you bastard!" he shouted.

In response, the Gustave twins simultaneously grabbed Tafur, throttling him. In a blink, six of Tafur's men jumped them from behind, beating them with fists, feet, and staffs. It was as if a pack of aroused dogs had attacked two bears. Those standing in their midst scattered as the fight broke beyond control until finally, after much effort and the drawing of swords, Walter Sansavoir and his knights managed to separate the combatants and hold them apart. "Stop this fisticuffs or take it elsewhere!" he bellowed.

DuLac, still ashen-faced over hearing the Saint-Germain name, looked at Sansavoir, shrugging. "Dammit," he said, "I simply asked this lout about this Bishop Saint-Germain and his brother, and he turned violent, by God!"

Sansavoir looked at Tafur, whom he had by now come to distrust since hearing about Zemun and Niš from Peter the Hermit. "True, Tafur?" he asked, sword in hand.

"No one lays hands on me, Sansavoir," snarled Tafur. "Not *this* jackass, nor those two hulking bastards at his side. We Tafurs fear no one!"

Seeing that Tafur would not settle, Sansavoir turned back to DuLac. "Well then… what is it biting at you about Bishop Saint-Germain and his brother?" he asked.

"Are they from northern France?" asked DuLac.

"Yes, born near Saint-Germain-en-Laye," nodded Sansavoir. "When they were boys their father was executed by William the Bastard of Normandy for treason. His name was Roger de Saint-Germain. Have you ever heard of him?"

"Yes," said DuLac coldly. "He was my… *brother*."

At this, Sansavoir nodded awkwardly, falling silent. Gathering his thoughts, and after some recollection, he continued. "Your brother? Ah, then I now recall who you are... according to the story, it was you who helped turn your brother in to the Bastard, then married your brother's wife, the beautiful Asta of the Danes." A look of puzzlement then filled his face. "But then... Bishop Saint-Germain and Guillaume Saint-Germain are your– *nephews?"*

"They're *nothing* to me!" snapped DuLac. "I've despised them both since their birth, and upon marrying Asta of the Danes, I sent them away. Who in hell wishes to raise another man's seed, huh? But my wife Asta became obsessed about the loss of her sons, and it eventually cost me my marriage."

"But then... they're also your *step-sons*, though you denounced them?" said Sansavoir with a tilt of his head, further dissecting the relationship.

"As I said, they're nothing to me, dammit!" retorted DuLac. "I'd as soon see them both dead, as well as my wife, and anyone belonging to my wife's old Danish Guard!"

"Ah, and I see the venom of it in your eyes!" hissed the Hermit, who had been listening with disgust to every word DuLac had uttered. "Shame on you, Sir, for denying a woman her sons back then, but even more so for betraying your brother. Oh, but what breed of snake on this earth turns in his own flesh and blood?"

"My brother was a traitor, conspiring with the King of France to overthrow the Bastard in Normandy," retorted DuLac, swelling with anger. "He *earned* his fate."

"But you are French," said Sansavoir, "not Norman. So why would you take William the Bastard's part over the king of France? And where have you been these past years?"

"Though it's none of your damned business," sneered DuLac bitterly, "I swore allegiance to the Bastard because the king of France treated me ill. Later, I fought for the Bastard during his invasion of England so he awarded me several large estates there after we defeated the Saxons at Hastings."

"We've heard England refuses to participate in the crusade," said Sansavoir, "because the Bastard's son who is now king of England continues his deceased father's hostility toward the Gregorian Papacy. So how is it you've come to Constantinople from England?"

"Again, though none of your affair, I've come to fight the Turks in the name of the cross, same as you," DuLac lied.

"Very well, then," Sansavoir nodded, looking at Tafur and the Gustave brothers, "if we're all here to fight the Turks, then let's quit fighting each other! We in this camp have turned into a nest of scorpions, it seems, with tails raised. And if it continues, the Turks shall make short work of us all!"

## Chapter Fifty-six

### An Act of Kindness

Tristan had been asleep at Mala's palace during the ceremony being held to welcome Peter the Hermit. Even had he been awake, he might well have chosen to forego it as he was still seething over the butchery of Jews, as well as over Zemun, Belgrade, and the debacle at Niš.

As for Handel, Guillame and the Danes, they refused to attend the ceremony, remaining in camp instead. Honoring and welcoming such a man after all the misery and destruction his crusade had inflicted upon others offended their sensibilities. Their mood soon elevated, however, when Tristan returned to camp and informed them of Mala's offer to host the Tuscan battalion within her palace at the top of the rise overlooking the harbor. The long march from Tuscany to Cologne, then on to Constantinople, was more than any had ever previously endured, thus the very thought of finding accommodations beneath a solid roof and sleeping in beds sent a ripple of satisfaction through the entire ranks of the Tuscan battalion.

Guillaume, alone, was reticent in accepting the offer. Feeling a nascent rise of apprehension, he pulled his brother aside. "Tristan, you vowed years ago that you'd set Mala aside, and I believed you. I still do, but I'm not as certain about her. How is it she just *happened* to be here in Constantinople as we arrived? I smell more than coincidence working here. I hope you've not forgotten your suffering over her, or the child lost in the Alps, or your bout with drunkenness and melancholy. Above all, I pray you remember the horrid penance you endured at Monteluccio to cleanse your sins, and your climb back into the graces of the Church."

"Guillaume," Tristan replied, taking that tone adopted by older brothers when brushing a sibling aside, "she is a huge trading presence here in Constantinople. She just happens to be currently renegotiating contracts out of concern for how the Pope's crusade might affect the future of her eastern trade network with the Byzantines, as well as with the Turks who might now choke off access to other Asian shipping partners. She is here for *business,* just as we are here for a *different* kind of business. The crusade is causing movement and concern in every quarter, Guillaume, not only our own."

Possessing little understanding of commerce and trade, Guillaume accepted his brother's explanation, though still unable to shed all misgivings. For the sake of his men more than anything else, he issued orders to break camp and begin moving munitions and supplies into the city and up the rise to what his men quickly termed 'Paradise.'

That the Tuscans were allowed to move into the city naturally raised the ire of many of the other crusaders, Burrel and Tafur in particular. "Look at those privileged bastards!" growled Tafur, watching them march through the gates and up the rise.

Upon entering Mala's palace and realizing what they had fallen into, the Tuscan troops quickly forgot previous hardships and made themselves comfortable. None were more satisfied than the Danes. Though they had been privy to the luxury of Mathilda Medici's grand estates, Mala's palace was far more opulent, spacious, and exotic.

"Swine's head!" howled Orla, "I suddenly feel like a prince of the city!"

"Ja," agreed Crowbones, "I've never seen such craftsmanship or detail in my life. Bones of God, these people here in Constantinople know how to live, eh? Back in Italy we're but poor, primitive peasants."

"Ja, w-we are but p-poor, pri-prim... primitive peas…ants!" stammered Guthroth, struggling with the tricky alliteration presented by Crowbones' final three words.

Hroc, too, was impressed. Taking more interest than the others, he and Guthroth set about together examining the details of the massive scrolled columns, the exquisite and endless frescoes covering wall after wall, and the minutely detailed tile mosaics appearing everywhere one turned. "Such *wealth* this woman, la Signorina, possesses," Hroc marveled. Experiencing one amazement after another, he finally turned to Guthroth and asked, "How is it then that Uncle Tristan knows this woman, la Signorina of Genoa?"

Guthroth knew the history, but had his entire life honored the secrets of others. "It d-does not m-matter," he said. "And d-do not ask again, Hroc… it is a p-poor question."

There was a trace of scolding in Guthroth's reply, but Hroc took no offense. He understood the message.

Handel was pleased by the accommodations also, but was even more impressed that Tristan possessed such a powerful connection in Constantinople. Moreover, he was surprised to learn it was a woman who possessed such wealth, and upon meeting her, was fairly swept from his feet. Stunned by Mala's youth and exotic beauty, he could barely collect words to issue a greeting. He had never during his travels throughout Europe with the Underground, nor within his entire existence, beheld such a beautiful creature as Mala. He fell immediately beneath her thrall... yet, somehow, sensed something queerly familiar about her.

Perceiving his puzzlement as they met, Mala embraced him with affection, kissing him on each cheek. Having had little experience or contact with women of any thread, Handel flushed purple, paralyzed by such an unexpected gesture from this woman of unmatched beauty. This quickly drew the unwanted attention of Tristan, Guillaume, and the Danes who found Handel's uncharacteristic awkwardness comical; each knew that Handel retained his calm, even under murderous fire, and could turn ruthless within the blink of a cold eye.

"Ho! The Bavarian Iceman blushes!" yowled Orla, poking his brother.

"Ja, ja!" brayed Crowbones. "Handel, brought to his knees by a little peck on the cheek!"

This further embarrassed Handel, causing him to back away from Mala, who then reached out and took his hand, pulling him back. "You don't remember me, *do you,* sir?" she smiled.

"N-no," Handel stammered, "though I thought for a moment we might have met before, perhaps."

"Indeed we did," said Mala, thinking back. "Do you not remember leading a military wagon train across the Alps to Tuscany some long years ago during the Investiture War?"

"Yes, I led several actually," nodded Handel. But why do you ask?"

"Do you not remember on one of those journeys coming across a small wagon and two ponies, half buried and frozen in ice atop a mountain pass? There were four people in the wagon, two of whom had frozen to death, a man and an infant."

Handel threw himself back in time, gradually reconstructing the catastrophe he had encountered one particular morning in the Alps years ago. "*Y-e-s*, yes, I remember now. As we broke through the ice to get into the wagon, I thought all four people were dead. As I attempted to enter, one of the women moved." He laughed a little then and shook his head. "Ah, I thought it was a ghost risen from the dead, and nearly shit my breeches! Anyway, yes, I remember dragging two women from the very doorstep of death itself from the wagon, one young, the other old."

"Yes, the young one was *me*. I still remember your kind face as you warmed us, checked on us, prayed over us, and fed us all along the rest of the way to Tuscany. I recognized you the moment you arrived here at my palace, though that was many years ago."

Shocked, Handel whispered, "*That was y-o-u*?"

"Yes, I fear I looked a fright that day— frostbitten, starved, near death. After you dropped us off at Canossa I learned your name, but was unable to learn anything more. I've for many years now tried to locate you. I've wanted all this time to thank you for your kind deeds, and for saving my life... but you're an impossible man to track down, Jurgen Handel. And in speaking to Bishop Saint-Germain, I now understand why."

There are multitudes of acts in life that bind humans together forever. Offering an act of kindness is on the short spectrum of this scale, whereas the saving of a life is at the high end. Handel, therefore, stood at both extremes in Mala's eyes. She had never forgotten that a Bavarian stranger by the name of Jurgen Handel had saved her life, which in the end, opened bridges to a new existence.

Handel had long since put the incident behind him. During that time he had been working an important mission upon the grand stage of the Investiture War. Little did he suspect back then that his small act of kindness to Mala would, in actuality, create a far greater impact on the future than did that single delivery of arms to Mathilda Medici that winter.

"Well, I must say, you look much changed since then," Handel nodded, finally working up a smile, clumsily returning Mala's embrace. "*Much, much* better, I'd say."

"Yes, I *am* much changed since then, Brother Handel," said Mala, lowering her eyes and tipping her head to him. "Indeed, *everything* has changed for all of us since then... has it not?"

## Chapter Fifty-seven

### A Simmering Pot

As various groups of crusaders had begun to inundate his capital in July and August, Emperor Alexius insisted they camp outside the city walls, allowing only limited entry into Constantinople. Incoming reports of disturbances caused by these crusader groups in Germany, Hungary and Bulgaria disturbed Alexius, causing concern for the security of his capital to grow. The savage incident in his own city of Niš by the Peasants' Crusade only exacerbated matters. In the end, his solution was to strictly regulate foreign traffic in and out of the city gate until after his meeting with Peter the Hermit. Once this was accomplished, he decided to finally open the city gates to all.

As a precaution he ordered first that the foreign masses assemble outside the walls of the capital to attend a briefing, the purpose of which was to explain Byzantine law and his expectations of crusader behavior while in Byzantium. This presentation was to be given in both French and German by the city's chief magistrate who was to be backed by a complement of Byzantine cavalry and footmen. Alexius did not actually anticipate trouble, but felt an armed presence would make more of an impact on the mobs of Latin crusaders waiting to enter the city– especially since mixed with the Peasants' Crusade there was now a large, mixed confederation of foreign military troops.

Impressed by stories passed along to him about Peter the Hermit's ability to ignite and bind a crowd to his will, Alexius further insisted that once his chief magistrate completed his speech, Peter the Hermit should preach to the masses about godly behavior and the sanctity of the crusade itself, focusing on the value of a solid alliance between Roman Catholics and Greek Orthodox Christians. It was a well conceived plan, and more than reasonable in all respects considering the huge numbers of foreigners who were now about to set foot inside Constantinople proper.

But alas, the most cleverly devised plans wither in the face of conspiratorial conditions. Despite his forethought, the Emperor miscalculated.

To begin, most of the non-military crusaders outside the walls that morning, which constituted the majority, had lived their entire existence in squalor beneath the merciless foot of Western European aristocracy. While thus strangled by their own culture at home, these people had been compliant for fear of violent reprisal from ruthless European nobility. Yet now these peasants and paupers had been on the road for over four months, roving freely, imposing their will on others for the first time in their lives by sheer force of numbers. In other words, they had lost their fear.

A second inevitability at work was the bigotry and condescension of the crusaders, both military and civilian, toward foreigners. Despite plainly witnessing the wealth, power, and sophistication of Byzantium on crossing its border, they still felt themselves culturally and spiritually superior; such arrogance quickly fomented a toxic brew. The Catholic arrivals also remembered that in 1054 during the Great Schism, Byzantium had broken from the Roman Catholic Church, which the Latin crusaders perceived as the only 'true' Church of God.

Although they little understood every detail of the Great Schism, the Catholic crusaders did know there were three issues of dispute: the true date of Easter, the infallibility of the Pope, and Rome's use of statues and other religious icons during worship. That the Greek Orthodox Christians would refute the Roman Catholic position on these three inviolable practices was anathema. Moreover, Greek Orthodox clerics continued to marry and have families. So it was that most Latins already considered the Byzantines to be but one tiny step above heathenism.

Above all, the greatest liability at work was the fact that so many within the crusader masses were simply poor and ignorant–two conditions thrust upon them by an overly rapacious Western European aristocracy. Thus fueled by resentment and hopelessness, and easily incited by the talk of demagogues, the Latin masses had arrived at that point when it would take but a spark to ignite an eruption.

As the Byzantine magistrate began his speech, he was able to garner the crowd's attention for only about ten minutes. After welcoming them, he launched into a tedious drone about Byzantine law. Shortly, certain members of the crowd began to twitter and rudely guffaw. This inspired others to adopt increasingly clownish behavior, ultimately leading to open shouting and ridicule of Byzantine law. There were those within the crowd, of course, who genuinely wished to hear what the magistrate had to say, but these were quickly drowned out by the others.

Soon it became impossible for the magistrate to be heard at all. In frustration, he stormed from the raised platform that had been constructed for the event while motioning for Peter the Hermit to take charge. Taking the stage with confidence, the Hermit motioned for order. "Oh, but settle yourselves, fellow travelers and soldiers of God!" he scolded. "Constantinople welcomes us today, and will soon open its gates, so listen, I pray, and be civil!"

"*They've not been civil to us!*" rang a voice from the crowd.

"Oh, the bastards treat us like prisoners!" shouted someone else.

"To hell with the Byzantines!" shrilled yet another. "Just tell them to open the goddamned gates!"

Moments later Peter heard himself being cursed, then felt himself being pelted with pebbles, plums, and other objects. Growing frightened, dodging missiles, he vacated the platform.

The commander of the attending Byzantine military had been gauging the crowd's abominable behavior with disgust, but as Emperor Alexius had anticipated little trouble, he had not actually issued instructions should disruption occur. Seeing that both designated speakers had left the platform, being uncertain how to proceed, the commander signaled to the ramparts and yelled, "Open the gates!"

This precipitated into a mad rush as thousands and thousands of Latins pushed and shoved their way through the gates of the city, fanning out in every direction, having no concept of where they were going, and most having no means of acquiring or paying for things they needed or wanted.

Further aggravating the situation was the fact that the thousands of soldiers who had arrived with Rainald of Broyes and other independent military leaders had been offended by what they perceived as a cool reception by the Byzantines. In particular, they were incensed over the emperor's restriction of their movement, allowing only allowed limited numbers of knights to enter the city gates at a time. The crusader commanders themselves had fanned the flames of this issue from the first day of their arrival, and in spite of now being given free access to the city, the commanders still simmered from the earlier sting of resentment.

In short, fifty-thousand discontented foreigners possessed of condescension, entitlement, bigotry, and violence throughout their journey to Byzantium unceremoniously stormed the gates of Constantinople. Predictably, mass chaos and pandemonium broke out within minutes. Constantinople, being a huge metropolitan port city, was accustomed to hosting foreigners from all over the world, including many western Europeans. Nonetheless, the citizens of the Byzantine capital had never been inundated by such vast numbers of visitors at once, not only lacking means, but also lacking all sense of social propriety and tolerance for different cultures.

Shocked by this flood of barbaric foreigners rushing through their gates, many residents stood with mouths ajar while others fled in terror. The merchants of the city had at first been contentedly expectant, knowing that multitudes of prospective customers awaited outside the city gates. As they now witnessed these foreigners pouring into their shops and storming over vending stalls, the merchants found themselves fighting off mobs of thieves who quickly began emptying inventories without payment. Next, many of the crusader men-at-arms, including the Tafurs, began harassing and molesting Byzantine citizenry. When residents attempted to ward off the mob or defend themselves, crusaders pulled weapons and openly attacked them in retaliation. Seeing what had befallen them, the complement of Byzantine footmen and cavalry sent to monitor the chief magistrate's presentation began to intervene. Hopelessly outnumbered, they were simply swallowed up by rampaging rioters.

Tristan and his circle were enjoying a lavish meal atop the breezeway of Mala's palace when the riot broke. It was Orla who first heard something. Gazing down toward the clamor arising from the city, he pointed and said, "Look there. What in thunder's going on down there?"

Staring down from the breezeway, it only took Tristan and Handel a short while to surmise what was happening. They were aware that Emperor Alexius had graciously arranged a briefing for the crusaders that morning, but had chosen not to attend, thinking the briefing would be both tedious and uneventful. Now, watching from the rise, they realized their error.

"Guillaume!" implored Tristan. "Assemble your troops! If nothing else, we must show the emperor that *we*, at least, honor his gestures of hospitality in the name of the Pope!"

"Yes!" agreed Mala, motioning to Salvetti. "Have Captain Moreno alert my Guard to accompany the Tuscans."

Handel's fuse went afire as he witnessed the bedlam below, and he was tempted to insist on abandoning the mob to Byzantine retribution at the hands of the emperor's Royal Guard. Nevertheless, knowing such a maneuver to be foolish, he grasped Tristan's line of reasoning. Running after the others to the stables, he shouted, "Aye, *we*, at least, had best remain in Alexius' graces!"

"Do we take lives?" shouted Crowbones, saddling his mount, throwing his hauberk over his head and down his shoulders.

"Hell yes!" replied Handel. "Teach these thugs a lesson, else they'll kill you!"

"No, just break it up! Kill only to defend yourselves!" countered Tristan, who had neither weapons, chain-mail, nor helmet, yet mounted and joined the others.

Within minutes the combined cavalry of the Tuscan Knights and Mala's Genoa Guard were thundering down the rise, splitting onto the streets of the marketplace. It was easy enough to differentiate the crusader masses from the Byzantines, so the horsemen immediately put crusaders to flight using the flats of their swords and the ponderous onslaught of their war horses. Unaware who the mounted men were, not understanding they were actually refraining from butchery, the men belonging to Rainald of Broyes, Geoffrey Burrel, and Desmond DuLac drew their weapons, violently repulsing the Tuscan and Genoan effort to break up the riot. Within moments men from both sides lay dead in the streets as Guillaume's intended attempt to instill order swiftly turned into a fight for survival. Although lacking horses, the crusaders numbered in the thousands whereas the combined forces of Guillaume and Mala numbered less than eight hundred.

In the midst of this conflagration, Orla and Crowbones found themselves surrounded, attacked by a dozen or more Normans of DuLac's contingent from England. The two Danes managed to hold them off by wheeling their horses about while wildly flailing their axes to and fro. Regardless, by sheer force of numbers, the Normans managed to pull them both from their mounts, taking them to the ground. Seeing this, Guthroth kicked his horse in the flanks and skillfully charged into the midst of the Normans, somehow scattering them without injuring Orla and Crowbones. Knowing they had narrowly escaped death, Orla and Crowbones jumped to their feet, recovered their weapons, and resumed fighting on foot.

In the chaos, Crowbones failed to notice a wild-eyed Norman coming at him from his flank, sword raised, just at the point of dropping his blade onto the meat of the Dane's lone arm. A blink later Crowbones caught sight of the descending sword. It was one of those flashing instants when one realizes what is about to occur, but is unable to stop it. Cursing in Danish, unable to halt the blade's deadly arc, Crowbones closed his eyes to brace for the very thing of his nightmares, the loss of his only arm.

Just as he thought to feel the blade against the chain-mail of his hauberk sleeve, he heard a loud clang and felt– nothing. Opening his eyes, he glanced up, spotting Hroc who had emerged from nowhere, miraculously hooking his ax beneath the Norman's descending blade. Reversing its downward motion, Hroc sent it flying in the distance. In one swift down-swing, Hroc then dropped his ax back and buried it within the stunned Norman's neck at the shoulder joint. "Get on my horse, Uncle!" Hroc cried. "And pull the sword from my belt to defend yourself!"

Guthroth, meanwhile, had cleared the Normans from around Orla and was holding them at bay while Orla pulled back, swearing at the top of his voice at the pack of men coming at him. In the midst of this savage rampage, he froze, suddenly struck dumb. Shocked, his eyes flared as he stammered, pointing at one of the Normans in the pack attacking him. "Oh, you *goddamned bastard!*" he screamed, erupting forward with complete disregard into the entire oncoming mass of Normans, trying to get at the man who had drawn his attention.

"G-get b-back, Orla!" shouted Guthroth, leaping from his horse to come to Orla's aid.

But Orla was now a man possessed. Charging forward, he flung one Norman aside after another with the fury of an enraged bull until coming upon two massive Normans who roughly repulsed his assault and threw him back; he had run into the Gustave twins.

"Get b-back, Orla!" hollered Guthroth, intervening as the two hulking brothers advanced on Orla.

Unphased, Orla charged again, blind with rage, pointing his sword toward the object of his fury. "It's *DuLac*!" he screamed. "It's *goddammed Desmond DuLac*!"

Crowbones, who had by now managed to climb atop Hroc's horse, heard Orla while simultaneously himself recognizing DuLac. His eyes going ablaze, he flung himself from the saddle of Hroc's horse and charged toward his brother and the Normans. Guthroth, still trying to pull Orla back, then also caught sight of DuLac. Seized by the same fury now possessing Orla and Crowbones, he too charged into the tangle, ignoring all other fighting surrounding them.

Orla's second charge against the Gustaves was like driving his body into a granite wall. As Orla bounced off them, repulsed, the combined force of Crowbones' and Guthroth's charge hurled him back into the two massive Normans, and in the ensuing tangle, it was impossible to tell who was getting the best of whom.

DuLac, who during the mêlée caught sight of Orla and recognized him, immediately cowered behind his two hulking lieutenants, knowing they could stop the Dane. Then he spied the ensuing attack of Crowbones and Guthroth, and his confidence flagged. He was well familiar with the ferocity of these three Danes in battle, and also feared their blind hatred of him.

The Gustave twins, equally as large and strong as Orla and Crowbones, were younger by twenty-five years, and managed to repulse the two Danes. Then, as Guthroth joined the fray, the Norman twins found themselves fighting for their lives, neither of them understanding why the three men before them seemed so driven to get at their master.

Just as the Danes began to reverse the momentum of the fight, a blare of trumpets split the air as the thundering clatter of thousands of hooves pounding the cobbled street set the ground atremble. Seconds later all fighting ceased as a battalion of Byzantine cavalry in full armor and battle array descended onto the marketplace. It was Emperor Alexius' Royal Guard, and they quickly fanned out, thrusting lances to the chests of any foreigner holding weapons. "Drop your arms, all of you!" the commander of the Guard bellowed. "And fall to your knees!"

"*Go to Hell!*" shouted one of Rainald of Broyes' Germans standing several feet away. "I take no orders from–"

Before the man could finish, five arrows from different directions whistled into him, piercing his torso from throat to belly. This quickly garnered every foreigner's attention in the plaza, and all immediately dropped to their knees except Orla, Crowbones, and Guthroth who were still trying to get at DuLac. In desperation, Guillaume and Handel grabbed at them, pulling them back.

The brothers complied, but glaring over at DuLac, Orla hissed, "Oh, but there'll be another time, you filthy bastard!"

The commander of the Guard rode about for a minute or so, surveying the damage to the market area, gazing at the dead littering the streets, which included Byzantine citizens, civilian and military crusaders, Tuscan and Genoan troops, and many of the Byzantine troops who had monitored the briefing outside the gates that morning. Noticing Tristan's bishop's garments, the commander rode toward him.

Tristan was still dismounting his horse to kneel as instructed, and had not been involved in the fighting as he had no weapons. Once the conflict erupted, he found himself helplessly watching the fray going on around him without being able to do anything.

"Are you not Bishop Saint-Germain, envoy of the Pope who held audience with Emperor Alexius several days ago?" asked the commander.

"Yes, Commander, I am," said Tristan, recognizing the man as one of the military men who had been in attendance during his and Handel's meeting with the emperor.

"What started this upheaval, Bishop?"

"Excitement, I suppose," Tristan replied, struggling to regain his calm. "These people were overly anxious to enter the city and… lost their senses." Pointing to Mala's palace on the hill overlooking the harbor, he said, "Some of us were there on the rise at the palace of la Gran Signorina. When we saw pandemonium break out, we thought we had best try to restore order amongst our own Latins, but they took up arms against us and things turned violent."

"With all due respect, Bishop, it's not your duty to restore order here in Constantinople," said the commander, looking displeased, "but *mine,* as City Commandant." Looking about at overturned stalls and the dead lying about the streets, he continued. "I'll be reporting this to the emperor within the hour, of course."

"These people are guests here in the city and he has extended his welcome to them," said Tristan contritely. "On behalf of Pope Urban II, we sincerely regret this incident, which is why we became involved in trying to stop it. Unfortunately, my brother and I have become all too familiar, since following them from Germany, with the atrocious behavior of many here in the square. Commander, if we overstepped our bounds, we regret those actions. We were thinking to help."

Nodding, the commander's scowl faded a bit. "Yes, and I'll report such to the emperor, Bishop. But you'd best remember, you tread on *Byzantine* ground now. You possess no authority here other than diplomatic privilege. It's not your prerogative to raise arms within our capital, regardless of intention."

"We understand," bowed Tristan respectfully. "It won't happen again."

At that the commandant swept his finger across the marketplace at all who had taken to their knees and exclaimed, "Should any one of you ever raise arms within this capital again, you'll be given the choice of execution or the severing of both hands. Consider my words carefully, each of you, for they're not a threat, but a promise." He then signaled his men to withdraw their lances, instructed two of his contingents to clean the streets and remove corpses, and instructed his other men to confiscate all weapons except those belonging to the Tuscans and the Genoa Guard, whom he determined posed no threat to the city. "You other men," he declared, "we'll store your weapons in the city armory and return them to you on the emperor's orders." Leaving half of his troops in the marketplace to ensure order, he turned and led the other half of his Guard back to the imperial palace to report to Emperor Alexius.

"My, *that* certainly went well," chortled Handel, walking up to Tristan, carrying a sword in his hand. "I'm not a prophet, but I'll bet the crack of my ass we can soon expect another audience with our host, Alexius, in the near future, eh?"

"Yes, undoubtedly so," replied Tristan, thinking it unusual to see Handel with any form of weapon other than a dagger. "You know, Handel, you look rather odd with that sword in your grip. When we arrived at the marketplace from the hill a while ago, I found myself in the midst of this mess without weapon or even shield. Even had I had them, I wouldn't have known what to do with them. It's only through good fortune, I suppose, that I survived. You must have been caught in similar circumstances as you had nothing save your dagger in your boot."

"Yes, but I quickly dispatched a man with it and took his sword, which I now possess."

"Like me, though," said Tristan, "you are unaccustomed to handling such a weapon, are you not?"

"Oh, not in the least," said Handel, spinning the pommel of the sword in his palm, then giving it a tricky twirl beneath his arm so that it flipped over his shoulder and slipped back into his fingers. "And I feel equally comfortable with cudgel, morning star, and hammer… when given the chance."

## Fifty-eight

### A Fermenting Bitterness

Licking their wounds, the Latin crusaders vacated the plaza and filed back to their camps, seething with anger at the emperor and his Royal Guard. Amongst the military crusaders, this anger also spilled over to Bishop Saint-Germain and the Tuscan force as several of the leaders assembled by Peter the Hermit's tent.

"Oh, once again Bishop Saint-Germain attacks Christian crusaders!" growled Tafur. "He's a pox to us all!"

The Hermit shook his head in objection. "No, this debacle wasn't his doing!" he declared. "The emperor welcomed us, only asking that we behave in a civil manner. But a curse on all of you trouble-makers, I say!" His stare then travelled from one man to the next, his lips trembling with scorn. "Your antics shame this crusade, and shame the Pope! Oh, but what's happened to your thoughts of God since traveling east?"

"Aye!" agreed Walter Sansavoir, who had for a while now felt uneasy over many of the military crusaders who had been congregating in Constantinople since his own arrival there. "Though I've had my own disagreements with the Bishop, I understand his actions today. You're here to take the part of Christianity, yet you behave like a pack of ravening dogs!"

"Bah!" retorted Rainald of Broyes. "We're being kicked about like the enemy, Sansavoir, and we'll not cow-tow to these people, nor to this damned Bishop Saint-Germain!"

"I agree!" shouted Geoffrey Burrel. "Bishop Saint-Germain clearly took a stand against us today, and set his brother's swords against fellow Latin Christians."

DuLac, who had narrowly escaped the retribution of the Danes just hours earlier, was listening carefully to the fiery denunciation of Tristan de Saint-Germain. Though his initial fear centered around the three Danes who once suffered beneath his boot in England, he now saw Tristan and Guillaume as equal threats. "Aye," he declared, "who would have ever thought a representative of Pope Urban himself would order an attack on Christian crusaders? Truly, this stands as an act of treason, I say. Guillaume de Saint-Germain's also a traitor despite apparent ties with both the Pope and the Countess Mathilda of Tuscany. Although these traitors are my nephews by blood, they're like serpents underfoot, and I doubt that either the Pope or Countess Mathilda understand their true nature!"

Innocenzo and Fazio had been standing in the background listening, but each interpreted the developing dispute differently. Innocenzo was in agreement with his uncle and Sansavoir, having long before determined that the Peasants' Crusade had turned savage. He had developed a fear of Tafur and his hoodlums since leaving Amiens, but now this vile talk about Bishop Saint-Germain by these new military vigilantes frightened him even more.

Fazio, conversely, took comfort in hearing these growing charges against Bishop Saint-Germain. In his heart, he felt the high cleric was an evil presence thriving within the very heart of the Vatican itself. Despite never having made a public stand against Bishop Saint-Germain since joining the Peasants' Crusade in Cologne, he now stepped forward. "I must agree with Desmond DuLac about Bishop Saint-Germain!" he declared boldly in his little elfin voice, which generated immediate snickering. Ignoring it, Fazio continued. "Yes, the Bishop is a serpent, I tell you, and is not what he appears to be!" Looking at the Hermit and Sansavoir, he said, "Though you both defend him, you don't know the depth of his deviousness, nor the extent of his wickedness!"

"What are you saying there, Fazio?" said the Hermit, becoming agitated. "I've known the Bishop since he was but a lad at the monastery of the Black Monks at Cluny. Whether I agree with him or not, he's *blessed* by the Holy Ghost!"

"Yes, yes, we've all heard the stories about the little Wonder of Cluny and about the so-called miracle at Monte Cassino," responded Fazio, "but there other things, *dark* things, that he's concealing from the world."

"Well, dammit, speak up then, man!" shouted Rainald of Broyes. "What the hell are you talking about?"

Fazio looked at the men before him, then looked over at the Hermit who was shaking his head, refusing to believe that Tristan de Saint-Germain could be guilty of anything but serving the Church. Seeing this, and perceiving the look of shock on Innocenzo's face, Fazio backed off. "This is neither the time nor the place," he said. "But know this... *all* men have their reckoning, and the Bishop of Ostia's time will come. And when it does, all you pikers laughing at little Fazio here will swallow your damned tongues!"

"Aw, bullshit!" hissed Tafur, flapping a hand at Fazio. "This little titmouse is speaking in riddles. The simple truth is, Bishop Saint-Germain has betrayed this crusade first at Cologne, then at Zemun, and now yet a *third* time today, which means there'll come another time, and another. He's not to be trusted, and we need to deal with him!"

"Agreed!" sniped Geoffrey Burrel.

"Aye, me also," shouted Rainald of Broyes. "We'd best keep an eye on him and his brother, too. Let's make a pact here and now that those two are to know *nothing* of our actions or intentions, and that we'll not heed a word they say."

"But he directly represents the Pope!" objected Peter the Hermit angrily. "Though I've disregarded his counsel in the past, I'm now of the opinion that his final interest lies in the success of recapturing Jerusalem... and isn't *that* why we're all here? Or have your motives changed, I ask? Aye, or possibly God was never your driving force from the very beginning!?"

"Indeed," said Sansavoir, "I now ask the same! Have you lost sight of our sacred mission here? There's already been too much fighting amongst ourselves here in this very camp, and now you try to drag Bishop Saint-Germain into your reptile pit!"

The others had already turned, and were not listening, breaking instead into huddles of discontent over Bishop Saint-Germain.

*Ah*, thought Fazio, watching with satisfaction... *the wheel finally begins to turn.*

## Chapter Fifty-nine

### The Danes

Just as emotions were running high within the crusader camp, they were also simmering atop the rise overlooking the harbor. "Oh, but who'd have imagined the gods would actually deliver Desmond DuLac to our doorstep!" exclaimed Orla, his cheeks flushing with anger.

"Ja, and were it not for those two Norman hulks, we'd have skewered him like a hog!" agreed Crowbones.

Guthroth said nothing. The color of his face spoke for him.

"You were all three foolish today," scolded Guillaume, disturbed by their rashness in trying to get at DuLac. "You could have gotten yourselves killed!"

"Oh, but I'd give my life quickly to end *his*," said Orla.

"Ja, me as well," rankled Crowbones, waving his stub in the air, having forgotten that he had nearly lost his good arm just hours earlier.

"Yes, but foolish nevertheless," said Handel.

This angered Orla, coming from Handel, more so than coming from Guillaume who was his nephew and commander. "What the hell do you know of our relationship with DuLac?" he said with heat. "We were like slaves to his whims for eleven years, as was Lady Asta. It's because of him that Tristan and Guillaume were orphaned, Handel. Add to that the death of my wife, and Crowbones' wife and children as we fled England to get away from him, not to mention other members of the Old Danish Guard and the thousands of Saxons he slaughtered during the Harrying of the North. He's a rabid wolf and needs to be put down! Yet here he is, alive and well while his victims molder in their graves!"

"Do you *really* think yourselves the only ones who've lost loved ones at the hands of rat nobility, or watched innocents fall like rotted fruit in their wake?" declared Handel. "As Guillaume said, you were foolish today. I don't begrudge you your fury, but be wise about it at least and live to fight another day! We need you. This mess we've been thrown into is far from finished, my friends. Hell, we haven't yet even seen the first Turk!"

Though Hroc had heard the bitter stories of DuLac, sons don't always absorb their father's poison. Hroc was more concerned about the carelessness that had swept his father and uncles into peril than about the past. "Ja," he said, "DuLac's not worth an injury to a one of you. There'll be opportunities to balance the scales in the days ahead. And I myself will help, but Handel's right... be wise about it."

This was the first time Hroc had ever challenged either his father or his uncles, and neither Orla nor Crowbones were pleased. "Your own mother, aunt, young cousins, and even your brother, Knud, in the end, no longer exist because of this man!" fumed Orla.

"Father," said Hroc, not backing off, "don't you think I know who this man is, or what he's done? Don't you think my belly burns? Still, I wish you and the uncles to live!"

The manner in which Hroc said this quenched Orla's fire a bit, as it did also for Crowbones. "Hroc is r-right," shrugged Guthroth, "and s-so is H-Handel."

Tristan had been listening to this exchange with mixed feelings. Despite having never seen DuLac since being refused by him at age seven and sent away, he had never forgiven him, nor forgotten the cruelty he had inflicted on his mother. That aside, he also agreed the Danes had endangered themselves. "I loathe DuLac," he said, "but he is little more than a burr beneath the saddle in the grand scheme of things right now. The crusaders have once again done the inconceivable, and we are caught in the middle. The Byzantines are angry, the emperor is angry, and we can count on the crusaders also being angry… at *us*."

"Indeed," nodded Handel, "best we keep an eye to our backs from this point forward. It's the hotheads who've now taken over the Hermit's march, and with these other fools like Rainald of Broyes and DuLac now in the mix, the boiling pot could tip any moment."

Mala had been listening, and though she knew very little about Desmond DuLac, her womanly intuition foresaw that imminent peril was tossing its shroud over the group with the appearance of DuLac in Constantinople. She had learned long before that the hot, blistering emotions of men often drove them beyond the boundaries of reason and caution; she sensed, one way or another, this business with DuLac was not going to end well. "Step back and listen, Orla," she said. "Heed Handel's advice. Don't let yourselves get caught in the midst of these crusaders with your guard down, especially DuLac. Today's riot has suddenly changed the climate here in Constantinople." Then, drawing down her eyes, she thought back to an earlier time. "And don't think I fail to understand retribution… I killed the man who mangled my mother's face, destroying her life with a dagger. I punctured his frame a hundred times, cut deep lines across his face and throat in the name of hatred and vengeance. But be *judicious*. Don't let revenge lead you to your own early grave."

# Chapter Sixty

## A Shifting Tide

That next day Handel found himself with the others gazing down at the crusader camp sprawled beyond the walls of Constantinople from atop the breezeway. "Judas Priest," he grunted, "that rabble down there never seems to learn, do they? Next thing they'll be setting the whole goddamned city afire like back in Zemun and Belgrade."

"This is not Belgrade," replied Tristan, his mood having turned foul by simply watching the crusaders below milling about their camp as though nothing had occurred the day before in the city plaza. "Should these people continue to behave like banshees, their end will arrive far sooner than imagined… and well it should, perhaps! Think of all the corpses piled in their wake, and the hatred bred with each step taken forward– Cologne, Zemun, Belgrade, Niš, and now the very streets of Constantinople. Oh, but life plays such tricks at times… they came to fight for God, yet perform Satan's labor! My dear father in this life, Odo de Lagery, has grossly miscalculated these people, and yoked us with protecting this filth. But they are not the ones needing protection, it's those in their path who need to be shielded."

As he spoke, Handel and the others detected uncharacteristic bitterness in his tone; the quiet rage that had been welling up in Tristan these past months was breaking to the surface. Every word he now breathed about the Peasants' Crusade was tinged with acid, and though his tone had barely risen, it was evident he was restraining himself through clenched teeth. It was not something they were accustomed to, and the very tone of it caused them to fall silent.

Handel had been the first to sense Tristan's first steps toward self-transformation, from watching his facial expressions over the past month, and most poignantly, having heard him blaspheme back in Niš for what Handel was certain was the first time in Tristan's life. He had also watched the ebbing of Tristan's implacable calm, the very trait for which he was most renowned. Tristan's current plaintive diatribe about the crusade was something Tristan would have never openly voiced prior to Cologne. No, these were things that Handel himself would say, but never Tristan. As Handel thought about this, he became conscious of how much he admired Tristan, not only as a cleric and a model of civility, but as a friend.

*He's our anchor*, thought Handel… *and should he ever lose hold, then we are all bound to drift.*

Guillaume and the Danes had also sensed change in Tristan, particularly after Zemun. Guillaume, since birth, had looked up to Tristan as the better half of his own soul. Upon their abandonment at Cluny Monastery as children, Guillaume had depended on him while also idolizing his academic brilliance, his frightening perception, and his penchant for grasping concepts, whether concrete or abstract. He was now also proud of Tristan's rise within the Church and his invaluable service to the Vatican. But as with Handel, Guillaume had recently become attuned to Tristan's shifting sensibilities. Despite a lifetime of concealing and restraining his emotions, Tristan now seemed to be disassembling his own walls. Understanding the complexity of current circumstances, Guillaume suspected this was not good.

That evening Tristan stayed up late working on his Papal Crusade Report. With blistering commentary, he documented in detail the brutal activity of the Peasants' Crusade in Hungary and Bulgaria, the Hermit's impotency in controlling his flock, and events since their arrival in the Byzantine capital. At the end of his night's work, he added something else… a commentary on Odo de Lagery's misjudgment of the so-called 'innocents.'

After midnight, discovering Mala alone on the breezeway, he shared in detail his litany of frustrations with her, including the fact that he now realized that Odo de Lagery had sent him on a fool's mission. "Oh, but why did he send *me* of all people within the Vatican," Tristan complained. "I was to travel with Bishop Adhémar and the southern French army, but instead I have been ordered to shadow the trail of this violent rabble which he so sorely misjudged!"

Mala had always hoped that Tristan might one day break free of Odo de Lagery's iron spiritual grip. In hearing Tristan's lament, she sensed a key slipping into a long locked door. Oddly, as she listened to Tristan question Odo's judgment for the first time in recollection, she did not feel the least sense of vindication. Rather, it caused her to reconsider Tristan and Odo's relationship… from a new angle. *Is it possible*, she wondered, *that Odo's hold on Tristan was actually less a matter of manipulation than a matter of Odo's own... dependence on him?*

The revelation startled her, forcing her for a moment to reassess Odo, the very man she had so bitterly resented for years. "Yes," she said to Tristan, "it well appears Odo could easily have burdened someone less valuable with the chore of Peter the Hermit." Then, placing her hand over Tristan's, she continued. "You know, I've been calling you 'Bishop' since your arrival here for the sake of appearances, but we're alone now, Tristan. I've been meaning to tell you just how overjoyed I am at seeing you again. I've missed you terribly this past year since your visit to Genoa, and with each day it seems I've thought of you more and more."

This touched a nerve in Tristan, causing him to look away a moment. "Yes," he said finally, "the same with me… and that frightens me a bit."

Mala smiled, but there was a sadness about it. "It's a bit more complex for you, I imagine," she said. "My own feelings are quite simple, but in your position with the Church, it must be maddening. I've complicated your life, I fear."

Tristan passed her a gaze, regarding her beauty, her exotic eyes darker than anthracite yet now agleam with reflection of torchlight. "Ah, but no more so than I have yours, Mala," he said. "Truly, it has made me wonder at times what God has done to us… and why."

"Oh, but God may have little to do with it, Tristan. I can't help but think that had you never fallen into the lap of Odo de Lagery, you would have never become a monk. Look at your brother. He was free of Odo's grasp, and never became a cleric."

This forced a wry smile upon Tristan's lips. "Oh, but he had our Aunt Mathilda who is more inflexible than even the most severe of nuns on the topic of God. Many say Guillaume should have been the monk, not me. At times, I agree." Then his smile dissipated. Lost in her eyes, his expression dissolved a bit. "Do you ever think of… our son, Mala?" he said, struggling with the words.

She looked away, drawing silent. As a slight tremor overtook her lips, she said, "Yes, but it hurts me so profoundly… I chase the thoughts away. I barely saw him, you know. He passed so quickly, frozen to death atop my belly, there on that damnable pass in the Alps. Yet I remember every tiny detail of his beautiful face. He looked so much like you… pure grey eyes, light hair, though his skin was darker, like mine. Such a beautiful child, Tristan, and it breaks my heart that you never had the chance to see him even, or touch him."

Tristan's gaze dropped, and he nodded. "Yes. And I suppose that was part of God's… punishing us, you and me."

"Perhaps. I used to believe our infant's death was God's wrath. Old Duxia de Falaise used to drone on and on about the merciless hammer of God, but now I sometimes think God had little to do with it, Tristan. The fact is, it was simply a horrid winter… my wagon got stranded on the pass, and a blizzard struck in the night. Duxia, Fernando, and I foolishly tried to cross the Alps in winter, and winter mercilessly claimed its toll. But please, I can't bear to talk about it without falling into tears."

"I understand. Oh, how very well I understand, Mala."

"An odd thing," she said, trying to construct a smile, "I vowed that once we were finally alone, I was going to tell you exactly how much you mean to me, and that I love you more than life itself. But as I've watched your eyes these past days, I realized I don't have to say a word… you already know. Nor do you have to say aloud what's in your heart about me. I, too, already know. And God knows, also."

"God?" shrugged Tristan. "Oh, but that is what has frightened me these past years, Mala," he said, shaking his head. "He has punished us once already, and I could not bear an even more severe punishment… nor could you."

"I could bear *any* punishment for you, Tristan. Yet there's another possibility you refuse to consider. Just as I said the death of our son might not have been God's doing but winter's doing, then perhaps it's not God that now keeps us apart, but our own imagined fear of God. Tristan, your mother was driven by God. From that foundation you were then placed in a monastery at age seven. Not just any monastery, but the monastery of the Black Monks of Cluny, the very nest of radical and strict reform Catholicism. Next, of all people, Odo de Lagery became your teacher, mentor, and father figure, not to mention you were later adopted by Mathilda Medici, perhaps the most inflexible papist alive."

"Ah, you continue to chip away at Odo and Mathilda," Tristan chided. "You forget my father was executed for treason and that the Saint-Germain family name was denounced. Odo and Mathilda actually saved me from a dreary end."

"No, I'm *not* simply chipping away at Odo and Mathilda," said Mala, her voice turning stern. "I'm once again trying to make you see that the three major influences of your life allowed you no choices. You were a *child*, Tristan, and you were shaped and molded to serve the Church! I know you can't help how you think or feel about God, morality or everything else in life, and because of that, I try to remain patient. I still hope one day you might yet shed the yoke you've shouldered since boyhood, though I neither expect it, nor will I plot to make it happen. I– "

"Mala," interrupted Tristan, "I possess free will, and intellect, and independent thought as well. Yet, you continue to act as though I am still driven by childhood influences. Give me credit at least for being a grown man, not some poor driveling soul still tied to his youth."

"Tristan, this damnable thing between you and Odo de Lagery holds us apart, and it always has. I've heard you this very night question him for the first time ever, and it gives me a flicker of hope. But I'll not manipulate your momentary disappointment in Odo, nor will I play the role of Sheba or Delilah. In just these past moments I've finally come around to realizing that Odo de Lagery does truly love you, and he needs you as much as I do. We *both* love you, Tristan, but he has maneuvered you into an impossible place." Then she shrugged. "Then again, so have I, perhaps. In the end, only you can choose. You're disappointed and hurt at the moment, in many things. You fought heart and soul for this crusade, but it's not turning out as expected. But know this, it's going to get worse… *far* worse."

"Well," muttered Tristan, wishing the conversation had not gotten so deep, "with everything else I've already endured, *that* is certainly encouraging."

The vacant expression on Tristan's face as he said this gave Mala pause, and she raised a hand to her mouth, covering it. "Well, well," she said, "just listen to me! A few days ago I would have given my right arm to simply *see* you, and now I'm ranting on and on." She laughed a bit then, at herself, and poured herself a goblet of wine. "*Bishop*," she said, "perhaps we should stop this bickering and simply enjoy the night sky and the lights of the harbor, the smell of the sea." She twittered then and held her goblet high. "Would you care for some wine?"

"Yes, Signorina," Tristan replied with mock formality, losing himself in Mala's smile. "Though I care not for its taste, it would do my heart good to share a taste with you on this most beautiful of nights." At that very moment he had to struggle to say no more, because he suddenly and helplessly felt himself on the edge of whispering… *Mala, I love you so.*

Mala sensed this faltering, and stared at him intently as he sat staring at her in silence. Then, nodding, she said, "Yes, I know, smart boy… I *know*."

## Chapter Sixty-one

### An Emperor's Ultimatum

As expected, Emperor Alexius soon summoned Tristan, Handel, and the Hermit to his palace to account for the riot. He was surrounded once again by his wife, his mother, Patriarch Nicholas and the three bishops of the first meeting, the Commandant of the Royal Guard and several military commanders. All seemed agitated.

"Would any of you wish of offer an explanation for what occurred yesterday?" scowled Alexius.

"No, Majesty," said Handel, taking on a look of agitation himself. "Bishop Saint-Germain and I made it very clear in the beginning, we are not in any way associated with the Peasants' Crusade, nor any of these other derelict armies arriving here before Bishop Adhémar's muster… yet you've brought us here like scolded children. I'll say it once more, we represent Pope Urban II, and he himself commanded that Peter of Amiens disband his crusade." Pointing to the Hermit, he said, "But this furry dimwit listens to no one."

"I see," replied Alexius. "Peter of Amiens, so what then do *you* have to say?"

The Hermit shrugged. "I can't be expected to control thirty thousand people, Majesty, let alone these other men-at-arms from Italy, France, and Germany who didn't march here with me. Even you yourself must deal with uprisings and rebellion within your own realm. One man can't keep his thumb on everyone else at all times."

"A weak excuse," frowned Alexius. "A good thing Bishop Saint-Germain and his brother's troops disbanded your mob yesterday, for had my troops intervened, we would have implemented Byzantine punishment. Any further offenses, and I will most certainly apply the law of the land– which treats civil disobedience with extreme severity."

"*Y-e-s*," hissed Augusta Anna, her icy glare set directly on the Hermit. "My son opened his arms to you despite *my* counsel, and that of others. Mass executions should be in order after yesterday's disgraceful outbreak, which is a point of discussion I will pursue later today in private with the emperor."

"Imprisonment might be a more reasonable solution, Majesty," interceded Tristan quickly. "Though Pope Urban disapproves of the Hermit's crusade, he sees these people as his spiritual responsibility. He may well consider your maiming or executing them as an offensive breech of the Catholic and Greek Orthodox alliance."

*"Offensive breech?"*said Alexius, sitting erect. "Ha! No more so than I found this *riot* offensive. Well, Bishop Saint-Germain… so you still maintain as does Handel here that you have no association with the Peasant's Crusade?"

"Yes, Majesty."

"Very well then. Truth is, I believe your actions yesterday are a testament to that response, therefore this is the last time I will summon you and Brother Handel in the company of Peter of Amiens. Handel, your earlier statement is well taken then. From here forward I will treat you and the Peasants' Crusade as separate entities. Bishop Saint-Germain, I will continue to recognize you as Pope Urban's official representatives here in Constantinople until the arrival of Bishop Adhémar. As to the Hermit's crowd, they will be regarded now as probationary arrivals."

"*Probationary* arrivals?" echoed the Hermit.

"Yes," snapped the emperor. "If from this point forward your motley herd will settle down and behave like human beings, they will be allowed to remain here until the Pope's armies arrive, after which time your followers can then proceed to the Holy Land with them to fight the Turks." He then shook his head. "You must understand, however, that I find the very thought of taking peasants, women, and children to war as *laughable*… and have no earthly idea how you came up with such a mad scheme."

"*God* Himself instructed me to do it," said the Hermit, reaching into his woolen tunic and producing his letter. "In this very letter of His own writing, delivered to me by the angels of Heaven."

This created a stir within the circle of Greek bishops, prompting them to mutter amongst themselves. Seeing this, Handel looked over at Tristan and shook his head. "Judas Priest," he whispered, "Here we go again."

"Put that nonsense of a letter away, Peter of Amiens!" commanded Alexius, cutting the Hermit off curtly. "Bishop Saint-Germain has forewarned me about it, and like him, I find your claim of God sending it to you to be preposterous, if not heretical. You have but one final chance to get your people in order. In light of what Bishop Saint-Germain said about Pope Urban's unfavorable interpretation of me maiming and executing your people, I will take a different action then should there be a continuation of horrid behavior."

At this, Augusta Anna's eyes lifted from the Hermit, gravitating toward her son. "A different action?" she asked, displeased that Alexius should make such a statement without having first counseled her or the Patriarch.

"Yes," said Alexius, not deigning to look at the empress, which seemed to greatly please Queen Irene. "Peter of Amiens, in the instance of further disruption, I will have the entire lot of you *deported* across the Bosphorus to the shores of Bithynia in Asia Minor."

"But, Majesty… isn't that immediately adjacent to Turkish territory?" asked Tristan, alarmed.

"Indeed. But Bithynia is under truce between us and Kilij Arslan," nodded Alexius. "I control the strip of coast there where many Greek Christians reside in peace alongside the Turkish border. There is an abandoned fortress of ours there at Nicomedia which can serve as a base. If the Hermit's lot remains peaceful there and does not create a stir, they will not be molested by Kilij Arslan's Turkish forces. Besides, as you know, Arslan is a Shia Muslim and is currently occupied in bitter fighting with his neighbors, the Danishmend Turks, who are Sunni Muslims."

"It is quite *questionable*, I venture to say, that The Hermit's people will remain to themselves," said Tristan. "Moreover, because of their shortage of food and supplies, they will surely be forced to range into Turkish territory."

"No need for that," replied the emperor. "I shall provide whatever is necessary by ferry to sustain these people until Bishop Adhémar's armies arrive."

This statement further irritated the empress. Issuing an audible sigh of disapproval, she looked over at Patriarch Nicholas who glanced back with a shake of the head.

"If deportation is deemed unsuitable," Alexius continued, "then the only other choice will be for the Hermit's people to turn around and march back home to Western Europe, which would be fine with me."

"My crusaders will most assuredly not turn around," said the Hermit. "They came to fight the Turks. The only option should there be more trouble then is to ferry us to Bithynia. If what you say is true about Kilij Arslan, then we'll be fine across the Bosphorus. As obstinate as some of these crusaders may be, even *they* will understand the wisdom of remaining within your borders along the coast. Besides, Walter Sansavoir has raised a sizeable army on his way east, and with these thousands of other soldiers who've recently arrived with Rainald, DuLac, and others, even should the Turks harry us, we'll be safe behind the walls of this fortress you mentioned at Nicomedia until the arrival of Bishop Adhémar. But let's see how the crusaders do in Constantinople first, Majesty, before considering Bithynia. I'll do my best to keep the peace."

"*Shit*," whispered Handel to Tristan, "that means we'll soon be in Bithynia. The Hermit's rabble wouldn't behave even should we threaten to set their asses afire! Alexius'll be deporting them before the week's out. And when these hooligans get shipped to Bithynia, they're damned sure not going to behave either. They'll be raiding across the Turkish border within a matter of days. Our whole damned mission from the very start was to protect the Peasants' Crusade from the Turks until Bishop Adhémar gets here, so you may as well warn Guillaume to get the battalion ready to deploy."

Tristan said nothing, but nodded with disgust, having already come to a similar conclusion.

"Very well," said Alexius, "now that we understand each other, Peter of Amiens, let time determine whether your so-called Peoples' Crusade can act like civil human beings or not. Otherwise, I'll begin preparing my ships."

***

As she stood and walked from her throne, Augusta Anna gestured to Patriarch Nicholas with a tilt of her head. Giving her time to vacate the throne room, Nicholas followed her path to a side corridor.

"Oh, but that son of mine!" rasped Anna as he approached. "Now he makes decisions off the cuff without even having the decency of forewarning me!"

Nicholas issued a theatrical shudder, grasping her hand with pathetic deference. "The young so quickly forget, my dear Augusta," he gushed. "If not for you, Alexius would have never had a chance at the crown. You've labored tirelessly on his behalf since his adolescence, yet he now acts as though he did it on his own." Shaking his head, he added, "By continuing to ignore your guidance, he shall soon slip– and all Byzantium shall pay the price!"

Augusta Anna was not listening. "These damnable crusaders, descending upon us like a horde of vermin," she gabbled, still brewing in discontentment over her son's decisions in the throne room. "Why Alexius insists on catering to and forgiving beggars and tramps such as this, I'll never understand. They're the filth of the earth, infecting our capital like swarms of starving insects! Worse yet, I do *not* care for the manner in which Alexius seems to defer to that young Bishop Saint-Germain. It seems my son is suddenly more concerned about Saint-Germain's opinions than my own!"

"Unacceptable," huffed Nicholas, trying to keep up with her brisk pace as she angrily made for her private quarters. He owed his patriarch position to Augusta Anna, and unlike Alexius, he had not forgotten. "As you suggested, Empress, mass executions would take care of the problem precipitously, and this riff-raff would soon make tracks back to their homeland where they belong!"

"It's a ploy, I say," muttered Anna, still hearing nothing of what Nicholas was saying. She stopped then, and nodded, almost with admiration. "That Pope Urban is a sly one, shipping off Europe's criminals and poor like this, dumping them in our laps in the name of God!"

"But in one thing, Alexius is correct, Majesty. With the Turks at our front door, we must not endanger the policy of détente with the Catholic Church. We need the Pope's troops"

"Yes, yes," I know," replied the empress.

"But then, what are we to do?" asked Nicholas nervously, acting more disturbed than he really was. Though he intended to stand by Augusta Anna as faithfully and for as long he could, he also clearly understood the Muslim threat… and was already beginning to realize that he might soon have to jump ship, especially now that Alexius had begun to assert himself more against the ceaseless encroachments of his mother.

Anna stood there in the stance of the aging who have become disturbed, her head shaking involuntarily, her lips riffling with tiny tremors. "I want this mob of worthless Catholic scum out of Constantinople, Nicholas," she finally said, squaring her jaw, looking at him directly.

Nicholas stared back at her, not knowing what to say.

"Alexius mentioned deportation," she said, taking on that distant gaze of calculation and manipulation. "See that it happens, Nicholas."

"Huh?" grunted Nicholas, confused. "But what can *I* do, Empress?"

"This rabble is easily agitated," she said, palming her chin. "See to it that we have people in the streets to… *agitate* them. Alexius will then be forced to carry out his threat of deportation… and once across the Bosphorus near Turkish territory, the *Turks* will take care of this rabble. Then, when the real crusader armies get here, they in turn can take care of the Turks for us. So, I place it in your hands, Nicholas."

"*Me*, Majesty?"

"Yes, *you*. It would be a job better assigned to the military, of course, but they listen only to Alexius. You and the bishops, however, possess a better grasp of my position."

This was, of course, a subtle reminder to Nicholas that it was she who had maneuvered the patriarch's crown upon his head. He had little difficulty deciphering the dig. "Indeed we do," he said, bowing.

Knowing Nicholas lacked the imagination or guile to actually implement her suggestion, she said, "Hire some ruffians to start a commotion here and there. In their present mood, the crusaders are a bundle of dry tinder and will be easily lit, Nicholas. *But*, be sly about it. If Alexius should ever find out, you will pay dearly… and I, of course, shall deny everything."

## Chapter Sixty-two

### The Fuse

Peter the Hermit carried the emperor's ultimatum back to camp, but was ill received. "The emperor's demands are reasonable!" he insisted. "He's willing to let us await the main crusader forces if only our people will settle down and follow Byzantine law. That's not too much to ask, I say!"

"Oh, but these Byzantine bastards are full of themselves!" exclaimed Rainald of Broyes.

"*Deportation*?" sniffed Geoffrey Burrel. "Ha, does the emperor think we're but children to be pushed aside?"

"Be reasonable," insisted the Hermit. "Despite the riot begun at your own hands, the emperor continues to offer markets and continues to allow us to come and go throughout the city in limited numbers."

"Agreed," assented Sansavoir, shoring up the Hermit's cause, "we should be at least as level as Emperor Alexius."

But the crusaders had long before lost adherence to reason and were not likely to rediscover it because of the emperor's ultimatum of deportation. In the meanwhile, Patriarch Nicholas set about his task of rounding up a corps of outlaws and hoodlums from the backstreets of Constantinople to carry out Augusta Anna's charge. His first step was to divest himself of all responsibility. This he did by passing the task along to one of his bishops, feeling the deed far beneath his own dignity. Besides, his only previous experience with criminals involved only members of the royal court, the church, and high Constantinople society, not lowly street thugs.

The bishop Nicholas tracked down to complete this task was a man of weak constitution, and accepted the commission without question. Being wary, however, he also quickly divested himself of responsibility by passing the command down to one of the monk superiors of the Hagia Sophia. This man was the first to find the order questionable, yet said nothing. Instead, he sought a particularly pliable young monk of his liking within the ranks of his care who was fresh from ordination, and hobbled him with the dubious chore.

Being naïve in nature, still burning with the altruism of godly faith, the young monk blenched with disbelief at first hearing what he was being asked to do. "But, Father," he said with wide-eyed innocence, "would God not frown upon such underhandedness?"

"Oh, no, no," replied the superior with soothing assurance, "tis for *God* that you do this thing, lad! Do you suppose for a single moment that He would approve of these filthy foreigners sullying our shores with their Catholic beliefs? Heaven forbid, they still worship icons and question the true date of Easter!"

This was enough to ease the young monk's concerns. Afire with the thought of serving God and upholding the tenants of the Greek Church, he accepted the chore with enthusiasm. Nonetheless, although this crooked ploy now presented no burden to his conscience, the task itself proved challenging; the young man had no association with criminal elements within the capital. After some investigation and forking out a pouch of gold bezants, he managed to hire his band of thugs.

Subsequently, within a matter of days, disorder reared its head again. The ploy of Augusta Anna and the efforts of the young Byzantine monk, however, may well have been for naught. Though the newly enlisted street thugs may have initially played a role in this rekindling of hostilities, in truth, the Latin crusaders needed no spark to continue their raucous, belligerent behavior. Within days the city magistrates and royal officials were documenting one abominable act after another as the Latins continued to disregard and defy Byzantine law. Citizens were pick-pocketed or openly robbed, and shops were vandalized or looted. Crusaders camped openly on city streets, urinating and defecating in public, often for the sole intent of offending their Byzantine hosts. They especially found pleasure in harassing Byzantine women and clerics, which in turn escalated into the proliferation of more civil disturbances. Certain Latins even became so bold as to set afire and pillage several city palaces belonging to people of influence. The final outrage, however, was the thievery of lead from the roofs of Byzantine churches to sell on the streets of Constantinople.

"God forbid!" wailed Patriarch Nicholas after receiving reports of his churches being stripped of roofing. "Bad enough these Catholic mongrels run the streets, but now they violate our most sacred edifices and attack the wealthy!"

Thus directly arousing the powerful Byzantine elements of both church and high society, the Latins had now gone too far. Infuriated by this continuation of lawless behavior by the crusaders, and having reached the limits of his patience, Emperor Alexius mobilized his Royal Guard and other military forces on August 7th and began rounding up all foreigners camped outside the city walls.

"Any of you wishing to return home are welcome to leave!" Alexius proclaimed. "The rest are to be deported as warned!"

Of the 50,000 Latin crusaders who had by now accumulated in the Byzantine capital, only a mere handful agreed to return to their homes. Alexius then had the rest herded aboard ships, reissuing the weapons that had been confiscated from them days earlier, and ordered his navy to ferry them across the Bosphorus and into the Gulf of Nicomedia where they were to be deposited along the isolated shores of Bithynia. This could have been a precarious operation had the crusaders organized themselves or decided to rebel, but the deportation was accomplished, surprisingly, with little objection or resistance from the Latin masses.

This was owed to the fact that the military elements among them had long been restless and were impatient to begin fighting the Turks, though they knew little of them. More critically, many amongst them smelled the scent of Muslim plunder and were satisfied to at last be pointed toward Turkish territory. Bolstered by such talk among the knights and footmen, the peasant population fell in line with this thinking, and within days Constantinople was vacated of Latin crusaders.

As the ships were being loaded, Peter the Hermit happened across Estelle Dupuis herding her older children across the gangplank, infant in hand. "Oh, but God in Heaven!" Peter exclaimed. "Estelle, disembark quickly, dear woman, and take your children back to France, I implore you!"

Gawking at Peter in disbelief, Estelle shook her head. "*Oh, but what's this you say?*" she huffed with indignation, her brows raising to the top of her forehead. "And lose mine and these childrens' chance of gaining eternal penance!? Was it not you who encouraged us to come this long distance for the salvation of our souls!"

"B-but Estelle, surely you–" sputtered the Hermit, stopping mid sentence. Seeing her iron resolve, perceiving that she was not about to leave the ship, his shoulders dropped and he hurriedly made the sign of the cross over the children as they scampered aboard, excited beyond belief; they had never in their life been aboard a ship. "*Oh... but dear God... what have I wrought?*" Peter murmured, shaking his head with self-flagellation as the pit of his belly knotted.

After crossing the Straight, the deportees disembarked onto a strip of Byzantine controlled shoreline adjacent to the Turkish border, and made camp at the abandoned fortress of Nicomedia. As this was occurring, Guillaume initiated preparations for his Tuscan battalion to accompany the Peasants' Crusade to Bithynia on Byzantine ships provided by the emperor.

Tristan, meanwhile, had to inform Mala of his own unexpected departure from the capital. "The entire reason Odo commissioned me to follow the Hermit here," he explained, "was to protect the Hermit's so-called 'innocent flock' from the Turks should the Hermit refuse to await the Pope's armies. The Hermit finally conceded to the wisdom of waiting, but his collapse of leadership and his horde's own lawlessness has now caused them to be deported and set down at the edge of Turkish soil… which means they may well soon be in peril."

Mala was stunned. She had been expecting Tristan and the others to remain there with her for another six months until Bishop Adhémar's arrival. Considering that everything she had planned and worked for over the past year had suddenly unraveled, she became distraught. "But Tristan," she pleaded, "could you not simply send Guillaume and the others? You're a bishop, and as a cleric you are prohibited from fighting or bearing arms. So what good can you possibly do in Bithynia? What purpose could you possibly serve there?"

"Though Guillaume commands the Tuscan force, Odo placed me at the head of this mission," Tristan said, no less distraught than Mala. "I could not possibly abandon the task. More importantly, I refuse to abandon Guillaume."

"You are not a man-of arms!" insisted Mala. "Won't you at least discuss this matter with your brother? Surely he knows you can contribute nothing should battle arise."

Mala was, in truth, correct, and Tristan knew she was. But there exists in men an inborn sense of honor and duty that often turns a blind eye to reason. Women fail to understand this peculiarity, and men refuse to walk away from it. So Tristan's answer came in a single word. "No," he said, refusing further explanation.

"Then you'll not ferry across the Bosphorus with the mobs," Mala replied. "They're not to be trusted, and they certainly hold no affection for you. You'll cross in *my* ships then, Tristan. And I'm coming with you."

"What?" said Tristan. "Absolutely not. I will not allow you in Turkish territory!"

"Oh, *Bishop Saint-Germain*," Mala said, her neck stiffening as color flooded her cheeks. "You may well be a high monk of the Vatican ordering other clerics here and there, but you don't order *this* woman anywhere! I've spent much time treading Turkish soil doing business these past years and will be far better off in their midst than you! Your entire Tuscan force shall cross the Bosphorus in the safety of *my* ships, not those of Alexius which will be spilling over with people who resent the entire Tuscan batallion. Furthermore, I shall be *on* one of those ships!"

As she said this, Handel and Guillaume had approached, hearing the end of this exchange. "Aye," said Handel, "we'd love to cross with your fleet rather than stow away with this damnable riff-raff of Latin crusaders." He detected that Tristan was growing angry, but also knew Tristan would lose the argument; Mala's face told him so.

"You have enough ships here to handle the Tuscan Batallion?" asked Guillaume.

"Yes," replied Mala, glaring at Tristan, "but I'll have to ferry you across in groups. "I'll get you to Bithynia, Guillaume, but I'm going with you, as is my Genoa Guard."

Guillaume, having been half raised by Mathilda of Tuscany who was a strong woman, as well as a warrior-woman who had led her own troops into battle throughout the Investiture War, thought little of Tristan's objection to Mala accompanying them. In fact, he saw her being of the same strain as his aunt, strong willed and fearless. "Excellent," he said.

"Guillaume," Tristan objected, "I'll not have it! She stays in Constantinople."

"Ho!" interjected Handel. "You have this backwards, lad. It appears *we* are going with *her* on *her* ships, she's not going with *us*."

"Brother," said Guillaume, "I agree. The Pope tasked you with turning the Hermit back, which we all knew would fail, through no fault of your own. Then he tasked you with following the Hermit across the continent and convincing him to await Bishop Adhémar, but that too has failed through no fault of your own. He then tasked me and the Tuscan Knights with protecting the Peasants' Crusade should everything else fail, and that time has come. We're soon to be on the Turkish border, and Mala shall take us there. And should she decide to stay once we arrive there, Handel and I both would like to see how you're going to stop her from doing so."

Outnumbered and outmaneuvered, Tristan could do nothing but give Mala a long look of disheartenment. *It might be dangerous*, his look said… *and I do not want you there because… I love you.*

Mala looked back at him, but there was no disheartenment in her eyes. Just as she had done that night they were alone upon her breezeway, she looked at him and said, "I know, Tristan… *I know*."

# Chapter Sixty-three

## An Assumption Exposed

The crusader exodus from Constantinople to the shores of Bithynia by ship was akin to the birthing of a new society of 50,000 people– without benefit of either amenities or collaboration. The coast of Bithynia provided a barren landscape for the most part, and was extremely isolated– two conditions that would shortly begin to cause problems amongst the diverse collection of crusaders who were now claiming it as their camp.

To begin, Rainald of Broyes' 3,000 men happened to be the first to arrive, and quickly staked claim to the abandoned fortress of Nicodemia which could accommodate only six or seven thousand people. Sansavoir's and Burrel's 7,000 troops arrived next, and feuding over possession of the fort became an immediate issue. Though outnumbered, the Lombards, Longobards, and Alemanni of Rainald refused to vacate the fort since they arrived first. This irritated the French and resulted in immediate squabbling. In the end, Geoffrey Burrel pitched such a fit that Sansavoir allowed Burrel's troops to claim the remaining half of the fort while Sansavoir and his men established camp outside its walls. As the final 40,000 crusaders arrived, they too established camp outside the fort itself. Their company was made up of primarily Peter the Hermit's Peasants' Crusade, but also included a dozen or so renegade military contingents from various parts of Europe along with remnants of several German peasant crusades.

As promised, Emperor Alexius promptly began to deliver shiploads of food and supplies, not so much out of concern for the welfare of the deportees, but because he had listened carefully to Tristan's counsel about jeopardizing the alliance with Pope Urban II. "If you will keep me apprised of your circumstances," Alexius told Peter the Hermit, "I will continue to provide your camp with reasonable assistance until Bishop Adhémar arrives. As leader of your new encampment, the best thing you can do is ensure your people maintain a low profile and refrain from crossing onto Turkish soil. If you do this, there will be no problems."

"Majesty, we thank you for your assistance and guidance," the Hermit replied gratefully, "and I will most assuredly remain in communication with you concerning our progress and needs."

Content to see the Latins depart his capital, Alexius was surprised and disappointed on learning that Bishop Saint-Germain and his party also intended to relocate to Bithynia. Hoping to dissuade him by leveraging Mala's assistance to reinforce his cause, Alexius summoned them both to his palace. "But this makes no sense," he told Tristan, "especially as you are not in any way associated with the Peasants' Crusade or any of these other early arrived, independent military units."

Without revealing the full array of instructions he had been given by Odo, Tristan simply replied, "Guillaume and I feel that with the Latin crusaders being so near to Turkish soil, any added military muscle we can contribute will be to their advantage... in case the Turks should become hostile over the landing in Bithynia. Then too, it would not hurt to have the Tuscan force there to keep an eye on the Hermit's horde."

The emperor shook his head, looking at Mala. "And Lady Mala, my Dear, what is this I have just come to learn about you also crossing the Bosphorus? The land is bare there, lacking all amenities for one such as yourself."

"Majesty," she replied, "I grew up in a tiny wagon traveling the roads of Spain and France with a band of Romanis who had nothing but the clothes on their backs and dreams of making a penny here or there. Trust that I'm more than capable of surviving Bithynia. Besides, I'll have my ships and my Genoa Guard. I'll be sailing back and forth between there and Constantinople as it's but a half day's sail. Mind you, I still have many business matters yet to finalize here in the capital."

"I simply don't understand either of you leaving Constantinople," the emperor insisted, "especially in the company of this violent mob calling themselves crusaders. In the end, I suspect that you shall have more to fear from them than from the Turks." But seeing that neither would budge on the issue, he shook his head and said, "Very well, I see your minds are made up, therefore I can only wish you the best. But remember, I will keep the channels of communication open, and should there be trouble, will send assistance."

That next day Mala's small fleet ferried portions of the Tuscan battalion across the Bosphorus. As it could not accommodate the entire force at once and would require several trips to ferry the entire force, she decided that Guillaume, Handel, and the Danes should go along with the first crossing; this would enable them to begin setting up camp while her ships continued ferrying the remainder of the Tuscan force, horses, and arms over several more trips. Mala and Tristan, it was decided, would remain in Constantinople and sail with the final crossing of her fleet.

As Tristan and Mala watched her ships depart the harbor from atop the rise, her palace seemed suddenly vacant and lonely in the absence of Guillaume, Handel, and the Danes despite the continued presence of Salvetti and the entire Genoa Guard. Still, an immediate comfort struck Tristan and Mala with this increased privacy now afforded them. Both reveled in this private time spent together, though they continued to address each other formally and maintained their distance in front of the ever present Salvetti, who seemed to be enjoying what he perceived as a growing state of happiness within la Signorina.

Salvetti assumed, mistakenly, that her elevated mood had been generated by the exotic surroundings and sunny weather of Byzantium since their arrival there. "Ah, Signorina," he commented several times, "this mild climate here along the Bosphorus favors you! I've never seen you so content or full of smiles!"

Tristan also entered a state of contentment, and though he dreaded having to deal with the Peasants' Crusade again in the near future, he decided to take full advantage of the pleasures afforded by Mala's company over the next several days– as well as of the entertainment and special soirée she decided to host during this precious period of tranquility. This soirée was an extravagant dinner gathering in which she invited Emperor Alexius, Patriarch Nicholas, and other dignitaries of the city, including several of her trading partners. Augusta Anna declined her invitation, as did Queen Irene; each had refused to go, thinking the other would be there.

On the evening of the dinner, Alexius exhibited an uncharacteristic sense of fun and humor. Even the dour Patriarch

Nicholas, in the absence of Augusta Anna, proved he possessed a taste for fine wine and other spirits, as well as an appreciation for a good story or two.

As the evening progressed, Tristan and Mala happened to be buried in discussion with Alexius and Patriarch Nicholas about the eventual arrival of Bishop Adhémar and Raymond of Toulouse to Constantinople. "I hear that Raymond of Toulouse continues to campaign to be appointed military commander of the Holy Crusade," said Alexius, "yet Pope Urban refuses him. And yes, I understand why the Pope has appointed Bishop Adhémar only as spiritual leader of the crusade, not military leader... after all, as a cleric, Adhémar is not allowed to fight. But this forces a question. Is the Pope's crusade, then, not to have an actual *military* leader?"

The question surprised Tristan, and he thought for a moment that he had misheard it. "Well yes, Majesty, of course it will," he said. "Pope Urban refuses to grant Raymond of Toulouse the post of military commander of the crusade out of deference to *you.*"

"*Me*?" said Alexius, perplexed. "But I certainly hold no objection to Raymond of Toulouse leading the military campaign."

This further confused Tristan. "But Majesty, Toulouse cannot be military commander in light of your position as emperor of Byzantium. Pope Urban reserves that position for *you.*"

Mala moved closer to Tristan as he said this, turning her back to the emperor to disguise her attempt at gaining Tristan's attention. Tristan, though, was so focused on Alexius, he missed her cue.

"*Me*?" said Alexius again, more surprised than before. "But that's absurd!" he laughed, dismissing the suggestion with a flap of his hand, looking at Patriarch Nicholas who also seemed amused. "I must remain here in Constantinople in the future. I certainly cannot be running about Asia Minor and the Holy Land chasing Turks!"

"Indeed," sniffed Patriarch Nicholas, shrugging as though Tristan's proposition was preposterous. "The emperor has an empire to run, Bishop Saint-Germain. He has no time for war."

The Gordian knot itself could not have confounded Tristan more than what the two men were implicating. "*But*, Excellency…

do you mean to tell me," stammered Tristan, "that you do not yourself intend to lead the military campaign against the Turks?"

Alexius looked at Tristan as though he had lost his mind. "Of course not!" he groused. Then his shoulders raised to his ears as he suddenly became aware of Tristan's own implication. "Bishop Saint-Germain, allow me to turn the question. Do you mean to suggest that Pope Urban believes that *I* shall be leading the fight against the Turks?"

The answer seemed so obvious at first that Tristan did not reply. After an uncomfortable silence, Tristan said, "Why yes... of course."

Alexius appeared stunned; it was his turn to appear as though he had taken a blow to the head. "I have n-e-v-e-r suggested that I would personally lead the fight against the Turks, not here in Constantinople, nor in Piacenza when I sent Patriarch Nicholas to Italy over a year ago to petition Pope Urban and the College of Cardinals for assistance against the Turks." Casting a glance at Patriarch Nicholas, he said, "Am I *misspeaking*, Patriarch, or am I correct?"

"You are most certainly correct," said Nicholas flatly, having now lost all trace of previous good humor. "At no time *whatsoever* has that idea ever been given consideration here in Byzantium. And if it had, it would have been brought to the table by the emperor in writing. I then would have presented such written communication when I visited Piacenza, and so would have the score of Byzantine envoys who have circulated back and forth since!"

Mala, having listened carefully to every word that had been said, nudged Tristan's elbow, forcing eye contact. *Stop this discussion now*, her eyes said.

Tristan understood, and though he felt confusion and anger swelling in tandem, he nodded politely and said to the emperor, "Ah, it appears that perhaps it is simply me who has made some inappropriate assumptions here, Majesty. Certainly, Pope Urban has never told me *directly* that you would be leading the armies against the Turks." This in fact was true, but it had definitely been implied by the Pope. It had also certainly been assumed, if not taken for granted, by the Pope. After all, since it was the Byzantines asking for military assistance, it was a given that they would also be fully participating in the war– with Emperor Alexius taking command.

Nonetheless, Tristan quickly changed course, and with Mala's assistance, moved the discussion into other channels.

## Chapter Sixty-four

### A Secret Exposed

Later that night after the guests had gone, Tristan sat on the breezeway with Salvetti and Mala, dissecting his shock about the earlier conversation with Alexius. "God forbid," he said, "how is it possible Alexius has no intention of taking the lead in this war? After all, the Turks are *his* enemy, and knocking on *his* door!"

"It makes little sense," agreed Salvetti, who had not been privy to the discussion, but like everyone else in Western Europe, had always assumed that Emperor Alexius would orchestrate and be heavily engaged in the fighting once the Pope's crusaders arrived to reinforce the Byzantines.

"Oh, but *Salvetti*," said Mala, "you have such a short memory. Don't you remember me telling you back in Genoa that the emperor would leave the war to the western knights, and that he wouldn't dirty his hands with the fighting?"

Salvetti thought back, as gradually, Mala's previous discussion about the political landscape surrounding the Holy Crusade knitted itself back together. "Aye, indeed, you did say exactly that, Signorina."

"Likewise," Mala continued, "I predicted that Alexius and the Byzantines would undoubtedly continue to carry on their sea trade across the Bosphorus with the Turks despite the war. Or have you forgotten that also?"

"Si, si, I remember… though I did not believe it at the time."

"Continue trading with the Turks?" said Tristan. "Ah, no! That simply *cannot* be!"

"Yes," Mala nodded, "Alexius' commerce officials and trade envoys of Turks further east of Kilij Arslan's territory renegotiated the pact yesterday, and Alexius himself approved it. How do I know? Because I was there!"

"What? exclaimed Tristan, stung to the bone. "But what form of treachery is all *this*?"

"It's not treachery, Tristan," said Mala, "it's business. The Turks to the east are not involved in this war, nor are they even in the path of the Christian march. And lest you be shocked even more, let me forewarn you... bad enough that I'm about to be forced to severe trade ties with Kilij Arslan and the Rüm empire, but I'll not cut my ties to the Turks east of Rüm! I've been trading with them since my move to Genoa nearly ten years ago– and have no intention of ceasing now, regardless of this Holy Crusade."

Struck speechless, Tristan sat back in his chair, setting aside his goblet of wine. Shaking his head, he said, "But what of loyalty and Christendom, Mala? Does it not matter to you that all Turks, being Muslim, are the enemy? Does it not matter that we are about to be at war?"

"The Turks are not *my* enemies, Tristan," said Mala calmly. "They are Pope Urban's enemies... and yours. This crusade is not about commerce or business, which is *my* arena. It's about religion. As you know, though I love God and attempt to support the activities of the Church, I've also had a bitter relationship with the Church and refuse the precept that it's infallible. Nor do I accept that the Pope is infallible, despite what the Vatican preaches or what *you* might believe, Tristan de Saint-Germain!" With each word she spoke, her face gained more color and her voice elevated. "Oh no," she continued, "Odo de Lagery is far from infallible, and this so-called Holy Crusade is entirely Odo de Lagery's war. The Seljuk Turks have no fight with Rome. And to this very day they still don't realize massive armies are forming in the west to fight over religion, otherwise they'd be uniting and mobilizing their own armies in preparation for war. But they're not. They don't even realize war is coming!"

Mala was speaking with such passion that Tristan realized that she not only had no heart for the crusade, but opposed it… a fact he had never considered. There had been cardinals of Rome who had opposed the crusade, and Handel himself opposed it, but Tristan had always assumed Mala to be in favor of it. Then again, he had never asked directly about her feelings on the issue, nor had she volunteered them.

"Oh, but I hope your opposition to the crusade is not centered simply on your distaste for Odo de Lagery and Mathilda of Medici," he said, his tone becoming defensive. "Yes, it *is* his war in a sense, but it is also *my* war as you well know, for you were there in Italy when I was preaching the crusade, Mala, and even accompanied me from place to place in Genoa as I preached it."

"No, my sentiments have nothing to do with Odo de Lagery, nor Mathilda, Tristan," said Mala, feeling bruised that he would think her so shallow. "I simply see no future in a war such as this."

"But why did you not speak up, Mala? Why did you not let me know how you felt?"

"Oh, and what earthly good would that have done?" Mala shrugged. "Would you have abandoned the cause then?"

Tristan shook his head. "No, of course not. I *believed* in it!"

"And *now,* after all you've endured with the Peasants' Crusade? And what about these other military groups who've shown up here in Constantinople, and the remnants of the two Jew-hating German peasant crusades?"

Tristan gave no response.

Salvetti, who was sitting between Mala and Tristan as their words crossed, fell still, feeling the onset of discomfort. Wishing to leave, he began to shift about in his seat, seeking the right moment to escape.

"Salvetti," Mala queried, trapping him, "did I not tell you in Genoa that *nobody* wins a war such as this– a war involving religion, race, and culture?"

"Signorina," stammered Salvetti, "I don't know enough about these things to talk about them, really... and it's not for me to get entangled in this dispute between you and Bishop Saint-Germain. I'm not smart enough to–"

"*Salvetti*!" snapped Mala, taking on heat. "Did I *not* say that nobody can win such a war as this, that it would only breed more wars?"

"S-si," groveled Salvetti, shrinking in his chair, unwilling to look Bishop Saint-Germain in the face. "Th-that's exactly what you said, Signorina… though it confused me a bit."

"*There*, Tristan!" huffed Mala, shooting an acrid look at him, her face flushing. "So now you finally know how I *really* feel about this crusade, and how I've felt about it for some time. You'd have known far sooner had you ever had the courtesy to ask! And *yes*, I accompanied you as you preached this war in Genoa, and yes I've kept my mouth shut about my true feelings all this time, but only because I… *love you, dammit*!"

As these words escaped her mouth, Tristan and Salvetti both sat erect, as suddenly stung by hornets. Looking at each other, then over at Mala, their jaws dropped. Neither could find words to speak. Salvetti, so disturbed at being witness to such an announcement from la Signorina, jumped from his seat and fled the breezeway crying, "Non ho sentito nulla! I heard nothing! May God cut off my ears!"

Tristan, too, jumped from his chair in an attempt to grab Salvetti and offer some sort of explanation as to what he had just heard. But Salvetti was too quick and had already fled from sight. Tristan's face had flushed when Mala uttered "I love you," and as he now turned to look at her, he saw that she, too, had turned crimson.

This was the first time either Tristan or Mala had ever spoken such a thing in the presence of another person, and it violated their unspoken understanding that such a thing was never to be uttered publicly. Staring at each other blankly, each wilted a measure, shrugging with mutual uncertainty and embarrassment.

This exchange of bewilderment continued a moment longer, but then they both shrugged – breaking into laughter.

## Chapter Sixty-five

### Bithynia

As the Latin masses settled in around the deteriorating fortress at Nicomedia, the immediate loss of their common cause against the hosting Byzantines of Constantinople began to generate a parasitic effect on the competing factions of crusaders. Within days bickering between Rainald's and Burrel's troops within the fort escalated into the outbreak of frequent fisticuffs.

Desmond DuLac played both ends against the middle, allying himself and his Normans with whichever side happened to favor his own whims at any particular moment. Moreover, in the face of Rainald's challenge, the French began to also bicker amongst themselves as Geoffrey Burrel and Tafur became increasingly belligerent in the face of Walter Sansavoir's moderation. Peter the Hermit, allied to Sansavoir, tried to squelch this discord now devouring the crusader camp, but his efforts fell on deaf ears as rambunctious military leaders struggled one against the other to hold court around the confines of the abandoned fortress.

The arrival of Guillaume, the Danes, and the Tuscans to the shores of Bithynia inflamed matters. After landing and assessing circumstances, Guillaume determined that he wanted to keep the Tuscan camp a cautious distance from the other Latins. Accordingly, he picked a site a mile and a half from the fort, midway between it and the small port town of Civetot.

As the first elements of the Tuscan force established their camp down the beach, Tafur and DuLac began suggesting the possibility of attacking the fledgling camp. Mention of such action, however, met violent resistance from Peter the Hermit who still held the strong support of Walter Sansavoir. Also, the splinter military groups in the mix felt it unwise to attack representatives of Pope Urban himself. The camp being thus equally divided on the subject, Peter the Hermit managed to neutralize Tafur's and DuLac's intentions.

"Oh, but such treachery against Bishop Saint-Germain would cause Sansavoir and I both to call for arms against the lot of you!" warned the Hermit. "He represents Pope Urban directly, by damn!"

Deciding it best to wait for more opportune timing, Tafur and DuLac nonetheless continued to stoke the fires of discontent against Bishop Saint-Germain and the Tuscans among the camps of Rainald and Burrel, though both acted less than enthusiastic about such overtures.

Emperor Alexius faithfully continued to ferry supplies to the shores of Bithynia from Constantinople, although this in itself did little to halt the escalation of infighting amongst the Latin crusaders. So it was that by the end of their first month in Bithynia, a hopeless rift had opened as the French separated completely from the Italian and German troops under the command of Rainald of Broyes. Despite being splintered, Peter the Hermit and Sansavoir against Geoffrey Burrel and Tafur, the French crusader forces, including DuLac's Normans, marched westward along the Gulf of Nicodemia and settled into the small port of Civetot. Though the original purpose of the Tuscan battalion, as devised by Pope Urban, was to boost the military security of the Peasants' Crusade against the Turks, Guillaume's immediate concern was now the hostility of Tafur, DuLac, Burrel and Rainald after the conflict within the plaza of Constantinople several weeks earlier. Handel held these same concerns, thus both were pleased to learn that the French had separated from the Germans and Italians.

"Ah, Guillaume," said Handel, "these imbeciles can't even cooperate with each other despite being stranded at the edge of enemy territory. Though they profess to be great military leaders, they split their forces in the gaping mouth of a potential Turkish threat! Yet, all the better for us at the moment, huh?"

Guillaume agreed. "Our camp sits between the two of theirs, far away enough to provide security and close enough to keep an eye to them both."

Within two weeks time the two divided crusader camps, the Italians and Germans remaining at Nicodemia and the French at Civetot, began to operate independently, sharing neither contact nor interaction. Even so, two issues soon became a major matter of complaint for both camps. The first was the increasingly oppressive heat of the summer climate. As the crusaders were from Germany, northern France, and northern Italy, they were unaccustomed to the draining effects of the sweltering southern sun, which conspired with the extremely sparse rainfalls of the area to make conditions unbearable for Europeans from northern regions. The second issue, which proved even more intolerable to the crusaders, was... boredom. After experiencing challenges, dangers, and adventures throughout the exhaustive journey to Constantinople, the inactivity of the isolated shores of Bithynia began to take its toll on many. In particular, this nagging idleness infected the military men of both camps who had envisioned glory through the conquest of Muslim territory and wealth. With time, it was the troops who especially fell victim to disillusionment and impatience. The heat, then, coupled with boredom and idleness, exacerbated an already existent atmosphere of irritability amongst the crusader masses, particularly amongst the leaders.

In the French camp, Walter Sansavoir and his troops continued to support the Hermit on most issues, and as time progressed, Sansavoir became the sole voice of reason amongst the French military. Tafur, who still professed religion to be his driving motivation, continued to loosely tie himself spiritually to Peter the Hermit though he and his fanatic peasant warriors had long ago split from him militarily. Tafur found himself now gravitating more and more toward the militancy of Geoffrey Burrel, whose intention of fighting the Turks had always been far more mercenary than spiritual. DuLac, also quick to use the guise of religion to shroud his intentions, actually lacked any interest whatsoever on the issue of God. Having been stripped of his noble status in England and living under a proclamation of banishment from that land, his only hope for reclamation was to acquire territory and wealth from the Muslims– through conquest. Recognizing that the declining authority of Peter the Hermit still possessed the support of many, DuLac continued to play the middle by now respectively manipulating the loyalties of the Hermit, Sansavoir, Tafur, and Burrel. Although he believed in no one, he also chose not to completely alienate one camp or the other until he figured which way the pendulum of power would ultimately sway.

## Chapter Sixty-six

### The Beach of Bithynia

The Tuscans were having a far better time dealing with Bithynia than the other two crusader camps. To begin, they were not burdened with bickering and infighting. The circle of leadership including Guillaume, Tristan, Handel, and the Danes, was a tightly knit group bound by both friendship and a common vision. Adding yet more cohesion, the Tuscan men-of-arms were extremely loyal to both of the Saint-Germain brothers, and lacked the mercenary ambitions of weasels like DuLac, Rainald, and Burrell.

Another advantage held by the Tuscan camp was access to Mala's small fleet. Since the Tuscan battalion was still in the good graces of Emperor Alexius, they were welcome to return to Constantinople as they wished. This opportunity they took in shifts as Mala began sailing back and forth across the Bosphorus to conduct business in the capital. In the end, this ability to periodically enjoy access to the amenities of Constantinople did much to combat the eroding effects of boredom and isolation suffered by the opposing camps.

Yet another factor favoring the Tuscan battalion was the fact that there was no sense of immediacy driving them. It had been the original intent of Tristan, Guillaume, and the others to march against the Turks with Bishop Adhémar's armies, but his arrival was still many months off. Unlike the fractured groups beneath the command of Rainald, Burrel, and DuLac, the Tuscans were neither pressed, nor haunted by visions of plunder; their interest in capturing Jerusalem centered solely on the interests of Christendom.

Subsequently, the sole specter hanging over Guillaume's camp was the possibility that the other Latins would encroach upon Turkish territory. So it happened that the Tuscan location a mile and a half between the brewing caldrons of Civetot and the Nicodemia fortress developed into a tolerable, if not somewhat pleasant period of inactivity and tranquility along the beaches of Bithynia.

More than others of the Tuscan camp, Mala and Tristan reveled in this new environment. They soon became lost in sharing conversational and platonic intimacy while walking the beaches together, especially late in the evening when the two would disappear for hours on end. As time elapsed, they became more and more absorbed in the private, idyllic settings of the Bithynian coast, and in each other. Before long, the sonorous bustle of their respective former lives in Rome and Genoa began to fade from memory, as did even the Holy Crusade itself.

In life, times arrive when humans want a thing so desperately, and strive so tirelessly to acquire it, that this unattainable thing abandons the world of reality– drifting instead into the vaporous realm of dreams. From there it evolves into a ceaseless obsession in both the conscience and the sub-conscience, never allowing one a moment's peace. But there comes a twist with this foible. In the rare instance that this unattainable thing, or dream, should actually become a reality, it continues to remain dreamlike despite being real. Thus the term 'living the dream,' and thus the nagging fear of the dream soon ending– which in the end, as with all things, must happen. It was in this state that Tristan and Mala cautiously cherished each day in Bithynia, taking nothing for granted, squeezing every moment of precious time together to its tenth degree.

The question arose, however, of how others interpreted this blossoming interplay between Bishop Saint-Germain and la Gran Signorina. It became evident to all within the Tuscan camp that the two adored each other despite the complete absence of open signs of affection or intimacy. The Danes thought little of it; they had never been able to grasp the concept of vows involving celibacy and chastity for anyone– not even holy men. Although Guthroth had taken the water and was now Christian, even he found the concept too unnatural to embrace.

As to Handel, he wondered at times more out of curiosity than concern, whether Tristan was respecting his vows or not. Ultimately, he was of the mind that it really was none of his concern. Despite being Benedictine, he had never adopted actual zeal for rigid reformism, nor did he necessarily frown upon those who did not adhere to it; his interest had always inclined more toward helping the weak, the poor and the dispossessed. Thus, having never adopted Gregorian fanaticism as related to celibacy and chastity, his thoughts on the topic were actually rather neutral though he himself had never pursued women nor enjoyed the pleasures of the flesh. In Handel's defense, it must be acknowledged that the moral rigidity imposed upon Catholic clerics by Pope Gregory VII was still a somewhat nascent philosophy, and many within the Church had still not accepted it. Outside of the reform nest itself, many Catholic priests and monks had continued to maintain carnal relations with women, or marry and raise families.

Mala's faithful financial adjutant, Salvetti, had been utterly shocked at hearing Mala's open profession of love for Bishop Saint-Germain on the breezeway several weeks earlier, and had fled that confession, confounded. Still, content to see La Signorina in such a state of bliss, he had by now resigned himself to the fact that la Gran Signorina and Bishop Saint-Germain were such powerful figureheads in Europe that they deserved the same right to break convention as other exalted aristocrats of the world. Like other men of Salvetti's low wrung on the ladder in life, he knew aristocrats broke every rule conceivable, at all times. Respectfully, he went about his business as did all men realizing this– by acting deaf, dumb, and blind.

It was only Guillaume, then, who became disturbed about the appearance of impropriety between Tristan and Mala, though nothing had yet, in reality, actually occurred. His inflexible faith and unshakeable adherence to Gregorian dogma allowed him no room but a firm stand against carnal relationships outside of marriage. Although he loved Tristan more than any person on earth, he now began to worry about his brother's soul. "You're a high bishop of Cluniac reform roots, Tristan," he would say in private to Tristan. "Beware of temptation, for God is ever present, Tristan. He knows all things. Have you so easily forgotten the bitter lesson and suffering of your penance at Montelucio ten years gone by?"

Tristan dismissed Guillaume's warnings; he had for the first time in life begun to appreciate the simple act of acknowledging his own emotions. He, as taught by his mother, Asta, had lived an existence of self-imposed restraint. She had taught him to conceal his joy, his anger, and his passion. "Never show your hand," she had preached time and time again, 'for that is to give away your position, placing yourself at disadvantage.' She had tried to teach these same lessons to Guillaume, but he lacked Tristan's sensitivities and possessed a far greater sense of play and rambunctiousness. Furthermore, he had only been four years old when Asta had sent her two sons to the Black Monks; she had not had time to make the same impression on him as she had on Tristan.

Granted, Tristan's ability to mask his heart and not show his hand in all but the most extreme of circumstances had become his strength. Forever holding one's passions in check, however, extracts a profound inner toll, which he was only now beginning to discover… because of Mala. She was magnifying and amplifying every aspect of each thing he now experienced in Bithynia, whether it was simple conversation together, sharing the sunset, listening to the surf crash against the shore, or walking the beach. The simplicity of it all was overwhelming, he decided… like the small farm next to the brook at the foot of Canossa in Tuscany.

It was the same for Mala. "I've never been so happy in my entire life!" she exclaimed with abandonment as they meandered the beach toward Civetot one dusk. Laughing, she took a playful swipe at him and said, "And yes, I shall now finally confess that I truly *did* connive to be here when you arrived in Constantinople, Tristan. But you've no idea the trouble I went through to make it happen!" Thinking back, she looked at him with impish eyes. "I even had a little man following you around as you made your way from Rome to Cologne to find out where you'd end up!"

"What?" queried Tristan. "You *spied* on me?"

"Yes, of course, because wherever you may be, there lies also my heart. Besides, did you not have certain agents of the Underground tracking down my whereabouts when you first joined their ranks? Come now, fess up! Isn't that how you first found my Romani camp along the Loire River shortly after you were ordained?"

Tristan, who had never admitted to such, tried to stifle a grin, but the effort failed. "Ah, but aren't you the clever one, Mala?" Then he took her hand, which is something he had only recently begun doing in the absence of others during their evening walks along the shore. "And wherever you are, my heart also resides," he said.

They walked along in comfortable conversation for another several minutes, lost in the warmth of each other's words; both feeling as lost in the midst of a short dream; both desperate to savor and enjoy each moment of that dream while it lasted; both knowing very well that dreams are a slippery, fleeting thing. Thus lost in each other, they came nearly to edge of Civetot before realizing how far they had wandered.

"We best turn about," said Tristan, reluctantly. "Dark has fallen, and I am despised here."

But as they started to change direction, they noticed two figures moving toward them along the shoreline, one tall, the other short. Seconds later a voice rang out. "Bishop Saint-Germain! It's me!" Moments later Innocenzo ran forward to greet them. "Aha, I *thought* that was you, Bishop!" he exclaimed. Then, peering intently through the light of the full moon, he said, "Oh, and who's *this* beautiful woman at your side?"

Tristan did not reply immediately– so Mala answered for him. "My name is Mala, and I'm visiting Constantinople from Genoa. I'm an acquaintance of the Bishop, and receiving news of his presence in Byzantium, have come to visit him here in Bithynia." She pointed then to the shadows of three ships anchored in the distance just offshore from the Tuscan camp far behind her. "I'm a merchant, and my vessels are anchored just there."

Though captivated by her beauty, which was evident even in the sparse light, Innocenzo turned to Tristan and embraced him, unable to constrain that childlike affection he had always possessed for the Bishop. "Oh, my uncle and I have missed you so," Innocenzo said. "He speaks of you often, and often quotes your counsel in Civetot."

"Ah, but I wager my words are ill received in his camp, n'est-ce pas?" said Tristan, deciding by now that he, too, was pleased by this unanticipated encounter. He had always liked Innocenzo.

"Your name isn't a favorite amongst *some* folk there," shrugged Innocenzo, "but even Sansavoir speaks on your behalf, despite what your brother did to him back in Cologne." As

Innocenzo finished these words, the shorter figure approached, and his eyes chanced to fall upon Mala in the half light, and hers upon him. They looked at each other, and as both mouths dropped, Innocenzo said, "This is my friend, Fazio, who also happens to be from Genoa."

Tristan looked down at the little man, recognizing him, and recalled the strange feeling he had about him during their encounter at Niš. Meanwhile, Fazio and Mala, their mouths still ajar, both blurted a burst of incomprehensible words.

"My God," stammered Mala, finally making sense, "*Fazio?*"

"*Signorina?!*" cried Fazio, his mind muddled.

"But what are *you* doing here?" asked Mala, still dumbstruck at coming across him in the midst of nowhere.

Fazio then recognized Bishop Saint-Germain, which caused him yet more consternation. Gathering his wits, he said, "I-I joined the Hermit's Crusade in Cologne after meeting Innocenzo. In fact, it was Innocenzo who passed along to me all the information about– " He halted mid-sentence, confused by this sudden situation he had now fallen into. Recollecting his conversation with la Gran Signorina back in Genoa and her violent reaction to the story he had conveyed to her from his jailer friend, he fell silent and only stared at Mala, his eyes full of questions.

"Fazio," said Mala, "I thought you intended to return to Genoa after your work in Cologne."

Fazio shrugged, keeping an eye to the Bishop. "Ah, Signorina," he said, "my pockets were full of money, I've no family left, and there was little for me back in Italy. It seemed the Hermit's crusade held promise, and I became good friends with Innocenzo here. So when I finished in Cologne, Innocenzo begged me to take to the road with him."

"You were in Cologne with the Hermit then?" said Tristan, still trying to put two and two together.

"Yes."

"Ah, perhaps it was there, then, that I first saw you, and not with the Hermit as he prayed over the dead crusaders at Niš. Yes, I seem to recognize you from somewhere else but..."

Mala laughed at this. "Oh, Tristan, if you saw Fazio in Cologne, then he's not nearly the slippery fish he claims to be. Though the chances are one in a million that you should ever meet, Fazio here is the very man I had following you about back in Italy and Germany!"

"*What?*" Tristan exclaimed.

"Yes, yes, Fazio has been in my employ from time to time, but his work ended in Cologne," Mala said, still caught in her own laughter. "Imagine my surprise at now seeing him in Bithynia!"

Fazio and Tristan looked at each other suspiciously, neither catching humor in the night's circumstances. Fazio felt only bitterness rising in his chest as he looked at the Bishop. Not only did the Bishop's handsome appearance hark back to bouts of previous envy in Fazio's mind, but the memory of the crimes this man had committed according to his jailer friend gave rise to visions of eventual justice. *After all*, thought Fazio, *if God truly delivers justice upon this earth, there would be no more deserving candidate than this wicked Bishop of Ostia.*

"Ah, but we must return the other direction," said Tristan. "Innocenzo, please tell your uncle he is welcome to visit our camp down the shore. Even when Mala here is not with me and is back in Constantinople, I stroll the beach each night for reflection or prayer. He would be most welcome to join me."

As Tristan said this, Fazio's eyes narrowed, wondering how one who had committed such crimes as the Bishop could even utter the word 'prayer.'

"Aye, I'll tell him," replied Innocenzo, grasping Tristan's hand. "Again, Bishop, as always, so good to see you! I've never forgotten how you saved my uncle from Lord Truffault's gallows back in France, nor has Uncle Peter."

As Tristan and Mala began their trek back to camp, Tristan was content to be alone with Mala once more, and took her hand in his again. And though the night, the beach, and the luminescence of the moon could not have been more perfect at that moment, the little farm in Tuscany came to mind for some reason. "You know, Mala," he said, "I have this recurring dream. Years ago at the foot of Mathilda's Canossa fortress, I came across a small farm set near a brook with sheep, goats, and fowl running everywhere. In the midst of this little pastoral paradise sits a small stone cottage, old but quaint and clever in design. Whenever I pass through Canossa, I stop there."

"Oh, so now you suddenly dream of being a *farmer*?" chided Mala, pushing him playfully with her shoulder. Laughing, she added, "Yes, actually, I think I might know the place. It came to my attention several months back when I went to see your aunt, Mathilda of Medici."

Surprised, Tristan sputtered, "You– *went to Canossa?* But... what of the bad blood you have so long carried for Mathilda?"

"I felt it time to bare myself of it. Besides, I had some things to express that... I've held with bitterness since first meeting her."

Tristan shook his head. "I dare guess, then– things turned ugly?"

"It wasn't exactly pretty, if that's what you mean... but my purpose was accomplished, at least. But enough about Mathilda. Tell me more about the little farm."

"Yes, yes... the place keeps coming to me in my dreams, for some reason," said Tristan. "And in those dreams... you and I live there together."

"Ha!" snarked Mala. "But then, in those dreams– are you still a high bishop of the Vatican?"

"No... of course not. It is but *dreams*, Mala."

"Is there more to them?"

"Yes. Mala, while living together on that tiny farm, you and I have a son… and we are all three sitting on the steps of the house as a loving and happy family."

"A *s-o-n*?" said Mala, her voice wilting. "Is it… the son we lost so many years ago?"

"Yes, I imagine so, perhaps. You know how disconnected dreams can be. Anyway, I just wanted to tell you. And when I find myself with you and our child in this dream, it is so very *real*… and when I wake up, I can still feel the dream. It lingers with me for hours, making me feel homesick even though I know it was but my imagination."

Mala, squeezing his hand a bit, said, "Yes, I have dreams too, not unlike that, but as you say, they're only dreams." Then she pushed against him again, less playfully, and led him away from the water. Dropping his hand, she then wrapped her arms around him and stared into his eyes. In the ethereal light of the moon, their pale grey essence reflected with startling clarity, such that she could see her own reflection. “Hold me, Tristan,” she whispered. “and don’t let me go, for this moment will never come again. Kiss me. Love me here, like in our dreams… before we awaken.”

Taken aback, Tristan hesitated. Though he had ceaselessly thought of a moment such as this during his many bouts of solitude, reflection, and regret, as it was now actually unfolding, it seemed neither possible nor real. Like a man who at that very moment between sleep and awakening shudders, not knowing which world he is in, Tristan shuddered. Admiring her face in the bluish luminescence of the moon, her thick raven hair aswirl in the breeze, and feeling the full press of her ample breasts against him, he leaned down and kissed her. It was a soft kiss at first, but then he began to feel a surge in his loins, and the kiss became more intense.

Returning his passion, Mala slowly tightened her arms around him and whispered in his ear. Then, without stepping back, she slowly dropped the top of her tunic, baring her breasts, and placed his hands over them, moving them gently over herself. “It’s been so long ago that you touched me like this, Tristan, but I’ve thought of it endlessly, night after night. I love you more than life itself, and would have surrendered my very life for a single moment as this. This very moment itself seems a dream, here alone on this beach in the shadow of God’s stars. I’m afraid that at any moment someone will roust me by the shoulder, and I’ll awake. Oh, but I love you so much, smart boy.”

The very ring of ‘smart boy’ sent a swell of emotion through Tristan, peeling away layer after layer of time and sentiment. “I love you too, Mala,” Tristan whispered. “I have loved you since that night we met as children, though I did not realize it then, and have loved you ever since. And with every year that passes, though I have fought it, I begin to realize it more and more.”

Mala kissed him again. Then, placing her lips to his ear, she said, “Very well then… come with me into the dunes, Tristan… and let’s allow this dream to fulfill itself before we both wake up.”

She turned, holding his hand, leading him away from the shore… and the two of them melted into the night.

## Chapter Sixty-seven

### Tafur's Sortie

Emperor Alexius, upon ferrying the crusaders to Bithynia, had made it very clear that the Turkish city of Nicaea, stronghold of Sultan Kilij Arslan, was a mere two day march from where the crusaders were disembarking at the abandoned fortress of Nicodemia. Repeatedly, he cautioned the crusaders to remain to themselves and not cross into Turkish territory, as that would alarm and agitate the Turks. "If you tend to your business," he counseled, "there will be no problems, as Kilij Arslan is currently engaged in battle to the east against the Danishmend Turks of the opposing Sunni sect." Contrary to his intention, this final bit of information only had the effect of emboldening the crusaders to ignore his other points of counsel.

Tafur was the first to stray from camp, over Sansavoir's objections. "Oh, we're simply going to take a look around at the surrounding countryside," insisted Tafur, "and I'm taking only ten men with me." Before Sansavoir could make report to Peter the Hermit, Tafur had already slipped from Civetot and was leading his pack on foot over the hills. He was little interested in sight-seeing, though, as his only hope was to come across Muslim shepherds who were known from time to time to stray with their flocks onto Byzantine pastures. After an hour's search, failing to come across such, Tafur's pack spied a farm nestled into the side of a draw. The farm, as were all farms surrounding Civetot, was inhabited by Greek Christians.

Approaching the barn, they spotted a young woman holding an infant in the crook of one arm while attempting to fill her pitcher from a cistern. "We've been walking for hours and we're thirsty," Tafur called to the woman. "Move aside so we can get at your cistern there."

The appearance of so many strangers took the woman by surprise, and as she stood before them, the brands burned into their foreheads frightened her. Not understanding French, her eyes widened and her face grew pallid, feeling suddenly threatened by the foreigners. Setting her pitcher aside, pulling her infant to her breast with both hands, she backed away a few steps, keeping an eye to Tafur. Then, when the men did not move but continued only to stare at her, she turned, quickly stepping toward the shanty behind her where her husband and father were splitting wood, out of view.

Having noticed that the young woman was pleasing in appearance, as she moved away Tafur whistled. "Come back here, bitch!" he laughed. "Let's have another peek at you!"

Though this was said in a language she failed to understand and carried the tone of a playful lilt, the woman detected something horrid in his voice. Her apprehension was confirmed as his comment was followed by a chorus of snickering and lurid comments. Again, she could not comprehend what was being said, but the tone was clear. Shuddering, her heart racing, she tightened the grip around her baby and hastened her pace toward the shanty. Seconds later she heard the sound of footsteps directly behind her, and let loose a scream for her husband and father.

"Not so quick, little dearie!" said Tafur, pulling her back roughly by the hair, driving her to cry out in pain as tufts of hair separated from her skull at the roots. Tafur then spun her about. Holding her by the throat, his eyes bore directly hers, which is what had first struck his fancy about her. Laughing, the men surrounding him groped at the infant, pulling it from the woman's grasp as Tafur, without warning, snatched at the top of her tunic, exposing one of her breasts. This caused her to scream again as other men closed in about her, cackling and grunting while pawing at her clothes. Tafur jerked her upper tunic again, baring her other breast, and began to roughly knead them both, squeezing and pulling at her nipples as the other men gathered around.

As they stripped the tunic completely from her body, the woman's husband and father come into view from behind the shanty. Their chore of splitting firewood interrupted by the commotion on the other side of the shanty, each happened to be holding an ax in hand. In a blink, recognizing what was occurring, both men raised their axes and ran at the circle of men despite being hopelessly outnumbered. "Let loose of my wife!" shouted one of the men in Greek, his eyes wide with fury.

As the husband ran into their midst, one of Tafur's men swept across the ground with the razor-sharp blade of his scythe, swiftly severing the man's right foot. Not realizing what had happened to him, the husband continued his forward motion for two or three steps without feeling the wound, then faltered as the now mutilated stub of his ankle threw him off kilter. Shrieking in agony as the pain inflicted by the scythe pierced the entire run of his leg, he stumbled onto the ground. "*Ahhggh!*" he moaned, spotting his severed foot lying to the side.

The woman's father, unaware of what had occurred to his son-in-law, continued his run at the intruders. An instant later his charge was abruptly halted as he ran full thrust into the prongs of three pitchforks to his chest and belly. His eyes flared, rattling in their sockets, then his head slumped onto his chest as the three Tafurs, holding their forks by the handle, raised him in the air as hoisting a hunting trophy. Aghast, the young woman issued a howl of dread, screaming her infant's name as it, in turn began to squeal. Then, unable to fathom how quickly her simple existence had turned to horror, she collapsed to the ground.

"Hold her down," said Tafur calmly, "and throw that squalling baby into the cistern," he added, as he and several others loosened the cinches holding up their breeches. "Aye, we'll take a bit of pleasure with this little bitch, and her husband can watch before we take his other foot and hands. Then we'll set this place afire and haul off the goats."

As Tafur pulled his breeches off and mounted the young woman, punching her in the face to quell her flailing limbs, one of the other men got down on his knees to watch. "Too bad Marcel Dupuis isn't' around anymore to laugh at because his staff won't get stiff, huh, Tafur?"

Looking up as he positioned himself between his frantic victim's thighs and violently thrust into her, Tafur puzzled. "*Marcel?* Who the hell's Marcel?" Then, continuing to ravage the peasant girl, he said, "Oh, yeah… Dupuis. Indeed, he'd be good for a laugh about now! Poor bastard's never had anything as fine as this little bird… only that fat-assed wife of his, Estelle!"

Thus began the particularly horrific reputation of the peasant Tafurs during the First Holy Crusade, the very mention of whom would soon spread terror throughout the Middle East and the Holy Land amongst Jews and Muslims alike.

## Chapter Sixty-eight

### An Unholy Alliance

Returning after dark to Civetot with a full herd of goats, a dozen oxen, and eight horses which they had taken from a succession of Greek Christian farms that day, Tafur and his men were eagerly questioned by many in the French camp concerning the surrounding countryside.

"What's out there?" they asked, curious about the territory beyond Civetot which Peter the Hermit and Sansavoir had declared forbidden.

"Did you see any Muslims?" asked others.

"No Muslims," replied Tafur, "only Greeks."

"So how did you acquire all this livestock?" people asked.

"Gifts from Greek farmers, grateful that we've come to battle the Turks," lied Tafur, mentioning nothing of the three rapes that had been committed that day, or that anyone else who happened to be on the farms they had plundered was either mutilated or murdered, including babies and children.

The Hermit and Sansavoir, smelling trouble, became irrate. "Oh, but you tempt fate, Tafur!" exclaimed the Hermit, "We were told to keep to ourselves, but now you place us in jeopardy by roaming the countryside and thieving from the locals. They're Christians, you know, not Muslims!"

"*Thieving*?" said Tafur, perfidious as ever. "Did you not hear me say this livestock was given to us?"

A scowl creased the Hermit's brow and his face drew up like purse strings. "You're lying, Tafur. This is barren countryside and these farmers of Bithynia have next to nothing. You've been raiding, damn you!"

Hearing this, Sansavoir put a hand to his belt, ready to draw his sword. "*What's this?*" he growled. "*You've raided fellow Christians*?"

Tafur stepped back, striking an aggressive stance, thrusting his staff in a defensive position. "They're *Greek Orthodox,* not true Christians," Tafur snarled.

"Hold you sword, Walter," said the Hermit, gesturing him off with a hand.

As Sansavoir complied, Tafur stuck the point of his staff into the ground and laughed, seeing that Sansavoir was no longer a threat. "These damned Greeks are no better than Muslims or Jews," he said, "so I'll take what I like... and there's not a damned thing you two can do about it! And next time I'll take a hundred men, or more."

"Have you not a speck of decency left in that black soul of yours, Tafur?" fumed the Hermit, quaking with agitation. "There'll be trouble, you know!"

Tafur laughed again. "And just what do you think these Greek farmers can do to us... turn to their neighbors for help, the Turks?"

"No, you fool, but word will get back to Emperor Alexius," growled Sansavoir. "These Greeks along the coast are his subjects, after all, and he's pledged to protect them!"

***

That next morning after Geoffrey Burrel and Desmond DuLac received word of Tafur's sortie into the countryside, they summoned him. "Did you cross into Turkish territory, or come across Seljuk scouts while you were out there?" asked Burrel.

"No, nothing like that," said Tafur. "Besides, I don't know where in hell the border lies exactly."

"So then, you raided Christian farms, eh?" said DuLac, knowing that farmers do not willingly release their livestock to strangers. "And probably killed a few?"

"What's that to you, DuLac?" asked Tafur, his eyes drawing down with suspicion.

"I couldn't give a damn," replied DuLac. "We were shabbily treated in Constantinople, so I've no affection for these damned Greeks one way or another. But know this, Burrel and I talked to a couple of Greek farmers ourselves yesterday, right here in Civetot's market."

"Yeah," nodded Burrel, "and the discussion was quite interesting. We wanted to find out about Nicaea. It's Kilij Arslan's capital, they said, lying only several day's march from here. According to the farmers, it holds Arslan's main treasury."

"I'm little tempted by wealth," mocked Tafur. "I've taken a vow of poverty. Or haven't you noticed my dress?"

"Ah, yet you thieve livestock?" smirked DuLac.

"There's a difference between eating and *hoarding*," replied Tafur. "Besides, the city of Nicaea is large, I hear, and well fortified. So don't dwell on foolishness."

"Oh, but Tafur, it's not the city of Nicaea that interests us at the moment," said Burrel.

"True, we couldn't lay siege to Nicaea with only half a camp," interjected DuLac, "but these farmers we spoke with yesterday… they claim Nicaea's surrounded by a series of small outlying towns. More interestingly, each maintains its own smaller treasury. After all, Nicaea itself is a major hub of Muslim trade for the entire Sultanate of Rüm."

"Did you not hear me?" said Tafur. "I'm not looking for treasure. I came on this crusade to–"

"*Recapture Jersusalem*?" interrupted DuLac, completing Tafur's thought with scorn. "Yeah, yeah, we've all heard you preaching that tripe to your men," said DuLac dismissively; he found men like Peter the Hermit, Sansavoir, and even Tafur to be faith-obsessed imbeciles, and thought their fervor to be ridiculous. "Nevertheless, we may still be able to help each other a bit here, my friend."

"How's that?" asked Tafur.

"I notice there's one man in our midst here in Byzantium you seem to despise more than others," said DuLac, drawing nearer. "I, on the other hand, have five. But the *head* of my little five-headed serpent is the same man *you* abhor."

"Bishop Saint-Germain," said Tafur with certainty.

"Exactly," nodded DuLac, "and my feelings toward the man are no different than your own, Tafur. Oh, I've seen the look in your eye any time his name is spoken. He's humiliated you personally, I've heard, and been responsible for the death of a good number of your beggar troops. Aye, your inclination to see the man fall is no different than my own."

"Perhaps so," said Tafur, growing impatient. "But get to the damned point, DuLac. What are you leading to?"

"Quite simply," replied DuLac, "Burrel and I have been in discussions about launching some raids on the outlying towns surrounding Nicaea. Whether you're interested in treasure or not, we could well use the help of your men. You claim you came all this distance to kill Muslims… so here's your first opportunity to take a few heads."

"Right," nodded Burrel, "We'll take the treasure, you can take heads. And if you should change your mind about the treasure, hell, we'll *share*. Moreover, we'll help you get back at Bishop Saint-Germain."

"Indeed," agreed DuLac, "and that'd be in your direct interest as well as mine. Of course, I'll need your assistance with the others of Saint-Germain's group also."

"And what of Peter the Hermit and Walter Sansavoir?" asked Tafur. "They'll not abide by harm coming to the Bishop of Ostia."

"A little detail," shrugged DuLac, "that we can easily work out later. Besides, Sansavoir doesn't hold any particular ties to Bishop Saint-Germain, he simply parrots the Hermit. But we'll talk about that later. Our first interest is to look toward the towns around Nicaea… agreed?"

Tafur said nothing as his eyes began to roll about in thought for several seconds. Closing them, he seemed to drop into muted conversation with himself. Finally, his lids slowly opening, he nodded. "Aye... and I'll take my part of any Muslim plunder," he said.

## Chapter Sixty-nine

### Into Turkish Territory

That next day Tafur and several hundred of his henchmen set out again for the countryside, joined by DuLac and Burrel, along with several contingents of their cavalry and footmen. Within hours the Tafurs raided several more Christian farms, leaving a wake of death and destruction while once again hauling away livestock. Burrel and DuLac were little interested in such paltry game, however, and left Tafur's group to amble about on horseback into Turkish territory where they eventually came across a small town.

Just as a leopard lazily considers his prey, DuLac gazed down upon the town from his position atop a hill, gandering about for signs of a military presence. "Oh, but this is easy pickings, Burrel," he said. "It appears these lambs are ready to be fleeced."

"Fleeced and *butchered*," grinned Burrel, turning to signal the troops behind them.

Without further discussion, the combined French and Norman cavalry attacked, streaming into the town like foxes scattering chickens, whooping and bellowing at the top of their throats. A short while later the footmen arrived, quickly joining knights as they teamed to plunder the town, going from house to house and shop to shop, hoarding anything of value.

"And what about these damned townspeople running amok?" shouted DuLac to Burrel.

"Kill them all," replied Burrel coldly, "they're goddamned heathens!" Spinning the young boy about that he already had in a choke-hold from behind, he plunged his sword through his throat, then broke into chase after an old woman who moments earlier had tried to spring the boy free.

Within the hour the entire town had been decimated. The only inhabitants left alive were goats, sheep, oxen, and horses– which were summarily herded and directed toward Civetot.

"Not a bad sortie," said DuLac as they crossed back into Greek territory, "though I was hoping for a bit more gold and silver from the commercial quarter. And dammit, no signs of a treasury as hoped."

"Bah, it was but a tiny town, DuLac," replied Burrel. He was about to suggest that the next town they hit would be more profitable, but before he could gather his words he spotted a swirl of dust approaching their direction. "Shit," he muttered, "riders coming at us…"

DuLac strained to identify the oncoming force. "Turks, maybe?" he snorted with apprehension, turning to warn his troops which were coming up behind him.

Burrel said nothing at first, but moments later sighed. "*Christ*," he muttered, "it's just that damned Rainald and his bunch."

Ten minutes later Rainald of Broyes galloped up at the head of a platoon of Longobard and Allemani horsemen. Riding next to him was a certain Captain Benini, Rainald's second in command. "Well now," Rainald said, "where in hell have you damned crows been?" Pointing behind DuLac's and Burrel's formation, he added, "Looks like you're coming back from Muslim territory?"

"Maybe," smirked DuLac, "or perhaps we've simply been out for a little ride in the countryside. Either way, it's none of your damned affair."

As DuLac said this, the men herding livestock came into Rainald's and Benini's view. "Ho there, then" exclaimed Rainald, "what's this booty you're dragging back with you?"

"Yah, yah," nodded Burrel, his mouth curving into a surreptitious grin, "we've been in Turkish territory. So what?"

Giving no answer, Rainald happened to notice blood splotching the chain-mail and hauberks of both DuLac and Burrel. Benini noticed it also, and exchanged a look of suspicion with his commander.

"Aye, and it looks as though you butchered some of the livestock back there, too, huh?" said Rainald, already guessing what had really happened.

"Aw, cut the horse shit, Rainald," said Burrel, his smile broadening. "Yeah, we did some butchering back there, but it wasn't livestock."

Benini shook his head. "Not smart," he said. "We were told to keep to ourselves. Yet now you're stirring a hornet's nest."

"No hornet's nest," said DuLac. "It was like robbing a sparrow nest, and not the first Turkish man-of-arms to be seen all day."

"Aye," added Burrel, "and we intend to return, making our way closer toward Nicaea where the towns are said to be more prosperous than what we came across today."

"Huh?" swallowed Rainald. "But what of Kilij Arslan? Don't you suppose he'll put a quick stop to such business?"

"As Alexius told us, he's off fighting the Danishmends," said DuLac, showing little concern. "But an interesting thing. Alexius told us Arslan was only temporarily occupied with them. We learned today though from several Turkish prisoners, may their souls rest in peace, that Arslan's been thus engaged nearly this entire past year. Better yet, it seems the Danishmends are enjoying a successful counter attack and will be keeping Arslan occupied for God only knows how long. So to our way of thinking, the towns around Nicaea are like an orchard ready to be plucked, and we intend to fill our saddlebags!" DuLac then reached inside his saddlebag and pulled out a small pouch of gold coins. "And this," he gloated, "from only the first town… and a small town at that. Burrel's saddlebag holds an equal amount."

Masking his envy, Rainald eyed the pouch. "Well now," he said, looking over at Benini, "we'd best get back to our camp at Nicodemia… just in case these louts *have* raised the hornets."

During the ride back to Nicodemia, Rainald said little, and it seemed to Benini that his commander was growing more cross with each lope of his horse. Finally, after reaching the fort, Rainald slid off his horse and grumbled, "Those bastards, getting the jump on us like this!" Turning to Benini, he said, "Send some scouts out to the border to make sure no Turks come across in chase– but also have them keep an eye to the activities of DuLac and Burrel, by God."

***

Over the next week Rainald's scouts reported no trace of the Turkish military. They also reported that the French and Normans were continuing their forays into Turkish territory, gradually edging closer and closer to the major city of Nicaea. More critically, they were hauling in substantial plunder while encountering feeble opposition from the conquered towns themselves. Evidently, according to the scouts, there had been no response whatsoever from the Turkish army, or what remained of it, in Nicaea.

"Well, I'll be goddamned if we're going to leave all the Muslim wealth to the Franks!" exclaimed Rainald, feeling scalded. Summoning Benini, he declared, "Mobilize the troops and have them ready to march at dawn."

"We're not taking on Nicaea, are we?" asked Captain Benini.

"No," replied Burrel, "but we'll match the French and Normans in raiding some of its surrounding towns!"

## Chapter Seventy

### Xerigordos… Harvest of Greed

At dawn, Rainald of Broyes marched out of Nicodemia with his full force of three hundred knights and three thousand foot soldiers dressed in full battle array, and made for the direction of Nicaea. Shortly before dusk they arrived at their first Turkish town, and easily overwhelmed it. Terrified by this sudden assault by thousands of foreign troops, Muslim residents fled for their lives but were quickly overtaken by Rainald's cavalry, who gave no quarter. "Dammit," Rainald had mandated, "we've no means of dealing with prisoners for God's sake, so take none!"

The town was sacked throughout the night as Muslims who hadn't escaped were tortured, mutilated, and killed, many being tied to posts and cruelly used for target practice by German and Italian archers. Women were molested and raped by the hundreds before being put to the sword, and children were summarily executed. In all, nearly a thousand Turkish men, women, and children met their end.

This act of decimating his first Turkish town did little to slake Rainald's thirst for blood, so he determined that over the next days he would move his troops even closer to the environs of Nicaea in search of larger towns and more plunder. Burrel, Tafur, and DuLac also continued to range freely across Turkish territory. Before long, reports spread rapidly throughout Turkish territory that bands of murderous foreigners had materialized from nowhere and were ravaging the land, engaging in wanton slaughter of the native population.

Although the knights and footmen of Rainald were equally merciless as the knights and footmen of Burrel and DuLac, it was the Tafurs who proved to be, without question, the most bloodthirsty of the entire lot. Muslim survivors streaming into Nicaea from the hinterlands told ghastly stories of men dressed like paupers with crosses branded on their foreheads, behaving like wild dogs loosened upon lambs. "These feral beasts mutilate every victim they get their hands on, and even eat human flesh," terrified Muslim refugees insisted. "They roast newborns upon spits, then devour them in some sort of perverse ceremonial rite to celebrate their victories!" Incredibly, these horrific claims were true. Tafur and his men, in now coming across Turks, had descended to new levels of bestiality and inhumanity.

The crusader raids continued, and still there came no response from the Turks. Gaining more confidence then with each raid, Rainald's Germans and Italians ranged deeper and deeper into Turkish territory. As September came to a close, they traversed a wide but shallow stream and happened upon the small fort of Xerigordos

A tiny garrison of Turkish troops along with the fort's citizenry had been watching the approach of Rainald's much larger force. Having heard the horror stories about these brutal foreigners, the Turkish troops and citizens decided, without exception, to flee out the back gate of the fort.

As it happened, the weekly market of Xerigordos had been in full operation that particular morning; when Rainald's troops entered the vacated fort, they were elated to come upon an entire plaza filled with plump fruit and vegetables, roasted meats, fresh fish, and hares and geese hanging broken-necked by scores from tethers. There were also stalls and booths brimming with gold, jewelry, fine fabrics, exotic incense and fragrances, copper and bronze castings, and a plethora of other valuables.

"Oh, but God in Heaven, Benini," proclaimed Rainald as his eyes raked over the marketplace, "we've slipped into a fortune here! How envious those bastard Franks would be could they only see us now!"

Knights quickly dismounted to join the footmen who were already exultantly storming stalls and booths of the marketplace, running about like hungry crows grasping at anything they could gather. Minutes later, as some of the men began to search homes and businesses, more shouts of elation broke the air as crusaders came running out of a building that proved to be the fort treasury which was brimming with gold and silver coinage, jewelry, and other valuables.

Thus the entire afternoon was spent by men rejoicing in newfound wealth and devouring the abundant fare of the marketplace. So complete was their celebration that they neither saw nor heard the distant approach of a massive army of Seljuk Turks advancing on the fort from the direction of Nicaea.

Since the Seljuks had emanated from the steppes of Asia, this army was heavily filled with fierce Turkish horseman known as gazis, wielding lethal composite bows. These gazis were deadly, and especially touted for laying down withering archer fire while expertly maneuvering their horses in swift, devastating cavalry charges. Only Muslim commanders wore any form of armor other than helmets, so the gazis were not weighed down with chain-mail and heavy shields, and were thus able to maximize the speed of their horses.

As Kilij Arslan himself was so heavily occupied by the fierce Danishmends, he had not returned to Nicaea after receiving reports of invading foreigners threatening the lands surrounding his capital. Instead, he quickly dispatched a force of fifteen thousand warriors from the territory of Chorosan to deal with this new trouble. This force was actually comprised of two armies, one led by a General Kareem Soliman, an aging but trusted veteran of many campaigns against both the Byzantines and the Danishmends. The other was led by an especially vicious and merciless fanatic named Mahmoud Malik, a favored Persian mercenary who filtered in and out of Kilij Arslan's employ.

Mahmoud Malik was also referred to as the 'Butcher of Medina.' Three years earlier, during the outbreak of civil strife between Shia and Sunni factions in that city, Malik had rounded up two thousand Sunni insurgents and had them beheaded in a public ceremony. He next went after the entire families of the executed, and one month later after rounding up over six thousand insurgent relatives, also had them beheaded. To crown this callous act, he had their severed heads impaled by lances and staked all along the full length of Medina's major avenues as a warning to others.

As Sultan of Rüm, Kilij Arslan had found the services of Malik to be especially effective in his fight against the Danishmends. Although Arslan himself was, for the most part, a civilized ruler and war lord, he had come to rely heavily on the obsessively sadistic and bloodthirsty Malik, who struck fear in the ranks of even the most brutal of enemies. A huge, glowering man with a noticeably oversized skull which he had elected to shave, Malik made for a frightening presence. The very stare of his dark eyes from beneath abnormally bushy eyebrows unnerved even the most audacious of warriors. Commanding an especially fierce band of renegade gazis, Malik was so dreaded that he even intimidated Arslan's regular troops, especially in the aftermath of victory when he satisfied his bloodlust by wreaking havoc on the captured.

Soliman and Malik, despite being tied together by Sultan Kilij Arslan on this mission to eliminate this foreign threat to Nicaea, shared little in common; moreover, each held the other in low regard. For his part, Malik thought Soliman to be tepid in battle and overly merciful to the vanquished. Soliman, on the other hand, found Malik to be a bestial creature of the lowest order, as well as a Muslim of false faith. Nonetheless, the two commanders had remained civil toward each other during the march back to Nicaea. Now, as their combined forces came into view of the fort at Xerigordos, they ordered their respective columns of horsemen and footmen to separate and form into wide ranks facing the fort.

It was at this point that a lone Lombard standing on the ramparts noticed the vast array of Turks assembling in the distance. "Shut the gates!" he shouted, bolting to action, spreading the alarm. Rainald's troops, gorged with food and wine, were sluggish to move at first, but as word spread that a massive Muslim army had appeared from nowhere, they came alive. Locking both gates, they scurried for weapons, taking positions along the ramparts. From there, gawking at fifteen thousand Seljuk Turks in full battle dress, all previous celebration and sense of good fortune amongst Rainald's troops quickly evaporated.

"Damn," muttered Captain Benini, discouraged, "we're in deep straights. We number but three thousand against that frightening horde yonder."

"No, we're in good stead here inside the fort," said Rainald confidently, looking down at the Turks. "Look there, they've no siege equipment… and the walls of this stronghold are solid. The best they can do is set the gates afire to break in, but we'll block them from the front and butcher them in the bottleneck from atop the ramparts with arrows. We'll be able to wait these bastards out for weeks if we have to, or until we can get word to the Franks. Their twenty thousand crusaders combined with our own could easily run these Turks right back to Nicaea."

At the very moment Rainald was recounting these advantages to Captain Benini, Mahmoud Malik's face turned crocodilian as he said quietly to General Soliman, "These foreigners are done, and don't yet realize it."

"We'd hoped to catch them in the open, but we're ill provisioned to oust them from a fort," disagreed Soliman. "We lack rams and towers, as well as trebuchets and ballistas. They can hole up in there as long as they wish."

"I spent time in this fort several years ago," replied Malik, "and we won't need war machines in this case," replied Malik.

"How's that? They'll never come out." Then a light broke across Soliman's brow. "Is there some secret access to make our way in?" he asked.

"No, even better. There's no *well* in the fort," Malik replied, his eyes overcome with that blank glaze that enters the eyes of predators when falling across already wounded prey. Pointing to the side of the fort, he added, "The stream lies well away from the fort, and the only cistern lies over a hundred yards outside the walls there to the west. A man can only last so long without water, Soliman… then he begins to go mad."

"Ah," nodded Soliman, shaking his head, "then no need to storm the walls."

"No, we'll wait them out, and send out a scouting party to make sure these foreigners stand alone here. But advance the archers and have them sling a steady hail of arrows over the walls these next few days to harry the men inside the fort. Afterwards, we'll set fire to the gates. That way we'll keep them stirred up, running about, and in a state of tension. Between that and the blazing sun, their thirst will accelerate. In the end they'll be begging to surrender, and then we'll help them end their misery… one man at a time."

## Chapter Seventy-one

### Thirst

That night the thought of water never crossed Rainald's mind. Even that next morning as his men finished the last of the fresh fruit, vegetable harvest, and wine supply left behind by fleeing marketers, no one inside Xerigordos was concerned about water; their full attention was diverted to the massive Turkish military force that had converged outside the fort. But by mid-afternoon as the blistering sun positioned itself straight above, casting its withering heat into the fort, the crusaders began to search for the fort's well. By early evening, having searched every nook, cranny and crevice, they had not found it. Only then, as the sun began to settle over the hills, did they notice the small cistern standing well beyond the walls of the fort between them and the Muslim legions.

"What the hell kind of construction is this, with no well inside?" complained Captain Benini.

"It's just a goddamned look-out outpost," concluded Rainald. "It was never intended to hold back a siege or even hold back the approach of an enemy! I figured that out as soon as we so easily overran it and those inside took flight. But who in the shit expected a goddamned Muslim army to show up like this the minute we entered? *Son of a bitch!* We're locked in now like rats in a snare, and vastly outnumbered."

Minutes later as dusk fell, the sky filled as a deadly rain of arrows began scudding into the fort, forcing crusaders to cower, seeking refuge within the cover of the sparse out-buildings and sprinkling of houses within the fort. It stopped after about ten minutes, but then resumed at odd, unpredictable intervals, keeping the men within the walls wary and nervous throughout the night.

That next morning the sun resumed its own punishment, as there stirred not even the slightest breeze. Even the shade of building interiors offered little solace to the trapped crusaders, except from the continuation of scything arrows dropping from above. By late afternoon their tongues were parched, and they stared longingly at the cistern a hundred yards away, and the stream beyond, filled with Muslim troops horsing about while bathing.

Physiologically, as pertains to humans and thirst, the body is comprised of roughly sixty-five percent water and cannot tolerate dehydration, which occurs when fluid loss exceeds the amount of fluid ingested. Without fluid balance, the human body is simply incapable of performing or maintaining normal functions. Symptoms of dehydration vary according to the severity of fluid loss, and worsen as moderate dehydration progresses into severe dehydration. Rainald's troops at first experienced dry and sticky mouths, fatigue, dry skin, and dizziness. As time dragged into the third and fourth day, their now intense thirst caused cracked lips, sunken eyes, rapid heartbeat and breathing, and their urine turned extremely dark. Their resulting craving for water was generated from central processing in the brain. Left unsatisfied as it was in this case, it led to confusion and disorientation. By the fifth day, panic overtook the crusaders, and on the next day this panic evolved into sheer desperation.

"Bleed the horses!" rasped Rainald, watching the deteriorating condition of his forces. "Surrounded and outnumbered as we are, they're of no use to us now!"

Moving lethargically, the hardiest of his men began to slay horses, which were in the same declining condition as the crusaders themselves. Then, laying atop the beasts and sucking at their necks and joints like nursing piglets, the men eagerly tried to quench their thirst. But blood is thick and viscous, and does little to satisfy swollen tongues and throats. By the next day the horses had all been slaughtered and drained, and a third of Rainald's three thousand men lay strewn about the fort, dead from either arrows or dehydration. Too tired even to remove the corpses from where they fell, the living were now surrounded by dead compatriots lying in every position of agonizing repose, their tongues chewed raw by their own teeth and their eyes bugging out in froggish, hideous stares of death… ceaselessly reminding the remaining survivors how they would look in a day's time, or perhaps even within hours.

Many of those still breathing lay about in a motionless daze, praying for their last moment to finally arrive while others slashed their own wrists and throats, too impatient to further tolerate their own misery. There were those also who tottered about aimlessly within the merciless shower of arrows, talking to themselves. Some even began to urinate into each others' hands, trading turns slurping the urine in desperate attempts to quench their maddening thirst, while yet others dropped rags down into the fort's privies. Poking them about in piles of recent defecation so as to absorb its sparse moisture, they then fished the rags out and chewed and sucked at them like thirst-crazed dogs.

Captain Benini was laying beside Rainald and hadn't spoken or moved in two days when, like a drunkard, he finally wobbled to his feet and pointed to the ground, muttering.

"Wh-what is it?" whispered Rainald hoarsely, struggling to make himself heard.

"W-w-wat-er," muttered Benini, his eyes widening. Stumbling forward, he threw himself to the ground and begin stuffing sand in his mouth, believing that God had miraculously brought forth a spring bubbling from the very earth at his feet.

"N-no, B-Ben-ini…" mumbled Rainald, his blistered eyelids slowly closing, "it's b-but hot s-sand..."

Though the gates to the fort had been successfully burned to ash by the fourth day, Malik waited until the seventh day to make his move.

"General Soliman," he nodded, "we're now ready to enter Xerigordos."

Riding slowly forward through the gate at the head of two hundred advance gazis, Malik's eyes raked over the inside of the fort. Of Rainald's original three thousand knights and footmen, twenty-five hundred were now dead. The survivors lay about muttering to themselves, not even aware of their own breathing, or knowing whether they were alive, dead, or dreaming.

Only one man, Rainald, was aware that the Muslims had entered the fort. Through the fog of his failing vision, he watched Malik dismount and walk toward him. Rising, Rainald staggered forward one disjointed step at a time, sword hanging low in his grip. "G-God-d-damn y-you!" he hissed, trying to raise his sword.

But his arm hung flaccid, its muscles paralyzed, and he could not lift the hilt of his sword beyond his belt. Then he fell forward onto Malik, who pushed him gruffly aside. Collapsing, Rainald closed his eyes as his cracked and bleeding lips continued to mutter incoherently in low syllables and growls.

"Gather the living!" instructed Malik. "When you come across those of fair skin and comely appearance, give them water and shackle then for sale for the brothels of Medina and Baghdad. Noblemen there who are lovers of men will pay highly for the meat of their white asses! Those who are big, muscular, and stout of frame, revive them also, but remove their testicles on the spot and seal the wounds with hot sand. We'll sell them as eunuchs."

"And what of the rest?" asked his men.

"Take the knights, slash their throats, and hang them from the walls of Xerigordos in their hauberks and helmets to serve as a warning to other foreigners! And the footmen, shackle them and bring them to camp for our amusement tonight."

Knowing that all of these footmen would be sadistically tortured by Malik and his men, laying disfigured and dead by morning, General Soliman said, "Are we not going to offer them the choice of conversion to Islam so they can live and be sold into slavery? That is, after all, Sultan Arslan's preferred method of dealing with heathen prisoners."

"Praise to Kilij Arslan," sneered Malik, "but after these seven days of boredom, tonight I seek entertainment."

## Chapter Seventy-two

### The Hermit Returns to Constantinople

Several days before Rainald of Broyes' foray into the fort at Xerigodos, Peter the Hermit learned that Burrel and DuLac had joined Tafur in raiding the countryside and were now looting Turkish territory. Furious, he summoned the three men for a meeting with him and Sansavoir. The three renegades quickly became belligerent, however, disregarding all the Hermit and Sansavoir had to say, going so far as to even castigate the two for their hesitancy in now attacking Muslims.

"Oh, but you both were in such haste in the beginning to take on the Turks, yet now you bitch at *us*?" barked Burrel, who had since Constantinople become openly defiant to the Hermit.

"You once heeded my words," said the Hermit, "but I see Tafur's thirst for violence and DuLac's greed has turned you, Burrel." Turning to Tafur, his look of scorn deepened. "And whatever happened to that burning desire of yours to serve God with humility, Tafur? I once thought you a pious man, but you've been infected by an insatiable, dark disease!"

"I still serve God," replied Tafur coldly, "but you've for some reason turned slack in this war on Islam, just as you became slack with the Jews in Germany, then the Hungarians. Look at this cross branded on my forehead, Hermit. Do you not see God's mark on me, as well as on my men?! It's *you* who now turns his back of God, and *you* who's become faint in the face of Christianity's call to eradicate Islam."

"No, we remain in good stead with God," growled Sansavoir. "But you three, you've become bloodthirsty fanatics, and now attack anyone standing before you whether they be Jews, fellow Christians, Greek farmers, or Turks! Yes, I'm still good for fighting the Turks, but not Turkish farmers and town dwellers. And in the name of God, Tafur, it's *you* who especially violates

God's decency! Peter and I have learned about the atrocities and horrors you and your men commit. It sickens both of us, just as it sickens God! These Turks you, Burrel, and DuLac attack aren't the scourge I came to fight. I came to take down the Turkish army that's swarmed over the Holy Land and Byzantium. *They* are the enemy, not helpless Muslim infants, mothers, and old women."

"And foolishly, you're directly violating the instructions of Emperor Alexius by raiding across the Turkish border before Bishop Adhémar arrives," interceded the Hermit. "Mind you, this plundering you've taken to is becoming more and more abominable! It's but a matter of time before the Turks send an army swarming down to consume us all."

"Oh, but let them come," sneered DuLac. "They're a dark, primitive race, these Muslims, and between our forces and those of Rainald, we'll make short work of them!"

Bobbing his head in exasperation, the Hermit's eyes began their characteristic circuitous motion, darting back and forth. "Bah, very well then," he snapped, "since I'm setting sail for Constantinople in the morning to request more supplies, while I'm there I'll also petition the emperor to send a battalion or two of his troops back with me!"

"To what purpose?" said DuLac, suspicion darkening his brow.

"Because you've attacked Turkish towns and we may be in peril, you fool!" retorted the Hermit. "I'll be back in a several days, and God willing, the emperor will provide assistance should Kilij Arslan show up."

An hour later the Hermit sought Innocenzo, but could not find him. Coming across Fazio seated atop a bench surrounded by thick brush near the Civetot plaza, he inquired about his nephew's whereabouts. Turning red, Fazio looked about awkwardly, but said nothing.

"Well, did you not hear me?" asked the Hermit, growing impatient. "*Where is he?*"

"I'm not sure," stammered Fazio.

Fazio had no more than finished his denial when a girlish squeal issued from behind the bushes at his back. Innocenzo's laugh followed. "My God, you sweet young lamb," he twittered, "you have such a tender, comely little crack!"

Turning crimson, the Hermit grabbed Fazio by the collar. "Oh!" he wailed, "So now you serve as my nephew's little lookout, Fazio!?"

The bushes promptly fell silent, but too late. Shoving branches aside, the Hermit caught Innocenzo, naked, squatting before a young girl of thirteen or so, also naked. Innocenzo's position indicated he had been about to mount the girl as he heard his uncle cry out and grab Fazio. Dumbfounded, Innocenzo looked up foolishly at his uncle, then made a wild scramble for his clothes. Not allowing Innocenzo to even get his breeches over his feet, the Hermit dove on top of him and began beating him mercilessly. "Angels of God!" he shrieked, rolling about with Innocenzo on the ground, holding him from escaping. "Can't you for one moment keep that damned worm of yours in your breeches, Nephew!"

Three minutes later, exhausted, the Hermit gathered himself as the battered Innocenzo finally managed to struggle into his trousers. "Y-yes, Uncle Peter," stammered Innocenzo, taking on the look of the innocent. "*W-were you looking for me?*"

His eyes ablaze, the Hermit began pulling at his long beard with slow, deliberate strokes. He did this for a full minute before a change of expression fell over his face and his tone changed, as though nothing at all had occurred between the two of them. "Innocenzo," he said, "you told me you came across Bishop Saint-Germain a night or so along the beach. I feel the need to inform him of what's going on here in Civetot, so I'm going to his camp. I want you to accompany me. He's not overly fond of me at the moment, I expect, but he does seem to be fond of you for some reason, so come along."

Making their way down the beach toward the Tuscan camp, Innocenzo tried to fabricate several excuses to explain how he had ended up in the bushes naked with an equally naked girl. He also tried to explain away her tender age, but each time he sputtered an opening word, the Hermit slapped him and began pounding him about the shoulders. "Be silent, Innocenzo!" he would exclaim each time. "And rather than invent stories, pray that God will one day undo this hopeless disease that causes your testicles to drive your feeble brain!"

Half an hour later they entered the Tuscan camp. Tristan and Mala were seated at one end of a long camp table across from

Guillaume and Handel, and the four Danes sat at the far end of the table filing axes and sword. "Well, look what the devil's dragged into camp," sniped Handel, scowling, "the very wellspring of our troubles!"

Tristan dismissed Handel's comment, offering a smile. "Ah, we certainly couldn't have expected such a visit, but you are welcome here, Peter, be seated." Then, greeting Innocenzo, he noticed bruises beneath his eyes and a cut lip. "What's this?" Tristan asked. But Innocenzo flagged off the question with a furtive gesture– and the look of humiliation on his face told Tristan he should inquire no further. "So then, Peter," Tristan continued, "to what do we owe the honor of this visit?"

"I've come as a friend, Bishop… and to warn you."

"Ah, about the fires of Hell, no doubt?" mocked Handel.

"No Handel, about certain men in my camp," said the Hermit. "You already know about Tafur's violence by now because of the Jews and Hungarians, but know now that he's been raiding Greek farms in the surrounding area for several weeks … and left many dead in his path."

"*Byzantine* farmers?" asked Guillaume. "But that's… outrageous!"

"Oh, but there's more," said the Hermit. "Then Burrel and DuLac joined the raiding, but crossed over the Turkish border, killing and plundering their way toward Nicaea."

This caught Tristan's full attention, and he looked at the Hermit, dismayed. "The very thing Alexius warned them not to do..." he murmured.

The Danes, overhearing DuLac's name, also turned and set their eyes on the Hermit. "That damned DuLac's a bastard if ever one was born," said Orla. "Wherever he goes, a trail of misery follows."

"Ja," agreed Crowbones, "especially if there's something to be gained."

Guthroth said nothing, but the file in his hand quickened its motion against his ax blade, and his cheeks flushed.

"Oh, such *fools*," said Mala, shaking her head. Through her heavy trade with the Muslims, she had come to know their temperament better than anyone at the table. She well understood the implications of what the Hermit was telling them.

"Yes," continued the Hermit, "and Rainald has also now joined the hunt for Muslim riches. In any case, I thought you should know what's going on around us now. I fear trouble's not far off." Drawing his aging face into an expression of remorse, he looked at Tristan and said, "Bishop… Tristan, lad… I pray each night for forgiveness. As you told me on the plains of Niš while we watched piles of our Catholic corpses being set afire by the Byzantine militia, my pride has given rise to one dread after another. This was never my intention... please know that."

Tristan was touched by this confession, as were all at the table except Handel who could find no forgiveness in his heart for this little preacher in the wake of all that had occurred since the Tuscan force had arrived in Cologne. No, too many innocents lay moldering in their graves to feel pity for this man, and there was no penance on earth adequate to nullify this perversion of a Peasants' Crusade the Hermit had birthed.

Tristan made the sign of the cross over the Hermit. "God forgives those who seek forgiveness, Peter," he said. "We thank you for warning us."

"We'll double the guard and send scouts out to keep an eye to movement, whether from crusaders or from Turks," said Guillaume, motioning to the Danes. "We're over five hundred strong in this camp, Peter, and should trouble arise, we'll come to your assistance in Civetot."

"Very well, then," said the Hermit, motioning to Innocenzo. "I'll be on my way for I leave in the morning for Constantinople to see the emperor."

"Oh?" said Mala. "I planned to set sail myself this evening for Constantinople for a meeting with the city's Harbor Commission in two days. But what business do you have with Alexius?"

"He needs to know that Burrel, Tafur, and DuLac have violated his counsel," said the Hermit. "The truth is, I'm hoping to talk him into sending Byzantine troops here to help control the fanatics of my camp. And if worse comes to worse, we might need his troops also should the Turks suddenly rise up."

Mala thought the Hermit's plan a good idea in light of Bithynia's now compromised position. More critically, she was concerned about the security of the Tuscan camp, and in particular, Tristan. "Well then," she said, "why don't I wait until morning to sail, and we can go together, Peter? My ships are certainly more comfortable than those little skiffs at Civetot. Besides, I hold Alexius' ear. Perhaps I can support your cause."

"Ah, yes," smiled the Hermit, "your words might well carry far more weight than my own." Standing, he reached over and grabbed Innocenzo by his hair. "One thing more, Bishop… if I might ask a slight favor?"

"Yes, Peter?" said Tristan.

"Might you be willing to hear Innocenzo's confession? I'd hear it myself, but I might strangle the lad in the process."

"Yes, most assuredly," replied Tristan, looking at Innocenzo. "Innocenzo?"

"Yes, Bishop," implored Innocenzo, struggling to free his head from his uncle's grip. "Please hear my confession, for though I never intend to, it seems I commit sins of the flesh again and again… indeed, it's as though Satan has taken up residence between my legs!"

## Chapter Seventy-three

### Mala Speaks

As Mala's vessel set sail that next morning, she stood along the ship's railing sharing conversation with Peter the Hermit. Her sole interest in helping him at the moment, of course, rested on Tristan, not on the Peasants' Crusade. In truth, Mala held many suspicions about Peter based on his history– as related to her by Tristan. As for Peter, he knew little to nothing about Mala other than what he had heard through vague discussion of her reputation as an extraordinary entrepreneur. Consequently, he readily accepted the story about how she and Tristan originally befriended as children and had continued this bond into adulthood.

"Aye, Tristan was but a child when I first met him, also," said the Hermit, thinking back. "An unusual boy to say the least... gifted, with frightening talents. When he was about nine or ten, I told him he was destined for greatness within the Church, though he had no desire to become a monk at the time. I also told him he was destined to sow the seeds of war against those opposing Christianity. Indeed, and it was Tristan himself as Vatican First Counsel who swung the Pope in favor of assisting Alexius against the Turks and declaring this Holy Crusade. Handel was against it, you know… and still is."

"Ah," said Mala, "so you must have impacted Tristan then, as did Odo de Lagery, the Black Monks of Cluny, Mathilda of Tuscany, and even his own mother who ended a sister of means at the convent of Marcigny-sur-Marne. I've often thought Tristan never had a chance to be anything *but* a cleric of the Church– that he was bridled as a child by the adults surrounding him… no, *shackled* by these adults, and forced to become a monk. Who knows what he might be doing now had he not been pressed into serving the Church?"

Surprised by these words, the Hermit shrugged with objection. "*Pressed?*" he said. "Oh no, no, my dear... it was his destiny. God rarely fills one soul with so many gifts. God placed him on this earth for one purpose only! And he's serving that purpose *brilliantly*. Don't you see?"

Mala looked at the Hermit thoughtfully. Through Tristan she had been warned of Peter's inviolable beliefs, but his comments now drove her to challenge him. "Ah, but isn't it possible that God Himself had other intentions for Tristan? That the adults around him conspired to mold his future? After your admission at the table yesterday about your own pride, you surely now agree that clerics are not infallible, including the Pope."

This disturbed the Hermit a bit, and his eyes began to shift a bit in their sockets. "I thought the Pope wrong about my Peasants' Crusade, and I disobeyed him," he said. "But the clouds have parted since then. So you see, the Pope *is* infallible. This Holy Crusade, as everything Odo de Lagery has done, is righteous. It was *me* who distorted the thing, not the Pope. *I'm* at fault, and many of the disasters surrounding the Peasants' Crusade are of my own prideful manufacture… which is why I now heed the Pope's advice and am trying to get the crusaders to wait on the main armies of Europe. But alas, I've lost my flock's ear and they defy me now." Closing his eyes, he added, "God's further punishment on me, I suppose."

"Ah, *God's* punishment again," sighed Mala, shaking her head. "The Church confounds me at times, Peter. It has cleverly established a ploy that can't lose. When good occurs, it's God's blessing, when evil occurs, it's God's punishment. Yet, by the same token, the Church claims that God gifted man with free will. It can't be both ways. Either God drives all things, or man drives his own decisions and causes his own punishment. When man's decisions go awry, such as what has happened to you, then the blame falls on the shoulders of man. Either God drove you to call for this unfortunate pauper crusade, or you drove yourself. As you spoke of pride yesterday, I felt you saw that *you* had driven this wheel, not God. But tell, Tristan informed me that you believe God speaks to you directly. Is that true?"

"Yes, most certainly! But at times I… misinterpret His meaning. He speaks in parables and riddles, you know."

"No, I *don't* know," insisted Mala. "Why would he not speak in *simple terms?* Why must everything be a mystery? Or perhaps, in reality, it's men who create the mystery, not God at all. In truth, I've begun to question the Church, Peter, and am no longer afraid to confess it."

This drew a scowl from the Hermit, and he pushed himself back from the rail, giving Mala a stern look. "Oh, but beware, young woman, God is listening to you this very moment."

"I said I've begun to question the *Church*, Peter, not God," Mala replied, returning her own stern gaze. "Just as you misinterpreted God's word, so have others. And when those high on the pedestal force their interpretations on others through threats of damnation and eternal fires of Hell, the ignorant become fearful. By ignorant, I don't mean the stupid, I mean those who blindly trust in authority. There's no authority on earth greater than God, so when men profess to speak for God, such talk *moves* people, just as you moved tens of thousands to join this Peasants' Crusade, and just as Odo de Lagery has moved tenfold that number. The Muslims are no better, putting non-Muslims to the sword, conquering lands and slaughtering in the name of Allah. You're preparing to do the same, accusing *their* interpretation of God as being false while adamantly clinging to the righteousness of your own belief. Meanwhile, people will die by the thousands on both sides. God didn't place us on this earth to murder each other in his name, Peter. He gave us life as a gift. It is *we* who take life away."

With each word she spoke, the Hermit became more and more alarmed for her soul. "Ah, you bash this crusade, yet you're willing to petition the emperor with me for assistance in Bithynia?"

"Yes," said Mala, "because of Tristan."

The Hermit rolled this about in his head a moment, then said, "You met as children, so I took you simply as youthful acquaintances… but why do I now suddenly suspect there's a bit more to it, *eh*?"

"Yes... there is," said Mala with firmness. "And I'm no longer ashamed of it, though he still runs from it… but only because of the Church, Odo de Lagery, Countess Mathilda, and everyone else who robbed him of free thought and free will as a child."

"Oh no, young woman," objected Peter, "it wasn't others, but God himself who always intended for Tristan de Saint-Germain to be a man of the cloth. Beware, you may be taking a crooked path with the Bishop, especially if you have personal designs on him along the way. And if that be the case, may the saints of Heaven forgive you!" He reached into his tunic then and fished for his prayer beads. "Ah, yes, I now see that I'd best pray for you."

"I don't need your prayers, Peter," Mala said, leaving the ship's railing. "Nor do I want them. Prayer has done little to shape my existence. Like everyone else, I've made my own mistakes and misjudgments. But unlike others, I blame myself and choose not to blame God."

## Chapter Seventy-four

### A Plea for Assistance

As Mala and the Hermit stood before the throne of Alexius for the second time in three days, Augusta Anna cast her gaze over at her son, lifting a brow. "And so," she huffed, "I hesitate to question your judgment openly, Alexius, but everything I foretold has now come about. I warned you not to allow this rabble into the city, yet you did… they rioted. I advised you to force them back from where they came, but you agreed to a second chance, allowing them to stay in Constantinople… they caused yet more disturbances, thieving even the metal roofing of our cathedrals. So rather than sending them home, you shipped them across the Straight to Bithynia... where now they pillage our own subjects there. Worse yet, they now attack the Turks– endangering the ever fragile truce we've maintained along that coastline for years. And here you are listening yet again to this hairy little monk who has been the root of our problems since the first days of August! Do you not see that sending troops to Bithynia is as good as an open declaration of war against Kilij Arslan? And we are not yet ready for that until Pope Urban's knights arrive in full force."

"Empress, we don't ask so much for the Byzantine troops to deal with the Turks or violate the truce," said Mala, "but to keep order and rein in the most militant of the crusader leaders from crossing into hostile territory."

"Yes," said Peter, "we simply need–"

"Oh, but shut your trap, you filthy tramp!" hissed the empress. "Though I might patiently sit here and listen to Signorina Mala, we in this court are quite weary of you, little man! I forbid you to speak further!"

Displeased first by his mother's open criticism, then further agitated by her uncharacteristic outburst demonstrating loss of royal demeanor, Alexius looked at her crossly, flapping a hand her direction, as if to say '*enough!*' Queen Irene, though exhibiting no reaction, was pleased by this gesture, and even more pleased that this continued plea for help in Bithynia was causing such dissension between her husband and the empress. She had perceived of late that Augusta Anna's authority over her husband was eroding, and the unexpected early arrival of the Hermit's crusaders had seemed to accelerate this process.

"I well appreciate that Peter the Hermit has informed me of the illegal activity across the straight," said Alexius firmly, "as it is what I commanded him to do." This sounded quite different from his tone of the first meeting when he had flown into a rage after learning that certain crusaders had killed Greek Christians, then crossed the border and attacked Turkish towns surrounding Nicaea. In fact, had Mala not been present to quell his fury during that initail visit, the Hermit might well have been dragged to the pillory for flogging. Fortunately, her calm line of reasoning had settled Alexius, which was the only reason he had agreed to this second meeting. "You assure me then, Peter," Alexius continued, "that at least Walter Sansavoir and *his* army along with many of your own followers have obeyed my instructions while in Bithynia?"

"Yes, Majesty," replied the Hermit, averting his eyes from Augusta Anna though she sat directly beside Alexius. "It's only a handful of instigators who keep the pot stirred, leading others awry. Though these thugs ignore me and Sansavoir, a strong hand such as yours would turn things about. But time is of the essence. As the outlaws of the crusade become bolder, the more I fear retribution from the Turks."

"I understand," said Alexius, "but there are implications and complexities that will launch into motion if a large Byzantine force lands in Bithynia, an action in direct violation of my truce with Kilij Arslan. Both sides have agreed to keep the area clear of our own troops, thus creating a buffer so to speak between Byzantines and Turks."

"You have *already* violated that term of the truce, Alexius," blenched Augusta Anna, "by landing the crusaders there. They *are* a large military force."

"Yes, but not a Byzantine military force," Alexius replied, struggling to hold his irritation at his mother in check. "Besides, they were instructed by me to remain to themselves."

"But they *did not…*" Augusta Anna insisted, glaring at the Hermit, then glaring at her son.

"Emperor," said Mala, "I well understand your hesitancy in sending troops, but there's another issue here that I failed to discuss during the first meeting."

"And what would that be, Lady Mala?" asked Alexius.

"The issue of Bishop Saint-Germain," Mala replied. "He is the Pope's First Counsel. Should anything happen to him, then I fear to think of the consequences in Rome, especially if they learn you had the opportunity to help him, but failed to do so. Pope Urban took him in as a boy of seven and has kept him at his side ever since. Tristan is like a son to the Pope, and he holds no person on this entire earth closer to his heart. If the crusader pillaging continues, or should the Turks rise up, Tristan's safety will be in jeopardy."

Although no one seemed to take notice that Mala had twice referred to Bishop Saint-Germain as 'Tristan,' this detail had for some reason caught Queen Irene's attention. She said nothing, however. Instead, setting her eyes intently upon those of Mala, she searched for something of which she was as yet unsure. Then, for some reason, the face of the young captain of the Royal Guard who had years ago set her heart afire came to mind. This surprised Irene and she gasped, as pricked by a thorn. Envisioning the handsome young captain's face, a surge of regret washed through her, causing her heart to break rhythm several beats.

Upon Irene's forced marriage to Alexius, Augusta Anna had sent the young captain to the Turkish front and arranged for him to meet his end. Learning of this, Irene's heart had descended into a trough of regret from which she had not even to this day completely withdrawn herself.

"The Bishop is there in Bithynia of his own volition!" insisted Augusta Anna with defiance. "If harm comes to him, it will be his own undoing, not ours!"

"Indeed," agreed Patriarch Nicholas, speaking for the first time. "As he's openly declared that he is not associated with the Peasants' Crusade, there was no reason for him to go to Bithynia in the first place."

"Oh, but there *was*," said Mala. "He follows Pope Urban's directive."

"What?" asked Alexius, surprised by this declaration.

"In private conversation," said Mala, "I learned that the reason the Bishop ended up following the Hermit from Germany was to help protect the poor and weak should they refuse to wait for Bishop Adhémar, or should they imperil themselves with the Turks... which is exactly what has now occurred."

Augusta Anna considered these words carefully, closing her eyes. When she opened them, she sat erect. "Oh, but the Bishop has *lied* then!" she snapped. "He vowed to us that he and the Tuscans simply happened to be taking the same route south as the Peasants' Crusade, which is how the two groups happened to arrive together at our border. Other than that, the Bishop insisted time and again that there was no connection whatsoever between him and the Hermit's traveling circus!"

"Bishop Saint-Germain did not lie," replied Mala, her eyes turning to embers as her tone grew cold. As a foreign dignitary and woman of substance, she was unafraid of the empress. "He merely maintained the integrity and confidentiality of the Pope's intent," she fired back. Then, pointing at Patriarch Nicholas, she asked, "Would you not do the same for your emperor, Patriarch? And in doing so, would you consider such a lie, or a *loyalty*?"

Not wishing to contradict the empress, Patriarch Nicholas stared vacantly at Mala, but said nothing.

"If the Patriarch was any kind of man," said Queen Irene, speaking up to everyone's surprise, "yes, he would maintain his loyalty to the emperor at all times and at any cost. But he sallies back and forth to curry favor with Augusta Anna... which is why he fails to understand there lies a great difference between *lying* and withholding delicate information out of loyalty. There also lies a great difference between political *expediency* and loyalty, though some in this court cannot seem to differentiate." The tone in which she said this was so emphatic, so succinct, that it drew everyone's eyes. So rarely had she ever spoken while seated between emperor and empress that this declaration by her awed all within the imperial hall save the Augusta Anna herself. Queen Irene then demurely folded her hands in her lap and said, "Husband, Lady Mala is correct. If nothing else, you must ensure the safety of... *Tristan*." As she pronounced this name, her eyes settled directly on Mala's, and she tipped her head the slightest bit– with such subtle inference that only Mala noticed. Then she faintly smiled.

*Oh, but what's this?* wondered Mala, confused.

"Very well," said Alexius, reaching over and placing his hand over that of the queen. "Yes, Irene, you are quite right." Turning about, Alexius motioned for his generals to advance. "Call in the ships from all neighboring ports," he commanded, and begin preparations to transport a full battle battalion to Bithynia. That should be more than adequate to collar this ring of rabble rousers causing disruption across the Straight."

"Yes, Excellency!" the generals replied, snapping to attention.

As he dismissed all in the imperial hall and they began to disperse, Queen Irene stood to leave also. Looking at her directly, Mala bowed. She wished to thank the queen, but felt it untimely with the Augusta sitting there. But Irene inconspicuously gave Mala a slight gesture– moving her eyes toward a side corridor, then receding down that corridor herself. Moments later the Augusta stood and walked to a different corridor with Patriarch Nicholas, and as soon as they were out of sight, Mala made for the corridor the queen had taken. Entering it, she found Irene waiting for her.

Mala grasped her hand and started to thank her for her assistance, but before she could open her mouth, the queen placed a finger to her lips, indicating silence. "Say nothing, but only listen," she whispered. Then, in a nearly inaudible voice, she continued. "My imagination caught something in your eyes a moment ago, though I saw nothing. My heart told me you were feeling something, though you were masking it. And your expression says much, though you suppress it. But one woman who has suffered unattainable love detects even the invisible... in a kindred soul. God bless you, Lady Mala, and may your fortunes be kinder to you than they were to me."

Irene turned then and left, leaving Mala wondering what it was, exactly, that the queen had just said.

## Chapter Seventy-five

### In the Hermit's Absence

The Hermit's warning to Tristan and his departure across the Bosphorus Straight with Mala to petition for Byzantine troops set the Tuscans abuzz. Their encampment had become rather complacent due to what they had mistakenly perceived as inactivity amongst the crusader factions of Nicodemia and Civetot. Their first order of business was to station scouts near the Turkish border for purposes of extending warning time should the Turks appear over the horizon. Next, Guillaume established several manned outposts about halfway between the border and the Tuscan camp for defensive purposes; Orla and Crowbones were charged with oversight and implementation of this strategy, and given command of forty Tuscan knights to assist. Also, as Guthroth, Hroc, and Handel were the most skilled riders of the camp, Guillaume sent them as advance scouts into Turkish territory to reconnoiter for a Seljuk military presence. And finally, Guillaume determined that he would remain in camp to commandeer the remaining four hundred or so troops of the Tuscan force, and Tristan would remain at his side.

The Hermit's departure to Constantinople also incited activity within Civetot itself. DuLac and Burrel began to work on Sansavoir, hoping to goad him into switching alliances. Sansavoir, despite being weaker standing alone in the absence of the Hermit, continued to repel their advances.

On the second day of the Hermit's absence, DuLac called for Tafur. "It's time to hatch our plan," said DuLac. "I've happened across some useful information these past two days. The Tuscans have sent many of their riders from the camp to establish lookout outposts. But of greater interest, it seems Bishop Saint-Germain takes strolls each night on the beach around dusk with some female merchant, an acquaintance of the emperor, I'm told.

They often walk our direction, though taking care not to come too close to Civetot knowing the Bishop's got many enemies here. It's a good time to set a snare, I think."

Tafur looked at DuLac, puzzled. "And how's it you've acquired this information?" he asked.

"Ah, a little sparrow passed it along. He and a friend happened upon Bishop Saint-Germain and this woman several nights ago. Saint-Germain happened to let it slip that he walks the beach at night with her, and when she's back in the capital, he walks it alone… for reflection and prayer, he said. As to the information about the Tuscans,' my little sparrow got that information from his friend who's been visiting the Tuscan the camp since the Hermit's departure."

The 'sparrow' was Benito Fazio and the 'friend' was Innocenzo, who as always, had shared his activities with Fazio. Innocenzo had no idea Fazio harbored such ill feelings toward the Bishop, nor did he imagine that Fazio would share their private conversations with anyone of DuLac's character. Innocenzo, unwittingly, was played as the dupe.

"If this woman you've mentioned is a friend of the Emperor Alexius," said Tafur, "then we'd be playing with fire by kidnapping her and the Bishop."

"Ah, but according to my source, she's back in Constantinople at the moment. She's sailed there with the Hermit, apparently. With her gone, the Hermit gone, and the Tuscan camp keeping an eye to outposts, there'll be no better time to take the Bishop, or simply kill him right there on the beach and bury him in the dunes. His disappearance will be a mystery. Aye, I'll send my two lieutenants, the Gustave twins."

"No," said Tafur, shaking his head. "I'll send my own men. I don't want yours anywhere near Saint-Germain."

"Huh?" huffed DuLac. "What in hell's that supposed to mean?"

"Simple," replied Tafur. "You'd like to see the Bishop dead right now… but I don't want such a quick end for that bastard."

"Dammit, Tafur," said DuLac. "Sometimes you're confusing as hell. I thought you hated the man as much as I do."

"Oh, I do. The Bishop's been in my way for over half a year now, showing up at every turn to discredit me and my men, or defy us in battle. He stands for everything I despise in this life. He's a high cleric, he's had everything handed to him in life, and continues to ascend. For just *once* in my life I intend to pick a man like him apart… bone by bone."

"Shit!" said DuLac, exasperation taking hold. "I'll have the Gustave twins dissect him, and I'll make sure they deliver the goddammned bones to you on a platter *personally*, Tafur. Then, dammit, we'll done with it and can move on to the others."

"Oh, though you're a nobleman yourself, DuLac, you little understand your own stinking breed," grunted Tafur, his face contorting with ridicule. "Men like you and Saint-Germain operate on prestige and position, unlike we poor who've had your damned boot on our necks since the day we first saw light. No… I'd far rather undo Saint-Germain my own way.

"And just what the hell way is that, Tafur?"

"Public *humiliation*... to begin with," said Tafur. "Aye, to be discredited, stripped of all honor and pride. He should have a good dose of my own bitter medicine before leaving this life, DuLac... learn what it's like to have absolutely nothing, and no one… know how it feels to stand alone in the face of a world that's turned against him."

"*Christ, Tafur,*" DuLac heaved, "and just how do you propose to accomplish that?"

"A trial… right here in Civetot."

"A *trial*? Have you lost your goddamned mind? There are those who respect the Bishop within this camp– the Hermit and Sansavoir for starters. And what about their followers?"

"They won't respect him by the time *I'm* done with him. I'll pick the judges, and I'll pick the witnesses. And I'll also pick the men to snatch Saint-Germain. And if I hear your bastard twins have laid a finger on him, then it'll be war between the Normans and the Tafurs right here in Civetot. Best not forget, DuLac, I've got you far outnumbered here."

DuLac's expression soured, knowing Tafur was right– the Beggar King's trump card lay in vastly superior numbers. "You're complicating things, Tafur! My solution's far simpler, far quicker. Nevertheless, I'll play along… to a point. But if your little game falls apart, then you can bet I'll step in, outnumbered or not!"

## Chapter Seventy-six

### Malik's Strategy

On the morning Mamoud Malik and General Soliman marched away from the fort at Xerigordos, Malik tasked a score of his horsemen to take custody of the eighty-five slaves who had been spared for the brothel and eunuch markets and make for Baghdad and Medina. He and Soliman, meanwhile, directed the main army toward the coast. Less than two miles out of Xerigordos, they encountered the scouting party they had sent out two days earlier.

"There's a large foreign camp at Civetot," reported the lead scout. "A strange thing though. It's a military camp, yet filled with as many women and children as there are soldiers, maybe even more."

"Women and children?" asked Malik, who could not have imagined that a vast peasant army including women and children had marched all the way from western Europe to make war on the Turks. "*Foreign* settlers?" he then said, looking at Soliman. "Surely they don't intend to settle in Bithynia with their families. The truce between Emperor Alexius and Sultan Arslan forbids further settlement. We've agreed to leave Greek farmers and shepherds already there to go unmolested as long as they remain on Byzantine soil… but now foreign armies and their families are settling in? Daring to pillage Muslim communities?"

"It makes little sense," said Soliman. "But if they're not Byzantine, where did they come from?"

"Though it sounds odd," replied the scout, "some of the Greek shepherds we encountered along the way told us Alexius' ships unloaded them here over a month back. These same shepherds are terrified of them, too, claiming the foreigners have murdered Greek farmers within the Byzantine strip of coastline."

"Alexius' ships unloaded these foreigners, yet they're killing Alexius' own Greek farmers?" said Soliman, as the mystery reported by the scout seemed only to deepen.

"And there's another thing, General," the scout continued. "The old fortress of Nicodemia is also occupied, but with only military men. Stranger yet, there's a third little camp sitting between it and Civetot. Why the smaller camp sits there alone, we couldn't determine, but it's got a small military bivouac set up also."

Malik shook his head, shrugging. "You say the old fortress at Nicodemia's occupied?" he asked.

"Yes sir," replied the scout, "a force of several thousand, the shepherds told us… yet, when we went to investigate, the fort was empty as far as we could tell."

The scout failed to understand that the Nicodemia fortress had been the camp where Rainald's Lombards, Longobards, and Alemanni had been encamped before getting trapped at Xerigordos. He and the other scouts had assumed that the missing troops reported by the Greek shepherds were perhaps in Civetot at the time.

"But why would these foreigners settle in the port of Civetot which has no walls and stands wide open when they could have opted for the walls of the old fortress?" puzzled General Soliman.

"Oh, the old fortress is like Xerigordos, sir… far too small to accommodate such vast numbers," replied the scout.

"Damnation," muttered Malik, "just how many foreigners *are there* at Civetot then?"

"I estimate at least fifty or sixty thousand in all… maybe more. The town's filled to bursting, and people are camped all about its fringes, half a mile or more."

This sounded inconceivable to Malik and Soliman both, but seeing the other scouts nodding with agreement, the two commanders looked at each other, stunned. "Perhaps we had best withdraw and call for reinforcements," said Soliman. "When Arslan sent us back to Nicaea, I'm sure he had no idea this foreign threat was so enormous in numbers. Nor would I have ever guessed such a thing."

"Fifty or sixty thousand," muttered Malik to himself, giving the numbers some thought. "No," he said, "we'll not withdraw. Though the numbers are vast, with women and children in the mix as reported, they couldn't have more than twenty or twenty-five thousand men-at-arms."

"Still," Soliman said, "attacking Civetot itself could be risky. I'm not worried about footmen, but we've no idea how many knights they have."

Malik, still rolling numbers in his head, looked up after some additional thought. "Soliman," he said, "about two hours march from Civetot near the village of Dracon, the plains turn into hills, and the road leads into a valley which gradually works itself into a narrow pass, creating a bottleneck... and that road is the only route to Nicaea. If we could set up an ambush in the gorge, we'd quickly even the odds. As the enemy marches into it, we'll let them come toward the end, then close the trap. We'll unleash our archers on the knights at the head of the column and from both sides. Once they're decimated, we'll send our horsemen in after the footmen."

"But how do we get them to march into the valley?" asked Soliman.

"Spies, Soliman. We'll send in spies posing as Greek shepherds who'll tell the foreigners of the massacre at Xerigordos. We'll also have these same spies tell them our army has withdrawn back east to continue reinforcing Kilij Arslan against the Danishmends, and that Nicaea now lies unprotected and ripe for plunder again. These heathens have been raiding and pillaging every Turkish town they come across, which tells me they're only after treasure. Everyone knows the big prize is Nicaea itself where Kilij Arslan's treasury stands. They'll not resist such a temptation. So come along then, Soliman, let's make for the valley of Dracon."

## Chapter Seventy-seven

### Night Skies

It is a peculiar trait of man that, as he gazes at the moon and the celestial arrangement of stars, they stir in him the need to find 'meaning'– thus often launching him into the realm of imagination, fantasy and the supernatural. Such was the case of Peter the Hermit and his followers who interpreted the celestial signs over Europe's night skies during the years 1094-1095 as signs from Heaven directing them to Jerusalem.

On a lower plane, celestial bodies also fuel the human heart toward simple reflection, in particular a night sky bursting with the illumination of a full moon and constellations of glimmering stars. So it is that a fully lit night sky so often lures us into gazing at the splendor and majesty of the universe, whereas a dark night keeps us under roof.

On the first night that the four Tafurs were instructed to conceal themselves amidst the dunes to await Bishop Saint-Germain's anticipated night walk, he failed to show. Despite the phase of the full moon, a heavy cloud cover had advanced over Bithynia, shrouding the moon, threatening rain– causing Tristan to remain in camp that night. By the next evening the sky had cleared, the stars were afire, and the full blaze of the moon cast a pale blue hue over the landscape, setting the sea afire with bright specks of light that danced about in a riot of shimmering motion. Awed by the clarity and wonder of the night sky thus reflecting against the sea, Tristan was prompted into movement. He took to the beach alone in the direction of Civetot.

Losing himself there in profound reflection and supposition about Constantinople, his crumbling faith in Odo de Lagery's judgment about protecting the Peasants' Crusade, and in thoughts of Mala, the world dwindled to the narrow scope of his mental ramblings. Finally, seeing the torches of Civetot in the near distance, he turned about, making back for the Tuscan camp. Moments later everything went black, and he felt himself being suffocated by a blanket forced over his head and shoulders. "Keep him quiet!" hissed an urgent voice, "and *quickly*, tie his damned feet!"

Startled, but unable to cry out, Tristan struggled to escape. Unable to break free, he next heard more voices, and felt himself being trussed– and shortly felt himself being dragged across the dunes, then hoisted to the back of a braying donkey. Striking the beast on the rump, his abductors broke into a trot across the sand. Twenty minutes later they were in Civetot.

Pulling Tristan from the donkey, his captors tore the blanket from his head and struggled to free his feet as he kicked and protested. Gasping for air, Tristan glanced about, infuriated. "*Oh, but what is this!*" he shouted.

Standing before him were four Tafurs, each bearing the brand of the cross on their foreheads, each glaring at him menacingly. Then, from behind them came a familiar but unwelcome voice. "Welcome to our humble camp, Saint-Germain," sniggered Tafur.

"Yes, indeed, welcome to our humble camp" echoed a second voice. It was Desmond DuLac, his eyes dull with hate, staring coldly at him. Tristan stared back and the two men measured each other carefully then, their eyes narrowing as each took on that expression of abhorrence that strikes men when, after so many long years, coming face to face with an elusive nemesis.

Despite already knowing that DuLac had arrived in Byzantium, this was actually the first time Tristan had set eyes on DuLac since being separated from his mother as a helpless boy of seven. Nonetheless, it took but a blink for the bitterness of that crushing, hurtful memory from the long buried past to overwhelm him; he felt himself suddenly filling with stark aversion and enmity. "And so, *Uncle*," he hissed, "after so many years we meet again!"

"Yes... yes," muttered DuLac, vaguely recalling the face of a seven year old boy, remolding it into the face of the grown man now hobbled before him. But then, involuntarily, his heart pulsed out of rhythm and he found himself struggling to mute the gasp rising in his throat ... because in seeing Tristan's face, he could not help but see the replication of the delicate, stunning features of beautiful Asta of the Danes, the wife who had fled their marriage and England a decade earlier. Her flight had cost him far more than a marriage, however. Indeed, despite his greed-filled heart and penchant for wickedness, losing her had nearly broken him. Asta, all things aside, had been the only person in life that Desmond DuLac had ever loved.

He had become hopelessly enraptured by her innocence and beauty at first sight during her forced marriage at age twelve to his brother, Roger de Saint-Germain, a man of forty. Eight years later, after being complicit in Roger's betrayal and execution for treason, DuLac had then quickly offered marriage to Asta; she accepted, but only as a means of financing a high Cluny education for her two sons at the hands of the Black Monks of Burgundy and securing the future of her personal Danish Guard and their families. DuLac had gladly paid this extreme toll, and for the first time in his entire existence, thought himself happy. But she had shunned his affection, turning against him, which was the greatest wound he had ever suffered in life. And that wound had never abated over time. Indeed, it had by now festered into abject hatred and a single-minded obsession to inflict retribution. Truly, he had dreamed for years now of finding her again... to punish her in the most hurtful ways conceivable for leaving him.

Collecting his composure, DuLac took a step forward, shaking a fist. "Oh," he growled, though I've hoped for years to get my hands upon your goddamned mother, now at least I've gotten my hands on you! And when I'm done with you, it will be my life's goal to find Asta again, only to let that goddamned bitch know that it was *me* who brought you to your end!"

Seething at hearing DuLac blasheme Asta's name, Tristan felt an inner eruption– the unearthing of an entire lifetime of repressed and subdued hatred against the man standing before him. Without wishing it, those injuries of the far past began slicing at him like razors, carving bare his heart as forgotten emotions hemorrhaged forth, one after another. Suddenly, he understood the vitriolic hatred held by Orla, Crowbones and Guthroth against DuLac. "Oh, but you short, rat-faced bastard!" he rasped, straining against the hold of his captors, so fury-filled that he could scarcely breathe. "You there," he screamed, straining forward, "with your stubby, short little arms and squinty eyes– tis no wonder those who despise you call you the 'mole!" Surging forward so furiously that it took the full squad of Tafurs to restrain him, Tristan was finally pulled back and held in check. In frustration, Tristan spat at DuLac, and shouted, "You'll never get to my mother, DuLac," he said, "for she is untouchable now... locked behind the stone walls of the Benedictine Convent at Marcigny-sur-Loire!"

Hearing this, a glimmer slipped into DuLac's eye. "Ha, you damn fool! I've sought for years to ferret out her whereabouts," he crowed, "*and now you simply reveal her hiding hole?* Marcigny lies in Burgundy, and I'll extract her from there, by God, even should I be forced to storm the goddamned convent walls with my troops!"

"She is untouchable now," repeated Tristan, spitting again at DuLac though DuLac had backed well away. "Aye, try as you may, you'll never set hands upon her again, for her soul is now with God! Only her *body* resides at Marcigny-sue-Loire... buried deep within the graveyard there!"

As struck by a blow to the head, DuLac convulsed. Jolted by this information, his face flushed scarlet as dark blue veins began pulsing up and down the length of his neck as he attempted to issue a sharp retort. But this unexpected, unimaginable news of Asta's death had stunned him to the bone; he was struck speechless. Standing there, mouth ajar, he froze– appearing suddenly crippled.

"Enough of this happy reunion horse-shit between uncle and nephew, or whatever the hell it is that ties you two together!" barked Tafur, who had been taking in the exchange impatiently. Jerking his thumb toward a ramshackle stone structure to his left, which was the former dungeon of Civetot, he said, "Let's drag him in there for now, but you fellows there, take care not to damage his clothes. And don't abuse him yet either for I'll want his face and body unmolested so as not to garner sympathy when I put him before the mob tomorrow!"

## Chapter Seventy-eight

### Aftermath of Xerigordos

On the night the Tafurs snatched Tristan from the beach, Guillaume had already fallen asleep. That next morning when he awoke before light, it never occurred to him to check on his brother. He and several other knights had decided at dawn to check on Orla's and Crowbones' progress setting up their observation posts, which meant Guillaume would be gone for several days. Tristan's absence, therefore, went unnoticed.

Handel, Guthroth, and Hroc, meanwhile, had ridden far beyond the look-out perimeter and were two days deep into Turkish territory scouting for traces of Muslim troops. As they approached the top of a rise, from the other side of its crown, Handel spotted what appeared to be a huge spiral of dust rising in the distance. "Look there," he said, "horses on the move... in large numbers I'd say."

Guthroth nodded with certainty as Hroc replied, "Ja, footmen don't create such a disturbance. Let's clear the hill and take a look."

Slipping over the rise, they happened onto Malik's and Soliman's forces just as they had made the first mile from Xerigordos and were beginning to disappear over the horizon. "Judas Priest," exclaimed Handel, "a full Turkish army on the march!" Then, looking the opposite direction, he spotted the fort of Xerigordos. Squinting, he took a closer look and said, "Christ Almighty… is that… *men* hanging from the walls and ramparts?"

"Can't quite tell," said Hroc, but Guthroth nodded again with certainty and made for the stream twisting its way around the foot of the fort.

Within twenty minutes all three men were circling the walls of the fort, shocked at seeing them strung with the eviscerated bodies of crusaders. "Rainald's men," said Handel, recognizing remnants of German and Italian hauberks and gambesons hanging from the partially stripped corpses.

Entering the fort, they looked about but found nothing. Then, after taking to the road and crossing the stream, they saw signs of ash and refuse from the large Turkish encampment that had been established earlier. It was here they discovered mound after mound of naked crusader bodies, as identified by their fair skin, each horribly mutilated in one way or another. Many were missing ears and noses, others had been gutted, and still others were missing hands, feet, or testicles. These heaps of mangled remains, smothered with hordes of flies feasting and crawling between bodies and into human cavities, stunk of fetid rot. And from beneath this horror, a nearly imperceptible but repulsive sound emanated with constancy. It was that supping, mucous-devouring sound peculiar of millions of maggots hungrily feasting on human flesh.

"Goddammit," muttered Handel, 'this is beyond brutality… it's perversion."

"Ja, and looks as though the Turks we spotted are now headed toward Bithynia," Hroc replied. "We'd best get word to the outposts and have them withdraw– and let Guillaume know as well back at camp."

"And w-warn C-Civetot, also," muttered Guthroth.

Although Handel felt that Burrel, DuLac and Tafur deserved neither consideration nor quarter, he knew the small town was brimming with women, children, and elderly. "We'd best stay off the roads and ride as the crow flies for the coast," he said, "then make our way along the beach so as to circumvent the Turks and–"

Before he could finish, Guthroth had already kicked the flanks of his horse, setting it at a gallop across the plain. "H-hurry!" he shouted, not looking back to see whether Hroc and Handel were following.

## Chapter Seventy-nine

### The Prisoner

As Malik and Soliman moved toward Civetot and began concealing their troops within the thickly wooded valley two hours march from the town, Tristan was being stripped of his bishop's garb. Several Tafurs then forced him to face the dungeon wall and shackled him to it.

"Oh, but it's good to have you in *my* house for once, Saint-Germain," gloated Tafur, his body trembling the least bit, like the spider spying the fly freshly snared in the web. "You'll pay, finally, for the death of my men in the Jewish quarter of Cologne. And in Hungary, too. Aye, and you'll pay for all the crimes of the high clergy feeding off the poor, kissing the asses of the nobility." As he said this, Tafur's thoughts reeled back to Archbishop Duchamps who had betrayed him to Lord Cartier back in Lyon so many years ago. Feeling these old hatreds resurrecting themselves, he slapped Tristan across the back of the head. Though Tristan was shackled face toward the wall, Tafur then shouted, "And turn around when I speak to you, you bishop bastard!"

Tristan twisted his head about, as ordered, but rather than cower, he leveled his eyes at Tafur. "Oh, but just look at you, Tafur… you long ago ceased to be human, and know it even yourself. The hate I perceived in your eyes since our first encounter is to be pitied, for it has made you immune to the feelings of others. Butcher of Jews… killer of Christians. Even prayer itself would fail to spare one as you."

"Ah, but spew your worthless tripe," Tafur hissed, his eyes cold and serpentine. "No adoring crowds to hear it, no Pope or College of Cardinals at your back. You're alone now, with no one here to applaud your sanctimonious drivel but the walls."

Tristan's eyes flared at hearing this, as the glacial gaze of Tafur's eyes dissected him with the precision of a razor. Tristan had never in his entire existence witnessed such hate and animus contained in a single gaze, not even during his earlier exchange with DuLac. Knowing nothing of Tafur's history, he failed to comprehend that the full weight of the Beggar King's tortuous past was now focused directly at him. For Tafur, however unjustified, Tristan de Saint-Germain had become the sole embodiment of a lifetime of revulsion aimed against high clerics and nobility.

Likewise, blinded by the unmitigated loathing in his prisoner's eyes, Tafur knew nothing of Tristan de Saint-Germain's history. He was ignorant of Tristan's own suffering at the hands of nobility, his future having been cast to the winds as a child by his own aristocratic but treasonous father, then further ruptured by the treacherous actions of Desmond DuLac and the merciless politics of the Bastard of Normandy. Nor did Tafur imagine that Tristan de Saint-Germain had always possessed a heart for the poor and an inclination toward the dispossessed, or that he had struggled against the injustices of life's cruelties.

"Do you not even, at least, believe in *God*, Tafur?" said Tristan, returning Tafur's icy stare. "Do you not acknowledge there is a Hell, and those who commit atrocities shall end there, suffering for their terrible judgment while here on this earth?"

The parasitic blight of Tafur's alienation and hatred had long since dismissed all acknowledgment of God *or* Hell, infecting him instead with a blinding obsession for cruelty and destruction. Yet, Tristan's last words infuriated him, as they accosted Tafur's veiled pretenses of piety and performing God's labor. Flushing red, he was sorely tempted him to lay into Tristan with a sound thrashing.

Sensing this, one of Tafur's men smiled. "We'll work him over for you, King Tafur, and take the whole damned night doing it!" he said.

Tafur shook his head. "No, he needs to be in one piece for the trial tomorrow, primped in his fine clerical vestments for all to see. I don't want to present him mashed to a pulp, lest others begin to feel pity, so as I said before, keep your hands off him… at least for tonight."

Tristan turned toward the wall, relieved at learning he would not be brutalized throughout the night as he had expected. Still, the mention of a trial took him by surprise. "A trial… *really*?" he said, refusing to either turn about or dilute the scorn seeping into his tone. "And just what *laughable* charges have you trumped up against me, Tafur?"

"Oh, there's nothing laughable about the charges against you, Saint-Germain," Tafur clucked with satisfaction. "I'm about to expose you for what you really are, and when I'm done, every heckling voice in the Hermit's camp will be calling for your goddamned head at the end of a rope… and deservedly so.

The tone in which Tafur said this puzzled Tristan; there was a certainty to it. Dismissing the thought, he began reciting Latin aloud.

"What the hell are you doing?" asked Tafur.

"Praying for your black, lost soul," Tristan replied.

"Spare me your prayers, monk," growled Tafur, "for you're the one who'll soon need them, not me!"

Tafur then gestured to the other men. "Keep a close eye to him," he said. "And remember, no one's allowed in– especially DuLac or any of his Norman goons."

"And if they should show?" asked one of the guards.

"Then raise the damned call, you fool!" Tafur replied.

"Then you'll be near, huh?" pressed the guard.

"Look, I've got a hundred of our men posted within the block, so quit pissing your pants about the Normans."

Satisfied, the guard nodded and saw Tafur to the door. As he stepped out onto the street, Tafur encountered a flurry of activity as Norman and French captains carrying torches seemed to be moving toward the Civetot plaza. "What's going on here?" said Tafur, grabbing a soldier running past, headed that direction.

"Burrel's put out a sudden call for assembly!" the man said, sounding harried, pulling his arm from Tafur's grip. "Something's in the wind, I heard… Turks maybe."

"*Turks?*" said Tafur.

"*Shit*, I don't know, Tafur! There's all kinds of rumors flying around… seems some damned shepherds happened into town a while back, then all hell broke loose."

***

Well after midnight, Tristan heard someone approaching his cell. "I've come to see the prisoner," a voice said.

"No visitors, you know that," snarled one of the guards.

"I'm Peter the Hermit's nephew," replied Innocenzo, his voice more insistent than Tristan had ever recalled.

"We know who the shit you are," said the guard, "but Tafur said no visitors, so piss off!"

"Search me, strip me," said Innocenzo, "I've nothing on me but… *this*… for you guards." Innocenzo withdrew a leather pouch from his tunic and handed it to the lead guard. "Twenty Byzantine besants," said Innocenzo, extracting one of the coins and holding it to the torch light. "Five year's wages for each of you within this pouch. All I want is to talk to the prisoner for a few moments… share a prayer with him."

The other guards gathered around Innocenzo as the first guard dumped the besants onto a stool top. "Yah, yah, Innocenzo," snorted the guard, "but what the hell's to keep us from simply taking these coins and turning you in to Tafur?"

"Oh, very unwise," replied Innocenzo quickly. "I'll claim you stole them from me when my uncle returns from Constantinople with the emperor's troops. These besants were gifts from Alexius to my uncle when he arrived in the capital. The emperor would be furious, and each of you would lose your hands for thievery. Come now, I'm not asking for the world. Take the besants and just give me a few moments with Bishop Saint-Germain. I'm no threat."

"Yeah, it's a simple thing," urged one of the other guards, his eyes alight with greed.

"Aye," agreed another, "we'll never in our lives see this kind of coin again!"

Innocenzo was allowed to pass, but on entering the cell fell into immediate distress at the sight of Tristan shackled naked to the wall. "Oh, dear Bishop… this is disgraceful! Uncle Peter would be furious!"

"Does he not know of my imprisonment?" asked Tristan, surprised that Innocenzo had managed his way into the cell.

"No, most certainly not! That's why I came here tonight. I suspected you thought he might be involved in your capture. But no, his hands are clean, Bishop! As you know, he's in Constantinople with la Signorina. No, he had nothing to do with this!"

"Thank God," sighed Tristan. "It shames me to confess it, but in the back of my mind I feared he had a hand in this, perhaps even using his departure as a ploy to appear innocent."

"No, Bishop, these cowards waited until he left for Constantinople to petition Alexius for troops. And for good cause, come to find out! My uncle's fears are coming about. A little while ago two Greek shepherds entered town and gave reports that Rainald's Lombards, Longobards, and Alemanni were trapped at an old fort in Xerigordos, and have been mercilessly slaughtered there by a Turkish army!"

"What? Rainald's army… lost?"

"Yes, three thousand nearly to the last man. Several hundred survived by converting to Islam and then being sold into slavery, the shepherds claim, but the rest were butchered."

"God in Heaven," Tristan whispered. "Where is this Turkish army now? Is it marching on Civetot?"

"No," replied Innocenzo. "Apparently they think Rainald's men are the only ones who've been raiding their territory, so having wiped them out, they're on their way back to join Kilij Arslan in his fight against the Danishmends."

Tristan shook his head. "That makes no sense, Innocenzo. That would leave Nicaea unprotected again as it has been these past two months, and invite more pillaging."

"You don't understand," insisted Innocenzo. "The Turks seem to think Rainald's army is the only foreign army in Bithynia. Evidently, they're ignorant of the much larger force here at Civetot. But, there's another problem now that the Turks are withdrawing."

"*If* they're withdrawing, you mean," said Tristan, unconvinced, "but go on."

"Because of the way these shepherds described the butchering of Rainald's men, the hotheads in camp like Tafur and Burrel are proposing to seek revenge by attacking Nicaea within the week. Apparently, the bodies of Rainald's men were deliberately and horribly mutilated because they were Christians. Even DuLac who had no interest in avenging Rainald, wants to attack Nicaea… for plunder, especially since the Turkish army that butchered Rainald's bunch has withdrawn and returned east to fight the Danishmends."

"And Walter Sansavoir?" asked Tristan. "What is his position?"

"Sansavoir stands alone against all of them, insisting they wait at least until my uncle returns with Byzantine troops."

"Does Sansavoir have enough troops to hold the others back?"

"I don't know. Burrel, Tafur and DuLac combined have many troops, Bishop."

"Oh, the wreckless fools!" Tristan exclaimed. "Even if the Turkish army *has* vacated the region, they will now leave a good sized reserve force at Nicaea. Besides, neither Burrel or DuLac have siege equipment, and I'm told the walls of Nicaea are formidable."

"The men are building ladders as I speak now," said Innocenzo.

"*Ladders?* None of these imbeciles have ever fought the Turks, Innocenzo. Do they actually think the Seljuks are so incompetent at defending their own capital that ladders will do the job?"

"Yes, they do," nodded Innocenzo. "Since the raiding they've committed against Turkish towns surrounding Nicaea has been so easily overcome, they seem to think the Turks are spineless."

"But, Innocenzo, all the towns surrounding Nicaea are small, and defenseless at that! The Seljuk military is an entirely different story! I'm telling you, Innocenzo, if Rainald's entire force has been massacred, the Turks are still about, and probably have their eyes set on Civetot as we speak!"

Innocenzo shook his head, confused. "In any case, Bishop, the crusaders are talking even now about taking the entire military force of over twenty thousand men and making a frontal assault on Nicaea in several days… as soon as they finish the ladders and get mobilized."

"And what of the women, children, and others?"

"They'll remain here in camp, apparently. Tafur wanted to take them as fighters seeing as that's why they came, but DuLac and Burrel finally agreed on something and refused, insisting the women and children would only get in the way."

"Oh, God in Heaven!" Tristan moaned. "Innocenzo, it will end in massacre! The Turks are far more clever than the likes of

Tafur, Burrel, and DuLac! And think... after the crusader military forces are decimated at Nicaea, what will then become of the thirty thousand women, children, and elderly they've left behind here in Civetot?"

"Oh, I shudder to think of it if our men-at-arms are defeated…" shivered Innocenzo, shaking his head.

"Hey, in there!" shouted a guard. "Time's up, Innocenzo!"

"Y-yes, yes, I'm coming," Innocenzo replied, grasping Tristan about the shoulders, embracing him. "Oh, Bishop, I'm so sorry. I don't know how things will end in the morning for you in this hostile climate. Word's spread there's to be a trial and that you'll be charged with high crimes against the Peasants' Crusade because of Cologne, Zemun, and the riot in Constantinople. But on my word, Bishop Saint-Germain, I'll be there for you. I may be a sinner, but I'll be praying for you nevertheless. Perhaps the Lord will give ear to an errant soul such as myself!"

"Yes, you have sinned Innocenzo, but so have we all… so God has not forsaken you," whispered Tristan, "just as you have not forsaken me. Your prayers will be most needed, though, for I feel a darkness approaching me. But you know, Innocenzo… in my wildest imagination, I could have never expected to meet my end like this… at the hands of *Christian* crusaders."

Hearing this, Innocenzo's eyes filled with tears and he crossed himself. Turning, he left the cell, disappearing down the narrow stone corridor crying aloud, "Oh God, Savior in Heaven, where have You gone? Where have You gone!"

## Chapter Eighty

### Four Witnesses, Ten Judges

That next morning Tafur and DuLac appeared in the dungeon cell with the Gustave brothers and a large troop of Tafur's men, one of whom was carrying Tristan's bishop garments. "Unchain him and dress him up properly," snapped DuLac.

"Yes, we want him in his Vatican *finest*," said Tafur, "so those serving as judges and all the rest can well see the gulf dividing men such as the Bishop here and we poor of the world."

After dressing him, the Gustave brothers placed manacles about Tristan's wrists and led him with Tafur and DuLac outside to the plaza adjacent to the Civetot harbor. "Oh, if only your goddamned mother could be here with us to witness your end," smirked DuLac. "But if Heaven is all that they claim, then sure as Hell, she's watching now from above, huh?!"

Tristan was led to the center of the plaza where he faced ten judges seated behind a makeshift table, their backs facing the harbor, their eyes facing thousands upon thousands of onlookers packed all about the plaza. Those spectators to the front were seated, crammed thigh to thigh, and behind them stood others packed so tight that they could barely move. Tristan turned to gaze at the carping mob behind him, perceiving there a dark mood of expectancy. Although spotting sympathetic faces among the nuns, monks and a handful of other, he but could not help but feel the chill of hostility from all others.

"Turn back around and face your judges, Saint-Germain!" commanded Tafur.

Tristan turned about, looking into the eyes of the ten people seated before him, five Tafurs and five other men in Norman uniforms. "Ah, Tafur, I see you and DuLac have somehow managed to acquire a most objective and fair selection of judges," said Tristan, looking from one judge to the next with disdain. "I need not fear trumped up charges then, I suppose?"

Several guffaws broke the air at this remark, but searing stares from Tafur and DuLac squelched them. "I'll be serving as your interrogator today, Saint-Germain," declared Tafur loudly enough to be heard by all, "and you'll serve as your own defense. At trial's end, the judges will issue a verdict… and if you're found guilty–a sentence."

"*If* I'm found guilty?" mocked Tristan, also loud enough for all to hear. "Oh, come now, Tafur… why not spare everyone's time and allow these judges to issue their verdict now, for I'm sure they've already been instructed on how to vote! This is no trial, but simple theatre for purposes of your own entertainment. As with all hypocrites, you seek retribution to sanctify your own filthy misdeeds! But a trail of blood follows you, Tafur, so even this trial will change nothing in the end. God has kept a close accounting of you!"

"Oh, don't become righteous with me, Saint-Germain, for all here today will shortly learn that you're an imposter, a false monk! Aye, while purporting to save the souls of others, you've wallowed in sin by being responsible for the death of Latin crusaders!" As Tafur said this, Tristan detected that same pontifical certainty in his accuser's voice that he had heard from him the previous night. It seemed, in fact, that Tafur actually believed his own words. "Our first witness is Henri Descartes," crowed Tafur, "a good peasant of Flanders who has bravely served this crusade as a fellow Tafur. Descartes, come forward!"

A barefoot man dressed in the sackcloth of the Tafurs stepped forward, pointing proudly at the brand on his forehead. He was large in size, and though not old, was toothless. As he stood before Tristan, the rich fabric of Tristan's clerical vestments looked imposing and authoritative in contrast to the peasant's filthy, ragged garb.

"Yes, I'm Henri Descartes," the man said awkwardly, grinning foolishly at the crowd. Having never had occasion to speak before an assembly of others, he was bursting with oafish self-inflation. Lacking all realization of his own clownish mannerisms, he glanced about, stooping and bending, to see who of his few friends he might recognize within the crowd. "Yes, I'm Henri Descartes," he repeated. Then, pointing to Tristan, he recited as rehearsed, "I accuse Bishop of Ostia Saint-Germain of being a traitor to Pope Urban's Holy Crusade!" As whispers ensued, spreading through the crowd, he added, "Yes, *that man* right there! He's the one!"

"Explain yourself," coaxed Tafur, crossing his arms.

"It was at Cologne when we were cleaning that German city of Jews," said Descartes, making his best effort to sound official. "This man and his group of Tuscan bulls, five or six of them, turned their weapons against us, killing many within our ranks!"

"Killing *Christian* crusaders, to save *Jews*?" queried Tafur, feigning surprise.

"The edicts of Pope Urban II mandate the humane treatment of Jews throughout Western Europe!" declared Tristan. "The proclamations of King Heinrich of Germany are also compatible with these same edicts concerning Jews. These Jewish pograms in which many within this crowd have participated are ecclesiastically illegal, and immoral as well. What you did in Cologne was a crime against the Church and a crime against God!"

This caused a wave of complaint to ripple through the crowd, but an old nun who was sitting near the front shouted, "The Bishop is correct on this matter!"

The man seated next to her, a Tafur, turned, then delivered his fist to her jaw. "Shut up, you hooded bitch!" he snarled.

"But tell us, Descartes," continued Tafur, "did the Bishop wield a weapon that day in Cologne?"

Descartes closed his eyes a moment, his shoulders sagging with confusion. "Uh, I don't remember. I d-don't think so." Then, seeing the look of impatience directed at him from Tafur, as well as from the row of judges before him, he straightened himself. "No, he had no weapon, but that makes little difference because it was *him* who ordered the others to attack us! My own two cousins were killed right there on the streets of Cologne in front of the Benedictine monastery at the hands of Bishop Saint-Germain's hooligans!"

"Thank you, Descartes," said Tarfur.

Descartes, enthralled by the instantaneous commotion he had generated by his accusation, grinned toothlessly, wishing now to say more and extend his time on the stage. Sensing this, Tafur cut him off. As Descartes was a member of the Tafurs, Tafur had made his acquaintance and knew him to be a fool. "That's all we need from you, Descartes," said Tafur, dismissing him.

Disappointed that his moment in the light had lapsed so quickly, Descartes shuffled dejectedly from the center of plaza. "Yes, King Tafur, he's *guilty*!" he shouted, pointing to Tristan as he vanished into the crowd. "Guilty, I say!"

Tafur, remaining grim-faced, gauged Descartes' effect on the crowd with satisfaction. Striking the ground three times with his staff, he announced, "I need Estelle Dupuis! Will Estelle Dupuis now step forward?"

From the midst of the crowd a heavy peasant woman holding an infant in her arms and surrounded by a huddle of children began making her way to the plaza center. The crowd opened before her, then closed behind her, many shouting her name and applauding: she had gained a bit of celebrity back in Cologne during the Hermit's rant in the town meeting with the burgermeisters.

"I am Estelle Dupuis!" she proclaimed, motioning her children to follow. Attaining her position before Tafur, she extended her arms outward, circling them about her as a mother hen gathers her chicks.

"Tell us your story, Estelle, as concerns Bishop Saint-Germain," said Tafur.

"My husband, Marcel, and I saw the celestial signs last year in Amiens, France," began Estelle, "so we took to the road to follow Peter the Hermit on this crusade against the heathens. I was eight months pregnant at the time and gave birth to my fifth child on the road just outside the city of Cologne." Then, though she looked forlorn and defeated, a light broke over her face. "It's been a difficult journey, but Peter the Hermit vowed to me before a great gathering in Cologne that I shall stand before the heathen army and stop them in their tracks." Raising her infant high above her head, she said proudly, "This is Jerusalem, my newborn son, and he too shall fight the heathens!" She beamed then, and began returning waves to the many people who had begun chanting her name, and shouting words of praise and encouragement.

"And certainly, Estelle, with God at your side, that shall all come to pass," nodded Tafur, encouraged by the mob's response to Estelle Dupuis. "But tell, I don't see your husband here today… where is he, dear lady?"

"Oh, my poor Marcel… he's no longer with me, or with this crusade," Estelle replied, her eyes dropping. "He was slain in service to God… back in Zemun."

"Ah… fighting the Hungarians?" asked Tafur.

"No," said Estelle, shaking her head ruefully. "Though he started that day fighting the Hungarians, it was not the people of Zemun who took his life." Raising her eyes, setting her gaze at the accused, she lifted a finger toward Tristan. "My husband was murdered at the hands of the *Tuscans*, who were being led by the Bishop of Ostia!"

A ripple of anger shot through the crowd at this, and others who had lost friends or relatives at the hands of the Tuscans began cursing and shouting threats. Someone in the back of the mob shouted, "He's a traitor! Hang him now!"

"He kills Christians!" screamed another. "No need for a trial, I say!"

"The man's a saboteur and wants this crusade to fail!" yelled yet another.

Though pleased by the crowd's reaction, Tafur feigned objection. "Oh, but *silence!*" he commanded. "Let the woman be heard!" Pacing about a moment with his hand at his temple, projecting an expression of reflection, he looked at Estelle and continued. "Estelle… are you *absolutely* certain of this accusation you've just made?"

"Yes, as certain as I stand here, sir, because you yourself were at Marcel's side as this happened. It was you who relayed to me the events of Marcel's end, do you not remember? Oh, and he revered you so, King Tafur… lucky he was to have you standing so bravely by his side as he fell."

"Thank you, Estelle," said Tafur, concealing the twinge of cowardice slipping over him as Estelle said her final words. But it passed like a gleam. Gazing at the crowd, he said, "As you begin to see, time after time Bishop Saint-Germain has stood in opposition to our march east, which is in direct opposition to the Pope's very plea for Christians to reclaim the Holy Land! Thus he defies even his own master, Pope Urban! And the number of our people murdered under his leadership climbs with each witness speaking today. Now, we need to hear from another victim, Thierry LaGrone. Come forward, LaGrone!"

A young peasant boy of fourteen stood from the front row and slowly walked to the plaza center. He had no cross branded on his forehead, nor was he a follower of Tafur. Rather, he was timid– uncomfortable at being the focus of attention. His face red with modesty, he glanced about nervously. "Y-yes sir, King Tafur," he mumbled.

"Tell us about Bishop Saint-Germain," said Tafur.

"I had always heard he was a great man," said the young peasant, his voice low.

"Speak up, boy!" barked Tafur. "These people need to hear your story. Nothing to be afraid of, lad!"

"I had always heard he was a great man," LaGrone repeated, feeling the heat of embarrassment rising at his collar, "and that he came from the Saint-Germain-en-Laye area of France where I myself was born. He's a bit of a legend there now. Oh, and I heard him preach the crusade back in France over a year ago. Yes, I thought he was a godly cleric, and they say he might even become pope one day."

"That's all very good," blenched Tafur, "but you no longer feel such admiration for him, I'm now told. So what happened to change your opinion of the Bishop?"

LaGrone said nothing. Staring blankly at the ground, he shifted his weight from one foot to the next.

"Come along now, LaGrone," urged Tafur, impatience seeping into his tone. "Don't be afraid… Bishop Saint-Germain can't hurt you any longer."

Raising his eyes with reticence, LaGrone looked at Tristan. "A while back in Constantinople," he said, "the day Emperor Alexius opened the gates to us, my little brother and I entered the city. We were excited about seeing the monasteries and churches of Constantinople. We'd heard they were the most wondrous in all Christendom… especially the Basilica Hagia Sophia."

"And did you see these monasteries and churches, LaGrone?"

LaGrone shook his head. "No we were still looking at the wondrous wares the Byzantines were selling along the plaza. But then a riot broke out for some reason. My brother and I didn't see what caused it."

"It was the Peasants' Crusade who started the riot!" shouted Tristan, pointing at Tafur. "The Tafurs and crusader men-of-arms."

"Silence!" growled Tafur, casting angry eyes at Tristan. "Tell us what happened next, LaGrone."

"In the chaos of this riot, men on horses charged into the plaza with weapons drawn. They were Tuscans and Danes, I was told later, mixed with Genoese. My dear little brother was trampled by their horses during the mêlée!"

"Trampled to death? By Tuscans and Danes?" asked Tafur.

"Y-yes, sir."

"Ah, but was your brother… *armed?*" asked Tafur

"No, sir. He was but a young boy. We ran away together from Dijon to join the Hermit's crusade."

"Well then," said Tafur, gazing out at his audience, "two lads taking the road alone with the Peasants' Crusade, making it all the way across the continent to Constantinople… only for the youngest to die far from home and Mother France. But then, LaGrone, I must ask… though your little brother wasn't armed, did he at any time attempt to *resist* the Tuscans?"

"No, sir. We were both just... trying to get out of the way."

"And how old was your brother, lad?"

LaGrone shook his head as tears formed in the wells of his eyes. "He was but… *eight*."

Tristan looked at the boy, his heart swelling to bursting. Raising his manacles, he declared to all, "The Tuscans and the Danes do not kill children! There was bedlam in the square that day as you all know, bedlam that *this* crowd started. This young lad's poor brother fell victim to your own mayhem and violence!"

"No," objected Tafur, "rather a victim once again of your own opposition to our crusade!"

Still looking at the peasant boy whose tears were now streaming over his cheeks in streams, Tristan said, "I am heartily sorry for the loss of your young brother, lad, and will pray for him! He is yet another innocent lost at the hands of this wretched mockery of a Christian crusade!"

"Oh, you'll pray for no one!" seethed Tafur, "For your prayers mean nothing. Rather, *we* need to pray for you! *You* are the sinner here today!" Dismissing the boy, he then shouted, "And for our final witness today, I call... Benito Fazio. Fazio, come forward!"

*My friend!* gasped Innocenzo, who had been standing beside Fazio since the beginning of the trial. *But what's this?* he wondered, glancing over at Fazio – too stunned to speak.

Fazio caught Innocenzo's look, but averted his eyes, knowing Innocenzo's strong feelings for Bishop Saint-Germain. Lowering his hat over his head, he made his way through the mob as several people began to twitter and laugh. His tiny stature, pointy beard, and odd hat gave him the appearance of a goblin, creating a sudden stir of amusement amongst the onlookers.

"I am Benito, and yes, I am coming!" Fazio called to Tafur in his high pitched voice, knowing that Tafur might not see him advancing through the crowd due to his lack of stature. But the sound of his strange little voice only caused further ruckus within the crowd, which irritated Tafur. Tafur had himself ridiculed Fazio on previous occasions, of course, but now wanted the odd little fellow to be taken seriously– for purposes of undoing Bishop Saint-Germain.

Fazio was the first witness Tristan recognized, remembering him from the encounter with Innocenzo on the beach nights earlier, and on the plains of Niš when the Byzantines were burning corpses. Tristan also recalled that this odd little fellow had seemed to exhibit a strange hostility toward him, though he could not imagine why.

As Fazio took his position before Tristan and the judges, Tafur said, "Oh, all of you of the Peasants' Crusade, you've heard testimony of one witness after another about Bishop Saint-Germain's treachery, but after you hear what Benito Fazio has to say, you'll begin to see that SaintGermain has played at deceiving the entire world, and moved within a whisker of the very papacy itself by disregarding the laws of man and the laws of God! Fazio, tell your story and show these people who the Bishop of Ostia *really* is."

Desmond DuLac, who had been somewhat disinterested in the proceedings thus far, spotted something in Tafur's eye that caught his attention. *Ah, but Tafur's onto something here with this little dwarf,* DuLac thought, taking in Tafur's sudden surge of confidence.

"Though I'll not divulge my employer," began Fazio, "all of you here should know that I was commissioned to follow Bishop Saint-Germain this entire past half year, which is how I happened upon this crusade in Cologne. But I tell you this, he's a false monk, a faker– and hides a deep and wicked secret."

"And what *is* this secret, Fazio?" said Tafur, taking on that satisfied air of the executioner sharpening his ax.

"Years ago within a dungeon cell of Canossa belonging to Countess Mathilda of Tuscany," began Fazio, "a friend of mine served as a jailer there. His name was Antonelli, a good, honest man of strong Catholic character. While employed there, he happened to hear by chance the unsolicited confessions of a prisoner who was ranting and raving over the death... no, the *murder* of a woman and her newborn child." This, of course, was an over-stated version of what Antonelli had actually told Fazio back in Rome. Nonetheless, Fazio had for so long now thought Tristan guilty, he believed his own words.

Tristan looked at Fazio, stunned, as confusion and surprise colored his face. Seeing the Bishop's sudden drop of expression, the crowd sensed something momentous. "Oh look at him!" someone said loud enough for others to hear. "He now takes on the look of a rabbit caught in a snare as the little man begins to speak."

"Ah," said another, "see him wiggle… it's the look of guilt!"

"And who *was* this prisoner?" asked Tafur, measuring the intensifying focus of the mob.

"It was Bishop Saint-Germain, himself!" replied Fazio, pointing at Tristan.

This caused a stir, but from within the crowd, a lone voice shouted, "No! Impossible! It cannot be!"

Fazio recognized the voice, as did Tristan. It was Innocenzo. But within an instant, a flurry of Tafurs swarmed him, beating him to the ground, kicking and mauling him. Seeing this, Fazio shuddered, wanting to call out to his friend... but said nothing.

Shortly all fell still again as Innocenzo was left, bloody and unconscious, sprawled belly-down on the ground. The crowd refocused their full attention on Fazio then, but none within it were snickering any longer at his odd appearance and elfin voice.

"And why, precisely, Fazio, was the Bishop ranting?" asked Tafur.

"Because this woman," replied Fazio, "was his... mistress."

"His *mistress*?" queried Tafur, going nearly falsetto. "But the good bishop here is a Cluniac reform monk, an avowed Gregorian who espouses celibacy and chastity."

"Ah, so he claims," said Fazio. "But like everything else about the man, it's a false claim. According to my friend the jailer, not only did the Bishop *have* this mistress, but he was the one who later had her *killed!*"

This precipitated a loud chorus of grumbling and anger, and soon many within the crowd were slinging accusations. "Oh, false monk! Pretender! Murderer!"

Stupefied by this latest charge, Tristan began to protest, but was so appalled by the distorted accusation that he could only stammer incoherently. This made him appear even more culpable to those watching.

"But why would he have his own mistress murdered?" asked Tafur, pretending to be puzzled.

"Because she became pregnant… and bore his child!" shouted Fazio. "At the time, the Bishop was rising quickly within the Church– therefore he feared scandal would injure further advancement, I suppose."

"And what of this child you mentioned, Fazio?" said Tafur, raising his voice to be heard above the growing clamor of the crowd.

"*Murdered also!*" cried Fazio, spitting out the words, releasing the entire hoard of abhorrence that had been festering in him since first learning of Antonelli's suspicions about the Bishop's ravings in the jail cell at Canossa. Like Tafur, the crushing weight of life's cruelties on Fazio were now aimed at a single target– Bishop SaintGermain.

Fazio's false accusation precipitated an uproar as people began to shout and blaspheme the defendant, calling for his execution. Tristan stood there like some pallid statue, shocked into numbness by this new, preposterous accusation.

"And," Fazio continued to shout, spittle now flying from his lips, "that murdered child lies buried in an un-named grave at Canossa Fortress! Out of guilt, Bishop Saint-Germain goes there often to visit the grave, begging secretly for God's mercy and forgiveness, I can only imagine!"

"Do you *deny* these charges?" interrogated Tafur, glaring at Tristan.

"Yes! Yes!" shouted Tristan, seeing that the crowd was about to erupt into violence. "It's not true! A complete fabrication!"

"And do you deny having the mistress also, I suppose?" asked Tafur.

When one is so appalled at being falsely accused of the unimaginable, one becomes too overwhelmed to speak coherently, or offer explanation with any sense of clarity, especially if the issue is complex. "I do not deny having had a mistress!" Tristan shouted. "Yes, I have sinned, and God has punished me with the death of this child, my own son who is indeed buried at the Canossa Fortress! But this child Fazio speaks of was not murdered… he froze to death in the Alps! Nor was the mother murdered. She lives to this day! And yes, damn all of you here in this hellish nest of false accusations and distortions, I still love this woman though the Church forbids it! But she lives, I tell you! *She lives*!"

"Then where is she?" demanded Fazio. "And what's her name?"

Tristan shook his head violently, refusing to offer up a name. "Oh, the very mention of her name is too good to be uttered in the presence of you criminals and vipers! I would never give you her name though you set me afire or quarter me!"

This further inflamed the mob. They understood neither the depth nor the falseness of the story Fazio had presented. Nor did they wish to hear or believe anything more from the Bishop; everything that next came from his mouth was drowned out by their fury as they began to surge forward, trying to get at him.

Even Sansavoir's face filled with anger. "There's no fouler creature on this earth than a false monk who pretends to save the souls of others!" he shouted. "To the hangman's noose!"

Innocenzo gained consciousness just as Sansavoir, who was standing near, cried these words. Struggling to rise, he then saw a cluster of Tafurs positioned next to Sansavoir, which caused him to cower, dropping back to the ground. Yet, in his heart he refused to believe a single word his best friend in life, Fazio, had uttered. "N-no, this simply c-can't be," Innocenzo whispered to himself. "It's not possible that Bishop Saint-Germain has done such a thing! Something's twisted here!"

"Let's hang him now!" shouted DuLac, advancing with the Gustave brothers, pointing to the small ships in the harbor. "Right there from the mast of one of those ships for all to see!"

Stepping forward, Tafur quickly gestured to a full troop of his men standing beside the judges and stepped between Tristan and DuLac, shoving his palm into DuLac's chest. "Hold there, all of you!" he shouted, gathering an expression of righteousness as his men jumped to his side, flagging their staffs and pitchforks at the crowd. "This is a trial, not a lynching! We've yet to hear from the judges!"

"Guilty!" cried one of the Tafurs seated at the table.

"Guilty!" agreed another, pounding the table.

"Guilty!" shouted all five Normans, standing in unison.

"Guilty!" chimed the three remaining Tafurs.

"There now, get the damned rope!" DuLac demanded, advancing again with the Gustave twins.

"No!" objected Tafur. "Indeed, we'll hang him in due time. But DuLac, I've already told you how I intend to take my time with this bastard of a bishop. We'll have him dragged through the streets naked every morning and every evening for a week, and allow our crusaders to spit on him, and fling stones and refuse at him. Indeed, we'll strip him of every ounce of honor and dignity he possesses one day at a time. No, I say, I'll not hurry this thing along! I want him to ponder his crimes and his approaching end, languishing in chains and suffering over the crooked trail he's taken to the bishopric of Ostia and to the heart of the Vatican itself!"

This infuriated DuLac. "No, goddammit! Hang him now, I say!" he yelled as the Gustave brothers pulled their swords, signaling to other Normans within the crowd.

"No! Tafur's right!" yelled Sansavoir, motioning for his own men to advance. "Let the Bishop ponder his fate and suffer from the weight of his deceptions for a time! Before descending to the depths of Hell, let him suffer a while here on this earth which he's so craftily manipulated all these years!"

A struggle ensued then as Tafurs, Normans, and Sansavoir's men jostled each other, pulling weapons and going at each other. Sensing disaster, and being far outnumbered, DuLac shouted, "*Here, here!* No need to kill each other over this impasse! Very well, then, we'll do as Tafur says!"

It took a good while for the aroused troops to settle, but they begrudgingly withdrew from the fracas, sheathing and setting aside their weapons.

"Take Saint-Germain back to the dungeon then," commanded Tafur, "and let's now settle this goddamned business about Rainald and Xerigordos."

## Chapter Eighty-one

### Vengeance Prevails

Tristan was dragged through the seething mob, wincing, covering his face as angry spectators struck out, spat and kicked at him. "*I killed no one!*" he bayed hoarsely again and again, unable even to hear his own voice over the furor of the crowd.

Finally, clearing the crowd, bruised and battered, he was manhandled toward his cell by a squad of ruffians. "Keep an eye on him and triple the guard!" shouted Tafur. "Raise the alarm if any Normans approach, for DuLac wants him dead now, but I'll not allow it. I intend to take time and pleasure picking him apart, one day at a time, dammit! I've awaited my time to humiliate and repay the high clergy my entire goddamned life!" Then, calling for Burrel, DuLac, and Sansavoir, Tafur said, "Clear this rabble from here and gather our lieutenants to determine our reply to the Turks for their slaughter of Rainald and his men at Xerigordos!"

Half an hour later the leaders took seats on the stools where the judges had been seated during the trial, huddling their subordinates around them. Though it had been Tafur taking the lead during the trial, it was now Burrel who took charge. "Listen here, by damn," he said, striking a fist against the tabletop, "just as I said last night during the assembly, I say we mobilize and make ready to make for Nicaea first thing tomorrow morning! We should quickly avenge the massacre of Rainald of Broyes and his crusader forces, and at the same time sweep into Nicaea– take everything we can carry out, and set the damned place afire."

"Agreed!" chimed DuLac. "The Turks'll not be expecting an attack so quickly."

Sansavoir shook his head. "No, I say. The Hermit should be back within the week, hopefully with Byzantine troops. He's insisted on waiting for the armies of Bishop Adhémar as a matter of caution, and I now think he's correct on this point. Though I was impatient to get here, the butchering of Rainald's army convinces me the Turks may be more than we anticipated. Who would have thought Rainald would have been so easily put down? No, let's wait on the Hermit's return, at least, before attacking. Besides, everything you're planning is based solely on the word of two Greek shepherds." Pausing to look at Tafur, his face turning bitter, Sansavoir continued. "And because of you and your bunch of wild beasts, these Greeks inhabiting Bithynia despise *all* of us now. Who knows where their allegiance really lies at this point, eh? You imbecile, you murdered Greek farmers and plundered their farms, yet so quickly now believe what they've told you about the Turks. Why in God's name would they now deign to help any of us here after what you've done?! Aye, and those two shepherds you listened to so intently... their own families might have been included in your raids, huh? Who knows what truth there is in their blathering about Xerigordos and the Turks slaughtering Rainald's bunch? Or about their claim that the Turks have now withdrawn back east to fight the Danishmends with Kilij Arslan. Aye, it could all be lies– a pay-back for the massacre of Greek farmers at your hands, eh, Tafur? No, I don't think they're to be trusted! Take time, at least, to send out patrols and reconnoiter the landscape before jumping into this thing half cocked."

"Aw, to Hell with you!" snarled Tafur, feeling blistered by Sansavoir's charges. "Now your damned imagination's running rampant, I'd say. Ha, I once thought you a bold knight, Sansavoir, but no, I've come to learn different! The Turks are gone. I'm sure of it, you pious lout!"

"Hold on now, both of you," intervened DuLac. "Dammit, we need to work together at this point, for once, and quit this bickering. Let's look at the facts here. First, Rainald was a fool and simply ran out of water, according to the shepherds. Had he had water, he could have held the fort at Xerigordos indefinitely. As for us, we'll never make that damned mistake. After all, we're *French*. Secondly, Rainald had a small force of a little over three thousand while we number twenty-thousand men-at-arms here in Civetot. And thirdly, according to the shepherds, the Turkish army that butchered Rainald's crusaders numbered only about five or six thousand. Again, it was the lack of *water* that defeated Rainald, not the goddamned Turks!"

"Damned right," nodded Tafur, glaring at Sansavoir, "and if we can't defeat five or six thousand Turks, then the bunch of us should simply all grow cracks and become street whores!"

"Furthermore," barked Burrel, sticking a finger in Sansavoir's face, "I notice you've become more weak-kneed with each passing day since arriving to Constantinople, Sansavoir! Seems you've lost your taste for enemy blood. But something else here, what if Alexius doesn't offer up any troops to the Hermit? What then? We'll have waited for nothing, and lost the element of surprise!"

"Then we should wait on Bishop Adhémar as the Hermit's also advised," said Sansavoir, refusing to give way.

"Christ Almighty!" snapped Burrel. "We don't *need* Adhémar. Tell me, do you really wish to share Muslim spoils with the greater lords of Europe who're following him here?"

"Indeed," agreed DuLac. "Share with Raymond of Toulouse, Bohemud of Taranto, and Godfrey of Bouillon? Shit, they're already rich beyond measure, and once they get here, they'll take charge. We'll be stuck scrabbling about for crumbs!"

"I didn't come east for Muslim plunder," said Sansavoir, standing firm. Looking at Tafur with disgust, he added, "Nor did I think *you* did, Tafur!"

"I *didn't*," sneered Tafur. "But listening to you– sounds you're simply afraid to fight."

"I've never feared a fight in my life!" snapped Sansavoir, centering his eyes on Tafur with growing agitation.

"Perhaps so, Sansavoir," said Burrel, seeing that Tafur had hit a nerve. Baiting him further, he added, "But you damned sure don't sound like that bold Frankish warrior of record I heard so much about in France over the years!"

"What!?" objected Sansavoir, his blood beginning to boil. "Are you now questioning my manhood?"

"Damn right we are," huffed DuLac. "Seems your balls fell off somewhere along the road to Byzantium, Sansavoir. But there's nothing to fear in Nicaea, I say! Rainald had but three thousand men, and he ran out of water. We've seven times that number here in Civetot, with ten or twelve times as many horse as Rainald had. The Turks won't know what hit them once we arrive at their gates, unless they have time to prepare. The element of surprise, Sansavoir, that's our trump card here."

"And what if they refuse to come out from their walls?" asked Sansavoir. "What of our lack of towers and rams? I've little faith in these shabby ladders your men have been fashioning. God in Heaven above– have none of you ever engaged in a siege before? You've no idea what you're getting into!"

"Bah!" snorted Burrel. "*Of course* the Turks'll come out! And if they don't, we'll send in bait. When they chase it, then we'll pull the main force out of hiding and take them down on the open plains like lambs to the butcher!"

Sansavoir shook his head again. "The Hermit led us here. I say we should obey *him*!"

"The Hermit didn't lead *me* here," retorted DuLac, giving Sansavoir a sharp look. "But Sansavoir, another question then. What of your captains and lieutenants standing there? Are they in agreement with you?"

This caused Sansavoir to look at his men, moving from one face to another. Though some supported their commander, others spoke up in agreement with Burrel and DuLac. "We don't fear a fight," one of them said, to the assent of several others.

"Nay, certainly not!" agreed another, which brought further agreement.

"Sir Walter," said a third, "I do see the wisdom of a... surprise attack."

"Look," said Burrel, by now exasperated, "the timid by no means avail in war, as do the bold! Aye, we can pull this off without you, Sansavoir, but it'd be a hell of a lot riskier. With all of us together, victory is assured. We need our entire Civetot force to make this work properly!"

"If you've no stomach for a fight," smirked DuLac, "then so be it. I don't understand it myself, but you wouldn't be the first man to turn soft."

"Indeed," said Tafur, "you're now a man with two cracks, Sansavoir! One running up the back of your ass and one running up your front!"

This offended Sansavoir profoundly, sending a ripple of fury throughout his entire body. As a knight, he could endure any hardship or obstacle– except an open affront to his courage. "*I fear nothing!*" he shouted.

"Very well then," said Tafur, "do you stand with us, or do you choose to remain behind with the women and children?"

This was the final straw for Sansavoir, whose neck now sprouted pulsing veins at Tafur's suggestion of remaining behind with the women and children. "Oh, very well!" he cried, slamming his hand on the table, standing. "We attack Nicaea in the morning!"

When wild bulls get their blood up, the flush of testosterone runs through the herd like lightning. Accordingly, a cheer arose as all but Sansavoir threw fists to the air and began slapping each other on the shoulders and chests, their brains filling with visions of Islamic blood and Muslim treasure.

Then a single voice rang out, breaking the spell. "And what of Saint-Germain?!" shouted DuLac. "I say we hang him before our departure!"

"Damn you, DuLac!" shouted Tafur, stepping up to him angrily, standing nose to nose. "I'll not tell you again. And if need be, by God, we'll fight it out right now, once and for all! I intend to deal with him in my own way, so he shall wait until after we take Nicaea. On our return, we'll then take the entire Tuscan camp as well. After all, DuLac, was it not you who said the Bishop was but one head of a five-headed serpent?"

Turning sullen, DuLac refused to answer. Still, Tafur's words seemed to placate DuLac the tiniest measure. Turning toward the Gustave twins, he nodded. "Aye, I'll settle for that," he muttered in a low voice.

But his thoughts were not centered on Bishop Tristan de SaintGermain. Indeed, it was Asta's face he now envisioned...

## Chapter Eighty-two

### The Pass Near Dracon

On the morning of October 21st, the combined military components of Civetot marched from that city and noisily took their first steps forward to attack Kilij Arslan's capital of Nicaea. Morale was running high amongst the ranks of these twenty-one thousand men, as was confidence; every crusader within the march was swollen with that pulsing exhilaration men feel on being freed from the torment of slow waiting.

"Finally!" the men shouted. "On to war at last!"

"Islam be damned!"

Two hours out of Civetot the plains rose into hills, and the massive army entered the narrow mouth of a pass leading into an area of inclines growing steeper with distance, forming a narrow gorge. An hour later as Sansavoir and his men neared the end of it, he turned his head back, marveling at the sight following him. *Ah, it's been awhile since I've lifted the banner of war,* he thought. *Such a splendid march... aye, it was foolish to oppose this attack on Nicaea! It was weakness on my p–"*

From nowhere an arrow scudded through the side of Sansavoir's neck, just between the ear cover of his conical helmet and the collar of his hauberk. Instinctively, his hand shot to his throat, but feeling the shaft of an arrow, he was overcome by that dumbfounding shock that befalls men when encountering the impossible. An instant later, before he could even cry out, three more arrows perforated him from heart to belly, and he fell dead.

Next the entire sky darkened as thousands of arrows scythed down in a withering rain of armor-piercing points that pierced crusader chain-mail from a distance of 100 yards or more, fired by seasoned Turkish archers at a shot rate of ten to twelve arrows a minute. During those first minutes alone, over one thousand of Sansavoir's knights and footmen dropped, maimed or killed, before even realizing they were under archer attack from the front as well as from both flanks of the gorge. Those surviving knights who rode at the fore with Sansavoir, knowing they could not retreat due to the thousands blocking them from behind, determined their only hope of escape from the neck of the gorge lay in charging head-long out of the valley– into the gaping mouth of the enemy. Fighting their own panic, and that of their horses, they drew swords or tucked lances into their shoulders, blindly charging forward.

It was a rush to extinction. Five thousand Turkish archers standing in endless ranks atop the two surrounding slopes and at the mouth of the valley peppered the sky with deadly missiles, and every knight within Sansavoir's advance corps soon lay dead.

Sansavoir's footmen, to the rear of these knights, also suffered the lethal wrath of Seljuk arrows as barrage after barrage mowed down crusaders with murderous accuracy. Caught in this hellish rain of death, survivors turned to flee– despite now being blocked by thousands of Tafurs standing in their path.

In the ensuing pandemonium, the advancing Tafurs next began to feel the murderous assault of the Turkish archers, and bearing only tiny peasant shields for protection, they too began to fall by scores.

"Pull back!" screamed Tafur, realizing his entire force would soon be razed whether they advanced or whether they stood their ground. "Pull back I say!"

"We're blocked by Burrel's troops!" men shouted.

"Goddammit! Run them over!" wailed Tafur. "Kill them if you must!"

Three thousand Tafurs bolted then, bounding first into Burrel's horsemen, then breaking their way through his footmen who followed.

"*What's this!*" hollered Burrel, who was far enough back to not quite yet understand what had happened at the front of the crusader column. Shortly, however, Turkish arrows commenced to rain onto his own troops as Turkish archers extended their range. Craning his neck to peer through the chaos, Burrel spotted ranks of Turkish horsemen assembling at the mouth of gorge ahead, waiting for the archers to finish their deadly onslaught. "Turkish horse ahead!" he screamed, alerting his knights. "Retreat! They're coming at us!"

Turning their horses about as arrows continued to arc into their midst, Burrel and his knights trampled over their own footmen to escape the bottleneck. Running them over, they next encountered DuLac's cavalry and footmen blocking the way.

"What in hell's going on?!" screamed DuLac as he and the Gustave brothers tried to steady their mounts against the wash of Burrel's knights sweeping through Norman ranks.

"*It's a goddamned trap!*" hollered Burrel. "Retreat, DuLac! And get your goddamn men out of the way!"

Spotting desperation on the ashen, panic-ridden faces of Burrel and his knights, DuLac spun his horse about, followed by the Gustave twins, and began to ride over and crush his fellow Normans. "Back to Civetot!" he shouted, digging spurs so deeply into his horse's flanks as to draw blood.

"No! Head for the old fortress at Nicodemia!" shouted Burrel, spotting Tafur fleeing his direction.

Tafur, seeing Burrel, flung himself onto Burrel's horse, grappling to hold steady. "Get off, you bastard!" shouted Burrel, slinging his elbows backwards to ward off his unwelcome rider.

"Damn you!" screamed Tafur. "*Ride, you fool or we're both dead!*"

Recognizing their mutual plight, Burrel kicked his mount in the flanks, galloping wildly through Dulac's Norman footmen–sending them flying to both sides of the terrified beast. DuLac and the Gustaves followed closely behind, flaying their horses' haunches in a savage rush for survival.

As the five cleared the final ranks of foot soldiers and galloped out of the gorge, they made straight for Nicodemia, giving no regard whatsoever to the women, children, and elderly they were abandoning at Civetot. Behind them at the other end of the valley, thousands of Seljuk gazis whooped with abandon, whipping their mounts, launching their sweep through the gorge. Most of the crusader knights now lay slain at the bottom of the gorge, as did over two thirds of the footmen, so the gazis simply rode rough-shod over them, mangling their corpses to an unrecognizable pulp. Ahead of them fled five or six thousand crusaders, mainly footmen, desperately struggling their way out of the confines of the gorge. On making the plain, though, they quickly found themselves caught in the open as Turkish gazis thundered into their midst from the rear.

Slashing crusaders to ribbons with their sabers for nearly an hour, the Turks then moved to the outside of those who had survived and circled them, trapping two thousand Tafurs and footmen into a single cluster. Malik issued a signal and the Turkish horsemen sallied around them again and again in dwindling circles until not a man stood. Turkish footmen then rushed into the fallen cluster, slashing throats of the dazed and wounded.

Satisfied that all foreigners near the mouth of the valley had been decimated, Malik pointed to those in the distance who were fleeing toward the coast. "On to Civetot!" he ordered, motioning his gazis forward.

## Chapter Eighty-three

### Civetot

Two hours later the Turks were nearly there, and as the outline of Civetot arose in the distance, Malik suddenly halted the Turkish advance, confused by what lay ahead. "*What?!*" he cried, glancing over at Soliman.

There at the edge of Civetot stood thousands of women and children formed in deep ranks.

Several Latin knights, forsaking the haven provided by the walls of Nicodemia, had fled back to Civetot to warn the people of the Turkish advance. Guillaume, Handel, and the Danes had already arrived half an hour before them and were already trying to round them up to make a run for the fortress at Nicodemia. Incredibly, instead of fleeing, most gathered shovels, forks, and staffs, following Estelle Dupuis to the edge of town. Once there, Estelle stepped out ahead of the others, surrounded by her four children. Holding her fifth child, the newborn Jerusalem, high above her head as the Turks approached, she screamed, "In the name of God, behold this Christian child named Jerusalem!" Shaking him then, as one would rattle a sword, she shouted, "Jerusalem! Jerusalem! Behold him and fall from your horses, you heathens! Be then devoured by the earth as it swallows your godless souls!"

The two youngest children standing in her shadow clung to her tunic, unaware and unafraid of what was occurring around them. But then, seeing their two older siblings trembling and fighting back tears of terror, the two little youngsters began to bawl uncontrollably.

"Don't be afraid!" Estelle scolded. "I'm but fulfilling the Hermit's prophecy! Upon the Turkish charge, I'll turn them back! Don't cry, children! God shall be your shield!"

General Soliman, as puzzled as was Malik by this sight, refused to believe his eyes. “Who’s that madwoman, and all those behind her?” he asked. “Is she a holy woman of some kind? Or has she simply lined these people up and is– begging for mercy, or signaling their own surrender, perhaps?”

“Ah, but there’ll be no surrender today, Soliman,” replied Malik, gesturing to his bugler. “Make your music, brother,” he commanded, “and blow the battle charge!”

Placing the trumpet to his lips, the bugler issued his call. Seconds later ten thousand ghazis drove forward, crouching low in the saddles of their dashing mounts, sabers at the ready. The ground trembled as forty thousand steel-shod hooves then rumbled across the plain leading to Civetot in a rumbling, sweeping wash of horseflesh.

“Oh, my God, here they come!” cried a woman standing behind Estelle Dupuis, falling to her knees, crossing herself. “We’re going to d-die!”

“Jerusalem, hold them back!” screamed Estelle, her face scarlet with passion, her throat shredding. “In the name of God Almighty, fall from your horses, you dark heathens!”

The thunderous advance of thousands of ghazis quickly drowned her out. As her children looked frantically up at her, they could no longer hear her voice through the deep rumble of oncoming hooves; they only saw the trembling movement of her lips, still declaring doom over the Turks racing toward them.

Death, like birth, brims with inequity; when either arrives, there are the fortunate, and the cursed. Those slipping into death gradually and peacefully are graciously afforded time to reflect about their existence on this earth, to weigh regrets, to make amends, or to cherish for a final moment the victories in life. At the other end of the spectrum, those discovering themselves standing before the jaws of annihilation with little time to think, receive no such accommodation. These unfortunate souls, rather like the trembling mouse freezing beneath the fatal gaze of the coiled serpent, simply stand paralyzed… and their minds fall blank.

So it was for the twenty-five thousand women, children, and elderly who had assembled at the edge of Civetot with Estelle

Dupuis... one moment standing there propped up by their burning faith... then the next moment– *extinguished.*

As the vast wave of gazis dashed forward, Estelle Dupuis, her children, and all those standing about her disappeared into a swirling storm of dust, crushed beneath tons and tons of rampaging horseflesh. Likewise, to both sides of her, thousands of other women and children were trampled and crushed by the oncoming surge of gazis who by now had raised their sabers and were butchering anyone who remained standing, or even moved upon the ground.

When the gazi charge was done, Malik called for his captains, shouting, "Now, into the town! Those children and women of pleasing appearance, set aside for the slave markets and harems, as well as the unshaven boys of sweet face– all others, put them down!"

Charging forward, he led the hunt for foreign prey in the streets and buildings of Civetot... which were shortly awash in blood.

## Chapter Eighty-four

### A Loyal Face

Shackled to the dungeon wall, Tristan heard the sudden outbreak of footsteps, shouting and pandemonium beyond his cell. The hysterical wailing of women and children began to ring in his ears, mixed with the clatter of hooves and the stampede of men, some in flight, others in pursuit. Still, Tristan had no earthly idea what had caused this outbreak, or what was occurring out on the streets.

Struggling against the manacles and chains binding him to the wall, he began to wear the meat of his wrists raw, but to no avail. "What's happening out there?!" he cried. "Release me! Does anyone hear me out there?!"

As the sound of chaos and footsteps racing hither and yon escalated, Tristan next heard voices shouting– in Persian. *The Turks have arrived*, he realized, instantly certain that disaster had befallen the crusader military force and now the Turks were ravaging Civetot, exactly as he had warned Innocenzo. *Best not to cry out* he thought, as the thud of boots thumped in the corridor, coming his way.

Soon a shadow loomed against the wall he was facing. Turning his head, Tristan saw a Turk approaching him, saber in hand. The man appeared puzzled at first, perhap due to Tristan's bishop garments, or perhaps by the fact that he was being held prisoner by these Western foreigners who had settled in Civetot. But then the Turk came closer and raised his sword, determining that this foreigner should be given no more consideration than the others.

"*Allahu akbar!*" shouted Tristan in Arabic, in his panic forgetting that the Turks had adopted the Persian tongue. "God is great! La ilaha illa llah! There is no God but God!"

Hearing this, recognizing this celebrated Arabic proclamation to Allah, the Turk halted, confused. "What? Are you Muslim?" he asked in Persian.

"No," replied Tristan in the same tongue, "but on this day I am also not your enemy. I am a prisoner here!"

The soldier, impressed by Tristan's Persian, stood back a moment. Thinking back to Malik's habit of taking fine-looking foreigners to market in Baghdad and Medina, he took a close look at Tristan's fair skin, blonde hair, and piecing grey eyes. *Ah, but this one will bring high bids, and Malik will be pleased,* he thought, quietly appraising the prisoner.

While he was thus calculating his bounty, a different shadow broke– but against the corridor wall. Next, a hand raised from nowhere, plunging a knife into the back of the Turk's neck. Dumbstruck, the soldier's eyes flared, staring vacantly at Tristan as his body broke into a brief spasm of lurching. Sprawling forward, the Turk collapsed to the ground at Tristan's feet.

"Innocenzo!" shouted Tristan, seeing that in one hand Innocenzo held a bloody dagger, and in the other, manacle keys.

Innocenzo heard nothing. Standing there, he trembled and shook as though enmeshed in the threads of some hideous nightmare. "*M-my God, my G-God!*" he blubbered, horror etched across his contracting face. "*I've just k-killed a man!*"

"Innocenzo!" Tristan shouted. "Quickly, release me!"

But Innocenzo, unable to take his eyes from the corpse of the man he had just murdered, failed to move.

"Innocenzo, *quickly!*" repeated Tristan. "We have to get out of here, find Guillaume and the Danes!"

Still Innocenzo's feet remained nailed to the floor.

Frustrated, Tristan fired a leg back and kicked at him, breaking his trance. Innocenzo, pale with dread, finally joggled forward to undo the manacles binding Tristan's hands, but his fingers trembled so, that the key chattered all about the lock, refusing to engage.

Losing patience, fearing more Turks might appear at any moment, Tristan worked his fingers into Innocenzo's and tried to extract the key from Innocenzo's trembling grip. "Here, give me the damned key!" shouted Tristan with exasperation, twisting his wrists about and pulling the key from Innocenzo with his fingers. Next, managing to release himself, he grabbed Innocenzo by the arm and wrestled him toward the corridor. “Get a hold of yourself!” he demanded, cautiously sticking his head around the dungeon door. What he found was sheer mayhem and slaughter as women and children ran about like stampeding sheep bleating in terror while Turks pursued them, mercilessly hacking them to shreds, then moving on to new victims. “Innocenzo, there are two horses across the way, there!” Tristan pointed. “Though the plaza is full of Turks running about, we might be able to get there.”

“N-no!” Innocenzo protested. “I’m a-afraid!”

“Innocenzo, we shall surely die if we remain here. Come now, we have to make a dash now or all is lost!”

“Y-yes, Bishop…” stammered Innocenzo finally, “but y-you go first… and I’ll f-follow!”

## Chapter Eighty-five

### Retreat to Nicodemia

As Turkish gazis were annihilating the peasant masses standing with Estelle Dupuis, Guillaume, Handel, and the Danes were racing about Civetot trying to get those who had remained in town to flee to the fortress at Nicodemia. Handel, Guthroth, and Hroc had intercepted Guillaume at the look-out outposts with Orla and Crowbones on Guillaume's second day there, and after informing him of the slaughter at Xerigordos, all of them made haste for their Tuscan camp. Arriving there, Guillaume and the others were shocked to learn that Tristan was absent and had not been seen by the Tuscans for several days.

"God in Heaven!" shouted Guillaume. "Where could he be?"

"Perhaps he's headed into Civetot to warn them of the Turkish advance," said Handel.

"No, impossible. How could he possibly even know of it?" insisted Guillaume.

"Dammit then, I can't imagine where else he'd be," said Handel, his face knotting with concern. "Anyway, we'd best warn those in Civetot about what's happening and get them the hell out of there and into the fortress down the beach. Come on!"

Turning their horses, they quickly made for Civetot hoping to herd as many people as possible toward Nicodemia– but on arrival, met sheer chaos. Those who had not followed Estelle Dupuis were now wildly running in all directions, seeking hidey-holes, nooks, or crannies in which to stuff themselves and their children. Having witnessed from a distance the murderous decimation of the thousands who had gone out to the outskirts of Civetot to confront the Turks, those in town had now fallen into blind panic. Undaunted, Guillaume, Handel, and the Danes set about the task of directing anyone willing to listen toward the fortress.

"And keep an eye out for Tristan!" instructed Guillaume in desperation. "He's got to be somewhere in this mess!"

"Aye," cried Handel, "check the buildings!"

At that same moment Tristan and Innocenzo charged from around a corner, galloping into their midst. "There he is!" shouted Hroc.

"Tristan!" cried Guillaume, his heart stopping for an instant. "Thank God you're alive! I was thinking the worst!"

The two exchanged an instantaneous nod of fraternal solace as Tristan pulled alongside Guillaume. "The Turks are coming!" Tristan warned.

"Alright, let's go!" ordered Handel, flagging the Danes to follow. "Herd anyone you can toward the beach! We might yet be able to get some into the fort!"

As these words escaped his mouth, a retinue of gazis loped around the corner at full gallop. Halting their horses only momentarily upon catching sight of Tristan's circle, they then spurred toward them.

"They're on us!" shouted Handel. "Go!"

Bolting ahead, Tristan, Innocenzo, and Handel made for Nicodemia, driving women and children ahead of them toward the beach. Guillaume and the Danes wrenched their horses back, turning them to gain time for the others, and charged headlong into the oncoming stream of Turkish horsemen. "Take this!" bellowed Orla in Danish, sweeping his ax horizontally, cleaving the head of the gazi leading the attack. "*Tage dette!*"

As Guillaume parried with the next oncoming Turk, Crowbones crushed another with his hammer. Meanwhile, Guthroth kicked his mount in the flanks and boldly ran his horse headlong into a fourth Turk's horse. As the animals collided, Guthroth's horse raised up on hind legs braying furiously, and sank its teeth into the snout of the other horse. Then, at the very moment Guthroth's horse dropped its front hooves to the ground, Guthroth leaned over with a deadly rake of his sword and opened the Turk's belly.

Simultaneously, Hroc charged into a bevy of three gazis coming at him at once. Using techniques taught to him by Guthroth, he swiftly spun his horse about, using the velocity of its spinning hind flanks to bowl over one gazi's horse while attacking the other two gazis with his hammer. After mauling them both, Hroc noticed that the Turk he had knocked from his horse, still dazed, was struggling to stand. Without hesitation, Hroc leaned out and swept down with his hammer, crushing the man's helmet so its metal construction bent inward in jagged points, piercing the man's skull, forcing blood to effuse from the wound like water from a fountain.

Seeing the ferocity with which these four foreigners had slain their comrades, the two remaining Turks turned to flee. Guillaume, meanwhile, managed to stick his adversary through the ribs just as they escaped, and exclaimed, "They'll be back with more! Quick, head for the beach!"

## Chapter Eighty-six

### Beach of Blood

As Tristan, Handel, and Innocenzo gained the bedlam of the beach, it was now streaming with terrified people fleeing for their lives. "Keep driving them forward!" shouted Handel, continuing with the others to flush the innocents of Civetot before them. But the elderly could not keep up, and began straggling aside, as did many women carrying or dragging children along.

Handel was in full flight beside Tristan and Innocenzo. Turning his head to measure the advance of the oncoming Turks, he happened to catch sight of an old nun tripping on the hem of her trailing habit. On her heels rode an advancing Turk, saber raised. Reaching into his belt, Handel reversed his horse abruptly and flung his dagger into the Turks's chest, killing him instantly– but the Turk's stallion continued its charge, dead rider still in the saddle, rumbling over the old nun. Handel thought her dead and was about to take flight again, but her head raised and she glanced up at him with imploring eyes, weakly reaching out an arm. Turning, spurring his horse headlong into the advance of charging gazis, Handel reached down to her. "*Grab my hand, Sister! Be quick!*"

The old nun couldn't make the reach. Struggling to rise, she collapsed. Handel started to dismount as another ghazi approached, but just as he slung his right leg over the saddle, an arrow whistled into the back of the nun's neck, its point breaking through the front of her throat. Unable to make a sound, her eyes frogged and she slumped flat-faced in the sand.

"*Goddammit*!" Handel cursed, hastily making the sign of the cross over her corpse before mounting to flee. But before he could swing his right leg back over his saddle and plant it into his stirrup, an arrow scudded from nowhere into the back of his left shoulder blade– and the point exited through his front, just below the collarbone. "*Argh!*" he groaned, feeling all breath escaping him as he felt himself going into a slow slide off his saddle.

"Handel!" exclaimed Tristan, who came from nowhere alongside Innocenzo, both riding full gallop toward Nicodemia. Just as Tristan cried his name, another arrow caught Handel in the back of his ribcage, puncturing a lung. "*Handel, my God!*" screamed Tristan, watching Handel slump forward over his saddle horn, barely breathing, about to tumble from his horse. "Handel, can you hear me!?"

Handel heard nothing, saw nothing, and felt nothing. Bleeding profusely, struggling to breathe against the collapse of his lung, he no longer knew where he was or what was happening around him.

With the Turks nearly on them, Tristan pulled alongside Handel at full gallop and grabbed at the reins of his horse. "Get on the other side of him, Innocenzo," Tristan yelled "and help hold him up between us so he doesn't fall!"

"Yes, Bishop!" shouted Innocenzo, his eyes white with terror. He wished desperately to bolt directly for the safety of the fortress which was drawing near, but something within held him from abandoning Tristan and Handel. Indeed, despite the cow-towing and gutlessness that had ruled his entire existence, on this one day, it seemed, he had reached down into an untapped spring of audacity, pulling from its depths the courage to make up for a lifetime of cowardice.

## Chapter Eighty-seven

### The Gate

Struggling to hold Handel in place, Tristan and Innocenzo awkwardly drove their mounts toward Nicodemia, feeling behind them the hot breath of Turkish horses flaring from inflamed nostrils as their gazi riders whipped them forward.

"*Ride, Innocenzo! Ride for your life!*" shouted Tristan, hoarse with desperation.

Approaching the entrance to the fort, whose gate had long since rotted to ruin, Tristan and Innocenzo saw people shoving and pushing in futile efforts to beat each other inside.

"It's jammed!" wailed Innocenzo.

A moment later a Turk attacked him from behind, sweeping his saber across Innocenzo's back, lacerating it from the top of his left shoulder to the bottom of his tailbone. Innocenzo's body lopped open in one blow. So sharp was the blade, Innocenzo felt nothing at first; yet, somehow, he knew that his entire back had been carved open. "*B-Bish-op…*" he gasped, his eyes agog.

Seeing this, Tristan kicked at Handel's horse, sending it sprawling into the mass blocking the gate, hoping it might force its way through the clogged opening. Next he turned, grasping for Innocenzo's reins, but before he could grab them, the Turk who had opened Innocenzo's back was now parallel with them. Sweeping his blade across in another vicious arc, he slashed at Innocenzo's head. This blow would have decapitated Innocenzo, but as the Turk's saber slashed across, his horse was jostled by Innocenzo's own terrified horse. The Turk's aim missed. Only the very tip of the blade made contact, but it slit Innocenzo's face diagonally from his forehead to a corner of his chin, mutilating forever the handsome countenance of his appearance.

"*B-Bishop!*" shrieked Innocenzo, his face running scarlet with blood. "*I-I-m d-done!*"

"No!" Tristan cried, grabbing at Innocenzo, pulling him from his horse onto his own in an act of miraculous agility; in hopeless moments such as this, the howl of survival rears its head and wails for life, enabling men to do the impossible. Tristan next somehow managed to heave Innocenzo onto the front of the saddle and charged into the knot of people blocking the fort entrance.

Guillaume and the Danes materialized from behind him, bursting through masses of pursuing gazis. Making the gate, they dismounted and began flinging people aside until an opening was made. Instead of rushing through, Guillaume and the Danes then pulled their weapons, forming a wall to keep the opening clear so people could enter without choking the gate and trampling over one another.

By now all fighting centered around the chaos of the fort entrance as from the ramparts DuLac's and Burrel's archers fired volley after volley into enemy ranks as Turks continued to stream forward in waves. On the ground, Guillaume and the Danes continued to defend the gate breech as Tuscans from within the walls worked their way out to join their commander and the Danes. Tristan, meanwhile, threw the bleeding Innocenzo from his saddle into the midst of this bedlam and dragged him to the opening. "*Here!* he shouted, handing him over to one of the Normans who was feverishly stacking barrels and other heavy objects to block the fort opening from the Turks. "Get him inside!"

"But he's dead," the Norman objected.

Enraged, Tristan balled his fist and struck the soldier across the jaw. "*Goddammit*!" he bellowed, "*I said get him inside*!" Then turning, he began searching for Handel, shouting his name above the din. The gate area was a blur of weaponry, men, and horseflesh, but within moments Tristan spotted Handel in the chaos. Having somehow regained consciousness, Handel was staggering about– just beyond the Danes, in the midst of Turks. "Handel!" shouted Tristan.

Lost to a moment of selfless courage despite being unarmed, Tristan broke from the safety of the wall of defending Danes and Tuscans and made a wild dash for Handel who was surrounded by the enemy. Ignoring his own safety, Tristan reached out to him, hoping to reel him in. The very instant he got a hold on one of Handel's arms, a Turk stepped forward and flayed at Handel's other arm with his saber, severing it at the shoulder.

Already too disoriented to know where he was or what had happened, Handel's eyes failed even to flinch, and he continued to stumble about like a man overcome with drunkenness, not even noticing it was his own dismembered arm lying there at his feet.

"*My God!*" shouted Tristan, still tugging at Handel's good arm, dragging him into the midst of the Danes and Tuscans. "*Oh God in Heaven, spare this man I beg you!*"

It was then that a lone Turk, seeing Tristan's bishop garb and identifying him as a man of significance, singled him out and took a run at him just as he was slipping back into the Tuscan ranks. The Turk plunged his sword forward, aiming at the middle of Tristan's spine. In the wild scramble of the gate, the sword glanced off its mark and pierced clean through the meat of Tristan's right arm and right side, driving to within an inch of his heart. Feeling the cold steel of the blade point ripping through him, Tristan shuddered– then went black, tumbling to the ground.

"Tristan!" shouted Guillaume, seeing his brother fall. "Get him!" he screamed to Orla who was fighting nearby. "He's down! Save him!"

Spotting what had happened, feeling the desperation of Guillaume's eyes, Orla dropped his ax and picked Tristan up in his huge paws, bulling his way through the Normans still trying to fortify the gate. "Come on, *breathe*!" Orla whispered hoarsely, looking into Tristan's dull eyes as they lolled about aimlessly in lethargic sockets. "Dammit! Come on, Boy, *breathe*!"

## Chapter Eighty-eight

### The Time of Reckoning

The Danes and Tuscans withdrew hurriedly into the fort, dragging Tristan, Handel, and Innocenzo with them. At the same time, the Normans managed to complete their push to block the entrance by dragging wagons, carts, stray timbers, and anything else they could get their hands on to close the breech.

"Over there!" shouted Guillaume, pointing the Danes toward a roofed corner of deteriorating ruins to escape the incoming shower of arrows. "Lay them out and get back to the breech! I'll stay and get help!"

The fort had by now become a seething mass of armed men dashing about defending the gate and taking rampart positions where crusader archers fired a withering barrage of arrows into Turks assaulting the impromptu barricade blocking the gate. Though many crusaders fell from opposing fire, they were effective in holding the gazis and Muslim footmen below at bay.

Malik, approaching the gate with General Soliman, watched for a short as the futile Muslim effort to break into the fort began to fracture. Turning to Soliman, he said, "Let's pull back. As we've no siege machinery, we'll wait them out like at Xerigordos."

"Is there no water in Nicodemia as at Xerigordos?" asked Soliman.

"There *is* an old well within Nicodemia," Malik replied, "but no food supplies as reported by the scouts we sent from Xerigordos."

"Ah, just as well then," said Soliman, calling for his bugler. "It'll take a while longer, I suppose, but in the end will be equally effective."

As those within the fort continued to scramble about, Guillaume seized a monk who was assisting the wounded and dragged him to the corner where Tristan lay. "*Tend to these three men immediately!*" he shouted at the startled monk, who happened to be a Benedictine infirmarian from the monastery of Rouen. "The one in the middle is my brother, and he's the Bishop of Ostia!"

"Y-yes, I see," stammered the monk, recognizing Tristan. "But all three look nearly dead..."

"Dammit, I know that, but do what you can!" shouted Guillaume. Taking a lingering look at Tristan as he lay there bleeding and unconscious, he then broke away, running to defend the breech.

Pulling a rag, the infirmarian forced it into the gaping hole beneath Tristan's right armpit to block the profuse bleeding, then pulled another which he wrapped around Tristan's perforated arm, thinking there was little else he could do for the Bishop. Next, looking at the one-armed Handel who had been placed on his side due to the two protruding arrows, the monk snapped them off at the back and front, leaving only splintered shards poking from Handel's shoulder and ribcage where the arrows had fully perforated his frame. As this was a rough maneuver, Handel screamed in agony; each movement the monk made sent shocks of pain searing throughout his entire torso. "*Kill me!*" he wailed. "*I can take no more!*"

Having no more rags, the monk reached down and grabbed a fist of hot sand and began pressing the grains against the bleeding stub of Handel's severed arm and around the base of the tips of the broken arrow shafts to discourage the bleeding. Though the arrow shafts themselves had somewhat sealed the two wounds, blood still streamed from both, mixing quickly with the sand, turning into a bloody murk. Knowing that was the best he could do for Handel, the monk then looked at Innocenzo whose slashed face was black with caked blood. Thinking the face wound severe, but less lethal than the wounds of the other two men, the monk noticed that the entire ground beneath Innocenzo was pooling in blood.

"*What?*" the monk muttered to himself, turning Innocenzo. A moment later the monk shrank back in horror, sickened by the gaping laceration that ran the entire length of Innocenzo's back, exposing the entire spine where the Muslim blade had opened his back. "*My God*!" the monk shivered.

Innocenzo had blacked out, but on being moved and hearing the monk's cry, his eyes flittered open. The monk had turned him toward Tristan, and seeing him, Innocenzo sobbed, "*B-Bishop! Pr-pray for m-me--- for I'm... d-dying!*"

Tristan himself had been fading in and out of consciousness, but now slowly managed to incline his head toward Innocenzo. "In-no-cenzo…" he whispered.

"B-Bishop," whimpered Innocenzo, "I am a hopeless s-sinner… and a l-liar. Forgive me my s-sins… for I will surely be c-cast into H-Hell."

"N-no," Tristan replied, struggling to make his words. "Y-you are a good h-heart, lad… and G-God will account for that."

Innocenzo shook his head, and the tears welling in his eyes began to stream down his cheeks, loosening the thick, mottled scabs of black blood covering his skin. "N-no… I c-can already h-hear the Devil l-laughing… I tr-tricked Peter the Hermit into th-thinking I w-was his nephew… but I'm… *n-not.*"

Tristan tried to smile, to reassure Innocenzo this was no crime, but he was too weak. "Inn-o-cenzo…" he simply rasped.

"Please, n-never tell him f-for it m-might break his heart," Innocenzo gasped. "He l-loves me like family… and has no one else… nor… do I." Then, struggling for air, he closed his eyes, not wishing to see the expression of the Bishop's face as he said, "And I-I am g-guilty of sodomy, Bishop… with my g-ood little friend F-Fazio… a sin against G-God…" Then a tremor seized him as a slow, extended rattle issued from his throat– as he left life behind.

Tristan wanted to weep then, but when excruciating pain takes all possession of the body and consciousness hangs by a thread, one can only stare ahead as the heart sends bottomless hurt to the temples and brain. "*In-no-cenzo*?" Tristan ached.

Knowing that Innocenzo had passed, Tristan thought for a moment about Innocenzo's many acts of courage during his last days on earth. He had boldly come to the prison cell and bribed guards. And though Innocenzo had never hurt another human being during his entire life, he had summoned the wherewithal to kill the Turk who had come upon Tristan shackled to the wall. And finally, he had tried to shoo the Hermit's flock toward the walls of Nicodemia and help save Handel at his own peril.

*Oh, Innocenzo...Innocenzo...* prayed Tristan silently, struggling to remain conscious. *May God keep your gentle soul…*

Then Handel stirred, calling out to him. Tristan had thought Handel already dead after seeing what had happened to him outside the gate. But recognizing his voice, Tristan struggled to turn his head aside at the very moment Handel's eyes met his own. "*Tr-Tristan,*" moaned Handel, painfully dragging his tongue over his parched lips. "S-so we meet death t-together, l-lad. I d-did not expect… s-such an ending."

"N-nor I…" rasped Tristan.

Handel stared straight up then, and closed his eyes, drawing a deep shuddering breath. "I n-never feared death all these y-ears… but now am suddenly afraid, my fr-friend."

"You have n-nothing to fear, Handel. You are a true and l-loyal soldier of God."

"I tried my b-best, lad," Handel wheezed. "But it n-now occurs to m-me... my end comes in a cr-crusade that I opposed, protecting people who b-butchered others, at the orders of a man who cl-claims infallibility… y-yet was wrong fr-from the very beginning… and continues his mistake w-with each step f-forward of this crusade. So pray for m-me… as I n-now know I sh-shall descend to the depths of H-Hell with Innocenzo… who is already there w-waiting for me."

"*No, no,*" Tristan objected. "You of all people, with your sense of justice and y-your blunt truth… G-God will p-pull you up, Handel, for He is a *forgiving* God."

"N-no," Handel moaned, his eyes growing cold. "I've t-taken the l-lives of others in God's name… but not at *His* request. I've m-murdered at the orders of th-those who profess to speak for H-Him… the men who drive the *Church.* I will now p-pay for this c-confusion of mine, Tristan. Though I thought I was pursuing a r-righteous path… it has all b-been so f-false… so very *f-a-l-s-e.*" His eyes closed then, and stared blankly ahead.

"H-Handel?" whispered Tristan. "*Handel,* can you hear me?"

There came no response.

Staring hard, Tristan's eyes searched desperately for movement– but there was none. Handel's soul had passed.

## Chapter Eighty-nine

### Island of Hope

In the face of the savage Turkish onslaught, all bitterness existing between the peasant crusaders, the French, the Normans, the Tafurs, and the Tuscans vanished. The original force of 50,000 Latins who had landed in Bithynia two and half months earlier had within the course of this single day dwindled to little more than three thousand. Only sparse remnants of each of the four contingents remained now within the fort, not counting those back in Civetot who were being murdered or sorted and shackled for Muslim slave trade. The only salvation, then, for the three thousand stuck within the walls of the abandoned fortress of Nicodemia now laid in clinging together. Even DuLac and the Danes momentarily lost all memory of previous enmity, as did Tafur toward Tristan.

While the Turks began withdrawing, DuLac and Burrel stood atop the ramparts and watched them pull back to Civetot. "Goddamn," said Burrel, "we've lost our asses, but at least we're alive!"

"Yeah, but what now?" grumbled DuLac. "We're like cornered rats."

"Yeah, maybe, but don't forget the Hermit. Have you forgotten he's petitioning for troops back in Constantinople?"

"Aye, maybe so," DuLac sighed, "but we pissed in our own goblet back there, remember? Alexius deported us, refusing to tolerate us anymore. Christ, what have we gotten ourselves into, Burrel? Shit, we're down to a handful of men. So much, then, for conquest and glory."

"Yeah, but unlike Rainald, at least we've got water," said Burrel, as Tafur walked up.

"But what the hell are we going to eat?" shrugged DuLac.

"The horses," said Burrel.

"What then?" shrugged DuLac skeptically. "Each other?"

Having heard the tail end of this conversation, Tafur gazed at them derisively. "You two have had the maggot of vainglory eating at your brains your entire lives," he said, "thriving on the broken backs of others. Damn right, if the time comes, we'll eat the dead."

"What?" objected Burrel, rankled by the remark. "Have you gone mad?"

"My men have been roasting Muslim flesh for two months now, to terrify the Turks and spread news that the Tafurs have arrived. It's how we celebrate the murder of heathens. But in the end, I don't imagine Christian flesh tastes a bit different… so if it keeps us alive, then so be it." He passed his tongue over his top lip then and made a licking sound for the express purpose of nettling the two noblemen, as if to assuage his own old resentments.

Below them as they talked atop the ramparts, Guillaume and the Danes had huddled around the infirmarian monk. "These two here died in the night as expected," the monk said, pointing to Handel and Innocecenzo. "The Bishop still clings to life, though I don't know how. He's lost too much blood and there's no telling what damage has been done inside." Looking up at Guillaume, he reluctantly added, "What I'm trying to tell you, sir, is that he'll not make it through the day."

This drove the color from Guillaume's cheeks, and as his eyes dropped, his face began to swell with emotion. He started to say something, but his throat lumped and the incomprehensible thing the monk had said then seemed to hang in the air as Guillaume felt his temples go numb. Slipping to his knees, he began to pray as faint traces of blue veins surfaced beneath the skin of his neck. "Save my brother, Lord," he implored, "for he has served you faithfully since the day you placed him on this earth. He's a good man, and he's been a loyal brother."

Guthroth, his heart already heavy from hours of vigil fretting over Tristan, watched Guillaume's fraternal grief with sadness. Going to his knees beside Guillaume, he folded his hands in prayer also. "Y-yes," he stuttered, "Boy has been y-your servant in all th-things, God." As he said this, he felt someone move to his side.

It was Hroc. Kneeling, Hroc made the sign of the cross. Looking over at Orla, he said, "Father, though Handel has passed and Uncle Tristan now lays here dying, and countless others have been slaughtered, I've also today been witness to many miracles of survival… including our own. As I think about it, it's occurred to me that someone, a greater power, has been watching over me, you, Uncle Crowbones, Uncle Guthroth, and Uncle Guillaume. We should every one of us be dead in light of what happened here and in Civetot. I've decided therefore, I wish to be baptized in the Christian faith, Father."

Orla considered his son's words a short while. "So be it, Hroc," he said. "I shan't oppose it, son. Ja, it's a miracle any of us are still standing." But thinking of the prophesy set out by his brother's bird bones in Cologne, he added, "But it's not yet done, either, Hroc. We may well all be dead within days. I've not mentioned this to any of you before, but Crowbones took out his bones back in Germany… they prophesized that most of us will never reach Jeruslaem. But as you all are my witness, should we at least escape Bithynia, then I too shall agree to baptism."

This surprised everyone listening, especially Crowbones. "Ah, but Brother," he warned, "Bithynia is not Jerusalem. If we survive Bithynia only to die a short while later on the way to the Holy Land, then surviving Bithynia means little. Why would you take Christian baptism upon escaping here, only to die shortly thereafter on the arrival of Bishop Adhémar, Raymond of Toulouse, and the others?"

"Perhaps it may mean little," nodded Orla, looking at his brother, "but at this very moment I'm well satisfied. After all, I'm still alive and able to speak to my son one day longer, and he's able to answer, unlike so many others who now lay dead. I suddenly feel I've been given a gift from somewhere, by *someone*." As he said this, he looked skyward. "And should I receive a further gift of even just a few more days with Hroc and the rest of you, then I accept the water."

"I've rarely heard such thoughtful words coming from your mouth, Brother," said Crowbones. "And good words they are." His shoulders raised then as he looked over at Guthroth and Hroc. "Indeed, I stand with Orla. Should we manage to walk out of this place, I too shall have the water poured over me."

## Chapter Ninety

### Waiting

DuLac, taking an accounting of his Normans, was shocked to discover that of his original 585 knights and footmen, there remained less than a hundred. Coward that he was, however, he had abandoned most of his troops at the onset of the ambush, even trampling over his own footmen as he, the Gustave brothers, and a number of Norman captains fled. Looking about the fort, he further realized, to his dismay, that the Tuscan force had fared far better than the Normans the day before, and now doubled his own numbers.

"Whatever you do," he warned the Gustave twins, "don't agitate that bunch for we're now slim in numbers and they could easily overcome us if they so decided. We'll hope Tristan de Saint-Germain dies where he lays in their little Tuscan corner there, but best that we kiss Guillaume de Saint-Germain's ass since he's the only one that can keep the Danes off our backs. They're already following every move we make like scavenging crows!"

The Danes were little interested in the Gustave brothers, of course, but as a point of self-preservation, DuLac wished to make the twins feel as endangered as himself. Even as DuLac was speaking to the Gustaves about the Danes, Orla and Crowbones were quietly watching DuLac from the distance. "Oh, but look at that little weasel hiding behind his two Norman wolfdogs," muttered Orla.

"Ja," responded Crowbones, "too bad the Turks didn't fill his ass with arrows in the gorge with the rest of the Normans that didn't make it out. But then, the sorry little snake was probably slithering away too damned fast."

"I'll tell you what," Orla said, "You and I could gather up Hroc and Guthroth late in the night and take him by surprise–

force him to look into our eyes before we slit his throat, and be done with him, eh?"

Crowbones considered his brother's words, but shook his head. "No… we'll wait, Orla. There'll be plenty of time once we're not in such straights with the Turks."

"What makes you think any of us will ever walk out of this place alive?" asked Orla. "I tell you, should I die without killing DuLac, I'll die for naught."

"Me too, Orla. But consider this, every man-of-arms counts at the moment, so we don't need to stir division at the moment. But I propose a pact between the two of us. Should the Turks make their way into the fort, we're doomed anyway, huh? So let's agree… if that happens, then our final act together will be to corner DuLac, make him look us both in the eyes, then slit his wormy throat. Agreed?"

"Ja," Orla nodded. "Agreed."

***

The Tuscans and Normans aside, a little over a thousand of Burrel's troops had made it out of the valley. Sansavoir's troops, on the other hand, had been decimated to the last man due to their position at the head of the formation as they had been trapped in the gorge. As for Tafur, his ranks had also been severely thinned. Though Tafur had managed to raise the number of fanatic peasant warriors to 4,000 men by the time he led them into the pass at Dracon, only eight hundred survived to make it to the fortress walls. The remaining survivors of the 3,000 total within the fortress of Nicodemia were women and children of the Peasants' Crusade. All the elderly who had remained in Civetot had been massacred. Of those elderly who tried to flee to the fortress, all were also slain; their aged limbs simply unable to outrun the swift chase of Turkish gazis pursuing them.

The knights who had fled the pass had retreated into the fort on horseback; as the days dragged on, the three thousand survivors, lacking food, set about butchering these faithful steeds. "We'll kill only a few each day, and ration their flesh sparingly," declared Burrel, showing a rash of sense for the first time since his departure from France. "The sooner we run out of horse meat, the sooner we perish!"

So began the wait as crusaders watched from atop the ramparts while the Turks kept guard, sending contingents out to surrounding forests and woodlands to gather timber for the construction of ladders, rams, and towers.

"The day after tomorrow," said Malik to General Soliman, "we take the fort."

## Chapter Ninety-one

### Darkness

Guillaume and Guthroth had been keeping vigil for two days over Tristan, who had fallen into a coma after Handel's death, never recovering consciousness. Shortly after midnight of the fourth day trapped inside Nicodemia, both Guillaume and Guthroth fell asleep as Hroc stood guard outside the ruins the Tuscans had claimed as their haven within the fort. As those within the fort were nearly dead of exhaustion, and the Turks had withdrawn to construct assault machinery, it was an especially sepulchral silence that hung over the fort that night; within the walls, nothing moved.

Yet, something was stirring. Within the conscience existence of every person born onto this earth, there seems to run a parallel existence that surfaces only during moments of unconsciousness brought on by either sleep or black-out induced by accident or injury. As the body reposes in dormant unawareness during such times, this parallel existence resurrects itself. Rising from the blackness of the subconscious, it knits itself together in disjointed and disconnected images, and though it seems surreal and ethereal, the threads of its reconstruction are real, representing actual faces, voices, and events.

This phenomenon, labeled a multitude of things to include dreams, visions, apparitions or premonitions, has been the source of infinite mystery throughout the ages– and to this day remains unexplained, and misunderstood. Yet, all humans know of its existence, and experience it during their lives in one vaporous form or another. While Tristan de Saint-Germain lay dying in an abandoned corner of the fortress of Nicodemia, his parallel existence slowly began to rise from the blackness of his comatose state.

Though unconscious, he felt consciousness, *thinking* himself dead, yet clinging to life. He sensed his soul rising and drifting from the shell of his deceased body. Then, from nowhere, the thunderous toll of a great cathedral bell rang out, slowly arcing its way upward, reverberating with such force that Tristan felt his very soul shudder and quake. Peering about the blackness in terror, in the milky distance he saw his mother, beautiful Asta of the Danes, sitting on a divan teaching him languages as a boy while he stood there in obedient adoration. "*Mother! Mother*!" his floating soul called out, desperately reaching to recover and preserve that precious moment of mother-son affection and innocence… but as he reached out, the vision dissolved, leaving him with that unbearable hollowness he first experienced when she had sent him away at the age of seven.

Then came the thunderous toll of the bell again as it changed direction, swinging back in a plodding track of descent, resonating with a second deafening call. In place of his mother, Odo de Lagery slipped into view; he was teaching Tristan how to document and dispense the vast Benedictine wealth flowing into the Cluny treasury tower from throughout Western Europe. But Odo seemed incredibly young, nearly boyish, in this vision, and Tristan marveled, remembering that exact point in time as though it occurred only moments ago. Tristan reached out again, crying, "*Prior Odo*!" But the image dismantled itself as the great bell reversed its descent and now began to rise again, issuing yet a third murderous call as its huge clapper thundered against thick bronze walls, sending out a rumble that shook everything before it in violent waves…

That was when he saw Mala sitting before him, a baby boy in her lap. Both were laughing and singing, lost in each other's playful joy. Tristan thought this to be their lost son at first, but then suspected it to be a different child. On closer examination, Mala was not the girl of twenty-one who had given birth in the Alps, but looked as she had when he had seen her only days before he had been taken prisoner by the Tafurs. Tristan next saw himself then appear, and after embracing Mala and their new son, the three turned and walked off, slipping into the film of a mist-laden, shadowy landscape. Mesmerized, he followed, thinking they would vanish as had the first two apparitions. But they did not. The shadows parted then, like voluminous, billowing stage curtains, and he followed their figures to a cottage next to a winding stream– where geese and swans were dipping their beaks into the water, snatching minnows or poking bills beneath their open wings to preen. There were sheep and goats nearby in an adjacent meadow, bleating and tugging at the rich carpet of clover at their feet spreading into the distance as far as one could see. It was only then he realized the Tristan of this vision was not wearing clerical garments, nor was his crown shaved in the required tonsure of the Benedictine order. Instead, he wore a white blouse with the ballooning sleeves of a gentleman farmer, along with woolen breeches and boots.

*I am dead... and this is Heaven,* thought Tristan's fading soul.

## Chapter Ninety-two

### Mala

The Turks had removed themselves from view of the crusaders trapped inside the fortress, and were engineering the construction of siege equipment in Civetot. For their part, the crusaders were well aware of the Seljuk scheme, and bracing for a full assault within the next day or two. Prayer, then, took on new significance within the walls of Nicodemia, even amongst those of dubious spirituality who had committed atrocities against Jews, Hungarians, Greeks farmers, and Turkish civilians.

Hroc took the sacrament of baptism from the very infirmarian monk who had been assisting the Tuscans with medical matters, and both he and Guthroth began to take impromptu religious instruction from Guillaume during the idleness of waiting. Hroc soon discovered why Guthroth frequently found himself in a state of confusion concerning the details of Christianity. Like Guthroth, though, Hroc listened attentively, struggling mightily to accept whatever he was told.

Though things were peaceful inside the fort and the Turks were nowhere to be seen, a shroud of doom hung over the fortress; all within knew that very soon the Turks would assault the breech and set it afire while simultaneously attacking the walls with ladders and towers. It was a dark time–each and every person in the fort began to ponder his own end.

Unbeknownst to those within the fortress, during the Turkish slaughter of those standing at the edge of town with Estelle Dupuis, many of the original Greek inhabitants of the small Greek port slipped aboard fishing skiffs and hurriedly evacuated Civetot. They knew the Seljuks would show no mercy and quickly navigated their tiny fleet across the Bosphorus Straight to the safety of Constantinople, a distance of twenty miles. Landing, they reported the massacre immediately to Emperor Alexius who was already in the process of mobilizing a moderate force to send across the straight as Queen Irene had recommended, despite Augusta Anna's and patriarch Nicholas' vehement objections. Considering the news of the crusader debacle in Civetot and the flight of many to the abandoned fortress at Nicodemia, he accelerated his mobilization and quintupled the number of ships and troops he originally intended to send to the Bithynian coast.

Realizing that he would now undoubtedly have to evacuate survivors, and having no idea what that number would be, Alexius was forced to await the arrival of additional warships from other ports. Once they finally arrived, Alexius ordered his naval commanders to set sail with a combined fleet of over one-hundred warships. Each was only half loaded with men-at-arms to allow room for evacuees on the return voyage. His greatest concern, nonetheless, was the safety of Bishop Tristan de Saint-Germain due to his personal significance to Pope Urban II.

Peter the Hermit, hearing the news of Civetot, fell into a fit of prayer, beseeching God for merciful intervention– though God had had little to do with creating this latest plight of the Peasants' Crusade. The Hermit also began to fret over Innocenzo, and could not help but wonder about Estelle Dupuis. "Oh Father in Heaven, save my poor naïve nephew, Innocenzo! And I pray also that Estelle Dupuis did not heed my prophecy in Cologne, for I now see it was my own foolishness that put her, her husband, and her children on the road to cleanse the Holy Land of Islam! I should have left that chore to PopeUrban's knights!"

Nobody was more upset by the news of Civetot than Mala, who fell victim to abject panic knowing she might lose the one person on this earth she loved most. "My life will be meaningless should anything happen to Tristan!" she confessed aloud to Salvetti, who had by now accepted the fact that Mala and the Bishop loved each other beyond words, and beyond Benedictine convention. "I'm taking my ships and the Genoa Guard when the emperor's ships launch, Salvetti. Say a Jewish prayer for me that Tristan's not already been slain, or I will surely take my own life just to be with him in the next!"

Salvetti adored Mala above all else, and began to worry as she agonized over her one true love. "If you sail the Bosphorus Straight," he announced, "then I'm coming with you to fetch him, Signorina!"

***

Three hours after Alexius's ships set sail from Constantinople, just across the Straight, the Turks had begun to assemble for their attack against the fortress. Lining up their towers, hitching them to oxen and forming into battle ranks, they began the short march down the beach to Nicodemia. Less than an hour later they came into view of the crusaders standing guard atop the ramparts.

"Here they come!" the guards shouted, sending those below into a flurry of activity gathering weapons and posting themselves in final defensive positions along the walls.

Guillaume, standing beside the unconscious body of Tristan, knelt at his side. "Exactly as we vowed as boys, Brother," he whispered, "we stand together until the very end. And though you cannot rise, I shall stand for you… and as we promised, we shall end together in spirit, at least." He made the sign of the cross, kissed Tristan on the forehead, then led the Danes to the breech. "To glory in the name of God!" he shouted.

As the Turks advanced to within half a mile of Nicodemia, the fortress fell silent as men crouched and braced for the Turkish onslaught. But suddenly, startling all, this silence was broken by a piercing cry from the west rampart. "Sails on the horizon!" someone shouted. "Coming from Constantinople!" Scarcely believing what they were hearing, all within the fortress exchanged looks of hope, then stared back up at the ramparts where the voice had rung out. "My God!" the voice came again. "There must be a hundred ships at least, maybe more!"

Shouts rang out from every quarter of the fortress as every man along the ramparts ran to the west wall to stare out to sea while many on the ground ran up the gangplanks to join them. "Salvation!" they exclaimed. "It's the Greeks!"

From shore, Malik and Soliman also spotted the sails. "Ships coming from the south… must be Alexius's ships," said Soliman, unperturbed. "Probably come to take these miserable foreigners from this shore."

"Or to make war on us!" declared Malik, anger swelling as his face pulsed red.

"No, not likely."

"I say we attack the fortress before they come ashore. We easily have time to scale the walls and wipe out those inside. By the time the Greeks come ashore, we'll have control of the fort and can cut them down as they land."

"To what purpose?" asked Soliman. "If the foreigners leave, then our mission is done. Besides, Sultan Arslan hasn't issued approval to fight the Greeks. This territory remains under truce."

"Dammit, the truce has been broken!" Malik insisted, his fuse shortening. "I say attack!"

"Then you'll do it with your half of the troops only, Malik," said Soliman with certainty. Having said that, he gestured to his signalman to trumpet a withdrawal. Then, without another word to Malik, he turned his horse for Nicaea as his troops did an about face and followed.

Malik simmered there for another ten minutes. Finally, conceding that to attack by himself would be fruitless, especially with the Greeks about to land, he also turned his army toward Nicaea.

***

The first dingy to disembark was Mala's, and as she stepped ashore, she ran to the gate, which was still barricaded. "*Tristan! Tristan, are you there?*" she wailed.

Guillaume and the Danes, standing at the other side of the barricade, recognized her voice and began slinging the obstacles blocking the breech aside. "Mala!" shouted Guillaume, embracing her, which was something he had never done before. "Oh but you're a sight for sore eyes, as are those ships there!"

"Where's Tristan?" she pleaded, unable to suppress her apprehension.

"He's… *hurt,*" said Guillaume with hesitancy. "He was run through, Mala, and he's been unconscious for days. The infirmarian says his time is short…"

"*Oh, my God!*" Mala bawled, turning white. "Take me to him quickly!"

When she got there, catching sight of his ghostly face, she dissolved. Grasping his hand, she snuffled, "Tristan, can you hear me? It's Mala! I've brought help!" He did not answer, which only made her more frantic. "*Tristan!*" she shouted, shaking his hand violently, as if that might force him awake. But it did not. Looking up at Guillaume, she cried, "Quickly, get him aboard my ship, Guillaume! We've got to get him back to Constantinople. The emperor's physicians are the finest in the world. They can save him!"

"Get that old remnant of a door there as a stretcher," ordered Guillaume, motioning to the Danes, "and lay him on it!"

Within the half hour Mala's ship set sail without waiting for the rest of the fleet and made quickly for Constantinople. They had placed Tristan onto the bed of Mala's cabin, and she sat there beside him the entire time with Guillaume and the Danes, holding his hands distraughtly while staring into his eyes for signs of movement. None came. An hour later his forehead began to feel cold. Startled, Mala shrieked, "*My God... we're losing him, Guillaume!*"

"Is he still breathing?" asked Guillaume anxiously, placing the side of his cheek to Tristan's nostrils to feel for breath. Looking at Mala, he said, "Yes, but barely… and slower than before."

Owing to a stiff wind, Mala's ship landed in the capital's harbor within just over three hours of travel. Tristan was quickly taken to the Imperial Palace and placed in the care of Alexius' physicians who immediately cleaned his deep wounds and began administering herbs and salves of various concoctions. They also siphoned secret potions of their own invention down his throat in reed tubes. Most of it came right back up, but occasionally they would take, and on two occasions this caused Tristan to lurch upward, gagging.

"Ah, he's improving by degrees," said the lead physician, smiling at Mala after hours of laboring over him. "But we need to leave him in peace now for a time."

Everyone left the room then but Mala, who refused. Sitting at his bedside, she recited every prayer she knew, holding his hand throughout. A few minutes past midnight, she started talking to him… as though he were listening, and might even reply. Still, he remained motionless and silent.

In the wee hours of morning, Mala heard the approach of soft footsteps entering the room. It was Queen Irene. She moved beside Mala, placing her hand on Mala's shoulder, and said, "I dedicated a mass in the Basilica Hagia Sophia for him last night, my dear, celebrated by Patriarch Nicholas. And though I despise the Patriarch's politics, he carries great weight within our Church here in Byzantium. Perhaps God will listen."

"Thank you, Majesty," said Mala, understanding somehow that in this woman she had found a kindred heart– one who had felt the torment and endured the sorrow of unrequited love.

The queen looked down at Tristan. "I noticed how handsome your bishop was on the day he first came to the palace," she said. "There was something in his posture and movements that reminded me of someone I once loved… and still care about. His death was like a knife to my heart." She studied Tristan's features then, and placed her hand to his hair, running her fingers through it gently. "Oh, he is far too handsome to be celibate and chaste, I imagine. And if some woman could convince him to abandon his vestments, she would be fortunate indeed." Then she smiled at Mala, and as quietly as she came, she left.

The sun broke over the horizon an hour later. Mala had finally fallen asleep, laying next to Tristan with one hand holding his and the other draped across his chest. But in her dream, she felt something stir gently. Then it came again with more force. Opening her eyes, startled, she realized it was not in her dream at all, but right there at her side. Tristan was shifting the least amount beside her, which was the first movement he had made since Mala had found him in Nicodemia. Sitting up, she stared down at him. His eyes were open. "*Tris-tan!*" she whimpered, placing her palms flat against his cheeks, kissing him.

He looked at her, confused. "I w-was just now at... our farm," he muttered, his words barely audible.

"What did you say, Tristan?"

"I w-was at our farm by the brook... sitting with you and the boy… then everything went bl-black."

"The boy?"

"Yes, our baby son." Then his eyes moved from side to side as seeking something. "Where is h-he, Mala?"

This confused Mala, and she swept the question aside, hurt. Sitting back, stung by the words, she whispered, "Tristan, you *know* where he is. He's gone… lying in a grave within the fortress of Canossa."

"No," Tristan insisted. "He is alive. We were j-just holding him a moment ago, you and I… and he was laughing. Where is he? I wish to hold him again."

At this, Mala suspected Tristan was suffering from delirium, yet the insistence of his voice pierced her heart. She had to struggle to hold back tears. "He's *gone*, Tristan. He lived but a very short while, only a few days… then God took him from us in the Alps. Don't you remember?"

"No," Tristan said, shaking his head weakly. "God gave us another son, Mala. And another chance. We were there just a moment ago in the midst of it on our farm… you, me, our boy." Gazing about the room, disoriented, he said, "Wh-what is this place, and how did we get here?

"*Oh, Tristan*," Mala said, shaking her head as a single tear gathered itself in the corner of her eye, then slowly streamed down her cheek, "there *is* no… farm, my love."

"Y-yes," Tristan asserted, urgency growing in his expression, "We w-were just there, the three of us…"

## Chapter Ninety-three

### The End… of the Beginning

Under the care of the Emperor Alexius' palace physicians, Tristan began to heal. Throughout his first two full days of consciousness, to Mala's distress, he persistently begged her to bring their baby boy to him. When the child never appeared, Tristan thought himself somehow ensnared within the web of some hopeless nightmare in which the child was just within reach, but being kept from him.

On the third day, his fog began to clear and he gradually began to regain his senses. It was on this day that he finally assented he was not dreaming… rather, the other thing was the dream. This cold realization crippled Tristan for nearly a week, crushing his will, smothering his heart. Worse yet, the image of himself, Mala, and their son sitting on the steps of the small cottage beside the brook continued to appear in his subconscious day after day; it seemed so real, he thought at times he might reach out and touch it.

The clarity of this recurring vision eventually grew filmy with time, but the hurt of it refused to go away. Regardless, he found comfort in Mala. Although he could no longer reach out and touch the farm in Tuscany, or their son, he could reach out and touch her, at least. So as he began the long wait for the arrival of Bishop Adhémar and the Pope's knights, his love for her continued only to grow.

For Mala's part, she remained at his side every day until his release from the royal physicians' care in early November. She then took him to complete his convalescence at her palace where Salvetti helped her nurse him back to full health. Guillaume, the Danes, and the surviving Tuscans troops were there also, having returned after the withdrawal from the Nicodemia fortress at Mala's invitation.

Peter the Hermit suffered an immediate mental and emotional collapse in the aftermath of the Civetot massacre, and prayed daily for Innocenzo, Estelle Dupuis, and the tens of thousands of others. He fell into a bleak period of dementia over the winter, sorely tempted to slink back to Western Europe after this disastrous debacle of his own devise called the Peasants' Crusade. As history records, he remained in Constantinople although it has never been clear whether he did this of free will or whether he might have been forced to remain by Emperor Alexius, or even by his own surviving crusaders. According to certain Byzantine reports, he did attempt to flee Constantinople on two occasions, but was forced back ashore upon being discovered.

Regardless, Peter the Hermit would end by awaiting the arrival of Bishop Adhémar of Le Puy and the sanctioned crusaders of Pope Urban II, and would later play but a minor role in the main crusade which would launch in late spring of 1077. Afterwards, he was to eventually return to France and open a tiny monastery where he would live the remainder of his years in obscurity within the back country of France, far from the grand stage of world events and religious politics. How or whether he ever reconciled himself with the slaying of so many innocents who abandoned all to follow his charismatic preaching has never been determined. It would seem impossible that one could ever find peace after serving as the actual wellspring of such wanton slaughter and destruction. Yet, stranger things have happened.

Desmond DuLac, the Gustave brothers, Geoffrey Burrel, and the other surviving military elements of the ill-fated deportation to Bithynia were allowed to remain in the area. Emperor Alexius allowed this concession on a probationary basis only on condition that the lot of them never enter the walls of Constantinople again, and remain inconspicuous wherever they happened to find accommodations. This they were able to do, being small in number and fearful of having their hands and feet severed. Tafur and his men found menial labor on the many farms surrounding the capital. Though their branded foreheads frightened the Byzantines, the Tafurs clearly understood it was in their interest to remain civil and on the right side of Byzantine law.

However, like DuLac and Burrel, Tafur and his men were only biding time and waiting for the continuation of the fight against Islam when the main crusader force arrived. DuLac kept the Gustave brothers at his side at all times, knowing that should Orla, Crowbones, and Guthroth come across him, they would slay him on the spot. Reciprocally, DuLac's own hatred of the Danes, Tristan, and Guillaume never waned either, and he continued to hope for the day he might devise their end.

Little Benito Fazio, incredibly, had been spared in Civetot owing only to his highly unusual appearance and voice, the very things he had cursed since birth. Having fled into a wine cellar as the Turks invaded Civetot, he was quickly apprehended, shackled, and lined up for the executioner's block. Several of the Turkish gazis watching the executions were struck by Fazio's comical appearance as it was his turn to be beheaded. Seeing his tiny frame and hearing his elfish voice as he pleaded for mercy, they laughed uproariously, having never before witnessed anyone quite as amusing as the tiny man quaking and bleating before the executioner.

"Ho, this little gnat is funnier than a court clown and might bring an exorbitant price in Baghdad!" shouted a gazi captain,

"Truly," guffawed another, "some of the emirs and shahs there would find him as amusing as we do! A court pet, perhaps!"

So it happened that Benito Fazio was excused from the executioner's ax and removed to the overland slave caravan, bound for a life of captivity in a foreign land for the entertainment of the wealthy. Yet, fortune smiled on the elfish little man. Like the Biblical character of Joseph with the coat of many colors, Fazio's future would not turn out as either he or the Turkish gazis scoffing at him could have possibly foreseen. Indeed, little Fazio would reappear as the Holy Crusade unfolded... under the most unlikely of circumstances.

Orla and Crowbones both took the water of Christian baptism just as promised after their rescue from Nicodemia. Soon thereafter, they joined Guthroth and Hroc in being puzzled, confused, and befuddled by Catholic doctrine and practices. Asking few questions for fear of appearing foolish, they both made better than feeble attempts to accept whatever they were being told, though at times they found it preposterous. In the end, they too were biding time and waiting for the second wave of crusaders to arrive in Constantinople. But as time would tell, and as the desiccated bird bones had already prophesized, neither Orla nor Crowbones, nor Hroc or Guthroth, would actually ever make Jerusalem. Rather, God had already determined a different destiny for the Danes.

Guillaume, perhaps more than anyone in Constantinople, impatiently awaited the arrival of Bishop Adhémar. Driven by his burning desire to serve God and his dream of freeing the holy city of Jerusalem from the grips of Islam, his childhood vow to become the purest of Christian soldiers had not waned a single measure since leaving Tuscany. He clearly understood that the Peasants' Crusade was but a sad footnote in Pope Urban's Holy Crusade, and that the real crusade would begin once the real armies arrived.

Mahmoud Malik, the Butcher of Medina, would reappear within the year as the scourge of the East, and his sadistic lust for blood would only be further fueled as the scope of war would begin to spread. He would help establish yet new parameters in horror and cruelty as he and his renegade gazis swept through one town after another, killing Christians, Jews, and Muslims alike. Malik would also encounter Bishop Tristan de Saint-Germain, and the two would become visceral enemies as the fortunes of Christianity and Islam swung back and forth in a ceaseless tide of blood and hatred until one finally prevailed over the other.

The ever faithful and altruistic Tristan, having barely survived the Peasants' Crusade, would soon be driven into new dilemmas and torn by even greater challenges as he, Mala, Guillaume, and the Danes struggled their way closer to Jerusalem in the face of improbable odds and impossible circumstances.

But the arrival of new crusader hordes, the advance toward the Holy Land, the merciless war between great Christian and Muslim armies, and the final outcome for all these characters just described is yet an entirely different story… called God's Scarlet Fury.

THE END

## FINAL NOTE

As December of 1096 rolled in January and February of 1097, the true knights of Western Europe began to appear in Constantinople… by the tens of thousands. Bearing the scarlet cross emblazoned across their tunics, carrying the finest of weaponry, and riding the most fierce horseflesh in existence, this second wave of crusaders arrived in sweeping torrents led by celebrated figureheads of Western Europe such as Bishop Adhémar of Le Puy, Raymond of Toulouse, Godfrey of Bouillon, Bohemod of Taranto, Tancred of Hauteville, Baldwin of Boulogne, Robert of Flanders, Stephen of Blois, and Robert of Normandy. Indeed, the knightly forces of Christianity would soon be sweeping across the Holy Land in numbers that Kilij Arslan, General Soliman, Mahmoud Malik, and Emperor Alexius Comnenus could never have imagined.